CW00497496

Huge thanks to my friend Stuart White who not only took the time & trouble to proof the manuscript off his own bat but whose enthusiasm and kind words spurred me to take the leap of faith which brought me here.

Marilyn Nash

DARK HORSES

AUSTIN MACAULEY PUBLISHERS™

LONDON · CAMBRIDGE · NEW YORK · SHARJAH

Copyright © Marilyn Nash 2022

The right of Marilyn Nash to be identified as author of this work has been asserted by the author in accordance with sections 77 and 78 of the Copyright, Designs and Patents Act 1988.

All rights reserved. No part of this publication may be reproduced, stored in a retrieval system, or transmitted in any form or by any means, electronic, mechanical, photocopying, recording, or otherwise, without the prior permission of the publishers.

Any person who commits any unauthorised act in relation to this publication may be liable to criminal prosecution and civil claims for damages.

This is a work of fiction. Names, characters, businesses, places, events, locales, and incidents are either the products of the author's imagination or used in a fictitious manner. Any resemblance to actual persons, living or dead, or actual events is purely coincidental.

A CIP catalogue record for this title is available from the British Library.

ISBN 9781398483361 (Paperback)
ISBN 9781398483378 (ePub e-book)

www.austinmacauley.com

First Published 2022
Austin Macauley Publishers Ltd®
1 Canada Square
Canary Wharf
London
E145AA

A special thank you to my son Grenville Nash who produced the initial cover design and didn't need all that much prodding

Part I
"April Is the Cruellest Month"

Monday, 19th April

7.15 pm

My name is Fiona Hamilton, I am 42 years old and recently I have begun to dream about young men.

I know what you're probably thinking. Here we go, classic cougar syndrome, some sad Mrs Robinson wannabe who's hit that dangerous age, fantasising about taking a young lover before time takes her looks.

And of course, that would seem perfectly reasonable except that these aren't those sorts of dreams. My young men are fully clothed and simply going about their daily lives, as though glimpsed briefly and in passing, from the window of a moving vehicle. In fact, as far as I'm aware, they don't even exist though I suppose it's possible that I may have actually seen their faces somewhere, in a shop, on the street, on television. At any rate, I don't think I recognise them. So why do they haunt my sleeping hours?

A Freudian psychologist would probably say it was sex, or rather the lack of it. Michael and I don't sleep together, you see—we've had separate bedrooms, pretty much separate lives, for years. I know how odd that sounds but there are all sorts of marital arrangements these days, some Bohemian, some rhapsodic, some morganatic, some convenient and quite a lot mutually inconvenient. Ours is probably no more outré than many others but I'll let you be the judge as you read on. Ergo, it's not that I have anything against sex per se, you understand, just not with him, so no, that's not it. Something more than usual is out of kilter that I haven't yet quite put my finger on.

Who's Michael, did you say? Well, technically he's my husband, sort of, but more of that later. Regional Director for one of those big new soulless hypermarket chains that people apparently like to shop in these days. At least I assume they must do because Michael assures me that every one of their stores turns over at least half a million a day and he'd know because he's forever on the computer or on his smartphone checking up on them. Works ludicrously long hours so that one day they'll give him a permanent seat on the Board and then he can work even longer hours.

'It's not frustration that's fuelling your dreams, Fiona. That's not why that procession of the flower of England's youth parades through your head every night this time of the year and you know it. You just won't admit it.'

'You think you're so smart, don't you?'

'Well, you are over 40. And those men you're subconsciously conjuring up are scarcely older than your own daughters: Young enough to be your son, in fact.'

'Don't say that.'

'I just did. Why can't you?'

And there it is. See, that's the issue I've been trying to skirt round. If it were lust, that would make me as bad as Jocasta. Worse, even. At least hers was an honest mistake. This is far more serious.

'Stop it, Fiona. Whatever are you thinking? That way madness lies.'

"Feef? Must you park your heap of junk in front of the garage? It's blocking both entrances."

In case you hadn't gathered, that's Michael arriving home. And I know it is. Maybe that was the idea.

Better pack my thoughts up and stuff them in the cutlery draw. Take out a potato peeler while I'm about it. I was supposed to be preparing supper but I got distracted. That's another thing I do a lot these days.

"God, I'm exhausted. What's for supper?"

We're all tired, Michael.

"Mince, mashed potatoes, and carrots. That's all the veg I could find in the fridge."

I have to 'fess up right here. I'm no Nigella Lawson, neither the foodie nor the sexy siren side. I bet she can whip up an Eton Mess at a moment's notice and she wouldn't necessarily serve it out of a sundae glass. Whereas I could only manage the mess, full stop

"Oh, for heaven's sake, Feef. Why didn't you call me? I could have brought something back from the store. You know what Sarah's like."

Yes, Michael. Thanks for reminding me. I do know what Sarah's like. Sarah, our elder daughter. 17, supermodel slim and permanently on a diet which she tries to cover up by claiming to be vegan. Mealtimes have turned into the frontline of the battle of the bulge. Sarah leading the rabbit food rebellion, ably assisted by younger sister Jude, part-time foot soldier in the greens regiment. And on the other side me, the oppressive frankfurter and fish finger Fuhrer, force-feeding plates of calories, carbohydrates and carcasses to the conscripted troops.

Michael, of course, is all for unconditional surrender.

"Where are the girls, anyway? Is it too much to expect someone to be around occasionally when I get home?"

You forget that no-one ever knows when exactly you will be home, Michael.

"Sarah's upstairs in her room. Doing her homework, she said."

Which would be a first.

"And Jude's at the stables."

Jude, our younger daughter, aged 16. Less of a picky eater but the pickiest of dressers. Won't wear anything that hasn't come from a charity shop, jumble sale or council skip. She calls it recycling. Michael calls it revolting.

Now he's rummaging through the fridge, much like his daughter rummages through piles of old clothes, looking for incriminating evidence, proof positive of my incompetence as a housekeeper, as if further proof were needed

"Have you seen the sell-by date on this milk, Feef? And those potatoes are going green."

I thought you said you liked green vegetables?

"I'll cut the green bits off. And I'll leave a note for the milkman."

Good job he didn't check out the carrots. They look like orange bendy toys. I'll have to hide them under the potatoes. That'll really get Sarah counting calories.

After his scintillating attempt at a conversational gambit Michael goes off to his study to check the FT, GDP and god knows what other acronym-ed indices on the worldwide web and I'm in the doghouse as usual. It's a bit of a sore spot with him, you see, this cooking housekeeping thing.

Some men have trophy wives. Michael has a trophy kitchen.

Seventy five thousand it cost, the year before last. Not that there was anything wrong with the old one. Not as far as I was concerned, anyway, but since when did my opinion count for anything around here? No, it was just, well, old. Unbefitting the area manager of a large soulless hypermarket chain where every store has a daily turnover of half a million.

So out went the chipped white tiling and in came the marble and malachite inlay. Out went battered aluminium and singed earthenware and in came

13

gleaming copper and colour-co-ordinated Le Creuset. Out went the ancient Tricity with the broken oven doorknob and only two plates that worked properly and in came the cooking island with the German cool-touch hob and two wall-mounted ovens. And out went the enemy of the ozone layer, circa 1985 and in came the Italian double-door fridge freezer with built-in wine rack and automatic icemaker. All very Euro-trendy and friendly, come to think of it. And now here it all sits, totally ignoring me and waiting for multilingual instructions from Nigella Lawson.

Well, two can play at that game. I don't need you either. Two years and I've never even used any of the pots and pans, all strung up and hanging from a rack on the ceiling like so many dead pheasants in a butchers shop. Never turned on either bit of the wall-mounted double oven, never found out how the icemaker works. And practically all that's in that great huge fridge are a few festering carrots, two bottles of white wine and a six-pack of diet Coke. Oh, and some eggs that I have every expectation may hatch any day now. I did manage to hang on to the original black-leaded stove, even though it's just for show and I swear it smirks at Michael when he passes by to plug in his fancy espresso machine.

That's why the kitchen's a bit of a sore spot with Michael.

"What's that funny smell?"

Jude The Obstreperous is back, crashing in through the back door like the CIA on a drug bust.

"It's supper. Mince, carrots and mash."

"Mum, how many times have we got to tell you, Sarah and I have given up eating meat?"

She means she's given up eating anything prepared by me and Sarah's given up eating. So is it any wonder that I don't bother filling up the fridge?

"Well you can both have the carrots and mash, then. Is that veggie enough for you?"

"Great. Sarah's vegan. She doesn't do dairy. And there's practically no protein or amino acids in that, either? Don't you know anything about basic nutrition?"

I know I'm starved of a lot of things in this house. Will that do?

"Not as much as you and your sister, apparently. First off I said 'mash'— you just assume I care enough about the end product to add butter or cream.

And second, I wouldn't recognise an amino acid if it jumped out of the pan and burned a hole in one of your father's marble worktops."

I am rewarded with a look part withering, part pitying, part contemptuous. I swear all those expensive imported Euro-appliances are glaring at me too, nodding in agreement with my dress-down, dressing down daughter. I bet Nigella Lawson doesn't smoke in front of her cool-touch hob. But then again I bet her cool-touch hob doesn't give her dirty looks all day. Until they left I never realised how close the old appliances and I had become. We seemed to speak the same language. Oh dear, does this make me a Euro-sceptic? Not that I care much one way or the other but it gives Michael something else to worry about. Half the stuff in his stores comes from Le Continent and whether in or out of the EU, he's always convinced there are new and evermore ominous trade barrier clouds on his horizon.

Jude is still giving me the disapproving eye. I decide that a proactive approach is called for.

"While you're upstairs give Sarah a shout and tell her supper will be about half an hour."

There, now I've really done it. Set myself a time limit. Ah well, better stub out the fag, kick the tyres and light the fires. I can do this.

8.00pm

"Ugh. I'm not supposed to eat this, am I? It's got milk in it. And cheese. I thought I told you last week, Jude's the lacto-vegetarian. I'm vegan. And macrobiotic. Are these carrots organic?"

Uh oh. The peasant is revolting. The veggie liberation war has begun in earnest. If she ever decides to join forces with the anti-smoking lobby I'm really in trouble. Sarah is now scraping the sauce of the carrots, kilojoule for kilojoule. What the hell is a kilojoule, anyway? Is it more or less than a calorie? Perhaps it's more or less a calorie? All I know is that it always needs to be less rather than more as far as Sarah's concerned.

"Of course. As if I'd ever try and feed you anything inorganic."

"Mum, inorganic is not the opposite of organic."

Watch out, troop reinforcements. Jude the Obtuse climbing into the fray with that look again.

"Point scored there, Feef."

15

Clearly broad linguistic skills are not one of the requirements of a regional manager of a large, chain of soulless hypermarkets, each with a daily turnover of half a million. Neither is an intimate acquaintance with exact definitions of the over-priced stock of his gourmet, fancy, fresh produce section. This ignorance, however, will not prevent him from backing the fruit of his loins to the hilt, whatever the issue, though I doubt he'd know whether said fruit was organic or otherwise.

"Actually, meine kleine professorin, it is. Don't they have any English dictionaries at that expensive social club you hang out in every Monday to Friday? For all your information the word 'organic' when used as part of the phrase 'organic vegetables' refers to the method of cultivation and not to the constitution of the plant matter itself. However, all fresh food, be it fish, flesh, fowl or vegetable, is classified as living matter and is therefore, by definition, organic. Ergo, even those carrots, half dead though they may be, still qualify. And the only inorganic matter at this dinner table are the three brass monkeys still sitting around it."

Leaving 3 mouths gaping wider than they have throughout the consumption of what was undoubtedly one of my greatest culinary failures to date, I get up, walk into the garden and throw the leftovers to the birds. Feeling that I've done my bit, even if my bit clearly wasn't good enough, I leave them all to load the dishwasher, pausing only long enough to call out

"And it was cheese and milk free, there being neither in the fridge."

Replenishing my wine on the way through, I retire to the conservatory to smoke and fume lightly.

Tuesday, April 20th

8.00am

The magic witching hour when I get to escape to work. Ink-an' Abulia, an antiquarian and second-hand bookshop, just off the High Street, quaintly closed on Mondays; purveyor of all manner of past works, fiction and non-fiction, including dictionaries. No half a million daily turnover there. Some months I suspect we don't even take enough to pay my wages which actually wouldn't worry me too much. I'd happily work for nothing. I just love being there. Sifting and sorting, buying and selling, searching and finding and, of course, reading. And every couple of months going along with George to auctions, jumble sales, car boot sales. Anywhere to restock and perhaps occasionally chance upon something rare and prized - a first edition or a much sought-after and long out-of-print literary treasure.

George Fitzsimmons. At seventy-nine, even older than most of our stock. Impeccable old-world manners and almost always dressed in the same old tweed jacket set off with one of his extensive collections of silk ties; lives in a small flat above the shop with a Bakelite radio nearly as old as he is; brews up a different blend of fine tea every day of the week in an old Crown Derby teapot which he insists must infuse for precisely five minutes, no more, no less, then it is strained through his Georgian silver strainer into china cups and saucers, after which the milk and sugar may be added (as well as a liberal lacing of single malt or five-star Napoleon brandy on late winter afternoons when the weather turns chilly). Sheer hedonism. Is it any wonder that I love my job?

8.15

I'm out of the house first. Having been informed that vegans can't have milk on cereal unless it's soy and knowing Sarah, she'd refuse to touch that unless it came with a personal note from the sharecropper guaranteeing the purity of every single bean, along with a detailed breakdown of its calorific content, I leave her nibbling away on a scant teaspoonful of dry muesli; Jude scrutinising the list of contents on a packet of cereal, accompanied by a well-rehearsed monologue on the debilitating accumulative effects of food additives; and Michael still moaning into a cup of black coffee about the sell-by date on the milk in the fridge. At the front door, I am tempted to leave the fresh milk sitting where it is but relent, bring it inside and place it in the fridge, refraining from offering it to Moaning Michael, and walk outside again.

Ensconced in the driving seat of my old Beetle, in vain do I press the starter button. Bugger! My usually trusty bug is letting me down. That means I'll have to ask Michael for a lift. I can hear him already.

For heaven's sake, Feef, I've told you before. Get rid of that ugly old heap and get something more reliable.

17

By reliable he means newer, more upmarket, more suited to the wife of the Area Manager of a big soulless hypermarket chain with a turnover of half a million a day. He'd like me to join the posse of four by four poseurs that he sees in the supermarket car park every day. Four by fours? That's a laugh. The closest any of those silly bitches ever get to off-roading is when one of them drives their luxury SUV onto the kerb by mistake; which happens quite a lot because most of them aren't mentally equipped to handle anything larger than a shopping trolley. Or maybe Michael sees me in a nice sporty little urban run-around from a factory somewhere in Western Europe. That way I could blend in with the appliances.

"For heaven's sake, Feef, why do you insist on keeping that old wreck. Tell Joe to hang on to it and sell it for scrap."

Told you.

"You know I won't be able to bring you home. You'll have to find your own way."

In case you're wondering, the reason he can't give me a lift home is that the bookshop closes at 5 or thereabouts, depending on what the weather's like and how busy we are, whereas Michael's hypermarket is open twenty-four hours. And he never gets home before 7.

Come to think of it, recently it's often been quite a bit later than that.

"It's a bit girly for you, isn't it?"

"Sorry?"

"Your air freshener. It smells like a Parisian tart's boudoir in here."

"I can't smell anything."

But he opens the windows all the same, simultaneously hooting loudly for the girls.

Jude flies out of the house wearing a pair of Victorian high button boots and a navy skirt that looks like part of a World War 2 Wren's uniform. At least it's in the school colours, I suppose. Not that I really care. Actually, it looks rather fetching with the striped blazer and straw boater.

"I hope they're not going to send you home for wearing that outfit."

Clearly, Michael doesn't share my view.

"I rather hope they are. I could do with a day off. I haven't finished my English essay and it's due in today."

"Christ, Jude, have you any idea how much that school costs me a year? What on earth is the use of me forking our all that money to send you there if you can't even make an effort? Why do I bother?"

"Yes, I do, you've told us often enough. None at all, I suppose. Haven't a clue. Nobody asked you to. In that order."

Michael is about to climb onto his privilege and private education soapbox when Sarah comes out of the house, hugging a pile of books to her chest. The dark blue uniform makes her look thinner than ever and the way her blazer hangs puts me in mind of the tattered coat upon a stick in Yeats' poem. She really is beginning to look very thin.

I too wind down my window and light a cigarette. I know it will annoy everyone but suddenly I feel the need.

Michael glares but says nothing. He puts the car in drive and we glide off in an uncomfortable silence.

As I walk in the shop, the bell on the door tinkles cheerfully. The silence is broken. George comes through from the back and I note that today is red with a thin black stripe.

"Ffion, a very good morning to you. The kettle's on. A Prince of Wales morning, I think, don't you?"

As George bustles off to make the tea, I sift through the post. Two circulars listing forthcoming sales, one request from a customer in Edinburgh for an early edition of Alice in Wonderland, a christening present for a niece apparently, and a mail shot from Michael's hypermarket advertising the week's specials. This latter item I throw straight into the bin. I know that we have several volumes of Alice and looking them over I select an attractive 1890 edition bound in red with gold leaf lettering on the cover and containing superb examples of the Tenniel plates. I wrap the book in tissue paper, write out an invoice, pop it and the book into a cardboard box and address it to the customer. Then I mark the sales dates in the diary. One of them looks very promising, an auction of the contents of a large estate not too far away, Featherington Hall. Shortly to be transmogrified into a number of bijou yuppie pieds-a-terre, leaving what promises to be a delightfully eclectic library of old books to be disposed of. When George comes in with the tea and a packet of digestive biscuits I tell him about the sale. His eyes light up.

"Capital, Ffion, capital. Who knows what little gems could have been lurking on the racks there? It's early Stuart, you know, Featherington Hall.

19

Built by Charles Bartholomew, 3rd Earl of Richfield. Did they send a catalogue, by an chance?"

"Nope. Just the flier. I'll phone them up and ask if one's available. Otherwise we'll just have to wait till the preview."

The shop bell tinkles as the door opens to admit an elderly lady. Mrs Barnes. One of our regulars and always first in on Tuesdays. I think she smells the tea brewing. George has already fetched another cup and saucer. They sit together on the battered old sofa and are soon onto their favourite topic. Agatha Christie—better in print, on the box or on the big screen. Discuss. You can see why George chose the name of his little literary establishment, can't you? Part book club, part Bloomsbury salon, part gossip circle and who cares if the customers never quite make up their minds about their purchase before closing time—there's always tomorrow. Leaving them happily tut-tutting about the current crop of remakes peppered with four-letter words, I begin to catalogue and stack a box of old Penguin paperbacks that Jude found in a charity shop over the weekend.

And my mind begins to wander.

And wonder.

I wonder, for instance, why Michael seems to have suddenly developed a taste, or should that be a nose, for scented air fresheners. He always claims to revel in the smell of his meticulously maintained leather upholstery which someone from the warehouse has to clean weekly with expensive dressing. No point in asking him. He'll only say it's to mask the odious odour of my tobacco.

And I wonder what to do about Sarah. She's clearly getting thinner and thinner. Is it just dieting or could it be something more serious? I try to recall articles I've seen in magazines about eating disorders. What do other mothers do in such cases? I conjure up images of skeletal teenagers, hospital beds, psychiatric wards. The images depress and frighten me. But surely Sarah isn't that bad? I know she doesn't eat much but then I don't cook much, do I? I just have to learn to come up with the sort of stuff she wants to eat. Which if I remember rightly is macrobiotic, organic, non-dairy, non-animal, non-existent. Mind you, I bet Michael's poncy chain must have a section that caters for picky eaters. All those tarted-up stick insects that parade around his aisles every day looking like they've never seen a square meal in their lives—surely they must ingest something other than diet pills and designer coke occasionally? He must have something suitable there somewhere. I'll ask him tonight.

And maybe I'll ask Jude if she thinks Sarah might have a problem. Then again, maybe not.

And while I'm berating myself for my apparent bad parenting, I glance at the calendar and know with certainty that it's true. A bad parent, a bad person and Sarah is the penance I must pay.

1pm

George is upstairs heating up a tin of mulligatawny soup for us. I decide to nip around the corner to the bakery and buy some fresh rolls. I call to George to listen out for the shop bell, slip on my jacket and walk quickly to Simmonds. It's an old family firm, part of the fabric of the high street. A very flimsy fabric these days. Shops like Simmonds just can't compete with the big boys. Big boys like Pricerite, Michael's hypermarket. They claim they have a bakery but it's not quite the same, somehow. Even fresh from the ovens you can smell the con. Cottonwool with a crust. Still, the 4 by 4 poseurs seem to like it, fawning over the focaccia ("Shall we have rosemary and garlic tonight, Basil?"), humming and hawing over the hamburger buns ("Sesame or poppy, poppet?"), raving about the rye ("Dark or light or would somewhere in between be more politically correct?")

Leaving the shop with a brown paper bag containing two warm, floury baps, I pop into the newsagents and search through the women's magazine section. Not my taste in light reading normally but today I'm looking for something in particular. Ah, this one looks promising. Mother's Monthly. "I nearly lost my child". Readers' heart-breaking stories of the power of a mothers love. I pay for the magazine and fork out for 40 cigarettes at the same time. I've a feeling I'm going to need them.

4pm

Joe, the owner of our local garage, phones. Apparently the bug needs a new carburettor. Joe says it's taken him all day to track one down so I won't have the car back till tomorrow afternoon. Will that be a problem? Only to Michael I think, but don't say. That'll give him something else to sulk about. Thanking

Joe, I put down the phone. The shop is quiet so I open the window, pick up the magazine and surreptitiously light a cigarette.

5pm

I've finished the article about Joan from Abingdon relating how she had to stand by helplessly and watch as her daughter battled a life-threatening eating disorder and I'm only on my third secret cigarette which all things considered I think is pretty good going. Just as I feared it seems that Sarah is showing all the classic early signs of anorexia. Food fads, obsessive exercising and calorie counting, a recent switch from tight to baggy clothes. Apparently experts are still puzzling over what turns a fairly normal teenage desire to weight-watch into a wasting disease which the victim is powerless to control or cure. But the one thing they all seem to agree on is that it's all the parents' fault. Now why doesn't that surprise me? I say goodbye to George and leave to catch the bus.

I've always liked buses, especially double-deckers but today I'm not in the mood to enjoy anything much. I find a seat on top, right at the front and settle back to worry and watch the world go by. And as the bus pulls onto the dual carriageway, past Pricerite I catch a glimpse of Michael in the car park, standing by a small, silver hatchback. He's talking to the driver, a blonde woman of indeterminate age. One of his high rolling customers, no doubt. Platinum store charge cards and on-line ordering. I don't bother to wave. He wouldn't see me. People on buses don't have faces as far as Michael's concerned.

5.45pm

Jude is out at the stables as usual and there's a message on the answering machine from Sarah saying she's gone to the gym. She's been doing that a lot lately. Just socialising and keeping fit, I'd thought, before I read the Woman's Monthly article. On an impulse I decide to go up to her room. I hardly ever do that and I feel guilty, like I'm spying or something. I expect a tip but surprisingly the room is almost clinically tidy. Bed made, DVD collection neatly stacked, books tidily arranged next to the laptop. On the bedside table is a magazine with some waif-like teen model on the cover, along with a free gift that came with it, a little pocket calculator called 'Your Handy Calorie

22

Counter'. Next to that is a notebook which I glance at. It appears to be some sort of a diary with what I take to be her total calorie consumption recorded every day. I note with anxiety the entry for yesterday. Monday, 17th April. 'Did really well. Only 360 ALL DAY! Farewell fat Sarah forever.' I have no idea where 360 calories comes in the scale of normality and I turn to the Handy Calorie Counter for assistance. Alas, it is of the digital kind, like those little hand-held computer games and as with the games I fail miserably to score. I put it back on the bedside table and resolve to try the shop stock for more information.

Moving across the room I open the wardrobe door and suddenly recoil, feeling faint. Pasted onto the inside of the door is a collage of pictures of stick-thin models. Models in swimwear, models in the latest lingerie, models in summer t-shirts and shorts. All of them bony, emaciated, skeletal clothes hangers. And where the room is barrack room presentable, the wardrobe is in total disarray. Clothes strewn all over the bottom of the cupboard, some items in shreds. I pick one of them up, a cotton spandex top that I know she only bought a couple of weeks ago at a trendy Birmingham boutique. It's been cut to ribbons with a pair of scissors. I stare at it bewildered and then I fall to the floor and cry my eyes out.

6.15pm

I slip my jacket on, clip a leash on Cromwell's collar and walk to our local shops. There's a greengrocers, a delicatessen cum mini mart, a post office, a hardware store and an off-licence and they know me by name in all of them. The greengrocers has tables of fresh produce outside and I select button mushrooms, peas still in the pod, green beans, purple calabrese and carrots of the non-bendy variety, all of which I pack into small brown paper bags for weighing. Once inside I take a tin of plum tomatoes, a packet of wholemeal spaghetti and a loaf of brown bread. Not up to Simmonds' standards but it looks nutritious enough. At the off-licence I buy 2 bottles of Chilean Cabernet Sauvignon which John, the owner, recommends. Then home via the common, where I let Cromwell off the leash and let him run and sniff while I sit on a bench and smoke. Before leaving I break off a piece of the loaf and feed it to the ducks. I know they don't really need it and the fowl police will frown but it's nice to see something I serve up being eaten.

23

7.15

I prepare pasta primavera with fresh vegetables and love, irrationally hoping that a sudden and probably long overdue metamorphosis into earth mother might cure my sick child. I will nurture her with good, wholesome vegan food, and she will eat and grow strong and healthy. And my younger daughter will be transformed into Jude the Amenable, Michael will turn into Steve, Philip will step in from the wings and I'll have no more need of my nocturnal cast of fantasy, 20-something extras. Then all the Euro appliances will stand around like the chorus in a Greek tragedy as the deus ex machina in the form of the kitchen god descends to chide us mere mortals for our silly human foibles. And Sarah will offer up a prayer of thanks to the kitchen god for his benevolence and beneficence and bless the Euro appliances for guiding me along the path of maternal righteousness. And as the kitchen god ascends to take his place on the Euro butter mountain, the curtain will descend on a cowed and chastened group, all of whom have learnt the error of their wicked mortal ways.

Pasta vincit omnia.

What was that? 'Who the hell are Steve and Philip?', you ask. All in good time, after I've swallowed a few bravery pills.

7.45

The girls are both back. I screwed up my courage to ask Sarah about the ripped clothes but one look at her pursed lips and dead eyes as she pushed past me and it failed me. She went up to her room to shower and change and I shrank from confrontation as I always do. Jude, arriving a little while later, could not contain her surprise as she walked through the kitchen on her way upstairs and found me julienning carrots—the fresh, crisp variety—and dicing peppers.

"You finally found where the knives are kept, then?"

A cutting remark. I would expect nothing less from my razor-witted youngest. And these thoughts bring me back to the dark secrets of Sarah's wardrobe. On an impulse I hear myself asking

"Jude, have you noticed anything odd about Sarah lately?"

"What do you mean, odd?"

That's right, answer a question with a question. Jude the Evasive. I knew it would be a waste of time asking her anything about her sister. They can be thick as thieves when it suits them and it usually suits them whenever it's a 'them and us' situation. Even when they were toddlers they used to cover up for each other. I wonder if boys are easier?

That's something I'll probably never know now.

Michael's car pulls into the drive. Suddenly I don't want to be caught in the act of cooking when he comes in, don't want to face the inevitable sarcastic remark. So I leave the pungent aroma of garlic and herbs and slip upstairs to Sarah's room. I knock lightly and call 'Sarah, it's me', but enter without waiting for a reply.

She is on her bed watching something on her tablet. She scarcely bothers to look up as I enter.

"Sarah, you are all right, aren't you?"

"Of course I am. Why shouldn't I be?"

Her tone is harsh, belligerent.

"No reason. I just thought you were looking a bit peaky this morning. I wondered if you were coming down with something."

"I'm fine. Just getting some 'me' time"

She glares at me pointedly.

"Sorry. Didn't mean to interrupt. I'm making pasta for supper, vegetarian. No dairy products, especially for you."

"I'm not really hungry."

"Well, maybe your appetite will improve when you see it."

"Maybe"

I am dismissed. She has now returned her full attention to the social media feed on the screen. Telling myself that Rome wasn't built in a day, I go downstairs. Michael is in the kitchen. As I walk in he asks

"What's going on? Have we hired a housekeeper?"

He has more in common with his younger daughter than either of them would care to admit.

I ignore the barb.

"Michael we need to talk."

"Not now, Feef. I need a shower. I've had a helluva day. One of the warehouse refrigeration plants broke down last night and this morning we had to junk an entire consignment of fresh fish. Salmon, turbot, bloody Beluga

25

caviar. The lot. Then just before I left one of our lorry drivers phoned from a police station in Folkstone. Apparently the police did a random check on his truck this side of the Channel Tunnel and found 5 illegal immigrants hiding in the back. I'm going to have to drive down there first thing tomorrow morning and try and sort it out. They're nearly all perishables, wouldn't you know it."

"Where did they come from?"

"France, of course."

"No, I meant before that."

"What do you mean, before that? They're all French—cheeses, charcuterie, soft fruit. It's the seafood I'm really worried about."

"Not the stuff in the lorry. The illegals. I wonder where they're from."

"Who the hell cares? All I know is they've got my lorry impounded and my driver in chokey. And if I don't get them both released first thing tomorrow that's a very expensive consignment of fresh food I'm going to have to write off. Two in 2 days. The insurance company's going to love that."

Shedding his jacket and loosening his tie, Michael heads out of the kitchen and upstairs to wash away the sins of today. Would that it were that easy for all of us.

Supper is hardly the catharsis I'd hoped for. Michael is still bemoaning the loss of the fish. Listening to him anyone would think he'd been out on a boat catching every one of them personally. Not to mention his captive lorry driver and the truckload des fruits et fromages.

Jude the Obsessed gives us all a long lecture on the indignities and iniquities of being a political refugee and quizzes Michael at length on their fate. His only reply is 'They can all go to hell as far as I'm concerned'. Fairly understandable under the circumstances, I suppose. I hope my younger daughter is not planning on a career in public relations.

And Sarah pushes her food around the plate so much I feel dizzy watching. Which I do surreptitiously. And I notice that not much of it is actually consumed. After a quarter of an hour of this pasta PE she throws her napkin onto her plate in what I assume is an effort to conceal the uneaten portion, picks it up and scrapes the leftovers into the dogs' bowls, telling us that she's off upstairs to finish her homework. Funny, I didn't know she'd started.

Michael drains his third glass of wine and heads off to his study to make some phone calls.

Jude grabs her mobile and also takes off upstairs, dialling as she goes.

I suppose that means it's my turn to load the dishwasher? Instead, I open the second bottle of wine and drink a silent toast to a young man who will have his twenty second birthday in a few days' time. And as ever I won't be there to celebrate, to hug him, tell him how proud I am of him and that I'll always be there for him, no more than I was on all his other birthdays. Because I won't, will I? I never was.

I met Michael in my second year at uni. I went up to Bristol the year after I left school and I tried very hard to be a carefree student. I partied and pub crawled, studied and smoked dope and tried to forget. Some days I almost managed it. Almost. At weekends I went up on the Downs and rode and when I rode I thought of Philip. And then I went home and tried not to think about him. Sometimes it even worked.

Michael was a graduate student, doing an MA in Business Studies. I met him at an arts cinema screening of Cousin, Cousine, in the bar at the interval. I was waiting to be served and I couldn't catch the bartender's eye. He was a lot taller than me and he saw me struggling so he just lifted me up and elbowed his way to the front. I got my half pint of lager and Michael at the same time.

He was the complete antithesis of all my other uni mates. He knew all the best pubs in the city where they had live jazz or real ale or both and all the most picturesque hostelries for miles in all directions. And it didn't hurt that he was incredibly good-looking. Only problem was that he didn't have too much in common with my old friends, particularly my roomies, Patti and Pip, which did cause a certain amount of froideur when they met up. They were both reading English with me and we hung around together all the time. Patti was from The Smoke and had that air of big city sophistication that only comes from being brought up in the capital while Pip, real name Alan Naseby, was from the Yorkshire Dales and the big city lights of Bristol completely dazzled him. He was a pretty good amateur guitarist and the three of us spent a fair few nights in our poky little flat in Clifton, smoking weed and consuming copious amounts of lager, him strumming one of his compositions and Patti and I chipping in with un-harmonious singing. Michael made no secret of the fact that he disapproved of the weed smoking, the late-night drinking sessions and my choice of companions. In his opinion it, and they, were extremely juvenile. Patti, ever the perspicacious one, expressed reservations.

"He's a Grade A Asshole, Fee. He's pompous and there's something about him I just don't like. I can't quite put my finger on it but he gives me the creeps."

I told her he was just more mature.

"He accused me of going off the rails. I told him 'We're students. That's what we're supposed to do.'"

There was no love lost between them, even then.

He taught me to drive his German coupé, gritting his teeth when I crashed the five-speed gearbox, and he couldn't understand why I wouldn't teach him to horse ride in return.

"It's because your name's not Philip", I told him, if pressed. And let it go at that.

And when I went riding I pictured my baby learning to crawl, taking his first tentative steps, speaking his first word. I read somewhere that nearly all babies learn to say 'mama' first. It's an easy sound to make, you see. But you're not his mama, I wanted to say to the woman who had my son, the woman who was bringing him up as her own. And I told myself 'he'll never be yours really'. And I hoped that somewhere deep inside she was telling herself the same thing.

By the start of my final year Michael and I were sort of an item. I moved out of the Clifton flat and into his much larger place off Whiteladies Road. Sometimes on Saturday mornings, we'd shop for furnishings. His tastes ran to white wood and Swedish chrome modern while I was all for trawling the second-hand stalls down the Gloucester Road for anything that took my eye—Victorian mahogany furniture, art deco ornaments, Edwardian kitchenware, all of which Michael would wrinkle his nose up at but he left me to it. He was working so hard on his thesis(which I gathered was something to do with how mobility and modern communications made multi-nationalism an inevitability) that I doubt he really noticed.

Looking back I can see that the Pricerite seeds had been sown a long time before. Also that I probably should have been a bit more assertive, not to mention perspicacious but then hindsight's a wonderful gift, as they say. At any rate, with his being so engrossed in his studies, that left me plenty of free time to hang out with Patti and Pip, away from his disapproving, black looks.

I was hoping for a career in publishing. Most of the big houses were in London but there were one or two good-sized ones in Bristol. By now I felt *really at home there so I thought I'd give the local ones a go first. I mentioned it once or twice to Michael but each time he seemed rather non-committal: A bit vague, dismissive even. I ignored him and wrote off to them anyway. Patti, at least, was supportive.*

Friday, 21st April

5.45am

Michael is up already, anxious to be on the road to Folkstone as soon as possible. I tell him I'll be fine on the bus and ask if he wants a cup of tea. He declines and says he'll pick something up on the road. I hear his car pull out of the driveway and I turn the radio on to catch the news and boil the kettle. The girls won't be up for another couple of hours yet so I can light my first cigarette of the day without fear of recrimination.

7.45am

I go upstairs and ask the girls if they want to come with me on the bus. You'd have thought I'd asked them to accompany me into the jaws of hell.

"Nobody takes the bus, mum. Honestly, what would people think".

Jude the Upstart. People would probably think she needed a ride.

"The bus stops miles away from the school. You can't expect us to walk all that way with our books and stuff."

Sarah. The same Sarah who exercises obsessively at the local gym in order to lose more of what little weight she still has. Clearly walking is not on the list of approved aerobic exercises.

"Well, how are you going to get to school, then? You know the bug's still at the garage."

"As if we'd be seen dead driving up in that thing. Anyway, how do you think we're going to get there?"

Jude is already on the phone, making an arrangement with one of her friends for a lift. Her tone of voice suggests hardship, parental cruelty, social humiliation. Then she bounces upstairs, calling to me that Amanda and her mother will be here any minute and not on any account to smoke in front of them.

I'm in the kitchen, writing a note for Jenny, our three times a week daily, with one hand and trying to button my jacket with the other when their ride arrives—a silver Mini with a very glamorous blonde woman in the driving seat whom I recognise vaguely from school functions and Jude's friend, Amanda, sitting next to her. I walk into the hall and shout upstairs to Sarah and Jude, at the same time opening the front door and greeting the occupants of the car.

"You must be Fenella", says the glamorous blonde.

She knows my first name, well, sort of. This surprises me. I certainly don't know hers.

"I'm sorry. Have we met? I've got a memory like a sieve for names."

"I don't think so. But Jude and Amanda ride together and she often talks about you."

This doesn't surprise me. More like amazes. I refrain from a cynical rebuttal and instead smile politely and comment on the lovely car.

She giggles lightly and manages to look even more embarrassed. I'm missing something here.

Jude and Sarah come out of the house together and Amanda swivels around to greet them as they climb in the back.

"Right, we'd better be off or we'll be late. Can we drop you anywhere? It'll be a bit of a squeeze in the back but I daresay we'll manage, won't we girls? I'm Louise, by the way. But everyone calls me Lulu."

"No, don't worry. I can take the bus. The stop's almost right outside the main gate. Door to door, easier than driving really."

For this babbling I am rewarded with dagger-like looks from both my daughters and I think, not for the first time, that it is a great pity that Michael didn't choose a school with boarding facilities or even better, the local comprehensive. I watch the sexy hatchback glide out of the drive, vaguely wondering why it looks familiar. Then as soon as it's out of sight I light my third cigarette of the day, pick up my handbag and walk to the bus stop.

1.30pm

"Feef, listen, something's come up."

I'm still at work and it's Michael on his cell phone. There is traffic noise in the background and the signal isn't very strong. I struggle to hear him.

"Are you having problems with the police?"

30

"What? Oh, no. That's all sorted out. The driver's out on bail and on his way back now. It'll have to go to court eventually but the company can deal with it. No, it's not that. It's Paul Matthews."

"Who?"

"The Pricerite area manager down here. He was taken ill a couple of days ago. He's still off sick and Francis asked me if I'd fill in for him. His deputy's away on leave and it's a bit chaotic with all the building work going on."

Francis Weston. Chairman of Pricerite. Numero uno. The biggest fromage in its fancy delicatessen. Thinks the sun shines out of Michael's backside and uses him as the corporate trouble-shooter whenever it suits him. And Michael plays along because he knows that ultimately he'll be rewarded with a seat on the board.

"Where will you stay? You didn't even take a change of clothes with you."

"They do have hotels here, you know. And clothes shops."

"I suppose so. But we do need to talk. How long do you think you'll be there?"

"Talk about what?"

Is it my imagination or does he sound suddenly defensive? Hard to tell with this line.

"Whatever it is, I'm sure it can wait for a couple of days. Three or four at the most."

"I suppose it'll have to. I don't want to discuss it over the phone."

"That sounds serious."

He manages an unconvincing laugh. I think I was right first time. He does sound guarded. Guilty even. I'm not sure why. It's not the first time he's been away from home on company business. In fact this must be at least the fourth or fifth time this year. It never seems to have bothered him before.

"Look, Feef, I've got to go. I need to pick up a suit and a couple of changes of clothes and get out to the store. I'll give you a buzz when I know what's happening."

The line goes dead.

A couple of customers are browsing happily in the shop and I idly pick up the copy of Mothers' Monthly again. This time I turn to read about Susan from Glasgow and her reunion with her long-lost daughter. And as I take in the article my heart skips a beat. Susan had a daughter when she was only sixteen and her parents forced her to have it adopted. And after years of self-

31

recrimination and grieving she finally made contact with her through some website. Apparently it's completely confidential. You just register and then you can leave a message giving all your details and asking your adopted son or daughter to contact you in confidence through the site. Or vice versa, for adopted kids desperately seeking their birth parents. And then by mutual consent you can even arrange a meeting. My hands are shaking as I copy down the site address. And for the first-time ever I wish that we had a computer in the shop.

I called my son Philip, lover of horses. I wonder if he is? But how would I know? I've had no contact with him for twenty two years, ever since the day he was born. They took him away from me straightaway. Said it was better that way. A fleeting glimpse of some straw-coloured hair and a little crushed red face in a blue receiving blanket and he was gone. My son. The child I had carried for nine long months, never allowing myself to feel connected, never daring to dream of motherhood. I was only seventeen myself, then, you see. Starting my final year at school and looking forward to my first year at Uni, reading English at Bristol, with sights set on a career in publishing. And my parents were horrified. How will you be able to study with a young baby, they kept asking. It'll ruin your life. And your career. On and on, right through my second trimester while I tried to come to terms with what was happening. All my friends were working for their A-Levels and making plans for their fresher years while my life was on hold. My due date was mid-April so I finished the first term, went back to school briefly in the New Year for my mocks, then went away. In the end I took the line of least resistance. My parents, the local Catholic priest, they even sent my headmistress around one day and they all said the same thing.

"Give the baby up. You're still young. There'll be plenty of time for a family later. After you've finished your studies. Think of all those poor childless couples out there dying for one of their own. You can make them so happy."

But what about me, I thought, as I finally capitulated under the barrage of well-meaning advice and allowed myself to be bullied into putting him up for adoption Does anyone care if I'm happy?

The father was someone I'd met through a friend of a friend while I was in the Lower Sixth, from Shropshire, originally. Everyone called him Jack but his real name was James, James Daniel Greville, and he was reading astrophysics at Liverpool Uni. We met at a party while he was staying with the afore-mentioned friend of a friend and dated casually for all that year and into the next, whenever he was in the area. He was cute and clever and we had fun. I was a bit smitten but I always assumed he was probably seeing other people when he was back in Liverpool. So when I found out I was knocked up, I couldn't bring myself to tell him. Somehow I thought he might think I'd done it on purpose—I hadn't, of course, but that's teen angst for you. Ergo, he had no inkling till he came down in December. I was 4 months and hardly showed, he wanted to have sex, I didn't and eventually I had to tell him why. I remember the look of shock on his face.

"Filly, why didn't you tell me? Shouldn't we talk?"

"What about? Family planning? Bit late for that."

My sick sense of humour was alive and well, even back then.

"No, about us, this."

"There isn't really an 'us', is there? We're just part-time casual. As for 'this', I have to make a plan. Till then it's probably better if we don't see each other for a while."

"Just let me know if you need anything."

There's an awkward pause.

"I mean it."

But I didn't. I walked away from him and swore the friend who'd introduced us to secrecy. This was something I had to deal with myself. I never contacted him or saw him again. I missed him but it just would have made a tricky situation even worse.

Philip was born 4 ½ months later and the next day he too was gone.

I never told another soul who the father was. Apart from Patti, of course. We told each other everything.

Monday, 24th April

7.15am

I hardly slept all night. No healthy young men this time but images of death. Flowers and funerals, coffins and cemeteries. Dead daughters, dead babies, dead lovers, dead relationships. This is always a bad day for me but this year I have other things to worry about as well. Sarah, who may be starving

33

herself to death and who will not let me close enough to help her. Philip, or whatever his name is now, twenty two today who probably never so much as spares me a passing thought. And Michael on a business trip and it seems a guilt trip too. I suppose I should feel grateful for Jude the Acidic, no hidden agenda there, just a quick wit, a nice line in sarcasm and the pithy put-down.

On an impulse I phone Michael.

"I've got the bug back. It only needed a carburettor."

"It needs putting out of its misery."

I ignore the sarcasm.

"I was wondering if I should come down on Sunday."

"No, don't do that."

He didn't give that much thought.

"We really need to talk. Undisturbed."

"Whatever it is you want to discuss, I'm sure it can wait. I'm up to my eyes at the store sorting out the mess that Paul's absence caused. The whole system here needs overhauling to cope with the expansion. I need to be on hand. Plus I'm dealing with contractors from morning to night. The re-vamp's supposed to be finished by the end of the month and as far as I can see it's nowhere near ready. I'm going to be working 25 hours a day."

Where the hell did that come from, anyway? You know how much you hate confrontation. Get a grip.

"I'm heading on over now. I suppose it's just as well you've got the car back. At least you can run the girls to school."

"Hardly. They won't be seen dead in it, apparently. They've arranged a lift with some woman called Louise, silver Mini Clubman, very affected. Calls herself Lulu, for god's sake."

"Amanda's mother."

How on earth does he know that? I suppose he just takes more of an interest in who's who in the zoo than I do. Which wouldn't take much.

I sit at the kitchen table and light another cigarette. It's going to be a long day.

I've managed to keep quite busy, thank goodness. The Featherington Hall sale catalogue arrived in the morning post so I went through it with a fine tooth comb, marking all the lots I think George will be interested in. Apart from all the usual bound collections you'd expect and some first editions which will be probably fetch far too much, there are several lots of loose books which are unlisted. These are always worth bidding on—you get a lot of mundane stuff but there's nearly always a gem or two tucked in amongst them. Then while I was going through the catalogue, 2 second-year English students down for the summer break come in with their next term's list They're doing the Romantic poets, one of George's areas of expertise. I call him over and they wander happily off with George detailing the complicated and somewhat debauched lives of the major Romantics, who, in the fashion of the day, indulged in remarkably decadent and bohemian lifestyles which to a large extent precipitated to the Victorian era of virtue and chastity shortly to follow.

"Though even Wordsworth", he whispers conspiratorially, "wasn't the model of respectability he's often assumed to have been. He had a rather, er, close relationship with his sister"

Their presence leads my thoughts right back to where they've been on and off all day. Is my son at university? Which one? What is he reading? I hope it's not the sciences, like his father. And definitely not business studies. He might even have graduated by now. Where is he? What's his name? What's he doing? A thousand questions and not a single answer.

Pushing these thoughts aside I walk over to our cookery section and run through what we've got. 'Basic Nutrition for Dieticians'. That looks promising. I flick through the pages, stop, read, re-read and get that sick feeling again. According to this, a healthy, active, adolescent female should have a daily calorie intake of 2000—2500. And I recall Sarah's diary entry saying that hers was a mere 360. There must be some mistake. I vaguely recall that calories have been re-valued sometime. Or was that kilojoules? The date on the book is 1979. That's quite a long time ago. That must be what it is. Calories were different then.

I close the shop and drive to the local library. Normally I'd walk but the rain Michael was complaining about has moved up to us with a vengeance. The bug's wipers can hardly keep up. Actually I'm glad. Sunny wouldn't suit me at all today.

Once inside the rather austere Victorian façade I go to the front desk. A young man with spiky bleached hair and a nose stud is standing behind. He looks up as I approach.

"Um, I need to use one of the computers."

"Help yourself. They're all free. It's the rain."

"I want to get onto the internet."

"They're all on-line. Anyone'll do."

"I'm a bit out of practice." I look at the row of space-age, flat-screen models and a mild panic sets in.

"I've never used one of those."

He looks up at me in surprise.

"Got a Mac at home, have you?"

I find the question incongruous but assume he is politely referencing the inclement weather.

"I always keep a coat in my car. But I didn't bother putting it on. I managed to park right outside."

He is looking at me rather oddly, sizing me up. He makes a decision.

"I'll help you boot up."

I smile gratefully, ingratiatingly.

He comes out from behind the desk and I follow him through to the computer section, marvelling as he glides his fingers over the keyboard, as practised as a concert pianist.

"I just want to look up a website I read about."

"Browse as many as you want. It's so quiet there's no rush. My name's Brian, by the way.

"Thanks, Brian."

He saunters off, hands in his pockets, master of the cyberspace universe. I wait till he's gone and pull the magazine article out of my bag, carefully noting the website details. Then I gingerly type in the name and suddenly, there it is. 'Welcome to Mother & Child Reunion', accompanied by a chorus of the Paul Simon track of the same name. The burst of music in the quiet library causes Brian to glance over in my direction and I give him two thumbs up. He responds in the same vein and turns back to his work. As the site comes up there's an on-screen introduction and a few details on how it works with all details cross-referenced using a sophisticated algorithm, I click on the button marked 'Mothers' and a new page comes up, inviting me to leave details of my child's birth and adoption—place of birth, name of the hospital, date, sex etc. And underneath there's a little box where you can leave a personal message. I think for a moment, then write 'I called you Philip. I hope you really do love horses. I hope you love your adoptive parents. And I hope you can find it in your heart to try and forgive me.' Then I click 'finish'. A message tells me that my details had been stored and would be posted on the site and suggests I check in weekly to see if any response has been received. It also cautions that not all searches are successful.

It's almost 2. I wave goodbye to Brian at the desk and make a dash for the car. Is it my imagination or is the rain easing off just a little?

Saturday, 29th April

"Mum, is it okay if Amanda stays for the weekend?"

I'm in the kitchen making toast before work and Jude's question takes me a little by surprise. She's not usually one for bringing friends home. She's afraid they'll catch me smoking, drinking or generally letting the side down.

"Shit!"

I burn my hands on the toast, lifting it out of the toaster and in doing so I drop it and it ends up on the kitchen floor. I pick it up, dust it and put it on a plate.

"You're not going to eat that, are you?"

"That was the general idea, yes. You and Sarah might be able to exist on fresh air and principles but I can't."

"I would eat if you'd buy some decent food. Anyway, please don't do anything like that in front of Amanda. It is all right if she comes, is it?"

"I suppose so. What's the occasion?"

There's a horse show in Fairfield this afternoon. We're going to ride over together and it'll probably finish quite late. Oh, and can you pick us up from the stables afterwards?"

This last remark is thrown in casually but I'm not fooled. Jude has now turned her back and is apparently studying the fruit bowl intently.

"In the bug, you mean?" I try not to smile. "I thought it was beneath your dignity?"

"It's not that. It's just not very reliable, is it?"

I ignore this sudden volte face towards my people's wagon.

"What about Amanda's mother? Won't she pick you up?"

"She can't. She's out of town for the weekend. And her dad's on an overseas trip. Won't be back till the middle of next week"

"Well, if you think the bug can be trusted to get us back in one piece, I suppose I can. What time do you need picking up?"

"I'm not sure exactly. We're both jumping in the last class. It depends on how big it is and if they start on time. Plus if either of us gets placed we'll have to stay till the end. I'll phone you when we get back to the yard."

"Fine."

I pause and Jude is halfway out of the door.

"Jude"

She catches something in my tone of voice and stops.

"What?"

"Do you think Sarah is eating all right. She's looking awfully thin. Actually I'm a bit worried about her."

Jude turns round.

"I know. I've noticed."

"Noticed what? That she's getting thin or that I'm worried?"

"Both."

"Well, do you think I'm right to worry?"

She studies her feet more intently than the fruit bowl.

"I suppose she has lost a bit of weight recently."

Jude the Embarrassed.

"How much, do you know?"

"A bit. I don't know. I haven't asked her."

Jude the Evasive is creeping back.

"I really am worried, you know."

"It's a bit late for that, isn't it? All this earth mother stuff you've been coming up with. It doesn't fool anyone. Sarah thinks…"

She stops abruptly. She obviously feels she's gone too far.

"Sarah thinks what? You might as well tell me."

"Well, Sarah thinks you're having some sort of mid-life crisis. She thinks it's you who's been acting oddly lately."

I open my mouth to refute this accusation but stop before the words come out. Perhaps she's right. Maybe that's what it's all about? A mid-life crisis. All this fantasising over young men. One in particular. And now maybe putting my name on that website will be like lighting a powder keg? What will the girls think when they suddenly discover they have a half-brother they've never even heard of? And how will Michael react when he finds out I'm trying to make contact with a child that isn't his and whom he has airbrushed out of existence? I think I can guess the answer to that one.

Jude looks at my stricken face and misinterprets.

"I shouldn't have told you that. Sarah will kill me."

I make an effort to smile.

"I won't mention it if you don't. Look Jude, I've got to get to work. Try and get Sarah to eat some breakfast when she gets up. Toast and honey. There's a loaf of organic wholemeal in the fridge. And a small pot of Manuka honey I bought for her specially."

"She doesn't usually bother with breakfast."

Lately she doesn't seem to bother with any meals at all, I think, but don't say.

"Can we talk more about this later? Maybe I have been a bit distracted lately. I've got a lot on my mind. But I really am desperately worried about Sarah's weight. You read so many awful stories."

Jude says nothing, just studies her feet and frowns. I pick up my jacket and handbag and head out.

Michael proposed just before graduation. He had suggested we go out for dinner, though I had no idea of the significance of the occasion. He took me to a very expensive restaurant called La Vie en Rose. All the waiters wore black dinner jackets and white gloves, the chairs were covered in burgundy damask and the lighting was discreet. This wasn't our usual bistro sort of eating joint and I started with paté and a curious sinking feeling in my stomach. When the waiter arrived with a bottle of Moet et Chandon it sank still further. I now had a good idea what was coming. The main course was lobster quenelles, a speciality of the house. I struggled to swallow and struggled even harder to keep smiling. When dessert arrived (mousse au chocolat avec l'eau de vie) I gave up the fight and just scraped my spoon around the sundae glass, waiting for the inevitable. Michael was a bit distracted. He didn't seem to notice that

39

the mousse was more re-arranged than consumed. He finished his dessert, reached across the table and grabbed my free hand.

"Feef."

"What is it?"

As if I didn't know.

"Feef, I have something to ask you."

"Well, don't look so worried. It can't be that bad."

Oh yes, it can.

"You must have thought about it."

"Thought about what?"

"You and me. What's going to happen to us."

"Well, what is going to happen to us? You're being very dramatic, Michael."

"After graduation, I'm talking about. We'll have to move."

I look up sharply.

"Why? I like it here."

"Thing is, I've been offered a job."

"Me too."

It's his turn to look up.

"You never mentioned it."

"Neither did you. And I did at least tell you I was applying for one. You kept yours quiet enough."

"When did you tell me?"

"Months ago. I told you I was going to write off to a couple of publishing houses here. Well I did. And I had an interview with one of them last month and they've offered me a job. I start in September."

"Well, that's just great."

Michael let go of my hand at this point.

"So what is this job of yours that you've been so secretive about?"

"It's an amazing opportunity, Feef. Pays well, brilliant prospects. I go in as entry-level management trainee. Fast tracked. I'll do a couple of months at Head Office in Manchester then they send me off the Harvard Business School for an intensive 3-month course in retail economics and psychology of management. That's in October. All expenses paid. Then back to Manchester and I should be Deputy Manager at one of their stores by spring."

Michael is looking more animated than I've ever seen him.

"One of whose stores?"

"Pricerite. That's what so exciting. They're in the process of turning all their stores into hypermarkets, one by one. They'll be the biggest boys in the market pretty soon. And I'll be in right at the ground floor."

"You're going to work in a shop?"

I can't help myself.

"Selling baked beans and soap powder?"

I burst out laughing.

"4 years of university education and you're going to be a glorified grocer."

I'm nearly falling off my chair now, I'm giggling so hard.

"Feef. Pack it in. Everybody's staring."

They were. Clearly La Vie en Rose was not a giggly sort of place.

"I can't understand you. I thought you'd be pleased for me. And for your information I won't be selling soap powder. I'll be running an organisation that sells soap powder. And a hell of a lot more besides. "

"Sorry."

I choke back the next wave of giggles and take a sip of champagne.

"That's why I brought you here tonight."

I can't help myself.

"To tell me you're going to be a shopkeeper?"

Another fit of the giggles.

"No, you silly bitch. To ask you to marry me."

He reaches into his pocket and pulls out a small, velvet-covered box. Inside is a white gold ring set with a very large, diamond solitaire. Michael may be many things but mean isn't one of them.

"That's a bit of an ungallant way to ask for a girl's hand, isn't it?"

"I'm sorry."

His tone is conciliatory.

"It's just that I wanted everything to be perfect tonight and it seemed to have all gone wrong."

He stops and takes my hand again. He tries the ring on the third finger.

"You will say yes, won't you? Come with me. Manchester, Harvard, the whole thing?"

I pull my hand away gently and remove the ring, offering it back to him.

"I can't marry you Michael. It wouldn't be right. We're very different. We want different things. And we hardly know each other."

"Feef. How can you say that? We've been living together for nearly a year."

"That's just sharing a tube of toothpaste, Michael. There's a lot more we haven't shared."

"Like what, for instance."

"Well, this job of yours, for a start. You've never even mentioned it till tonight. And you must have known for months."

"I wasn't trying to keep it a secret. I just didn't want to mention it till I was sure. I only got the letter of confirmation last week. That's when I bought the ring. Your ring. I want to you to have it, Feef. We don't have to get married right away. You could stay here for a few months, if you wanted. Then join me wherever they send me. We could get married next summer."

"No, Michael."

That sounded much louder than I'd intended. People were staring again.

"Well, at least think about it."

"I don't have to. I can't marry you. Why couldn't you just have left things as they were? Why did you have to go and spoil everything?"

I'm crying now. I push my chair away from the table and rush outside. Michael's car is parked quite close but I just start walking blindly. I'm half-way down the road when he catches up with me. He stops the car and opens the passenger door. We drive home in silence.

2 months later I graduated and the week after that I missed my period. I couldn't believe it—not again. I thought I'd been so careful with my pills. I brought a pregnancy test kit and as I feared, it was positive. I kept it to myself while I tried to work out how, when and what to do till one evening when Michael came home laden with flowers, balloons and a wicker bassinette. I just looked at him, speechless. How the hell could he possibly have known?

"I saw the test kit."

I was taken aback. I had thrown it in the bin outside.

Right there was the first red flag—how did I miss it?

Then he said he couldn't be happier and produced the ring, the one from the restaurant.

I had been outmanoeuvred. We married in September, more or less the same time I should have been starting work as a sub-editor with Brunel Publishing, and Sarah was born on April 15th.

6.30pm

The house is quiet. Jude is obviously still at the show and Sarah is probably using the school gym. Michael, of course, is on the job. In Folkstone. Which means he won't be using his home computer, will he? So he couldn't possibly mind if I do, could he? Well, not if he doesn't know about it. His spare laptop is in his study, you see, a room he treats as his sanctum sanctorum. That and the wine cellar in which he stores select bottles for his most select clientele as well as his personal collection of rare wines and spirits. He belongs to some sort of club and the members buy and sell on auction or amongst themselves. These 2 areas are technically not off limits but there's an implication of restricted access to me and the girls.

I slip inside, carrying my cigarettes and an ashtray. I know it's also supposed to be a smoke-free zone but what the eye doesn't see the lungs won't cough over. Then sitting at his desk, I light a cigarette and boot up the machine, typing in a general search under 'calories'. This should yield some more up-to-date stuff than the old textbook in the shop. Dozens of site listings appear and I choose one or two at random. I learn that there are calories and kilocalories and joules and kilojoules. This is not enlightening. Another site tells me that to lose weight a woman should reduce her calorie intake to around 1500 per day. And my daughter is consuming a mere fraction of this amount. I click on 'search' again and type in 'anorexia'. Again, a multitude of listings. I click and read, select another, then another. By 7.30pm I probably know about as much as I need to on the subject and I am certain that my daughter is in the throes of this eating disorder. What I don't know is what to do about it. I learn that sufferers are always initially in denial, much like drug addicts, so confrontation will not lead to confession, much less to control and cure. And that they suffer from an unhealthy and distorted conception of their body image: That they generally come from comfortable middle-class households and are often high achievers at school: That ultimately hospitalisation is the only answer: That a complete recovery is far from certain:

And that many young women ultimately die from its effects.

My thoughts are interrupted by the phone ringing. It's Jude, back at the stable yard with Amanda and wanting a lift. I tell her I'll see her in twenty minutes.

Sunday, 30th April

3pm

"When they put that oxer up two holes in the jump-off I nearly died of fright."

"Well, you got over it, didn't you? So what are you moaning about?"

"Only just. And then to get a quarter of a time fault after all that effort. Honestly, there's no justice."

We are all in the kitchen drinking tea. Jude and Amanda are on the sofa, critiquing their performances at yesterday's show. Sarah is sat at the table. Her tea of course is black with no sugar. Even so, she sips it very slowly. The weather is unseasonably cool so I turned the central heating on but she is wearing a thick winter sweater, two waif-like wrists protruding from the baggy sleeves, long bony fingers wrapped around the glass of tea.

"I think I'll take one of the dogs for a walk and pop to the shops at the same time? What does everyone feel like for supper tonight?"

"No animal products and no additives." (Jude)

"I'm not fussy. I eat anything." (Amanda).

"Nothing, I'm not really hungry." (Sarah).

At this remark I glance at Jude and briefly catch her eye. Then she quickly looks away and goes back to drinking her tea.

"Sarah, why don't you come with me? A bit of fresh air might do you good. Perk up your appetite."

"All right. I might as well." She gets up and empties the remains of her cold tea down the sink.

Good lord. I hadn't expected an answer in the affirmative; at least not without an argument.

"Right. It's Dottie's turn. Why don't you root out her lead while I go and put my jacket on? What about you? Are you going to be warm enough?"

"No, I think I'll put a coat on. It's pretty chilly."

Sarah shivers as she says this, although it's as warm as toast in the kitchen. I grab my jacket from the stand in the uncloaking room as she rummages in one of the dresser drawers for the dog's lead. Then she too takes her coat from the stand, her thick, calf-length, navy school greatcoat, Calling Dottie from somewhere in the garden we set off together for the shops. Even inside her coat Sarah looks chilled to the bone. She walks slowly and I find myself constantly having to re-adjust my pace so as to keep alongside of her. I want to ask questions but instinctively feel that this is not the right time and I bite my tongue. A first for me. So we chat desultorily about more mundane matters— the damp weather, the dogs' imminent annual vaccinations, summer holidays. Then Sarah asks me if I've heard from Michael this weekend.

"He probably hasn't had time. He's very busy down there."

"I bet he is."

Something in Sarah's tone makes me turn and look at her but she avoids my eye and looks away.

"Let's go back by the lane behind Lockitt's Farm. Then we can let Dottie have a run around in that empty field."

When we reach Chanterelles, the little delicatessen, we tie Dottie to a post outside and leave her chatting to a Jack Russell similarly incapacitated. Once inside I confess to being at a bit of a loss. You've probably gathered that I'm not much of a cook, though I can grill a chop or two with the best of them but my daughters have issued their edict. Nor flesh nor fowl must pass the kitchen door. I wander around the shelves looking nonplussed.

"It's no good. I'll have to buy a book."

"Well, you work in the right place. What sort of book?"

"Vegetarian cookery. If you and Jude have both given up meat I'll have to learn to change my ways."

"Meat-free cooking? You? You'll have to learn to boil an egg first."

Sarah is laughing and it suddenly occurs to me that it's a long time since that happened. More companionably than I would have expected, we wander around the shop together and pick out wild rice, sun-dried tomatoes, Portobello mushrooms and red peppers which my eldest daughter assures me will make a vegan Italian risotto. At the fresh food counter she selects a wedge of Parmesan cheese.

"I thought vegans didn't eat cheese?"

"This is for everyone else."

I nod. I'm puzzled but pleased at this apparent resurgence of interest in food.

Then we collect Dottie and set off for Lockitt's Farm. On the way I take a deep breath.

"Sarah, you would tell me if anything was wrong, wouldn't you. I know I'm not the world's most maternal creature but I do love you both dearly."

"I don't know what you mean."

"Well, you've been looking awfully peaky lately. Not your usual self. Perhaps we should make an appointment at the surgery for a check-up? It couldn't hurt. Maybe you need a tonic, or a course of vitamins or something."

"Stop fussing, mum. Please. There's nothing wrong with me. I'm fine. Just a bit worried about end-of-term exams, that's all. Next year it'll be my mock As in November and then the real thing. You've forgotten what it's like."

The aggressive, defensive tone is back in her voice and an invisible shutter has come down. I let it pass and decide not to pursue the idea of medical help right now. So we stand for a while watching Dottie sniff out unseen rabbits and run around in that purposeless, pleasurable way that dogs have. Then we make our way home.

I know what you're thinking about me. Two unplanned pregnancies and then a shotgun wedding. What's the matter with this woman? Hasn't she ever heard of contraception? What can I say? Philip was a mistake, pure and simple. A close encounter of the sexual kind at the wrong time of the month and a condom that clearly wasn't failsafe. But when I moved in with Michael I went on the mini pill and I honestly don't know what went wrong. I spoke to my doctor who just shrugged and said those low-dosage pills weren't completely reliable. If I'd been sick, had the runs or just somehow missed taking one, that would compromise the effectiveness. Well I hadn't been sick, hadn't had the runs and took my pill religiously last thing at night when I cleaned my teeth. Yet there I was pregnant. I still couldn't work it out.

Anyway I told myself I had to do the right thing this time. Anyone who's never gone through what I did when I gave my child up for adoption, gave away my own flesh and blood to strangers, can never really understand the hurt, the doubts and most of all the guilt. That never goes away, never lessens, just gnaws away at you day after day like some insidious cancer. You push it away, try and bury it but it's still there, a malignant tumour, eating away and growing inside you. With Sarah I had to make a better choice.

Michael, predictably, was over the moon. He'd got what he wanted, hadn't he? A fast-tracked job, new wife (very corporately sound) and the prospect of becoming a father filled him with delight. Just before the hastily arranged wedding I sat him down and told him about Philip. And I said he could still change his mind if he wanted to. Single motherhood probably wouldn't be so bad. I was older now and I still had the chance of the job at Brunel's. He was clearly shocked and went very quiet for a while. Then he said it really didn't matter, what's past was past (trouble was, it wasn't, was it?), that he understood these things happened and he really didn't mind. Which I took to mean that he really didn't care. Philip, after all, was another man's child and apparently out of the picture, whereas this one was here and now and all his own work. I had nowhere to go. Checkmate.

On the eve of the wedding I met Michael's parents, Charles and Diana (Yes, really!), for the first time. His father, Charles, was a captain of industry, owner of a paper mill somewhere in the highlands of Scotland. And his aristocratic mother, Diana, looked like she spent most of the profits on her wardrobe. They breezed in with a couple of crates of French champagne in the boot of the Bentley and professed themselves to be 'absolutely delighted' that Michael was going to settle down with such a lovely young woman.

Diana asked to see the wedding dress, an ivory silk flapper affair from an antique clothes shop in Clifton, which she described, unconvincingly as 'charming'. And Charles whisked Michael off to the hotel bar to celebrate 'man to man'. Left alone, Diana and I lapsed into an uncomfortable silence, then she brightened up and suggested 'going shopping'. Though clearly more used to negotiating a Landrover around the country estate, she braved the downtown traffic in the Bentley, finally straddling three spaces in an underground car park. She then proceeded to drag me from one bridal department to another, pulling out more and more variations on the net curtain theme, all the while cooing 'Oh, look, Fiona, isn't this just darling?' or 'It's not too late to change your mind, you know. I've got my gold card right here with me'.

It was a nightmare.

And just when I thought it couldn't get any worse, it did. My parents motored down from Chester, arriving in the late afternoon. Fortunately by that

47

time Michael and Charles had vacated the bar and when mum and dad arrived we were all sitting in the lounge of the Harbour Hotel taking tea. And Diana being Diana that meant cucumber sandwiches, petit fours, Earl Grey as well as Ceylon, the lot. Mum didn't say anything but I could tell she was shocked at the extravagance of the whole set-up, Dad too. It's not that they were short of money. Back then dad still had the business—a medium-sized electrical appliance shop just off the Rows with lots of very loyal customers. But they'd always been careful. Dad was constantly lecturing me on the importance of 'putting something by for a rainy day'. So fancy hotels, extravagant meals and large tips were outside their sphere of experience. Whereas to Charles and Diana it was second nature.

"So after the wedding we thought we'd take the Dunloghaire ferry and motor round southern Ireland for a few weeks. It's ages since we've had a proper break. And of course Charles absolutely insists on paying for the honeymoon so we've booked them two weeks in a simply scrumptious hotel in Nice we stayed in last year. Nice is so wonderful this time of year, don't you think, Audrey? I may call you Audrey, mayn't I? Mrs Dobson sounds so formal. And after all, we are going to be family."

My mother smiled weakly at this verbal onslaught and I looked over at Michael and mouthed 'Nice?' He smiled back conspiratorially and pulled the corner of two air tickets out of his back pocket to show me. The first of many decisions Michael would take without consulting me.

Dinner was even more painful. Charles was at his most expansive best or worst, depending on your point of view. He insisted on ordering for everyone, expense no object, though to be fair he did know his way around a menu and a wine list. Mum was even more uncomfortable. The idea of spending a week's housekeeping on one restaurant dish, never mind drinking vintage wine at a hundred quid a bottle shocked her puritan sensibilities to the core. And dad's protestations that he didn't smoke fell on deaf ears when cognacs and cigars on the balcony were called for.

Somehow we got through the meal and Michael and I promised to meet back at the hotel in good time tomorrow. We went back to the flat where all I wanted to do was crash. I finally got to sleep at two am, praying I didn't turn into Diana in a few years' time.

Sarah has taken over the kitchen. She's welcome to it as far as I'm concerned but I confess to a certain puzzlement. This same young woman who for weeks now has been demonstrating an extreme aversion to food in all its forms is now bustling around preparing a vegetarian risotto with an attention to detail at which I can only marvel. A printed-out recipe off the internet is propped up on the work surface and our shopping is neatly lined up and laid out in small bowls. She chops tomatoes, peppers, garlic and onions while butter sizzles in the newly christened copper skillet. I open a bottle of white wine and sit at the table to watch. As far as I'm aware she has never so much as heated up a takeaway before yet here she is deftly dicing and slicing, sautéing and stirring like an experienced professional. Clearly this is not an inherited skill. My ineptness in the culinary arts has been well documented and as for her grandmothers, I'm sure Diana wouldn't know where to even find the kitchen in her huge Scottish mansion and my mother, though competent, is strictly meat and two veg.

The door opens and Jude and Amanda stroll in. Jude takes in the scene with undisguised amazement. She opens her mouth to say something I know will be scathingly sarcastic but I catch her eye in time and shake my head. She looks sceptical but quickly revises the script.

"Finally giving mum some lessons then, Sarah?"

Sarah looks up and smiles.

"I hope you're all hungry. There's going to be masses."

"Want a Coke?"

Jude is opening the fridge.

"Yes, please"(Amanda)

"Is it diet?" (Sarah)

Jude checks.

"Yes."

"Okay then."

I light a cigarette and Sarah ostentatiously switches on the huge, copper-covered extractor fan above the cooking island. I endeavour to stay down wind.

"What have you two been up to this afternoon?"

"Nothing much. Watched tv in my room then we went out to the stables. Amanda borrowed Sarah's old bike. We went out for a hack. Mattie came with us."

Mattie, short for Matthew. Quite cute in a gawky, adolescent sort of way and worships the ground on which Jude walks. She in turn treats him with utter contempt and complete disdain. Jude the Imperious. I am surprised he was allowed to accompany them. Clearly the surprise shows in my face.

"He was all tacked up the same time we were. We couldn't really say no."
Amanda chips in.
"Don't know why you're so hard on him. He's quite sweet really."
"He's not sweet. He's pathetic. Like a stray dog that keeps following you home. Anyway 'sweet' is hardly a compliment."
"It's not his fault. He's nuts about you. And do you know how many girls in our school would pay to go out with him?"
"I've got better things to do with my money. Anyway are you saying you want me to go out with a male prostitute?"
"When you two have finished maybe you could make yourselves useful and lay the table. I'm nearly ready."

Jude and Amanda pull faces at Sarah behind her back and giggling, set to, pulling cutlery out and finding placemats. And I can't help thinking that this is the lightest the atmosphere has been at suppertime for as long as I can remember.

Is the difference in Sarah or is it the fact that Michael's not here? Maybe it's a bit of both.

With a flourish Sarah places the copper pan on the table and lifts the lid. The dish smells wonderful. She hands out pasta bowls to everyone and passes around the parmesan cheese and a small grater. Then she fusses about making sure everyone is served, insisting that we fill our bowls.

She serves herself, a very small portion, and declines the cheese.

Jude and Amanda eat as though it was their first square meal for months. With my cooking it probably is, as far as Jude's concerned. I taste mine. It's delicious and I say so.

"Sarah, this is superb. I wish you'd cook for us more often. Give the dustbin a break."

Sarah looks both pleased and embarrassed. She is watching us all eat like a mother hen with a brood of chicks but so far she hasn't touched her own food.

I smile and try to keep my voice light.

"Eat up"

"I was just waiting for it to cool down a bit."

Sarah picks up her fork and begins relocating grains of rice in that familiar fashion. At once I am confused and depressed. I thought we'd turned a corner but we seem back on the same long straight road leading nowhere.

Monday, 8th May

Amanda stayed the night again. Both parents were away for the weekend, apparently. At half past eight, the silver Mini screams into the drive and hoots outside the front door. As before, all three girls pile in and I hover around just to be polite. As she gets in, I hear Sarah ask Louise how she'd enjoyed her weekend.

"Tremendously, darling. Lovely break."

"Where was it you said you went?"

"France, actually. A quick trip across the channel to do some shopping."

"It's a pity Mr Sinclair couldn't have gone with you." (Sarah)

"Oh, I think he'd have been bored silly. He hates traipsing around the shops with me."

"So you went on your own then?"

"Er, well, actually I was with a friend."

"Someone from around here?"

"Actually, yes"

"And when is it Mr Sinclair's getting back?"

God, Sarah, this is beginning to sound like the third degree.

Louise puts the car into gear.

"Em, Thursday, I think he said. Do you remember, Mandy?"

"Wednesday evening, isn't it? He said he'll catch the last flight after his meeting."

'You're probably right. I could never keep up with his schedule so I gave up trying. I just expect him when I see him."

She turns her attention to me.

"Darling, it was sweet of you to take care of Mandy for me. You must let me return the favour some time."

"It was no problem, really. She made herself at home. No trouble at all."

51

'Well, thanks anyway. Must go. Don't want the girls late for assembly."

She drives off and I go back inside.

12 noon

In a mood of virtuous resentment I've vacuumed the house, done some dusting and thrown two loads of laundry into the machine, even though I know Jenny's coming in tomorrow. And now it's no use. I can't wait any longer. I again sneak into Michael's study and turn on the computer, wondering what he'd say or do if he caught me. Sometimes I even think he locks the door though I've never been able to prove it.

I log on and wait nervously while it searches for the Mother and Child Reunion site. A little icon in the corner of the screen tries to tempt me take a holiday in Cyprus. Right now I wouldn't take much tempting. Eventually the site comes up, greets me by my first name in a sinister Big Brotherly fashion and I click on 'mailbox'. It's empty. Well, they warned me that it could take a while. Part of me is disappointed but there's another part that's relieved. I don't have to tell the girls just yet then.

The phone rings. It's Michael.

"Feef. Listen, can you pick up my other suit from the dry cleaners and courier it down to me?"

"I thought you'd only be down there for a few days?"

"The plan's changed. I'm up to my eyes here and Francis is flying down on Wednesday. He wants to check on progress on the renovations first hand so it's pretty urgent."

"Easy to see where your priorities lie."

"The man relies on me. That's why I'm paid a six-figure salary. That's why you live in that big house. That's why I can afford to send the girls to private school."

"As I recall, Michael it was you who chose and bought this house. It was you who decided the local grammar wasn't good enough. And it's you who thinks that money can solve everything."

"What on earth do you mean by that?"

"I mean you bury your head in your business and assume that your big salary and inherited money will solve everything."

"What's the matter with you all of a sudden? Wrong time of the month?"

"Oh, that's right. Make it my fault. And of course I'm a woman so it must be hormones, mustn't it?"

"I haven't the faintest idea what you're talking about. I left the house a week ago and everything was fine. Now all of a sudden I'm in the doghouse and I don't even know what it's supposed to be over."

"Everything was fine? God, Michael, I'm speechless. We sleep in separate bedrooms, live virtually separate lives, our elder daughter has a potentially fatal eating disorder, the younger one spends as much time out of the house as she can, and who can blame her, and my son's grown up without me even knowing him. I don't even know what he looks like."

"For heaven's sake, Feef. I thought we'd put that behind us years ago. Must you be continually raking over the past? And what the hell do you mean about Sarah? She looks all right to me."

"How would you know? You're never here. And when you are your mind's always somewhere else. I said we needed to talk but you told me you were too busy."

"Oh, was that what that was all about?"

"What did you think I meant?"

"Nothing. I don't know. There's just no pleasing you these days. I even offered to buy you a new car."

"There you go again, thinking that money can solve everything. I don't want a new car."

"Well, what then?"

"A new life. A new deal. This whole arrangement was a huge mistake, Michael."

"You're making no sense at all. Are you sure it isn't PMT? Or the menopause? Perhaps you should see a doctor? A psychiatrist, even."

"You stupid, stupid man. It isn't me that needs the psychiatrist. It's Sarah. She's the one who needs help. Serious help. She's anorexic. If she doesn't get it soon she could die."

"I think you're being overly dramatic."

"And I think you're being overly arrogant and patronising, as usual."

"We'd better talk about this when I get back."+

"And when might that be?"

"I'm not sure. Friday, maybe."

"Let's hope she makes it till then."

That last remark comes out before I can stop it and of course I regret it immediately. Playing right into his hands. But I couldn't help it. I'm worried sick about Sarah and he thinks it's all in my mind. Or my uterus. We say our goodbyes and I put the phone down. And like the dutiful wife that I signed up to act like, I back the bug out and head first for the dry cleaners.

"There you are Mrs Hamilton. There's the suit, the other jacket and trousers and just the three shirts this time."

Yes, that's right, shirts. Michael favours the fine linen cotton variety for work and naturally he won't trust me to launder them. Just as well. I can't iron properly to save my life and they're hell to get right.

"So let's see, that's fifteen seventy five altogether. Oh, and I found this in one of the pockets."

She hands me a top of the range smartphone which I know isn't Michael's because he has his with him. I assume it belongs to a colleague and he must have forgotten about it.

Back in the car I drape his things over the back of the seat next to me and drive to the local courier depot. Pricerite has an account there and the girl behind the counter is used to strange requests from Michael. She obligingly finds a box about the right size and we carefully pack up the suit and two of the shirts. She assures me it'll be delivered to the hotel before breakfast tomorrow morning. On an impulse I drop in the phone so he can return it. If I hold onto it I'll probably lose it before he gets back.

Monday, 15th May

Michael's still away. I'll expect him when I see him. Not that I care one way or the other.

Anyway, it's sale day. George doesn't drive so we'll go together in the bug which means an early start. The girls are getting a lift to school with Louise again so I set my alarm and I'm out of the house by seven, load George into the passenger seat and stuff his wicker picnic basket under the bonnet by seven thirty and within minutes we're out into the country.

It's bliss. In complete contrast to the dull weather over the weekend the sun is shining from a near cloudless sky and it promises to be a perfect day weather-wise. And it's wonderful to be out of town, away from the house, away from thoughts of Michael and Sarah, away from everything for a few hours. I wind down the window and smell fresh grass and assorted countryside smells. Sheep are grazing in open fields, ripening wheat is waving in the breeze and cows are herded from byre to meadow. I spread the map on my knee and plot a back road route which will take a little longer than the main roads but will give me more of a chance to enjoy the drive and clear my head.

Beside me, George is perusing the sale catalogue again. There's a Jane Austen first edition of Emma as well as an extensive selection of much older treatises on the medicinal uses of herbs, all of which I know he badly wants for his own collection.

"I've decided to push the boat out, Ffion. After all, how often does an opportunity like this present itself, right on our doorstep, practically? So I suggest you have a look at the mixed lots and bid on them. And I'll go and view the reserves. Imagine it, Ffion, a first edition of Emma. That will complete the set. I bought the first one nearly forty years ago. That was Mansfield Park. I paid five hundred pounds for it, a fortune at the time. And it took me years to track down Pride and Prejudice. And now Emma is within my grasp. I absolutely must have it at any price."

"Steady on, George. The bidding could go quite high, you know. And if you bankrupt yourself buying it I'll be out of a job."

"Don't you worry. I've quite a bit put by, you know. And that book will make me a very happy old man. Oh, I know life isn't about possessions. Heaven knows, I have precious few of them. But my books mean a lot to me. And when I die I mean them to be put to good use."

We reach an intersection and I check my map.

"If my navigation's right it should be just down here, about five miles on the left."

The house is more beautiful than I could ever have imagined, weathered red brick covered with ivy and Virginia creeper, mullioned windows and acres of landscaped gardens surrounding it on all sides. We drive up and over a brick and grass ha-ha decorated with stone urns and make our way up the drive. It's eight thirty and the auction is due to kick off at nine but according to the catalogue the kitchen artefacts will be the first to go. We park and I note that there aren't too many cars there yet. Maybe bidding will be slow and George will pick up a bargain.

Inside I locate the ante room where the general books are stacked. I walk up and down the shelves and then pick through the boxes, noting their contents and making a few notes on my programme. That done I head off to find George. He's in the library where the rare books are on display. He sees me and looks over his shoulder conspiratorially.

"It's over there. I had a quick look but I don't want to appear too keen. Walls have ears, you know. It's magnificent. In remarkable condition considering its age. I was going to go to ten but I might be prepared to make it twelve. And look at these."

He takes my sleeve and pulls me across to view the collection of herbal treatises, the earliest dating back to the fifteenth century before the house was built. The illustrations are breath-taking in their detail and I can understand his passion.

"And just imagine. I read somewhere that those dreadful Americans come and buy them up and then rip them to pieces so they can put the illustrated pages in a frame. Just because they have no history what right have they to come and destroy ours? Philistines, every last one."

The rare books are going to be sold in situ so I leave George and wander off. The others won't come up till after lunch so I decide to have a look at some of the furniture items. As we came in I spotted a beautiful refectory table which I think will just fit in the kitchen and I go to see if there are any chairs which might go with it. I view what's on offer and finally decide that the sturdy Victorian ones which were used below stairs would be perfect. I note some sale numbers and wonder with a smile what Michael will think when he sees his designer kitchen defiled with old wood.

It seems I was right about the turn out. There's only a smattering of people in the sale room and when the refectory table comes up the bidding ends up between me and a middle-aged lady in a faded, multi-coloured kaftan. It goes to four hundred pounds and she loses interest. The chairs are in a set of twelve. Far too many really but I can use the rest on the patio. This time I'm bidding against a scruffy-looking man who I'm sure is a dealer. At three hundred pounds I'm about to give up but he suddenly drops out. Obviously his profit margin was disappearing. I cross to the recorder's desk and give my details and the helpful lady there lets me have the phone number of a local haulier who can deliver for me.

That done I wander around the ground floor, drinking in the details. My low heels tap on the bare wooden floorboards and I pass workmen in overalls rolling rugs and climbing ladders to lift tapestries from the walls, whilst others take down measurements in dog-eared notebooks. I try to imagine what the house looked like only a few months ago, period furniture still in place, probably in patterns not changed for centuries and what it will look like soon, parcelled up into strange little sections, each reflecting the new owners' differing tastes and lifestyles? It saddens me, this carving up of England's historical treasures, this egalitarianism, this bringing down to size of what was once great and glorious.

There's still no sign of George and I don't want to go and disturb his concentration so I make my way outside again, into the car park, lift out the picnic hamper from the car and look for somewhere to sit. The day is now quite warm and through a group of trees I hear the sound of water. I follow the noise and find myself looking at an eighteenth century pond of Olympic pool proportions. Stone urns like the ones on the ha-ha but filled with flowers and shrubs dot the side of the water feature and at the top end, water tumbles from a fountain of a stone cherub, emptying an ornate ewer. There are lichen-encrusted stone benches alongside and I select one nearest to the fountain where I sit and have my lunch; tea from an ancient heavy metal thermos, and one of George's thick ham sandwiches And I wonder idly how much a small apartment in the house would cost and realise how lucky the new residents will be to wake every morning and have all this beauty right on their doorstep. Some small birds are drinking from the fountain so I throw the remnants of my sandwich on the floor for them and leave them fighting over the crumbs.

Back at the car I replace the picnic basket and as I close the bonnet lid I see a familiar silver Mini drive in and park. So remembering my social graces I walk up to the driver's door.

"Louise, fancy seeing you here."

The occupant jumps.

"Feef."

'Feef'? I'm a little taken aback too. Nobody ever calls me that except Michael.

We both regain our composure.

"You startled me for a minute there. I didn't think antiques would be your sort of scene."

"Incanabula."

"Sorry?"

"Books. Old ones. I sell them. Only today I'm buying them. And you?"

57

"Er, just looking really. I saw the sale advertised in this morning's paper and it seemed such a lovely day for a drive."

"It is glorious, isn't it? The grounds are magnificent. Is your husband back yet?"

Is it my imagination or is she looking at me rather oddly?

"No, not yet. This evening, I think. Or is it tomorrow? He's always chopping and changing"

"Yours too! I keep my tone light."

"Oh yes. The girls said Michael was out of town for a few days. Brighton, wasn't it?"

"Folkstone. Still the seaside though. Could do with a bit of that myself."

She giggles incongruously.

"Quite. Well, I must get inside and have a wander around. See what's left."

"Me too. They're going to start on the boxes of books soon and I don't want to miss anything."

Together we walk over to the house and I let Louise ramble on about how difficult it is running such a large house with her husband away so much of the time and how you can't find any decent help these days and how her cleaning lady absolutely refuses to come in at weekends. I'm quite relieved when she eventually picks up a catalogue and heads off for the furniture auction.

The boxes of books are a steal. No-one except an eccentric few apparently read anymore so I bid on all the ones I wanted and then a few more as well. On impulse I also bid for a huge box of assorted old clothes that I saw and which I'm sure Jude will kill for. It goes for a tenner. And just as I'm finishing up George appears. He looks beatific.

"I've done it, Ffion. Emma is mine."

He holds up a tissue-wrapped bundle triumphantly.

"Well done, George. How much?"

"More than I wanted but rather less than I expected. And I rescued these."

He indicates some heavy botanical tomes tucked under his arm and toddles off whilst I go to see about the job lot books. I can take most of them in the back of the car and the rest can come with my table and chairs, along with Jude's antique clothes collection. As I carry them out George carefully places the priceless edition on the passenger seat, along with the botanical collection, then looks in the hamper for something to eat. I tell him about the garden.

"Charles Bridgeman. I did some research on the house in anticipation of our little excursion. He re-designed the entire exterior in the middle of the eighteenth century. Including that delightful little ha-ha we crossed on the way in."

Leaving me strict instructions to keep the car locked at all times he too meanders off to view the gardens.

Just then Louise appears, followed by 2 khaki-coated lackeys, staggering under the weight of three or four heavy cardboard boxes. She opens the door of the car, presses a switch, the back opens up and the rear seat back folds down. As this is taking place, she moves some carrier bags emblazoned with the name Maison de Marie, Calais. Then with some gesturing and pointing the lackeys stack the boxes in the back. She sees me watching.

"Feef, there you are. I was looking for you inside. I've had the most marvellous time. Bought some simply super conversation pieces. And a huge sixteenth century settle. It's so big I haven't a clue where I'm going to put it but I expect I'll find a spot. They said they'd bring it on later."

"There were some beautiful things, weren't there? I've bought a kitchen table and far too many chairs."

"I thought you said you were here for the books."

"Those too, of course. More than I planned actually. It'll take me days to catalogue them all."

"Don't you mind working in that funny little shop? It can't be for the money, surely? And how do you find the time to run that lovely big house of yours?"

"We've come to an arrangement. I don't interfere with it and it doesn't make too many demands on me. We just muddle along on parallel tracks till the points need changing. Bit like me and Michael, really."

She laughs nervously.

"I'm sure you don't mean that."

"No. I think I probably have more of an understanding with the house."

That nervous laugh again.

"Look, I really must run. I promised to take Amanda and Jude out to the stables after school and I'm going to have to get rid of this lot first. Otherwise there'll be nowhere for them to sit."

She jumps into the front seat, starts the engine and glides off down the gravelled drive.

I can't resist another look around the grounds so I head off through the trees and find George almost in the same spot where I sat for lunch. I join him on the bench.

"Ffion. Isn't it exquisite?"

"Utterly gorgeous. When I first thought about dividing up such a lovely old house I was appalled. But then I came and sat out here and thought how lucky people would be to be able to enjoy all this beauty every day."

"Quite so. I was talking to the agent inside and he tells me there's still one ground floor set of apartments available."

He pauses, staring into the pond.

"I said I might be interested."

He looks sideways at me.

"For my retirement, you understand."

"Retirement? I'd never thought of you retiring."

"Don't look so startled, Ffion. It won't be for some time yet. And in the meantime I'll be able to sort out this place. Buy some bits of furniture. Maybe I could spend the odd weekend there so it doesn't become too neglected. Of course I'd need some help. Not driving anymore is a bit of a disadvantage."

"Well, I'm always available. You know that. So long as the bug keeps going. Did I mention that Michael offered to buy me a new car?"

"And what did you say?"

"I said I was happy with the bug. Something new and soulless wouldn't suit me."

"I read somewhere that when husbands offer to buy their wives expensive presents it's usually the sign of a guilty conscience."

George is chuckling.

"I read that book too."

"And is there any truth in the theory, do you think?"

"Beats me. I'm no psychologist."

"Perhaps not. But I think you're a very astute young woman all the same."

I pack up laughing.

"Darling, George. Only you would be gallant enough to call me a young woman."

"Everything's relative, my dear Ffion. Come, let's have a last look around and get back before the traffic builds up."

Companionably we stroll off through a bower at the far end of the pond to find a beautiful flower garden on the other side, a little neglected but the design still recognisable. An array of floral scents is starting to rise in the late afternoon air and the colours are a joy to behold. I wish I could stay here forever.

6.45 pm

I'm in the kitchen again, trying to think of something for supper that will offend the least number of people when the back door opens and Jude walks in with a young man I recognise as Matthew. They're both dressed in jodhpurs and smell vaguely horsey. I'm surprised but endeavour not to show it. This bringing home of friends is beginning to be a habit. She coughs a bit, looks at her feet.

"I hope it's okay. I said Mattie could come for supper."

If there ever is any supper it'll be fine.

"No problem. I haven't started cooking yet."

Shit. That means I'll definitely have to come up with something edible now.

"And then he's going to help me with my chemistry homework."

"Ah, not just decorative. Useful too."

"Mum!"

Jude the Impervious is blushing.

"Where's Sarah?"

"Gym."

Only one word but she manages to sound guilty, apologetic and disloyal, all at the same time. I change the subject.

"So you've been riding? Hasn't it been a gorgeous day?"

"Really nice, Mrs Hamilton."

"We're all going to watch a three-day event next month."

"Sounds like fun. Where's that being held?"

"Beecham Abbey. Just outside Gloucester. It's a really tough course. Mark Philips designed it."

"The abbey?"

"Ha, ha. You're so funny, mum'

"Maybe I should come too."

61

"We don't need a chaperone."

"I wasn't thinking of that. I just thought it would be nice to get away somewhere for a couple of days."

"You'll be bored."

"No, I won't. I was riding before you were born, remember. And I used to event."

Before I got pregnant the first time. Before your brother was born, I want to say. But this is hardly the time or the place. I wonder what is? I settle for a safer subject.

"Mattie. Any food fads or allergies?"

"He's a human dustbin."

Jude the Incorrigible.

"What a refreshing change."

He grins and the pair of them go off to shower and change. I take the easy option, lift 2 pizza bases out of the freezer and while I'm waiting for the oven to heat up I find some passata, slice up some mushrooms and make a salad.

Sarah arrives just as I am popping it in the oven.

"I'm not eating any of that."

"It's completely vegetarian."

"It's got cheese on it."

"No, it hasn't. I thought everyone could grate on some of that Parmesan at the table."

"Well, anyway, I'm not hungry. I had something while I was out."

Patently untrue but short of calling her a liar there's not much I can say.

"Well, sit and keep us company, anyway. Jude's brought Mattie home for supper. Do you want to lay the table while I finish up here?"

"Can't. Homework."

She goes upstairs and I set the table for three and a half, just in case.

Wednesday, May 24th

I'm in the shop, unpacking the boxes of books. I wasn't kidding about how long it would take me to catalogue them all. I've just emptied the first one when the phone rings.

"Mrs Hamilton?"

"Yes."

"This is Melanie Forbes."

Pause.

"I'm the headmistress at the Priory."

"Oh yes, of course."

"It's about your daughter."

"Which one. I have two."

"Sarah. Mrs Hamilton. I've had several of my staff bring it to my attention and I thought it was my duty to pass it on to you."

"Pass what on?"

"The fact is, Sarah is looking thin. Very thin. We're very concerned."

Not half as concerned as me, I want to say but don't. Somehow I don't want to discuss it with this woman.

"Have you ever heard of a condition called anorexia nervosa?"

Where does this woman think I come from? A Martian cabbage patch?

"I think that's what Sarah is suffering from. It's very serious, Mrs Hamilton. She needs to see a doctor."

"Mrs Forbes,"

"It's Ms, if you don't mind."

"Ms Forbes, I don't think Sarah would be very happy to hear that I'd been discussing this matter with you. I agree she's looking rather thin and I have spoken to her about it. She told me it was just stress. Pressure of work. And you know what girls are like these days. They all like to stay slim, work out."

"That's just it, Mrs Hamilton. I do know what the girls are like. And believe me, your daughter has a serious problem."

I want to end this conversation, get off the phone.

"Yes, well thank you for bringing it to my attention, Ms Forbes. I'll have another talk to Sarah."

"What about your husband?"

"What about him?"

"Have you spoken to Mr Hamilton about this? I tried to get hold of him this morning but they told me at work that he was away for a few days. I find him to be very level-headed and sensible."

Great. She tried Michael before me. Michael head-in-the-sand, hand-in-his-wallet, pass me the rose-tinted spectacles, Hamilton.

"Well as you seem to be aware my husband is out of town on business for a few days and it's not the sort of thing I'd want to discuss over the phone. But

63

when he gets back I can assure you that I'll make sure that he's well aware of the situation. Now if you'll excuse me Ms Forbes I really must get back to work."

I put down the phone and get back to categorising the books. But I can't concentrate properly. I'm annoyed with myself for being so short with that woman. I know she was only trying to help but I didn't like her patronising manner and the fact that she thinks Michael is some sort of walking panacea for all that ails the world. And I'm even more annoyed with Michael for trivialising the issue and being so smug and cynical.

"George, I have to go out for half an hour. Can you manage on your own?"

"Of course, of course, my dear Ffion. Take as long as you like."

I drive to our local GP's surgery. It's a group practise and you never seem to see the same doctor twice but I figure it's a start. As always in these places there's a snotty young receptionist in a short skirt and a low-cut blouse and an even snottier old matron in a British Home Stores-style twin set and a pair of ugly clip-on earrings. The waiting room is empty apart from an old man and a young woman with a baby and a toddler.

"Yes, can I help you?" (short skirt).

"I'd like to see one of the doctors, please."

"Which one?"

"Whichever one's free. It doesn't really matter."

I'm afraid they're all busy. You'll have to make an appointment."

"No, it can't wait. I need to see someone as soon as possible."

"Is it an emergency?"

"Yes."

"What exactly is the problem?" (Twin set).

"If you don't mind I'd rather discuss it with the doctor."

"Yes, but I have to have some idea."

"It's confidential and I'd really need like to speak to a doctor as soon as possible."

Twin set's lips purse.

"Are you a patient here?"

"Yes. At least I was. Do you get expelled for poor attendance?"

The purse gets tighter.

"What's your name?"

"Hamilton. Fiona."

Twin set turns her back and begins rummaging through some brightly coloured files on the wall behind the desk.

"Miss White. The nurse can see you now."

The young woman collects up her brood and walks down the corridor.

Twin set locates the file and turns back to me.

"Mrs Hamilton. I see you have private health insurance."

I don't reply. There doesn't seem much point.

"Well, if you'd just like to take a seat you can see Dr Patel when she's free."

"Thank you."

So Michael's fringe benefits do come in useful sometimes.

I sit down and pick up a magazine. It's full of stick insects modelling summer fashions. No wonder young women like Sarah have problems. But what is it that turns a diet into a death sentence? What pushes them over the edge?

"Dr Patel is free now, Mrs Hamilton."

Twin set is smiling. Or giving what passes for a smile in her world.

I put the magazine down and follow her down a corridor. She stops at a door with a white plastic name plate reading Dr Meera Patel, knocks and opens the door.

"Mrs Hamilton to see you, Doctor."

"Thank you, Betty. Do come in, Mrs Hamilton."

Twin set aka Betty steps aside and lets me pass. Then she shuts the door behind me. I wouldn't put it past her to be listening at the keyhole.

"And what can I do for you today?"

"Actually I need some advice. Some medical advice."

Well, you've come to the right place."

Dr Patel smiles.

"What sort of advice, exactly? What seems to be the trouble?"

"It's about my daughter, Dr Patel. I'm very worried about her health."

"Wasn't your daughter able to come with you?"

"Well, that's really the crux of the matter. She doesn't think she has a problem. Or maybe she does but she won't accept it. I suggested we come along to the surgery together so that she could have a check-up but she refused. Said she didn't need it."

"And what makes you think she does, Mrs Hamilton?"

65

"She's lost weight. A lot of weight."

"What do you consider a lot?"

"Enough to make her look like a walking skeleton. Enough to have her headmistress on the phone to me this morning, saying that she and a lot of the staff are seriously worried."

"How old is your daughter?"

"Seventeen."

"And how long do you think this excessive dieting has been going on?"

"It's hard to say. About a year ago she and her sister both decided to become vegetarians. I didn't think anything of it at the time. It's the sort of thing teenagers do."

"And what about her sister? Is she losing weight too?"

"No, Jude's fine. It's more of a socio-political statement as far as she's concerned. But with Sarah it's different. She claims to be vegan. Won't touch dairy products either. Even that would be okay. It's just that lately I don't think she's eating much of anything. She counts calories obsessively and I think she's trying to eat no more than about 350 a day."

Dr Patel had been doodling idly on a pad as she listened but at this her head shot up.

"350? Are you sure?"

"Fairly. I saw a diary where she was keeping a record of her calorie intake and that's what she wrote down."

"Mrs Hamilton, if what you say is correct then I think you're right to be worried. It certainly sounds as though your daughter could be in the throes of an eating disorder. But there's nothing much I can do until she comes to see me. Even then I can tell you it won't be easy. If Sarah is anorexic she'll have a very distorted body image. No matter how much weight she loses she'll still think she looks fat. And she'll resist any attempt to encourage her to eat. Usually hospitalisation is the only answer in cases like that. And there's no quick cure. Sometimes, I'm afraid, there's no cure at all."

It's my turn to look up sharply.

"I'm sorry to be blunt but I'm trying to impress upon you the seriousness and the urgency of the situation. It's imperative that you try and persuade your daughter to come in and see me. That would be a start. Then we can take it from there."

"And if I can get her to come in, what then?"

"Well, I can assess her condition properly though from what you tell me there seems little doubt. Then we have to try and persuade her to seek psychiatric help. It's the only way. I know an excellent man I can recommend. But really it's up to Sarah."

"That's pretty much what I thought. Well, thank you for your time, Dr Patel. I'll see what I can do."

"Good luck. And if you do manage to talk her into coming tell the ladies at reception that she doesn't need an appointment. I'll see her any time."

"I appreciate that. Goodbye."

7pm

"How many times have I got to tell you, there's nothing wrong with me. I don't need a check-up and I'm not going to see any doctor. Okay?"

"Sarah, I'm desperately worried about you. Look how thin you're getting. You're not eating properly and I don't want to see you getting ill. Your body needs vitamins."

"Fine, I'll take a vitamin supplement. Will that satisfy you?"

"There's other things as well. Carbohydrates, protein, you're a growing girl."

"Oh, look who just turned into an expert on nutrition. If you're so keen on healthy eating how come there's never any food in the fridge? And how come dad's always complaining that he doesn't get fed properly?"

"Okay, so I'm not a domestic goddess. But I do my best."

"Hah!"

"Sarah, my cooking skills aren't really the point."

"Wrong, mum. It's exactly the point. You say I'm not getting enough nutrition. Well, whose fault is that?"

"Sarah, even when I do cook you just don't eat anything."

"Well, what about Jude?"

"What about her?"

"She won't eat any meat. And she hates your cooking too."

"Yes, but Jude isn't losing weight the way you are. Look, this isn't getting us anywhere. Just come to the surgery with me. The doctor can have a look at you and maybe make some suggestions about what you need. And then perhaps I could get a book on vegan cooking. We've probably got one in the shop somewhere. Perhaps we can try it together. I can see you quite enjoy messing about in the kitchen. That meal you made for us at the weekend was wonderful."

"Okay, fine. If it'll make you happy, go and find a book. But I'm not going to any doctor. I'm not ill and I hate the smell of those places. And doctors are all the same. Always thinking you should be worried about nothing. I don't think I'm that thin. Anyway it's better than being obese like loads of kids today. How would you like it if I stuffed myself with junk food all day? You think that's healthy? That's what some of the girls at the comprehensive live on. Chips and burgers and chocolate. All that grease and fat. Yuck. Not for me, thanks. Now if you don't mind I have homework to do. I do have exams coming up, if you hadn't noticed."

Sarah flounces out of the room. That conversation got us nowhere. Obviously if I'm going to get her to a doctor it'll be kicking and screaming. And that's just me. I turn to my trusty filter cigarettes and wonder what I can find for supper that will vaguely constitute 'vegan'. Not that I think it'll make much difference.

I'm making a salad with some leafy things from the kitchen garden and a can of cannelloni beans when the phone rings.

"Feef? Just to say I should be back on Friday evening. Don't know what time, exactly. Depends on the traffic."

"Good. We really need to sit down and talk."

"So you keep saying. And I got the phone, by the way."

Is it just me or are we straying off the point? What's that got to do with us needing to talk?

"It was in your suit pocket. The lady at the dry cleaners found it and gave it to me. Anyway, I'll see you Friday evening. I'll hold supper till you arrive. That way you can see for yourself what Sarah's like."

"I still think you're exaggerating."

"I spoke to a doctor about her. She agrees with me. She has all the classic signs."

"Such as?"

"She cooked for us on Sunday. Made a wonderful risotto."

"Doesn't sound to me like a girl in the throes of an eating disorder."

68

"I said she cooked it. I didn't say she ate it. She pretended to—pushed it around the plate a lot, then scraped it into the waste disposal. You'll see for yourself when you get back."

"I'm sure it's nothing. Anyway I'll see you on Friday. Bye."

Discussion closed, presumably. I wonder, not for the first time, what the hell I'm still doing in this 'marriage'. I promise I'll explain more about this later.

Thursday, 25th May

The haulier phoned early and said he'd be able to deliver the stuff this morning so I waited in for him and his mate. It took a bit of manoeuvring between 3 of us but now the huge refectory table is installed in the kitchen, along with eight of my Victorian chairs. I hunt around under the sink, find a tin of beeswax and spend the best part of an hour rubbing it deep into the old wood. At length, satisfied with my efforts, I pull an old Crown Derby soup tureen out of one of the cupboards, a relic from my Bristol junk shop days, fill it with fruit and dried flowers and place it in the centre. A couple of potted plants at either end complete the look. The other four chairs I take into the conservatory and arrange around an old bentwood and glass table that apparently started life a century or so ago on a tea plantation in Ceylon. They look surprisingly effective together. While I'm on a roll I drag the box of clothes up to Jude's room as a surprise, then it's off to work.

1pm

George and I are sitting having lunch—cheese and tomato rolls and fresh cream éclairs from Simmonds—and discussing his apartment at Featherington Hall.

"I'm going in to sign the papers next week, Ffion. Apparently there are a few finishing touches still to be done in the kitchen and bathroom and I can move my things in any time after that. You will help me pick out some furniture, won't you? I'm absolutely no use at that sort of thing. Besides, I can't even remember the last time I went inside a furniture shop. All the pieces upstairs I've had for years."

"Of course. I'll enjoy it. It's fun spending someone else's money! And it won't be just furniture, you know. You'll need curtains, crockery, all sorts of things if you're going to be keeping two places going."

"You know, Ffion, it all sounds very exciting. I'm really looking forward to it. I was hoping that if it wasn't too much trouble you might drive me down on Friday afternoon to spend the odd weekend. Then since we're closed on Mondays you could maybe fetch me in the afternoon. If it's not too much of an imposition, that is."

George looks at me anxiously.

"Don't be silly. It's a lovely drive. We can do it as often as you like. Every weekend, if you want. If we leave straight after the shop closes I can be there and back by seven. And there's never anybody at home then. No-one's going to miss me."

"Surely not? I certainly don't know what I'd do without you."

"Nor me, you. This job's a lifesaver, you know. How about starting on Monday? Looking for furniture, I mean. Have you thought what sort of them you want?"

"Period, definitely. Something very much in keeping with the history of the house. It's a clause in the purchase agreement."

"Very well. Old English it is. We'll start with a tour around all the local antique shops and if we don't find what we're looking for we'll go farther afield. You know, I'm getting as excited as you are. I can't wait to get started."

George smiles and begins to clear the lunch things. I go back to my cataloguing and sorting.

Friday, 26th May

6.30pm

"What the hell is that?"

Michael is back, though whether semi-permanently or just for the weekend I have no idea.

"It's called a table."

"I'd call it a monstrosity. We didn't need a new one, did we?"

I'm sitting at my new old table, studying a second-hand macrobiotic cookery book from the 1970s that I found in the shop.

"Actually it's a very old table. Late eighteenth century. I bought it in a sale at Featherington Hall. The chairs too, but they're not quite so old."

"What were you doing there?"

"Books. I went with George to buy some and he ended up buying a piece of the place. Oh, and guess who I bumped into there?"

His head jerks up.

"Who?"

"Louise. She was there spending her husband's money. Bought most of the contents of the house, as far as I could see. I left her organising a pantechnicon to haul it all back."

"She does have a reputation as a bit of a shopaholic."

"You're not kidding. The back seat of her car was full of carrier bags from some fancy French boutique. She said she hopped across the Channel a couple of weeks ago. Week-end shopping trip with a friend."

He studies the surface of the table minutely.

"Well lots of people do."

Then he looks up.

"Where are the girls?"

"One out, one in. Jude's been riding. She just phoned to say she was getting a lift home from the stables with Mattie."

"Mattie?"

"A horsey friend."

I omit to say that I think she's quite smitten. Also that he's a thoroughly likeable young man

"And Sarah?"

"Back from the gym half an hour ago. She's in her room watching tv."

"I'll pop in and say hello before I shower."

He picks up his overnight bag and heads for the door.

"Michael, it's a good thing you're finally back."

He turns.

"Er, yes. It's nice to be home."

"That's not what I meant."

But he has already turned away, headed down the hall. I hear him going upstairs and turn my attention back to the cookery book, looking at recipes for beans. Apparently you have to 'pick them over', whatever that means, and then they need to soak overnight so clearly pulses are off.

7pm

"Wow! That looks great. Makes the place feel really warm."

Mattie and Jude have arrived home and he's admiring the table and chairs.

"Glad you like it."

"What are you cooking, mum?"

"Meatloaf without any meat."

"Do you need a hand?" (Mattie)

I love this boy!

"You can lay the table, if you wouldn't mind."

"Okay. Just let me wash up first. He makes for the cloakroom down the hall and Jude heads off upstairs for a bath.

Five minutes later she bounds back into the kitchen.

"Those clothes in my bedroom, was that you?"

"Mmm. I found them in the sale at Featherington Hall when I went with George last Monday. I thought you might find a use for some of them."

"They're wicked. Flapper, Edwardian. And some of that stuff's a lot older. There's hats, shoes, even a real ostrich feather boa. I'm going to show Mattie and Sarah."

She flies out again and I hear her calling their names. Sounds like they're going to get a fashion show.

We christen the new old table, all five of us. Michael produces a case of a chateau-bottled claret from the boot of his car. He says it's a new line for Pricerite which came over with the impounded lorry and he wants to try it himself. That prompts Jude to quiz Michael about the illegals but Mattie defuses a potentially explosive discussion by turning the talk to taking horses over the channel to shows in Europe, a much safer topic of conversation till someone mentions Brexit and how it's made animal movements much more complicated and that in turn sets Michael off on the whole EU thing. This time Sarah saves the situation, telling Jude and Mattie that if they're going anywhere interesting she wouldn't mind tagging along. Michael opens a bottle of the wine and we all have a glass, even Sarah, though she professes she'd rather have white. Lower in calories, I think, but don't say. When the food is put out she helps herself to the minutest portion of the meatless meatloaf, spreads some salad around the rest of the plate and spends most of the meal cutting tomatoes and radicchio into ever smaller segments, occasionally popping a piece into her

72

mouth where it takes her several minutes to chew and swallow. I glance surreptitiously at Michael to see if he's noticing but I don't want to be too obvious. After fruit and cheese and biscuits Mattie and Jude clear up and stack the dishwasher. I want to ask Mattie what he's done with my other daughter but I bite my tongue. Jude the Uncooperative transformed into Jude the Obliging. Then all three of them troop off upstairs to hang out.

Leaving Michael and me alone.

Michael pours us both more wine and pushes his chair back.

"You wanted to talk."

"Well, mostly it's about Sarah. You must have seen how she was at dinner. She hardly ate a thing."

"Not as much as the rest of us, I grant you."

"Trust me, I was watching. She did her usual trick. She takes a tiny amount, spreads it around her plate to look like more, then she just plays with it for half an hour. Hardly any of it goes in her mouth. And I told you about the call from her headmistress."

I fill him in about my visit to the surgery.

"Have you spoken to her about it?"

"A couple of times but she just denies there's anything wrong and flies off into a temper tantrum. And the doctor says that she has to go along voluntarily. It's no good trying to force her."

"Well, we'll just have to see if we can talk her round. Meanwhile there's nothing we can do."

"But she's getting painfully thin, Michael. I don't know how much longer we can put it off till she's seriously ill."

"I still think you're blowing this out of proportion. I'll have a talk to her myself. See if she'll listen to me."

"I don't think it works like that."

Michael picks up the tv remote.

"I want to catch the news. I feel a bit out of touch."

"Michael, there's something else."

He looks up sharply

"I thought there might be."

I don't know what to make of this remark so I let it go.

"It's about Philip."

"Philip who?"

73

"Philip I don't know. My Philip. My son."

"Jesus! That was years ago."

"It doesn't make any difference to me, Michael. It doesn't matter how long ago it was, it never gets any easier. I lost my child and it hurts."

"I thought we'd agreed to put that behind us. You have two daughters now. And that boy has grown up with new parents. He's not yours anymore. Let it go. There's nothing you can do anyway."

"There might be."

"What do you mean?"

"There's this website. It re-unites birth parents and adopted children."

"No, Feef. I won't let you. Think what it would do to the girls. If Sarah is a bit depressed that could just push her right over the edge. And what about me?"

"You? Where on earth do you come into it?"

"I should have thought it was obvious. What do you think it would do to my career if something like that got out?"

"Oh, don't be stuffy. Nobody cares about things like that anymore. And don't be so bloody selfish. It's all 'me, me, me' with you, isn't it? What about me? How about my feelings for a change?"

"Feef, I absolutely forbid it. It could have untold consequences."

"Forbid it? Just listen to yourself. You sound like some Victorian pater familias. You don't control me and anyway, it's too late."

"What do you mean? What have you done?"

"Nothing much. I just registered on the site that's all."

"Well, bloody well unregister."

"No, Michael. I want to go through with it. I want to find my son again, if it's at all possible."

"I just don't understand you. What good could it do? The boy's how old now, twenty, twenty one?"

"Twenty two. Last month."

"Well, that just proves my point. He's not a boy anymore. He's a man. With his own life to lead. Leave him alone, Fiona. Let sleeping dogs lie."

"Never exactly one for the 'mot juste', were you?"

"Don't get clever with me. You know what I mean."

"Yes, Michael. I know exactly what you mean. Philip is something nasty and sordid from my past. From before I met you."

"This is ridiculous. I'm going to bed. We can talk about it some more tomorrow."

He flounces out of the room, Jude-style, and I'm left alone again. Making a desultory effort to tidy up the kitchen I empty what's left of the case of wine into the wine rack and put the box outside for the dustmen. It's stamped 'Roget et Cie, Rue des Soldats, Calais'. Well, well, well. The French Connection.

Michael went off to do his stint at Pricerite Head office in Manchester for 3 months while I stayed on in Bristol. Patti had landed herself a job with BBC Bristol, just gophering but with a promise of better things to come. I was mildly envious of her burgeoning career while the only thing burgeoning in my life was my belly. Still, at least I could shop for baby things with her, knowing that I was going to be able to keep this one.

In complete contrast to my rather nihilistic state of being, Michael's mood on his return was what I could only describe as ebullient. Apparently Frances had taken him under his wing and sent him off to gain some first-hand experience in their stores around the greater Manchester and Merseyside area. "One-stop shopping is the future, Feef. And Pricerite is cutting edge." Seriously? What could be so exciting about joining a chain of supermarkets? He brought back what looked like a set of encyclopaedias which he told me was the corporate operational handbook and style bible which was for his eyes only. He insisted on going out and buying a safe in which to store them, a small, portable grey, steel affair with a combination lock, a combination he kept strictly to himself, I noted.

From Manchester he was sent straight off to Harvard Business School, arriving back a day too late for Sarah's birth at Bristol Royal Infirmary. "Our first baby", he declared, when he saw her. My unspoken thought was "Yours, maybe but not mine." And when I looked at him, at his challenging expression, I knew I don't have to say it. He produced a very professional-looking camera bag which he opened to display an even more professional camera with an array of lenses and lighting attachments, proclaiming that such high-tech items were too cheap to pass up over the pond. He then proceeded to take reel after reel of his new daughter. There were even one or two photographs in which I featured. The following day Mum and Dad came down and fussed over Sarah as though neither of them had ever seen a baby before and of course the subject of Philip was taboo. And Charles and Diana insisted on wetting the baby's head with a magnum of Bollinger and congratulating their son for being such a successful sperm donor. That's not exactly how they put it but it was what they meant. Cue more family portraits, with Sarah centre stage

I suppose it wasn't too bad at first. After Harvard Michael was sent to Reading as Assistant Manager. The new Pricerite store was on the outskirts of town and we bought a lovely old 16th century farm cottage a few miles away, courtesy of a huge down-payment from Charles and Diana, which I painted and papered right up till Sarah was born. Michael was in his element in the new job and he insisted we needed to entertain several times a month— Pricerite management, suppliers, big clients. That was when he found out I couldn't cook. Well, I suppose if I'm honest 'wouldn't' would be more appropriate. Up till then it hadn't been a problem. In Bristol he'd usually taken care of that side of things but now he didn't have the time. And anyway he saw it as part of my new role in life. Stepford wife.

Not that I didn't try. I signed up for a cordon bleu course at the local poly but I abandoned it half-way through. For one thing I thought it was boring. For another it was still a lot more interesting than my fellow students. A couple of young women who wanted to be chalet girls and thought they needed to learn some cooking skills first, some assorted au pairs who just wanted a break from childcare, young middle-management wives about my age who actually took the corporate entertaining thing seriously and a bunch of middle-aged matrons who hadn't got anything better to do. All seriously depressing. And every class was followed by a visit to a local pub or coffee shop where the chalet girls and the au pairs discussed their love lives, the young wives talked about Ikea furniture and baby formulae and the matrons planned chichi dinner parties and cruises in the Caribbean.

Oddly enough, considering how things turned out, Sarah was an easy baby. I bought her a really rugged buggy and together we took long walks in the countryside surrounding the cottage. And she sat and gurgled and smiled and took an interest in everything. And I couldn't help but wonder every time I looked at her how Philip had been at that age. Was he so placid and happy? When did he first smile? Walk? Talk? And the other mothers and staff at the baby clinic when we went along for jabs and suchlike would smile back at this contented child and ask me "Is this your first?", to which I always replied "Yes". It seemed simpler.

Even in those days Michael worked long hours. He enjoyed his work and he was very ambitious. So it was no surprise that only a year later he was promoted. I was pregnant again. Michael doted on Sarah and he pronounced himself keen on a larger family. Almost as soon as she'd taken her first steps he persuaded me to throw away my packet of birth control pills. Well, he thought he did. Actually I thought it was far too soon and I kept on taking them secretly. He couldn't understand why it was taking so long for me to fall pregnant. After three months he was puzzled about my apparent reversal in fertility. I told him it was early days. After six he started making noises about me going to see a doctor to check that everything was okay. After nine he made an appointment with Diana's Harley Street gynae and just the thought of keeping it panicked me into coming off the pill and as usual with me, I missed my next period. Michael relaxed, I threw up a lot and then came his promotion.

And a move to Maidstone. Pricerite was concentrating on the south east that time, far away from Cheshire and even further away from Scotland, thank goodness. I could only cope with Charles and Diana in very small doses and to be honest although I knew my own parents doted on Sarah it irritated me a bit. They'd been very instrumental in persuading me to give Philip up and in some irrational way I saw their devotion to their granddaughter as a sort of betrayal of my son.

So just outside a pretty little village in the Kentian countryside we bought an old oast house with 2 acres of garden. I painted and papered again and Jude arrived, screaming in protest on the 1st August. Michael declined to attend the delivery room but was on hand with the camera once mother and baby were cleaned up and presentable and yet more happy family snaps were captured once we were home with Jude and Sarah posed together prettily, to the strict instructions of the photographer.

Thursday, 1st June

1am

I'm in bed, dog-tired but I can't sleep. I lie awake and fret or sleep fitfully, tossing and turning and finally give in to a craving for caffeine and nicotine somewhere in the early hours and go downstairs to make tea and smoke. That's the way I handle stress—narcotic abuse and addictive crutches.

When I go back upstairs at an hour later I pass Michael's room. His door is slightly ajar and he is fast asleep, his breathing rhythmic, his dreams untroubled. He has always had that ability. Whatever problems beset him during the day, professional, domestic, philosophical, he can turn them off like a television set at night. Just clicks the remote and they're gone, at least till tomorrow. I don't know if he's beginning to share my concern over Sarah but the Philip thing infuriated him. I know him well enough to see that something else is rankling him but as soon as his head hits the pillow the programme is finished till he tunes in again tomorrow.

Friday, 2nd June

I finally managed to fall asleep but not for long. I rise at 6am, shower and go downstairs where Michaels is already drinking coffee and speaking on his cell phone. He breaks off abruptly when I enter.

I keep my tone light.

"Did you speak to Sarah last night?"

"Mmm."

"And?"

"She says she very stressed out with her end of term exams. Says it's nerves and she can't eat much when she's worried. But she'll be back to normal as soon as they're over. I thought that'd be it."

"And you believed her?"

"Well, let's wait and see, shall we?"

It's like talking to a brick wall.

"Do you want some toast?"

"No, thanks. I've got a breakfast meeting with the store manager. I need to catch up with what's been happening while I've been away." He depresses the plunger on the cafetière and pours himself coffee.

"About that other thing."

I turn away so as not to catch his eye.

"It's quite ridiculous, you know. Totally absurd after all this time."

I say nothing, just put on the kettle for tea and put some of Sarah's wholemeal bread into the toaster.

"Are you listening to me?"

I heard what you said, if that's what you mean.

I watch the toaster till the bread pops up. It hasn't browned very well but I butter it and take it over to the table, just as Jude comes down in a tearing hurry as usual. Today the school uniform is augmented with a cream, lace-trimmed blouse from the twenties and black, heeled flapper shoes from the same era.

"Thanks, mum. You must have heard me coming."

She commandeers my plate of toast, then twirls around to show me the outfit. "What do you think? They're both from the box."

Grabbing a knife, she rummages in the fridge, emerging with the pot of Manuka honey. At least one of my daughters is still eating.

"Very attractive. Whether the formidable Ms Forbes will agree, I'm not sure."

I pop a couple more slices of bread in the toaster and this time I get to eat it. Sarah walks in. I consider offering to make her some then decide against it. It's too early for confrontation.

"Time I was off. I take it you two are going with your father?"

Michael has been glaring at me throughout but now he attempts to smile.

"I hear Lulu's been ferrying you two back and forth while I've been away? Perhaps you should get her a card or a gift or something?"

'Lulu' as in 'My friends call me Lulu'?

I turn to the girls.

"Maybe you can have a look for something suitable over the week-end."

To Michael.

"What do you think she'd like?"

"How should I know?"

His tone is sharp and his response a little too quick.

"I just thought you'd know the type. You get women like her in the shop all the time."

He looks at me and I look back at him. Then I pick up the keys to the bug and leave.

Sarah was three and a half and Jude nearly two when I first starting suspecting that Michael was having an affair. It wasn't the unsociable hours he kept. I was used to those. It was something in his manner that I just couldn't put my finger on. Up till then we'd shared news of our respective days when he

79

got home in the evenings. Not that mine was exactly scintillating stuff. Dropping off Sarah at nursery school and picking her up again in the afternoon and most of the rest of the day spent trying to find ways to keep Jude the Inquisitive and the Irascible amused. She was as difficult as Sarah had been easy, grizzling constantly unless there was some new distraction to gain her attention. I had found a job of sorts, reviewing books on a freelance basis for the local paper. Reading them wasn't too much of a problem. I managed that late in the evenings, after the supper dishes had been cleared and Michael had either disappeared into his study or gone to bed. But writing up the reviews was a bit trickier. I put my antediluvian computer in a corner of the kitchen and hastily fitted in my writing between the very short peaceful interludes when Jude would finally consent to sleep for half an hour or so. And when both the girls were finally in bed and asleep and Michael and I could sit down to supper I'd tell him about the book I was reading and he'd talk about Pricerite, expansion plans for new stores, contract negotiations with new suppliers, land deals and the like. And I honestly tried to take an interest. This was the man I married after all and if that was what made him tick I had to accept it. But deep down I think I really despised it: The garishness of their store décor, the uniformity of their stock, the undermining of the small shopkeeper, the philosophy that bigger was better. And although I thought I hid it well, perhaps Michael suspected? At any rate he began to change. On more than one occasion he suggested that I was wasting my time with the book reviews. "It's not as though we need the money", he said dismissively one evening. "But I do", I replied. "I need to feel that I'm not just sponging off you the whole time. I need to feel that I'm making a contribution, if only to my self-respect." And he just laughed in a sneering sort of way and told me that what I earned wouldn't even keep me in cigarettes. He still professed to take an interest in the girls but it was always in a distracted, detached sort of way. And once or twice he even forgot to look in on them when he got home and he'd always done that.

And about that time his business trips grew more frequent.

Part II
"Blow, Winds, and Crack Your Cheeks! Rage! Blow! You Cataracts and Hurricanes, Spout Till You Have Drenched Our Steeples, Drowned the Cocks!"

Saturday, 10th June

8am.

Michael left at the crack of dawn again, though whether eager to get back to the office or just to get away from me and/or home, the jury's still out. Jude is also absent. Mattie came over half an hour after Michael left for work and the pair of them went riding. So with Sarah still in bed there's nothing to stop me using Michael's computer. I pull up Mother and Child then my stomach lurches. There's a message!

'I may know your Philip. Please give more details.'

My hands are shaking and I don't know how to respond. The message doesn't say it's from Philip but any lead would be a start.

So I type back 'Philip was born in Chester General at 1.45pm on April 24th **** . He had blonde hair and weighed 6lbs 11ozs. He went to his adoptive parents the following day. If you think this is the same person please get in touch.' I click 'send' and sit staring at the screen for a few minutes. Then I log off, heart pounding.

As I come out of Michael's office Sarah is coming down the stairs.

"Naughty, naughty, mum."

"I don't know what you mean."

"Yes you do. It's written all over your face."

"What is?"

"Guilt. You've been in the study and I bet you've been smoking in there as well, haven't you?"

If she only knew what I'd been up to and why I was apparently looking so furtive.

"There'll be hell to pay if dad finds out."

You don't know the half of it.

"Is it that obvious? I'd better open the window."

I keep my tone casual.

"Do you want some breakfast?"

"No, thanks. Just tea. No milk, no sugar."

We both go into the kitchen and I put the kettle on.

"Can I have a lift into town with you? I want to go shopping."

"Of course. Do you need any money?"

"No. Dad gave me some. He said I looked like I needed cheering up. You know, exams and everything. So he said I should go around the shops this morning and find something nice. Then I'm meeting him at work and he's taking me for lunch."

"Where?"

"The Butter Cup. It's an old houseboat moored on the river just outside town. It's been converted into a restaurant."

"Sounds lovely but what about the menu? Are you sure they do vegetarian food?"

"Vegan. Try and get it right."

"Do they cater for that?"

"Dad seems to think so. He says he's been there quite a few times. I told him I don't eat much at lunch."

Or any other meal, I think but refrain from vocalising.

"Well enjoy the shopping, anyway. You can tell me all about it this evening. Finish your tea. I'm just going to clean my teeth and then we can go."

I feel sick with anticipation all morning. What if it isn't Philip at all? What if I'm working myself up into a state of anxiety for nothing, a false trail, a different baby? And then again what if it is? Then what happens? And what if it's someone enquiring on his behalf and when he finds out he doesn't want anything to do with me? I could hardly blame him, considering the way I've blamed myself all these years. My son. It even sounds strange. All these years talking about 'my daughters' and trying to forget that I ever had a son. Not that I ever succeeded. And now maybe it's possible, just possible, that I might one day get to see him again.

Fortunately the shop is busy till closing time. Dealing with customers' enquiries is easier than dealing with the questions racing around my head. But as soon as the 'Closed' sign is put up on the door I grab my bag and head out.

"Ffion. It's not like you to be in such a hurry."

"Sorry, George. I have to get home and check something on the computer. I'll tell you all about it on Monday. Don't forget we're going shopping. I'll pick you up at half-past nine."

"Computers, is it? Ffion, my dear, mark my words, nothing good will ever come of messing around with machines like that."

"I certainly hope it will in this case."

84

Smiling at his puzzled expression I rush out of the shop. I'm frustrated by Saturday traffic as I drive home. Dozens and dozens of people with seemingly nothing better to do on a warm July afternoon than swarm around the shops spending money. As soon as I get in the door I make a beeline for the study and switch on the computer. As the site comes up I sit for a moment, take a deep breath and then click on my mailbox. There's a reply. I click again, cross my fingers and begin to read.

'The time, date and place fit in with the information I have. Please send some details about yourself.'

I'm elated and disappointed at the same time. I still don't know if the message comes from Philip or a third party. But it's a start. It takes me a long time to compose my response and I type and delete till at last I'm satisfied.

'My name is Fiona. I was seventeen when my son was born, unmarried and was just finishing school. I allowed myself to be talked into giving my baby up for adoption and not a day has gone by since when I haven't regretted it. It's my dearest wish to make contact again with the boy I called Philip.'

I clicked 'send', and sit and smoke two cigarettes, one straight after the other, trying to control my shaking hands. Then I take the dogs' leads, call Cromwell and Dottie and set out for a walk.

We walk for miles, past Lockitt's Farm, through a small copse at the edge of their property and then along the riverbank. And I play through different scenarios in my head. If the person who sent the two messages isn't Philip then who could it be? Surely not one of his adoptive parents? But who else would know? A friend he's confided in, perhaps? But in that case surely it meant that Philip himself wanted to make contact with me? Then again, perhaps not. Perhaps the friend was acting out of good intentions? Misplaced good intentions. But if it is Philip then surely it's a positive sign that he replied and asked for more details about me? And just suppose it is, how do I break the news to the rest of my family? Michael's reaction the other week told me all I need to know on his opinion but it's nothing to do with him—never was. And I've no idea about the girls. Jude will probably just raise her eyebrows and make some scathing remark about still waters and family skeletons. But I'm not at all sure about Sarah. I can't get into her mind these days like I used to. There's a space between us that I can't close and this might turn a short distance into a light year. And what about her anorexia? What effect would such news have on a condition like that? There's no way of knowing. Some of the information I read on the subject seemed to imply that the disease is triggered by background insecurity but other articles said that the causes are far from clear. I decide to take it one day at a time as far as my elder daughter is concerned. Then there's the parents. Mine will be baffled. In all those years since, they've never once mentioned it, not even when the girls were born. As far as they're concerned it was over and done with years ago, an embarrassing incident that's best forgotten. But Charles and Diana? I've never asked but I'd lay bets that Michael has never told them. Not that they're exactly related to Philip, of course, but there's definitely a family connection, one something tells me they wouldn't be too happy to hear about. Especially Diana. Unwanted teenage pregnancies don't really figure in her world, even today.

I sit for a long time on a tree stump on the riverbank with all these thoughts running through my head. And in the end I know that whatever happens I have to carry this through because I've wanted it for so long. Thought about it, dreamed about it and now the opportunity may at last be presenting itself, I have no choice. Nothing else and no-one else matters, except Sarah, of course, and I resolve to tread very carefully as far as she's concerned.

And once it's clear in my mind I call the dogs and we walk home.

Back in the house I have to summon all the willpower I can muster not to go into the study and log on to Mother and Child. It's way too soon and I don't want to be disappointed. There's nobody around downstairs but there are sounds of life upstairs. I walk up and find Jude, Matt and Sarah, all in Sarah's room, binge-watching some weird drama series. When there's a gap between dialogue I ask

"How was The Butter Cup?"

"Okay."

"Just okay?"

Sarah pauses and half turns away so I can't see the expression on her face.

"It's all cosy little booths, like those old chop houses they used to have in London."

"The ones in the Hogarth prints."

She nods, then pauses

"Dad must go there lots. The staff all know him. Are you sure he hasn't taken you there?"

"Positive."

"Funny, I thought you must have done. I wonder what gave me that idea?"

I don't know quite what to make of this remark but don't press it in front of the others. Cosy little booths? I can't remember the last time Michael took me anywhere like that to eat.

"At least you got out. You needed a break. I'm going downstairs to start supper. Are you staying, Mattie?"

He exchanges looks with Jude.

"I've asked him to stay over, if that's all right with you."

"Yes, of course it is. He can have the blue room. I'll take some clean towels in."

Another look I can't quite fathom exchanged.

'Them as ask no questions isn't told no lies'

I find a couple of towels and fluff up the duvet. Then I go down to the kitchen, make tea and take it out to the conservatory, along with a packet of cigarettes. Dottie joins me and flops down at my feet and I idly stroke her head with my free hand. Sarah seems brighter but I'm not convinced that it's any more than temporary. Some of the stuff I read talked about mood swings from deep depression to near euphoria and all points in between. And often in a very short space of time.

"Is there any more tea in that pot?"

Jude and Mattie have joined me.

"If there is it's probably gone cold. Why don't I make some more?"

I start to get up but Jude interrupts.

"It's okay, stay there. We can do it. Are there any biscuits?"

Jude the Amenable.

"I think there's a packet of shortbread somewhere. Try the cupboard next to the fridge."

The pair of them bustle around the kitchen and bring out a fresh tray of tea and biscuits. Mattie refills my cup and we all sit companionably around the colonial table in my new old chairs. John Burton who comes to do the garden a couple of afternoons a week has just mowed the lawn in lovely cricket pitch stripes and I can't help thinking that from the outside, looking in, we must look like an advert in Country Life for gracious living.

Appearances can be deceptive.

'Should we take some tea and biscuits up to Sarah? Lots of sugar and milk."

Jude the Acerbic shatters the illusion. I glance at Mattie, a little embarrassed.

"What's the matter, mum, don't like letting family skeletons out of the closet?"

Mattie's trying not to smile.

I'm trying too. Unsuccessfully.

"Sick jokes aren't funny, Jude."

All of a sudden I let out a girlish giggle. I can't help it. Jude joins in. The pair of us laugh till tears pour down our cheeks. Mattie looks on a little bemused but too polite to comment. Eventually we both subside.

"Seriously, it's not a laughing matter, you know, Jude."

We sober up.

"I know, mum. Sorry. I just couldn't help it."

"Me, neither. I think it's all been such a strain, the last couple of weeks. I'm worried sick about her and I just don't know what to do next."

"She told me you tried to get her to see a doctor."

"Fat lot of good that did."

"Thin, you mean."

We giggle again but this time keep it under control

"She just flat out refused. Said there was nothing wrong with her, just exam stress."

Mattie, looking slightly embarrassed, chips in

"She really believes that, you know. She can't help it. It's like alcoholism. Sufferers are always in denial."

"Alcoholism? I hadn't thought of it like that but I suppose you're right."

"Trust me. I've seen it at first hand."

I look curiously at Mattie but he doesn't elaborate.

"You have to get her to admit she has a problem and I don't think it'll be easy."

Jude nods.

"It won't. I've tried too. Told her she was looking too thin and she shouldn't lose any more weight. She just quoted that silly Wallace Simpson thing about never being too rich or too thin. As if she was any sort of advertisement. Ugly old stick insect with a big nose."

88

"So what do you two suggest?"

"We could get Mattie to hold her down while we phone for the men in white coats and get her committed."

"I'm serious."

"Who said I wasn't? I don't see you're going to get her admitted to a hospital or whatever any other way."

"She'll have to decide for herself and it'll probably take some sort of crisis."

"Like what?"

"Hard to say. But that's what usually happens with alcoholics. Collapsing in the street, getting fired from their job, something like that."

"Just wait and see. Is that what you're saying? That seems a bit passive."

"That's all any of us can do for now, mum. Come on. Let's go and start supper. I've got an idea. We'll count how many forkfuls she swallows and take bets. Loser loads the dishwasher. I say three. What about you, Mattie?"

"Four, but I bet they're all lettuce."

They pick up the tea things and carry them through to the kitchen. I follow with my ashtray. I can't afford to be too far away from it these days. As I'm walking inside I hear Michael's car coming up the drive. Come to think of it a glass of wine sounds like a good idea, too.

Sunday, 11th June

I lay awake last night thinking of the conversation with Jude and Mattie. I know it was wrong to laugh but it was harmless really. Just Jude's wicked sense of humour. Mattie might have brought about a miraculous metamorphosis in her manner but there are some things he'll never change, thank goodness. And at least I'm not the only one who realises that Sarah has a serious problem, even if Michael refuses to acknowledge it. That was an interesting comparison that Mattie made with alcoholism and anorexia. Both of them diseases that creep up on the sufferer gradually. One starts with a little social drinking, the other a little social dieting and bit by bit they take the person over, destroying personalities and destroying lives. And Mattie's right. You can't start treating either of them till the sufferer admits that there's a problem. Perhaps anorexics need their own victim support groups, like AA? Maybe there is some help out there? I suppose that's something else I could look for online. For a computer-phobic Luddite, I seem to be undergoing some sort of sudden conversion and I'm not sure it's a good thing.

Good thing or not, all day I'm dying to log on to Mother and Child but with Michael around the house I don't dare go into the study. It'll only cause more friction and I don't feel up to it at the moment. So I allow myself to be persuaded to go along to the stables with Jude and Mattie instead. I'm given a guided tour around all the stalls and when they've tacked up I watch them schooling over some jumps in the outdoor arena. And again I think it might be nice to get back on a horse.

Monday, 14th June

Today's the day I promised to take George shopping for furniture. As soon as I'm up and washed and dressed I phone him to confirm when I'll pick him up. Then I sit in the kitchen drinking tea and making lists of what he'll need. Michael comes in, pours tea from the pot and disappears off into his study without saying a word. I've been getting the silent treatment ever since I told him about trying to trace Philip. Not that he could have been accused of being a chatterbox before. Anyway I won't be able to get on to his computer while he's in the study and I doubt he'll come out till I've gone so I'll have to curb my impatience yet again.

One by one Jude, Mattie and Sarah appear. Jude's been fishing in the box again, this time for a Flapper-era felt cloche hat onto which she's sewn a school badge.

"Where's dad?"

"In his study."

"I'd better go and drag him out. Otherwise we'll be late. He's got to drop Mattie off as well."

"I'm going into town to take George shopping for antiques. I can take you."

"Well you've got the right car for it. I don't think Mattie'd appreciate you driving into school in that thing and dropping him off. Someone might see him."

Jude the Embarrassed. Some things never change.

"Drop me off in what?"

Mattie has walked in and caught his name.

"Mum's VW Beetle, circa 1990. She refuses to part with it."

"It's a classic. Convertible, too. Very cool."

The look on Jude's face is priceless.

"Can I drive?"

I turn away so June won't see my face, on the pretext of getting my keys out of my bag. I fish them out and throw them to Mattie.

"Fine by me. Why don't you go outside and warm it up for us? Just watch the clutch when you back out. It's a bit vicious. Sarah, go and tell dad that I'm taking you to school so he doesn't have to bother."

Sarah is sitting at the table listening to her iPod. She doesn't hear me. I go over and tap her on her shoulder. Even through her school shirt I can see protruding bones covered with a thin layer of skin. I have a sudden vision of Mattie putting the top down on the car and Sarah just flying out of the back seat as we drive along, like a cardboard cut-out. I shake my head so that the picture disappears and repeat my message. Sarah skips off to Michael's study with more energy than I would have thought possible on her calorie intake and I follow Jude out of the back door.

George and I are treating it like a holiday. I show him my list and he adds a few things to it. Apparently he wants a tallboy for the bedroom and a hat and coat stand for the vestibule. I tuck him into the passenger seat of the car and ask him if he'd like me to put the hood back up.

"Certainly not. It's a beautiful day. Let's enjoy it."

He pulls on a tweed cap, lights his pipe and I wait for a gap in the traffic and pull out. We head first for a large antique mall on the outskirts of town. It's in a converted barn and there are dozens of booths to browse around. We find a lovely Edwardian dinner service which George sets his heart on. I tell him it's far too expensive, we haggle with the stallholder and eventually agree on a price which I still think is too much. Then we pick up lamps and pictures and lots of things for the kitchen, stuff them into the bug and head out for a shop I know in a nearby village. There we find, as I thought we would, some of the larger items of furniture that George wants, even a very handsome cherrywood tallboy and we arrange to have them delivered to his new apartments.

Buoyed by our success we repair to the local pub for beer and an early ploughman's lunch which we eat at a wooden bench in a very pretty garden. Once again I'm struck by how wonderful it feels to be out of town and far from home for a few hours.

Filling up our glasses, the publican tells us of a local auction at a house in a neighbouring village. It's scheduled to start at 1pm so we forego our second halves and set off once again.

The sale is in a tall redbrick Georgian house, right in the centre of the village. Apparently the owner had recently died with no living relatives and the entire contents are being disposed of. Here George bids successfully for two large Persian rugs, a chaise longue and a job lot of curtains, some with a botanical flower motif, the others variously plain and regency striped. They are ridiculously cheap and by unpacking them from their box and spreading them around we manage to pack them all into the bug. And though we are now rapidly running out of room I also buy a box of unframed prints that no-one else seems interested in. There are 4 charcoal racehorse sketches that I thought I'd have framed and give to Jude on her birthday, some pastoral watercolour scenes and a number of very charming pictures of wild field animals—rabbits, badgers, stoats, game birds, all of them obviously done by the same hand and which I propose to hang around the kitchen to complement the new table.

Finally I try and talk George out of buying a Victorian dining table and eight chairs but he is very insistent and so gets his own way. I have to say that it is very handsome. We make a few enquiries and are directed to a local garage where the owner says he'll be happy to take George's purchases to Featherington Hall, which done, we squeeze back into the bug and drive triumphantly back to the shop. I drop George off, telling him I'll see him tomorrow and make my way home through the evening traffic.

"Where the hell have you been?"

Michael is standing in the entrance to the drive as I pull in.

"I've been trying to call you all afternoon but the phone's just been ringing and no-one answered. And your cell was on voicemail."

"I left it at home. And I don't work on Mondays. You know that."

That is to say I should have thought you would. I've been working at the shop for years.

"You can't expect me to remember stuff like that. So where've you been? Why didn't you tell anyone where you were going?"

"Christ, Michael, I'm not a bloody child. I don't have to account for my movements. Anyway I did tell someone. Jude, Mattie and Sarah all knew I was going out for the day. That's how I was able to take them to school."

"Well Jude hasn't come home yet and Sarah's not in any position to tell me."

"What do you mean? What's happened?"

"She collapsed at school. Melanie Forbes tried to get hold of you and when she couldn't she called me."

I feel sick.

"How is she? Where is she?"

"They sent her to the local A & E but I managed to transfer her to the Avon Clinic. The A & E doctor said she was severely dehydrated so they put her straight on a drip. I said we'd be along as soon as possible."

"God, Michael, this is awful. I should have expected it. Seen it coming. Shit, I did see it coming. I just didn't do anything. How is she now?"

"She's very weak. They're keeping her on the drip and they say they've going to keep her in and run some tests."

"I need to get over there."

I put the car into reverse.

"Don't be stupid. Put that wreck away. I'll drive you."

"What about Jude?"

"She's got a key. She can let herself in."

"Does she know what happened?"

"No, I told Melanie not to worry her. I said we'd tell her when she got home."

"She needs to know what's going on. Let me run into the house. I'll call her on her mobile."

"I've tried. She doesn't answer."

"She's probably riding. Look, let's go. I'll call her from the clinic when I've seen Sarah."

I park the bug in the garage and we both get in the BMW. That floral scent is there again but I say nothing. Just open the window and light a cigarette.

"Why don't you give up that filthy habit? It's not good for you, you know."

"Maybe not, but I'm not the one in the clinic, remember. Perhaps you should worry a bit more about what's good for your children."

"I do worry. That's why I pay for them to go to a private school with an excellent academic and sporting record. That's why we live in the house we do. That's why they have all the money they need. That's why they want for nothing."

"I wouldn't say that."

"What's that supposed to mean?"

"Well, for starters a bit of attention from you wouldn't go amiss. Maybe if they saw a bit more of you, Sarah wouldn't be in that clinic right now."

"You don't know that."

"No, I don't. But there has to be some reason."

"How about having a mother who's so obsessed with finding some young man she hasn't clapped eyes on for over twenty years she neglects the people on her own doorstep. How about a mother who can't boil an egg, let alone make sure her daughters are getting enough to eat? How about a mother who insists on embarrassing both of her daughters by driving round in a rusty pile of scrap that's over thirty years old, even though her husband has offered to buy her a new one? Shall I go on?"

"No, I think you've probably said quite enough."

I light another cigarette from the stub of the one I've just been smoking, as much to annoy Michael as to satisfy a craving for nicotine. We continue the journey to the clinic in stony silence.

Michael parks the car in the car park and we walk in the front doors together. Once inside he pointedly draws my attention to a 'No Smoking' sign in the foyer. A nurse at reception taps in Sarah's name into a computer and we are directed to a private room on the second floor.

Sarah is asleep when we enter which is just as well. At least she can't see the look of horror on my face. She looks dreadful, her face devoid of colour, a bony hand and skeletal forearm lying on top of the coverlet, attached to a drip. An electronic monitor next to the bed beeps rhythmically. A nurse is next to the bed making a small adjustment to the drip. She looks up and smiles as we enter.

"Hi. I'm Nurse Dakin. I've been looking after Sarah since she was admitted."

"How is she?"

"She's come around a few times and she has spoken a few words but she was a bit incoherent. She may have a mild concussion so we're just keeping an eye on her. But she was severely dehydrated so we've put her on a saline drip. I'll leave you with her for a bit but I'll be right next door if you need me."

She goes out, leaving the door open.

I approach the bedside and take hold of her hand. Michael brings over a chair and places it next to the pillow. I sit down and he perches close by, on the edge of the bed. Her breathing is shallow but rhythmic.

We sit like that for some time, an arm's length away from each other and neither saying a word. At about seven o'clock the door opens and a middle-aged man in a white coat enters.

"Mr and Mrs Hamilton? I'm Professor Turner. You can call me Stephen."

He picks up Sarah's chart and looks at it as he speaks.

"I'm Head of Department and the clinic's Consultant Psychiatrist. I was called in by the A & E staff as they were a little bit concerned at her condition. I'll be having a proper look at your daughter tomorrow. Meanwhile, perhaps we could have a little chat?"

He replaces the chart and looks up at us.

"My rooms are just down the hall."

He walks over to the door and holds it open. Michael and I walk over and then follow him down a pastel-painted corridor and into a room with the Professor's name on the door. Inside the walls are painted pale blue with dark blue shutters. Several Lowry and Hockney prints hang on the walls. A comfortable-looking sofa and easy chairs are arranged in one corner and in the opposite corner there's a desk and computer. Professor Turner takes a seat on one of the easy chairs and gestures for Michael and I to sit on the sofa. We sit down one at each end, scarcely glancing at one another.

"I'm told your daughter collapsed at school today and that's why she was admitted."

"Yes. They phoned me at work and by the time I got to the school they'd called an ambulance and taken her to Stratford General. I wasn't too happy about that so I had her brought here."

"Sarah is severely underweight for her height and age. That's why I was consulted. The ER doctor suspects she might have an eating disorder."

Professor Turner pauses here and looks at both of us.

"Well, I think she's probably been skipping a few meals. You know what young girls are like. And I know she's under a lot of stress at school. She's been studying hard for her mocks."

"Skipping a few meals? Don't be so ridiculous, Michael. You've seen what she's like at mealtimes, just playing with a few bits of salad and then shoving the rest in the dogs' bowls when she thinks no-one's looking."

"It sounds like you have some concerns of your own, Mrs Hamilton?"

I tell him all about the photo collage and the cut-up clothes and about my talk with Dr Patel. He asks if I've mentioned any of this to Sarah and I say not in so many words, but that I had tried to get her to go along to the surgery for a check-up.

"I think it's probably best if we keep her in here for a few days. We can run some tests to make sure there's no physical reason for her weight loss and I'd like to have a chat with her myself, find out more about what's going on. If she does have an eating disorder, and it certainly sounds as if that night be the case, then we'll have to decide what best to do next."

"What are the options?"

"Well, it largely depends on the individual. We do see some on an out-patient basis but I find it's better if they stay with us for a while. We have a small psychiatric unit on the top floor with a wonderful team who are all used to dealing with such illnesses. And it's a very friendly, relaxed atmosphere. It used to be the case that victims of anorexia were subjected to a very harsh routine, isolation, loss of personal privileges if they refused to co-operate, that sort of thing. It's still done like that in some places. But here at the Avon we take a more sympathetic, holistic approach. We try to find out in each individual case what triggered the problem in the first place and then work from there."

"And no doubt it'll all be blamed on the parents? Never mind that Sarah's never wanted for anything in her life—private education, a wardrobe full of expensive clothes, her own tv and laptop. What more could she possibly want?"

"I'm afraid it's not that simple, Mr Hamilton. It's true that many of these girls' problems have their root causes at home. But it rarely has to do with material possessions, either having them or not having them. Eating disorders have their root in severe emotional problems but we're not quite sure what triggers them. After I've had a chat with Sarah and been able to examine her properly I'll be able to assess her condition. If, as it seems, she does have a food-related issue we can start trying to find out what caused it in her case. And what we can do to reverse it. I have to tell you that it's a long, painful journey for these girls, for their families too. And there's no guarantee of success. Treatment is entirely voluntary and we find that many regress several times before they fully recover. I'm afraid statistically one in five never do."

He pauses and looked at both of us. Michael has turned his head away with a sceptical look on his face. I feel queasy.

"Our own rate is above the national average, I'm glad to say. Do either of you have any questions?"

I shake my head. Michael stands up and walks over to the window.

"I'd better phone Jude. She'll probably be wondering where we are."

"Here, use this."

Michael turns away from the window and hands me his cell phone.

"I'll leave you to make your call in peace, Mrs Hamilton. I have to go and do my rounds now. I expect you'll want to look in on Sarah again before you leave. I'm hoping she'll have a good long sleep. She seemed a bit incoherent when she was brought in but that may be confusion about her surroundings and how she got here. It'll probably all come back to her when she's awake. I'll phone you tomorrow after I've made my initial assessment."

He leaves the two of us alone and I call Jude.

"Mum, how was your day? Did George find anything he liked?"

The shopping expedition. It seems like a lifetime ago now.

"Very successful. But listen, Jude, I've got some bad news. It's Sarah."

"I wondered where she was. Is she okay?"

"Apparently she fainted at school this afternoon. She's been admitted into the Avon. They say she's severely dehydrated and they want to keep her in for observation. Your father's here with me."

"I'm coming over right now. Mattie'll drive me."

"No, don't do that. The doctor thinks she'll probably sleep till morning. I saw her earlier and I'm just going to look in on her again."

"Why didn't anyone tell me sooner?"

"Your father told Melanie Forbes not to worry you. I think he thought it'd be better coming from one of us. And he tried to call you a few times after school but your cell phone was off. Listen, darling, I'm going to pop back to Sarah's room now. I promise I'll ring you if there's any change."

I give the phone back to Michael.

"Are you coming with me?"

"I suppose so."

We walk back down the corridor to Sarah's room. Nurse Daklin is taking her pulse which she notes on the chart at the foot of the bed.

I walk over to Sarah's bedside and stroke her cheek. It feels cool to the touch, like very fine porcelain. As I touch her she moves her head and opens her eyes.

"Mum. What's going on. Where am I?"

She tries to raise her head and sit up. The effort proves too much and she flops back down onto the pillow.

"You fainted at school this afternoon, sweetheart. You're in the Avon. The staff here are worried that you might have hit your head when you fell so they're keeping you in overnight for observation."

I refrain from mentioning the 'A' word.

"I'm fine. Honestly. Can't I come home?"

She makes another attempt to sit up and with quite an effort this time manages to pull herself onto the pillow.

"I really think you'll be better off here for now, Sarah. I'm sure it's only a precaution but they don't want to release you till they're sure you're okay."

"Dad, can't you do something?"

"Well, like your mother said, it's just to be on the safe side. We can sort everything out tomorrow morning after you've had a bit of a rest."

"But I hate hospitals. I want to go home." Her voice rises hysterically.

I look at Nurse Dakin. She comes over to the bedside.

"Sarah, your parents are quite right. We need to keep an eye on you for the next few hours, just to be sure. Why don't you lie back down and rest?"

With a supreme effort Sarah flings back her bedclothes and tries to stand up. As she does so, her legs buckle underneath her and she falls back onto the bed, pulling out her drip line as she does so. Nurse Dakin moves round, swings Sarah's legs back onto the bed and efficiently re-attaches the drip line.

"Sarah, you're obviously very weak. Try and be sensible, darling. Just for tonight."

"I don't want to stay in this place. It smells funny."

But she lies back just the same and allows the nurse to pull up her sheet.

"Sarah, absolutely nothing's going to happen. All we want is for you to get some rest. Your father and I will stay as long as you want."

"What for?"

Sarah turns sulkily away.

"Because we love you and we don't like seeing you like this. Please just try and get some sleep. We'll sort everything out in the morning."

"Can I go home then?"

I think about what Professor Turner told us and glance quickly at Michael and Nurse Dakin.

"Professor Turner promised he'd look in on you first thing."

"He better had. I'm not staying in this horrible place a minute longer than I have to."

"Right. I'm through here for now so I'll leave you three alone for a while. Just give me a shout if you need anything, or you can press that buzzer there by the side of the bed."

Nurse Dakin leaves, this time closing the door behind her.

Michael and I sit for a long time. Sarah says nothing, just stares at the ceiling. Sometime around nine she finally falls asleep. I slip next door to the nurse's station. Nurse Dakin tells me she'll keep an eye on her and suggest we go home and then come back first thing. I ask if I can stay and she says that I can but warns that that would be liable to keep Sarah awake and fretful. I return to Sarah's room and have a whispered conversation with Michael who is keen to leave. He's clearly uncomfortable in this alien environment too. I'm reluctant to abandon Sarah but I'm outvoted. I tiptoe over to the bed and kiss her lightly on the cheek.

"Bye, darling. See you tomorrow."

As Michael and I step outside the door and walk past the nurse's station Nurse Dakin looks up briefly from her paperwork.

"She's come to the right place, you know. Professor Turner is wonderful with cases like your daughter's. He's got a remarkable success rate."

"Thank you, Nurse. If Sarah does wake up and starts panicking please phone me straightaway."

"Of course, Mrs Hamilton. But let's hope she sleeps through. A good night's sleep will do her the world of good. The lack of calories and nutrition that girls like her put themselves through make it hard for them just to get through the days. They all suffer from complete exhaustion and we find that for the first few weeks all our in-patients spend a lot of time just sleeping and relaxing, gradually regaining a bit of strength.

I glance anxiously at Michael but his face is a mask. Only his eyes reveal a look of scepticism and indifference. We walk to the car in silence but as soon as he backs out of the car park he lets out a tirade.

"Sanctimonious, jumped-up sod. Who the hell does he think he is telling me my daughter has emotional problems? What does he know about her home life, her background? Has he any idea how much her school fees are? The size of her clothing allowance?"

"From what he was saying, Michael, I gather those sort of things don't count for much in this sort of situation."

"What sort of 'situation'? What's that supposed to mean. You're beginning to sound just like him. Sarah is under stress at school from her exams. Because of that she hasn't been eating properly. And today she was feeling a bit light-headed at school and she fainted. That's all there is to it."

"Light-headed? She's a walking skeleton. Have you really looked at her recently? This has been building for months. And I blame myself for not doing more to prevent it sooner."

"You may very well blame yourself. If Sarah is unhappy about anything, and I'm not saying she is, then it can't help having a mother like you. Out working when you've no need, obsessing about a sprog you gave up twenty-odd years ago. Sarah's not the mental case. You are."

I'm stung by his words but determined not to show it. It's neither the time nor the place.

It's gone 10 o'clock by the time we get home. Jude and Mattie are still up and in the kitchen when we get back.

"Mum, how's Sarah? Do you want a cup of tea? I can put the kettle on. Or a glass of wine."

"A glass of wine sounds marvellous, thank you, darling. Sarah's being well looked after. She's on a drip and resting and they're going to run some tests in the morning—find out why she fainted."

Jude is opening the fridge and lifting out a bottle of Chardonnay.

"I think we all know why that was, don't we?"

"Probably but they have to make sure. And this way we know that Sarah's finally going to get some professional help."

Jude and Mattie have cooked supper—macaroni cheese. They've left it in the oven on a low light and it smells wonderful. I suddenly realise how hungry I am. Jude pours my wine, lifts a bowl of salad out of the fridge and sits with me at the table. Mattie lifts the dish out of the oven.

"I'm just going into my study to make a phone call."

"Why not use the phone in here?"

"Can't. It's too noisy. I won't be long. Start without me."

Mattie joins Jude and me at the table and I serve myself.

"Jude, this is great."

"Thank Mattie, not me. All I did was make the salad."

"Well, whoever's responsible, it's wonderful. Such a nice surprise."

"Mum, after you phoned I was thinking. All those jokes we were making about Sarah at the weekend and now this happens. It's like a sort of punishment."

I smile wryly. I know I deserve punishment but not for the reason she thinking.

"I do feel guilty about Sarah but not because of that. I should have been more insistent. I knew she had a problem but I just wasn't pushy enough. It's not that I didn't care. I just didn't know what to do. It's as much my fault as anyone's."

Mattie speaks up.

"It's nobody's fault. Sarah couldn't help what happened to her and there's absolutely nothing you or Jude could have done to stop it happening, believe me. Sarah's an addict. Only in her case she's not hooked on drugs. She gets high on abstinence."

"You'd know, would you?"

Michael sits down and looks at Mattie.

"Well, I've seen something similar fairly close up."

Mattie looks embarrassed and glances away.

"I take it you're not planning on going to work tomorrow?"

It's my turn to be confronted.

"Why? Are you?"

"That's you all over. Answer a question with a question."

"If you must know I'm going to drive to the Avon over first thing and then I'll stay as long as she needs me."

"It's a bit late to start playing earth mother, isn't it."

"For God's sake, Michael, can't you just try and be civil for once. Have you got any idea how upset I am about all this? Just because I'm not crying my eyes out and having hysterics doesn't mean I don't feel anything. I love my children, all of them."

"Don't you mean both?"

Jude misinterprets and leaps to my defence.

"Dad, don't be so pedantic. Can't you see mum's really worried about Sarah?"

"Sarah will be fine. Everybody's blowing this way out of proportion. I'm sure all she needs is a few days rest and she'll be right as rain."

"A few days rest? Exactly what planet are you from? Sarah's anorexic. She's seriously ill."

Jude the Accusatory. I've never heard her so angry where Michael's concerned. Fortunately Mattie intervenes before all-out war is declared.

"I'd better get some shut eye or I'll be useless tomorrow. You coming?"

"What? Oh, yeah. I suppose it is getting a bit late. Are you okay to clear up, mum?"

"No problem. Off you go."

The two of them go upstairs and Michael finishes his food in silence. Then he announces that he's going for a shower. I wait till he's safely out of the way then rush to his study and quickly turn on the computer. Cursing its slowness as it boots up I log on and sign in to Mother and Child to check my messages. Nothing. I'm disappointed but I try to tell myself that these things take time. As I log out something lying next to the wastepaper bin catches my eye. It looks like a rail ticket. I pick it up and examine it. It's a Eurostar ticket for 2 passengers, dated last month. I put it in my pocket and decide that before I leave there's one more thing I have to do. I push the re-dial button on the phone. The device at the other end rings a few times and then an answer machine cuts in. "This is the Sinclairs. If you want Lulu or Neil, leave a message. If it's Mandy call her mobile.".

I now know nearly all I need to. You start with a suspicion or an intuition. You gather intelligence and evidence. You sift through it physically and mentally, putting the pieces together like a complex jigsaw puzzle. Then just as you put the last piece in place, suddenly the whole picture becomes clear. Steve taught me that.

I still haven't told you about Steve, yet, have I?

I will.

When Michael comes downstairs I've cleared the table, loaded the dishwasher and helped myself to a last glass of wine and a cigarette. We pass in the hallway as I go up for a long and much needed soak in the bath.

"Did you get hold of whoever it was you needed to talk to so urgently?"

"What?"

"The phone call. Just before supper."

"Oh yes. I needed to confirm a few details about the new store opening with Francis."

Of course you did, Michael.

After my bath I make a quick call to George to let him know I won't be in tomorrow, then I go straight to bed. I set the alarm for six to make sure I get to the clinic as early as possible.

Tuesday, 15 June

5am

I needn't have bothered. I'm woken at five by the phone ringing insistently. It's Sarah calling on her mobile.

"Mum, what the hell's happening? I can't believe you left me here on my own. When are you coming to pick me up? Who said I needed to come here in the first place? Some stupid nurse said dad signed the admission form. I don't believe her. And I know my rights. They can't do anything without my consent and I'm definitely not giving it. I want out. Now. I'm not staying here. I need you to come and pick me up immediately. And if you won't do it let me talk to dad."

"Sarah, calm down. We explained everything last night. Don't you remember? You passed out at school yesterday. I was out with George so Ms Forbes called your father. He was so worried he had you taken there. And when I spoke to the doctor last night he said he'd like to run some tests. Just to make sure there's nothing seriously wrong. Look, just hang on in there. I'll be along as soon as I've got dressed."

"Well, bring me some clean clothes. All I've got is my school uniform from yesterday and this stupid hospital gown that doesn't even fasten properly."

"I'll pack some things and be right along. Okay?"

She hangs up abruptly. Clearly okay is what she is not.

"Who was that on the phone?"

Michael is outside the door, fully dressed for work. I'm out of bed and rifling through the wardrobe for something to wear.

"It's Sarah. She sounded hysterical. Blames us for booking her in to the clinic and insists on coming home immediately."

103

"Well, maybe she should, then. We can't force her to stay there against her will. I didn't like the sound of that idiot doctor anyway. She'll probably be better off at home."

"How can she be? Neither of us is equipped to deal with her problems. We have to persuade her to stay there for a few days at least. It's for her own good. I need you to back me up on this one, Michael. Next time she collapses it could be much worse."

"God, what did I ever do to deserve all this?"

Michael stalks off down the corridor and I jump into the shower. I wash and dress and then go into Sarah's room with a small overnight bag into which I shove a few sets of day clothes and underwear, some sleep shorts and tops and toiletry items. By the time I get downstairs Michael is up, showered and shaved and the kettle is on.

"I haven't got time for tea. I need to get there before Sarah does something silly."

"I'll come with you."

"What about Jude? How's she going to get to school?"

"Damn, I hadn't thought of that. What if I call Lulu and ask her to give her a lift? I think I've got her number somewhere."

I've got your number too.

"No, I don't think that's such a good idea."

"Why not?"

"Michael, it's not even half past five in the morning. She'll be asleep."

"Well, I'll call her from the clinic. I'm sure she won't mind."

"No. She's done more than enough recently."

My voice sounds sharp but I'm certainly not planning on apologising.

"I'm going now. On my own. You can take Jude to school and follow on then if you want to."

I pick up my car keys and leave the house before he has time to reply.

So early in the morning the roads are nearly empty and it only takes me half an hour to reach the Avon. I go straight to Sarah's room to find her up and pacing about. On her bedside table is a tray with tea and toast on it. It looks untouched.

"Are my things in there?"

She takes the bag from me and begins rummaging inside for her clothes.

"I don't want to stay in this place another second. It's horrible."

"Sarah, you can't leave before they've examined you. Don't be silly. The doctor said yesterday you might have had a mild concussion from when you fell."

"I'm fine. Well, I will be when I get out of here. Where's my clean uniform? I thought you could just drop me straight at school. Now we'll have to go home so I can get changed again."

"School?"

"Yes, school. You know, that red brick building I hang about in from Monday to Friday. The one dad's always complaining costs him so much. You may have forgotten that I have exams coming up. I can't afford to take time off. I need to get back."

She disappears into the bathroom with her underwear, a pair of jeans and a top. A nurse enters the room. It's a different one from the night before.

"Morning. You must be Mrs Hamilton. I'm Wendy Parks. I'm afraid Sarah's a bit upset and I see she hasn't touched her breakfast."

She picks up the tray.

"Nurse, can you tell me when Professor Turner will be available?"

"He usually comes in at half past seven to do his rounds upstairs. Then he has his counselling sessions and workshops from nine. I'm sure he'll want to look in on your daughter as soon as he arrives. He always likes to introduce himself to his new patients first."

I check my watch. It's six fifteen. Somehow I'll have to talk Sarah into staying put for the next hour or so. Then hopefully Professor Turner can take over, talk some sense into her. I say the words to myself but I don't really believe them.

Nurse Parks picks up the tray.

"Is that tea still warm?"

"I shouldn't think so. It's been here a while. I'll get rid of this and see what I can organise for you."

She takes the tray away and as the door closes Sarah comes out of the bathroom, fully dressed. The jeans only emphasise her thinness and she looks deathly pale.

"Who was that you were talking to?"

"A Nurse Parks. She says Professor Turner will be here in a while so we won't have long to wait. I'm sure you'll like him. He seems very nice."

"I'm bloody sure I won't. I hate doctors. Hate hospitals. They're depressing. They all smell of death."

"Well, this isn't really a proper hospital. It's a clinic. More specialised."

"In what?"

She sounds suspicious.

"I don't know exactly. Paediatrics, physio, oncology. I know there's a maternity unit. A friend of mine was in here a couple of years ago."

"In case you hadn't noticed I'm not pregnant."

"You're not a child either. So that's two departments you won't be visiting. Can we interest you in a bit of physiotherapy?"

"Mum!"

She's smiling. That's a step forward.

The nurse comes in with two cups of tea on a tray.

"There you go. And I found you some biscuits too."

"You're a star, Nurse Parks."

"Wendy, please."

I spoon sugar into one cup and offer the other to Sarah.

"No thanks. It's got milk in it. I don't touch dairy products, remember?"

"Suit yourself."

There doesn't much point in arguing just now so I drink both cups myself.

"Can we go now?"

"Not yet. I told you I want you to wait and see the doctor. Just to make sure you're okay and this sort of thing isn't going to happen again."

"It's not."

"You can't be sure."

Sarah picks up her mobile and starts dialling.

"Dad, I'm stuck here at this stupid clinic and mum's insisting I stay and wait for a doctor to have a look at me. I've said I'm fine but she won't believe me. I need to get to school."

She pauses and listens.

"Okay. And don't forget my uniform. See you."

She clicks off her phone and give me a look that says 'I went over your head'.

"He's coming right over."

"What about Jude? He's supposed to be taking her to school."

"He said Louise could take her."

106

I'm suddenly very angry but I don't want Sarah to see it. All the same, she looks at me very curiously.

In the end Michael and Professor Turner arrive at about the same time.

"Dad. I thought you were never coming. Can we go? If we leave now I can still be at school by nine."

"Well, I—"

Professor Turner interrupts him. "Sarah, I think it'd be a good idea if I had a look at you first. Just to make sure. Especially since you're here now."

Sarah moves over to Michael defensively.

"I'd rather you didn't. I just want to leave now. I need to get back to school."

"It won't take long. I'm sure you can spare a few minutes."

Sarah looks at Michael, then me.

"Then can I go?"

"Of course. So long as the doctor says you're okay."

Professor Turner goes to the door and calls for the nurse. When she arrives he asks if Michael and I could wait outside for a while.

"There's a visitors' waiting area just along the corridor, past the lift. It's got a tv and a coffee machine. Just go and help yourselves. I'll give you a shout when we're finished."

We follow his directions and I sit down and pick up a magazine for want of something better to do. Michael pulls out his cell phone and makes a call.

"Jude? I'm at the Avon with your mother. Sarah was in a bit of a state and she wanted me here. I don't think I'm going to be back in time to take you to school so I thought Lulu could take you. Do you want me to call her?"

He pauses and listens.

"Well I suppose it's okay. I'll see you later."

He switches off the phone.

"She says she'll call Mattie for a lift"

"Good"

Michael picks up on the tone in my voice and looks at me curiously. Then he turns away, pours coffee from the filter machine and switches on the local news channel. I get up and walk over to the window. The Avon is set in enormous, well-tended grounds, lovely rolling lawns, dotted with weeping willows and silver birches and stretching right down to the river and far in the distance I see people walking their dogs along the opposite bank as a few skiffs

107

and other small craft drift past. The sun is up and it promises to be another glorious June day. The irony isn't wasted on me. The pathetic fallacy turned upside down.

After about half an hour we're joined by Professor Turner. He too helps himself to coffee and sits down next to Michael.

"So how is she? Ready to go home?"

"I'm afraid not, Mr Hamilton. As I thought Sarah is quite definitely a fairly late stage anorexic. Her periods have stopped and she's beginning to develop some downy hair on her stomach and upper arms, both classic symptoms. If the situation is allowed to continue without professional help your daughter will most probably die."

Michael is looking at him in open disbelief.

"My daughter is a healthy seventeen year old. What are you talking about, 'die'?"

"Mr Hamilton, your daughter is extremely unhealthy. Her body weight is dangerously low, she has a BMI of 13 and she's running the risk of major organ failure. It's entirely possible that she may already have inflicted serious damage—I can't tell until I've run some tests. But I have to make you understand how crucial it is that Sarah gets the help she needs without delay."

"Does Sarah understand?"

"I told her pretty much what I told you. I find in these cases that the young women are usually in a state of denial and that the only way to get them to face facts and admit they need help is to be brutally frank."

"How was she after you told her?"

"She was very upset. But that's a good sign. I'd have been a lot more concerned if she'd seemed indifferent."

"Should I go and have a word with her?"

"I'd leave her for a while, Mrs Hamilton. Nurse Parks is with her. She's very experienced in counselling these girls and she'll stay with Sarah and answer any questions that she has. I've already explained to Sarah all about our rehabilitation unit upstairs and the sort of treatment we recommend in cases like hers. When she's ready Nurse Parks can take her there to have a look round. You can go with her then. Do you have any questions yourselves?"

"How long will Sarah have to be in here for?"

"That really depends on your daughter. Usually around six months but as I said a lot of the girls don't stay the course. They check out, relapse and have to be re-admitted. It can be a long, painful process for them and for their relatives. But let's hope Sarah manages to stick it out."

"And what exactly are you planning on doing to her"

"Nothing drastic, I assure you, Mr Hamilton. We don't force feed them, if that's what you mean. What will happen first is that Sarah will see our dietician and together they devise a realistic goal weight and a sensible eating plan so that she can work towards achieving that weight. In the mornings all the girls have a group counselling session where they're encouraged to share their problems and talk openly about their illness. In the afternoon they might have a one on one with either myself or one of the other doctors where we can go much deeper into the root cause of their own anxieties and slowly work through them. Meals are taken on their own to begin with. That's because it's such a difficult task for them. They're obviously reluctant to eat anything at all at first and we find that trying to do it in front of others just doesn't work. Later on when they're feeling more comfortable they can come along to the dining room."

"What about the rest of the time?"

"Well, if they're students like Sarah we encourage them to keep up with their studies. There's a small library and computer room where they can work. Otherwise they're free to join in one of our group activities. Some of the girls like to get out and help in the garden. We have a couple of sculls so they can get out on the river. A couple of them help out on Radio Avon—that's our internal hospital channel. There are all sorts of things they can get involved in. Again in the initial stages we like them to stay on the premises at night, watch tv and so on. But once they've been here for a few weeks they're free to go off to the pub or the local cinema, wherever they want. One of the staff members tags along for supervision on the first outing but it's just a formality."

"What about visiting?"

"We usually recommend that families stay away for the first week. No visits, no phone calls. Give the girls time to settle in to the routine and used to being away from home. After that you're pretty much free to drop in whenever you want. And once we feel the patient is beginning to recover we encourage the odd weekend visit home. They can also 'earn' a free pass if they hit one of their weight milestones. It's a good way of seeing how they cope out of this environment so that we can assess when they might be ready to leave us completely. You know, in a way it's lucky that Sarah fainted like that yesterday. Getting the girls here is always the most difficult part and the longer it takes, the harder it is to treat."

His cell phone goes off and he answers it.

"Sorry about that. They're wondering where I am upstairs. I'd better go and put in an appearance. I'm sure I'll see you up there later. I told Nurse Parks to come and find you when Sarah's ready."

"Thank you, Professor Turner."

"Stephen, please." He smiles and moves away

After he leaves Michael stands up.

"I never thought I'd see the day when one of my daughters was admitted to a psychiatric unit."

"I suppose you're going to say that that's what comes from having a mad mother?"

"You said it, not me. But I hope this means you're now going to give up your insane idea to trace that son of yours."

"Why?"

"Isn't it obvious? If Sarah's going to have to stay in this place you're going to have to start acting like her mother and give her a bit of attention. Give up that stupid job of yours, for a start. It doesn't even pay enough to keep you in cigarettes anyway. I can't see the point."

"Why is it that everything with you comes back to money? And do you really think Sarah's problems have got anything to do with the fact that I go out to work? I'm always home by the time the girls get back and they're not exactly kindergarteners anymore. They're teenagers with their own lives to lead. They'll be leaving home in a couple of years."

Until I'd spoken those words I hadn't really thought about it but suddenly I realise it's true. Always assuming we can get Sarah through this okay the girls will both be going off to university soon. And that means Michael and I will be left on our own. The implications of which I don't have time to deal with right now. So I tuck that thought away in the back of my cigarette packet and save it for later.

Nurse Parks appears.

"Would you like to see Sarah now? And then when you're all ready I'll show you upstairs."

She accompanies us to Sarah's room and holds open the door.

"Sarah, your mum and dad are here."

Then she turns back to us.

"I'll leave you three alone. Just give me a shout when you're ready."

Sarah's eyes are very red. I cross the room, sit down on the bed next to her and put my arms around her.

"Mum, he said I might die."

She begins crying again.

"Oh, Sarah, that's a worst case scenario. It's not going to come to that. Professor Turner is here to help you. We all are. The important thing is that you stay here till you're better."

"But I want to come home. I don't want to stay here."

"But Sarah, we're not the right people to help you, even though we're your family. You know that, don't you?"

She mumbles something, through her tears.

"Look, sweetheart, dry your eyes and try to not to worry too much about anything at the moment. Your father and I will come with you and see you settled in. And then we'll just take things one at a time. It's not forever and we'll be able to come and see you."

I pass her tissues from a box on the bedside table. Michael is hovering in the doorway, clearly embarrassed by the whole scene.

"Michael, why don't you see if you can find Nurse Parks and then we can all go up together."

"Fine."

He makes it sound like anything but.

The four of us make our way back to the lifts and up to the fifth floor. The décor is dusky pink and burgundy. There are picture windows with views of the grounds and the river and the whole floor feels light and airy. We turn off into a side corridor and Nurse Parks opens the door of one of the bedrooms. We all troop in except for Michael who stands awkwardly in the corridor.

The bed has a plum-coloured bedspread to match the carpet and curtains and there's an easy chair covered in the same fabric. On one of the walls, which are painted in a shade of dove grey, there's a mounted television set. A remote control sits on the bedside table. On the facing wall to the left of the door is a large, felt-covered pin board, under which stands a bookcase. The third wall is completely taken up with a bank of built-in wardrobes and cupboards and the fourth is half-filled with a large window. The overall impression is that of a hotel rather than a hospital. I cross to the window and open it—it only allows for a few inches.

"Oh, Sarah, look at the view. You can see for miles. And the river looks beautiful."

"I'll leave you to settle in for a bit and then I'll come and show you around."

Nurse Parks leaves. Michael remains outside.

"Right, let's unpack your things. And whatever else you need you can let me know and I'll bring them along."

I try to keep my voice light as I open the cupboard doors and start stowing cosmetics and clothes. Sarah is staring silently out of the window hugging herself tightly as though she were cold.

"Sarah."

She slowly turns round.

"It'll all work out okay, I promise. You'll stay here for a while, get better and then you'll come home. You'll be able to keep up with most of your schoolwork so you won't miss much. Think about it. If all goes well you'll be better by Christmas. Sooner, maybe."

"It's like a prison sentence and I haven't done anything wrong."

"Of course you haven't, darling. But you've been ill and you need help. I know it seems like a long time now but I'm sure it'll pass much quicker than you think."

A tear forms in the corner of her eye. She wipes it away with the palm of her hand. There's a tap on the door. Nurse Parks is back.

"Right, if you're ready let's go and have a look round."

Once again we follow her, Michael taking up the rear. As we cross through a large central seating area we pass a group of young women. All of them are thin and emaciated, some worse than Sarah, but they're chatting and laughing together. As they catch sight of Sarah they turn.

"Hi, you must be new. Welcome to Anorexics Anonymous."

This sets them off laughing again.

"Well, this is as good a time as any to meet our group. Sarah, this is Kim, short for Kimberly."

"Hi, Sarah. My name's Kim and I'm an anorexic."

The group packs up laughing again.

Nurse Parks points out a girl with short spiky hair the same colour as the curtains in Sarah's room and a matching belly ring.

"And this is Jo, Lisa, Akhila, Petra and Nessie. Girls, where's Anna?"

"Haven't seen her. She must still be in her room finishing breakfast."

"Okay, Well, you lot carry on. Christine's taking your session this morning."

She turns back to us.

"Christine Fisher, one of the nursing staff. We're all on first name terms here. I'm Maggie, by the way. The reason I was asking about Anna is that she's new to the programme too. It takes a while."

She doesn't elaborate but I assume she's referring to the problem of trying to encourage the girls to eat. We walk on a bit further.

"Right, this is the television lounge. All the rooms have their own tv but a lot of the girls like to get together to watch their favourite programmes. And through here is the library and computer room where you can catch up with your studies. That room the girls just went into is where we hold our group sessions. And the doctors' rooms are all down this corridor. That's for private counselling sessions in the afternoons. But most of the staff are around the rest of the time if you ever need to talk to someone. My little office is here and the nurses' station is right next door. We're all here to help you, Sarah, so just come and find one of us if you ever need a chat or some advice. And through here is the kitchen. Meals are prepared in the big kitchen downstairs but we all use this for snacks and tea or coffee. And through there's the dining room. We all eat together, staff and patients. Right, I think you've seen just about everything. It all probably seems a bit strange right now but don't worry, you'll soon settle in. Why don't I take you along to meet Christine now and you can join the other girls for the last bit of this morning's session."

Sarah looks startled.

"Er, I'm not sure. I mean…"

"Don't worry. You won't have to do or say anything if you don't want to. Just sit and watch and listen. It'll help you to get to know the other girls in the group and see what goes on. Have you got a cell phone?"

"Yes, it's here."

Sarah takes it out of her jeans pocket.

"I'll look after that for now."

Sarah looks at me, panic-stricken.

113

"Sorry, house rule. You can have it back in a week."

She takes the cell phone then gently shepherds Sarah away from my side.

"Right, say goodbye to your mum and dad and we'll get you started."

"Bye, darling."

I give her a hug.

"Remember, we're here if you need us."

Nurse Parks looks at me and shakes her head with a small gesture that Sarah can't see. I remember the rule about no contact for a week. Now I'm fighting back tears too. Michael is dry-eyed but visibly shell-shocked by the whole process. He also hugs her.

"Bye, Sarah. If you need anything, anything at all, you let me know."

"Bye."

Sarah's voice comes out as a whisper. And then she's gone.

Michael and I make our way back to the lift, down to the ground floor where we fill out some admission forms. Then we go back out to the car park. As soon as we're outside I light a cigarette. Michael shoots me a dirty look.

"You know, what Mattie said the other day. That anorexics are like alcoholics. Those girls reminded me of it just now when they introduced Sarah to AA. It's just a different addiction, you see. Alcohol or abstention. And I'm just as bad, only in my case it's nicotine. Sarah's going to go through a rough few months but she's braver than me because I'm still smoking."

"You could stop if you wanted to."

"Maybe. But I'm not sure I do, that's the thing."

"Then what do you want?"

"I don't know."

"It's nothing I can give you, is it?"

I turn and look at him.

"I'm not for sale for the price of a new car, if that's what you mean."

He looks at me oddly and something in his expression brings me up. Of course, the silver Mini. Perhaps he'd get me a matching one if I asked.

He takes my keys and opens the door of the bug for me.

"I may be late home. There's a lot to organise with the new Edinburgh store. I need to fly up before the end of the week."

"Fine."

I climb in and he closes the driver's door. Then he walks across the park to the BMW. I watch him for a few seconds, put the car into first and drive out.

114

It's such a relief to be back in the shop. I tell George everything that's happened and how awful it was having to leave Sarah, especially not being able to see her or talk to her for a whole week."

"Well, my dear Ffion, it sounds like it's for the best, you know. She's in good hands now and these things are better sorted sooner rather than later. Now, how about a nice cup of tea? Irish breakfast, I think. You need something strong."

The sun is shining strongly through the shop front, highlighting the particles of dust in the air. I pick up a feather duster and some furniture polish and set to dusting the shelves and the books. And though I tell myself it's terribly disloyal and hardly the time or the place I find myself wishing there was a computer in the shop. Then I chide myself for even thinking about it, as though my subconscious was trying to replace a lost daughter, albeit temporarily, with a found son. Fair exchange is no robbery.

At lunchtime I rush off to Simmonds for ham and cheese rolls. I'm tempted to go to the library and use the computer there but I feel guilty about leaving George again when I came in so late. I console myself with the thought that I'll be home hours before Michael so I can use his then. Back at the shop I give Jude a call in her lunch break.

"How's Sarah?"

"As well as can be expected, isn't that what they always say? When I first got there she was insisting on coming home straightaway. She thought it was some sort of conspiracy getting her there in the first place."

"So she has to stay?"

"Her doctor said it's the best place for her to be right now. He had a long talk with her and persuaded her that if she didn't stay for treatment she could die....diet."

"Diet? Isn't that what she's already doing?"

"Yes. I meant she could overdo it. And it's better for girls in Sarah's condition to stay there to make them face up to reality. I suppose it's a bit like an alcoholic finally admitting to themselves they're got a drinking problem, like Mattie said the other day. He seems to know a lot about it."

"It's his mother. She's been on and off the bottle for years. Been to all the best clinics but apparently she dries out for a few months then she has another relapse."

"Poor kid. It's a wonder he's as level-headed as he is."

"Well, he's very close to his father. And I know he loves his mother but he says it can be hard sometimes. That's why he's so good at cooking and stuff. He's always had to fend for himself. Look, mum, the bell's just rung. I've got to go. I'll see you later."

"Okay, darling. Bye."

After lunch George goes out to sort out some paperwork for his new apartment, leaving me alone. At half past three the shop door opens and Louise walks in.

"Feef, you poor thing. I've just heard. Mandy sent me a text message telling me about Sarah. How simply dreadful. You must be devastated. I think it's so brave of you to come into work. I'd be a complete wreck if anything like that happened to me. I'd just go to pieces. Is there anything I can do?"

I keep my voice icily polite.

"No thank you Louise. I'm sure we'll manage."

"Well, I'm sure it's no-one's fault. No-one could blame you. It must be difficult keeping track of things with you working all the time. I suppose you just didn't notice anything was wrong. And what about poor Micky? I know he dotes on those girls. How's he taking it?"

Micky?

"Why don't you ask him yourself next time you see him?"

I smile sweetly as I say this.

"And now if you'll excuse me I really must get on with some cataloguing. I walk to the door and pointedly open it."

"Oh, right. Well, I've got some shopping to do in town. But I meant what I said. If there's anything I can do, anything at all, just give me a ring."

Well, actually, Louise, there is. You could stop screwing other people's husbands in your own backyard. Not that I really care, it's just a matter of principle.

"I'm sure we'll be fine, thank you."

"Give me your number, just in case."

She produces a Samsung phone from her handbag. The one from the dry cleaners. The penny drops about Michael's cagey reaction.

"Mandy's got my number."

"Oh yes, of course."

And I've got yours.

"That looks expensive, Aren't you worried you might lose it?"

She gives me an odd look and I smile sweetly. Then I stand by the door waiting. She takes the hint and exits, leaving a trail of expensive scent behind her, the same one I've smelt so often in Michael's car. I shut the door behind here and lean against it, trying to compose myself. My hands are shaking. In fact I'm trembling all over. The bare-faced cheek of the woman. I stay like that for a couple of minutes and then the phone rings.

"Fifi, I've just heard about my darling grand-daughter."

What is this, the bush telegraph? Is there anyone in the whole of the British Isles who doesn't know?

"Michael phoned me at lunchtime. Poor boy. He's beside himself with worry."

He hides it well.

"So naturally he phoned me. And I've had a chat with Charles and he thinks it would be a good idea if I came to stay for a few days."

God, no.

"We were planning a little trip to Tuscany. Some very dear friends of mine have a villa there and they've been pressing us to come and stay for ever. But I daresay we could postpone for a few weeks."

A few weeks? If this morning was like a bad dream this is turning into a nightmare.

"Diana, dear, it's very sweet of you to offer but really we'll be fine. There's nothing you could do. None of us are allowed to see Sarah just yet anyway. She has to have time to settle in to her treatment."

"But what about Michael? You know what men are like in situations like these. No good at all. They just go to pieces. And poor Jude. Her only sister struck down by a wasting disease that could kill her. Anything could be going through her mind. She needs someone to keep an eye on her."

"Well, she's got me, Diana."

"Well, that's no good, is it? Not with you spending all your time with those dirty books."

Dirty books? What does she think this is, a porn shop?

"Jude will be fine, Diana. We all will. It's Sarah we need to worry about now and I can assure you she's in excellent hands. Michael arranged for her to be admitted to a wonderful private clinic, lovely surroundings, very

117

experienced staff. She's in the best possible place and we'll all be giving her as much support as possible. So there's really no need for you to change your holiday plans."

"No, I absolutely insist. Charles and I will set off first thing Thursday. I'll probably stop in Edinburgh on the way. Pick out something nice for Sarah to cheer her up. Anyway we should be there sometime early evening."

I resign myself to the inevitable.

"Fine. Well, we'll see you both the day after tomorrow."

The shop door opens again. I'm relieved to see it's only George back from his meeting with the agents.

"Signed, sealed and delivered, Ffion. What the young people call 'a done deal', I believe. But I'm sure you don't want to hear about that at the moment. You must have other things on your mind."

"Actually, George, it's a change to hear about something normal. I've just been told that my in-laws are arriving on Thursday which is just about all I need."

"Then you'll want some time off work to look after them. Take all the time you need. I can manage on my own for a few days."

"Good lord, no. This job is the best excuse I have for avoiding them as much as possible. They're Michael's parents. He can look after them."

The shop door opens again and a middle-aged woman in a turquoise jogging suit enters.

"Hello, there. I was wondering if you had any Barbara Taylor Bradford paperbacks. Only I'm off to Spain tomorrow and I always like to pack a few in my bag when I go on holiday. She's a marvellous writer, isn't she?"

George raises his eyes heavenwards and goes off upstairs. I smile.

"Very popular. They're over here. I think we've got pretty much all of them in stock. Did you have a particular one in mind?"

She follows me over to the far corner where we keep our romances and beams delightedly at the choice. She spends some time making her selection and by the time she's paid and left it's just after five. I call upstairs.

"George, I'm off. I'll see you tomorrow."

Then I rush out, locking the door behind me. I'm anxious to get home and check my messages as soon as possible but the first thing I see is Michael's car in the drive. The study computer is out of the question, then. I consider asking Jude if I could use her laptop but that would inevitably lead to a barrage of questions I don't want to answer so for now I'll just have to curb my impatience.

Lipstick on his collar. That would have been too easy. There was nothing I could really put my finger on. Even his trips away seemed genuine enough. As soon as he'd joined Pricerite, Francis had been grooming him for greater things and it was about the time that he started shooting up the corporate ladder. Which meant that he was quite often summoned up to the head office in Manchester at a moment's notice, or sent around the country to site meetings whenever a new store was being built. So he was away for days at a time and of course there was hardly any cellular network in those days so it wasn't easy to get hold of him. And when he was at home he just seemed sort of distant, somehow. Distracted. Sex became perfunctory at best. And when one day I asked him outright if anything was wrong he looked startled and utterly offended and said "No, of course not. Why should there be?"

So naturally I knew there was. I just didn't know what exactly.

Then one week he went down to Devon to find a suitable site near Barnstable. He said he'd probably be away for a week. And I don't know what made me do it. Jude was just getting over a cold and still at the niggly stage and I hadn't been away anywhere since she'd been born. And on Friday morning I suddenly thought we could pay Michael a surprise visit. A couple of days at the seaside for the girls and change of scenery for me. So I threw some things into a bag, stuffed Jude's buggy into the Beetle and headed south. Michael had phoned me on Monday evening when he arrived and told me he was staying at a small hotel called The Splendide on the front. The girls and I arrived about half past three and it wasn't hard to find the place. I knew Michael wouldn't be there but I was sure I could talk the hotel staff into letting us into his room. And that's when all the wheels fell off.

I parked right outside, gathered up the girls and went into reception. There was a young woman behind the desk and I went up and introduced myself as Mrs Hamilton.

"I thought we'd surprise my husband. I know he's out at work but I thought you'd probably have a pass key so I could drop my things off and get cleaned up."

"Mrs Hamilton?"

Her tone of voice and the look on her face both said she thought I'd recently escaped from the local mental institution.

"Er, perhaps it would be better if you waited till your husband came back."

"Hardly. I've got two children under five, one of whom needs changing. We've been three and a half hours on the road and I need to sort them out, have a bath and then get them something to eat and drink. So if you wouldn't mind just letting us into the room."

"Wait there, Mrs Hamilton. I'll just go and get the manager."

"Oh, for heaven's sake."

She backed away, clearly flustered, and disappeared into a back office. Irritated I looked around for the loo and took Jude off to change her while Sarah amused herself on the floor with her new colouring book. And it was when I was coming back out that I saw her. Cindy Prince. A young woman from Pricerite's marketing department. Power suits, high heels, short skirt, long blonde hair and silly, affected voice. I'd met her at a couple of store launches. She was coming down the main stairs and when she saw me she stopped dead in her tracks. She tried smiling but it froze on her lips. For one second she looked about to come over to me, then she turned on her heels and rushed out of the front door, looking like Crystal Carrington on speed. And just at that moment the receptionist returned with the manager. He took in the fleeing figure of Cindy Prince and me with Jude in my arms, stood stock still outside the ladies and I could see him making a mammoth effort to compose himself. He stepped forward with an artificial smile fixed on his face.

"Mrs Hamilton, I'm Mr Compton, the hotel manager."

But I'd seen enough. Had enough. How could I have been so blind and stupid when the signs had been there all along. Her all over my husband like a bad rash, gushing his praises in that silly, high-pitched voice of hers. Mind you, she was all over everyone, that was the way she was, so no wonder I didn't take too much notice. But the frequent trips away, the store launches, the meetings at Head Office. Suddenly it was all clear.

"Mr Compton, I think there's been a mistake. I must have the wrong hotel. I'm sorry to have bothered you."

And with that I scooped the girls back up and left with as much dignity as I could muster. I strapped them both into the car. Sarah was asking when we were going to see daddy and why we were leaving.

"Daddy's not there, sweetheart. Mummy's got the wrong hotel."

"Are we going to another one?"

"I'm not sure. Just be quiet for a minute, Sarah. Mummy's concentrating on the traffic."

I pulled out and headed off down the road with no clear idea of where I was going. I was trying desperately not to burst into tears. After twenty minutes or so of aimless driving I came up to a set of traffic lights and a big sign said left for Bodmin and Truro and right for Exeter, Bristol and Bath. I went right.

It took about 2 hours to reach the outskirts of Bristol. Patti had stayed on there, still working for the BBC. She'd married a local news producer called Ross Badger and I knew they were living in Bath. I skirted the city and took the A3 and arrived in Bath about half past six. It was a warm evening and the town was alive with students and visitors strolling around the streets and sitting drinking coffee and beer outside pubs and bistros, looking carefree, happy, normal. It was like watching a film. I left the town centre and on a side street pulled over and fished in my handbag for my address book, hoping that I'd remembered to write Patti's new address in it. I had. Flat 1, 31 Covington Place. Where the hell was that? I pulled out again and drove around for ten minutes till I saw a Police Station. By now both of the girls were fast asleep so I left them in the car while I ran in to ask directions. I remember the sergeant at the desk looking at me rather oddly and saying "Are you all right, love?" I told him I was fine and did my best to smile reassuringly. I'm not sure I was very convincing but anyway he took me over to a big street map on the wall and pointed out Covington Place and the one-way system.

It was the ground floor on a street of Georgian townhouses. There were pots of red geraniums on either side of the front steps and the solid, black front door looked freshly painted. I got out of the car and rang the doorbell. No-one answered. God, I was thinking. What am I going to do if she's out? Or worse still, away on holiday. I rang again. Then I heard footsteps and the door opened. It was Ross.

"Sorry. We were in the back with the tv on and it's hard to hear the bell."

He stopped and looked at me.

"Good heavens. Fee. You're the last person I was expecting. What brings you here?"

"Em, I was in the area and I thought I'd drop in. I hope I haven't come at an inconvenient time?"

"Not at all, no. Come on in."

121

He opened the door wider and shouted through to the back of the flat.

"Pats, we've got a visitor. Come and see who's here."

I hovered in the doorway, looking back at the car.

"I brought the girls with me. They're asleep."

Patti came out from a door at the back of the hall.

"Fee. What a lovely surprise."

She rushed up and gave me a hug, then she also looked out at the car.

"Is Michael with you?"

"No, just the girls."

I tried to keep the tone light as I said it but it was a waste of time. Patti was always too good at reading between the lines. She'd been the only one who told me right out that Michael wasn't the right man for me. We'd almost fallen out when I told her I'd turned down the publishing job to get married.

"You're a fucking fool, Fee. He won't make you happy and you're not cut out to be a corporate wife."

"I'm pregnant."

"Get rid of it."

"I can't. Won't."

And that's when I told her about Philip. She was the only other person in the world who knew.

And now she looked hard at me and I waited for her to say 'I told you so'. But all she said was

"Ross, help Fee with her bags. And let's get the girls inside."

I picked up Jude, still fast asleep while she unstrapped Sarah and lifted her out. Then I followed her and Ross into a big bedroom at the back of the flat. There was a chintz bedspread on a big double bed, with matching curtains.

"I think there's a camp bed somewhere if you need it."

"We'll be fine, don't worry. We can all squash in here."

"Look I'm sure you want to wash and change. The bathroom's through there. Sort yourself out and then come and join us in the kitchen. I'm just about to start supper."

"Thanks, Patti."

I unpacked the holdall and fielded a thousand questions from Sarah. 'Where was daddy?', 'Why had we come to see Auntie Patti?', 'Was daddy

122

coming to join us?', 'How long were we going to be here', 'Would she be back in time for school on Monday?', 'When could she have something to eat?'. Jude had woken up too so I marshalled them both into the bathroom and ran a quick bath. Then with all of us clean and changed I took them into the kitchen.

"The girls must be starving. Shall we feed them first. How about a boiled egg and soldiers?"

"That's for babies."

"Well, Jude is a baby. What would you like?"

"Please can I have a sandwich?"

"Of course you can. Ham or cheese?"

"Both."

Nothing wrong with Sarah's appetite in those days.

Ross laughed.

"A young lady who knows her own mind. Right, sit down here, you two."

He pulled out 2 chairs and sat them both at the kitchen table, grabbing a couple of cushions from an easy chair for Jude.

"I'll see to the sandwich and the boiled eggs while you big girls have a chat."

Patti picked up an open bottle of wine and two glasses and we went outside. There was a small paved patio with a table and chairs and after we'd sat down Patti poured the wine.

"Okay, do you want to talk about it?"

"Not really. You'll only say 'I told you so'."

"Well, that's a given. What's he done? Screwed his secretary?"

I told you she was perceptive.

"Marketing assistant. Leggy, blonde thing with an affected voice."

"How did you find out?"

I explain all about his late nights and trips away and the embarrassing incident in the hotel.

"So you left?"

"I thought it was a good idea under the circumstances."

"I s'pose so. She'll have told Michael, of course."

"Of course."

"So what now?"

"I'm not going back."

"Good for you. Pity it took you so long."

123

"Is it okay if we stay here for a few days, just till I can sort something out."

"Fee, you're my best and oldest friend. Stay as long as you need."

"What about Ross?"

"Oh, don't mind him. He'll be in his element. He's always on at me to throw away my pills and have a couple of kids. He's dying to be a father. He'll adore having the girls around."

"Thanks, Patti. I really appreciate it."

"Hey, what are friends for? Now, come on. Let's go and rustle something up for supper. You must be starving."

It took about two weeks for Michael to work out where I was.

Patti and Ross had been great. No pressures, no questions, just stay as long as I wanted. Thursdays were Patti's day off so she offered to babysit and give me some time to myself. I used the time to try and find somewhere to live and to start looking for a job. I'd seen a couple of likely places on the noticeboard at the local paper shop so the first thing I did was walk around and get the details, then I went around to check them out. A couple of them turned out to be no more than bedsits, hardly suitable for two children. And one was a dingy, plasterboard, partitioned affair with a shared kitchen and bathroom. Then I had a bit of luck. The ground floor of a small, terraced house with a tiny little galley of a kitchen and a small strip of garden at the back but completely self-contained, clean and fairly cheap. 'I'll take it,' I told the owner. I wrote out a cheque as a deposit and pocketed the keys. I went back to tell Patti and then I went and sat down with a copy of the local paper, going through the sits vac column with a fine tooth comb, marking anything I thought looked promising. Unfortunately after several futile and frustrating phone calls I realised that with no hands-on experience and no practical qualifications to speak of, it wasn't going to be easy. I drove to the local Job Centre where they pretty much told me the same thing though they did send me along to a couple of places looking for what they called a 'Girl Friday'. No luck at either of them. I don't think I was exactly what they had in mind—late twenties and two small children to consider and my only work experience as such was my part-time book reviews at the Chronicle.

I was sitting having a cup of tea outside a little café a few streets away from the city centre when I looked across the road and saw a sign on the building saying 'Bath and Avon Gazette'. And I suddenly thought 'Why not?'. So after my tea and a fortifying fag I walked over the street and into the offices of the Gazette. A young girl was sitting at a scruffy desk just inside the door, simultaneously talking on the phone and typing something on an old computer. Beyond I could see half a dozen desks, all empty except for the one at the back where a middle-aged man in a tweed jacket with leather elbow patches was performing the same double feat as the receptionist. I hovered, not wanting to interrupt. As I waited a man who looked to be in his early thirties came out of a small office with a glass window facing into the corridor. His sleeves were rolled up and he kept pushing a lock of blonde hair out of his eyes.

"Sorry, Classifieds closed at twelve o'clock. If you come back tomorrow morning it'll be in Monday's edition."

He moved off in the direction of the man at the rear.

"Em, actually I'm looking for a job."

"Job? What sort of job?"

"Anything."

"Have you got any experience?"

"Well, I have done book reviews. For the Kent Chronicle."

"Don't really need anything like that at the moment."

"Oh, right. Well, it was just a thought. I saw the sign, you see. From the café over the road."

"Wait a minute. I've just had a brainwave. Have you got a car?"

"Yes."

He looked hard at me.

"Come through here."

I followed him into his office. His desk was a tip, littered with papers and overflowing ashtrays. He pointed to a hard wooden chair in front of the desk.

"Take a seat. I'm Steve, by the way. Driscoll."

"Fiona. Fiona Hamilton. Pleased to meet you."

"That sounds Scottish but you don't."

"No, I'm from Chester, actually."

"But you've been writing for the Kent Chronicle."

"I moved."

"And now you're in Bath?"

"I moved again."

"Well I might be able to offer you something if your copy's any good. I'm two reporters down at the moment. One's sick and the other's on holiday. So we've got a temporary vacancy. The one guy does sports but I think I know

someone who can cover for him. Which leaves local events. Fêtes, funerals,
marriages, christenings, the odd court hearing. Interested?"

"Definitely."

"Right. How's your shorthand?

"Short."

"You can type, I take it?"

"Two fingers. But I'm quite fast."

"Fair enough."

He leapt up from his desk and bounded into the outer room. I picked up my
bag and followed him. He stopped at one of the desks and pulled out the chair.

"This is Eric's desk. He's the guy on leave. Just type me something off the
top of your head. You said you've done book reviews. Write me one on this."

He threw the phone book across the desk at me. I smiled.

"So long as I don't have to read the whole thing."

"Nope. Just the juicy bits."

He turned away to shout something to the man at the back who was still
typing away on a keyboard furiously. I thought for a moment, flexed my fingers
and began. Half an hour later I was finished. I hit 'print', collected the sheet
from the machine and went through to Steve's office. He took the paper and
leaned back in his chair while he read.

'This is a cracking read. From first to last the pace never lets up. Right at
the start Police, Fire and Ambulance are all on the scene and on the next page
you're whisked from one emergency medical centre to another. Local
government and big business are both involved but the main protagonists are
identified only by their last names and an initial which leaves the reader with
more questions than answers. Open it at any page and you're exposed to a
slice of humanity at its most raw and basic. A name, a number, tantalising
clues to the identity of the person. And then the trail goes cold. It's a mystery
worthy of Hercule Poirot. The story starts with the mysterious Aaron, B. How
and why is he linked to Abbey, H.? And why has a page been torn out, right in
the middle. If we could find it, would this prove to be the missing piece of the
puzzle?"

He read on to the end. Then his face, deadpan throughout, lit up.

"If you want the job you can start now."

"Goodness."

I checked my watch.

"I suppose it's okay. What have you got in mind?"

"We've been running a few articles on traffic congestion in the city and what's being done about it. Why don't you drive around the city centre a few times. See what it's like, how easy it is to park, that sort of thing. Stop a few people in the street and get their views. Then come back here and file it. Little filler—only about 200 words. I'll need it by six."

"Can I make a phone call first?"

"Help yourself."

I called Patti and asked if she'd mind having the girls till I'd finished. Which of course she didn't. Then I took the notebook and the little Dictaphone Steve gave me and set off for downtown Bath on my first ever journalistic assignment. It proved fairly easy. Traffic was at a crawl at best and a complete standstill at worst around much of the city centre. I did three circuits, just to get the feel of it, then I went looking for a parking place which took forever. When I finally found a space in a multi storey I took the machine and canvassed a couple of people who were just leaving or getting back to their cars. They weren't impressed, to put it mildly. And they were even less impressed with the way the city council was handling it, especially the constant hold-ups from road works and the never-ending contra-flows. Then I strolled around town, stopping a few people at random. Same story. Finally I paid a visit to the municipal offices where I spoke to a very pleasant young man in the roads department. He told me that the root of the problem really lay in Georgian streets trying to absorb new-age Elizabethan traffic. Also people still preferred to use their own transport rather than take advantage of the Park and Ride scheme. He wasn't quite so forthcoming on the subject of roadworks and admitted that it was a constant problem, especially in the holiday season. He photocopied plans of the current contraflow system for me and gave me a brochure with details of the Park and Ride timetable. After that I decided that I had enough material so I drove back the Gazette offices and sat down to type it all up. I finished just after six, gave it to Steve and asked if he minded if I left to relieve my babysitter.

"No probs. Come in tomorrow around twelve. I'll give you a couple of other assignments and we can talk about money. Welcome to the team."

He smiled, then returned to his PC, typing furiously.

Driving back to Covington Place I felt happier than I had done since walking into the hotel nearly two weeks ago. I had a job, albeit temporary, and

127

it promised to be quite enjoyable. I'd be able to move into the flat and start re-building my life. The only problem would be the girls. I could enrol Sarah at a local school but I'd have to find a decent day-care centre for Jude. I wondered who to ask. No good talking to Patti about that sort of thing. I was still pondering on all the variables when I arrived back at the flat. I rushed in, called out to the three of them and then went through to find them in the garden. Patti was drinking tea and the girls were playing on the small lawn with a dolls' tea service, obviously copying 'Auntie Patti'. I bounded up to the table, beaming all over my face, and full of my news said

"Guess what?".

One look at Patti's face wiped the smile off my face.

"What is it? What's happened?"

She poured me a cup of tea and without looking up said, "Michael phoned."

Wednesday, 18 June

The atmosphere in the house is even more fraught than usual. Michael is grinding beans and teeth in one corner of the kitchen, I'm doing tea and nicotine under the extractor fan and Jude is eating a bowl of cereal, her undivided attention on an open copy of 'All's Well That Ends Well' propped against it.

"Shouldn't you have finished that last night?"

"No, I was supposed to have learned Act II by last Friday."

"So why didn't you?"

"Too busy."

Michael makes a noise halfway between a snort and a grunt and turns his attention back to the cafetière.

"What time did they say they'd be here?"

"Early evening."

"I'll try and get away early but I can't promise anything, not with the organised chaos up north. I may have to stay up there for a few days."

"Can't you cancel now your parents are coming?"

"It's business. They'll understand. Did they say how long they'd be staying?"

128

"Overnight, I was hoping, but I don't think that's what your mother's got in mind."

"You never really liked her, did you?"

"I like her better when she stays in Scotland. And I'm not really up to house guests at the moment. I've got enough to cope with. Anyway, I'm off to work. Jude?"

She doesn't look up from the Shakespeare.

"Mmm?"

"Nothing. Bye."

On the way to work I'm struck by the fact that not one of us so much as mentioned Sarah. It seems disloyal but what is there to say for now? It's out of all our hands and part of me is guilty, the other relieved that at last she's getting the professional help she needs. I have promised myself I will only call twice a day—it'll be an effort not to do so more often—and so far I have basically been told she's 'settling in' she's 'coping as well as can be expected', with which scant and non-informative bulletins I have to content myself. George bustles in with tea, English breakfast, he tells me, so I can keep my strength up.

"And a little of this, I think."

He picks up a bottle of brandy from the tray.

"George, it's only just gone nine o'clock."

"My dear Ffion, I think from what you tell me that it's going to be a very long day and you're going to need all the help you can get. And it's strictly medicinal."

He tops up my tea with a generous tot and waits till I've taken a sip.

"Better? Now, I've been doing some thinking and I believe I might be able to ease the situation."

I look at him sceptically over the rim of the cup.

"Well, from what you've told me, Charles and I have a vaguely similar background. So the chances are, we'll find something in common, school, regiment, club."

"Regiment? You were never in the army, George."

"Aha, my dear Ffion. That's just where you're wrong. Officer cadet at school and then two years in North Africa and Israel in the sixties. My sort all had to then, you know. The family expected it."

"All right, assuming you can find some common bond with Charles, how's that going to help?"

"Elementary, my dear Hamilton. I use Charles to get to Diana. Compliment her on her exquisite taste, lead the conversation around to interior decorating, drop a few broad hints about how a colour-blind old bachelor can't be expected to know about such dilettante pursuits, how the new apartments need the feminine touch and so on and Bob's your uncle. I guarantee she won't be able to resist. We can take her out to have a look at the place, show her what needs to be done and I suspect that after that she'll be practically camping out there."

I give him an old-fashioned look.

"George, you wily old trout. It might just work. Cheers."

I pour some of the brandy into his tea, we clink cups and I feel moderately more cheerful and not on account of the eau de vie. After that a steady stream of customers keeps me occupied till lunchtime. Then I tell George I'm going to have to skip lunch and go shopping. I jump into the car and head off for Pricerite, the first time I've been there for as far back as I can remember. The car park is fairly full so I drive around the back to the employees' area and there's no mistaking the silver Mini parked next to Michael's BMW. I grit my teeth and march past his secretary into his office, ignoring her feeble protest that

"He's in conference."

Michael is sitting behind his desk, with Louise perched on the corner nearest his chair. As I enter, the pair of them leap to their feet like a couple of teenagers caught smoking behind the bike sheds.

"Louise, fancy seeing you here."

"Er, I was just leaving actually. I was in the shop and I thought I'd pop in and say hello. See how Sarah is."

"And how is she?"

Louise gives an embarrassed, girly little giggle.

"Mandy and I are so worried. It's simply dreadful. Anyway, I must dash. I'm sure I've taken up enough of your time, Micky, love. Don't forget, Feef. I'm right here if you need me."

"How kind."

And right there if my husband needs you too. She picks up her handbag, smiles sweetly at both of us and exits.

"Well, this is a bit of a surprise. So what brings you here?"

"Shopping. I thought that's what people did in places like this?"

"Not people like you."

"Oh, people like who, then? Louise?"

"Well, yes, I suppose so. She's one of my regulars."

"Yes, I'd heard that."

I keep my face impassive.

"Actually I'm here on account of your parents. I didn't think Diana'd be very impressed with my usual culinary repertoire. I was thinking of something that will heat up easily in a cauldron. What does Louise usually buy?"

"Louise is quite a gourmet cook. Very professional."

"I bet she is. Look, I'd better get on with the shopping. I don't want to be too late back to work."

"I'll come with you."

He leads me through the executive offices and into the back of the store. Once inside he collars an employee and sends her off to fetch a trolley. Then we walk over to the fresh produce section. Michael picks up a couple of bunches of asparagus and holds them till the trolley arrives, at which point he begins to fill it in earnest. From fresh produce we walk over to 'cook chill', then 'dairy produce', the butchery department and the fresh fish counter. This feels bizarre. It's years since Michael and I have been shopping together. By the time we get to the check out the trolley is filled to bursting so another minion is commandeered to pack them in a strong box, the entire lot is bar-scanned and Michael signs the till slip.

"You won't have room for all this in your car. I'll get it delivered this afternoon."

"Thanks."

He walks out to the car park with me.

"I'll see you this evening. I should be back about seven."

"Fine."

He opens the car door and I get in. He tries to give me a perfunctory kiss on the cheek, for appearance's sake, no doubt but, Di-style, I duck away and put the car in gear. He shuts the door and I drive back to the shop.

As soon as I'm back I pick up the phone, dial the number of the clinic and ask to speak to Maggie, hoping she's still on duty. She is.

"It's Fiona Hamilton. I just wanted to see how Sarah's doing."

"I thought you'd call around about now! Sarah's not too bad. We keep them very busy for the first few days so they don't have too much time to worry about home or their new surroundings. She was very quiet in the first couple of group sessions but that's to be expected. I sat with her at lunch again. It took a while but she did manage a couple of spoonfuls of soup. And when that was finished she had a one on one with Stephen—Prof. Turner."

"How did that go?"

"We usually have a staff meeting at half past nine when we go through all the cases. So that'll be tomorrow morning and we'll probably map out a fuller plan for Sarah then."

She paused.

"It does take time."

"I know. Sorry."

"Don't apologise. She's your daughter."

"There was one other thing. I know it probably sounds trivial but she'll need things—clothes, stuff like that. I hardly brought anything with me for her this morning."

"Just pack it all up, whatever you think she'll need. You can drop it off downstairs. They'll make sure she gets it."

"I'll get her sister to help me. She'll know better than me what Sarah uses. Won't you tell her I'll drop if off for her as soon as I can?"

"Of course. And you can phone me anytime. I'm usually somewhere around."

"Thanks."

I put the phone down and suddenly want to cry.

I get home just after five. The groceries are stacked outside the back door, so the first job is to take them inside and unpack them. I've never seen the Italian fridge looking so smug. 'Just don't get used to it', I think. As soon as everything's stowed away I shoot off to the study, shut myself in and log on to Mother and Child. There's a message flag and my stomach lurches, till I remind myself not to get my hopes up. Quite right, too. It's just another platitudinous update from site management telling me that the membership is growing exponentially and my chances of finding my lost family are getting better by the day. I mark it as read and am about to log off in irritation when another flag icon pops up. I'm tempted to ignore it after the last one but then decide I might as well check, just in case. I double click and the message comes up on the screen.

'Hello, Fiona. I may have some information for you. Are you on social media?'

Social media? As if! What a cryptic message. I wonder if I'm being taken for a ride, someone playing a joke. I can't think why they would but you read so many stories of people being duped on these sort of sites. I ponder for a moment and decide on my response.

'No, I'm not but I can give you more information about myself and the person I'm looking for if you can be more specific about what you want to know'

I hit 'Send' and immediately regret it. That sounded so terse and impersonal. What if this person really is just trying to be helpful and I've basically blown them off? What if it's Philip and I've come across as a cold, hard bitch, the sort of cold, hard bitch who'd give up a baby with scarcely a second thought? I feel slightly sick. Oh well, it can't be unsent so let's wait and see. Reluctantly I log off and get up. Then still with a horrible sinking feeling I head for the kitchen.

Jude and Mattie are already there, sitting at the table drinking tea. Mattie fetches another cup and pours for me.

"I didn't hear you two come in."

"I stuck my head around the door of the study but you were so intent on what you were doing on the computer you didn't notice. Since when have you been so computer literate? What are you up to?"

"I'll tell you another time."

"So it is a secret?"

"Sort of. But I will let you into it soon. Promise. And whatever you do, don't say a word to your father. In the meantime there are more pressing issues. Namely the imminent arrival of the dreaded Diana."

"She's not that bad. I quite like it when she comes. She always throws a lot of money around."

Jude the Avaricious.

"Gold digger. For that you get to help me cook supper."

"What are we having?"

"Stuffed trout. I know you don't eat fish. You can have an omelette."

"Nope. Fish is fine. Mattie says it's really good for you. It's not veggie but it's sustainable. How do you stuff a trout anyway?"

"I haven't a clue. These are pre-loaded. Pricerite's answer to haute cuisine for the harassed housewife or the inept daughter-in-law."

"So why exactly are the old folks gracing us with their presence?"

133

"Blame your father. Apparently he rang Diana and told her about Sarah and she suddenly took it into her head to play the ministering angel. And I wouldn't use the phrase 'old folks' in her hearing, if I were you."

"Duh! I'll tell her how fab she looks and ask what's her secret. That should be worth a few quid."

"You have a seriously greedy streak that must come from your father."

"Some girls collect dolls. I collect dosh."

Jude grins and then the two of them start setting the table while I stick the fish in the oven.

Michael, Charles and Diana arrive almost at the same time. Mattie took one look at the Bentley sweeping into the driveway and raced outside for a better look, Jude close on his heels. I dutifully follow as Michael also pulls up and gets out. Regal as ever, Diana waits for Michael to open the door for her, then steps gracefully out. She embraces Michael and 'my darling Jude', holds me at a slight distance and kisses the air somewhere behind my ears, steps back and says 'And who's this handsome young man?' Mattie introduces himself, steps around to the back of the Bentley to help Charles with the bags and is rewarded by a beaming smile, Diana's equivalent of the royal seal of approval.

So far so good.

We troop into the house and bags are carried upstairs. Talking non-stop to Michael and Jude, Charles and Diana go up to their room to wash and change, leaving Mattie and me in the kitchen. I pull a bottle of Chardonnay out of the fridge and give it to him to open.

"Quite something, isn't she?"

"Your mother-in-law or the Bentley?"

"Both, I suppose. They've got quite a lot in common, when you think about it. They both come with a high price tag, they both cost a fortune in refurbishing and maintenance, they both turn heads and they're both high-class status symbols."

"Mrs H, you're a bit of a rebel on the quiet, aren't you?"

"Not much to rebel against by the time I was old enough to care. Except capitalism, I suppose. I did have a 'Cuba Libré' poster on my wall as a teenager."

"Free Cuba?"

"Rum & coke! And now Jude wants to free battery chickens and Asian sweat shop workers. What about you? What do you want to liberate?"

134

"Right now? The cork from this bottle'll do."

He grins at me with that very disarming smile of his and with a deft twist of the wrist he opens the Chardonnay.

"Years of practise. Long story."

"I'd like to hear it sometime."

The upmarket, oven-ready fish from Pricerite were so easy even I couldn't stuff them up. That came out as a bad pun but it wasn't meant to be. When everyone was seated and served and heaping compliments on the chef, I decided that discretion was the better part of valour. Not that I proclaimed them all my own work, I just forbore to mention their retail origins. There was one nasty moment just after we started eating when Charles said he wondered why I hadn't asked him to tell his ghillie to catch me a few fresh ones from the burn on their property which I managed to pass off by saying that I hadn't wanted to put anyone to any trouble. But on the whole the conversation jogged along on fairly safe grounds. The paper mill, the new Pricerite store in Edinburgh, how Jude was getting on at school. Then as we cleared the plates from the main course Diana made some patronising remark about it being high time I learned to cook properly. I thought it was a fair cop and opened my mouth to confess but Jude jumped in with "Mum's great in the kitchen, isn't she, Mattie?"

Michael snorted but Mattie re-joined with, "Certainly is. Makes a kickass cup of tea."

Diana winces at the language and I got up to clear plates and fetch the dessert—Pricerite Superior Selection Tiramisu, pre-decanted into sundae glasses, the packaging tied up in carrier bag and deposited in the dustbin. Hiding the evidence—it strikes me that I have quite an attention to detail that would prove very useful were I to choose a life of crime.

"Hear that Diana. I may not be able to boil an egg but I can boil a kettle."

"Well you know what Michael thinks, don't you?"

More or less but I'm sure you're going to tell us anyway.

"He thinks if you'd spent a bit more time in the kitchen Sarah wouldn't be that hospital now and none of this would have happened."

The table falls quiet. I carry on adding wafers to the pudding.

"That's not really true, gran. Sarah's illness has got nothing to do with mum. It's just one of those things."

"Nonsense, Jude. And please don't call me 'gran'. My name is Diana."

"Mattie, Jude, pass the pudding around, won't you?"

135

I hand them the dishes, lift a bowl of whipped cream from the fridge and sit back down at the table.

"He has a point, you know. You've always been more interested in your work than in your home. And what sort of a job is that anyway? Handling all those nasty old books. You don't know where they've been."

Someone else's bookshelves, mostly.

"You've got a library full of old books at home, Diana."

"That's not the same thing at all. They've been in the family for years, generations some of them."

"Well, we do have some very valuable volumes in the shop too. You know, I should introduce you to George Fitzsimmons, my boss. I know he'd love to hear about your library. He's a collector, you know."

"I have no intention of selling any of them if that's what you mean."

"No, no. Of course not. George's collection is very specialised, anyway. First edition botanicals, and Jane Austens mostly. It's just that books are his whole life and I know he'd love to hear what you've got. He's from an old Irish family, himself."

Charles looks up.

"Would he be one of the Dublin Fitzsimmons?"

"I think so."

"I was at school with one of them. Archie. Ended up in the same regiment."

I love it when a plan comes together.

"Well, you can ask him when you meet him. Why don't you pop in sometime tomorrow?"

Diana's face was looking decidedly frosty. It always did when she felt she was losing control of a situation.

"I rather thought we'd spend the day visiting Sarah. That is why we're here, you know."

"She's not allowed any visitors right now, Diana. I did explain that to you on the phone."

"Nonsense. We're her grandparents and we've travelled a long way to see her. I'm sure they'll make an exception."

I raise my eyebrows in Michael's direction. It's his turn.

"I don't think so, Ma. They seem very strict on that point. Absolutely no visitors or home contacts for the first week."

"It's utterly barbaric. Are you sure these people know what they're doing? Why don't you speak to my man in Harley Street? He could recommend somewhere."

"Well, let's see how she gets on first, shall we? At least the Avon is close."

"What use is that if they won't let you visit?"

"Only for a few days."

"How long do they think she's going to be there?"

I look first at Michael and then Jude, Mattie and I all exchange glances.

"Well? Is someone going to tell me."

"They're not sure, Diana. But if all goes well she should be home before Christmas."

"Christmas? But it's only June. How can it possibly take that long?"

"Anorexia is a very difficult condition to treat, Diana. Very complicated."

"It seems perfectly simple to me. Sarah hasn't been eating properly so she's lost a lot of weight. All she needs is to follow a proper diet so she puts it back on again."

"Would anyone like some coffee?"

Mattie to the rescue again. If he didn't exist I think I'd have to invent him.

"Good idea, Mattie. Do you want some help?"

"Jude and I'll manage. And we'll load up the dishwasher while we're about it, won't be, Jude?"

"We will? Oh, right."

"Thanks, you two. As it's such a lovely evening why don't we go and sit outside for a while. Diana, you must see how lovely the rest of these chairs look with my old bentwood table. I bought them a couple of weeks ago at an auction at Featherington Hall. And I know you're quite an expert on these things."

"I hope you didn't pay too much for them? They're very below-stairs. About 1840, I'd say. Though they are in remarkably good condition."

The moment has passed for now. We troop outside where Charles lights a cigar and I have a much-needed cigarette while we wait for the coffee and Diana launches into a long lecture on the changing styles of English furniture through the nineteenth century. Safe ground.

Michael and I are bickering about who should stay at home and entertain Charles and Diana who are both still in bed.

"They're your parents."

"Yes, but you can afford to take off work. I can't."

"How do you work that out? If I'm not there it leaves George all on his own."

"Well, you're not exactly W.H. Smiths, are you?"

"That's not the point. George isn't a young man. He can't manage everything by himself."

"Look, this is ridiculous. You know how busy I am with the new Edinburgh branch. I've decided to fly up tomorrow morning. There's a red eye from Birmingham which means I can be there by eight."

I stare, open-mouthed.

"You are joking, aren't you? With Sarah in hospital and your parents in situ. You're planning on dropping everything for a jaunt to the Scottish capital?"

"I told you I'd have to go. And it's not a jaunt, as you put it. It's a bloody site meeting. Make sure everything's in order before we open the doors. And check on the arrangements. Francis is cutting the tape at this one personally. It's a big thing for Pricerite. Largest hyperstore north of the border. I'm not leaving anything to chance."

"Except possibly your daughter's health."

"Oh, here we go with the histrionics again. Sarah's in excellent hands, she's not allowed visitors so I can't see it'll make any difference whether I'm here, there or in Timbuktu."

I can't pretend I'm surprised at this turn of events. I capitulate.

Michael takes his coffee and disappears into his study. The subject is closed.

Friday, 20th June

7.30am

Diana doesn't appreciate being woken too early so I tiptoes around getting ready and I'm in the kitchen toute seule, drinking tea. Jude breezes in dressed in the boater and the button-up boots and wearing a very self-satisfied smile.

"You look like the cat that's got the cream."

"No, I'm the dude that's got the dosh. Look what Charlie gave me."

She produces two fifty pound notes from her pocket.

"Well, that should more than cover the cost of your school lunch."

"I'm not wasting this on anything so mundane as food."

"Careful, you're beginning to sound like your sister."

"Ha ha. Very funny, mum. Not! Are you taking that extra stuff to Sarah tomorrow?"

"It'll have to be Monday."

"Can you take her this as well? I thought it might cheer her up."

She produces a small, digital photo frame.

"I couldn't send them by phone so I dug this out and put it together last night, after you all went to bed."

She turns on the power and flicks through the album to show me. There's one of Cromwell and Dottie trying to climb a tree in the garden after a neighbourhood squirrel sought refuge there, one of the three of us at a horse show last year when Jude won a cup for her show jumping, a couple of Sarah and some friends from school, a few taken at a party they both went to last Christmas and a couple of recent ones with both girls and Mattie. There are no pictures of Michael.

"I couldn't find any of dad. Well, nothing recent, anyway."

"No, I suppose not. Not to worry. I'm sure Sarah will appreciate it. I've picked out some books from the shop for her. I was going to buy some magazines but I wasn't sure if it was a good idea."

"Why on earth not? Oh…. right."

"Let's you and I pick out Sarah's stuff this evening. You'll probably know better than me what she needs."

"Okay."

Michael comes out of his study, talking into his cell phone.

139

"So we've fixed on the Friday after next. The shuttle'll get us into Prestwick about nine thirty. David Tennant will meet us there and we'll all transfer by helicopter to the store. The PR people tell me they've got full press coverage organised, terrestrial and satellite TV coverage. You'll give your speech at ten, David will say a few words and unveil the plaque and we'll open the doors to the public after that. The film people will follow David around the store, he'll chat to some of the shoppers and sign autographs while you meet the manager there, Iain McAlistair, and some of the senior staff. Then we'll rescue David and the helicopter'll take the five of us off to Glengarry for a private lunch and back to the airport by four." He pauses and listens. "His PA? No, that shouldn't be a problem. The chopper's a six-seater, they told me. I'll tell Marketing to change the lunch reservation." He pauses again and glances at me. "No, That's not Feef's cup of tea. And with Sarah in ...er...hospital, you know what it's like." Another pause. He laughs, a little artificially, I think. "Exactly. Okay, Francis. Good to talk to you. I'll keep you posted."

He snaps his cell phone off.

"Right, Jude. Are you ready?"

"Have been for the last ten minutes."

He suddenly notices her outfit.

"I don't know how you get away with it. What's the point of having a uniform if you don't have to wear it?"

"Actually there's nothing they can do about it. The rules say navy skirt and black sensible shoes. Nothing about how old or new they've got to be. And a straw boater's optional in the summer. I checked."

Her father grunts cynically, pecks me perfunctorily on the cheek and the two of them leave.

Michael rang again later that evening, full of excuses and arrogance. Yes, he knew he was wrong but it didn't really mean anything and there was no need for me to have left like that. In fact how dare I take his children away. I must come home immediately and stop being so childish. We were both adults and these things happened. It was a one-off and it would never happen again so why didn't I just stop being so silly and get in the car and drive home. People were starting to ask questions. How did I think it looked, me just disappearing with the girls like that? What was he supposed to say to Sarah's teacher? And how was he supposed to cope on his own with all the cooking and cleaning and didn't I know how busy he was at work? On and on till it ended up sounding as though I was the guilty party. I waited till he finished.

"I suggest you tell Sarah's teacher that she won't be needing her place anymore and you put an advert in the Kent Chronicle for a housekeeper. The number's in the hall drawer. Goodbye, Michael."

I put the phone down. It rang again almost immediately.

"What about the girls? I have rights, you know. You can't take care of them on your own."

"Watch me."

I put the phone down again. It stayed quiet.

The three of us settled happily into our little flat in Bath, though Sarah was a bit puzzled by all the changes. Patti raided her boxroom for some extra bits of furniture and at the weekend we went out and bought pots, pans and dishes as well as towels and bed linen. A walk in the local park on Sunday yielded some useful information on day-care for Jude from a lady with twin boys about the same age. Only a few streets away and the lady I needed to speak to was Sally Carter.

So Monday morning saw the three of us up at the crack of dawn getting ready. I took Sarah to her new school first and stayed with her while she had a conducted tour and met her new teacher. The headmistress told me that children needed to be picked up before four fifteen and I wondered how that would square with the paper. As soon as Sarah was settled I took Jude around to First Steps Nursery to meet Mrs Carter. At the sight of so many other youngsters Jude seemed a bit overwhelmed at first but within five minutes she was being shown how to finger paint at one of the small tables with a few of her new peers.

So far so good. I headed off to the Gazette offices.

Tweed jacket was already there.

"We weren't introduced last week. I'm Bill Bailey."

"As in 'Won't you come home?"

"You've got it. My mother was a jazz fan and I've had to live with hearing that joke ever since."

"Sorry. I'm Fiona."

"I know. Steve told me. He said you were filling in for Eric for a while. He's had to pop out for a bit, Steve, I mean, not Eric, but he shouldn't be long. Fancy a cup of tea?"

141

"Love one."

I follow him to the back of the news room and behind a curtain where there's a tiny sink and draining board with some mismatched mugs and an electric kettle. Bill plugs the kettle in and pops a tea bag in two of the mugs.

"Sugar?"

"Two, please."

He picks up a milk bottle, smells it and pulls a face.

"Gone off. 'Fridge is on the blink. Won't be a tick. I'm just going next door."

While he's fetching fresh milk the kettle boils and I finish making the tea.

"Just in time, I see."

Bill's back with Steve in tow. He helps himself. I explain about the four o'clock curfew. He thinks a bit and says it shouldn't be a problem.

"Except on Thursdays. That's our deadline day and we usually end up working quite late."

I mentally thank my lucky stars that that's Patti's day off and hope she won't mind an extra bit of babysitting. Then we all take our tea and follow Steve through to his office.

"Fiona. First thing you do is ring the central police station. Speak to Sergeant Bryant. He'll give you all the low down on accidents and incidents over the weekend. You need to check in with him every Monday morning. Make a list of them and we'll go through it together. See what's worth following up. Then phone the Magistrate's Court, speak to the Clerk. Find out what cases are lined up for this week and bring that to me as well. Bill, what progress with that councillor and the call girl story?"

I leave the two of them to it and go off to work the phones. When I've got my lists I go back to Steve's office and he runs a practised eye over the paper.

"Okay. This MVA looks promising."

I look blank.

"Motor vehicle accident. See if you can find out any more information. The dead driver, follow up on the next of kin. Then go over to the hospital and find out the condition of the others. Try and talk to the relatives if you can and get some quotes from the nursing staff. And when the pubs open get over to the Admiral Nelson and find out about that fight there on Saturday night. It's getting to be a regular occurrence. Talk to the landlord and find out what the

142

story was. Then follow up any leads he gives you. That's probably enough to be going on with. Off you go. Oh, you'll need this."

He fishes in a desk drawer and pulls out a notepad.

My head's already spinning. This is a far cry from leisurely book reviews. I take a deep breath and head off into the unknown. Another phone call to the police station provides a list of names and addresses, as well as more details and the exact location of the accident which I check against the street map pinned up on the wall. A thought strikes me and I pop my head around Steve's door.

"Is there a camera around I could use?"

"Sure."

Steve reaches behind him and produces an old Nikon.

"Do you know how to use one of these? It's print."

"I think so."

"Good girl."

I take the camera, the notepad and the list of names, jump into the bug and head off for Bath Royal Infirmary. A little subterfuge and a few white lies in Casualty and I learn the condition of the other crash victims. I also manage a few words with the mother of the front seat passenger, a young woman called Susan Burgess, described as being in a critical but stable condition. I also learn from Mrs Burgess that the dead driver, John Wilkinson was her daughter's boyfriend and that he lived alone in a flat on the outskirts of the city.

"But his parents are only around the corner from us. Poor things. I can't imagine what they're going through. Losing your child so young."

At this point Mrs Burgess breaks down in floods of tears and at a loss what to do or say I fetch us both tea from the machine in the hall. As Mrs Burgess's sobs subside and she sips her tea she tells me more about her daughter and her boyfriend, how long they'd been going out, where they were planning their holiday this year, how John was a Bath United fan and the two of them never missed a match. Then she produced a photo of the two of them on holiday in Majorca the year before. A pretty brunette and a tall, suntanned young man seemingly with their whole lives ahead of them. I ask if I can borrow the photograph and she nods. I also ask if she'd mind if I took her photograph.

"Oh, I'm not sure. And I must look such a mess."

She wipes her face and brushes a lock of hair off her forehead.

"You look fine. And it will help to make the story more real for our readers."

"Well, I suppose it'll be all right."

I take the photograph and promise to return the picture as soon as I can. I decide against going around to the Wilkinson's house but I take his mother's phone number anyway.

It's now after eleven so I head off to the Admiral Nelson to investigate the fracas. The landlord turns out to be an ex-boxer from London, John Marshall. Very jolly and very streetwise. He attributes the fighting to drunken outbursts by rival Bath United and Bristol Rovers fans, especially when one or the other has performed particularly badly or well in a match. He says it's nothing he can't handle most of the time and I can well believe it but that sometimes it spills out on the streets after closing time and then he has no option but to call in the fuzz.

"A night in the cells soon cools them down."

"Until the next match."

"Oh, they're not bad lads, really. In fact I've persuaded a couple of them to come down to the gym with me. Take their aggression out on a punch bag."

"Is it working?"

"Well, looking at the way they performed last night, maybe a bit too well."

He laughs loudly and I join in.

"Well, thanks, John. I'd better get back to the paper."

"Anytime, darling. Pop in for a drink sometime."

"I might just do that. But perhaps not a Saturday night."

He flexes his impressive biceps.

"I think I can promise you'll be all right."

I laugh again and take my leave. Back at the office I type up my story on the car accident and file it with Steve. He looks it over.

"It's all right so far, Chester, but it doesn't go far enough. You've only given me half the story."

"How do you mean?"

"Well, you've interviewed the mother of the girl but what about the parents of the dead boy? And you need to talk to his work colleagues, some of his friends. Get some of their reactions to his death."

"I did get his mother's phone number but I didn't like to intrude."

"That's the first thing you've got to learn about journalism, my girl. Reporters spend their lives intruding. People's grief, people's secrets, every aspect, every detail of their lives. Especially the parts they don't want anyone to know about. You're just going to have to get used to it."

I go back to my desk and ring the number Mrs Burgess gave me.

By early afternoon I've spoken to a few people at the Building Society where John Wilkinson and Susan Burgess both worked. And I've phoned a few of their friends. At three o'clock I drive around to Mrs Wilkinson's house for a pre-arranged appointment. I'm not looking forward to it.

I ring the doorbell and it's opened by a middle-aged man whose face is ashen and whose eyes are glazed. I introduce myself and he shows me through to the living room. Mrs Wilkinson is sitting in an armchair, next to a coffee table holding a box of tissues. There is one tissue in her hand and several on her lap. Her face has the same pallor as her husband's. He explains who I am and I smile weakly, wishing myself a million miles away from this room.

"Mrs Wilkinson, I'm very sorry about your son."

She looks at me with red, puffy eyes and tries to smile politely.

"He was always such a good boy. Such a wonderful son. And now he's gone. Why? Why him? It's not fair."

She breaks down in tears. Feeling even more awkward, I sit down next to her and put my arm around her shoulder.

"Would it help to tell me about him?"

I listen while she recounts memories from his childhood. He was a long-awaited only child and clearly both his parents' pride and joy. While she's talking her husband leaves the room, returning a few minutes later with two family albums. I look at the photos they show me and begin to form a picture of John Wilkinson. He obviously loved soccer and there are pictures of him on and off the field from an early age. Later photos show him with fiancée Susan, including more of the holiday in Majorca and some from the engagement party, surrounded by both sets of parents and various friends and relatives. I point to one of the photos.

"Do you mind if I borrow this? I promise I'll take good care of it."

The both nod and I carefully remove the picture and close the book. Mrs Wilkinson is crying again. Clearly the memories are too painful.

"I know this has been very difficult. Thank you so much for seeing me."

145

There are tears in my eyes now. I busy myself putting the photo into my handbag and rise to leave. Mrs Wilkinson smiles wanly and her husband sees me to the door. I shake his hand and once more say how sorry I am, then turn and walk to my car. Sitting in front of the wheel I find myself shaking. That was one the hardest things I've ever had to do and it's only my first day at the paper.

I wonder if I'm cut out to be a journalist but before I drive off something prompts me to get out, take a photo of the front of the house and then to go and knock on a few of the neighbours' doors.

It's now nearly 4 o'clock and I drive to the school to pick up Sarah. Tomorrow I'll have to rewrite my piece but for now I can only reflect on how lucky I am still to have my girls. And that makes me think of my own son, lost to me in a completely different way. If anything ever happened to him I'd never even know about it. It's a depressing and disturbing thought.

"This is more like it."

It's Tuesday morning. As soon as I got into the Gazette offices I sat down and wrote a new story on the car accident from the point of view of the human tragedy, Mrs Burgess with her daughter in ICU, not even aware that her fiancée is dead and the Wilkinsons bereaved and childless for the rest of their lives. I've also had the film developed and when I take the story in to Steve I lay out my assortment of pictures for him to select a couple.

"Yeah, much better. We can definitely use this. Well done."

"It was hard. I felt I had no right to be there questioning those people. But oddly enough...."

"What?"

"Well, I got the feeling that they really wanted to talk, to tell me about it."

"Second rule of journalism. Everybody wants to tell their story. Tragic, comic, frustrating. They all want people to hear their side. And we're the means, the medium, the message. Remember Marshall McCluhan?"

"Who?"

"Canadian mass media guru of the sixties. Wrote a book called 'The Medium is the Message'. You should try and get hold of a copy. And Andy Warhol."

"The 'fifteen minutes of fame', you mean?"

"Exactly. As much as people pretend to hate us, they love us really. How else would they get their fifteen minutes?"

"I suppose you're right. I just hadn't thought of if it like that. Well, to be honest, I hadn't thought of it at all. This is all new to me."

"You'll learn. Now, aren't you supposed to be in court?"

I checked my watch, muttered a mild expletive and rushed off, pausing only to pick up my little spiral notebook.

Court reporting proved much easier than interviewing grieving relatives. The only drawback was having to hang around for hours, listening to the minutiae of a host of minor offences. I took copious long-hand notes and even found time to start writing them up in full during the boring bits, then cut the last case short to rush off to pick up the girls.

Patti proved a more than willing babysitter on Thursdays. She said it was better than the real thing cos she could hand them back before bedtime. Gradually as the weeks passed we all settled into a routine. With the paper out on Fridays that was an easy day at the office—mostly planning ahead for the following week or writing up the odd story which hadn't made that week's paper. Then the afternoons were pretty much my own so I could catch up with shopping, laundry and the like. Patti and Ross spoiled the girls rotten when they had them so every Thursday was like Christmas as far as they were concerned. And at the weekends we took drives into the Gloucester countryside, parked the car somewhere and walked or if the weather was bad we went over to Patti's, spent time in the city library or the girls all-time favourite, the Bath toy museum. Sarah still asked when daddy was coming but not very often and although she'd quickly settled in at her new school and made friends she still talked about going back to her 'real' school sometime. Jude didn't seem to notice anything had changed, though she took to nursery school like the proverbial duck to water and couldn't wait for Monday morning to come. Jude the Independent, even at that age.

And Michael still phoned Patti occasionally but all she'd tell him was that we were all fine and that I'd said I didn't want to speak to him. He even drove over there one Saturday—he must have got her address from that hall phone book - but not only would she not tell him where we were staying, she wouldn't even invite him into the house. Just left him standing in the street and shut the front door. And when he rang the bell for the second time she answered it and told him he was making a nuisance of himself and if he didn't shove off she'd call the police. Knowing the way Patti felt about Michael I know she really enjoyed that. She phoned me after he finally drove off and recounted the whole

147

incident with positive glee. Apparently he'd told her that it was all her fault that the girls and I were staying away and that he wasn't going to stand for her screwing things up. And she said she thought it was a very apt choice of verb and that he'd done a pretty good job of that himself "you and that that little secretary tramp of yours". And all he could counter that with was that she wasn't his secretary. "Oh, really? I heard she was pretty good at taking things down."

I was beginning to enjoy my new life but deep down I knew it couldn't last.

Friday, 20 June

6pm

Since his lordship is out of town there's nothing to stop me checking up on Mother & Child. There's a message flag! I click on the icon and can't believe what I see.

'Fiona—I'm fairly sure the person you call Philip is now named Alex. How do you want to take this forward?'

I'm stunned, excited, delighted, confused and terrified all at the same time. Is this Philip/Alex or just someone who knows him? It's a very impersonal message but so was my last reply. And is it meant to be cold or is it just naturally cautious? Either way, what's the right response? Just as I'm trying to formulate my answer Jude burst into the room and I guiltily shut off the site.

"Come on, let's do it."

"Do what?"

"Pack for Sarah, of course. Are you okay?"

Jude the Intuitive. She can read me like a book. I keep my face expressionless and don't rise to the bait.

"Of course. No time like the present."

"At least I'll be doing something constructive. I've been feeling really bad about Sarah all week. It must be horrible not being able to call us or anything. And stuck in that place with a bunch of sick strangers. Real 'One Flew Over The Cuckoo's Nest' sort of place."

I laugh.

"It's nothing like that but I know what you mean. I just keep telling myself it's all for the best. There was nothing we could have done here. She needs specialist help and hopefully she'll get it there. Maybe we'll have the old Sarah back with us soon. Come on. Let's go upstairs."

Jude and I go up to Sarah's room. Although it's only been a couple of days since she was last in it, it seems strangely forlorn. At the back of her wardrobe is a large holdall for her hockey kit so I lift that out. Jude rummages through her books and music and makes a selection while I pack jeans, tops, trainers and underwear. From the pinboard Jude also takes a couple of posters. The Handy Calorie Counter is still on her bedside. I pick it up and put it in my pocket and while I'm about it I surreptitiously remove the montage of the models stuck on the inside of the wardrobe door.

Saturday, 21 June

I come down to find the kitchen a hive of activity. Charles is up and dressed and sitting at the table reading The Daily Telegraph. Jude is slicing bananas into a bowl of cereal.

"You're up early, Charles."

"Always am, even at the weekends. Drilled into me when I was a boy. Have you heard from Michael?"

"No but I'm not expecting to. He'll be too engrossed in making sure everything's shipshape and Edinburgh fashion before the chief whip sees it."

"He tells me a full seat on the Board's almost certain. Probably before the end of the year."

"Very likely."

"And promotion. Apparently Francis wants to make him his second-in-command. It'll mean a move to Manchester, of course."

Jude and I both look up.

"Why?"

"Well, it stands to reason. That's where their headquarters are. And Francis'll want him on the spot. Too far to be commuting from here."

I look at Jude's stricken face.

"Well, maybe not. It's only a couple of hours on the motorway, after all. Anyway we'll cross that bridge when we come to it."

"Manchester's miles away. I'll never see Mattie or Amanda. And what about school? And where would I keep my horse?"

149

"Jude, there's no sense in worrying about something that may never happen. Let's wait and see."

"Your mother's quite right, Jude. Your father can probably commute. It wouldn't take him long in that car of his. Now, any chance of a cup of tea, young Fifi?"

"Coming right up."

"Splendid."

"And there's some Pricerite croissants in the 'fridge. Not exactly Parisian patisserie but quite edible."

"Capital. A continental breakfast."

"I'll have one as well, please. With some strawberry jam."

The Manchester moment has passed, thank goodness. I pour tea and heat the pastries in the microwave. Jude takes hers upstairs, with her while she finishes getting changed for the stables, along with a tray of Earl Grey for Diana and Charles and I carry ours out into the garden. Another gorgeous day is promised, weather-wise, at any rate. I sip my tea while Charles spreads copious amounts of jam onto a croissant.

"Has Michael actually talked to you about moving to Manchester?"

"Well, not in so many words. But I gather the promotion's more or less signed and sealed. It'll go to the next Board meeting as a matter of form but with Francis' backing it's in the bag. Hasn't he mentioned it to you?"

"To be honest we haven't had much of a chance to talk about anything recently, what with all his away trips and then this awful thing with Sarah."

"Quite so."

"Anyway I'm sure he'll tell me when he's ready. He usually does."

I make an effort to keep my voice bright.

"But don't say anything more to Jude, will you? I don't want her worrying unduly. She's got enough on her plate at the moment."

"No, of course not, my dear. I just assumed you both knew. But you know, I wouldn't fret too much about young Jude. Got her head screwed on right, that one."

Not trusting myself to speak, I nod and smile, then take the dirty dishes indoors and stack them in the dishwasher. Just as I finish Jenny arrives. She looks a bit surprised to see me as I'm usually at work so I explain about the in-laws staying and tactfully suggest she holds off on the vacuuming till her ladyship makes an appearance.

150

We neither of us have to wait long. Jenny has no sooner started on the kitchen when Diana sweeps regally in. I politely wish her 'good morning', shepherd her into the garden, then fetch a tray of coffee and croissants. As she busies herself with buttering a pastry I broach the subject of Ink-an'-Abulia.

"I really ought to get to work. I did phone this morning to tell George I'd be late and he insisted I bring you in and introduce you. I'm sure you'll like him. He's very charming."

Diana raised an eyebrow and said nothing. Charles said that work always came first and he'd be delighted to meet another of the Dublin Fitzsimmons. Diana said that in the present circumstances shouldn't it be Sarah who had first priority, Charles reminded her that she wasn't allowed visits or phone calls so there was nothing to be done for now and the two of them got into a squabble which ended in us finishing the journey in complete silence.

Fine by me.

When we reach the shop Diana says she'll wait in the car. I point out that I might be there a while and it'll be quite hot sitting outside so she reluctantly comes with Charles and me. I affect the introductions. Charles is his old affable self and George is old world charm personified. Diana shakes his hand politely and then stands awkwardly in the middle of the shop, her handbag clasped in both hands and dangling around her knees, Thatcher-style. At that point a customer came in so I left the three of them and went off to serve the young man. He turned out to be a fan of mid-twentieth century science fiction so I show him our fairly extensive paperback collection. While he was browsing I tidied up behind the counter and filed the week's receipts. By the time he finished and left, George et al had disappeared upstairs. I follow and pop my head around the door of George's small sitting room.

The three of them are sitting drinking tea—the Georgian silver service, no less, and the Crown Derby cups. Just as George predicted, he and Charles have found a common bond. They were both Oxford men, though at different times and colleges. George read English at Greyfriars whilst Charles read PPE at Balliol. They happily swap anecdotes about some of the more notorious student drinking houses they both frequented and about student life in general. Amused to learn of a side of George I didn't know existed, I pour myself a cup and join them since the shop is quiet.

Diana begins to look restless so this sly old bookworm cleverly brings the conversation around to antique furniture.

"Ffion tells me that you're something of an expert on the subject."

Diana feigns modesty, quite a feat for her.

"Oh, I wouldn't go that far. Of course one does pick up a little knowledge here and there."

"Well I'm sure you know a lot more than I do. Actually we've been doing a little buying together recently and I'd very much appreciate your comments on the pieces we bought."

Diana looks around the flat with a puzzled expression.

"Oh no, not for here. Of course it's very convenient living above the shop, both literally and figuratively but I've always wanted somewhere a little more rural, a sort of country retreat. And I've finally done something about it. Perhaps Ffion has mentioned that I've bought a small set of apartments in Featherington Hall?"

Diana is suddenly animated.

"Really? I did read in Country Life that it had been divided up. Such a pity really but only to be expected these days. So tell me about your accomodations. Are they on the ground floor?"

"Yes, the last unit available. I was very lucky, only came upon it by chance after another buyer had pulled out. So of course I have garden access. And the developers have managed to retain all the original wood panelling and flooring. Even the windows are original. And that's where the furniture has gone. I really would love you to see it and give me your expert opinion."

Diana beams.

"Well, I'm not sure if it's possible. Is it far?"

"Oh, no, not at all. How far would you say, Ffion?"

"About forty miles. And it's a lovely drive."

"The only problem is that I don't have a car these days. I'm afraid I've been relying rather heavily on Ffion for that sort of thing. She's been very kind."

"Well, that wouldn't be a problem. We could all go together in our car. And I dare say we could spare the time, couldn't we, Charles?"

"Of course. Absolutely delighted. No trouble at all."

"Well, that's settled. Shall we say Sunday? We could make a day of it. Stop off somewhere for lunch."

"Sunday would be perfect. And while you're there perhaps you could give me your thoughts on décor? I'm afraid I'm very ignorant in such matters. Probably make a complete pig's ear of it given half a chance."

George glances at me slyly.

Diana positively simpers.

"Well, I do have a little experience there, as it happens. Of course where we're living now isn't really my choice. A bit like this place, as it happens. You know, living over the shop."

I surreptitiously raise my eyebrow at George. Over the shop, indeed. An early Victorian mansion built at the same time as the original paper mill and a good two miles away from the actual plant.

"But my family home is just outside Edinburgh. The main house was built in 1542, though we mostly lived in the new wing."

1698, if I remember rightly.

"My dear Diana, it must be fate that brought you to me. You see, Ffion, out of poor Sarah's illness some good has already come."

Downstairs I hear the shop bell tinkle and I excuse myself quietly as Diana begins a lecture on Jacobean milk paint and tapestry restoration.

After the customer leaves and I'm finally on my own for the first time all day, I phone the Avon. Wendy Parks is off duty but I manage to speak to Professor Turner. He tells me that he's had another short session with Sarah but she's still largely in denial about her condition.

"But that's perfectly normal at this stage. Some of the girls take several weeks to accept that they need help. Months, in some of the worst cases. Actually that's where the group sessions really come into their own. It helps them to come to terms with it much quicker when they realise they're all in the same boat, so to speak. And the ones that have been there longer tend to be quite outspoken when the new arrivals keep denying that there's any sort of a problem and it's all been a big mistake in their case."

"So it sounds like it's going to take quite a long time before you can even start getting to the root of the problem. What pushed Sarah over the edge."

"Well that really depends on the individual patient. We try to persuade them to open up without putting too much pressure on them. But it's a big step forward when they do so the earlier we get an inkling of the root cause, the better. And meanwhile we try and treat the symptoms. Encourage them to begin eating small amounts of food under supervision and make sure they settle

153

in to the routine. Remember, they all start out like Sarah. None of them wants to be there and none of them wants to admit they've got a problem. Often we'll pick up a really useful clue as to what triggered the onset of their anorexia through the group sessions. They'll share something with the other girls or even just make some chance remark which we can pick up on and work with. But I'm afraid it all comes down to one thing, Mrs Hamilton. Time."

I tell him I quite understand, thank him for *his* time and hang up. At around one George, Charles and Diana come downstairs. Diana wants to know if there's a decent fabric shop I town and I tell her to try Cotton Pickin' just off the high street. She raises an eyebrow at the name but takes directions anyway. Although it's easy walking distance Charles asks apologetically if he might borrow the car. Apparently Diana wants swatch books and they're quite big and heavy. I hand him the keys, tell him to take as long as they need and say I'll catch the bus home.

"Are you sure? Won't that be rather inconvenient?"

"Practically door to door. I do it all the time."

As soon as they've driven off I around on George and throw my arms around him.

"You weren't in military intelligence, by any chance? That was brilliant."

George looks pleased.

"Very successfully executed, if I say so myself. And it's killing two birds with one stone. I really shall be grateful for any help Diana can offer in the decorating line. And meanwhile, you're off the hook."

I smile gratefully.

"At least that's one less problem to worry about."

George looks at me shrewdly.

"It'll all turn out for the best, you mark my words."

"I hope so. It's just that it's all so complicated. Everything seems to be happening at once."

'For what it's worth I think you deserve some happiness in your life, young Ffion. You don't seem to have had too much of that recently."

He looks at me in his insightful, understanding way and I know that he's not just talking about Sarah. We've never talked about Michael but between George and I there are some things that don't need to be said. Then he pats my hand and I return to my cataloguing to keep my mind off the time.

The afternoon is passed in helping a couple of art students select some course books for next term and a trickle of general customers. At five I shut up shop and head off home by bus. I sit upstairs as usual and all the thoughts I've pushed aside all day now flood back into my mind—Michael, Manchester, Sarah, her illness and of course Philip. I turn my problems over in my head, one at a time, examining them from every angle, not exactly plotting a course of action but more looking at the possibilities.

Michael is clearly in the throes of a heavy affair with Louise which is too close to home and therefore out of order. But is this the right time to make an issue of it? I leave this unanswered and figuratively move on to Manchester. Despite my light-hearted tone and easy words to Charles this morning I am surprised that Michael has not even mentioned the promotion or the possible move. He rarely does anything unintentionally so clearly it's a deliberate omission and how curious that he has chosen to keep this bit of information to himself. Several possible scenarios spring to mind. It is, of course, entirely possible that he could commute. Perhaps he could find a little pied-a-terre up there and come back at weekends. On the other hand, if he was thinking of a move en famille then he'd know it wouldn't win him any votes. Jude, and Sarah once she's recovered, would both have to change schools at critical times. And leave all their friends. Who knows, it might even push Sarah further over the edge. Not to mention George and my own job. It might even be Sarah's condition that was making him hold off mentioning it, though knowing Michael that seems unlikely. There is another possibility. Perhaps he hasn't told us because he has a rather different scenario in mind?

I wonder if Louise knows about Manchester?

And right there and then I realise that this farce of a 'marriage' has gone on long enough and it's me that needs to make a move, even if it's just metaphorical.

And that leads on to Sarah. I'm desperately worried about my daughter but at the same time I'm actually relieved that she's been admitted to hospital and will have to confront her illness. And oddly, considering what little I saw of her of late, I miss her physical presence in the house. But then again, in all probability I'll only have her at home for another year or so and Jude too. The nest will soon be empty.

Which leads me straight to Philip. I'm still mentally trying to compose a response to this morning's message and trying to fathom whether it's actually

155

from him or from a third party. Still deep in thought, I glance out and see I am almost home.

Once inside the house I head off to the study while I still have the place to myself. I log on and after a moment's thought I send the following message.

'I love the name 'Alex'. Is it short for Alexander? This is virgin territory for me too but I feel like a part of me is missing from my life and I really want to make contact with him. If you're sure that's him and he feels the same, I'd love to share details about my life and learn about his. Regards, Fiona'

I re-read it, decide it sets the right tone and hit 'send', metaphorically crossing my fingers as I do so.

I'm suddenly more optimistic at the prospect of finding Philip again and him getting to see his sisters, albeit somewhat vicariously. But the joy and excitement this thought invokes is tempered by my worries over Sarah. I'll hear soon as to what's been decided about her treatment and I'm very nervous, knowing how prickly and uncooperative Sarah might be.

After nearly 6 years of hamming up the part of a Stepford wife, Bath was blissful. Money was pretty tight but the girls and I seemed to manage somehow. Luckily we all liked baked beans and sausages and the bug was cheap enough to run and pretty reliable. And with Patti's help I juggled work, school and day-care without dropping any of them too often. The paper was tough. As the newest kid on the block I was expected to pay my dues so I was made to cut my teeth on all the dirty jobs no-one else wanted to do—more MVAs, not all of them fatal, thank goodness, endless court reporting on minor cases of burglary or possession of cannabis, traffic jams, dog bites, playground fights—nothing was too trivial or too tedious for Fiona's desk. But gradually Steve began giving me the odd little interesting assignment, though he made it quite clear that they were as well as, not instead of, the other stuff and that I'd just have to find time to fit them in. I knew he was testing me. He was like that. Nothing too exciting at first but then one day I was in his office while he was opening his mail and as he sorted out bills from letters to the editor and general correspondence, one clearly caught his attention. He handed it over to me.

"Sounds like sour grapes to me but you never know, there might be something in it. Why don't you check it out?"

I skimmed through the letter. It was an anonymous tip-off about possible sharp practices in the local meat trade which they accused of mislabelling

156

some meat products, misrepresenting the actual grades and possibly even covering up the country of origin. It specifically referenced a supply company called Gregson's and suggested that supermarkets, either knowingly or otherwise, were openly selling dodgy butchery produce.

"I don't know much about the other some of the stores but I wouldn't have thought Pricerite would risk that sort of sharp practice."

"You know something about them?"

"Enough."

Steve raised an eyebrow.

"Long story."

"Want to tell me?"

"Not really. Not now, anyway."

"Fair enough. But why don't you keep that and see what you can dig up."

I started the following Saturday. Telling the girls that we were going shopping we drove around all the supermarkets the informant named in the letter. Although there was only one Pricerite store in the area, just on the outskirts of Weston, there were a few other major chains in and around Bath and I checked them all out. It took all day and the girls were a bit puzzled that I kept looking at food but didn't buy anything.

"Haven't you got enough money, mummy?"

I laughed. We were now in our fourth store and I was picking up yet more packets of meat and Sarah thought she'd worked out why. I was trying to find something I could afford.

"No, sweetheart. It's not that. It's for mummy's work. You see, I have to look and see how much they all cost and then I'm going to write about it in the paper."

A bit of an oversimplification but it satisfied my five-year old. I noted the prices, chatted to the butchery manager, just a simple housewife looking for a bargain, how you could tell the difference between different meat grades, how to tell English lamb from New Zealand, what to look for in a pork chop and so on. And then we drove on to the next store.

I left Pricerite to the end so we didn't get there till early afternoon. Jude had been fast asleep in the car seat for most of the afternoon but as we pulled into the car park she woke up. Sarah recognised the Pricerite logo and got very excited.

157

"Mummy, mummy, look. It's where daddy works. Are we going to see daddy?"

Jude heard the word and took up the cry.

"Daddy, daddy."

Get out of that one, Fiona.

Having got nowhere with Patti, Michael had taken to writing to me via her address. I returned all his letters unopened. But 2 months after we moved into our flat, on one of our Sunday afternoon outings, this time to the Pump Rooms, I bought a postcard in the souvenir shop, scribbled a note saying that the girls were both well and addressed it to him at work. And a month later I picked them both up after school, took them back to the office and put in a call to Pricerite in Eastbourne. I asked to speak to Mr Hamilton without giving my name and when Michael came on the line I handed the phone over to Sarah so she could speak to her father.

She chatted on about her teacher, what she did and didn't like about her new school and about the new pink shoes that Aunt Patti had bought her and then she offered the receiver to me, saying that daddy wanted to talk to me. I shook my head and lifted Jude up so that she could also say something. I'm fairly sure she didn't really know who she was talking to but even at that age that didn't inhibit her loquaciousness and she launched into a long, rambling monologue about her friend Monty, what he ate and what he didn't, when she was allowed to play with him and when she wasn't and how she wanted to bring him home, all in all far more than Michael probably needed to know, except the one pertinent fact, that Monty was a pet rabbit at nursery school. When I thought he'd heard enough I told her to say goodbye and then I replaced the receiver and we all went off to find some ice cream.

Michael had obviously said something to Sarah because following that she suddenly decided that she needed to write to daddy. So every Saturday morning after that she would give me something she'd done at school, a picture or a paper shape or a little nature walk treasure which I had to pop into an envelope, and then while we were out shopping we'd call in at the main post office in town so that she could post her letter.

And now here we were outside Pricerite in Weston and she was quite convinced that we were about to see daddy. I explained as best I could that this wasn't daddy's shop, just one that looked like it. Very like it. As we went inside I could understand their confusion. All the Pricerite stores were identical. In

158

through the fruit and veg section, into the deli, on past the bakery, turn ninety degrees past all the chilled meat counters on the right, tinned goods on the left, then frozen foods, dairy, wines and spirits, household cleaners and right at the back, toys, automotive, housewares and electrical appliances. I could find my way around in the dark and I was having a nasty case of deja vu. I checked out what I needed and made a note in my notepad, bought crayons and colouring books for the girls and fled. I could phone the butcher from the office.

Back at my desk on Monday I began ringing around the supermarkets pretending to be an agricultural student preparing a paper and talking to the meat buyers about their suppliers and their selection policies. They all said they used approved local meat wholesalers either directly or through a middle man. Gregson's was common to all three so I gave them a call first and asked to speak to the owner, George Gregson, sticking to my student story. He had a West Country accent and when I asked him where his all his meat actually came from he sounded a bit cagey, saying something about 'here and there, depending on the time of year.' So I asked if it was all British and he said no, he sold some New Zealand lamb, Argentine beef and German pork, all excellent quality, he assured me.

"Anywhere else?"

He hesitated.

"Why're you askin'?"

A shot in the dark but apparently I hit the target. I fired again.

"Well, I'd heard that there were a lot of grey imports in the meat trade these days."

"What are you sayin'? I run a respectable business."

His tone was sharp, truculent. I was on the right track.

"I didn't necessarily mean you. There have been cases where they don't conform to EU regulations. Animals aren't vaccinated properly, dodgy feed, that sort of thing."

"Well I wouldn't know about that. My pork's all kosher, all my customers'll tell you that."

I stifled a giggle at his unintended pun. His tone was still serious, full of righteous indignation. I thanked him for his time and hung up.

Over the next couple of weeks I did a lot more research. I visited other supermarkets and butcheries and asked about their meat suppliers and if they ever bought from Gregson's. They all said no and the way most of them said it left me with the distinct impression that our Mr Gregson had a bit of a dubious reputation. I visited a few stores, hanging around the delivery areas in the back. On several occasions I saw refrigerated trucks marked 'Gregson's Meat Products' drive in and offload.

The next step was to pay a few clandestine visits to Gregson's. Their centre of operations turned out to be a warehouse in the Bridlington area of Bristol. I made a practice recce to get the feel of the place and work out how best to effect an entrance. I noted that all the staff seemed to disappear at lunchtime. Surely it couldn't be that easy? It was. The following day I arrived just before lunch and parked down the street, on a watch and wait mission. Just on noon a hooter sounded and several staff members began trickling out of the front gate. By half past twelve the place seemed quiet. I got out of the bug, walked around the outside and took some pictures. Then I walked in a side gate and into the main yard. There were a few of their refrigerated trucks parked on the far side, against the back of the warehouse building and a stack of heavy-duty plastic crates. Nothing out of the ordinary at all. Disappointed, I spotted a rear gate and left. Then quite by accident I hit pay dirt, as they say. Just outside was a skip overflowing with discarded cardboard boxes, several of which had labels in Cyrillic script. I thought that was odd so I took some general pictures and some close-ups of the writing. This was heady stuff!

Before going back to the office I had my films developed, then took the pictures, my notes and one of the discarded boxes into Steve's office. He looked over my little hoard.

"Good but not good enough."

He pointed at the Cyrillic writing.

'No idea what that says but I've got a contact in the modern languages department at Bristol. I'll give her a call and ask her to translate. In the meantime I don't know what you're still standing there for. I thought you were covering that break-in at the bookies?"

Okay, Fiona, reality check. I collected a fresh notebook and the camera and traipsed off to the tiny bookmaker's offices to take down the details of the reported cash heist. Turned out someone had made off with the petty cash box, containing all of about twenty quid. In other words, just up my street. I interviewed the manager and the rest of the staff, took some pictures of the scene of the crime, then went back to the office and wrote it all up for the paper, knowing full well that Steve would probably spike most of it and reduce it to a paragraph and a captioned photo.

I made one more surveillance trip to Gregson's. Sitting in the bug I photographed someone I took to be Mr Gregson himself—camel hair coat, suede shoes and newish Rover, the Arthur Daley of the meat trade.

Meanwhile Steve had got hold of his contact at Bristol uni and she confirmed that some of the writing was Serbian, some Croatian. She also helpfully identified a few words including 'pig', 'goat' and 'frozen'.

So I now had proof that some meat that came into Gregson's was from Central Europe, not Germany as claimed by the wily owner.

'So have you got enough to start putting your story together?'

'Almost. Just one more loose end.'

A couple of days later I tied it up. I drove to Bristol, to the faculty of chemistry to meet one of the staff who answered a question I posed in the affirmative. Then I popped into a couple of minimarts and a few more supermarkets, this time in the guise of an ordinary shopper and made a beeline for the butchery sections. There I picked up various packets of what was labelled as New Zealand or English lamb—chops, a small joint, some stewing meat cubes and a packet of mince, all of which I placed in a cooler bag, brought specially for this purpose and then delivered back to my tame professor who assured me that what I was asking would be an excellent project for a couple of his students. It would take a few days, he advised me, and he'd phone me as soon as he had a definitive answer.

One week later, true to his word, he called me up, outlined his students' findings and faxed over a series of lab results—DNA tests on the meat, identifying species and countries of origin. Most was lamb, from NZ and Britain but the mince undoubtedly contained a mixture of mutton and goat's meat, the latter of which being species native to Central and Eastern Europe. Gotcha!

In Steve's office that afternoon I laid everything out for him on the battered table we all sat around for our rare staff meetings—all the photos from Gregson's, the Croatian and Serbian labels, my purchase receipt and the university lab findings.

"So what does all this lot tell you?"

"Well, for starters I know that Gregson's is buying goat from Croatia and passing it off to supermarket as New Zealand and local lamb."

"And from a journalistic point of view, what don't you know?"

I'd given this a lot of thought.

"Well, I don't know if the Croatian meat is imported legally or illegally. It's probably black market but proving it would be difficult. Also I don't know whether anyone on the retail end even knows the meat isn't what Gregson's labels say it is. All they know is that it's cheap."

"Correct. So this is how we proceed. In the interests of fairness and full disclosure you'll have to tell those supermarkets what the lab tests revealed and see what they have to say then."

"But aren't they bound to deny all knowledge?"

"Of course they will and that may well be completely truthful but they'll still have some explaining to do to their customers after we go to print and they'll also be honour-bound to cut off all ties to Gregson's."

"And what about that side?"

"I'll handle Gregson personally. I'll be interested in his reaction when I present your findings and tell him we're going to publish and be damned."

"He might lawyer-up."

"He'd better. Because if necessary, I'll hand all this lot over to the police and let them take it from here."

I'm absurdly pleased. This is a real scoop and my name will be on the by-line. I had no idea journalism could be so exciting. Steve is shuffling the papers on the desk so I head off towards the door.

"Stroke of genius."

I stop and turn.

"Sorry?"

"DNA testing on the meat. Ingenious. Nice one."

I smile.

"Thanks."

He goes back to his papers and I carry on out of the door, feeling I may have actually found my metier.

All of that had taken me several weeks to ferret around and it took me another week of writing and rewriting to put the story together to Steve's satisfaction but it was worth it. It ran on the front page and so what if it was only the Bath and Avon Gazette? I felt like a real journalist, especially when Steve and Bill dragged me out to the pub down the road, tipped half a pint over my head and welcomed me to the club. I was on a high for the next two weeks,

162

even though I was back to reporting on chimney fires and vandalism in the local parks.

And then all of a sudden I came back down to earth with a bump.

6.30pm

As I sat in the office contemplating the possibility of making contact with Philip/Alex, the phone rang. It was Professor Turner.

"Mrs Hamilton? Sorry to call you at home but I've been swamped all week."

"It's fine. I'm assuming you've had another chance to talk to Sarah?"

"Yes, indeed. And to discuss her case with my staff yesterday morning."

"I see. So what do you think? Have you had any thoughts on her treatment?"

"Do you mind if I ask you a rather personal question? There's always a lot of soul-searching in these situations, I'm afraid, and sometimes tough questions have to be asked and answered if we want to get to the root of a problem."

"I'll do anything I can to help my daughter. I'm desperately worried about her and I want her to get well and come home."

"I was wondering, is everything all right between you and your husband?"

My mind flashed back to the night Sarah was admitted when Michael and I had sat in Professor Turner's office. I replayed our conversation in my mind and concluded that we probably hadn't presented much of a united front.

"Well, I think we were both a bit fraught that night when you met us. And you know how protective fathers are towards their daughters. I could see what was happening to Sarah but Michael was still in denial. It's understandable. And of course he's away such a lot. He doesn't see so much of Sarah as I do."

"Does he have to be away?"

What an odd question.

"It's his job, you see. He's regional manager for Pricerite and that means a lot of travel—visiting other branches, Head Office, you know."

"I see."

What does he see?

"That's hardly unique."

"By no means. But I do feel in this instance that it might be an adverse factor. It's just an impression I formed when I was talking to Sarah yesterday."

163

"I didn't know she noticed whether he was home or away. She spends most of her time in the school gym or in her room watching Netflix."

"Actually Mrs Hamilton, Sarah strikes me as a very perceptive young woman. She notices more than you think."

I'm starting to feel very uncomfortable at the direction this conversation is taking and I light another cigarette.

"So what are you saying? That Sarah's illness is some sort of psychological reaction to having an absentee father?"

"That would be a gross over-simplification even if I'd had more time to work with Sarah. No, it's just an impression I got, that something to do with your husband's work or his travelling is troubling your daughter. And she seems a little worried about you."

I can't help it. I laugh out loud.

"Sarah's worried about me?"

"As I say, it's just an impression. But I do think it would be helpful if you were to come and join in a few sessions with Sarah here at the clinic."

"Of course I will, if you think it'll help. Perhaps Michael should come too?"

"That might be useful."

He sounded dubious.

"But not just for now. For the first month or so we really have to concentrate on persuading Sarah to eat, try and get her weight back up to a level that's no longer immediately life-threatening. And while we're doing that we'll continue to work with her, try to find out more of the reasons behind her illness. And when we know that we'll have more of an idea of how to go about treating her successfully.

"I feel so useless. She's my daughter, she's hurting and I can't kiss it better like I used to be able to."

"You brought her here and that was the best possible thing you could have done for her. There's no quick fix but I promise you, Mrs Hamilton, we have a very high success rate. The national average is about eighty percent but ours is ninety five"

"That's still not a hundred."

"Unfortunately that's true. There are a few we don't manage to reach. But there's a very good chance that Sarah will be one of our successes. Hold on to that thought."

"I will. Thank you, Professor… Stephen."

Tuesday, 24 June

Charles and I have both been up for ages taking a petit déjeuner in the garden. Glancing at my phone I see it's time Jude was leaving for school and half-rise to give her a shout when at the precise moment, as if on cue, she bounces out into the garden. She has her school boater in one hand and the cloche in the other.

"Which one, granddad Charlie?"

She holds them both up, then puts them on in turn.

"Oh, the boater, definitely."

"Right, boater it is. This one's for you, ma."

She pushes the cloche down on my head.

"Actually, my dear, that looks rather fetching."

"Thank you, Charles. Maybe I'll wear it to work."

"Right, young lady, we'd better be off."

Charles stands up and dusts crumbs off his lap.

"Who did you say we were picking up first?"

"Mattie. His house is the closest. Then Amanda."

"Seems it's my lucky day. I get to ferry two gorgeous young creatures around."

I stay in the garden long after the Bentley makes its stately exit out of the drive. I am somewhat amazed to find Diana come out, immaculately dressed in a cream Jaeger suit, Gucci shoes, expensive-looking gold chain and bracelet and hair in a chignon. In her hands she is holding an open embossed leather personal organiser into which she is making notes with a gold fountain pen.

"Good morning, Fifi, darling. Have you seen Charles anywhere? I need to go out."

"He's taken Jude to school. He'll probably be back soon. Would you like some breakfast?"

"Just tea, thank you. Earl Grey. With lemon. What about Michael?"

"Still in Scotland, as far as I know."

She misses the inference and indifference in my words and tone.

"Oh yes, of course. What about you? Aren't you going to work? Surely the shop must be open by now."

"I didn't like to go out and leave you so I told George I'd be in late today."

"What nonsense. Charles and I are perfectly capable of occupying ourselves. In fact I have a lot to do today. As soon as he comes back we're going shopping. I have several projects which need taking care of. So off you go. Perhaps we'll call in and see you later. If I have time, that is."

It seems I'm dismissed. Feeling like a truant skipping school I mutter my thanks, gather up my jacket and handbag and head off to Ink-an'-Abulia before the clock strikes 12 and my Beetle turns into a pumpkin.

When I arrive, full of apologies, I set about cataloguing the new books on the old cardex system that George has used ever since the shop first opened. I try to imagine installing a computer in its place and the image is so incongruous I find myself smiling. The expression is not lost on George.

"Ffion, that's the first time I've seen you smile all week. What's amusing you?"

"Nothing, really. I was thinking about computers."

"Don't trust them, myself. I've heard they can, what's the expression? Freeze up. And then everything that was on them is lost. Imagine that. All your information, all your records, just lost. You mark my words, you're better off with these."

He grins and taps the box of file cards I'm updating.

"I agree. A lot more reliable. But I'm beginning to think that computers can have their uses. They have some at the clinic so the patients can carry on with their studies and keep in touch."

"And how is Sarah?"

"I phoned this morning and they said she's a bit chirpier. She's a bit more forthcoming in their group sessions and making friends with the other girls."

"That's a step in the right direction, surely? I'm sure she's in excellent hands there and the sooner she starts on her programme, the sooner she'll be home again, fit and well. You mark my words."

On an impulse I turn and give him a hug. George looks both pleased and embarrassed and he offers to go upstairs and make us both some tea.

"Prince of Wales is called for, I think. Don't you?"

I nod and smile and he potters off upstairs to put the kettle on while I return to my cataloguing

Just before five the shop door opens and Jude and Mattie come in. Mattie is carrying a copy of the local paper and Jude has a map in her hand.

166

"Mum, do you feel like going for a drive?"

"Do I have a choice? Where are we going?"

Jude spread the map out on the counter.

"This little village here. Fordham."

I checked the map. It was about twenty miles away, towards Stourbridge.

"And what's in Fordham? And don't say a ford."

"Second-hand horse box. Mattie's dad says he'll cough up for one, so long as it doesn't cost more than a thousand and they're asking eight hundred for this one. It's an old Renault, very tough."

"Well I suppose we can take a drive out there. I've got a feeling that Charles and Diana will be late. She phoned after lunch and said she was going to be busy so I wasn't to worry if they weren't there when I got home."

"I'm telling you she's up to something."

Mattie phones the number in the ad and after asking a few technical questions about the horse box, he covers the phone and asks me what time I think we can be there by. I check my watch and tell him about three quarters of an hour. As he rings off, George comes back in from the newsagents next door.

"Jude the Irresistible How lovely to see you, my dear. And who is this young man?"

'This is Mattie, a friend of Jude's. I've been roped in to going with them to look at a second-hand horse box.'

Mattie offered his hand and the two shook hands.

"Well, it's a lovely afternoon for it."

"Why don't you come along?"

"Oh no, I'll just be in the way."

"Nonsense. It'll do you good. Come on, it's after five. Let's lock up and be on our way. Mattie, do you want to drive?'

"Righto, Mrs H."

George fetches his jacket and I lock up behind us. Outside, Jude and I climb in the back and George gets in next to Mattie.

Mattie pulls out into the traffic and heads out of town.

"Goose neck or ball hitch?"

I look at George in astonishment.

"How on earth would you know anything about trailer hitches?"

"My dear young woman, don't forget I grew up in Ireland. My father bred hunters. Used to sell some of them on the mainland. Many's the time my

167

brother and I had to travel over with the groom to deliver them. That was in the late fifties. We still had one of the first post-war civilian Landrovers off the production line. Bottle green, it was. No heater so in winter we just had to wrap up as best we could and the seats were rock hard. Used to put a folded-up horse blanket on the front seat for long trips. Didn't make a lot of difference, as I recall."

"Doesn't sound like they changed much over the years, then."

Mattie explains that this is an all-in-one van and box which seems to both surprise and impress George. The two of them chat about hunters and horse breeding for most of the journey while Jude map-reads and I sit back and enjoy the scenery. As we get near to the village, Jude pulls out her mobile phone and calls the number in the advertisement to ask for directions. Ten minutes later we're pulling into the driveway of a weathered, red-brick house with a tidy gravelled frontage overhung with mature chestnut trees. Mattie parks the bug, gets out and rings the doorbell. No-one answers but a few moments later a middle-aged man in a tweed jacket and cavalry twill trousers comes around from the side of the house.

"Good evening. You must be Matthew."

He holds out his hand and he and Mattie shake formally.

"I'm Oliver Prentiss."

George, Jude and I all get out of the car and Mattie makes the introductions.

"Well, I expect you want to have a look at the box. It's in the garage around the back. Follow me."

We all troop after him. Behind the house is a row of buildings in the same red brick as the house, obviously the original stable block. There are still two horse stalls at one end with green half-doors, over which one grey horse and one chestnut are looking out expectantly. At the other end the half-doors have been replaced with large, wide wooden ones, painted the same shade of green. Producing a key and unlocking a padlock, Mr Prentiss swings them open to reveal a small green and grey horse transporter. It's an old-fashioned design but looks to be in good condition. In fact the paintwork positively gleams. Mattie walks around it, checking the tyres and looking underneath. Then he pulls the back down and walks inside. George also gets inside and gives it a practised eye.

"It looks like it's in really good condition, Mr Prentiss. Do you mind if I ask you why you're selling it?"

"Well, I don't really have any use for it anymore. It was really my wife's."

I pick up on the past tense but say nothing.

"Looks like you've been polishing it."

"Oh yes, every week, ever since we bought it in 1998."

"1998. Wow."

"Oh but it's perfectly roadworthy, I assure you. I have it serviced annually, just before its MOT. Even though it hasn't been used for some time."

"And you're asking eight hundred?"

"Well I wasn't quite sure what would be a fair price, what with it being so old. So if you think it's a bit much I'm prepared to come down a bit. Tell you what, let's call it seven."

Mattie looks embarrassed.

"Oh, I didn't mean to haggle, Mr Prentiss. I'm sure eight is very fair."

"On the other hand, it is getting on a bit."

We all three look at George in mild astonishment.

"There's always the problem with spares on such an old model. Also, these older vehicles are quite heavy on fuel and this young man is still a scholar. So all things considered six sounds about right to me. "

Oliver Prentiss smiles.

"Quite right, Fitzsimmons Six hundred pounds it is, then."

"That's great, Mr Prentiss. I'll just have to okay it with my father but I think we have a deal."

The two of them shake hands again.

"Splendid."

Mattie pulls out his mobile.

"I'll just go outside and speak to dad."

"Can I have a look at your horses?"

Jude had been uncharacteristically quiet up to now, content to leave the negotiations to Mattie but I can see she's dying to have a look around.

"Of course, young lady. Let me show you."

He leads the way back to the two stalls, stopping outside a small door next to the first loosebox.

"This is the feed room. It's time for their supper."

169

Two bowls of mixed feed stand on a rough wooden table. He picks up one bowl and Jude takes the other.

"Let me give you a hand."

"Thank you, Jade, is it?"

"Jude."

They carry the food bowls outside and Mr Prentiss opens the door to the first stall where the chestnut, slightly greying around the muzzle, is grunting impatiently.

"This is Captain Scarlet. He's getting on a bit now, like me."

Jude opens the second stall door and puts the food inside.

"And who's this?"

"That's Cloud Dancer. My wife bought him just before she...."

He turns away and busies himself collecting the feed bowls.

"Does anybody ride them?"

"Oh, I get on the Captain every now and then. I'm not much of a rider, but he looks after me pretty well. And a young girl from the village used to come out and exercise Cloud a few times a week but she went off to college last September. So since then he hasn't done much. I was thinking I might have to sell him. It'll be a wrench, I don't mind telling you but it's not fair on him, just hanging around getting bored."

Joining us, Mattie looks pleased.

"My father says fine, Mr Prentiss. He'll organise a cheque tomorrow and I'll make a plan to collect it next weekend."

We say our goodbyes and are about to leave.

"Would you like me to exercise him? Cloud Dancer, I mean. Maybe I could come out a couple of times a week after work."

The words come out of my mouth before I can stop them. Jude is halfway into the car but she stops, turns and stares at me open-mouthed. Mattie catches the look on her face and smiles with wry amusement and George looks positively approving.

"He'll probably be a bit fresh."

'That's okay. I don't mind a handful.'

"Mum, you haven't ridden for years. You'll never cope."

Jude the Untrusting.

"Thanks for the vote of confidence. I was riding before you were born. And very competently too, I'll have you know."

"And when exactly was the last time you were on a horse?"

"It's like riding a bike. You never forget."

I cross my fingers as I say that.

"Can I make a suggestion?"

We all turn to look at Mattie.

"Why don't Jude or I get on him for half an hour when we come to pick the horse box up? Just work a bit of his nonsense out."

It's a perfectly sensible suggestion, just what I'd expect from Mattie but I'm getting a little fed up with this 'child is father to the man' philosophy.

"I've got an even better idea. Why don't I come over with you both, get on the horse while you sort out the box and then I'll drive it back, just to see how it handles?"

Mattie now looks at his feet sheepishly, Jude raises her eyebrows skywards and George has to turn away to suppress a laugh.

"I'm sure you'll be fine, Mrs Hamilton. Tell you what, I'll put him on the lunge for ten minutes before you get here. I may not be anything like the rider my wife was but I can manage that. And I'm sure that's all he'll need. He's fairly well-mannered most of the time."

"That sounds sensible. Are you sure you don't mind?"

"My dear lady, I'm very grateful for your offer to ride him occasionally. He could definitely do with it. Just let me know what time you'll be coming and I'll make sure he's properly warmed up and tacked."

"I'm really looking forward to it. It's time I got some fresh air and exercise again."

I'm about to add that riding's also a wonderful way to push your problems out of your mind but I catch the thought and keep it to myself. As I do so I have an image of myself as a student, riding on the Downs in Bristol, every weekend no matter what the weather was like. Riding to forget the baby I'd lost. Riding to forget the mental photograph I took of his little face. Riding to suppress the guilt I felt the rest of the time. And what will I be riding to forget now? Sarah's illness? Michael's amorality? My long-overdue mental metamorphosis. I shake my head to clear these thoughts away and as I look up I see Mr Prentiss watching me. And I can see in his eyes that he understands, that he too rides to forget. I summon up the brisk, business-like Fiona.

"Right, we'd better get going. Don't want to take up any of your time, Mr Prentiss."

"It's been a real pleasure, Mrs Hamilton. I don't get many visitors these days. And it's Oliver, by the way."

"Fiona! I'll phone you and let you know exactly when we're coming for the box."

"Any time will be fine. You'll usually find me at home. I don't get out and about as much as I used to."

We all climb into the bug, Mattie puts it into gear and we drive out. Mr Prentiss waves in a farewell gesture and I wave back.

"What a lovely man. A real old-fashioned gentleman. And George, I'm sorry to say you shamelessly took advantage of his nice nature."

"Nonsense, my dear Ffion. Just a bit of horse trading, that's all."

"Sly, old Irish fox."

"You know, I think this calls for a little celebration. On me. Why don't you pull in at that pub just up there, young Mattie?"

He points to a country pub just up ahead and set slightly off the road. It looks like a converted Elizabethan cottage and there are slatted wooden tables and chairs outside, with large cotton umbrellas displaying the logo of the licensing brewery.

"Righto, Mr F."

As Mattie pulls into the car park the sky rumbles ominously.

"Oh oh. I think sitting in the garden's out."

Mattie pulls into a space and jumps out to put the bug's hood up. Then we troop inside, Mattie ducking to avoid hitting his head on the low lintel and George, good to his word, buys a round—a pint of Guinness for himself, half a pint of lager for Mattie, dry cider for me and Coke for Jude—and we find a comfortable corner to sit down. Naturally the talk is all of the horse box.

"I'll get dad to give me a lift on Saturday morning, then when I get it home I'll go out with him and get a feel of how it drives."

"You realise it probably hasn't been properly road-tested for years."

"I'll stick to the back roads and trust to luck. And do you realise that this means we'll be completely independent when we go over to Fairfield? No more waiting around for other people. No ringing around to see if anyone's got a space on their box."

"Brilliant.:

Jude's cell phone rings and she pulls it out of her pocket and clicks a button to read an incoming message. She pushes the phone across to Mattie and he

172

also reads the message. They exchange a look which I can't interpret and suddenly seem in a hurry to leave. Glancing at my watch I remember our house guests and have to agree that we'd probably be getting back. We finish our drinks and head out to the car park to be greeted by a flash of lightning and a loud crash of thunder. Then the heavens open. The spell of sunny weather has well and truly broken.

"You lot wait here. I'll bring the car up."

Mattie leaves us standing by the pub entrance and makes a dash for the bug. He drives up and we all pile in and drive back to town with the wipers on full speed. We drop George off back at the shop and then carry on home with the storm showing no signs of abating. The Bentley is parked in the drive and Mattie pulls in in front of it, as close to the front door as he can get.

"Mrs H. do you mind if we borrow the car for a bit? There's something we need to do."

"In this weather?"

"We shouldn't be long."

Sitting in the back seat I see them exchanging that look again.

"This wouldn't have anything to do with that cell phone message, would it?"

They glance at each other and look away guiltily. The rain beats down on the bug's canvas rood but other than that the silence is deafening.

"Jude?"

She stares ahead out of the windscreen. Jude the Inscrutable.

"Mattie?"

He turns to look at me, then looks back at Jude.

"You'd better show your mum."

"Sarah'll kill me."

"Sarah? What's Sarah got to do with this? You're not thinking of going to the Avon, are you?"

Jude fishes in her bag and pulls out her phone. She thumbs through a quick sequence and hands it to me.

As I suspected it's a message from Sarah asking Jude and Mattie to come and pick her up. She asks them to text her when they're on their way and she'll meet them outside in the grounds.

"Jude, I can't believe you were going to go through with this. You know how important it is for her to stay there. She has to get well."

173

"I wasn't. I just thought Mattie and I should go and speak to her. Talk her out of it."

"She's not supposed to have any contact with any of us for another couple of days. You know that as well as I do. Where the hell did she get another phone from, anyway? The nurse took hers."

"How should I know? Maybe she borrowed it from one of the other girls. Or maybe…"

She breaks off.

"Maybe what?"

"Well, remember what I was telling you about Diana. About her asking all those questions about mobile devices. Perhaps she was planning on buying one for Sarah."

In a split second I know she's right. That must have been what Diana was on about when she said she was busy all day. She must have quizzed Jude on different models and setting it up and so on, gone out and bought one and then delivered it to the Avon for Sarah. I fleetingly contemplate going inside and giving her what for, then decide against it. For now, at any rate.

"What are you going to do? You're not going to get Sarah into trouble, are you? It's all right for you but she'll blame me as usual."

"How do you work that out?'

"It was me she texted."

"Jude, I have to do something. For Sarah's sake."

"S'pose."

I jump out of the car, rush indoors and head straight for the study where I shut the door firmly behind me, sit at the desk and place a call on the Avon. A brief enquiry tells me that Nurse Parks is not on duty but I am put through to one of her colleagues, a Nurse Sims. When she comes on the phone I introduce myself and she asks how she can help.

"Actually I'm a bit concerned about Sarah."

"I can understand that. But I can assure you she's in very good hands here. And she seems to settling in quite well."

"I wouldn't be so sure about that, if I were you."

"What makes you say that?"

Nurse Simms sound puzzled

174

"I promise you. I looked in on the girls half an hour ago. Sarah was watching television with Kimberley and Amy. They were all laughing and enjoying the programme so I left them to it."

"Hmm. Well maybe there was another reason she was feeling buoyed up."

"Sorry?"

"Apparently she texted her younger sister."

"Oh, that's interesting. I wonder where she got hold of a mobile phone?"

Unexpectedly she laughs.

"Don't worry. It happens. I'll have a word with Sarah."

"Her sister's worried she'll know it was her that blew the whistle."

"Just tell her everything we do here is for the good of our patients. Sarah's with us because she's very ill and needs serious help. Letting us know what she was planning is part of that help. In America they call it tough love. Look, lots of the girls try these tricks in their first few weeks. It's hard for them to adjust and accept that the whole process is just something they have to go through to get better. So sometimes their friends smuggle in a mobile, sometimes they manage to sneak down and use one of the payphones on the other wards. And the computers are all line so they can make all sorts of plans by e-mail or social media. Heck, some of them just walk out and hail a taxi. And we're just medical staff. We're not the police or the Gestapo. At the end of the day they're not prisoners either. It's up to the girls themselves to make the decision to stay and get the help they need. And most of them do. Don't worry."

"So I can leave you to it?"

"Definitely. And don't worry. It'll be fine. I'll pop up and have a quiet chat with her and I'm sure we can sort it out. She'll feel a bit frustrated and probably blame me but I've got thick skin!"

I put the phone down, much relieved. I hear Jude and Mattie talking and the next hurdle occurs to me. How exactly am I going to handle the Diana situation?

You're probably wondering what went wrong in Bath when it all seemed to be going so right. Okay, money was a bit tight but we were managing. The girls were happy and settled, I'd found an interesting job which looked like it might turn into a career, I had friends around me who cared and for the first time in ages I was happy.

It all began quite innocuously. I was sitting in the office one morning typing up a story on a fire the previous evening at the Theatre Royal. Not very dramatic, just an electrical short in the lighting box during a performance of Equus. The fire brigade had been called, the fire was quickly put out and in true theatrical tradition the show went on. Steve had sent me around first thing and I'd interviewed the stage manager and the lighting technician and taken a couple of photos. The manager hadn't come on duty so I left my number and asked for him to call me at the office and there wasn't much else I could do. The damage was minor, a local electrical company was already busy rewiring and it hardly seemed worth a big exposé on public safety standards in old buildings so I was struggling to make it sound interesting. Three Silk Cuts later I was just about finished when a call came through to my desk. Thinking it might be the theatre manager I picked it up but it wasn't him. It was Michael.

My stomach churned when I heard his voice and my first instinct was to put the phone down. But something in the tone of his voice stopped me.

"Feef, is it really you?"

"It's Fiona now. It always was."

"It's wonderful to hear your voice again. I've really missed you,"

"What do you want, Michael? And how did you know where to find me?"

"It was your article on Gregson's and the Pricerite connection."

The by-line I'd been so pleased to see in print had clearly proved a double-edged sword. Fuck, fuck, fuck.

"We had no idea it was going on in the branch till you exposed it. Francis sent me down to sort it out and he told me to thank you personally. I've had to stay on for a few weeks to make sure everything was back in order."

My stomach turned again.

"Michael, where are you speaking from?"

"I'm in the Weston branch. I've been here since last week."

I grip the phone with both hands and took a deep breath. Michael in Weston-super-Mare, just a few miles away, it was a nightmare."

"I've been trying to pluck up the courage to contact you. I've seen you, of course."

"What the hell do you mean, you've seen me?"

Upset has turned to angry.

"You've been following me? You've really crossed a line, Michael."

176

"Not really following. I was just trying to screw up the courage to speak to you."

"It wouldn't be the first thing you'd screwed up. Or just plain screwed."

"Yes, I did screw up. And now my head's screwed up. So I wanted to put things right. I just needed to talk to you. Anyway I knew you were working for the Gazette. So I just drove around there a few times, hoping I could bump into you. Mostly I just parked across the street. A couple of times I spotted you coming out of the office but you always seemed in a hurry and at the last minute my nerve gave out. I know how you must feel."

"That would be a first."

"Oh, Feef, what I did was wrong, stupid. A fling. It didn't mean anything."

"It did to me."

"I know, I didn't mean it like that. Just that it wasn't serious."

"To whom, Michael?"

"Look, we need to talk. Properly, not like this. Have dinner with me?"

"You're out of your mind."

"Yes, I am. Totally. I've been out of my mind from the day you walked out. I miss you. I miss the girls. You were my life, Feef."

"Only a part of it, apparently."

"Look, just dinner, all right? No strings."

"No."

"Feef, please. I'm begging you. My life is nothing without you and the girls. I'm going out of my mind."

He started to cry. I put the phone down and found that I was crying too but not for the same reason.

He phoned again that afternoon, then the following morning and again the next afternoon. After a week, in desperation, I agreed to meet him in the café across the road for a cup of tea.

"Just tea, Michael. And absolutely no sympathy."

We'd agreed on eleven o'clock but I watched out of the Gazette windows all morning, with a sick feeling the in pit of my stomach that grew sicker and sicker as the witching hour drew near. Just after a quarter to eleven a silver Audi came into view, slowed down and parked outside the café. And a few seconds later Michael got out and went inside. It was the first time I'd seen him since he packed for that fateful business trip. The face of a familiar stranger. I stayed by the window and lit a cigarette with trembling hands. And at eleven o

177

clock exactly I picked up my bag, walked across the road and went into the café.

'Feef!'

Michael jumped up, knocking his chair over. For a horrible moment I thought he was going to touch me, I shrank back against the open doorway, Michael hesitated, read the body language and dropped his hands to his side.

"You look wonderful."

"Hello, Michael."

I was still standing semi-frozen in the doorway and heaven knows how long I'd have stayed there like that but a young man in biker's leathers was coming in and needed to get past. I stepped aside and now found myself standing awkwardly just next to the chair Michael knocked over. He picked it up and held it out for me. I ignored him and sat down opposite. The waitress finished serving the biker and came to take our order, a refill of coffee for Michael and tea for me. I lit another cigarette.

"Still smoking, then?"

"Seems so."

"I've missed you."

"I looked down at the table and flicked non-existent ash off my cigarette.

"I'm really sorry, Feef."

I kept my eyes on the table and concentrated on the gingham pattern of the tablecloth. With my free hand I traced the pattern with my fingernail, tiny square after tiny square, keeping my eyes down, it took all my concentration not to miss any out.

"I'll do anything."

"I think you've done more than enough already."

Blue square, white square, blue square, white square. Suddenly he grabbed my hand, interrupted my tracing. I glanced up at him, shook my hand free and continued where I left off.

"Excuse me."

A waitress was standing by the table holding two cups and saucers. Reluctantly I abandoned my geometric study and leaned back in my chair. She put the cups down and walked off and I busied myself with the sugar bowl and milk jug.

"You're not making this easy."

"I'm here, aren't I?"

178

"Yes, yes, you are. Thank you."

Now it was his turn with the sugar.

"How long was it going on for?"

His hand shook and sugar spilled into the saucer.

"Does it matter? It's over, I swear it."

"How long?"

"Six months."

I cast my mind back. It must have started just before last Christmas, round about the time he started keeping longer and longer hours. Pressure of work, he said. And I believed him. Well, no, if I'm honest I think I knew right from the start. It was just that I didn't find out her name till much later.

"And if I hadn't so rudely interrupted you, how much longer would it have gone on for?"

I looked up at him briefly. And saw he was crying.

"Oh for heaven's sake, Michael, grow up."

I stubbed out my cigarette and rose to leave.

"I have to get back to work. I'm on a deadline."

I walked to the door.

"Feef, can I see the girls?"

I didn't turn round, just opened the door and half walked, half ran back to the office, rushed into the loo and threw up.

The following evening Patti and I had a girlie heart-to-heart. We left Ross looking after the girls and went to a basement wine bar downtown where I filled her in on the phone calls and the close encounter of the fifth kind. I was adamant that he shouldn't have anything to do with Sarah and Jude but Patti put her logical, legal hat on and said I'd have to let him see them because if I didn't do it voluntarily he could take me to court for legal access. She was right, of course, and I didn't think I'd be able to handle that and I knew the girls certainly wouldn't. So we decided that the safest bet was to pick a Sunday and stick to safety in numbers. Patti suggested their place as a neutral venue but I didn't know how the whole thing would go and I didn't think that would be fair on them. Or their best china and ornaments. So in the end we decided on the park with Patti and Ross to come along for moral support.

I told the girls where we were going but I left out the bit about whom we going to see when we got there. Both of them loved the park but Jude especially. A small stream ran through it and whenever we went there we took

179

bread to feed the ducks and moorhens that swam up and down, sometimes hiring a little rowing boat so we could get closer and enjoy the water. On the far side was a bandstand where we sat on fine days, eating ice cream and listening to the music. And between there and the car park was the playground where Sarah sat on the see-saw with her arms around her baby sister and I half sat on the other end and pulled them up and down. And then a turn on the swings, Jude in the little baby chairs, only needing a gentle push, Sarah on the open ones, swinging herself, a little higher every time we went.

So I had no intention of meeting Michael anywhere near the river, the bandstand or the playground.

In the end I picked the gardens. There was a flower clock there, planted to bloom all year round, tulips in the spring, asters in summer, chrysanths in the autumn and ornamental cabbages in winter. It amused the girls for five minutes on our visits but wasn't top of their must-do agenda so I thought that would suffice.

At ten o clock the following Saturday morning the girls and I drove around to Patti and Ross's house and we all piled into their Range Rover. On the way to the park I made them stop at the corner newsagents so I could buy cigarettes, 60 Silk Cut for good measure, and I managed to get through 2 and a half on the way there. A 15 minute drive.

I smoked another as I dawdled and dragged my feet on the way to the clock garden. Ross and Patti decided to keep a discreet distance behind us but they promised they wouldn't be far away. The girls were skipping around, unaware of the significance of the occasion. To them it was just another Sunday morning in the park and there were certain rituals to be gone through—find a friendly dog for Jude to pat and Sarah throw a ball for, ride the roundabout for a couple of rotations every time we're anywhere in the vicinity, roll around in the grass if it's dry or splash through the puddles if it's been raining. This day it was a golden spaniel that was on the receiving end of Jude's cuddle and when Sarah produced the ball from her pocket he obliging ran after it a few times, each time returning and dropping it at her feet, much to her delight. We would both have been quite happy to spend more time in this harmless pursuit but unfortunately the dog's owner looked at his watch and cut things short apologetically.

"Sorry, we'll have to go. I'm supposed to be somewhere."

So were we. I looked around and saw Ross and Patti sitting on a park bench, Ross surreptitiously glancing down at his watch. I looked down at mine, took a deep breath and hurried the girls off towards the flower clock, resplendent in early October with variegated chrysanthemums in full bloom.

And just beyond the twelve o'clock bed I suddenly saw Michael.

Sarah, who was learning to tell the time and liked to point out the inaccuracy of the clock against my watch, spotted him next. At first I could see her struggling to place this at once familiar and yet strange face then realisation dawned. She squealed 'daddy, daddy' and took off straight across the clock face and into his waiting arms. Jude, alerted by her sister's animation and hearing the magic word, looked up and hurtled after her big sister. I watched the reunion from where the big hand is on the four. It was only twenty past eleven but it felt like high noon.

I watched the scene across the flowerbed play out like a bad home movie with the sound turned down. Michael scooped up the girls in his arms, then put them down on an adjacent park bench, from behind which he produced 2 enormous, brightly wrapped presents. The girls gleefully tore off the paper and examined their presents, a big Barbie house for Sarah and stable full of My Little Ponies for Jude. Anyone who didn't know him might have given Michael credit for an astute choice but more likely he just grabbed the biggest things he could find in Pricerite's toy section. So with Sarah stripping and re-dressing Barbie in an assortment of fashionable new outfits, Jude making galloping movements on her lap with her new herd of Neapolitan ice cream-hued ponies and Michael sitting beaming in the middle, an arm around each of them, they could have been an advert for an upmarket toy store.

And as the girls alternated between playing with their spoils and gazing up adoringly at the prodigal father, Michael looked over in my direction and smiled. I returned his gaze stone-faced but either he couldn't see or he didn't want to because he bent down and said something to the girls, then they all got up, gathered up the booty and walked towards me, skirting the flower beds this time.

As they grew closer I started to panic and looked around frantically for Patti and Ross but they were some way away, sitting on a blanket spread under a big horse chestnut tree, not even looking in my direction.

"Mummy, look what I got from daddy."

Sarah waved her new doll in the air.

"An' me"

Not to be outdone, Jude held up 2 of her ponies, one in each chubby little hand. I smiled indulgently at the girls as they ran up but the smile froze on my lips as Michael stepped up, put his arms around me and kissed me on the cheek.

"Feef, darling, I've missed you so much."

I wriggled out of his grasp, not wanting to make it too obvious in front of the girls.

"Your hair's different."

"A lot of things are different."

"The girls have both grown. Jude's got to be quite the chatterbox. And Sarah's very fashion conscious. I told her we could go shopping after lunch. She says she's seen a pair of shoes she wants."

"Yes, and I told her they were too expensive and she couldn't have them. And what's this about lunch? I promised to bring the girls to the park and I've kept my word but that's all. Anyway Patti and Ross are here. They drove us here this morning."

"Well ask them to join us. My treat. Please."

I looked at him and then at Sarah and Jude who were obviously delighted to see him and it occurred to me that I couldn't very well drag them away after ten minutes which was my original plan. On the other hand I had no intention of letting him take them anywhere on their own.

"Don't you think that might be a bit awkward under the circumstances?"

"They don't have to stay. I could take you and the girls home."

"Yes they do and no you absolutely couldn't. Come on, girls, let's go and find Aunty Patti and Uncle Ross. You can show them what daddy bought you."

Taking one in each hand I march them off towards my friends who are still keeping a discreet distance, playing Frisbee with a couple of teenagers. When we reach them I frogmarch Patti off behind a big horse chestnut tree.

'He wants to take us to lunch."

Patti checks her watch—it's quarter past twelve.

"He's had nearly an hour. How much time does he need?"

"Thing is, it's not him—it's the girls. I can't just drag them away now. Look at them. They're all over him like a bad rash. And there's no way I'm letting him take them anywhere on his own."

"God no. Well I suppose we could always do drinks and sandwiches in the beer garden."

"Brilliant. That way we don't have to go anywhere else and I don't have to say no to the girls when they ask if they go in daddys car."

Patti discreetly let Ross in on the plan and apart from shooting a somewhat dubious look in Michael's direction, I saw him nodding. I took a deep breath and marched up.

"We've all decided on the beer garden. It's over the other side of the river—it's walking distance but it can be slow progress. Jude's little legs don't cover much ground and there's always a lot of distractions along the way."

"No problem."

He turned round, picked Jude up and hoisted her onto his shoulders. Then he stooped down, scooped up Sarah and slung her piggy-back style behind him, the girls both squealing with delight

We all sat outside the pub on wooden benches drinking Vimto and Somerset cider and eating Cumberland sausage and mashed potatoes. Michael cut up Jude's sausages but when he tried to feed her he was rebuffed with a very forceful 'I a big girl now. Jude do it."

Jude the Independent, even at that age.

"She thinks she can do it but she makes a big mess and she needs a spoon. I can use a proper knife and fork. Look."

And Sarah proudly demonstrated her cutlery motor skills to her father, even managing to propel her potato onto the back of her fork.

"I've missed out on a lot."

"Your choice."

And I turned away and chatted to Patti and Ross about a movie which we'd all been to see the weekend before.

After the girls had finished eating, they ran off to the petting zoo behind the pub, their father following and taking pictures of them with an expensive-looking electronic video camera. Finally they all came back and he and Ross argued about who was picking up the tab. They settled on half and half and we prepared to take our leave.

"I could give you all a lift home."

"We'll stick with Patti and Ross, thanks."

"It's no trouble."

"I said no thank you."

He looked at my face and didn't push it, bent over and made to kiss me but I stepped smartly aside. Lunch was one thing, physical contact was entirely another.

"Maybe we can do this again sometime?"

"Maybe."

"I'll call you."

"I might not be around the office. I'm quite busy these days."

"I'll take my chances."

"That's your problem, Michael. You always have."

He hugged the girls and promised to see them again soon, Jude reminding him not to forget to bring a present, Sarah telling him that he needed to come to her school and meet her teacher and all her friends.

Then we parted company, Patti and Ross dropped us off at home and life returned to normal for the rest of the day.

When I said I was busy at work, I hadn't known the half of it. It was now about 2 months after my triumph with the Gregson's exposé and when I went into work on Monday morning Steve called me into his office, told me I had a permanent position if I wanted it and said I was now the Gazette's official crime correspondent. If I was interested, that was.

If? I was finally a full-time staff member and on top of the world. Even the fact that Michael was lurking somewhere in the vicinity failed to burst my bubble. The news necessitated another lunchtime visit to the pub with Bill and Sally, our girl Friday, but this time I didn't get drenched in beer—they just toasted my good health and welcomed me on board. Everything was falling into place.

When I emerged from the study I found Diana in the kitchen wearing a butcher's apron and matching oven gloves and checking something in the oven. She heard the door open and turned around.

"Fifi, Jude, perfect timing. The daube is done to a turn so if you just set the dining table and give me a hand with the potatoes it'll be ready in no time."

"I'm soaking wet so I'm going upstairs to bath and put on dry clothes."

Upstairs, I try, unsuccessfully, to wash off the blackness of my mood. When I finally reach a compromise shade of grey and I've soaked away most of my pent-up anger and mental exhaustion, I get out and walk into the bedroom to put some clean clothes on. Dressing for dinner, the wicked witch of the north downstairs would have described it. I'm towelling my hair dry when the phone rings. Thinking it might be the Avon I pick it up but it isn't the hospital, it's Michael. Clearly a call of obligation. He inquires perfunctorily about Sarah and I reply equally perfunctorily, saying that as far as I knew she's as well as could be expected. Jude is covered in even fewer words and by the time we get to Charles and Diana a grunt is all I can manage. There is a pause.

"I gather you're moving to Manchester?"

"Who told you that?"

His tone is odd. I'd expected guilty affirmation but what comes over is simultaneously evasive and probing.

"Charles. He seemed surprised that you hadn't mentioned it. Frankly, so was I."

"Well, nothing's been decided yet."

Again that slippery tone. What hadn't been decided? From what Charles said Manchester was a done deal.

Anyway, speak for yourself.

Politely I wish him well for the opening next week and ring off without even bothering to ask what time he'll be back tomorrow. As for being sent to Manchester, personally, Coventry would have been my preference.

Downstairs in the kitchen a small battalion of covered dishes is lined up on the table like soldiers on a passing out parade under final inspection from the Commanding Officer. As each passes muster it is ceremonially handed to one of the three dumb waiters standing dutifully by the door, namely Charles, Jude and Mattie. Diana herself carries through the piece de resistance and sets her casserole down in the centre of the impeccably-laid table with a flourish.

"I thought we'd eat in here for a change. So much more suitable than the kitchen, don't you think?"

Obviously we didn't or we wouldn't eat there as often as we did. I smile sweetly and bide my time.

Beaming at us all, she deftly ladles the stew onto my rarely used Limoges dinner plates. Come to think of it, it was she who'd bought them in the first place, bringing back an entire dinner service in boxes in the boot of the Bentley on one of her frequent continental jaunts.

The boeuf Bourguignon is surprisingly good. Well it's a surprise to me that Diana even knows how to light the oven since she's waited on hand and foot back home and all the cooking is done by the redoubtable Mrs McGregor. Jude is busying herself picking out the meat from the casserole but Mattie keeps the conversation light by telling Charles and Diana all about the horse box and the show he and Jude are planning on entering. And nobody mentions Sarah. Everything was going about as well as could be expected till the cheese course.

'Charles took me shopping today."

"So we noticed."

Jude's tone, both accusatory and recriminatory, is lost on Diana.

"I thought if I'm to help George decorate his little pied-a-terre I'd need a few things that I didn't bring with me."

"Like a mobile phone?"

"What was that, Jude, dear?"

"Never mind."

"So we went to Pricerite's electronic department and Charles insisted on buying something called a tablet. You know, like those ancient writing stones, He said I could use it to help me with decorating. Of course I thought he was pulling my leg but he assures me that there are special programmes you could get. I told him I'd never be able to get the hang of it but he said almost anyone can use them, these days. You should get one yourself, Fifi, dear. He says I can use it to transfer pictures of the flat from my phone. I just plug it into the tablet and really have a good long look at them before I make a decision on colours and what piece goes where."

"Just the tablet?"

"I gather you think we've been a bit extravagant, Jude dear."

"No, not extravagant, just..."

She sees the look on my face and uncharacteristically breaks off.

"I think what Jude is trying to say, Diana, is that whilst we're all impressed with your newly acquired grasp of technology and your evident enthusiasm to join the computer revolution. I just wish you'd told me you had bought Sarah a new phone."

Diana looks so completely taken aback, I wonder if I have misjudged her.

"No, dear. You weren't listening. Charles bought this one for me a few weeks ago. See."

She produces it like a magician pulling a rabbit out of his hat and raises it equally as triumphantly.

"And now I have the tablet."

186

The expression on her face is entirely guilt-free and suddenly I want the ground to swallow me up. I stammer out an apology.

"Sarah managed to get hold of a phone today. We assumed you must have bought it for her. I apologise for jumping to conclusions."

"Sorry, gran. I mean Diana."

There is an awkward silence for a few moments, finally broken by Charles.

"Diana could probably do with a few lessons from you youngsters."

"What do you need?"

"Perhaps one of you could teach me how to prose?"

"Prose?"

"She means text" (Mattie)

Jude giggles and I take the opportunity to mend fences.

"Personally I think 'prosing' sounds much better."

Charles smiles sympathetically in agreement. Mattie tactfully busies himself buttering a Bath Oliver and proffers it to Diana.

"I don't know about anyone else but I'd like some of that Stilton."

Charles holds up his plate.

"Me too."

Sarah must have sourced her phone from somewhere closer to home, just like the nurse said, and I've done my mother-in-law a bit of a disservice.

After supper Mattie and Jude disappear off upstairs to her room and Charles and Diana move in to the sitting room, Diana leading the way making little notes in her personal organiser as she walked, Charles the customary two paces behind for royal consorts and staggering slightly under the weight of Diana's swatch books and the new tablet.

Wednesday, 25 June

Sleep is once eluding me so I rise early, shower quietly and take tea into Michael's study. Then I type in the familiar address on the search engine, select Mother and Child and log in. Another message!

'Hello, Fiona. I'll try and give you a potted bio and yes, Alex is short for Alexander. That's my name'

It's him! My heart begins to pound and I have to stop and take a deep breath. Holding onto the edges of the desk to prevent my hands shaking, I read on.

'My father's a classics master and an admirer of Alexander the Great—lucky for me it wasn't Ptolemy!

I was brought up in a little village near Kings Lynne called Birchley. Dad is headmaster at a small prep school there which I attended till I was 9, then to the local grammar school. After that I read English at Oxford. Just graduated with a 2.1 and I'm trying to decide what next—maybe a Masters.

You asked if I liked horses—I did use to ride when I was at school but these days I never seem to have the time. I was on the varsity rowing team and I play a bit of rugger, mainly to keep dad happy. I also play the guitar a bit but I'm not very good. I leave that to others and just listen instead. My taste in music is pretty catholic but I'm a sucker for a bit of heavy metal or well-played classical concertos.

I prefer Gilbert & Sullivan to Italian opera and I like Renaissance art.

I'm also addicted to sausage and mash, draft Guinness and macaroni cheese which is one of the only things I can cook myself.

I hope that gives you some idea of the real me and I'd like to know a bit more about you. Also my birth father, or is that a sore spot?

Kind regards, Alex.'

Philip. My Philip. I've finally found him after all these years. And he sounds really warm and funny, the sort of young man any parent could be proud of. I hope his adoptive mother appreciates him and even thinking of another 'mother' causes a sharp pain in my chest. Yes, I'm unfairly jealous. I read and re-read the scant details and begin to compose my response, keeping it light in tone and in detail, mirroring his own.

'Hello Alex. I was thrilled to hear from you after all this time and to learn that you've had such a wonderful upbringing. You wanted to know a little bit more about me. I work in an antiquarian bookshop called Ink-an'-Abulia. That's a pun on Incunabula dreamed up the shop owner, George, on account of the length of time people take to select their books.

I now have two teenage daughters, Jude and Sarah, My younger daughter Jude tells me she's into 'Indie' bands, whatever that means! She's horse-mad and has a passion for antique clothes that drives her father mad, especially when she wears them instead of her school uniform. Sarah's taste runs more to contemporary and trendy. She's very fashion conscious. Must have inherited it from her grandmother—it certainly doesn't come from me!

You asked about your birth father and I have to be honest and say I haven't had any contact with him since before you were born but I do know he went to Liverpool University—he read astrophysics there. I read English like you but I was at Bristol.

Please send me some more details about yourself and your life whenever you have time. I've missed so much and I really want to get to know you at last. With love, Fiona Hamilton.'

I hit 'send' and experience a fleeting moment much freer and happier than I have for a very long time, which is immediately superseded by feelings of guilt and betrayal for taking attention away from poor Sarah. Still the only one up, I put in a quick call to the hospital and learn that as a result of having the illicit cell phone confiscated my elder daughter is sulking in her room and is refusing to eat any breakfast. I am concerned but the nurse assures me that her reaction is entirely normal and that it's only a temporary setback. I tell her to give Sarah my love and resolve to speak to Professor Turner later on the advisability of discussing the whole Philip thing with Sarah in her present state. He's a doctor so everything I tell him has to stay between the two of us and I know he'll have some sound advice as to how to broach the subject.

Hearing Jude pottering about in the kitchen I bring myself back to the here and now and I summon all the willpower I can muster not to spill the beans about Alex. I have to tell someone though and I resolve to call Patti as soon as possible—she'd kill me if I didn't anyway!

"The evil one not up?"

"Hasn't manifested herself in human form yet. But I did see a strange black cat with diabolical yellow eyes lurking in the bushes in the garden."

"That'll be the familiar. Probably poor old grandad."

"Yeah, wakes up every morning with a strange craving for kippers and milk." (pause) "Did dad say when he was coming back?"

"Not till later this week. Why do you ask?"

"No reason."

The speed and tone of her response says there is. I don't push it.

"I need a favour."

"Just the one?"

"You're so funny, mum. Mattie says he'll give me driving lessons. Can we use the bug?"

"I suppose so, so long as you're careful."

189

"Thanks."

She looks at me shrewdly. Jude the Insightful.

"What's with your sudden love affair with computers and the internet anyway? You haven't got a secret lover, have you?"

"No, not me."

The words are out before I can stop them.

"As opposed to?"

Jude the Interrogative. I attempt a quick cover up.

"As opposed to all those 40-somethings on TV these days who always seem to be having torrid affairs while their husbands are at work."

Not very convincing but the best I could manage off the top of my head.

"And what about the 40-something husbands?"

Jude the Astute. I'm definitely not comfortable with the turn this conversation's taking but I keep my tone bright. Too bright.

"Well, yes, them too, if you believe everything you see on tv."

"I'm not totally blind, mum. And neither is Sarah."

My stomach lurches but I endeavour to keep my voice even.

"Well, things aren't always quite what they seem."

"There's none so blind, you mean."

"No. I meant I'm probably seeing the bigger picture."

"It's not the first time, is it?"

"What isn't?"

"Mum, you know what I'm talking about. Sarah says that's why we went to live near Aunt Patti and Uncle Ross that time."

"She remembers?"

"It's not the sort of thing you forget, is it? She talks to me about it sometimes. And now she's seeing it happening all over again. I think that's half the reason she's in the Avon in the first place."

Jude the Analytical.

"Jude, we need to talk about all this but not right now."

"When, then?"

"Soon. I just have to work a few things out first."

"We're on your side, you know, mum. Even Sarah."

And now I'm completely taken aback. And very touched.

"Thank you, sweetheart. Finish your toast and I'll drive you to school."

190

Michael did such a good job with the Weston store that Francis decided to leave him there for a while. Pretty soon he traded in his hotel room for a furnished flat in a fashionable area of Bath, the ground floor of a listed town house with a balcony view of the Royal Victoria Park in the foreground and rolling hills beyond and it wasn't long before he began pressing me to allow the girls to stay over occasionally with him at weekends. For a while I refused, insisting that if he wanted to see them it could only be with me but gradually I found myself agreeing to let him have them for the occasional few hours, picking them up from school and taking them shopping, to tea or to the cinema. And of course they always came back laden with gifts, new clothes, toys, books and on one memorable occasion a new lilac-coloured bike for Sarah and a matching tricycle with trainer wheels for Jude. I was pleased for them though if truth be told I was also a little jealous of their avaricious delight, knowing that I couldn't afford such extravagances on my meagre hack's wages. I was also more than a little concerned that they would soon become spoilt and lacking in the proper values befitting our somewhat impecunious situation.

Then the deliveries began. I came home one evening to find a hamper of groceries on the doorstep containing the sort of things that I'd become used to living without—my favourite St Emilion wine, imported cheese, Parma ham and things for the girls as well, a huge punnet of out-of-season strawberries and a tub of Cornish clotted cream—Sarah's favourite treat—and a box of Belgian chocolate bears for Jude. And though my initial reaction was 'what a nerve thinking he can buy his way into our home' I rationalised my thinking by reminding myself that he was, after all a glorified shopkeeper and such a gesture was easy for him and signified nothing. So I brought the hamper inside, made Eton Mess for the girls after their sausage and bean supper, then after they'd gone to bed I indulged myself with pasta, fresh parmesan and strips of the ham, washed down with chilled white wine. If Michael belatedly wanted to put food on our table so be it. The following week another delivery arrived and the next and the next and the next. Each time I shared the spoils with the girls but never once did I ever refer to them to when Michael and I spoke on the phone or when he picked up or dropped off the girls.

Then he began to expand his repertoire. One week I found a gift-wrapped box of lingerie bearing the name of an expensive boutique in town. This, though sorely tempted to keep, I re-wrapped and gave to girls to return to him on their next outing. I did the same with the cashmere sweater and the Italian

191

leather boots that I'd admired for so long in a local boutique. I must confess that it was with great reluctance tinged with a dose of self-righteousness that I sent the gifts back. But I had no such qualms the day I found a small box containing a ruby and diamond eternity ring tucked in with the smoked salmon and fresh cream éclairs. I snapped the box shut, almost shaking with rage and immediately phoned him.

"That wasn't funny."

"What are you talking about?"

"You know perfectly well, you bloody hypocrite."

"Oh, you mean the ring."

"Yes, I mean the ring. And not just any old ring. An eternity ring. After what you did. You couldn't even last 7 years before you got bored and started screwing around. And now you expect me to believe that you can pledge yourself for eternity. Hah! You stupid, stupid man. Haven't you worked it out yet? You had it all—a faithful wife, two gorgeous daughters, a beautiful home and it just wasn't enough for you. You threw it all away on an easy lay. And just what were you trying to prove anyway? Christ, Michael, she wasn't even all that attractive, just layers of make-up and a skirt stopping just short of her arse. Is that all it takes for you? And what about me, us? Didn't you care how much you'd hurt me? That I'd never be able to trust you again? Did I mean that little to you?...."

"I can't undo it, can't pretend it didn't happen. I did it. Mea culpa."

"Extremely bloody culpa."

"All I can do is ask you to try and forgive me."

"Well I can't, so don't."

"Can't or won't?"

"Both, probably."

"Don't say that. You just need more time."

"Michael, the girls and I have built a new life here. We're happy. Don't spoil it. My job, the girls' schools, Bath, Patti and Ross. Oh, you wouldn't understand. It was our little world and there wasn't any room for anyone else only now you're here and you don't fit in. It's like when you throw a stone in a pond and it makes all those ripples and the whole surface of the water is affected. Well that's how it's been since you came to Bath. You keep causing little ripples and unsettling everything. The girls get confused—one minute they live here, next minute they're staying with you, I tell them we can't afford

something then you go out and buy it for them. They're getting spoilt and it's not good for them. You're over-compensating and if you think it impresses me you're wrong. You can't buy forgiveness and you can't make up for what you did with toys and clothes and smoked salmon."

On and on I went, venting months of pent-up emotion, bitterness and venom, finally admitting to myself how much he'd hurt me, that all my new-found independence and toughness was an amalgam of instinctive self-preservation and an absolute determination to do the best for the girls, till at last I ran out of words, out of anger, out of emotion.

"Just leave us alone."

And I put the phone down without waiting for a response.

And after that he did get a bit better. The girls came back with fewer and fewer goodies and they spent more time in the park than the shopping centre. Occasionally I even joined them and we played happy families with a picnic on the beach at Clevedon and a drive to Exmoor. One day we even took a trip to Bristol, showing the girls our old haunts around the university, eating lunch in a little street café in Clifton. Then we walked across the suspension bridge, Jude perched on Michael's shoulders and Sarah skipping along happily between us. From the outside we must have presented a picture of the perfect nuclear family.

And of course I still had my job. Exposés like Grigson's porkies about the lamb don't come along every day but in the meantime there were rumours of questionable hygiene practices in local school kitchens, possible irregularities concerning the awarding of local building and road construction contracts and evidence of the suppression of a report into a World War II unexploded bomb in the grounds of an old people's home to get my teeth into and to tell the truth having an extra child minder around did make the juggling act a lot easier. Also, uncharacteristically Michael wasn't putting any pressure on me or so I thought at the time. In retrospect however I could see that he had a carefully thought-out master plan all along.

At any rate it was all jogging along nicely till the day Jude fell off the Jungle Gym and had to be taken to hospital. I heard about it in a call from the nursery school while I was interviewing a local licensee about allegations of under-age drinking and drug-taking at his pub. I cut the interview short and raced over to Bath Royal Infirmary where Jude was in A & E waiting for x-rays with one of the teachers. I let her get back to the school and stayed around

193

with Jude for nearly three hours until it was our turn and by then it was obvious that we weren't going to get out in time to pick Sarah up from school. I knew Patti and Ross were away in South Wales for a few days so there was only one other person I could ask—Michael.

Anyway just as I expected the x-rays showed no fractures but the whole rigmarole had taken all day. I bundled Jude into the bug and battled the rush-hour traffic - delivery trucks, juggernauts and commuter cars - around the hospital and the city centre till we reached the historic district around Michael's fancy flat where it petered out into a stately trickle of Volvos, Jaguars and the odd Roller. Not to worry, we could hold our own. I found a spot on the park side of the street between a midnight blue Range Rover and a red Porsche, reversed deftly in and set about unstrapping Jude. She of course couldn't wait to tell her sister all about her big adventure so we made our way up the beige steps and rang Michael's bell.

He and Sarah were in the kitchen where she was instructing her father on how she liked her chips (no vinegar, tomato ketchup on one side of the plate, mayonnaise on the other so she could dip each end in a different sauce). I'd forgotten that Jude had only eaten half a sandwich since breakfast and at the sight of a plate of her favourite fried potatoes she couldn't contain herself—she scrambled up on to a stool and dived in, completely destroying her sister's carefully-laid out plate design, grabbing a handful of chips and cramming more in than her mouth would hold. Sarah shrieked in outrage and slapped her sister, knocking all the food off the plate, Michael grabbed a cloth and dabbed futilely at the blobs of cream and red and bits of half-chewed chips that were dropping all over his imported ebony counter-top, Jude was totally nonplussed and carried on eating the spilled food and I busied myself filling the kettle and plugging it in, all the while keeping my back to the little Dali-esque tableau behind me so they wouldn't see me laughing. Then, tea made and expression suitably restrained, I turned around and took charge, sweeping the remains of the food into the pedal bin, wiping first Sarah's angry tears and then Jude's ketchup-encrusted face and finally cleaning and polishing the counter-top, restoring it to its pristine, shiny black former self. Then I turned my attention to Michael who had retreated to the centre of the kitchen, hands hanging loosely by his side, exhibiting no trace of the senior retail troubleshooting abilities which made him so valuable to Pricerite.

"Tea? And I think we might need another packet of chips."

And Michael looked at me and said
"Come home, Feef. Please."

Thursday, 26 June

George is still upstairs in the flat and the shop doesn't open till 9 so I'm surprised when the phone rings just after I arrive. It's the last person on earth I want to speak to.

"I tried the house but no-one answered."

"What do you want, Michael?"

"How's Sarah?"

"You could have phoned the clinic to find that out."

"I didn't have the number to hand."

"Wrong answer."

"Look, Feef, I don't know what your problem is…"

"Maybe that's my problem."

"Jeez, I don't have time to play verbal gymnastics with you. I'm up to my eyes here with stuff for the opening and I'm trying to tie it all up so's I can fly back as soon as all the plans are done and dusted. I just phoned to see how things were going."

"Well let's just say as well as can be expected shall we?"

"Meaning?'

"Meaning under the present circumstance it's little wonder Sarah has unresolved issues."

"I have no idea what you're talking about but I don't like the way this conversation's going so let's just cut it short."

Well since you mention it I'd love to cut it short. And I don't just mean the conversation.

"I never asked you to phone in the first place."

And I slam the phone down. Very grown-up.

I stand in the shop, lost in thought, re-playing the conversation I had had with Jude. It never occurred to me that Sarah would have known what the separation was all about, much less that she still discussed it with Jude. I'd always made a point of never talking about it in front of the girls and anyway it hadn't been mentioned for years. And if Sarah's been worrying about it for all that time and if she's picked up on what's going on with Michael and Louise

195

it's bound to have had an effect on her. I think back to that time when Louise was giving the girls a lift to school and Sarah all but put matchsticks down her fingernails over her cross-channel shopping trip. That meant she must have guessed that she went to Calais with Michael even before I did. And from what Jude said they'd obviously discussed it amongst themselves. I wonder if they've said anything to Amanda. Or maybe that's who told them in the first place. And how about Amanda's father? Does he have any idea what goes on when he's off on one of his frequent business trips?

What a mess.

Feeling guilty, though for what I couldn't say, I phone the clinic and learn that Sarah has apologised for the mobile phone incident and is getting ready for her first sculling lesson. I then ask to speak to Professor Turner and in a very faltering voice, repeat the bare bones of my conversation with Jude, though omitting any overt reference to Michael's infidelity, just vaguely referencing that both girls are aware that all is not sweetness and light between me and him. As I anticipate, he's not surprised and says it confirms that that was pretty much what Sarah had revealed to him. He then asks me if we could meet confidentially and discuss the implications in detail. I promise to come in on Thursday and we agree a time. Then I tidy, dust and catalogue in a futile effort to distract myself till George comes through with the tea tray

At 11 Charles and Diana appear, Diana coming over charm personified and oozing paint and paper samples. The three of them troop off upstairs, George taking up the rear and tossing me a wink over his shoulder as he climbs out of sight. Left alone I phone Patti and fill her in on recent events. As expected she's thrilled about the Alex thing and assures me that my search was absolutely the right thing to have done. As for the infidelity issue, her initial response is 'I told you so' and her second is 'I'm coming up.' And even though we've already got a bit of a houseful, I tell her that's exactly what I hoped she'd say and can it be today and I don't really mind when she says no, she'll have to juggle her work schedule but she'll make a plan.

The thought of imminently seeing Patti gives me such a lift that I manage an almost genuine smile when Diana glides downstairs with the other two meekly in tow. Taking this as some sort of secret sign of sisterhood she brings her swatch book over to the counter and I am obliged to hold my false smile through her shortlisted selections of velvets and damasks and chips of matching paint. Finally, just before my lips go into spasm she slams the books shut, summons Charles and collects a politely protesting George, insisting that she might need his opinion. Even though we both know that's highly unlikely, George obliges, Diana and entourage sweep regally out en route to Cotton Pickin' and I'm left to my own devices.

Then since my watch tells me it's break-time, I call Jude. When I tell her Patti's coming for a visit, she spots the fly in the ointment.

"But mum, dad'll be back in a few days."

"So he says. And your point is?"

"I was thinking that, well, he and Aunt Patti don't exactly see eye to eye, do they?"

"I know. It's going to be bliss."

"Mum, you're wicked."

"Well, mildly mischievous, maybe. I'll pop out at lunchtime and pick up some things for a barbecue. The weather's so nice I thought we could all eat outside this evening. I assume Mattie'll be joining us?"

"Definitely. His mother's been on another of her benders recently so he's keeping out of the way."

"Poor him. It must be awful having to live like that all the time."

"It sounds callous but he's really counting the time till he goes to uni. He's tried his best to help her but she needs professional intervention…oh, the bell's rung. I'll have to go."

"Okay. See you later, sweetheart.

Okay, I admit it. I stayed the night though I probably shouldn't have and we had sex which we definitely shouldn't have. Especially as Michael cried as he came, burying his face in my shoulder and telling me again that he was so, so sorry. In response I dug my fingernails in his back, wriggled out from underneath him and resolved never to be so weak again.

The following day was Saturday and after a family breakfast, Michael suggested an educational trip around some of Bath's historical sites which I had to agree would be time well spent so we drove into town and wandered around the Roman Baths, then toured a nearby costume museum where Jude was very struck with the display of Roman dress—ever the historic fashion fascination, even then. Sarah, of course, was far more interested in the colourful contemporary clothing in the gift shop. And everywhere we went Michael kept grabbing at my hand, gripping it like a bounty hunter holding on to his prey and it was only with the utmost difficulty that I managed to pry him loose, keeping a fixed smile on my face while I inwardly berated myself with the thought of 'oh god, what have I done?'

By this time the girls were both desperately hungry so we stopped off in a small café for a light lunch, after which I decided it was time to extricate myself from the situation so I suggested it was time to go home. Michael readily agreed and we climbed into his car and he began to drive. As we approached a set of lights Michael moved over into the inside lane, indicating that he was turning left, whereas our place was to the right. I pointed this out, thinking he was just driving automatically.

"Wrong way."

"I always turn here. Otherwise you end up in the city centre and it takes far too long when the traffic's heavy."

"It's the wrong way for us, I mean. Completely the wrong direction."

"Why? Is there some stuff you need to pick up?"

He deftly changed lanes and turned right.

The penny finally dropped.

"Michael, I want to go home. It's been a long day, I'm dog tired and so are the girls. Just drop us off now please."

"But you are moving in with me, aren't you? I mean after last night…"

"Last night? That was just sex, Michael."

He looked at me, swung the car straight across the inside lane, nearly taking out a Ford Focus on the way and pulled off into a side road before coming to a complete standstill and turning off the engine. Then he turned to face me and took both of my hands in his.

"Feef, this is tearing me apart. Just tell me what you want me to do and I'll do it. Anything. Whatever it takes."

"Michael, I'm really trying here and right now I don't want anything from you and I can't give you any more. It just is what it is. Accept it."

"But what is it? Last night…today, didn't that mean anything?"

"Should it have?"

"Christ, Feef, can't you ever be serious?"

"Serious? How dare you say that to me, Michael? How serious was it when you were sleeping with the office junior? How serious was it when you were telling me all those lies about working late? How serious was it when I had to *find out in the worst way possible? How serious, Michael? How fucking serious? Just take us home."*

And embarrassingly, he began crying again.

I looked at him and made a decision.

"Come on, girls."

I got out, went around the back and helped them unbuckle their seat belts.

"Let's take the bus home. We can stop off at the mini-mart and find something nice for supper."

"What's the matter with daddy?" (Sarah)

"He's got something in his eye. That's why he had to stop the car."

And pre-empting any further inquisition, I take one in each hand and shepherd them briskly off down the road towards the nearest bus stop.

Friday, 26 June

Jenny offered to hold the fort in the shop for me to go to the Avon so at 1 o'clock I leave it in her capable hands and head out. I toyed with the idea of buying a sandwich to eat on the way but decide I'm too nervous. Just like anticipating a good wigging from the head, better to just get it over with as quickly as possible.

In fairness, the comparison to a stern teacher is totally unfounded. Professor Turner has been nothing but sympathetic, kindly, considerate and helpful and so it proves again.

"Mrs Hamilton, this is very delicate. I don't want to speak out of turn and I certainly don't want to breach doctor-patient confidentiality. It's just that I had already formed an opinion from what Sarah has been telling us that certain factors in her home life are troubling her greatly and you more or less confirmed that to me on the phone. Anorexics use their disease as a means of controlling their lives. On a subconscious level they feel that by exercising such strict control over what and when they eat they are somehow gaining control over other areas of their lives as well. And in Sarah's case I feel she's trying to influence something that's happening within her family circle and which she can't inhibit in any other way. Of course this is a gross over-simplification and unfortunately I can't be more specific, at least not without consulting Sarah first. I don't suppose I'm making much sense, am I?"

199

"On the contrary, Professor Turner, I know exactly that to which you are referring. You are alluding to the fact that my husband is having an affair to a woman known to Sarah and that she knows all about it, am I right?"

Only a slight raising of his eyebrows indicates that his composure is in any way disturbed.

"And given the closeness of the two sisters it can hardly come as a surprise that Jude knows all about it too and that they talk about it frequently together. You understand I only found that much out myself last night. Not that my husband was having an affair, I've suspected that for some time. And I also sensed that the girls knew something was going on if not exactly what. Turns out they probably know at least as much if not more than I do. And whilst Jude tends towards cynicism and a head far older than her years, Sarah is more emotionally adolescent and her illness is probably a direct result of the stress and trauma she feels about what her father is doing. Which she is powerless to exert any influence over. How am I doing so far?"

He allows himself a slight smile.

"In essence that is an extremely astute and concise précis of Sarah's problems."

"But you must understand, Professor Turner, that I'm just as powerless to wield any influence over the situation as Sarah is."

"You accept your husband's infidelity? Forgive me, Mrs Hamilton, but you don't strike me as the type of woman to stand idly by in such a situation."

My mind flashes back to Bath.

"No, I'm not. What I meant was that I'm sure my husband knows what he's doing is wrong yet he's chosen to go ahead and do it anyway. And I'm certainly not the sort of woman who would beg him to stop because that in itself would imply an emotional reaction that I simply don't feel. To be honest, Professor, I'm completely indifferent to anything the girls' father does these days. My only regret is the effect it's had on Sarah."

"Does he realise he's the underlying cause?"

"No, Michael is totally oblivious to anything and everything that goes on domestically. And he's in complete denial over Sarah's illness. It's his stolid Scottish aristocratic stock. Probably thinks all she needs is a couple of bowls of porridge and a good wigging and she'll be as right as rain."

He smiles again, a broader one this time.

"Perhaps we should put it on the breakfast menu here?"

My turn to smile.

"I can't speak for the other girls but I know Sarah'd run a mile at the thought of a mere teaspoonful."

I grow serious again

"I don't want to go into details but I have a feeling everything on the home front is coming to a head. Something happened years ago, before I even met Michael, and now my past is catching up with me. But it's at my own behest and it's something I had to do. I was sleepwalking for a long time but I'm waking up."

He looks searchingly at me.

"I'm always here if you want to unburden yourself, Mrs Hamilton"

"Fiona"

He smiles.

"Fiona. Fixing families is part of the job,'

"I've realised ours is just too dysfunctional to be mended."

'Not all the elements, I believe."

He looks at me shrewdly and kindly.

"I'm making a plan."

He nods and we leave it at that.

I stood my ground in Bath. I had my work, Sarah and Jude were settled at school, our little flat was looking and feeling like home and if we needed company Patti and Ross were just a short drive away. So I was immune to Michael's wheedling and cajoling and bribing, much more so than the girls. They revelled in the expensive gifts he showered them with and loved staying over in his huge flat with its park view and central heating, just like they enjoyed being dropped off and picked up from school in his executive company car with leather seats that moved every which way but loose. Little girls are avaricious little social climbers and Michael played that trump card as often as he could.

Don't get me wrong. I wasn't totally against a bit of spoiling myself. I had occasionally allowed him take me out for dinner at one of Bath's trendy restaurants or an evening at the theatre just as I, on that one occasion, had had sex with him afterwards. But now there was the added complication of Steve.

I hadn't mentioned that, had I? It started innocuously enough with the odd pub lunch, ostensibly to forward plan the upcoming paper, went on to working

201

suppers and finally culminated in the occasional post-coital business breakfast. Michael had no idea but then it really wasn't any of his business. All he knew was that the girls sometimes had a sleepover at Patti and Ross's place and as they clearly had a ball he could hardly object to that.

Steve was the very antithesis of Michael. He lived in a tiny cottage off the Tetbury Road which might have been quaint had it not been so cluttered. There were books and papers everywhere, bed unmade, overflowing ashtrays and inevitably a sink full of washing up, all of which I found incredibly easy to ignore. Supper was usually fish and chips or curry bought on the way, then we'd vacate to the bedroom and explore each other's bodies in between literary discussions, political arguments and lots of wine and cigarettes. The first lover I'd ever had who teased me physically and tantalised me mentally and brought me to simultaneous orgasm on both counts. I felt like a student all over again and more alive than I had in a very long time.

And if any of you disapprove, remember that he was only the third man I'd ever slept with.

Amazingly we were able to switch the lust off like a light bulb at the office, probably because we were both even more passionate about our work than we were about each other's bodies. I was working on a series of articles on the effects of the environment and urban pollution on the city's Roman remains which took me from the sites themselves to the Bath city council offices to Bristol University and even on day trips to other similar sites around the country and to other environmental research centres. I was in a great place professionally, the girls were sorted and settled, I'd finally worked through my anger at Michael and had put the whole incident behind me and I had a new man in my life. In short, I was happy.

And then came Christmas.

Michael went to town—designer-decorated tree with presents piled high underneath, bowls of nuts, candied and fresh fruit and imported chocolates everywhere, more candles than Westminster Abbey, hand-made crackers, everything straight out of the pages of the Christmas edition of Harpers Bazaar. And his çoup de grace—a family dinner on Christmas Eve where he presented the girls with matching designer purple velvet frocks and low-heeled pumps and a Dalmatian puppy in a satin-lined basket whose name, we learned, was Dotty.

You can see what his game plan was, can't you? My tiny flat and pathetic little strip of a garden was totally unsuitable to keep a dog, whereas Michael's flat came with an enormous walled and landscaped affair to the rear where a puppy could roam free to its junior canine content. It being Christmas Eve I opted not to make an issue of it, settling simply for acknowledging Michael as official keeper of the dog and telling the girls they could visit as often as time allowed, being careful not to be any more specific. And to an outsider looking in there we were the picture-perfect nuclear family again, grouped around Michael's circular, cherry wood dining table, complete with floating candles, gold and cream cloth and napkins and festive food courtesy of Pricerite's delicatessen. Michael expensively and expansively casual in imported beige chinos and crew-necked cashmere sweater, two daughters looking utterly adorable in their new frocks and me, wife, earth mother, and domestic goddess in full-length black silk shift and new ruby choker, the latter a Christmas present courtesy of Michael, presumably to match the baubles on his designer tree.

As deceptive a tableau as a Magritte canvas.

As January blew in, work became frantic but fulfilling and though I never admitted it to him it was quite handy to have Michael to call on to pick the girls up from school occasionally. Pricerite always had a driver available if he was tied up and they liked nothing better than being taken to the shop and running amok amongst the aisles or laying paper trails in Michael's office. At the weekends Dotty was taken for long, brisk walks in the park in front of the flat or loaded into the car for a run on the beach or in the country. And it was all so innocuous yet insidious it dawned on me too late that by occupying our Saturdays and occasional Sunday mornings in this manner Michael was effectively trying to cut me off from any sort of an independent social life.

And when I worked it out I decided that no longer would I keep Steve just for mid-week. Suddenly I found a myriad excuses for cutting short Michael's happy family Saturday jaunts too so I could of fit in more time with him. And ultimately that led to everything coming out in the open. Clearly Michael was puzzled by the truncated outings and my obvious reluctance to stay over on Saturday nights so in typical fashion he chose the most underhand way possible to get to the bottom of it—he grilled the girls. Not that they could tell him much, just that they often spent time at Aunty Patti's and Uncle Ross's house and sometimes at the weekends they stayed overnight. And when he finally pieced it all together he confronted me.

"So who is it, Feef?"

"Who is what, or whom? What are you talking about?"

"You know perfectly well. You're seeing someone. Sleeping with him too, otherwise you wouldn't have to farm the girls out at your friends' place."

"I don't see that that's any of your business."

"You're still my wife, or had you forgotten that?"

"And we're still separated, or had you forgotten that?"

'Christ, Feef, I thought we were getting past that. I thought eventually you were going to move back in with me."

"Where on earth did you get that idea?"

"All the time we've been spending together as a family. The night you stayed over."

"I told you before, Michael, that was just sex."

"There was more to it than that. You must have felt it too."

"Sometimes I wonder if there was ever any more to it."

And right there and then I realised that there was more than a grain of truth there. Remember, I turned down his proposal and only changed my mind or more accurately had it changed for me when I found I was pregnant with Sarah. Not the best basis for marriage.

"I could sue for custody, you know."

"Oh, don't be so ridiculous. On what grounds? What judge in their right mind would take 2 daughters away from their mother for no better reason than a fit of jealous pique on the part of their father."

"All right. I admit, I'm jealous. I can't bear the idea of another man touching you."

"That didn't stop you touching another woman. You have very dubious double standards."

"It didn't mean anything. It's you I love, Feef. You know that."

"Yes, I think on some acquisitive, Forsythian level you probably do. But honestly, Michael, I don't think I love you. I don't think I ever loved you. Not properly."

The words were out before I could stop them and they echoed around the emotional emptiness I felt about the man I had mistakenly married.

"I see."

And with that he turned and walked out of the door.

It was around that time we heard the devastating news that Pip Naseby had died very suddenly. After graduation he'd moved to Cardiff, bumming around with a fringe band called Carat and giving guitar lessons for a bit of ready cash. Last time I'd seen him on a visit to Bristol he'd seemed pretty chipper in spite of not exactly having found the elusive fame and fortune that had been the plan when the band was formed. They moved to London, hoping that might bring them their big break which clearly never happened but they were making a living and country bumpkin Pip seemed to be enjoying life in the big city. And then he died.

Patti had heard the news first, just a minor item on the newswires and she'd called me straightaway. The three of us had been so close and it was hard to accept that he was actually gone. It wasn't clear how he'd died but there were the usual rumours of substance abuse, given that he was a rock musician, but it was all a bit vague. Anyway his parents took his body back to Yorkshire for burial and Patti, me and a few other old mates travelled up to Hebden Bridge for his funeral and wake, as did his fellow band members.

I'd told Michael about Pip's passing over the phone but all he said was 'That dope head', conversation closed. I'd also said Patti and I were going up to Yorkshire for the funeral and suggested it would be a nice gesture if he also attended but his response was that Pip had been mine and Patti's friend, not his and he didn't think it would be appropriate. I retorted that I'd only mentioned it out of politeness and his presence really wasn't wanted anyway and put the phone down on him. So while Ross stayed behind, holding 2 forts and looking after the girls, Patti and I made the journey together.

It was hard to take it all in.

After that time, Michael took to waiting outside in the car and hooting whenever he came to pick the girls up. I stopped going to his apartment altogether which puzzled the girls more than a little but I always made the excuse that I had work to do. Actually it was more that I had the boss to do. Steve challenged me mentally, kept me on my toes. With the girls over at Michael's or Patti's we'd sleep late on Sundays and he wouldn't let me get up till we'd gone right through the Sunday papers and finished the crosswords. That would sometimes be followed by long, lazy lunches with friends, his and mine. He knew lots of local artists, writers and theatricals, quite a few of whom were also friends of Patti and Ross, and even a few new-money, barrow-boy *types whose source of income was vague in the extreme. The resultant mix was part-artistic, part-intellectual, part anarchic and wholly intoxicating and the conversation was always stimulating. At other times we went to art exhibitions in Bath or Bristol or even further afield, to avant garde plays or music concerts, classical and rock. His tastes were catholic, his mind like quicksilver and I felt more challenged and fulfilled than at any other time in my life. And very gradually he began to stay over at my flat during the week, his presence completely accepted and unquestioned by the girls who called him Uncle Stevie and knew him well enough from the office. I was aware that they would probably mention it to Michael and that he wouldn't approve but there really wasn't much he could do about it. It was the noughties, after all.*

It sounds so corny but I found myself liberated and in love. I had the girls, I had my independence, I had Steve when it suited us and I had my job which was becoming a career. What could possibly go wrong?

4.30pm

I arrive home to find the house empty, an unexpected gift. I make tea and carry a cup through to Michael's study, then log on to Mother and Child. I have a message.

'I notice you didn't answer my question about whether your two girls know about me. So I suppose that means they don't? Pity. I think I rather like the idea of having two half-sisters with there only being me at home. I was thinking of bumming round Italy but I've decided to put it off for a few weeks while I get a bit more money together so I'm working for a landscape gardening firm. It's good fun. Lots of fresh air and good honest toil. And it's inspired me to work my way through D.H. Lawrence! I'm toying with the idea of a Master's thesis on twentieth century British novelists next term so it'll give me a head start. How are you coping with the in-laws? Oh, and any tiny nugget about my birth father might help to put another piece in the jigsaw.

Best regards, Alex.'
I type my reply.

'Things are a bit tricky at the moment but I plan on telling the girls about you when the time's right. The in-laws are still in situ but my boss has put them

206

both to work to keep them out of my hair! Your birth father was quite tall, with light brown hair and his first name was James. He was pretty bright but we lost touch years ago so I can't really tell you much more than that. Sorry.

I always found D.H. Lawrence a bit depressing A sort of intellectual Catherine Cookson without the happy endings. All clogs and cloth caps and trouble at t'mill. Inevitable for the time, though, I suppose. You should try and get hold of the film version of Women In Love with Glenda Jackson. It gained a bit of notoriety when it first came out because of all the nudity. Glenda Jackson full frontal and a naked fight scene on the baronial hearth rug between Oliver Reed and Alan Bates—very ground-breaking for its time. Brilliantly acted and the cinematography is very artistic.

Gosh, this is beginning to sound like an A-Level essay. How's the gardening? And have you had any more thoughts about your holiday plans? Write when you have time.

Keep in touch. All my love. Fiona.'

I send the message and log off.

Monday, 30 June

After a terse phone call with Michael in which he said there were still quite a few last-minute adjustments to the new store and he really couldn't say when he'd be home, I'm about to run Jude to school when Diana puts in an unscheduled appearance, not only up but dressed to the nines. She's made a plan.

"Before we pick up George, we thought we'd like to see where Sarah is staying."

My heart sinks. She's using the royal 'we', of course and I can't think what this is going to achieve. I attempt a peremptory ploy.

"I thought you wanted to get over to Featherington Hall as soon as possible—get a head start."

I keep my voice light but I needn't have bothered. Diana isn't having any of it.

"A couple of hours won't make any difference. I want to see if it's suitable."

I groan inwardly and wonder what her definition of 'suitable', in terms of a private rehabilitation and convalescent facility might be but years of experience

207

have taught me further protest would be futile. Instead I decide that discretion will be the better part of valour and I offer to accompany them.

"I can show you the way."

"It won't be necessary. Charles has Satnav."

"Still, it might be better if I'm there. They know me."

Uncharacteristically Diana caves in and we all 4 pile into the capacious Bentley, drop Jude off at school and head off to the clinic. Despite its newness and landscaped garden setting Diana is scathing in her comments, likening it to a disinfected Holiday Inn. At reception she more or less demands the grand tour and of course she can't resist asking to see Sarah, even though she knows full well that's out of the question. The receptionist is nonplussed and flustered and Nurse Dakin is summoned.

"Mrs Hamilton, if you'll just let me explain."

"It's Lady Hamilton, actually. Twice over. My father was an earl and my husband was knighted 20 years ago for services to commerce and industry."

"I'm sorry. But you must understand that it's an important part of the patients' healing process. They need to be isolated from everything that might cause emotional upset, just at the beginning."

"Emotional upset? I'm her grandmother. I'm sure she'll be delighted to see me. We've always had a very close bond, you know."

I'm not sure if a card and a large cheque on birthdays and Christmas classify as an intimate bonding but diplomatically keep my thoughts to myself.

Fortunately just at that moment Professor Turner made an appearance. He took in the scene with a practised eye and walked up, smiling broadly.

"Mrs Hamilton. How are you? And this is?"

He was looking at Diana, still beaming.

"Lady Hamilton. Sarah's grandmother. My husband and I have travelled all the way from Scotland to be with her."

She holds out her hand and Professor Turner shakes it.

"Charles Hamilton. Pleased to meet you."

Charles also proffers his hand and they shake.

Nurse Dakin glanced over at Professor Turner with that desperate look in her eyes that Diana often induces.

"Lady Hamilton, why don't I show you around upstairs? And perhaps we could just pop in and have a very brief visit with Sarah? After all, her initiation week is up tomorrow and seeing her grandparents might be just what the doctor ordered. Come with me, both of you. We'll use the staff lift. It's always quicker."

Nurse Dakin shoots him a grateful look and sidles away. I decide that if I tag along with Charles and Diana it might upset Sarah to the point where she'd want to come home and that wouldn't help anyone.

"I'll wait in the café and have a cup of tea. It's probably better if Sarah doesn't know I'm here."

"Excellent idea."

After half an hour Charles and Diana re-emerge, having been given the grand tour.

"What a charming man. He clearly understood the situation and the bond I have with Sarah. She was so pleased to see us, even though it was really just hello and goodbye. But I promised her we'd be back again for a proper visit later this week."

Her tone is both conciliatory and mildly triumphant. This is a woman used to getting her own way and Professor Turner was canny enough to concede a little to gain a lot. I'm surer than ever that Sarah is in the best possible hands.

2pm

After dropping me off at the shop and collecting George, Charles and Diana head off to Featherington Hall. They have decided to 'camp' there for 2 days by which they mean they will spend the days organising and supervising some painting and decorating and the nights tucked up in a comfortable local hostelry which Diana read about in The Good Hotel guide.

It's with a huge sense of relief that I watch them all drive away, leaving me alone.

As it turns out it's a quiet day at the shop and on impulse I phone my mother. I haven't spoken to her much recently what with her always being more in Michael's camp than mine and considering the current state of play but she is my mother. I dial from the shop landline and wait for her to pick up.

"It's me. I thought I'd call and fill you in."

"How's Michael?"

See what I mean?

"Fine, as far as I know. He's in Scotland."

"Visiting his parents?"

"No, they're down here visiting us."

"Oh."

Her tone is puzzled and I decide not to elaborate.

"What about the girls? How is poor Sarah?"

"She's in very good hands at the Avon. But her doctor has warned us that recovery from a wasting disease is a slow process."

"And Jude?"

"Jude is Jude. She has a boyfriend but if you speak to her, whatever you do don't say I told you. How's dad?"

"Fine. He got some new glasses."

"That's good. Give him my love. And you."

"Love to the family. And remember us to Charles and Diana."

"Will do."

We say our goodbyes and I hang up. You can probably tell we aren't close.

Once home I head straight for the computer. This time there are 2 messages for me. I click on one sent late yesterday.

"This whole thing is getting to me much more than I thought it would. I was okay with the adoption thing till I hit puberty and then I did start wondering what was the matter with me that my birth mother didn't want me. I really worked myself up about it and honestly, if you'd tried to make contact with me then, I think I'd have probably been pretty rude. After I left school I learned to rationalise it a bit more and that's when I thought I'd try and track you down, really just to fill in a few gaps. But since I made contact I've realised it's a lot more than gap-filling—that your life is a part of mine, one way or another. I can't stop thinking about you and my two half-sisters. I've always wanted to be part of a bigger family and now in a weird sort of a way I am. I don't suppose you could send me some photos, could you? I'd like to know what you look like and Sarah and Jude. I'll do the same for you. I really hope you'll tell them about me soon. Yours, Alex."

Reading his words I'm immediately wracked with self-recrimination. My guilt about giving him up must have been nothing compared to how he felt, feeling that he wasn't wanted. As for the girls, so many times in their lives I've wanted to tell them about him but somehow the time was never right. And even now when I've found my long-lost son and we're in almost daily touch, now with Sarah in hospital and Michael and I mismatched, misaligned and irrevocably estranged, I wonder if it will ever be the right time.

Before I reply I click on the second message from Alec. It simply says 'As promised, see attached. Alex". I scroll up and down the screen but see nothing, apart from a strange symbol and the word 'Drive' which means nothing to me. I switch off the computer and resolve to discreetly ask Jude later.

It's just the 2 of us for supper which feels strange after weeks of what seems like feeding the five thousand. I make pasta with smoked salmon served with a small salad and we eat companionably. At an appropriate moment I casually ask

"Oh, I nearly forgot. What does this mean?"

I draw the little symbol I saw earlier.

"That's Google Drive."

"In English?"

She sighs heavily and shoots me a withering look.

"It's a file sharing or file hosting platform."

She glances at my uncomprehending face.

"Do you want me to do it for you?"

"No. I need to learn."

That came out rather too quickly.

"It's for when you want to send files too big for the recipient's server. You post it there and send that link. Then the recipient—that's you—can click on the link and download the file."

"I see."

Clearly I don't.

"With a mouse, mum."

Jude pantomimes moving a computer mouse around the table and tapping with her index finger. This is accompanied by much raising of eyebrows. I get it and I'm sure I'll work it out.

10.30pm

After she goes to bed I pull up Alex's last message and following Jude's instructions I click the mouse where it says 'Drive', wait while a little message comes on and tells me something is downloading, then something miraculous happens. I stare at the screen, hardly able to believe my eyes. A series of little pictures appear, like a reel of film, all of them showing either a young boy or a young man. Alex! I strain to get a better look at them and accidentally click the

211

mouse on one. Magically it opens up to almost full screen size and I realise that after 21 years, my son is right there in front of me. I see a baby bundled up in bonnet and jacket, my baby—the baby I gave up all those years ago, his face still so achingly familiar. After staring in wonder for several minutes I click again and a tousle-haired toddler building sandcastles on a foreign beach appears. My heart is pounding and my fingers are trembling so badly I can hardly work the mouse but I manage somehow and a freckle-faced 8 or 9 year old playing cricket on the school playing field is on the screen. Click. Now he looks about 11 or 12 and again the background looks foreign, possibly southern Spain. Click. A teenager with a group of friends at an amusement park. Click. A more mature-looking young man with a group of students on the lawns in front of an Oxford college. Click. The same student in a dinner jacket, an attractive girl with long blonde hair in an evening dress hanging on his arm. Click. Back to the baby. I run through the slide show again and again, smiling broader than the Cheshire cat.

Well clearly something did happen, didn't it?

Life with Steve was amazing. Every day brought some new delight. There was a little delicatessen just down the road from the office and quite often we'd stop in on the way home and pick up something to eat. When he could be bothered Steve was a great cook, if a little slapdash, and we ate Italian, Bolivian, Thai—whatever he felt like cooking—sometimes at his place when the girls were with Patti and Ross, sometimes mine. The girls soon grew used to tasting all sorts of exotic dishes and delivering their verdict which was usually either totally ecstatic or totally scathing, and I contributed by washing up. Sarah had such a healthy appetite back then—who could have foreseen how that would change? Once we stole a long weekend together. Leaving the girls with Patti and Ross, hopping on the Eurostar to spend an idyllic weekend in Paris, sleeping in a tiny little hotel room off St Germain du Prés, strolling around the Rive Gauche and sipping coffee and cognac at little pavement cafes. And then we went back to the hotel and had very cramped, multi-orgasmic sex and just before we fell asleep in the early hours of the morning Steve said he loved me, I said I loved him and we both thought we were going to live happily ever after.

And he was so brilliant with the girls and we were so much in love. The months passed by so fast as they do only when you're truly happy. We talked vaguely about marriage but I would have had to have become unmarried first and I didn't really want the stress right then but moving in together seemed like a good idea. Neither of our places were eminently suitable for our soon to be extended family and after hours of looking in estate agents' windows and wasted journeys looking at properties which ranged from the sublime but completely unaffordable to the ridiculous and slightly unaffordable, we put it on the back burner.

During this time Pricerite posted Michael to Taunton and I breathed a sigh of relief. His resentment of Steve was palpable—the man who had taken away a prized possession. Steve thought it was hilarious and took to referring to him as 'Gollum' and me as 'My Precious'! He kept the Bath flat on and still drove up to take the girls out on the odd autumn weekend but the visits were few and far between as his new appointment made increasing demands on his time.

Meanwhile work was still fun and life with Steve was idyllic. I'd read girly magazines that talked about 'finding your soul mate' and I'd always dismissed it as romantic drivel but now I realised it was actually possible—in Steve I really had found the missing bit of me.

And then just when it seemed that, difficult divorce aside, life was as good as it gets, came the divine retribution that I always knew was my fate for abandoning my baby and then selling my soul for a mess of Pricerite potage.

It was just after New Year, bitterly cold and Steve was working late. He'd had a tip-off about a scandal concerning the local MP and he'd arranged to meet the source in a country pub. If that sounds a bit cloak and dagger, it happens in the newspaper industry all the time. People don't want to come into the office in case somebody sees them and asks questions and often there's too much information for a phone call. Steve's meeting was arranged for 8pm in a country inn the other side of Bristol so he took the opportunity to catch up with some admin and said he'd go on from there and sleep at his place so not to expect him. I told him to give me a call when he was back and he said he would if he got home by a reasonable time. By 10pm I was dog-tired so I just went to bed and fell asleep. And when I woke next morning I didn't give it a second thought that I hadn't heard from him. Mornings were always a blur and a mad panic of waking the girls, washing them, dressing them, feeding them breakfast, packing lunchboxes, sorting myself out and finally rushing them to day-care and school; and even though this was a Monday and they'd had a sleepover at Michael's I still had to tidy up the flat, sort out the laundry and throw a few

213

ingredients into the slow cooker so I wouldn't have to make supper when we all got home. After that I went straight to the office. Steve wasn't in—nothing out of the ordinary—and I did try and call him on his mobile but it was switched off so I got stuck into an article on the problem of vagrants in the city centre. I have to stress that this was all perfectly normal and even what happened next was not exactly unprecedented. Just after 10am a police officer in uniform accompanied by another one in plain clothes came in to the office, looked around, caught sight of Bill and approached him. They had serious expressions and I assumed something had happened and they needed information from the public. I carried on typing. Not for long. A tap on my cubicle door, I looked up, took in Bill's grave face and knew something serious had happened. He said just three words

"I'm so sorry"

And everything after was far from normal. I was walking into a nightmare.

A body, thought to be Steve's, had been found near the car park of The Golden Goose public house on the A39 to Glastonbury. His car was in the car park with the keys still in the ignition and what appeared to be a recent dent in the driver's side rear fender. They said that the body had been taken to Bath Royal Infirmary and would be retained for a thorough post mortem but that they needed someone to make a formal identification. They also said they were following up enquiries at the pub with bar staff and patrons but that his injuries indicated that he may have been the victim of a hit and run. The pm would tell them more. Then they smiled wanly, patted me on the shoulder, shook hands with Bill and left.

I was in complete shock, scarcely taking any of this in. Bill offered to make the formal ID but I insisted on accompanying him. Part of me refused to believe it was true, that it was all a ghastly case of mistaken identity, that it was not him lying dead on a gurney but some stranger who had somehow stolen his wallet. That must be it.

It wasn't.

His body was covered in a white cotton sheet. The pathologist pulled back just enough to show his face. I flinched and felt my legs buckle underneath me but Bill had his arm firmly around my waist. There was a pale pink weal on his forehead but otherwise his face was unmarked. A tear welled up in one eye, we both nodded silently to the policewoman outside the room and then left, propping each other up all the way to the car park.

214

Telling the girls was the worst. Trying to explain the awful irreversibility of death to children so young is impossible. They didn't understand the finality, just that Steve had gone away.

"He'll come back. Like daddy."

Sarah

"I want him to come back now."

Jude.

I served them some supper and drank tea as I watched them eat and willed myself not to cry in front of them.

The phone rang. I went to answer it and heard Michael's voice.

"Feef. I just heard. It's terrible."

"Who told you?"

"It was on the news. I heard it on the car radio."

So soon?

"I can't talk to you right now."

I put the phone down abruptly.

The next few weeks passed in a blur. The police questioned everyone who was at The Golden Goose that night. They showed Steve's photo around but no-one remembered him coming in. Someone said they had heard a squeal of tyres sometime after 8pm but they put it down to teenagers messing around in the car park. Photos were taken of the tyre tracks and traces of red paint on Steve's car were sent off for forensic testing which would take some time to match. And they quizzed me and the other staff at the Gazette as to whom Steve might have been going to meet that night but none of us knew. Source confidentiality was a sacred vow to journalists and Steve was no exception. He took that secret with him to the grave. I told them Steve used burner phones for his confidential contacts but there wasn't one on his person and search as I might in the office and his cottage, I never found anything. The working hypothesis was that whoever it was had somehow knocked him over, whether by accident or design, and had driven off without reporting the accident.

"We'll keep on looking but it might take some time", the plain clothes detective told me,

Patti was an absolute brick throughout this period, cooking for Sarah and Jude when I lost track of time and reality, helping with the school runs and even force-feeding me occasionally when I was able to swallow.

And somewhere in the background, Michael hovered and havered. For the life of me I couldn't work out why. It's not as though he cared a jot about Steve, quite the opposite. He disliked him as much for our relationship as well as the fact that they were polar opposites in personality and interests. Yet there he was, popping up like the proverbial bad penny and making out he cared about the situation and cared about me. It occurred to me that he was probably perversely pleased to have his rival permanently out of the picture and his presence irritated me and inflamed Patti but still he hung around whenever his work schedule allowed. What with him and a cloyingly, sugary police liaison officer who had been assigned the case and who called in daily and clucked over me like a protective mother hen, I felt besieged. Besieged and utterly bereft.

Michael palled up with the policewoman—Sade by name—coming on as the supportive father and implying, I am sure, that he had been cuckolded but under the circumstances he was more than willing to forgive and forget. He would quiz her on the details of the case whenever he saw her and offer theories and suggestions. In fact he took an inordinate interest in the whole investigation, to try and impress me, I assumed. That and morbid curiosity. It certainly couldn't have been concern for the loss of Steve. He rang the police station incessantly, asking if they had traced the car, identified the driver, found any new evidence and seemed quite elated when they told him that miniscule red paint traces on Steve's Saab had been identified as coming from a Citi Golf, even though they said there were over 2,500 registered in the country at that time, of which over 200 were in Bath, Avon and the West Country. Suffice to say it was like looking for a needle in a haystack. I scarcely cared. Steve was gone and was never coming back.

We held a memorial service. Though not especially religious, Steve was a lapsed Anglican so it was in the local church, packed to the rafters with all his many friends and acquaintances. My parents motored down from Chester to offer moral support and the bad penny pitched up and sat in the row behind us. Afterwards we all repaired to a local park where we released white balloons, read poems and a group of his more musical friends played pieces and melodies that Steve had been especially fond of. Then we went to the wake, held in our local where everybody knew us both. How does it go?

'Where everybody knows your name
And you're always glad you came'

I sat with Patti and Ross and the girls while mum and dad fawned all over Michael like their long-lost son. I gritted my teeth and pointedly ignored him.

After a month I began going into work part-time, as much to try and distract myself as anything else but there wasn't much chance of that. The owners of the paper had appointed an interim editor, a pleasant-enough man called Tony but his presence just drew me back time and time again to Steve's absence.

Finally, in a major effort to emerge from my stupor, it occurred to me that what I should be doing was what Steve had taught me about investigative journalism. In other words, start being a bit more proactive and see what you can find out. If nothing else it would be cathartic.

I began with his phone log. There were some from unrecognised numbers which led nowhere and one from a mobile phone number that indicated it was no longer in use. Then I went to the Golden Goose to speak to anyone who was there that night, hoping they might remember something useful that they hadn't told the police. I did find a kitchen commie who'd gone out the back for a smoke around the alleged time of the accident and he confirmed he'd seen a small car, could have been red, tearing out of the car park and turning towards Bath but he didn't get a good look at the driver and he didn't notice the registration. He did think it was a man, not all that old.

Back in the office I scoured recent back issues of the paper, looking for a name or a lead to anyone who might have had a grudge against Steve due to adverse publicity. I came up with a couple of miscreants we'd reported on, including Gregson, and passed them on to the police to follow up on. I even hung around Gregson's a few times, thinking he surely would be pretty resentful and maybe even revengeful after our exposé but I never saw him driving anything but his beige Rover. And when I followed him home one afternoon I could see his wife's car parked in the driveway—a blue Volvo.

The police followed up on everything I gave them but all the leads led nowhere. At least it kept me busy.

After the memorial service Michael became an even more frequent visitor again. He was at the flat almost every weekend, bringing gifts for the girls, hampers of food, bunches of flowers and bottles of wine. Deep in the throes of *grief I suppose I just allowed it to happen. I cared little about anything, apart from Sarah and Jude and to be truthful, I blanked out his presence. He was considerate and conciliatory to the point of obsequiousness and frankly I couldn't have cared less if he came or stayed away, but the girls were glad to see him. He was probably better company than me.*

Tuesday, 1st July

Charles and Diana arrived back late in the evening, having dropped George off at the shop. Diana was in the afterglow of a job well done and regaled Jude and me with a detailed account of the progress to date and future plans for George's apartment, complete with pictures on her newly acquired cell phone. Jude and I make all the right oh and ah noises and for once the mood is upbeat and convivial. So if it's not their presence that's a damp squib, that only leaves Michael.

Wednesday, 2 July

2am

Jude and I spoke to Sarah on the phone before supper, the first opportunity since her purdah expired and we have been told we are welcome to visit at the weekend which we definitely will do. Sarah sounded fragile and unsettled.

"Please can I come home? I miss you and I hate it here. I can come in as an outpatient. I wouldn't mind that."

"Professor Turner says the girls who live in are the ones who have the best chance of recovery, sweetheart. Just give it a bit longer. We'll see you at the weekend and I'll bring Aunt Patti if you like. And Diana and Charles are desperate to have a proper chat with you."

"That's what I mean. I'm missing all the fun, stuck in here."

"We'll call every day, I promise. And we'll visit as often as we can manage. It will get better. And so will you."

Clearly she was not convinced. I handed the phone to Jude and left them chatting, feeling like the worst mother in the world. Nothing new there.

Lying in bed, fretting over Sarah but buoyed up by the thrill of finally knowing what Alex looks like, I contemplate how to proceed. Obviously I want to meet him but is it too soon? Or not soon enough? He has expressed an interest in getting to know the girls, which I think is a good sign but there is the minor detail of neither being aware of his very existence. And there and then I make up my mind to talk to Jude at the weekend when she'll have time and space to take it in. And she will know if it's the right time to let her sister in on this unexpected development. With that thought I fall into a deep, dream-laden sleep full of images of Alex, waking at the break of dawn feeling if not happier, at least more unburdened that I have in years.

Thursday, 3rd July

Patti rings up very early to say today's the day and she'll call me later. I'm over the moon at the thought of having her around—a confidante, sounding board and the only real friend I have in the world.

Once in the shop I hear the other side of the restoration story from George. Diana is a perfectionist par excellence—no surprises there—and George is highly appreciative, if a little overwhelmed.

"She could make a lot of money if she took up interior design and restoration professionally, you know, Ffion."

"Nothing so vulgar for our Diana!", I smile. "Besides, you must know she's merely reprising her Lady Bountiful role, doing her bit for charity with you."

We both laugh at this absurd idea.

At lunchtime I run out to do some quick shopping. With Jude & Mattie, Patti, Charles, Diana and me, that's 6 for supper so I take the easy option and decide we'll barbecue. I nip first to the butchers where owner, John, cuts me some lovely rump and weighs me some of his special home-made sausages, then next door to Simmonds for bread rolls. I don't want to leave George for too long so I resolve to pop into Dysons on the way home for everything else—a packet of veggie burgers for Jude, salad stuff and big potatoes. Oh, and I mustn't forget charcoal and firelighters.

At four Patti phones on her mobile and says she's already on the ring road so I tell her to come straight to the shop and we can go home together.

As soon as she arrives George insists that I leave work immediately so we drive through the sunshine of the late afternoon, dawdling in the slow-moving traffic which gives me plenty of time to bring her up to speed on the search for Philip/Alex, the Michael/Louise saga and Sarah, taking in Jude/Mattie and

Charles/Diana on the way. As I finish filling her in she gives one of her characteristic growl cum giggles.

"Shit, Fee. It's a wonder they didn't lock you up with Sarah."

"Shit, Patti. Half the time I'm sorry they didn't".

I direct her to Dysons so I can pick up the rest of the barbie stuff, then we drive home in comfortable camaraderie.

The first thing we see as we pull into the drive is the Bentley parked possessively in the drive, close to the house. Patti grins wickedly and pulls up alongside in her hugely expensive Italian sports coupé, just close enough to make it almost impossible to get in on the driver's side of the Bentley. Or out of mine, either, but I don't mind climbing out on her side—it'll be worth it later when Charles has to move it so Diana can get in. As we exit Patti strokes the side of the Maserati and says wistfully.

"I suppose I'm going to have to let it go soon. Pity."

I look at her in astonishment. Surely she and Ross can't be strapped for money? They earn a packet between them and they bought their place in Bath for cash when property there was still vaguely affordable.

"Patti, no, it's gorgeous."

"So it is but it's a bit on the small side. I'm probably going to have to trade it in for something sensible with fold-down seats and enough space in the boot."

I open the back door and turn round.

"Space for what? You haven't taken up golf, have you?"

"You are joking? Mind you, Ross did get a hole in one."

"Ross golfs now?"

She burst out laughing at my now completely baffled expression and pats her tummy.

"He knocked me up. I came off the pill a couple of months ago. I just felt like a break, you know. And the idiot didn't use anything. It only took one shot and one of those little tadpoles wormed its way right in."

"Tadpoles swim. Worms worm."

"Well they both wriggle and squirm. As did Ross when I explained the facts of life to him."

"So what did he say?"

"Oh, some Cosmopolitan crap about hormones and body clocks and Freudian slips. So after I punched his shoulder and had a tantrum we suddenly worked out that in some warped sort of agony aunt way he was probably right. Maybe I did have some subconscious hidden agenda coming off the pill and he probably accidentally on purpose forgot the condom for the same reason. And guess what? We're both over the moon. We've been stripping baby shops bare, painting murals all over the nursery walls and cross comparing the safety specs on every brand of buggy we see. I've even stopped smoking and started spritzing my white wine."

"Patti, that's wonderful. I'm so pleased for you. And bags I put my name down as godparent."

"Too late, you're already booked."

Cue for a really girly hug and when we pull apart we're both crying and laughing at the same time, though perhaps not for exactly the same reasons. I take her upstairs and show her which room she's in, we leave her case then go back down to the kitchen and Patti puts the kettle on while I rustle around for tea pot, cups and spoons. Just as the kettle boils, Charles and Diana chose that precise moment to come through from the sitting room.

Diana takes in Patti's lilac-streaked spiky hair, her short skirt, high heels, the wide expanse of midriff she is exhibiting plus her belly-ring which comprises a huge ruby, and looks at her as though she is something nasty that she picked up on her shoe. Charles beams.

"Aren't you going to introduce us, my dear?"

"Actually you've met before, a long time ago. This is Patti, my oldest and dearest friend. She was at the wedding"

"Hey, less of the old, if you don't mind. It's bad enough having my obstetrician refer to me as a primagravidas!"

"You're expecting?"

Only 2 words but Diana imbues them simultaneously with disbelief, distaste and dismay.

Patti pats her still almost flat tummy, much of which is on display.

"I know. At my age. I can hardly believe it myself. My husband, the one-hit wonder."

Diana tries to smile but manages only a rictal grimace, being one of the 'lie back and think of England' brigade as well as hereditarily opposed to any form of body-piercing, even ears. Patti feigns oblivion and puts on her best butler voice.

"Shall I serve tea on the terrace, your ladyship?"

She picks up the tea tray, I do the same with a plate of biscuits and we move out to my lovely old plantation table and a beautiful black country late summer afternoon.

As we sit Patti chats brightly about the tailback from the contra-flow on the M5, the best designs for baby car seats and the big new drama series she's working on. Charles endeavours to show interest but Diana's face is set with her glassy, finishing school fixed, false smile and I also pretend to listen when in reality I am playing and replaying Alex's picture display back in my head over and over again.

Just before six Jude and Mattie and Jude come around the back of the house to join us, along with Amanda and a boy they introduce as Jake. Jude and Patti fall all over each other with much hugging and kissing, somewhere in the middle of which Jude formerly introduces her proxy aunt to Mattie. Feathers ruffled at not being the centre of attention, Diana drags Charles off inside, ostensibly on the pretext of finalising arrangements for tomorrow. Left alone the entire atmosphere lightens immeasurably. Patti insists on opening a bottle of fizzy wine and since it's a special occasion I agree that everyone can have a taste so Jude gets out the glasses and I pour a small amount into them, Patti topping hers up with some sparkling mineral water she brought with her. She catches my look.

"Sacrilege, I know. But I promised my Obs & Gy I'd cut down."

We toast to a speedy recovery for Sarah and the health of Patti's baby. Jude the Ingenuous then raises her glass

"To happy families."

She smiles so seemingly innocently that it is only by summoning up reserves of self-control and avoiding Patti's eye that I refrain from laughing out loud,

And on that note Mattie volunteers to fire up the barbecue and Jake is roped in to assist, Jude says she and Amanda will lay the table and Patti and I take the empty glasses and bottle into the kitchen.

"You'll have to tell her."

"I know. I've sort of dropped hints that there's something I need to talk to her about but she hasn't a clue what and the time just never seems right.'

"How do you think she'll react?"

"Actually I think she'll probably be okay with it. She's very level-headed under all that clothing rebellion. And Mattie's an absolute brick. He's been brilliant with the whole Sarah thing and Jude knows she can lean on him for anything. It's Sarah I'm really worried about. A bombshell like that could just tip her right over the edge."

"Possibly."

"You sound doubtful?"

"Well it'll be a shock, sure. But if you come at it from the right angle I'm sure she'll understand."

"She might understand the baby out of wedlock thing but not hiding it from her and Jude for all these years."

"I wouldn't be so sure. Those two girls of yours are both pretty savvy and they really love you."

Her words remind me of the conversation yesterday with Jude.

"You could be right. Did you have any idea she knew what had happened with me and Michael that time? Jude said she told her all about it and they chat about it sometimes."

"Heavens. And she was only what, 5, 6 at the time?"

"That's right. And something else, Jude says they've both worked out what's going on this time and with whom and Amanda also knows."

"Sounds to me like nothing phases them and you might as well tell them everything."

"Well that's just it. Jude, maybe, but I'm almost sure that the whole thing with Michael is part of what set off Sarah's eating disorder. She's started hinting at it to her doctor and he and I have also had a bit of a heart-to-heart."

"Thing is, you can't really tell Jude and keep it from Sarah, can you? And these things have a horrible habit of coming out one way or another."

"You're right. We're going to see Sarah at the weekend. I can speak to the doc then and see what he thinks. She'd really like it if you came with me. You are staying for a few days, aren't you?"

"Right here, kiddo. Don't worry, we'll see it through together. You should have ditched him years ago, you know that, don't you?"

And I think back to Bath and know that as always on the subject of Michael, Patti is spot on. I had my chance and I blew it.

I know what you're thinking. How on earth did I get from there to here, back with Michael and far from Bath and Avon and the stupid answer is it was by default and I allowed it to happen.

It was like this.

223

The months passed by and I had begun to accept that I would probably never know exactly what had happened to Steve, by whom or why. My investigations had led nowhere and the police had more or less lost interest. I mourned his loss daily but only ever allowed myself to indulge my grief when I was alone and the girls were asleep or when Patti and I had a heart to heart and gradually I packed away my memories into a locked box inside my head to which I alone held the key. Life went on, just not Steve's.

One weekend Michael proposed a day out into the country to which I acquiesced as I knew it would do the girls the world of good—I had been trying my best to stay as cheerful as I could manage until they went to bed but I still wasn't exactly the life and soul of the party and I felt guilty—stupid, I know. Even the fact of Michael's still cloyingly ever-present presence washed over me, such was the slough of utter despond into which I had descended.

Anyway it was late September, something of an Indian summer and the weather was beautiful. We drove north, into the Black Country, through Stratford-on-Avon to a small village where he turned into an imposing driveway between two stone posts topped off with couchant stone lions, each bearing the inscription 'Lionsgate House' on brass plaques. The property had a circular driveway, leading to a large Georgian 4-storey house on which the same name was etched into the stonework above the lintel, along with the date of construction, The Year of Our Lord 1792. I assumed we were paying someone a visit and was irritated that Michael hadn't had the good manners to let me know beforehand. He must have known I was in no condition for social calls. Instead, he produced a bunch of keys and said 'Shall we have a look round?', getting out of the car and approaching the front door. Somewhat nonplussed I watched him as he approached the door, unlocked it and walked inside, followed by an excited Sarah and Jude, scrambling out of the car, eager for a big adventure. Reluctantly I took up the rear. We toured the ground floor, my low heels echoing on the polished, dark wood floorboards—three huge reception rooms, a large, formal dining room, study cum library kitchen, pantry, cloakroom, uncloaking room, butler's pantry and utility room. The girls were having a ball exploring. They had also felt Steve's loss deeply but Michael was still 'daddy' and they were enchanted with Lionsgate which they likened to a large dolls' house. Then Michael suggested we look upstairs, at which point I asked him what exactly we were doing there. I should have been used to his bombshells by now but this one floored me.

"It's my new house. I signed the papers last week".

To say I was dumbfounded was an understatement. I sank down on the staircase and he told me Pricerite had just opened their largest hyperstore to date not far from the village, along with a centralised admin centre. He implored me to move in with him and bring the girls and assured me that it could be on any terms I chose.

Still in the despondency of loss and living in a limbo of chaos and confusion, I refused point blank. He proposed we keep to separate bedrooms, nothing more would be expected of me and if it didn't work out I could simply walk away with the girls. I stood my ground.

Back in Bath he phoned constantly and not a call went by without him asking again and again. I said no, again and again.

The girls returned from regular visits to Lionsgate, imploring me to move there.

"It's lovely, mum. It's got 5 bathrooms."
Sarah

"Daddy's going to buy me a pony and he says I can keep it at the stables down the road. And Dotty likes it too"
Jude

And so it went on, grinding me down, wearing my resistance. It took just over a year till I finally caved in. During that time the girls had been back and forth between me and Michael in a sort of human pass-the-parcel game. In Bath for term time with the odd weekend away, then holidays in Lionsgate from where they had to be prised away, what with pony rides, shopping sprees and generally being spoiled stupid. I didn't just feel like the poor relation—I was. That December I agreed to bring them for Christmas, spending the day there and staying overnight, separate bedrooms and no strings. Unbeknownst to me, Michael also invited Charles and Diana and they did their usual Lord and Lady Bountiful bit, driving down with a Fortnum and Mason hamper, a brace of pheasant from their estate and a bottle of vintage Krug that must have cost an arm and a leg to toast our 'reunion'. I smiled through gritted teeth and glared at mine host. After all, it wasn't his parents' fault. How could they know?

I drove back to Bath on Boxing Day, leaving the girls with their father and grandparents. I spent New Year's with Patti and cried my eyes out when we sang 'Auld Lang's Syne'. I had never missed Steve more than at that moment.

That night I got very little sleep, just thinking over his loss, the girls' future and my utterly miserable situation and somewhere in the stilly hours I made up my mind that I'd move in to Lionsgate until I could think of a better idea. It would be my enduring punishment for giving up my first-born child. That was why Steve had been taken away from me and to make restitution I had to make further penance in order to free myself of the burden of guilt. If that sounds quite crazy there's a perfectly good explanation—I had lost all sense of reason and somewhere my childhood Catholic indoctrination of confession, punishment and absolution had never quite left me.

I told Michael that there were three conditions. The first that under no circumstances would we be sharing a bedroom. Ever. The very thought of sleeping with anyone other than Steve right then, least of all Michael, was anathema to me: the second that I could make no long-term commitment—I just couldn't think far ahead anymore and though right now it seemed the best arrangement for Sarah and Jude, if at some point in the future it clearly wasn't working, I would leave and take them with me: and the third that he was free to sleep with whomsoever he chose so long as he was discreet and he didn't bring it home out of consideration for the girls. I typed it out, printed two copies and said he had to sign them, so there was no misunderstanding.

"Anything."

He was smiling as he penned his name on the pages.

"This is serious."

He sobered his expression but all the same I knew that as far as he was concerned I had drawn up a treaty of surrender. Think what you like, Michael.

Patti railed and raged and told me I must be 'out of my fucking mind' when I coerced her into signing as a witness and of course she was spot on—I was. I had simply left sanity behind in my terminal grief. Oh, and did I mention I had turned into a walking Zombie?

Truth be told, I wasn't sorry to leave Bath, nor the Gazette. Too many memories, all of them of Steve. All the same, I had framed the small print pretty carefully.

"Come and see the pictures from Alex."

I drag her off to the study, close and lock the door, then boot up the computer, click on the link and scroll. Patti gets up close and personal with the screen, then takes the mouse, stopping, starting, back-tracking, proceeding till she comes to the end.

"He's a good looking kid."

"Hardly a kid—he's 22."

"Doesn't matter. He's still your baby."

We look at each other and smile and she instinctively puts her hand on her stomach. Then she switches on Michael' printer, presses a couple of keys and makes a print-out of all the photos.

I take the prints and we walk back into the kitchen. Hearing signs of life, I quickly stuff them between the pages of the macrobiotic cookbook I bought for Sarah in the vain hope that it might persuade her to eat something I prepared, making a secret 'Shhh' sign to Patti. Then we re-join the others looking like butter wouldn't melt.

Friday, 4th July

I'm up at the crack of dawn as usual and while I'm drinking my first cup of tea for the day I can't resist the temptation to pull out the photos from their hiding place. I am still gazing at them in wonder when Jude unexpectedly comes into the kitchen. I fleetingly contemplate trying to conceal them but I know already that it's too late. Guilt is written all over my face and I can hide nothing from Jude the Insightful.

"Quite a looker. Am I to assume that you've taken a toy boy to get back at dad?"

Oh God, back to images of Jocasta and Greek tragedy again. I can see how it must look but that had never occurred to me.

"Jude, no. It's not like that. There's something I need to tell you, talk to you about. Something you need to know about this boy. It's a bit complicated. Now's not a good time."

She is now examining the photos microscopically and looking at me in a manner I can't interpret. Jude the Inscrutable.

"When then?"

"Tomorrow. Promise."

She looks at me with that unfathomable expression again.

"Okay."

And she hands the pictures back to me.

Saturday, 5th July

George phones up at 7am and insists I take the day off. Says I've been holding the fort all week and it's his turn and besides, I have a new guest to take care of and he knows I'm dying to see Sarah. I tell him he's a brick and I'll see him on Tuesday. Then he drops a mini bombshell. He, Charles and Diana are taking a little trip across the Irish Sea, as the song says. George's brother has invited them all over to the family seat, Wellington House, in County Wicklow. For George it's a long-overdue visit to catch up with his family and there's the added bonus of the promise of a few pieces of furniture, some bric-a-brac and the odd painting to decorate his new apartment. As for Charles and Diana, they'll be in their element with the huntin', shootin' fishin' brigade so presumably a good time should be had by all. The trip will last a week or so, he'll keep me posted and is that all right? I tell him it's fine and the shop will be quite all right without him and he hangs up sounding absurdly pleased at the prospect of the impending reunion.

Not long afterwards, Jude appears and I decide to take the bull by the horns right there and then. I hand her a cup of tea, into which I have added extra honey. She sips it, pulls a quizzical face and I tell her it's for shock. She laughs but all I can manage in return is a weak smile.

"Remember I said there was something we had to talk about?"

She nods over the rim of the teacup and raises her eyebrows in an interrogative fashion but I say nothing, just turn and gesture for her to follow me. Walking into the study, I repeat the actions of the other night with Patti, booting up the computer, pulling up the site, clicking on 'My messages' and then up the last one from Alex.

"Get you."

"I've been practising. Quite a lot, actually."

"I'm impressed but confused."

"You'll see."

Whether fate or co-incidence I don't know but I now see there's another message waiting for me from Alec. I instruct Jude to click on 'open'.

228

"Did you manage to open those pictures? I tried to find ones that would let you know what I looked like and when. And you will reciprocate, won't you? I'd really like some of you as well as my sisters. Wow, that sounds weird when I write it but really exciting. By the way, I told dad I'd been in touch with you and he was cool with that. Said I had a right to know stuff. Oh yeah and I've ordered that movie from Amazon. Write soon, pics please. Love Alex."

I read the message, tears well in my eyes and I can't speak. So I simply turn the screen towards Jude so she too can look at the pictures of the half-brother she never knew she had. I sniff and dab my eyes.

"I called him Philip but his adoptive parents changed it to Alex. He's 4 years older than Sarah and he's your half-brother."

She spends a long time reading and re-reading the words on the screen, occasionally cutting to the pictures. Finally she moves the mouse and clicks on the 'reply' icon. She types some words, then turns the screen back for me to read.

"Hi, Alex. Bit shell-shocked at the moment so I can't say much. I'm Jude, one of your sisters and until 5 minutes ago I didn't even know you existed."

When she sees I have read her message she clicks on 'send', then drops her eyes and begins fiddling with her bracelets. We sit in silence for several minutes, then I pluck up courage to speak. My voice is breaking.

"It was never the right time."

Silence.

"I honestly never thought I'd ever hear from or see him again."

More silence.

"I didn't want to give him up."

"Then why did you?"

The words are half-shouted.

"I don't know, Jude. I shouldn't have let them take him away. All those years that I can never get back."

Now the tears are a total flood and I cry and cry and cry till my eyes and my cheeks ache the finally I subside.

"And he's not dad's?"

I shake my head.

"No, it happened while I was still at school. Before I met your father."

"Does he know?"

I nod.

229

"All this time, mum, and you never said a word."

"I couldn't tell you when you were small and then the longer it went on the harder it got."

"When did you get in touch with him?"

"A few weeks ago. I heard about this website and I thought it was worth a try. They say it can take ages and doesn't always work but I found him almost straightaway. And I wanted to tell you and Sarah but then she got ill and so even then it wasn't the right time. I was talking to Patti about it when I spoke to her last week. About wanting to tell you."

"Aunt Patti knows?"

"Patti's my oldest and closest friend. She's the only person I ever told apart from your father."

"And what does he think?"

"About what?"

"About you getting in touch with Alex."

"I haven't told him. Not about finding him. I mentioned the website to him. He didn't like the idea so I haven't discussed it with him further."

"Sarah will have to know. She has a right."

"Of course she does. But I don't want to upset her. Not now."

"Trust me, mum, she'll be a lot more upset if she finds out later and thinks you....we kept it from her."

"I was going to talk to Professor Turner about it. See if he thought Sarah was strong enough to cope with news like that. The last thing I want to do is set her back even further right now. She's got enough to cope with. How does Amanda feel about what's going on?"

"We've been talking about it a lot. Especially since Sarah went into hospital. With Mattie too. Amanda says her mother's done it before. The point is, what are you going to do about it, mum? You can't just ignore it. He's doing it right under your nose. With my friend's mother. Is that how you deal with everything, just push it to the back of your mind and pretend it's not happening? Like Alex?"

Ouch. That was straight to the point and cuttingly accurate, Jude the Intuitive. That's also how I dealt with the loss of Steve.

"What about Amanda's father? Does he know?"

"That's his business, isn't it? And don't change the subject. God, you're doing it again, avoiding the issue. Issues."

230

"Oh Jude, it's not that. It's just that I don't know what to do or what to say. Your father was horrified when I told him I was trying to trace Philip, I mean Alex. And that's another thing—he never mentioned it to Charles and Diana and somehow I can't see your grandmother taking it in her stride. You know what she's like. She'll probably see it as some dreadful blot on the family escutcheon and order me to never darken her doorstep again."

"See, there's always an upside."

A chink in the armour of Jude the Insufferable. Her sense of humour hasn't failed her completely. I smile wanly.

"Well we can cross that bridge when we come to it. I think you're right about Sarah. I'll phone Professor Turner this morning, tell him I need to speak to him."

"I'll get ready. I need to take some more stuff to Sarah."

"Of course."

I nod and we leave the study. Patti is in the kitchen brewing coffee and seeing our solemn faces she surreptitiously raises a quizzical eyebrow to me and I nod imperceptibly. Jude avoids her gaze and heads for the door.

"I'm going to get changed."

Once she's out of the room I turn to Patti.

"We've decided to tell Sarah together. Today."

"I think that's a good call. She needs to know, especially now Jude's found out."

"That's what Jude thinks. Says she doesn't think Sarah'd ever forgive me if I kept it back from her now."

"And what about Alex? Where does he fit in all this?"

"Well he's desperately keen to see pictures of us all. Apparently he's genuinely thrilled at the idea of suddenly being presented with an instant extended family."

"I suppose they'll do to be going on with till he can have the real thing."

I stare at her.

"Meet the girls, you mean. I'm trying not to think that far ahead."

"Time you did. And time you gave some thought about what you're going to do about that alley cat, quasi-husband of yours. I told you that you should have ditched him years ago. Why you ever went back to him that time in Bath I'll never know."

"It just seemed the only real choice I had at the time. For the girls' sake, anyway. You know what a mess I was after Steve. And I just didn't have a better plan. I'd lost my boss, my mentor, my lover, my whole life had come crashing down around me Christ, I was so bloody gullible and so vulnerable."

And I bang my hand hard down on his beloved marble counter top.

"Yes you were and I told you so at the time. But that was then and now's now and you'd better get it right this time."

I check my watch. It's half past eight.

"I'm going to speak to Sarah's physician. Jude and I want to fill Sarah in before Michael comes back."

"While the alley cat's away, the mice do play!"

I call Professor Turner on his cell and say only that I need to talk to him urgently and he advises me he'll be there till noon, no questions asked.

Back in the kitchen the ever-resourceful Patti has hatched a cunning plan. She's going to insist that Charles and Diana drive her over to George's Featherington apartment

"It's not just a ruse—I really want to have a look. Killing two birds."

"You're a brick. But Sarah does want to see you."

"Give her my love and tell her I'll be there as soon as I can. This is a family thing."

Jude is uncharacteristically quiet on the way to the Avon and I fill the silence by chain smoking. Once there we go straight up and immediately are ushered in Professor Turner's office. I introduce him to Jude and after exchanging pleasantries he proffers tea which I accept, feeling badly in need of another cigarette. An auxiliary brings in a tray and I busy myself with milk and sugar whilst preparing what I am about to say. Professor Turner also helps himself, leans back in his chair and smiles.

"So Fiona, what is it that is so urgent as to bring you to my office on a Saturday morning?"

I take a deep breath and try to relate the story briefly and chronologically, beginning with Alex's birth and adoption, right up to tracing him and telling Jude all about it and her insistence that Sarah should be told as soon as possible. He listens patiently without interrupting and when I subside he addresses a question to Jude.

"What about you, young lady, why exactly do you think that your sister needs to know now?"

232

"Because I know I would if it were me. And I know Sarah. She'd be really angry if she found out later that we'd deliberately kept it from her. She'd think that was patronising and really disloyal."

"Fair enough. And what makes both of you think that Sarah is strong enough to hear news like this?"

"We don't. That's what we're here to ask you."

"Mrs Hamilton, Jude, there's no way I can accurately gauge Sarah's reaction to such a portentous piece of news. I can tell you that she's in a very fragile emotional state at the moment and I can also say that it appears to have been largely triggered by recent events."

He breaks off.

'Jude, would you excuse us for a moment. I need to talk to your mother in private."

Jude looks at me quizzically. I look first at her, then at Professor Turner.

"Sarah and Jude share everything. You can speak freely."

"If you mean that dad's screwing my best friend's mother behind your back, then yes. Sorry, mum."

She shoots me an apologetic glance. I squeeze her hand reassuringly.

"If it was behind my back I wouldn't mind."

"Clearly two women who like to speak their own mind. No bad thing, that. And Jude, you're clearly very close to your sister."

"Mum's complained that we've been as thick as thieves ever since we were tiny."

"And you really feel strongly that Sarah needs to hear this piece of news and that you think it would have a worse effect on her if she were to find out later that you'd withheld it?"

"Trust me, I know her."

Professor Turner regards us silently for a few moments.

"I have to say that these are exceptional circumstances and on balance I'm inclined to the view that they require an exceptional response. I think perhaps you should trust your instincts and share your news with Sarah."

"Would you like one of the nurses to be in the room with you?"

"I don't think so. If we're going to let skeletons out of the family closet it should only be the family there to see them."

233

"Very well. You can use my rooms here—it'll give you a bit of privacy from the other girls. I'll ask someone to bring Sarah here and then I'll leave you alone."

He picks up the phone and presses a key.

"Linda? Won't you go and find Sarah Hamilton and bring her along to my rooms. Just tell her I need a quick word. Thanks."

I'm suddenly very nervous. What if we're doing the wrong thing? What if my elder daughter ends up resenting me as much as she resents Michael? But deep down I know that Jude's right. She has a right to know. There's a knock on the door and a nurse I haven't seen shepherds Sarah into the room. As she sees Jude and me she stops dead.

"Mum, Jude! You said you were coming after lunch."

She begins to cry and Jude and I get up and hug her. She is still painfully thin but I see more colour in her cheeks and her eyes seem brighter, though that might be from the tears. Suddenly she stops dead.

"There's nothing wrong, is there? Has something horrible happened, is that why you're here?"

"Oh no. It's nothing like that, darling. But Jude and I do have something important we want to tell you and we wanted to run it by Professor Turner."

"This is a little bit of an unusual situation so I'm going to leave you alone with your mother and sister and they can explain."

Sarah looks understandably baffled and still worried. Professor Turner and the nurse both leave the room, shutting the door behind them. I gently lead Sarah over to the sofa in the corner and the three of us sit down. Jude produces her phone, on which she has loaded the photo montage and I take a deep breath and begin to tell Sarah the story. When I finish she's quiet for a few minutes then asks

"Where does he live?"

"Norfolk, that's what you said, isn't it, mum?"

"Yes, a little village just outside King's Lynne. His father is headmaster of a prep school there. But he's studying at Oxford right now."

"What about his mum? His adoptive one, I mean?"

Jude the Inquisitive.

"You know, he's never actually mentioned her. Maybe he thinks it'd be a bit tactless talking about her to me."

"P'raps."

Jude sounds doubtful.

"I can't believe you never told us. Not a single word."

"Oh, Sarah, what can I say? I honestly thought I'd lost him for good. Everybody kept telling me that when it happened. I had to see some sort of social worker from the agency and she kept going on and on about how adoption was final and did I understand that I was waiving all rights to my child, that I could never expect to have any sort of contact with him every again. And if I think about it, I wasn't much more than a child myself, same age as you are now. I don't really think I properly took it all in. Of course, over the years, I did read about some mothers managing to trace their birth children and vice versa but it didn't happen very often and it was quite difficult. And if I ever brought the subject up, your father didn't want to know. He had his own two daughters so what interest would someone else's son be to him? It wasn't that I was trying to hide something from you two, it's just that it didn't seem worth all the upset it would cause if I told you.

"And then a few months ago, I read about that internet site and decided to give it a go. To be honest, I never really thought it would work, especially not that soon. I was so shocked when Alex got in touch with me. Shocked and excited and I did want to tell you both then but everything just seemed to happen at once. Your father and Louise..."

"I hate him, do you know that?"

"You don't mean that, Sarah."

"Oh, don't I? I've had time to think about it all since I've been in here. It's his fault I'm even here in the first place. I've seen them, you know. Quite a few times, only they never saw me. And then that day we went to the Butter Cup for lunch and the head waiter kept asking after Mrs Hamilton and asking me how my mother was and what a beautiful woman you were and how he just loved your car and I was totally buying it for a minute except that every time he said something dad, just completely changed the subject or buried his head in the menu. So finally I asked the waiter if he liked convertibles and he said yes and I asked him which he preferred, the new Beetle cabriolet or the original convertible bug and he said he'd never really liked the shape of either of them and then dad gave me a really funny look and changed the subject again and that's when I knew he'd been taking her there and passing her off as his wife. And then when I got back you told me you'd never been there. I did try to drop you a hint but you took no notice. And I knew it was going to be just like the

235

last time when you were crying in that hotel and then we drove to see Aunt Patti and Uncle Ross and we had that little flat in Bath only this time where would we go? I don't want to move, not even if we went back to Bath again. I like it here. All my friends are here and I even like that lame school. So I didn't want to go anywhere and it's just not fair and it's all his stupid bloody fault. And now I've ended up in this place and Professor Turner says it's my way of trying to control one aspect of my life cos the rest is so chaotic and I can't do anything about any of it. And that's why I hate him and it's not fair him hurting you all the time and you always putting on a front and pretending you don't care when I know you do. You deserve someone much better, mum, and you deserve a much better daughter than me. I've been horrible for months, just because of what he was doing and I couldn't tell you or do anything about it so I just took it out you instead. And now you probably hate me too."

Saran begins to cry and to my horror Jude, my little rock, is also crying. I put my arms around both of them, tell them I love them more than anyone or anything in the world and hug them tight and wonder if I too hate Michael but conclude that what I feel is what I told Professor Turner—complete indifference. And between sobs Sarah asks me if finding Alex is going to change things and if I'll end up loving him more than her and Jude and I tell her that could never happen but that meeting Alex would make me very happy and fill an emptiness in my life and that I really hoped we'd all end up thinking of ourselves as part of the same family and then we all three are crying our eyes out and clinging on to each other as though a tornado is about to tear through the room and part us.

Then when all our sobs have subsided Jude puts her phone down on the coffee table in front of us, displaying the pictures of Alex that she'd loaded up to show Sarah.

"Does he look like his father, mum?"

Both girls are focussed on my face, waiting for my response. And though I haven't given him a second thought for years, suddenly the boyish face of James, albeit a little fuzzy around the edges, flashes into my mind.

"Yes, I think he does, a bit. He has the same colour hair and the same jaw line. But when I look at these pictures I can see both of you too. There's a strong family resemblance—look at his eyes, Jude, they have the exact same shape and colour as yours. And Sarah, that's your mouth, you both have the same smile."

The girls both stare at the pictures, scanning them closely to see the resemblance.

"Sort of." (Jude)

"A bit." (Sarah)

They look from the photos to each other and exchange a silent message. It's a look I recognise from as soon as they were old enough to communicate with each other.

"Mum, Sarah and I need some space."

I take the hint.

"And I need a nicotine fix. I'll leave you two alone for a bit."

They look relieved but say nothing else, just continue scrolling and re-scrolling through the slideshow. I stand, walk to the door and exit, closing it firmly behind me. Checking the corridor, I see there is a door to a fire escape at the end so I head for that and fresh air. Once outside I light a cigarette and lean against the stairway, taking in a view of the car park and gardens beyond, wondering if I have just opened Pandora's box. Neither of my daughters looked exactly thrilled at this unexpected extension to the family, though I supposed on the plus side they didn't exhibit the shock-horror that their father displayed when I told him. I finish my fag, stub it out then linger for a few more minutes before once more tackling the fray.

Outside the office I tap lightly on the door

"It's me."

"Come in, mum"

I gingerly open the door and take in the scene. Sarah and Jude are huddled together on the sofa and it's clear they've both been crying. I step inside, unsure how to play this.

"I know it must have come as a shock."

Silence.

"You must hate me."

"No!"

This is semi-shouted by both of them, almost simultaneously. Jude takes the initiative.

"Sarah and I were thinking what if it had been one of us."

Sarah jumps in

"How could Grandma let you do it?"

"It was cruel."

"Her own flesh and blood."

"You mustn't blame her. Remember I was at a Catholic school and the staff convinced her it was for the best. You know how devout she is."

"That's no excuse."

"Even your grandfather thought it was the best thing. He wanted me to go to 'varsity. So did I. I was beside myself trying to work out how I could manage it."

"They could have helped."

"Perhaps."

I pause, thinking back to how difficult it had been at home—the atmosphere, the nagging, the recriminations, on and on till I was almost mental.

"It is what it is. I just need you to understand that I thought about him pretty much every day. Even after you two were born. I loved you both so much and I couldn't help wondering what it would have been like to have had you all grow up together."

The girls look at each other.

"Why does dad hate him?"

"I don't know that he does. He's just indifferent."

They look at each other again with an expression I can't interpret.

"He's lucky."

I look at Sarah in confusion.

"Alex? I suppose he has had a good life with his adopted parents."

This is not something I care to dwell on.

"That too. I meant he hasn't got any of dad's genes."

"He's treated you like dirt."

"I really don't mind about Louise, you know. Actually it makes things simpler."

"We've both decided we don't ever want to see him again."

I take a deep breath.

"Your father's a problem for another day. Right now it's Alex we're discussing."

I hesitate.

"I really want to meet up with him. If he wants to see me, that is. Can you understand that?"

Again, the look. They nod.

"And maybe even meet you."

Now the look is one of mild panic from Sarah and sibling sympathy from Jude. I choose my words carefully.

"But only when Sarah is more her old self. And only if you both want it."

The relief is palpable.

"We just…"

Jude looks at Sarah, then continues.

"We just wish you'd told us sooner."

They both tear up together and I move over to the sofa, sit in the middle with my arms around them both and shed a few tears of my own.

12 noon

"Always the glutton for punishment, my dear Ffion. What brings you here today when I explicitly ordered you to take the day off."

"I have some news to share with you."

"Oh."

The reaction is non-committal, typically George. He busies himself pouring tea into another cup.

"What if I told you once that Sarah and Jude weren't my only children?"

"Indeed?"

"Actually I also have a son. Philip, his name was."

He hands me my tea.

"It's Alex now."

"Oh, and how would you know that?"

George still keeps his voice neutral but this time he glances at me over the rim of his cup.

"He told me."

"You've seen him?"

"Well, no. We've just been corresponding. Over the internet."

I explain all about Mother and Child Reunion and how I traced Alex. Well, really how we traced each other. This is a new thought to me but it's obvious really. If he hadn't wanted to find me he'd never have registered on the site, would he? I'm absurdly pleased at this idea.

"My dear Ffion, that's wonderful."

"Do you really think so? I kept having, well not doubts exactly, just attacks of conscience. The girls didn't even know he existed until a couple of days ago and Michael found out that I was looking and he was livid. Ordered me to stop searching. He has no idea I've actually found him."

"Do you plan on telling him?"

"To be honest we're not exactly on what you'd call speaking terms at the moment."

He glances at me.

'I rather guessed as much.'

And I never doubted he had.

"But I have told the girls. That's where I've been today. Jude and I went to the Avon to tell Sarah."

"And how did they take it? It must have come as somewhat of a shock."

"I think they're still absorbing it. The one positive they seemed to find was that with Michael being persona non gratis right now as far as they're concerned, they're as happy that he's not his flesh and blood as anything else."

"Be grateful for small mercies."

He looks at me knowingly and we both smile.

"It's none of my business but it strikes me that Michael might not be too pleased about this turn of events."

"You're quite wrong. You're part of the family and it's every bit of your business. And no, he won't."

"So…?"

"Michael might not be that relevant."

We exchange a companionable look of understanding and I head for the door.

I had left Jude in the car, telling her there was something I needed to talk to George about. Now I smile in what I hope is a reassuring fashion, though I suspect it was more of the leer of an asylum escapee, put the bug into gear and we drive home. It's started to rain quite heavily and I hope it is not a portent of things to come.

Patti and Charles are in the kitchen engaged in a game of chess. I step inside, Patti raises her eyebrows and I shrug my shoulders noncommittally. I greet Charles who returns the salutation but scarcely looks up from contemplation of his next move, pick up the cook book in which I secreted the printouts of the photos and leave them to it. Diana is in the drawing room making elaborate sketches on a notepad. On the spur of the moment I go in and sit down adjacent to her.

"Diana?"

"Yes, dear?"

She is equally as engrossed in what she is doing and scarcely looks up.

"There's something I need to share with you. It's something that's happened rather suddenly and with you being here, it's bound to affect you so I feel I ought to fill you in."

Now she does look up, rather concerned.

"It's about you and Michael, isn't it? I knew something was wrong."

"No. That is, sort of but that's not what I want to talk to you about. You see…"

I hesitate, not knowing quite where to begin. I pull out the photos and spread them on the coffee table.

"Something happened in my life, a little while before I met Michael. I had a baby…"

She raises her head and an eyebrow simultaneously.

"…a son. He was given up for adoption."

"Did Michael know?"

"Oh yes. I told him before we were married."

"How curious he never mentioned it."

"I think he believes some things are better left unsaid. Anyway in the past couple of weeks I have caught up with my son—his name is Alex—and …."

I tell the story to date and explain that I am rather hoping that Alex will be able to come and visit in the not too distant future. Diana sifts through the pictures as I speak.

"A good-looking young man; and a definite family resemblance."

She breaks off as a thought occurs to her.

"And you'd rather Charles and I were out of the picture, is that it?"

"Heavens, no. That is, you are welcome to stay as long as you want, so long as you won't feel awkward. George would be completely adrift if you abandoned him now. And I know Sarah really wants to see you both."

"Naturally. I'm her grandmother. I'm sure she'll be delighted to see me. We've always had that very special bond, you know."

Diana looks pensive.

"Still waters."

241

"I'd put it behind me for so long, you see."

"I didn't mean you, Fifi, dear. Even as a child he could be very secretive."

She sets her sketchbook aside.

"Is there a particular reason you're telling me this now?"

I explain briefly about having made contact with Alex.

" 'All chickens come home to roost', as my grandmother used to say. As it so happens we were planning a short sojourn in Eire with George. His brother has asked us to visit and we accepted."

"George mentioned it. Sounds lovely. He never takes holidays. It will do him the world of good."

"I think perhaps I'd better have a quiet word with Charles. And we'll firm up out plans for Ireland and give you some space. Isn't that what they say?"

I smile gratefully and we both leave the drawing room together.

I go into the study and log on to Mother and Child. There's a message waiting from Alex.

"So now you know what I look like and I'm guessing that your daughter came across them by accident? Sounds like it came as a bit of a shock. I'm really sorry. I've been worrying about it all day. Is she okay? I know I've been pushing for you to tell them about me but maybe I was being a bit selfish. Anything I can do to help, I really feel bad. Yours, Alex."

I go off to find Jude, telling her there's something she needs to see. I turn the screen for her to read the message.

"Oh, god, mum. Now I feel really bad too."

She sits at the keyboard, hesitates for a moment, then begins to type.

"Hi Alex. This is Jude again, your stepsister, I guess. Mum filled me and Sarah in and you're right—it was a helluva shock. Sarah's not too well at the moment and mum's treading on eggshells so just give us some time. It's a lot to take in."

She looks at me for affirmation. I nod and smile wryly and she presses 'send'.

Sunday, 6th July

10am

"Do you know what ever happened to his real father?"

242

Jude is at the stables and Charles and Diana are busy making preparations for the trip to Ireland tomorrow so Patti and I are having a girly gossip on the patio.

"Funny you should ask. Remember, once I went off to uni I never went back to Chester, not to live. And I just never re-connected with my old friends from school. As for the father—James—I know he was at Liverpool when Philip, I mean Alex, was born, but I never saw him afterwards and I certainly didn't make any attempt to try and find him. What would have been the point? He was pretty good-looking, smart too, but we were never a serious item. The pregnancy was just one of those things. I think our relationship had pretty much run its course and I gave him short shrift the last time we spoke. I didn't even put his name on the birth certificate. And that worked both ways. I mean he never made any attempt to come looking for me. He probably doesn't even know if he fathered a son or a daughter."

"I wonder if he thinks about it?"

I pause to consider.

"I have no idea. I suppose it's possible. It's odd you should bring it up because Alex was asking after him last week."

"The next logical step after you."

Again I pause. The thought irritates me mildly.

"I suppose so."

Patti falls silent for a moment. She opens her mouth to say something, then closes it again.

"What?"

"Nothing."

She smiles unconvincingly, then changes tack.

"I had my P.A. on the phone yesterday. They have to re-shoot some scenes from the drama series I was working on so they're calling me back."

"When?"

"First thing tomorrow."

"So you'll need to leave today?"

"Actually not. We're shooting on location with a crew from Pebble Mill so I'll still be around. But I think I should pop back to Bath this weekend and spend a few days with Ross."

"It'll be good for you both. This is a very special time for you."

"We video chat every day."

243

"It's not the same and you know it."

"He'll fuss like a mother hen."

But she's smiling.

Tuesday, 8th July

Patti is out at the crack of dawn to make the commute to Birmingham and yesterday Charles and Diana, along with George, caught the 2pm ferry from Holyhead to Dunloghaire.

I'd promised Sarah we'd visit again today but with George away I can't leave the shop till after closing, though I have no doubt Jude will have phoned and/or texted her several times already today. I had a brief message from Alex on Sunday saying that he was pressing ahead with his plans to spend a few weeks in Italy. Apparently he has an Italian student friend, Paolo with whose parents they'll crash for a few days—they live in Padua—after which they plan on travelling around the country staying with Paolo's extended family and friends and picking up odd jobs along the way. He says he'll be away till September but has promised to keep in touch. To this end I have been instructed to sign up to several social media sites with messaging capabilities, there no longer being any need for Mother & Child.

I console myself with the thought that he has committed to staying in touch and message him along those lines, as well as telling him I hoped he would enjoy himself. The sub-text, of course, reads that I would much rather he stayed closer to home just in case the opportunity arose for us to meet, though in truth that seems unlikely in the immediately foreseeable future.

4.59pm

Almost on the dot of 5pm the three enter the shop. Jude pulls a face as she spots a few browsing customers, knowing full well this could mean a long wait. There's rarely any such thing as an impulse buy in a bookshop. Gradually, however, the stragglers make their final selections, I check them out and am finally able to shut up shop, literally and figuratively. Thereafter we all pile into the bug and head off to the Avon.

Sarah is in surprisingly good spirits. Jude confides in me later that a fellow sufferer called Alicia, an Avon resident of 3 months has taken her under her

244

wing and is helping her acclimatise. Also that she has given the Alex situation a good deal of thought and she thinks she understands why I didn't tell them sooner, given how dad is behaving and how he has treated me over the years. Ouch. I hadn't realised it was that obvious.

In the meantime, we repair to the clinic's cafeteria, a room on the ground floor with a picture window overlooking the river. I order tea and scones but resolve not to say a word if Sarah declines to join us. In fact she accepts a cup of Russian-style tea—black with lemon and no sugar—and does consent to a tiny morsel of dry scone from Jude which she cuts up into even more miniscule pieces, arranges and rearranges on her plate but finally allows a couple of crumbs to pass her lips. Baby steps, I tell myself.

The teenagers chat happily amongst themselves with me chipping in occasionally, phones are produced and pictures are taken till at last visiting hour is up. Sarah's face falls but we do our best to cheer her up with promises of another visit on Thursday. I hand the keys of the bug to Mattie and tell the three of them to wait for me outside while I have a quick last word with Sarah.

Once alone I tell her how proud I am of her and that the time there will pass much quicker than she thinks, especially now that we are able to pop in so often. In response she tells me everyone is really nice to her but it still feels a bit like a prison sentence. Instinctively I give her a hug.

"We all miss you dreadfully but more than anything we want you to get better."

"It's hard."

"I know. But you're in the best place you could be."

She checks a clock on the wall.

"I'd better go back upstairs before I turn back into Cinders."

We smile at her joke and hug again. She turns to go, hesitates, then turns back.

"Mum."

I wait.

"I wish dad would stay away forever."

Then she turns and hurries away, not looking back till she reaches the main staircase and starts to climb. And with her words echoing in my ears, I suddenly realise I feel the same way.

245

Friday, 11th July

10am

Jude announced at supper last night that Amanda's mother was taking another weekend break and asked if it would be okay if she (Amanda) could stay over, to which I readily agreed. It wasn't lost on me that this was the weekend of the big Scottish opening, the one with the celebrity tape-cutter, the helicopter transfers and the estate hospitality.

I mulled this over and just now sent Michael a cryptic text message which read simply 'Maybe you should have asked Lulu to open the hyperstore?'

Almost immediately my cell phone rings.

"I saw your message. What's the reference to Lulu supposed to mean?"

"She's a Scottish singer, very famous and very popular. I was just pointing out that she might have been a better choice than David Tennant."

There is a stony silence for several seconds, presumably as he wonders whether to retort or not.

"How's Sarah?"

"Funny you should ask.'

"Why?"

"Just a coincidence, that's all."

There is a minute's silence as he waits for me to elaborate and I decline. Then.

"I'm actually glad you called. There was something I wanted to say."

"Which is?"

"I don't want you back in the house."

"Are you out of your mind?"

"I was for quite a while but I'm right back inside now. And I need you to leave… We all need you to leave."

"It's Patti, isn't it? She put you up to this. She's never liked me."

"Which just goes to prove what an excellent judge of character she is, far better than me. But no, it wasn't her. I've given it a lot of thought, Michael, and I don't want you in the house anymore. In fact I don't want you in my life anymore either."

"Where the hell am I supposed to go?"

246

"That's hardly my concern."

"You've completely taken leave of your senses."

"I just told you I've finally regained them. And I'm not doing this just for myself. I have the girls to think about. Sarah still has scars from the first time you screwed around and now this. You're the cause of her eating disorder, you do know that, don't you?"

'Oh, that's right, blame me."

"Speak to the staff at the Avon if you don't believe me."

'That was years ago. Sarah can't possibly remember anything about it. She was still a baby. No, it's you that refused to let it go. You've never forgotten it and never forgiven me."

"How can I when you're still reminding me? How could you and with Jude's friend's mother too? And did you think they wouldn't know? They knew about it before I did and it brought it all back for poor Sarah. Can't possibly remember? She was 5, not 5 months."

"You're sounding hysterical and I haven't got time to deal with you right now. There's still a lot of loose ends I need to tie up."

"For me too. Do not come back here, Michael. I mean it."

His phone goes dead.

I feel no emotion at all bar an overwhelming sense of relief. Taking a deep breath I call Patti to tell her what I've done. She makes a single comment.

"Better late than never."

"I thought you were going to say 'I told you so'."

"It was implied in the sub-text."

We laugh but we also both know it's not really funny.

Saturday, 12th July

3am

I lie in bed but sleep evades me. I scarcely know what to think or feel, so much has happened in the past two weeks. It's as though someone took my life, tore it up into little pieces and tossed them high in the air. And now they are all fluttering to the ground and I'm catching them all and putting them back together, realising as I do so that some of them were in the wrong place to start with. And newly re-arranged, everything seems to look better somehow. I can

247

finally admit to myself what I think I knew for months—that to Michael I was merely a possession just like the house and his car and his vintage wines. That was why he was so jealous of Steve—because he could see that someone else really cared for me, because he thought he somehow owned me and because he was clearly losing me.

Also that I never loved him. In fact I never knew what the word meant till I met Steve. I married him out of some misguided sense of duty and returned to him for much the same reason. It was capitulation, compromise, resignation, surrender.

And that the situation has taken its toll on all of us but most of all on poor Sarah. And that if I had allowed it to continue. her recovery would have been all the harder. As it is I know she has a long way to go but at least now she won't have to carry around all that guilt, all that baggage, all that worrying on my behalf when all along it is I who should have been worried about her. And the end of the road for the biggest guilt trip of all. I have found the son I should never have given away, just doing what everyone else thought was right and not listening to the nagging voice inside me that said otherwise and went on saying it for the next 22 years. And most of all I am able to admit to myself once and for all that not only did I never love Michael, now I can't even tolerate him anymore, that I haven't for a long time and that finally I am free— free of him, free of guilt, almost free of worry and maybe even free to be myself once and for all.

At 6am Patti phones from Bath and wastes no time in getting down to business.

"You need a lawyer.'

"What on earth for?"

'Because this time you're going to divorce him, that's why. You should never have gone back to him, Fee. You knew what he was like.'

'I was very vulnerable at the time. And I had the girls to think of.'

'Damn right, you were vulnerable. You'd just lost the love of your life.'

'Yes, he was, wasn't he?'

I can see Steve's smiling face in front of me.

'You two were made for each other. I'd never seen you so happy as you were just before the accident.'

We both fall silent, each with our separate memories. For so many years I've hidden mine away in a little box, a box I only ever allowed myself to open

248

occasionally when I was alone and when I felt strong enough to peek inside. Now I knew I can take them out and separate the happy from the sad, can take strength from what Steve had given me instead of only mourning his loss and missing him so dreadfully, can finally be grateful for the time we had together.

Patti interrupts my reverie.

"I'll ask some of my Pebble Mill mates to suggest a good law firm. As soon as I'm done here we'll make an appointment and go together."

"I'm lucky to have you."

"Hey, what are friends for?"

We hang up companionably and I give up any thoughts of sleep and haul myself out of bed. I'm heading for the shower when the phone rings. It's Patti again.

"Call a locksmith."

"What?"

"A locksmith, today. Get the locks on the house changed. That's an order,"

"Yes, Ma'am." I pause, then add. "This is strictly 'entre nous' for now. Ross, excepted, of course."

"Understood."

I hang up. This is awfully grown-up.

7pm

I'm in the kitchen preparing supper—cheese and onion quiche with a side salad which shouldn't upset any of the assembled company. Jude and Amanda are setting the table and Mattie decides to turn on the evening news. I hear the word 'Pricerite' and look up to see that the store opening has been tagged on as a feature extra. Apparently it's a big deal north of the border and David Tennant always draws the crowds. The girls stop mid place-setting and we all stare at the screen. The newsreader gives a brief account of the event whilst behind her various clips from the ceremony are shown: Frances shaking hands with the Proctor of Edinburgh, David cutting the tape, a brief extract of Frances making the inaugural speech and a leaving shot of the group boarding the helicopter, the VIPs going up the steps first, accompanied by their respective PAs.

"I suppose we can expect dad home today or tomorrow."

Jude doesn't sound enthusiastic.

249

"Maybe not."

The girls turn their attention back to the screen and Jude blurts out

"Talk of the devil…."

I whirl around and realise she has spotted her father in the background, taking up the rear as the party heads off to the waiting helicopter. The camera is still on David and Frances but Michael can clearly be seen shepherding them in front of him but that's not all. The slim, blond woman in a floral frock and a fascinator on her head is almost out of shot yet even so she is easily recognisable.

"Sorry."

I turn to look at the girls as the picture reverts to studio and the newsreader. Jude and Amanda are both giving me an old-fashioned look.

"I knew where she was."

"Amanda, I'm sorry."

"We've all talked about it, mum. We're not small kids."

"I suppose not."

There is a silence. I want to ask a question but I hesitate.

"Amanda, does your father know?"

"Probably. It's not the first time. He just waits for it to run its course."

I digest this piece of information. Seems like he and I have something in common, just that in my case Michael has breached the most important clause in the contract—he brought his affair to my doorstep. Then I remember myself, the matter is in hand and with my best Mary Poppins smile and breezy casualness I announce``

"I'm starving. Let's eat, shall we?"

I pick up oven gloves, lift the quiche from the oven and place it in the centre of the table. Then I take the lead, sitting down and helping myself to salad. The three follow suit and happily the conversation turns to Sarah, her treatment and plans for the next visit and the elephant in the room is ignored.

11pm

Before I turn in I knock lightly on Jude's bedroom door. She answers with a "Come in" and I enter. She is in bed reading so I perch on the end.

"There's something else I need to tell you."

"Which is?"

250

"I spoke to your father this morning and I told him not to bother coming back."

She sets her book aside and looks hard at me.

"Probably best. Have you told Sarah?"

"I thought I'd go over in the morning. Do it in person rather than over the phone."

She nods, gives me another long, hard stare, then goes back to her book. Jude the Inscrutable. I turn to leave.

"At least we won't have to move to Manchester."

Her voice is a mixture of triumph, relief and typical Jude tongue-in-cheek.

"True. I hear it's always raining."

"We could get dad a brolly as a leaving gift."

I turn back and smile.

"Good idea."

Then I leave her to her book and her thoughts. No doubt there will be many questions but they can wait.

Sunday, 13th July

The three teenagers are up and out early for the stables. I'm told there's a mini show on and they're all competing which means grooming and plaiting for the horses and best bib and tucker for them. Once they're out of the way, I tart myself up a bit and head out to the Avon where I take Sarah for a walk in the grounds, along the towpath. There's a light drizzle falling which I trust will not metaphorically dampen spirits more than need be and after exchanging gossip, news and a progress report on her programme I repeat the news I gave to Jude last night.

"Not because I said I didn't want him back?"

I shake my head and turn to face her directly.

"Because I didn't. I can't cope with it anymore, Sarah. I've given it a lot of thought and I know we'll all three be better off without him."

"Don't you mean four?"

"Alex?"

She nods.

"Let's not get ahead of ourselves there. I'd love to meet up but it has to come from him. And he's in Italy for the next few weeks."

251

"Lucky duck."

"It does sound fun, doesn't it? Talking of ducks, this rain's getting heavier. Maybe we'd better head back?"

"I prefer getting wet to going back in there."

"Fair enough."

And we continue walking along, both lost in our separate thoughts yet probably thinking of the exact same thing.

Tuesday, 15th July

Amanda had a text message from Louise yesterday afternoon saying she was back home and she felt she ought to put in an appearance, though she didn't sound too happy about it. I wondered vaguely where Michael had gone in the meantime but only out of idle curiosity. I know there is a company VIP penthouse somewhere in Manchester CBD that Frances would be only too happy to place at his disposal.

Patti phoned very early to say that she was driving straight from Bath to Pebble Mill and that she'd see me at home this evening some time. I confess to having felt really guilty hogging her company for the past couple of weeks but now that she's working in Birmingham my conscience has eased on that score and I'm looking forward to seeing her again tonight.

I also had an email from Alex saying that he was in Florence, enjoying the architecture, the art, the food and the weather and that he was picking up quite a lot of Italian already, He even addressed me as La Bella Signorina, though whether that's more familial than plain Fiona I'm not sure. Jude reported that she also had a message from him, though she didn't elaborate.

And last but not least George phoned half an hour ago to say how much he was enjoying his own family reunion and being able to show Charles and Diana all the scenic spots and convivial hostelries that Dublin and County Wicklow had to offer and saying how impressed he was with all the superb new restaurants that had sprung up in his absence. I'm inordinately pleased for him. In all the time I've known him he's hardly ever taken a holiday and although never overtly stated, I always had the impression that there was a certain froideur between him and his siblings. If fences that side are being mended then he's also killing two birds. And before you mention it, yes, I know I'm mixing my metaphors.

All in all I'm feeling fairly upbeat which makes it all the worse when I drive home and not only see the navy BMW parked in the drive but also Michael at the front door attempting an entry. My stomach lurches at the mere sight of him and I silently offer up a prayer of thanks to Patti about having the locks changed; also that Jude and Mattie are riding. Desperately trying to pull myself together I park and get out of the car.

"I wasn't expecting you."

"What's that supposed to mean?"

"I didn't think you'd be coming back."

"And what the hell's the deal with the locks."

"In case you did."

"I need some stuff."

"Tell me what you want and I'll put it together."

"Don't be so ridiculous. I'm here now. Open the door."

"I can't do that."

"You mean you won't."

"Yes."

We stand there looking at each other like two pugilists in the ring, waiting for the bell. I honestly don't know what would have happened next if Patti's Maserati hadn't pulled in at that precise moment. Pulling in right behind the BMW she leaps out from her car with astonishing agility considering her age and condition.

"What's she doing here?"

"She' as in the cat's aunt? 'She' has a name."

Michael glares first at me, then at Patti who grins.

"'She' is staying with her friend for a few days. 'She' was worried her old trouble might be coming back."

She smiles, Michael glares and balls up his fists. The gesture is not lost on Patti who can't resist.

"You wouldn't hit a pregnant woman, would you?"

Michael's jaw drops and he stares at her still almost flat belly.

"Congratulations."

He couldn't sound less sincere if he tried.

"Thanks. Ross is hoping for a son. I suppose it's always nice when the first-born's a boy, isn't it?"

She leans languidly across the bonnet of her car, then looks directly at Michael and smiles so sweetly you'd think butter wouldn't melt.

"I'll move the car so you can back out."

She does just that and Michael, stymied, moves towards his car.

"I need to get in. There's stuff I need."

"So you said."

He looks daggers at me, then puts the Beamer into gear and drives off.

"Anyone'd think he had something to hide."

Patti grins wickedly as I open the front door and we enter the house companionably.

Saturday, 19th July

With Jenny having agreed to literally look after the shop we have arranged an afternoon visit en masse to see Sarah—me, Patti, Jude, Amanda & Mattie. It is a balmy summer day and we head out into the gardens, selecting a bench overlooking the river for Patti and me with the teens sprawling on the lush grass. Sarah had hinted at some good news and once we are settled she looks coyly around and announces that she has put on some weight. All patients are subjected to a weekly weigh-in every Friday morning after which any weight gain, no matter how small, is greeted with approval and even occasionally applause by the staff and fellow inmates; maintenance is considered acceptable on a sort of 'must try harder' basis; but any loss leads to a corresponding loss of privileges whereby inmates lose some of their daytime freedoms with extra monitoring during mealtimes. All of this I know and understand and even though on visits I have seen my elder daughter making a real effort on the food front, she is still stick thin and only managing to consume small amounts at a time so I have been careful never to reference the weigh-ins, nor ask any questions directly related to the subject of weight. However she is now displaying a triumphal look which the Victorians might have described as high cockalorum. Sarah, it seems has triumphed in her scales test.

"I've put on 370 grammes."

Amanda, Jude and Mattie make whooping noises, accompanied by pats on her back and hugs all round. Cell phones are produced and group selfies taken while Patti beams like a mother hen, if hens were able to smile. I make what I feel is a suitably enthusiastic response.

"Well done, darling."

Privately I translate that amount as less than a tin of baked beans or a pot of jam, neither of which substance would ever pass my elder daughter's lips. Baby steps, I chide myself inwardly again while outwardly maintaining an aura of admiration.

Jude whispers something in Sarah's ear, a look of panic briefly flits across her face, then she nods. I glance at Patti surreptitiously who shrugs her shoulders equally as imperceptibly. Jude, meanwhile, is fiddling with her phone. Now she looks at me somewhat sheepishly.

"I've sent a couple of pics to Alex."

"I'm sure he'll appreciate that."

Another baby step, I remind myself, this small acknowledgment of what? Friendship? Cyber acquaintance? Blood relationship?

"He's been sending us some from Italy."

She passes her phone over and swipes across the screen to show me a series of scenic pictures of Italy, Alex, another young man, presumably Paolo and an older man and woman, Paolo's Papà and Mamma, no doubt. I smile and make an effort not to overdo it. Inside I'm as pleased as Punch.

We'd gone to the Avon in 2 cars, partly because we were such a large party but also because Patti and I had some 'other business' to attend to. As threatened, she's quizzed some of her Pebble Mill colleagues for the name of a reputable law firm in Brum, preferably one specialising in divorce law. Off her own bat she also called up and made an appointment so that's where we're headed this afternoon. Taking our leave of Sarah, the three head off to ride whilst Patti and I turn in the opposite direction, headed for Birmingham.

We reach the outskirts just before 3pm, our scheduled appointment time. The offices of Finchley, Finchley and Stutton are located in a row of converted Victorian mews cottages on the Stourbridge side and our appointment is with a Ms Claire Rowley who turns out to be an attractive young black woman, immaculately turned out in a close-fitting cream shift with matching jacket and high-heeled black slingbacks, who ushers us into a small, tastefully furnished meeting room and indicates for us to sit down.

After enquiring as to whether we would like tea or coffee, which we both decline, she smiles and asks me to explain the situation. I deliver a précis of our chequered history, up to and including recent events, to which she listens attentively. I also hand her my copy of the paper I had us both sign before I moved into Lionsgate, which she studies carefully, then responds.

"No two marriages are alike, Mrs Hamilton, and companionship and consideration for the wellbeing of the offspring are as good as basis, if not better, than many."

She pauses.

'Your case seems very simple. Your husband is clearly the guilty party which he has demonstrated by conducting an affair with someone known to you and your daughters, thus clearly breaching the terms of the contract you drew up and signed. Furthermore, from what you tell me, his actions have had a detrimental effect on the mental health of at least one of your daughters and his choice of new partner has placed you all in an untenable position. One positive point is that he has left the family home.'

'Technically he didn't leave. I asked him, told him, not to come back."

'Of course you did. He had been committing adultery close to home, in direct contravention of both his marital vows and the conditions of your agreement. Perfectly understandable that you wouldn't countenance him under the same roof under the circumstances. He had made his remaining unworkable. Do you know if he has legal representation?"

"I'm sure you can contact the company lawyer for now."

I hand her a card with the Pricerite legal firm's contacts.

"Thank you. First thing Monday I shall contact them on your behalf and institute proceedings. I shall be asking for the marital home to be placed in your name and a fifty-fifty split of all other assets, including bank accounts. I shall also be seeking half of his future earnings to be settled on you in perpetuity and an additional allowance for your daughters' education and upbringing. Naturally we shall also seek full custody with visiting rights only for your husband, though given the age of your daughters, that might not be necessary. Do you have any questions?"

"Is all this absolutely necessary?"

"All what?"

"All this formality. And the money. It seems so greedy."

"It's no more than you are entitled to after 18 years of marriage, Mrs Hamilton. And you will need enough money to maintain your lifestyle. From what you tell me the salary you earn at the bookshop is scarcely sufficient to support yourself, let alone your two daughters."

"Lots of people live on much less."

"Possibly but there really is no need in your case. Your husband earns a very good salary and he can quite easily afford what we are asking. And remember that all this is completely of his own doing. Think of it as compensation—reparation, if you like."

"I'm not sure."

"Well, I am. Make the bastard pay, Fee. Face it, he owes you a lot more than a few quid."

"I think Ms Rowley has more than a few quid in mind."

"Well let me put it this way. If you don't get it, Louise will."

"There is that. Somehow I don't think our Louise will be exactly cheap to run."

"Seriously high maintenance, that one."

Patti and I begin to giggle. Ms Claire Rowley looks slightly bemused. When our giggles subside I try for something akin to a straight face.

"Very well, Ms Rowley. You may begin proceedings."

"She means go and screw the miserable bastard."

"I thought that was Louise's job?"

We collapse in giggles again, this time to the point where tears are streaming down our cheeks and finally the fearsome Ms Rowley cracks.

"Believe me, Mrs Hamilton when I've finished with a man he really knows he's been well and truly screwed."

Looking at this self-confident young woman I don't doubt it for a minute. Michael will never know what hit him.

Sunday, 20th July

I am sipping tea in the kitchen when Patti enters wearing a pair of dungaree shorts.

"I thought it'd be a good time to have a spring clean."

"It's mid-summer."

"Long overdue, then."

We spend the next couple of hours packing up Michael's belongings from the bedroom and bathroom and taking them out to the garage. It feels very good. That done we do the same in his study, filling cardboard boxes with books, files and papers. While I'm doing that Patti fiddles around on his

257

computer, discovering lots of images of Louise, some just of her and others of the two of them together. There are even some from the Eurostar and from Calais, each one date and time logged. The evidence had been there all along, right under my nose, if only I'd known where to look.

"She's a bit old for that thong, don't you think? And one of her breasts is completely lopsided."

The mildly pornographic images taken by Michael of his lover should have sickened me but all I feel is mild amusement at the idea of her having been photographed looking like a Penthouse centrefold a little past her pose-by date.

Patti, though, is in her element, printing them all out and placing them in a large box file, on the top of which she writes 'Hamilton v Hamilton' in red felt tip pen.

We collect everything collectable. Patti looks at me shrewdly.

"What about the deeds to this house?"

"I've never seen them. Actually it must still be his name."

"What!"

"It's just occurred to me. He bought it when we were living apart. I told you about it—remember?"

"And he never put it in joint names?"

"Not as far as I know."

"I suppose it won't make any difference."

We finish packing everything I don't want to look at and lug the boxes out to the garage to join the rest.

"What do you think I should do with the wine collection downstairs?"

She eyes me wickedly.

"Keep it."

"But it's not mine."

"Possession is nine tenths of the law. Or call it safe keeping."

"That's what he always said about the cellar. 'Safe as houses'. He's bound to want it back."

"I was always told 'I want doesn't get'!"

"You're wicked, you know that!"

"Practical."

I grin at her.

"I'll message Michael and tell him to send a van to collect the boxes."

"Do it through Claire. And make it clear he's not to come in person."

"Yes, ma'am!"

Patti nods towards a couple of cartons containing odds and sods.

"I can drop that off in a skip at on my way to work tomorrow."

"Not unless you do it in relays. Your car boot's only big enough for a little overnight bag."

"So you reckon Louise could squeeze in then?"

We both fall about laughing and once again I'm struck by how little I feel at the idea of Michael's infidelity. The first time it happened I felt sick and I remember my legs almost buckling underneath me when I caught sight of Cindy Prince. Yet now, thinking of Michael and Louise I feel no more than if I were watching a television soap unfold before me. The tenuous link we had maintained for the sake of the girls was well and truly broken. Michael had already been relegated to the category of 'just someone I used to know'.

8pm

Amanda having gone home, the four of us are in the kitchen eating supper—chicken and couscous courtesy of Patti—when Jude's cell phone rings and after checking the caller she excuses herself from the table and goes into the garden to take the call. It's a good half hour before she returns, mouths something to Mattie and they exchange a glance which I interpret as not good, then looks directly at me.

"Amanda says dad's at their house. Been there all weekend."

Patti and I exchange slightly raised eyebrows.

"Her dad's away on another business trip to Sweden. He's supposed to be back on Tuesday. She says her mum's going to meet him at the airport and tell him then. Anyway Amanda says it's really weird in the house at the moment and it's going to get worse when her father comes back so I said she could come and stay here. That is okay, isn't it?"

I hesitate fractionally.

"Of course it is."

"I hoped you'd say that. Mattie, can we go and get her now? I told her we'd come straight over and she said she'd pack a few things."

"Can we borrow the bug, Mrs H?"

I nod and the two of them head off out of the back door.

"You're collecting quite a house party."

259

"Well it's not as if we haven't got enough room. This place is far too big. Do you realise there are 7 bedrooms, not counting the old servants' quarters in the attic? And don't forget we've lost Charles and Diana now."

"Might be a bit awkward."

"I thought about that but it's not her fault, poor kid. And it can't be any more awkward than her staying there with her mother and Michael. God, Patti, just when you think the water's starting to clear a bit somebody wades in and muddies it up again."

"I thought he'd gone to Manchester?"

"So did I."

The sound of car wheels on the gravel drive breaks the silence.

The three of them troop in through the back door, Jude and Mattie protectively flanking Amanda on each side like emotional bodyguards, one carrying a lilac holdall, the other a large cardboard box. Amanda's eyes are very red and she looks a little shell-shocked.

"I haven't made up another room. I thought you and Amanda would prefer to share."

"Thanks, mum. Let's go upstairs, you lot."

And the two bodyguards usher Amanda through the doorway.

"Dunno bout you, Fee, but I'm bushed. I'm off to bed."

"Sorry, Patti. This is probably the last thing you need in your condition."

"Are you kidding? I'm having a ball. What are friends for if not to kick a man when he's down?"

She gives that wicked grin again and heads for the door.

Monday, 21st July

I've been awake since 4am, still trying to take in all the events of the past few days. The situation reads like the script of a bad soap opera but this is fact, not fiction. Looking back over the past few months I see now that there was an inevitability about it all—the increasingly overtness of Michael's infidelity and my utter indifference to it, the effects that it had on Sarah with her intuitive nature and heightened sensitivities, my gnawing guilt for having given away my son coupled with my determination to try and find him. Come to think of it, it's less like a soap opera script and more like the modern transcript of a Chekhov play. All the main characters are in place, summer visitors and year-

260

round residents of the country house—the strong-willed matriarch and her wealthy industrialist husband, the unfaithful husband and the long-suffering mouse of a wife, one daughter struck down with consumption, her sister impossibly cheerful in the midst of domestic chaos and familial anarchy, her stalwart suitor, himself hiding the scars of domestic tragedy, the fashionable friend from the city, the bearer not only of hope but of new life and last but not least, the long-lost son, still estranged but even in absentia an unwitting and unwilling catalyst in the unravelling and volatile situation. Not to mention the fact that I certainly put away enough tea to fill a good-sized samovar. So what should we call it, this commencement-de-siècle drama? 'Two Sisters and a Half-Brother in the Mulberry Orchard', perhaps?

Giggling inappropriately I rise, shower quickly and tiptoe down to the kitchen for tea and toast. I'm about to turn on the TV to catch up with the news when the phone rings

"Feef?"

My stomach churns and I feel suddenly sick.

"I thought we should talk."

What about, I think, but I say nothing.

"I'm moving to Manchester."

"I thought you'd already left."

"With Lulu."

He pauses, as though expecting a reaction.

"There's a company flat we can use while we look around for somewhere suitable. I'm driving up there after lunch and she'll join me in a few days, after she's had time to speak to Gerald and make a few arrangements. I thought you should know."

"Aren't you leaving it a little late to start taking me into your confidence?"

"And, em, Amanda. Lulu asked me to..."

"To what?"

"To make sure she'll okay."

"Why shouldn't she be? This isn't the Gingerbread House and I'm not the wicked witch."

"I didn't mean that."

"That's exactly what you meant. You've made your views on my mothering skills pretty clear. I pause briefly. "Your stuff's boxed up in the garage. Get someone to pick it up. It's in the way."

I slam the receiver down and light my first cigarette of the day.

Tuesday, 22nd July

Amanda confirmed that Michael and Louise had decided to drive straight up to Manchester and not wait for her father to return. Apparently Louise dumped her husband by text message and Amanda said that was a horrible way to do it but she said she'd thought about it and there really wasn't any nice way.

"I think he probably knew though."

"What makes you say that?"

"You did, didn't you? Maybe not all the details but you knew something was going on. And I think it was the same for him. He's been awfully distracted for the past few months and away on business such a lot. He never used to go away so often."

"When does he get back?"

"This evening. His flight gets in around 9 so he probably won't be home till 11. I've told him I'm staying here again tonight and I'll see him tomorrow. That is all right, isn't it?"

"Of course."

Poor kid.

Just before lunch George phones to say that they plan on cutting short their stay and returning at the weekend. Diana, he says, took the news of Michael's leaving very badly but like the true blue aristocrat she is she's putting a brave face on it.

'She must have been quite fond of you after all.'

'Rubbish. She's just worried about the scandal and any possible fall-out in her social set. Just remind her that now she knows how the Queen felt in her Annus Horribilis. That should cheer her up.'

'You really are extremely cynical for one so young, Ffion. I can quite see where Jude gets her feistiness from.'

We laugh and hang up amicably.

262

Thursday, 24th July

7pm

We're all in the kitchen readying for supper. Even Patti, whose days often finish late in the evening, caught a break when bad weather halted filming.

Amanda has been telling us that her father looks utterly defeated. Reading between the lines I suspect that the 'open marriage' was pretty one-sided. Her mother played around and her father turned a blind eye.

"He said he'll try and spend a bit more time at home. I think he feels bad for me but I feel really awkward. I know that sounds horrible. And he...."

She hesitates.

'He what?'

'Well, I think he wants to talk to you sometime as well. Because you're sort of in the same boat together, if you know what I mean.'

She glances at me quickly and looks away in embarrassment.

'Tell him it's fine. He can call me anytime and ask me anything he likes.'

'Thanks, Mrs H. You're really a very cool person. Sarah and Jude are really lucky.'

'Hey, don't cry.'

I give her a hug and wonder who died and made me Earth Mother all of a sudden. What a turnaround from a couple of months ago when I had the distinct impression that I should have been sterilised at birth.

Sunday, 27th July

Sarah rang last night in high spirits. Her weight gain was up to half a kilo which automatically meant she had a free 24-hour pass and I promised to pick her up at the crack of dawn so she wouldn't waste a second of her furlough. Even a dark and threatening sky couldn't dampen the atmosphere and the day was spent revisiting old haunts and catching her up on current events. I noted that only the most oblique references were made to either Michael or Louise, that Sarah still spent an age over her minute portion of wholemeal vegetable pie and salad at lunch but that even though she scraped all the topping off the pastry (the latter being surreptitiously passed to Cromwell under the table) she did eventually eat most of her salad and some, if not all, of the vegetable filling. Thereafter the heavens opened but she still insisted on visiting the stables with Jude, Mattie and Amanda and in the early evening I dropped them all off at the cinema in town.

Monday, 28th July

I had to rise very early again to drop Sarah back at the Avon. She blinked back a few tears as I left her at the entrance but told me she was determined to earn more day releases as soon as she could.

Patti, too, had a very early start, even though she'd only come back around 9pm after a long editing session the night before. I expressed concern, considering her condition, but she pooh-poohed my objections as 'fussing' and reminded me that she was used to keeping odd hours in her work.

On impulse, after dropping Sarah off, I decide to drive to Featherington Hall. I find the door to George's apartments open and a small army of painters and decorators hard at work with Diana firmly in charge of operations and Charles and George her downtrodden Aides-de-camp, the intrepid trio having arrived back from their sojourn beyond the pale. George is both delighted and surprised to see me and I to learn that a marvellous time was had by all and George's old family seat, Wellington House, now in the care of his elder brother, has been raided for a treasure trove of suitable antique artefacts and odd items of furniture, all of which will be packed and shipped across the Irish Sea in a matter of days, thence to be ensconced in the Featherington apartments which are a good deal more spacious than I had envisaged.

In contrast to George's enthusiastic greeting, Diana looks uncharacteristically nonplussed at my presence.

"Fifi, we weren't expecting you."

"No, I don't suppose you were. Actually it was you I really wanted to see. I thought we should chat."

"Pas devant les domestiques, my dear. Let's go into the kitchen and make some coffee."

Leaving the crew and the men to carry on she and I go off, and again, quite uncharacteristically, Diana puts the kettle on and busies herself grinding beans and lifting out cups and saucers, all the while making small talk about the choppy waters on the Irish crossing, the charm of the Irish countryside and the difficulty in finding reliable moving agents for George's family heirlooms. I let her ramble on for a few minutes and then gently interrupt.

"I wanted to come and see you in person rather than talk on the phone. Look, Diana, I know you're never really liked me and..."

She freezes with her hand on the top of the cafetière and looks at me in bewilderment.

"Never liked you? What an extraordinary thing to say. I liked you from the first moment I met you back in Bristol all those years ago. If I hadn't I would never have sanctioned the marriage, believe me."

I can scarcely comprehend what I'm hearing.

"But you never thought I was good enough for your son, did you?"

"Again, you couldn't be more wrong. I could tell you were a very capable, intelligent young woman, a good match for Michael and just what he needed if he was going to get where he wanted. Though to be honest, at times I found you a little intimidating."

"*You* found *me* intimidating?"

I find this thought so absurd I start laughing.

"You're a very strong woman. It must have incredibly hard to have given up your son and to endure all that unpleasantness in Bath. That's how I know you'll come through this current contretemps. You won't let it defeat you even though it must have come as quite a blow."

Hardly, I think, but I keep the thought to myself.

"Michael's my only son and I love him dearly but I don't for one moment condone what he's done. It's unforgiveable, abandoning his family like that for a married woman."

"Nothing's ever as black and white as that."

"Perhaps not but I was brought up to believe in the sanctity of marriage, sticking together, no matter what."

"Turning a blind eye, you mean?"

"If that's what it takes, yes."

"It doesn't really work like that anymore."

"Women's Lib, I suppose you're talking about."

'Something like that.'

"Well he's put you all in an impossible position and I told him so in no uncertain terms when he telephoned to tell me where he was and what he'd done. And I also told him that on no account was he ever to bring his fancy woman to my house."

Women's Lib? Fancy woman? I'm in a lexical time warp here, as if it wasn't hard enough trying to digest the bombshell that Diana hadn't apparently looked on me as the enemy and the outsider all these years. She just had a funny way of showing approval.

"That's very loyal of you and it brings me to what I came here to say which is just this. I know how fond you and Charles are of the girls and you're still their grandparents so you'll always be welcome at any time. In fact I'd appreciate it if you'd stay in all our lives. They have enough disruption to cope with at the moment and they need as much continuity as they can get. Which is why I plan on staying on in the house, even though it's really too big for the three of us. I just feel that a move would be the wrong move right now."

"Does that mean that we're still welcome to come and visit?"

God forbid!

"Absolutely, Any time you want."

"That is a relief. I was afraid we'd lose you all when you…"

"When we divorced, you mean? I don't see why. Even Michael will want to see the girls sometimes."

Not that the girls much want to see Michael as things stand at the moment.

"And this *other woman.* George implied you know her."

"Rather well, I'm afraid. Her daughter's Jude's best friend. You met her a few times—Amanda."

"Isn't that a bit awkward socially? How are the girls handling it?"

I refrain from stating that my two are actually over the moon.

"Well Amanda's been staying with us for a couple of days so they've all been muddling through it together and her father is back from a business trip so I hope that'll make things a bit easier for her."

"What a mess it all is."

She stands, lost in thought and seemingly lost for words. I decide I should fill the ensuing silence and adopt a bright tone.

"What about that coffee? I don't know about you but I could do with a caffeine boost."

As if by invisible signal George and Charles tap on the kitchen door and come and join us. If I didn't know better I'd say they'd been listening at the keyhole. Charles glances nervously at Diana.

"Is everything all right?"

266

"Perfectly. Fifi and I have talked the situation over and she's said we must visit as often as we can so the girls have...perpetuity."

I smile. "Continuity."

"Quite. In situations like this, it's important that the children have continuity and that means they need us around even more."

I only meant I didn't plan on selling the house.

"But we can't come back straightaway, Fifi, dear. We have obligations to dear George first but as soon as we're done here we'll be back. And we're getting on so well it shouldn't take more than a week."

Oh my God, they're not going home.

"No rush, honestly."

"Nonsense. The girls clearly need us—you too. I can see you're putting a brave face on it but at times like this you need your family around you. So that's settled, then. Shortbread, anyone?"

Later, back home I break the news to Patti who of course packs up laughing.

'You're far too diplomatic, Fee, you should have told her to take the high road back to Bonnie Scotland.'

"I know but I've always been a bit of a doormat where Diana was concerned."

"Mind you, there is one good thing about it."

"What?"

"Well just think how Michael's going to react. His own mother tells him on no account to bring his floozy home and never darken her door again and at the same time she can't do enough for you and the girls. I'm sure the irony won't be lost on him."

"Hadn't thought of that. Perhaps I should get Ms Rowley to write it into the divorce settlement. Court awards Mrs Hamilton full custody of her former in-laws. Mr Hamilton is denied visiting rights at present."

This time we both fall about in fits of giggles and once again I acknowledge just how glad I am that Patti's still around.

Friday, 2nd August

Driving home after work, my cell phone rings. I don't recognise the number but I pull into a lay-by to take the call.

267

"Mrs Hamilton? We've never met. It's Gerald Sinclair, Amanda's father.'

"Ah."

I try to keep my tone non-committal.

"Yes, a pity I couldn't have introduced myself under more pleasant circumstances."

"Quite."

"I was wondering if we could meet for lunch one day next week. I'm sure you agree we have a couple of things we need to discuss."

By 'a couple of things' I assume he's probably not referring to Michael and Louise. All the same I'm not sure I'm ready to meet the cuckolded husband just yet.

"I am a bit busy. There's a lot of stuff I have to take care of."

"Absolutely but I really would appreciate it, mostly for Amanda's sake. We had a long talk and she seems very fond of you, in spite of everything that's happened. And with us both in the same boat, so to speak, I just thought we should compare notes."

Compare notes? Does he think I kept a diary? Even worse, has he kept one and he wants to show it to me?

"How does Wednesday sound?"

Like a nightmare.

"Fine. Where did you have in mind?"

"I was thinking of The Butter Cup. Do you know it?"

I'm just about to tell him that's not such a good idea when the irony hits me.

"Yes, I do. Shall we say one o'clock?"

"I look forward to it. Thank you."

Before I drive off, I call Patti.

"I've just had a call from Amanda's father. He wants to meet up and compare notes.'

"And you agreed?'

"I tried to wriggle out of it but he was very insistent. And get this. He wants to meet at The Butter Cup. He obviously has no idea that was one of their favourite trysting spots."

"You're going to tell him, of course."

"Maybe."

There's a momentary pause, then we just pack up laughing. We're giggling so hard that it's all I can do to semi-compose myself.

"See you later."

I drive home, still smiling at the unintended significance of his choice of venue.

Wednesday, 7th August

The day of the Close Encounter of the Third Kind. I diplomatically decided to steer Amanda's father away from The Butter Cup but he is not to be dissuaded from the meeting so leaving the teens minding the shop and with a decided feeling of unease, I agree to meet him for a Ploughman's at the Pig & Whistle, just outside the village. We stand at the bar, collecting plates of bread, cheese, pickle and ham, plus 2 half pints of lager which we load onto a tray and he gallantly carries to a small, secluded booth. I take my plate, cut a triangle of the rough, brown bread, spread pickle on cheese, cheese on bread and cram it hungrily into my mouth. Across the table he fiddles with cutlery and crockery, picks up his glass, then puts it down again, then just as my morsel of bread and cheese is mid-way twixt plate and lip, he speaks.

"Bolt from the blue."

I raise a metaphorical eyebrow whilst popping the piece of open sandwich into my mouth so I am not obliged to answer.

"I had no idea."

Again, the eyebrow. I chew with relish. I really am very hungry.

"So what's to be done?"

A question. He has paused, expectantly, waiting for a response. I stall for time, whilst trying to gauge his train of thought.

"In respect of what, exactly?"

"The 'situation'."

His fidgety fingers make an 'apostrophe' sign, clearly glad of some occupation. I think of my own current 'situation' and decide I am in no position to comment so I merely nod my head and try and look concerned. I suspect I manage 'constipated.'

Still not touching any of the food on his plate he now launches into a soliloquy worthy of Hamlet at his most self-pitying. It was all his fault. His work kept him away too much. He had taken his wife for granted. She deserved to be treated better. Et al. As soon as he pauses long enough I jump in.

"Amanda seems to be accepting the situation quite well."

"Just like her to put on a brave face. But how's a teenage girl supposed to cope without her mother?"

"Have you spoken to Louise?"

As soon as the words are out I instantly regret them.

"She won't take my calls."

He chokes, starts to cry, tries, and fails, to check his emotions, then his chest begins heaving uncontrollably. I look on in horror, unsure what I'm supposed to do in such a situation. Definitely not eat. I abandon my bread and cheese and proffer paper napkins. Dry-eyed but still heaving, he waves my hand away.

"I'm the last person who should be giving relationship advice but honestly, I think you should just let the dust settle. Don't do anything drastic…"

He cuts in, shaking his head vigorously.

"I'm all right really."

"I didn't mean that. I just meant give the whole situation some space and reassess it in a few weeks."

He nods.

"You're probably right. It's just all been such a shock."

He visibly pulls himself together. It's an effort.

"Would you mind letting Amanda stay on for a bit?"

"Of course."

"I'm not too much use to her right now. And there's the business. I'm supposed to be in Prague the day after tomorrow."

"She'll be fine." I pause. "Sometimes life just doesn't happen the way we want it to."

My mind flashes back to Steve and Bath. I have to shake my head to clear the memory and with an effort I manage half a smile.

"I have to go."

"Of course."

I fish in my bag for some money but he shakes his head.

"I've got this. Thanks for coming." He pauses. "What you said makes sense."

He rises and in an uncharacteristic impulse I move around the table and give him a light hug. Then I hurry out.

Monday, 12th August

The postman arrives, bringing with him an embossed, foolscap, registered envelope from the redoubtable Ms Rowley. Opening it I find a letter of instruction for her to act on my behalf in the matter of Hamilton v Hamilton which I am to sign in duplicate and return one copy. This I do, then set them aside for later when I shall deputise a more than willing Patti as a witness signatory. Hopefully I can return them by registered dispatch first thing tomorrow morning.

Communication with Alex is now almost on a daily basis. He posts pictures and succinct updates on his travels and adventures on a social media site that he shares with Jude and Sarah and which Jude shares with me. For my part I receive rather more formal accounts of his Italian sojourn by email, not unfriendly, just not overly familiar or familial. All in good time, I tell myself. At the very least my son (!) is in regular contact with me and that is a lot more than I hoped for only a few short months ago. More than that, he is in constant contact with his two half-sisters which is even more unbelievable. So much has happened in just a couple of months that sometimes I wake thinking I have dreamed them all, like those anonymous young men who disturbed my slumbers on so many restless nights just before the summer saga kicked off.

Sarah diagnosed with a potentially life-threatening illness, now thankfully undergoing treatment; Michael about to be served with divorce papers and hopefully out of my life forever; Patti pregnant, newly back in Bath with Ross, house-hunting for a home in the country and good local schools; Alex lost and now found, like Milton's Paradise; Jude with her sharp edges filed off courtesy of Mattie; and George with his enviable new pied-à-terre which he has yet to use, though he assures me he plans on so doing any time soon; and a newly mellow relationship with Charles and Diana.

It was all going swimmingly then all of a sudden I find myself drowning.

Part III
"The Childing Autumn"

Sunday, 31st August

It had been a summer of beginning and endings—as Dickens so succinctly wrote 'it was the best of times, it was the worst of times' and with the season's change, today I woke feeling that we are on the cusp of just such a transition. Last night, via social media, Alex announced that he was definitely returning to Oxford to complete his Masters and that he was going to stay with his father for a couple of weeks beforehand, it being the right and proper thing to do.

I would be lying if I said I wasn't disappointed. I had fervently, if feebly, hoped that he might have decided on a face to face visit here before going up but in my heart I knew it was probably too soon. It's a crushing blow nonetheless.

The girls are starting their new school year in 2 weeks' time, and it's been arranged that Sarah will complete her 'A' Levels with a distance learning syllabus that Ms Forbes has drawn up. If all goes well, this will be her last year of school but it's too soon to say, anorexia-wise and study-wise.

6.45pm

I'm in the kitchen with an old Robert Carrier cookbook propped against the wall, attempting to prepare a Beef Wellington for supper. Alex let slip in a mail that it was one of his mother's specialities and a family favourite so I'm having a practice go in the event that I ever have the chance to prepare the fatted calf, or more accurately in this case, the lean cow. The phone rings and with no-one else in the house I sigh loudly and decline to clean off my beefy, floury hands to answer it, letting the answer-phone in the vestibule kick in. My pastry is now flaking where no flakiness is required, my beef fillet is so rare I suspect a competent vet could revive it and I feel I have almost literally bitten off more than I can chew. After some judicious gluing of the pastry cover with egg white and remembering to spread some paté on the bottom to soak up the worst of the haemorrhaging, I cover the resultant mound with a tea towel, prior to sticking it in the oven, hoping that it will look better when it comes out than when it goes in. Just in time. The sound of gravel on the drive outside the window tells me the stable party is returned.

Jude enters the kitchen breezily.

"Message for you on the answer machine. Don't you ever check it? The cops phoned. I think they want to talk to you."

"Are you sure?"

I can't think why.

"Not a hundred percent. They asked to speak to someone called Flora Hambleton."

"They're clearly confused."

"What do you expect? They're bluebottles. Here's the number."

She sticks a Post It note on the window of the microwave.

"I'm going to put my stuff upstairs."

She exits, just as upbeat as she entered.

Sighing at the intrusion, I dial the number on the wall phone.'

"Hello?"

"Is that Ms Hambleton? Ms Flora Hambleton."

"I'm Mrs Fiona Hamilton. Are you sure it's me you want to speak to?"

There's a rustling of papers on the other end of the line, then....

"I beg your pardon. I misread someone's handwriting. My name is Detective Inspector Leila Bhadri and I'm from the Bath and Avon Cold Case Squad. I'm contacting you with reference to the death of Steve Driscoll. We've been tasked with trying to clear up some old open cases and his file has come to our attention."

My knees are buckling and my stomach lurches. I steady myself by leaning my spare hand on the kitchen wall.

"I'm not sure I can help you."

"We, that is my colleague and I, would like to come and talk to you anyway. Just to go over what's known and bring us up to speed. It would really help if we could chat to you. Get your account in person. Would it be convenient for us to come and talk to you sometime? Shall we say next Monday?"

I can't think straight.

"I'm afraid I'll be a bit tied up for the next few days. Family stuff."

The week after, then?"

"I'm not sure."

"Perhaps I should give you a call next week and we can fix a time."

"Em..."

275

"There's also a Mr Hamble, sorry Hamilton, in the file. Would that be your husband?"

"Yes. Well, not exactly. We were separated at the time."

"But you're back together now?"

"Yes, I mean, no. It's complicated."

"I see."

She clearly doesn't.

"Do you know where he can be contacted?"

"I don't have an address. Just a phone number."

"That would be helpful."

I give her Michael's cell number, she thanks me and says she'll be in touch. Then she puts the phone down and after a few seconds I do the same. I look up to see Sarah, out on a precious day release, watching me anxiously.

"Are you okay, mum? You look as white as a sheet."

"Fine, darling."

I smile wanly.

"I'll be back in a moment."

I hurry out of the kitchen, not quite trusting my legs, and head for the study where I collapse into a chair, light a cigarette and try to digest this news. Steve is dead and buried deep inside me. Do I want to dig him up? Not really. That won't bring him back and it won't change the past. This rattling of skeletons seems to me both disrespectful and disturbing. Some drunken idiot, a hit and run, who cares who it was after all this time? Why do people talk about closure when it's the complete opposite? What would that be? Aperture, perhaps? Not for me—I'd rather not open that particular door with all its hideous memories. Concluding that I'm definitely not looking forward to what might come next, I stub out my cigarette, set my face in a mask of what I hope is inscrutable and head back to the kitchen to finish preparing the last supper.

In my absence Jude the Inventive has unwrapped my culinary abortion, fashioned some leaves from the pastry scraps and somehow affixed them to the top, giving it a somewhat more professional look than my amateur attempt. Instructing me to speed-read Carrier's instructions I call out that it needs a beaten egg glaze which Amanda literally whips up before my chastened eyes and Sarah artistically brushes over the pastry. The resulting, creditable representation of the colour illustration is ceremoniously placed in the heated

276

oven. The girls then set about preparing vegetables, Mattie sets to laying the table and I am relieved of my duties.

With this unexpected reprieve, I pour a glass of Nuit St George and light another much-needed cigarette.

45 minutes later, the Beef Wellington, smelling divine, is set triumphantly upon the table, alongside a store-bought quorn pastie for the non-carnivores. I have not revealed the significance behind it, save to explain that my culinary ineptitude had been tried and found wanting. Mattie deftly carves both dishes up into slices, Jude places them on plates and these are passed around the table for everyone to help themselves to vegetables. I note that Sarah has been served a tiny portion, from which she meticulously removes all offending pastry which is as usual surreptitiously passed to an eager Cromwell and Dottie under the table. She also shares half the filling with them but she does manage to eat some, declares it delicious and finishes all her vegetables, including a tiny boiled potato.

I smile inwardly. It may or may not have come up to Alex's mother's standards but if he ever does darken our door, at least I can claim a passable homage. I raise my glass.

"To my kitchen crew, for saving my bacon, or more correctly, my beef fillet!"

Tuesday, 2nd September

It seemed strange at first to be back in the shop, just George and I, as it was for so many years but we soon slide back into an amiable companionableness. Over morning tea I enquire about his plans for the Featherington apartment and he tells me that he hopes to put in a few autumnal weekend stays with more extended visits once spring comes round. He also drops a small bombshell of his own by announcing that he intends spending Christmas with his family in Ireland and that Charles and Diana will also be joining the house party. It appears that what began as a small conspiracy between the pair of us to keep my in-laws occupied during the summer is cementing itself into a firm friendship, something that pleases him and I tell him I'm pleased too. On a less pleasant note, I also fill him in on the phone call from the police and how much I dislike the idea of metaphorically waking the dead for no good reason.

277

"But Ffion, my dear, someone got away with manslaughter and that someone should be brought to justice."

"Will it bring Steve back?"

"Of course not but…"

I cut him off abruptly.

"Then it's a pointless exercise."

He looks at my face and though I try and affect a mask of indifference, he pats my hand, nods and says he'll put the kettle on for more tea.

The cup that cheers. How would we function without it?

Mid-afternoon Patti rings on the shop landline.

"Why have you always got your bloody cell turned off?"

"I'm fine, thank you."

"You probably shouldn't be."

"Why, in particular?"

"Because I had the fuzz on the phone last night. They were ferreting around and asking questions about Steve."

"Such as?"

"Did I know you? Did I know him?"

"What did you say?"

"I asked if the Pope was Catholic?"

"What did they say?"

"They must have thought it was a trick question so they changed tack and quizzed me about what sort of car I drove back then.

"They called me as well. They're from some cold case unit. I told them I wasn't interested in opening up old wounds."

"Keeps them off the streets, I suppose. Oh, wait, maybe not!"

I giggle. Trust Patti to make a joke of it.

"Oh, I've some news."

Her voice almost cracks.

"Apparently I'm not having a baby."

My stomach lurches.

"Oh, Patti, what happened?"

"I had a scan."

She pauses.

"If this was a script, it would read 'pregnant pause.!'"

Bizarrely she is laughing.

278

"I'm not having **a** baby. I'm having two!"

"Twins? Oh my God!"

"I know, right!"

"What does Ross say?"

"Never mind Ross, it's not him carrying this mini litter. I'm terrified."

"I'm sure you'll be fine. Have you got a good Obs & Gy?"

"The best. He's promised me a pain-free C-section at the first hint of a contraction, if not sooner."

"I should think so too at your age."

"Come here and say that!"

We are both now in fits over the phone. When we come up for air, I notice a customer who has just entered and who is looking at me somewhat oddly.

"Shop! Better go. We'll talk later. And congratulations. Really. A double-yolker!"

We laugh again and I ring off, glancing apologetically at the customer.

Thursday, 11th September

A slight hiatus today. On our regular evening visit to the Avon Sarah is looking less than sunny. When pressed on the cause of her mood, she clams up but I learn from Jude later that on her weekly weigh-in the reading indicated she had experienced no weight gain. With a depressing feeling of dèja vu, I inveigle her outside on her own. Walking around the gardens, I dive straight in.

"Remember when I used to read Pollyanna to you and Jude?"

She responds flatly.

"Sort of."

"So you know what the next line is, then. What she would have said."

She doesn't look up.

"You mean about finding something to be glad about?"

"Precisely."

"Which would be what exactly?"

Her aggressive-defensive tone has returned.

"Isn't it obvious? So you haven't put on any more weight in the last 2 weeks but on the plus side, you haven't lost any either. And that's......"

"....something to be glad about. Yeah, yeah. That's what the staff said too. But I'd been trying really hard."

279

"I've seen you. But there's bound to be swings and roundabouts. There's no such thing as a straight line in life. I should know."

She finally looks up and it's obvious she's been crying.

"I s'pose so."

"You'll get there, trust me."

"How do you know?"

"Because you want to, that's why. It's the same with alcoholics. They can only start to recover once they've admitted they have a problem in the first place. And you've already done that."

I pause and look her in the eye.

"You've come a long way in a short time, Sarah. You should be congratulating yourself, not beating yourself up. Just think what you, what we've all been through these past couple of months. And you had an extra burden. You're doing really well. Keep telling yourself that."

The ghost of a smile.

"Thanks, mum."

"Come on. Let's go back inside before they send out a search party."

The trouble with feeding an anorexic, even one in recovery, is that they have an encyclopaedic knowledge of the calorific content of every food item you're ever dreamed of and then some. And even though they're making a conscious effort to improve their eating habits and wean themselves back on to some sort of dietary normality, they still have serious inhibitions which will take a long time to conquer and overcome. So for example, salads are fine so long as they come undressed and on no account must any avocado be included, owing to their high calorie count. Or if they succumb to temptation and dare to consume a chip or two, there is a heavy price to be paid in terms of what else may not pass their lips for the rest of the day. And if, heaven forefend, they are morally obliged to eat a sandwich, it must be a diet loaf sliced very thin, a single slice of bread, no butter and preferably containing only a leaf of lettuce and a slice of cucumber. At the Avon, the staff spend a lot of time trying to push past these self-imposed barriers and the menus are carefully planned accordingly. With Sarah when she's home, we have come to a more family-friendly arrangement whereby she eats the same as us, only less of it and with any sauces or other embellishments surreptitiously scraped off to the best of her ability and fed to Cromwell or Dottie on the sly, such as last week's vegetarian pastie. When presented with something where this is impossible—a portion of buttery, creamy mashed potatoes, say, she reserves a teaspoonful for herself before the dairy produce goes in, then resorts to the chip-style tactic of foregoing any other food in that meal. I'd be lying if I didn't admit it was a struggle and thus it's no real surprise to me that she's not piling on the pounds too fast but I wisely keep my counsel. Baby steps.

9pm.

I am setting a tea tray in the kitchen for tomorrow morning when the phone rings. Assuming it will be Patti to take up where we left off, I snatch up the phone and pre-empt her.

"So tell me more about these two buns in the oven, then? When exactly are they going to be cooked?"

"Mrs Hamilton?"

Oops.

"DI Bhadri here. When we last spoke you requested some time for family matters."

"I remember."

Actually I'd managed to forget. I sober up instantly.

"I was hoping you'd have some time to sit down with myself and my colleague this coming week?"

"I really don't think I'll have the time to travel to Bath."

"You misunderstand. We'll be happy to come to you. It's just for an informal chat, you understand."

"Oh, I see."

I knew that really. I just hoped she'd take the hint.

"Shall we say Tuesday, 10 am? I have your address."

"I'm afraid I'll be at work."

"In the evening, then. Around 6pm?"

I want to say no but she'll just keep on suggesting dates and times. She is the persistent type.

"Very well."

I put the phone down with an impending sense of foreboding. This is going to hurt. A lot.

281

Tuesday, 16th September

I spent the entire day in a miasma of painful memories and sickening flashbacks. I confided in George who naturally offered tea, sympathy and a shoulder to cry on. His intentions were well-meaning but nothing distracted me for long so I kept as busy as humanly possible and took my time going home, in the vain hope that if they arrived and found the house empty they might just turn around and drive back to Bath.

Pulling into the drive at twenty past six I see a white Ford saloon parked to one side of the front porch. In the front, are two people, 1 male, 1 female, who immediately emerge from the vehicle and wait for me to park and do the same.

"Mrs Hamilton?"

The woman smiles and looks me directly in the eye. I nod and look towards her companion.

"We spoke on the phone. I'm DI Bhadri and this is my colleague, DS Cox.

I force my face into what I hope is a credibly apologetic smile.

"I was delayed at work. Please come in."

I open the front door and lead the way towards the drawing room. shepherding the fuzz inside.

"You have a lovely home."

DI Bhadri smiles again, as I motion for them both to sit down.

"Thank you. But I'm sure you haven't come all this way to talk about real estate and home décor."

It was intended as light humour but it came out a bit sharper than I'd intended. DI Bhadri appears not to notice. Smiling somewhat ruefully, she carefully removes a file from her shoulder bag and spreads it out on the coffee table, in front of the fruit bowl.

"We understand this may be painful for you but I assure you it is necessary. Just to give us a better picture of what happened."

"I don't care one way or another, you know."

"Excuse me?"

"I mean after all this time it doesn't much matter who did it. It won't bring Steve back."

"Perhaps not but most people do find that closure helps."

'I'm not most people."

Is that the merest hint of a raised eyebrow from her colleague? She certainly appears not to react as she skims the papers in the file and outlines the facts

"It says here you last spoke to Mr Driscoll on the afternoon of January 19th?"

The words bring Steve into sharp focus but I am determined not to show emotion in front of these two strangers.

"Early evening, really. It was a Sunday and my daughters were with their father. He left the house just before 6pm to go into the office and told me he'd be late home because he was meeting a source in the pub."

"He used that word. 'Source'?"

"Yes. He was promised some information about a Member of Parliament."

"Had he used the source before?"

"I had the impression it was someone he didn't know. When I made some enquiries later, I couldn't find any information to verify the story."

'So it's possible that the meeting was a hoax?"

"Not necessarily. Someone could have heard something and got hold of the wrong end of the stick. Or maybe just wanted to stir up trouble."

She shuffles her papers again.

"And no-one at the pub recalls him coming in with anyone?"

"He never went into the pub, as far as anyone remembered."

"So we can't assume he even met anyone?"

I shake my head.

"The police concluded that it was just a random accident. Steve was in the wrong place at the wrong time. Maybe someone had had too much to drink or just wasn't looking, knocked him down, panicked and drove off."

"And what do you think?"

"I think they were probably right."

"But the source never showed up?"

"Not as far as anyone could ascertain. But maybe he came, saw the commotion, put two and two together and left. It was supposed to be clandestine so maybe he just didn't want to get involved."

"You're sure it was a 'he'?"

"Nope."

DI Bhadri consults her notes again.

"And you were at home that evening?"

"I had no reason to go out."

"Is there anyone who could vouch for your movements?"

I stare at her.

"I suppose not."

"And did you own a car at that time?"

"Same one I have now."

"Which is?"

"A cream Beetle convertible."

She makes a notation in her file. I give her a look of disbelief.

"We have to cover all bases, you understand?"

She smiles but it doesn't quite reach her eyes. I smile back, equally unconvincing. Her colleague steps in to cover the awkward silence.

"It says Mr Driscoll's watch was missing."

"It wasn't with his belongings at the morgue. I suppose it was damaged. Must have fallen off somewhere."

"He wore it on his left wrist?"

I nod. DI Bhadri cuts in.

"But according to the autopsy..."

Her colleague hands her a sheet of paper and she scans it

"......there were no obvious injuries to his lower left arm."

"Maybe someone stole it. It was a Rolex. A present from his father."

"Someone?"

"A bent copper." I look at the two of them. "No offence. Or someone at the morgue."

"Possibly. And can you identify this?"

Her colleague hands me a sheaf of papers."

"That's a print-out of the mailing list of our out of town subscribers."

DI Bhadri nods.

"Well I think that's all we need for now. Thank you for your time, Mrs Hamilton."

"My pleasure."

I make no attempt to keep the sarcasm out of my voice.

They rise to leave.

"We'll be in touch."

"Thank you."

I lead the way back to the front door and let them out. Closing the door behind them, I exhale.

Wednesday, 17th September

Work is again a much-needed distraction. As soon as I arrive I pick up a feather duster and attack the book shelves whilst replaying my conversation from last evening with the filth and suddenly pick up on the questions as to whether Steve's source might have been female. Then I remember Patti telling me that they were also interested in the car she was driving at the time. Maybe she's on their hit list, no pun intended. I pause in the dusting and ponder the absurdity of the implications. If that's the tree they're going to bark up, they might as well give up now. Why can't they just let sleeping lovers lie?

With Jude, Mattie and Amanda all back at school I finally had time for myself and just as I did all those years ago back in Bristol I have been finding solace in riding, slipping off to Oliver Prentiss's place 2 or 3 times a week after work where he sometimes joins me on a gentle hack. Much needed food for the soul and virtual armour against the barrage of abuse I am receiving from Michael via his very expensive firm of solicitors.

- *I'm a neglectful and irresponsible mother, so much so that my elder daughter is now in a mental institution*
- *I'm a frigid wife whose cold indifference caused him to seek comfort in the arms of another woman*
- *I bore a child out of wedlock with whom I am now obsessed with reuniting, potentially alienating and mentally damaging both his children*
- *I have even manipulated his own parents into believing he is an unfit and unfaithful husband as a result of which they are now estranged*
- *I insist on working in menial employment in spite of his financial generosity, thus causing him social embarrassment*
- *I smoke too much and I am a borderline alcoholic both of which make me unfit to have custody of his daughters*
- *I left him for another man with whom I ran away to Bath to cohabit, taking his two daughters with me*
- *I drove him out of the marital home and have denied him access to his possessions*

- *I have denied him access to his daughters*

The list goes on and on, each postal delivery bearing a fresh accusation. Of course all correspondence is directed to Ms Rowley who gives his claims short shrift in vehement and succinct rebuttals.

"It's normal in such cases", she tells me. "It's all part of the parry and thrust of the initial skirmish, an attempt to lessen any settlement and spread the blame. But be in no mistake, Fiona, the fault is all his and I will take him to the financial cleaners."

She assures me I'm doing the right thing, Patti says the same but nonetheless I find it all a bit distasteful, somewhat unsettling and hugely uncomfortable. I can't wait for it all to be over.

Things in the opposite camp are very different, so I infer from Amanda and Jude. Gerald Sinclair is bending over backwards, in true English public school style, to receive a damned good, metaphorical thrashing from Louise. All the blame lay with him, he accepts full responsibility for Louise's perfectly understandable affair owing to his long work absences and his door is always open in hope of a future reconciliation. In the meantime he cannot lavish enough of his worldly goods upon her so she may think more kindly of him in the future.

Is it any wonder I need some me-time on the back of a horse?

Friday, 19th September

An email from Alex informs me he is flat seeking in Oxford. It also says that he intends capitalising on his new-found appreciation for Italian opera with as many visits to Glyndebourne as he can afford, that he has settled on the evolution of crime fiction from Wilkie Collins to the end of the last millennium as the theme for his Master's thesis, that he has taken a part-time job as a waiter in a local brasserie and that he has signed up again for his College's rowing team.

What he doesn't say is anything about his parents, though I know he had planned to visit as soon as he got back, nor is there even the remotest reference to the possibility of him visiting here anytime in the near future. He does, however, make passing reference to Sarah and Jude which makes it clear that he is in regular contact with them both which I take as a positive sign.

In reply, I too make no mention of a potential meeting, fearing rejection, and I wish him good luck in his endeavours to find suitable accommodations. I also tell him, super-casually, that I am in the process of divorcing Michael and that the girls are on board with the decision but then it occurs to me that he probably knows all that and more so I delete the last bit and tell him instead of my having taken up riding again.

I finish by reminding him that I have easy access to all sorts of literature, fiction and non, and that if he is looking for any particular books for his studies, he only has to ask.

I sign off with 'Love Guin'. He hasn't yet committed to giving me a familial title and instead, he has settled on Guinevere, shortened to Guin because apparently I look like the image of Lancelot's lover from a volume of The Once & Future King which he had as a child. I'm fine with that. I also add two lowercase exes.

Monday, 22nd September

I was overdue a meeting with Professor Turner so I have scheduled one for this morning. I have kept him abreast by telephone of our ongoing family situation and he has reciprocated with progress reports on Sarah but like all shrinks he places a lot of importance on eye contact and body language, though of course he never says as much. So like a junior employee on an annual assessment interview I duly present myself at his rooms in the Avon at the witching hour and am ushered in. He rings for tea, shepherds me over to his cosy corner where the armchairs and coffee table are and we sit. I adopt my neutral expression and sit, legs demurely crossed, face tilted at just the right angle and look at him attentively, remembering to lean slightly towards him in what I hope is an open and receptive attitude.

"It's turning decidedly cooler, isn't it?"

The opening weather gambit. A safe move. I nod and move my metaphorical pawn in response.

"Summer's lease hath all too short a stay."

"A quote from the Bard—well, we are at the Avon, after all."

He laughs, appreciating my literary reference. Then he puts on his professional countenance.

"I'm sure you're anxious to hear about Sarah's progress."

He smiles but somehow it doesn't quite reach his eyes.

"I can see she hasn't put on a lot of weight. And she's still counting calories like insomniacs count sheep."

Now he gives a genuine smile.

"I assure you that's perfectly normal. For an anorexic, the switch from a severely restricted food intake to what you might consider a 'normal' diet is an extremely slow process. And progress is rarely a smooth upward curve. It pitches and dips, levels out, backs up, often right back where it started. That's par for the course. And for many, the obsession with the calorific content of foods is something that never leaves them."

"Is this your way of telling me Sarah won't be home for Christmas?"

Again the half-smile.

"She can definitely have a home visit over the festive season but no, she will almost certainly not be ready to leave us by then."

"I rather thought not."

He pauses, as though impeded by a carpet of lexical eggshells.

"The terms 'psychiatrist' and 'psychic' are radically linked, as I'm sure you know. And I often feel I need a deal of the gifts of the latter to properly do my job."

"Like a vet?"

He pauses to consider.

"A good analogy. The difference is their patients can't tell them what's wrong whereas with mine, they sometimes can but often won't."

"And you think that's Sarah's problem?"

He shrugs, noncommittally.

"But surely everything is out in the open now? Michael's infidelities, past and present. The knowledge that she has a half-brother. I understand that's a lot to take in but I thought Sarah was handling it all quite well, working through it?"

"She was. Very open in her counselling sessions, happy to talk through it all and very relieved that it's no longer a skeleton in the family closet."

"I'm sensing a 'but'."

"More of a 'but what?'. There's something else that seems to be bothering her and it's something she won't open up about. If I or the nurses try to probe, we're curtly rebuffed and she clams up."

"And she hasn't dropped any hints?"

288

"I was going to ask you the same thing."

We look at each in silence for a few seconds.

"Do you want me to ask her?"

He shakes his head.

"Let's just play it by ear. Hopefully she'll tell us in her own good time."

"You don't think it's the slow pace of her recovery? I know that's been bothering her."

He pauses again.

"Therapy can be a double-edged sword. On the plus side it can bring some issues into the open and that allows the patient to talk freely in a safe space about things they have kept to themselves and haven't previously dared share with anyone."

"And the minus?"

"The human brain is an exceedingly complex organ. In cases of severe emotional or physical trauma, for example, it will often bury the incident so deep in the psyche, the victim will have no real recollection of the incident. The memory is so painful it's metaphorically been wrapped in cotton wool and tucked away in a secret place and there it can stay hidden for years. And sometimes, the forced introspection of a therapy course can peel back some of that cotton wool covering, revealing little glimpses of the painful memory. If the subject delves deep enough the entire covering can come away, revealing a raw, emotional wound that has never been allowed to heal."

Now I'm very confused.

"But surely Sarah has faced her demons? They're not festering anymore."

"That's certainly what we thought but....my gut instinct tells me there's something else that's gnawing away at her. Some half memory that's been triggered by her sessions, something she may not even fully remember just yet. Something that's just below the surface that is trying to force its way up."

He stops, looks at my stricken countenance and smiles.

"Oftentimes, a child will experience something its mind is not capable of fully comprehending so it goes into defensive mode quite unnecessarily. And when the secret finally comes out in the adult it turns out to be something quite trivial."

"You think that's what's going on with Sarah? It's something from when she was much younger, a molehill she turned into a mountain?"

289

"It's possible. Really, we'll just have to play the waiting game till she's able to bring up that memory and confront it." He smiles and stands up. I expect you'd like to see her now you're here?"

"Yes, please."

He glances at the wall clock.

"She'll be on her morning break. Let's try the library."

He rises and walks towards the door, waiting for me to catch up. As I do so he pats me lightly on the shoulder.

"Slow progress is still progress."

He smiles reassuringly, professionally and I feel slightly less anxious. Only slightly.

Wednesday, 1st October

Since their visit I have heard nothing further from the fuzz. So far, so good. Alex is settled back in Oxford, planning out his as yet untitled thesis.

Michael is proving surprisingly stubborn in the divorce proceedings, such as they are. He is refusing to commit to any terms of reference until his application for access to the house is granted and on the advice of Claire, the orders of Patti and my own instincts, his requests, nay demands, have all been rebuffed. Patti is more convinced than ever that the deeds to the house are still there somewhere and his solicitor's references to 'the retrieval of certain items of no value per se but of import to his professional activities' add fuel to the fire of speculation. He doesn't mention the wine collection downstairs which I find odd but frankly I don't give a damn what he's referring to. I just don't want him back in the house, now or ever. On one of our sessions with Claire while she was still here, Patti quizzed her as to the situation over the 'marital home' and Claire's opinion was that whoever's name is on the deeds as it stands would be irrelevant as any judge would almost certainly grant residence to me and the girls for purposes of continuity, particularly in light of Sarah's situation where any disruption might cause a medical setback. Furthermore she would insist that the house be a pivotal portion of the final settlement. She even went so far as to write to Professor Turner to that effect, referencing Sarah's fragile mental condition, to elicit a written response from him stating that in his professional opinion, her mother, sister and the home she had grown up in these past 10 years were the only anchors in her life right now, the loss of which could trigger a severe relapse. 'Such a relapse', he wrote, 'might have grave consequences.' That last sentence, Claire said, would carry great weight with a judge and I was not to concern myself over the possibility of losing the house. She therefore wrote to Michael's solicitor advising him of the same and enclosing a copy of Professor Turner's letter which was met with a resounding silence.

Although I have not said so to either Claire or Patti, all of this equivocation puzzles me somewhat. Under the circumstances I should have thought that Michael would have wanted the split to be done and dusted as speedily as possible. Louise has instigated corresponding proceedings against Gerald and I assumed that the indecent haste was due to a desire to formalise the new relationship—make an honest woman out of her, if you like. I know that sounds ludicrously Victorian but in many ways Michael's moral code is out of synch with contemporary views. Marriage to him equals respectability and stability and he would not relish the concept of 'living in sin' for long—what might Francis think, for one thing? And whatever it is that's causing him to stall and vacillate, it surely can't be the house per se. I know in his eyes it's a prime piece of real estate but I also know he has old family money being dutifully guarded by a few gnomes in Zurich, not to mention a massive investment portfolio I'd found in his study, and those factors, along with his elevated employment status, would mean he could easily raise more than enough finance to purchase something befitting his rank and requirements without feeling even the slightest pinch. I toy briefly with the idea that he just wants to get his hands on the vintage wine and spirit collection but if that's it, why not just comes out and say so? So if not that stuff or the house per se, what then?

This question niggles away at me somewhere in the back of mind, not enough to lose sleep, just enough to constitute a curiosity but until I can come up with an answer, I keep my counsel.

Saturday, 4th October

7pm

Mattie and Amanda both chose to return to their respective homes after riding this afternoon. Ironic how each in their different ways have ended up as

291

carers at home—Mattie taking charge and being the grown-up when his mother is on one of her frequent benders and Amanda having to give moral support for her poor, bereft dad who is still not handling the separation very well and is apparently a gibbering wreck at the prospect of the impending divorce. The pair flit in and out of Lionsgate but are now firmly established as part of our extended family. This evening, however, it is just Jude and me.

As usual around this time we are in the kitchen where, cookbook in hand, I am trying my hand at a Portuguese potato dish while Jude is doing something Spanish with 2 cod steaks. I also have a bottle of Rioja chilling in the fridge to complete the Iberian theme. I am just putting the lid on the potatoes when Jude turns to me with a slightly embarrassed look on her face. It's obvious there's something on her mind and she doesn't know quite how to put it.

"Spit it out."

She blushes.

"It's about Alex."

"What about him?"

"He says you've never actually invited him to come here."

I am somewhat taken aback and I pause to consider the implications of this statement. It confirms, as I had assumed, that he and Jude are in intimate contact and implies that their conversations are much deeper than the polite exchanges that he and I engage in. I am also somewhat shocked that he thinks I have not issued an invitation to him to visit. Surely that can't be true? Heaven knows, I've thought about him doing just that enough times. Have I really not said as much, even if only indirectly? And even so, surely he must know that nothing would give me greater pleasure than to meet up with him and have him come and stay with us. I choose my words carefully.

"I thought I had, at least in so many words."

As I speak I am desperately trying to recall the exact words I have used in our online exchanges.

"Sarah and I really want to meet him."

"So do I."

She looks me straight in the eye.

"I thought you must."

"I'll call him. Sound him out."

"Okay."

There follows a Pinter-esque pause. I shake my pan of potatoes and assume an air of general busyness whilst secretly waiting for the next instalment. A couple of minutes go by, then Jude once more downs her fish slice and turns to look at me.

"Does dad know about Alex?"

"Why do you ask?"

"You always tell us not to answer a question with a question."

Hoist by my own petard.

"He knows of him, yes. I told you."

"And what about now?"

"What about it?"

I genuinely don't know where this conversation is going.

"Does he know you tracked him down and you're in touch?"

"He knew I was looking. I told you that as well."

"That's not what I asked."

I choose my words extremely carefully.

"I think he thought it was a bit pointless after all this time."

"And does he know you've found him?"

"I don't think so."

Pause.

"What about Alex's father?"

"What about him?"

"Do you think he knows about you?"

"He knew Alex was looking for me and gave his approval."

I'm getting the distinct impression that Jude the Inscrutable actually knows a lot more than she's letting on and that someone's playing word and mind games here.

"It's not really any of my business."

"Of course it is!"

Jude almost shouts. I decide to jump in with both feet.

"What exactly am I missing here?"

"If you bothered to ask, you'd know."

Jude pulls a face, then turns back to her pan of fish. Apparently the conversation is over for now. I am secretly and silently mortified and slightly unnerved. Firstly, can the reason Alex hasn't come to meet up with me, us, be as simple as that he was waiting for an official invite? Or is that perhaps just the excuse he's given to the girls for not coming? I need to tread a bit carefully here. The one thing I've tried to avoid in all our correspondence is to be too 'smothering', to give any impression, however slight, that I was somehow trying to reclaim what was rightfully mine. Because of course he's not. I gave him away.

As for his adoptive parents, that's even more of an eggshell subject for both of us probably. I'd obviously love to hear whatever he wants to share but I don't want to come right out and ask; and from what Jude was hinting out, he presumably doesn't want to come right out and tell me.

After pondering for a moment I decide a casual email would be my preferred medium. I nod to myself imperceptibly and declare the 'papas â la paubre' ready to serve.

Monday, 13th October

1pm

Eating a solitary lunch, apart from Cromwell and Dottie at my feet, the phone rings. Rising to answer it I hear a familiar voice. DS Cox

"Mrs Hamilton? I hope I'm not disturbing you?"

"Not at all. I like cold soup."

"I've interrupted your lunch? Sorry."

"It's fine. What can I do for you?"

"I'm just calling with an update on the case. We think we may have traced the car."

"Oh?"

I try to sound like I give I damn.

"There was a report from Lowestoft about a Golf stolen from outside a block of flats in a suburb, 4 days after the incident with Mr Driscoll. The owner had been away on holiday and came back to find the vehicle missing and the date it disappeared was only guesswork so no-one ever made the connection at the time. But going back through the records we were able to find the VIN number and it seems it resurfaced about 5 years later. It was unclear where it had been during that intervening time but someone spotted it behind some lockups in Clacton and decided to restore it. So when it was roadworthy and

294

the guy applied to re-tax it, it came back into the system. I spoke to him on the phone and he confirmed the vehicle details. I'm pretty sure it's the right car."

"I see. Well thanks for letting me know."

"You seem remarkably uncurious if you don't mind me saying so, Mrs Hamilton."

"Call me Fiona. And yes, I am."

"Surely you'd like to know. The who, how and why, I mean."

"Not really."

"You may feel differently if we can pinpoint the perpetrator."

"Perhaps."

I pause.

"I do understand you're doing your best and doing your job."

"I've been in Cold Case for about 15 months now. I'm really enjoying it. It's very satisfying when you finally put an old open case to bed."

"I can understand that. It's just that in this instance I can't see what difference it will make. Chasing up an old hit and run. Who knows, the driver might not even have realised what he'd done."

"Or she."

"I suppose so. Either way, it won't fix anything."

"A man lost his life, Fiona."

"You don't need to remind me."

My voice suddenly chokes up and I cover the receiver.

"I'm so sorry. I know it's hard, opening up old wounds but I really want to be able to draw a line under it."

He hesitates for just a fraction too long.

"Another file off my desk, if nothing else."

He's adopted a light tone but somehow it doesn't ring true. He probably thinks there's something wrong with me and he's probably right.

"Anyway, I'll leave you to your lunch. I just thought you needed to be kept abreast"

"Thank you, DS Cox."

"Simon."

I put the phone back on the receiver and put my soup into the microwave. As I resume my meagre repast I replay the conversation in my head. It's entirely possible that he's just ticking boxes but something that he said, no,

295

something that he didn't say, has disquieted me. I wonder if he still thinks I somehow had a hand in it and that's why I don't want him digging to deep?

2pm

Lunch over, I load the dogs into the back of the bug for company and set off for Featherington Hall. As per the Master Plan, George is now spending the occasional weekend at his apartment there, with me dropping him off on Friday after work and collecting him at a mutually convenient time on Monday afternoon or early Tuesday morning. He has apparently exchanged pleasantries with some of the other residents and decided to undertake an historical botanical record of the Hall's gardens. Already he's unearthed the original layout and notes on the plantings from old family records in the still extant private library and has also found reference to an even earlier kitchen garden from an adjoining former abbey which had been all but destroyed on the orders of Henry VIII in his Dissolution of the Monasteries. He is now utterly in his element, a horticultural Sherlock Holmes, tracking, tracing, poring over his vast collection of old herbal and culinary treatises, unearthing clues and following leads. Thus it was that he had reserved this morning for a more detailed plod through the available family history and had requested me to only pick him up in the afternoon.

Arriving at the hall and parking the car, I allow Dottie and Cromwell to have a run around to let them also enjoy the sights and smells of the grounds, before putting them back in the car and making my way to the east side of the building and the private entrance to George's apartment. I find him in buoyant mood.

"Ffion. You'll never guess what I found."

He produces a copy of a hand-written monastic treatise which he tells me is part of a book of herbal remedies hand-written in the 12th century by monks at Featherington Abbey and detailing the plants, roots, nuts, berries and barks used in these ancient cures, all of which were either grown in the abbey kitchen garden or gathered from the woods nearby.

I have to confess it is impressive stuff and I can well understand his excitement and enthusiasm. I resolve to tell Patti all about it as it occurs to there's a fascinating documentary somewhere here, though I refrain from mentioning this to George.

On the way home, he pumps me for information on the divorce proceedings, on Sarah's progress and Jude's autumn competition schedule and of course Alex, whom he brings in at the end, like a casual afterthought, even though I know full well it was no such thing. I fill him in on his flat in Jericho and the basis of his thesis, then explain the dilemma of 'to directly invite or not to invite, that is the question'.

George says he takes my point about not wanting to incur rejection, though he opined that he thought that highly unlikely, but equally that he thought I should be less obtuse about my feelings.

"My dear Ffion, you work in a bookshop. What more natural an environment for an English literature student? And your house is large enough to accommodate a visitor and them not feel either intrusive or obtrusive."

"That's as may be but the last thing I want is for him to feel obligated."

"Then leave it open-ended. Extol the virtues of our extensive literary collection and the emptiness of your house and let him know he'd be welcome here anytime, if he feels like a break from the city of dreaming spires."

I ponder this suggestion for a few moments and realise that as usual the wily old fox is spot on. After all, a general invitation can instigate an equally general acceptance with no obligation or commitment whatsoever.

"You're absolutely right. I'll even do it by email so he doesn't feel put on the spot on the phone." Pause. "There's something else I need to sound him out on."

I keep my eyes resolutely on the road ahead, thus avoiding his gaze.

"His adoptive family, by any chance?"

I break off and turn to look at him.

"You must have been a great loss to military intelligence when you left the service."

He says nothing but the corner of his mouth twitches slightly and his eyes twinkle.

Thursday, 16th October

6pm

We are all at the Avon visiting Sarah, 'all' meaning George too. She seems happy enough in herself but Professor Turner seemed so sure that she was

297

holding something back, I keep a weather eye and ear out for clues as to who, where, what, how or why. Meanwhile the other three have made a plan that we will take a drive to a local riverside restaurant and spend the visiting period there. A look of mild panic passes fleetingly across Sarah's face when she is appraised of the itinerary so I put my arm around her and assure her that such places all have vegan and low-calorie menus these days.

The chosen venue is a converted boathouse called Rollocks and as the evening is fairly mild we opt for a table on a wide, covered deck right on the water's edge. George and I plump for steak and chips but the youngsters all agree to eat vegan in solidarity with Sarah, choosing the house special of three-bean paté and salad. And though I note that Sarah mainly eats around the paté, disguising her subterfuge by concealing it under a large lettuce leaf, she is at least eating something and even goes so far as to accept a couple of tiny chips from my plate. Baby steps, yes, but at least we are walking forward.

Later, on the way out, I manage to manoeuvre her to one side and explain to her that Claire and I have both read the metaphorical riot act to her father and told him never to darken our door again. I expect her to be relieved but instead a dark cloud passes over her face, then passes. Perhaps I imagined it?

Tuesday, 21st October

3pm

George is upstairs working on his garden research project and I am alone in the shop, save for a couple of browsing customers who have been in for some time and show no sign of leaving in the foreseeable future. The phone rings, rudely breaking into the silence. I answer it to hear the now familiar voice of DS Cox, AKA Simon.

"Fiona? I just thought I'd update you. I've arranged to poke around that Golf with forensics."

"Surely you don't expect to find anything useful after all this time?"

"Not really but you never know. I'm actually amazed it's still on the road. Those old Golfs were built to last."

"I suppose they must have been."

I try to sound mildly interested.

298

"It's changed hands a couple of times since the re-fit and it's now registered to a Mr Hassan in Eastbourne. He says he gave it to his son to use and he's been out of town for a few days but he's back on Sunday."

He pauses, presumably for a response. I duly oblige.

"That's amazing."

"Isn't it? He says we're welcome to go over it so I'm driving down on Monday morning with a couple of the forensic guys."

"What are you hoping to find?"

"Not much, if I'm honest but you never know. It's more about due diligence, really. I'm really pinning my hopes on re-interviewing the witnesses."

"Well, good luck."

I hope that sounded appropriate, bid him a polite farewell and replace the receiver, feeling somewhat disquieted. I tell myself that it wasn't the car that killed my beloved Steve, it was the driver but all the same I shudder as though someone has walked over his grave, someone not very nice.

To distract myself I wander over to our crime fiction corner and browse the stock, selecting a few volumes that catch my eye and making a few cryptic notes as I go.

Dorothy L Sayers. Ngaio Marsh. Agatha Christie. Josephine Tey, Ruth Rendell. Patricias Cornwell & Highsmith. Vera Caspary. Marjorie Allingham. Why so many female crime writers?

Inspector Lestrade. Inspector Japp. Inspector Parker. Relationship between detectives and police. Peelers. Penny Dreadfuls. Jack the Ripper. Victorian primness v sensationalist reading material.

I make more jottings and resolve to put them together in a more cohesive form when I get home and pass them on to Alex. Done with that, I pick up the phone again and call Patti.

"Wassup, home girl?"

I know she's working on a psychological thriller set in the American deep south but being filmed in south Wales so I let it pass, save to add the words 'Lizzie Borden' to my notes for Alex.

"According to the Fuzz they've tracked down the car that hit Steve."

"Persistent little beggars, aren't they? And what are they hoping to achieve?"

299

"Closing the book on open files, so they say. I'm sure they think it was me."

"That's stupid."

"I don't think they hire them for their intellect."

I pause slightly, then change the subject.

"How are the four of you?"

"I'm about to lose sight of my feet and the bosses insist on sending a car to collect me and drop me off from work."

"A chauffeur. Very nice."

"It is, rather. Poor Ross is quite beside himself and fussing around like an old woman. He's taken to whipping up disgusting concoctions in the blender which I'm supposed to drink morning, noon and night."

"I'm so excited for you. Do you know what you're having yet?"

"Nope. I've ordered my gynae to keep it to himself on pain of death. I'll probably succumb in the end, though."

"It'll make baby shopping much easier."

"I suppose."

She hesitates.

"It might not have been random, you know. It could have been someone who had a grudge against him."

"Like Gregson? The pork butcher. They cleared him, remember? And I did my own research. He'd moved on."

"Someone else, then."

"Does it really matter now? They might even be dead themselves."

"You're right. Listen, I'd better go. The Director and the leading man look like they're about to have a punch up."

"Go and stand between them. They wouldn't dare hit a pregnant lady."

"You haven't met our director."

We laugh and hang up.

11am

I am up to my eyes updating George's quaint Cardex stock control system when the shop door opens and the bell tinkles. I barely look up till the customer approached me and coughs politely. Guiltily I cease my admin work and look up to find not a customer but Gerald Sinclair. Although we've spoken briefly on the phone a few times, mostly concerning lifts and sleepover arrangements for Amanda, we haven't actually met since that time in the pub. I acknowledge his presence, smile politely and greet him whilst simultaneously scrutinising his facial expression for signs of further emotional distress. He certainly looks somewhat hangdog and haggard but I am relieved to see that he seems calm and in control.

"Gerald? How are you?"

"Fine, fine."

Looking at him I wouldn't go quite that far.

"So what brings you here this morning?"

"I wanted to chat to you and I didn't like to come to the house in case Mandy was there…Is there somewhere we can talk. In p*rivate*?"

This last phrase is spoken sotto voce.

"Of course. Follow me."

I come out from behind the desk and lead the way to the back, then up the staircase to the flat, with him following. Once upstairs, I usher him into the small kitchen and indicate that he should sit down at the table.

"Just excuse me for a sec."

I walk next door to the small dining room where George is working on his horticultural research, the dining table covered in various old maps, tomes and botanical prints.

"George?"

He looks up and raises a quizzical eyebrow.

"Amanda's dad has popped in for a quiet chat so I've put him in the kitchen. Would you mind going downstairs to mind the shop for 10 minutes?"

"Not at all, my dear Ffion."

He half-rises.

"You won't forget you promised to drive me over to Featherington Hall this afternoon?"

I smile.

"Of course not. We can leave as soon as I shut up shop."

"Excellent."

He walks off towards the stairs and I return to the kitchen.

"So … what was it you wanted to see me about? Tea?"

I put the kettle on as I speak. He nods.

"Yes please."

He pauses, as if to gather his thoughts, then begins.

"I've agreed with Louise's solicitor that the house will be sold and the proceeds divided equally between Louise and myself."

"That's a big step."

"And difficult. Amanda was 7 when we bought it, so it's really the only home she's ever properly known. I'm on my way now to call in on the estate agent to make the arrangements." Pause. "It's a wrench, I don't mind telling you."

Oh dear. He looks as though he's going to burst into tears again. In lieu of a paper tissue, I proffer a sheet of kitchen roll but he waves it away and takes a deep breath, while I turn away and busy myself with the teapot.

"Thing is, I haven't had the heart to tell Amanda about it yet. And she needs to know before the agent comes around to take photographs and put up a sign outside."

"Of course……and you want me to break it to her."

"Oh no. I think I ought to do that. It's just that I'll have to look for somewhere else to live. I think it's called downsizing."

He gives an embarrassed laugh.

"So I just wanted to forewarn you. It might mean Amanda spending more time with you till I sort something out. And from what I remember house-hunting can take quite some time."

I nod.

"You don't want to rush into it. What sort of place did you have in mind?"

"I thought a newish townhouse might fit the bill. As you know I'm away quite a lot and I need somewhere convenient for the airport and low maintenance."

He doesn't look thrilled at the prospect.

"Very sensible. And please don't worry about Amanda. She's practically part of the family now. No bother at all."

"Thank you. That's a weight off my mind."

I hesitate.

"Do you mind me asking? Hasn't Louise asked for custody?"

He shakes his head.

"We've talked about it and decided it's best that she stays here to finish her 'A's. Then she'll be off to varsity and she'll be able to make up her own mind where she spends her hols."

"That seems like a good plan."

I pour the tea and proffer a cup to him, placing the sugar bowl and milk jug on the table. We both busy ourselves with the English tea ceremony.

"I know it's a cliché but time really is a great healer. It does get better."

"That sounds like it came from the heart."

I nod, as the images of Steve and Alex flash through my mind. I push them away and feign a jollity I don't feel.

"Biscuit? I think George has got some chocolate digestives somewhere."

I push my chair back and rummage in the cupboard, then compose my face and turn round, smiling.

"Bourbons. Even better!"

We both take one and sit there at the tiny table, each lost in thought. Contemplative is the word that springs to mind.

4.55pm

As luck would have it, there are 7 customers in the shop, all happily browsing and in no hurry to leave which means it will be a late drive over to drop George off at his apartment and also I'll be late getting to Fordham where I'd planned a hack with Oliver before it got too dark. I pick up the phone and dial his landline number.

"Oliver? Just to let you know I won't make it in time this afternoon so go on without me."

"No problem. See you next week."

"Shame, though. After the week I've had I was ready for some chill time."

Then I redial, catch Jude on her cell and tell her not to worry if I'm a bit late home and to lift a quiche out of the freezer for supper.

303

That done, I wait for all the stragglers to make their individual selections, check them all out and finally shut up shop at half past five. George and I are soon on our way to Featherington Hall and using the back roads we make good time, even for a Friday. So good in fact, I think I'll carry on to Fordham anyway, just to give the horses a carrot and a pat at least. I message Oliver's cell to let him know and having taken my leave of George I set off.

It's almost 7.15pm and dark by the time I drive into Oliver's yard so he must be back from his ride. I see a couple of lights on downstairs in the house and I just drive around to the stable block at the rear. But even before I get out of the car, I sense that something's not quite right. Skipper, Oliver's Springer spaniel who always accompanies him on hacks, is lying down in the yard, his ears pricked at the sound of the bug. The main yard light is on and I see Dancer rugged up and swaying her head over her door in a fretful state. Captain's stall door, however, is open and empty which means that Oliver must still be out. A couple of possible scenarios present themselves. Maybe the horse went lame and the return journey had to be at a snail's pace; maybe Oliver had to get off and lead him back; and maybe Skipper went ahead though that seems odd. I get out of the bug and immediately hear the sound of hooves clattering on concrete. Approaching the stable block I now see that Captain is in his stall, right at the back, fully tacked up and jittering about in alarm. On closer examination I see that one of the leathers and irons is missing while the other is dangling, not run up and is caught up in the reins.

My stomach lurches. As unlikely as it seems, with Captain so sensible and well-mannered and the back tracks they ride on being pretty quiet, Oliver must have fallen. There's no other explanation for the scene in front of me. Obviously I need to go and look for him but I hesitate, undecided as to whether to go on foot, on horseback or even in the bug. I decide on the middle option, hoping that Captain might retrace his steps, pick up a heavy-duty torch from the tack room, lead the horse out into the yard, mount up using the remaining stirrup and set off going in the reverse direction of Oliver's usual route. On an impulse I call Skipper to come along with us which he readily does.

It's slow-going. The torch is of limited use and we have to tread carefully in the dark. We skirt around the edge of a fallow field, then onto a bridle path which leads to a narrow B road that loops around the back of the village. As we head up the road, Captain bristles slightly, stops and spins round. I turn him, kick him forward and shine the torch left and right, sensing that we must be close.

I almost ride past him but Skipper races ahead and whines. Slowing even more I shine the torch where Skipper is nosing about and can just make out the crumpled form of Oliver lying in a heap at the foot of a hedgerow. One of his legs is splayed at a strange angle and he is motionless. My stomach lurching, I spring down next to him.

"Oliver!"

I call out but there is no reaction. Kneeling down and holding tight to Captain's reins, I use my free hand to try to feel for a pulse. Nothing. Oh Christ. Wait, it's faint but it's there! I pat his arm and call his name again but still he makes no sound or movement. I reach for my cell phone, call 999 and frantically give directions. Then I remove my jacket and put it over Oliver's prostrate form.

It takes about 15 minutes for the paramedics to arrive, blue light flashing incongruously on the side of the rural road. After a lightning-quick assessment, Oliver is transferred onto a backboard, his neck placed in a brace, then onto a gurney which in turn is loaded into the back of the ambulance whereupon he is quickly hooked up to a drip and an electronic monitor. One of the paramedics informs me that his wrist might be broken, he has a head injury, a suspected collapsed lung and they're taking him to the nearest hospital in Woodbridge. I watch all this feeling useless, all the while clutching on to Captain's reins for dear life.

"I'll take these two back and follow you."

"That's just for triage, love. I've already called for an air ambulance for onward transfer to the nearest major hospital."

I feel sick. There's something they're not telling me.

"Can you call me. Let me know."

"Are you a relative?"

"A friend. He's a widower. Lives on his own."

He nods understandingly and takes my number. Then he shuts the rear doors and the ambulance pulls away. I mount up and we slowly retrace our steps, Skipper following reluctantly.

Driving home, I can't stop fixating on it all. I know falling off horses is part of riding horses—it happens. And the older you get, the harder you fall, I suppose. But the idea of serious injury at Oliver's time of life just doesn't bear thinking about.

Jude is waiting up for me at the house.

"There's a piece of quiche in the oven and some salad in the fridge."

"Thanks, sweetheart."

I have no appetite but I don't want to burst her balloon so I pour myself a glass of Pinot Grigio and dutifully sit at the place she's laid. She sits opposite me and as I force down small mouthfuls of food, I relay the events of the evening. She is just as horrified as me and presses me for details which I'm unable to supply.

"Such a nice man."

I nod and smile.

"Very nice."

"You don't mind if I tell Mattie?"

I shake my head and she immediately pulls out her cell phone and dials, walking away as she does so. I use that as a diversion and unobtrusively clear away my unfinished plate so as not to cause offence. Then I put my jacket back on and repair to the patio with my wine and a packet of cigarettes.

It's almost midnight when my phone finally rings.

"Mrs Hamilton? It's Dwayne. The paramedic."

"How is he?"

"He's been airlifted to the spinal unit at Edgbaston."

"That's bad, isn't it?"

"Not necessarily. They'll be able to properly assess him there. Till then we can't say one way or another."

"Hope for the best and plan for the worst. My grandmother used to say that."

"Wise woman. I'll text you the main switchboard number but there's no point in ringing tonight. It'll be too soon."

"I understand. I'll call them tomorrow. Thanks, Dwayne."

His phone clicks off and once again I am left alone with my thoughts.

Saturday, 25th October

9.15am

I am in the shop, mentally weighing up when I can reasonably call the Royal Edgbaston to check on Oliver when the phone rings. I am momentarily nonplussed, convinced it must be someone with news on his condition, then rationality cuts in and I realise no-one involved in his care knows of my existence, much less my work phone number, Dully I pick up the receiver, anticipating an early customer enquiry. Wrong again.

"Feef?"

"Michael, whatever it is you want, I can't talk about it right now."

"Who said I wanted anything? I just thought we should talk."

He sounds very full of himself. I'm assuming he must have got his leg over last night.

"It's not too late, you know."

"I'm sorry, what?"

I almost stumble over my words as I try to work out where this conversation is going.

"For us. It's still not too late. We could call the whole thing off. I could come home. This thing with Louise, it was never meant to go that far. She was just another desperate housewife. I thought it might make you jealous. You know there's never been anyone else for me, Feef. It was always you."

"Geez Michael. It was too late 10 years ago. I should never have left Bath, never moved back in with you. I was half out of my mind for a while and by the time I came to my senses it was too late. And I've no intention of making that mistake again."

"It was that man, wasn't it? That arty-farty hack without a penny to him name. You chose him over me!"

"Piss off, Michael."

I slam the receiver down before he can get another word in and find myself out of breath, heart and adrenaline pumping. I breathe and exhale deeply a few times, then pick up the phone again and dial the number Dwayne gave me. I mentally cross my fingers are the number rings, then find myself repeating my story about Oliver's widowhood and solitary existence before I am finally transferred to a Mr Reddy, Senior Orthopaedic Consultant in the Spinal Unit, who advises me that there is considerable swelling on the base of Oliver's spine, that he has been placed in a medically induced coma to allow time for the swelling to subside, only after which will a full assessment and prognosis be permissible. I thank him politely and am about to replace the receiver when he adds a codicil.

"Mrs Hamilton. Please understand that many patients are referred on an advisory or precautionary basis only. I never jump to conclusions."

His tone is kindly, reassuring.

"Thank you."

I replace the receiver, uncross my fingers and try not to jump to any of my own.

Sunday, 26th October

I rise early, make tea and carry up a cup to Jude. Lying in bed in the early hours I formulated a plan to take care of Dancer and Captain in their owner's absence, mentally designating the three teens as assistants. Somewhat nonplussed by the early arousal, Jude accepts the tea less than graciously. I fill her in on my plan and instruct her to call Mattie and Amanda and tell them to be ready at 7.30am whereupon we will all drive to Fordham. Leaving her to her task and telling her to get ready as quickly as she can, I head downstairs and make up a picnic basket of sandwiches and fruit.

At the stable yard both horses have their heads over their loosebox doors, waiting expectantly for their breakfast which Oliver would normally have given them by now. Dispatching the teens to the feed room I tell them to mix feed for the horses, then muck out the looseboxes while I go over to the house and sort things out there.

Inside, I am greeted enthusiastically by Skipper who must also be hungry so I root around for a tin of food, empty it into his bowl and put him and his food outside. Then I turn off the lights left on last night and pop upstairs. Identifying Oliver's bedroom, I find a small overnight bag, into which I pack toiletries, pyjamas, bathrobe, slippers, a framed photograph of his late wife and his laptop which is lying open on a small desk. I know he will have no use for any of these items for a while but I need to feel useful and it's all I can do for now. I take the travel bag downstairs and stow it in the bug, then join the teens.

With everything now in order, we all troop into the feed room and park ourselves on some hay bales for our picnic brunch. It is decided that I will sort out the morning feeds for the foreseeable future with the teens covering the evening time after school, fitting in grooming and stall cleaning as best we can. Skipper had better come home with us for now. That plan agreed, Skipper settled in the back of the bug and with a last check on the horses, we are ready to leave when my cell phone rings, reading 'unknown number'. I answer it and a male voice identifies himself as PC Wharburton.

"I found your number on an item of lost property and I was hoping you could identify the owner."

He then explains that the item in question is a cell phone which was handed in by a member of the public, having been found on the side of the B147, just south of the village and that there was a missed call and an SMS from my number. I explained the circumstances briefly, we agree that the cell had most probably been dropped in the fall and he asks if I could come and give him a brief statement on what I saw that evening, to which I readily agree.

10 minutes later and we are at the station and I am signing my name to a short statement detailing what I saw when I arrived on the accident scene. PC Wharburton, a young man who grew up in the village, knows Oliver slightly and promises to keep a weather eye on the house while he is in hospital, for which I thank him. He also says he'll take a look around where the phone was dropped to see if anything else might have been lost. From our side I advise him that the 4 of us will be looking after the horses daily and that the dog is coming home with us.

That done, it being Sunday, we set off for the Avon where it's a case of 'good news, bad news'. The good news is that Sarah has now put on another half a kilo since admittance which takes her to her next target marker weight gain. The bad news is that, according to Nurse Dakin, she's not happy about it.

"I thought I'd pre-empt her and let you know. Forewarned is forearmed."

"I thought she'd be thrilled. That a real milestone."

"Yes and no. You have to understand that on a rational level these girls know they have to put on weight and learn to eat what we think of as a regular diet. But on their irrational, anorexic side, they're fighting an inner demon the whole time, the one that sits on their shoulder and tells them that by gaining weight they're losing control of their bodies again. Eating is greed and weight gain is gluttony. Deep down, they want to go back to the way they were and every day is a battle against that desire."

I sigh deeply.

"And I thought she was doing so well."

"She is! She's a very strong young woman and she's doing her utmost to overcome her illness but it's taking every ounce of willpower and resolve she can muster."

"Which means that she's still a long way from acceptance?"

"She's not there yet but it's still early days. And right now, half a kilo seems almost gross."

"So I shouldn't say anything?"

"Not unless she brings it up. And if she does, just play it down. Tell her that's really positive but don't make a big thing of it."

"Thanks for the heads up."

She smiles and puts an arm around my shoulder.

"It's a long war, not a short battle. But try not to worry—I've seen dozens of cases, some successful, some recidivist and I've got a good feeling about Sarah."

As predicted, Sarah imparts her news more or less as a throwaway line. Jude's face lights up and she almost opens her mouth to say something but I catch her eye and surreptitiously shake my head. She twigs straightaway.

"We've got news too. Remember I told you about Oliver, the man who sold Mattie his horsebox?"

Sarah nods.

"He fell off his horse last night. Must have been spooked by something. And now he's in hospital and we'll have to look after the horses till he's out. We've got his dog in the back of the car. Do you want to see him?"

Sarah nods and we all troop out to the car park to see Skipper. On the way I bum a plastic bowl from the kitchen and fill it from a standpipe to give him a drink. That done, it's decided to take him for a walk along the river bank. Sarah fishes in the glove compartment, knowing there's always a spare lead for Cromwell or Dottie in there and deftly clips it onto Skipper's collar.

"I miss the dogs. Do you think the three'll get on?"

"Tough if they don't. But Cromwell's pretty sociable on his walks and Dottie's long past her fighting peak. I'm sure they'll be fine."

And without another word exchanged on the subject of weight gain, we all exit the Avon grounds and head for the river.

Wednesday, 30th October

As early as decently possible I phone Edgbaston and enquire about Oliver. I am told that the swelling on his spine is responding to treatment and that further x-rays will be carried out on Friday. All being well, he will be brought out of the coma and fully assessed then. I thank them for the update, tell them I will call again on Friday afternoon for further news and replace the receiver. Before leaving the house I receive a call from Patti.

"I'm officially off work from Friday. Oh, and my gynae has booked me in for a C-Section on December 28th. Put it in your diary and please, please come and hold Ross's hand. He's panicking about it already."

"Wouldn't miss it for the world. That's quite a Christmas present you're getting."

"Don't I know it! I know it's insane at my age but honestly, Fee, I can't wait."

"I'm thrilled for you both."

I fill her in on the Oliver situation, and Sarah's big milestone, then remember another bit of news I have to share.

"By the way, you'll never guess who phoned last week?"

She doesn't need to be told.

"Toerag. What did he want."

"To come back."

"Jesus Christ. I hope you told him to eff off."

"With himself!"

"I wonder if that woman knows?"

"Shouldn't think so for one minute. He was always good at keeping things to himself."

"That's putting it mildly."

"What about the husband? How's he taking it all?"

"Still a bit shell-shocked but trying to move on. Listen, I've got to go. I have to go over to Fordham and sort out the animals, then collect George."

"And I'd better get to work. Don't forget. The 28th."

"I won't."

"Oh, and I think we've found a house. I'll email you a link to the listing. If all goes well, we could be in by the end of November!"

"Moving in your condition? You're completely barking, you know that."

"Probably."

She laughs and cuts the connection.

The dogs having palled up, I load them all into the bug, then head off to Oliver's place where they run riot in the garden and I feed Captain and Dancer and clean out their stables. I noticed a pint of milk on the front doorstep so I take that in and scribble a note for the milkman cancelling the order till further notice. I also pick up the post and put it on the hall table, along with the morning paper. That done, I head off to Featherington Hall, reversing my route on Friday evening. Only a couple of days ago but it seems like an eon.

On the way back George advises me that he's pulling out the big guns, planning to carry out some further research at the Bodleian. I ask whether he'd like me to drive him but he says he'll be happy with the bus and train. Only then does it occur to me that subconsciously I may have been seeking an excuse to take a trip to Oxford and possibly engineer a meeting with Alex so perhaps it's better if George does use public transport.

No point in trying to force the issue, Fiona—you'll meet Alex in his own good time.

"I'll probably need to make several trips so I wouldn't want to put you out. Of course, it will mean leaving you single-handed in the shop."

I smile. A mad rush in the shop would be even rarer than some of George's incanabula, though we do have our moments when we've got our pre-Christmas clearance sale on.

"I'll cope."

"I may even stay over for a night occasionally. My old Master is long gone but the current incumbent was a contemporary of mine and I have an open invitation."

"You're getting to be quite the gadabout, George Fitzsimmons."

"Time's winged chariot, dear Ffion. So much left to do and so little time to do it. I've been festering far too long in my little bolthole. It's time I came out into the sunlight."

312

I glance sideways at him and he looks content; no, that's not it—he looks happy. It was a propitious day when the Featherington Hall catalogue dropped through the letterbox.

"We had a Tenant's Association meeting on Saturday, you see, and I proposed a project to try and restore the gardens to their original state."

"And?"

"The motion was passed unanimously. I explained that the current layout is largely as it was but that many of the plantings have been changed. Also the vegetable garden has fallen into disuse so my idea is to track down as many of the plant and vegetable species as I can, along with their precise locations, and persuade them to grow again, precisely as first envisaged. Oh, and to reincarnate the abbey herbal garden."

"That sounds ambitious."

"The opposite of which is aimless."

He admonishes me mildly with a joshing, old-fashioned look.

I smile.

A short silence.

"Young Alex is also at Balliol, isn't he? Would you like me to look him up?"

His tone is casual but I am sure he has given this a lot of thought.

I shake my head.

"I don't think that's a good idea."

"Too soon?"

I shake my head.

"Far too late, really." I glance sideways at him. "And that's why it has to come from him."

"Understood. Still, should the occasion arise…"

He leaves the question hanging.

"Before I forget, I'm going to need a few days off myself in December. Patti's got a due date for her C-Section and I've promised to be there."

"Quite right, too."

He pauses.

"I have rather a soft spot for that young woman. She may be a little eccentric in her habits but there's a good head on her shoulders."

"She's the best."

We drive on in companionable silence, me wondering when exactly Alex might suggest a face to face meeting, George no doubt relishing the idea of all the Bodleian resources for his restoration project at his disposal in the near future.

4pm

I am in the study composing an email to Alex, telling him all about George's Bodleian project and desperately trying not to make it sound like a fat hint, yet hoping equally as desperately that he will take it as such, when I am surprised by a delegation. Jude, Mattie and Amanda tap on the door and enter as a threesome, a sort of Reservoir Dogs pastiche in school uniform. I look up with raised eyebrows, then Jude pipes up.

"We've been thinking...."

She stops and I am left none the wiser. Mattie takes up the tale.

"Thing is, Mrs H. we were talking about the Oliver thing over lunch and if he's going to be in hospital for a while we thought it'd make more sense to bring his horses to the stables in the village. Save all that driving back and forth."

I ponder this for a few seconds. It certainly makes sense and even though I love being behind the wheel of the bug, I seem to have spending a lot of time driving recently.

"Are there any spare stalls there?"

"A big double one has just opened up. That's what made us think of it."

"And have you spoken to Bethany?"

She owns the local yard.

"She says it's fine, so long as you're okay."

Jude pauses.

"It'll mean two more liveries on the bill. But it's a bit cheaper because they're sharing."

I do a quick mental calculation.

"I'd say it was a justified expense. It'll save time and petrol money and be way more convenient."

"So is it okay if we go and box them over now?"

I nod.

"Do you want me to come with you?"

"We'll be fine."

"Okay. Drive carefully."

I am rewarded by a withering look from all three. I hear them heading off upstairs, presumably to change and I continue my email.

'Hey, Alex, how goes the research? I've been setting aside a few books in the shop that I think you might find helpful.'

I deliberately don't offer to post them. I just leave that hanging and continue.

'I expect Jude has filled you in on Oliver's accident? She and her friends have decided that it would make more sense to stable his horses nearby in the meantime so they're going over there now to collect them. Actually I don't even know why I'm telling you that because you probably already know!

The other news is that George has undertaken a huge restoration project of the gardens at Featherington Hall and he'll be making a few trips to Oxford to the Bodleian for research purposes. Who knows, you might even bump into him! I'll have to send you a couple of pictures so you'll know him if you see him. Otherwise he'll just blend right in as a stray dog!

Oh and I hope I don't have to tell you there's an open invitation if you ever want to come and spend a few days. Lionsgate was built on generous Georgian gentry lines so there's heaps of space.

Let me know about the books.

Love

Guin'

There. Now the ball's in his court about the books, the cat's out of the bag re George's impending visits to Oxford and I've baited my visiting hook in the hope that he'll bite.

I wonder if English is so full of metaphors and idioms because as a race we are so reticent and reluctant to come right out and say what we mean, or did it happen the other way round?

Friday, 1st November

3pm

With immense difficulty I have resisted the urge to call Edgbaston any sooner but hopefully they will have some news by now. I tentatively dial the

315

number and ask for Mr Reddy. He advises me that the swelling around the spinal cord had gone down sufficiently to bring Oliver around and to do an MRI scan.

"The scan confirms severe trauma to the 1st and 2nd cervical vertebrae, 3rd and 4th in the coccygeal. Nerve testing on Mr Prentiss was inconclusive which is not unusual at an early stage in such cases. So it's still just a question of 'wait and see' but he is alert and talking."

"When can I come and see him?"

"You can pop in anytime on Sunday. He's still in ICU so there are no formal visiting hours. I'm sure he'll be happy to see you. Just remember, he's on strong medication and he might tire very quickly."

"Thank you."

I put the phone down and tell myself that no news is good news. I just wish I could believe it. I set that thought aside and prepare to drive George to his apartment for the weekend.

Saturday, 2nd November

7am

I am surprised by the phone ringing early on a Saturday morning and my first thought is bad news, either about Oliver or Sarah. As I swiftly cross the kitchen to answer it, my second thought is Michael. Either way, it can't be good.

In fact it's neither. It's DS Cox on the line asking if he can come and see me today as he has what he refers to as 'some new evidence.' I explain that I will be working in the shop but he is welcome to call in so long as he understands that customers come first. I also decide to say what's on my mind.

"It wasn't me, you know, and if you still think that, you're either barking up the wrong tree or barking mad."

He makes a noise that could be him clearing his throat or possibly him suppressing an oath—hard to tell.

"We have to consider all possibilities, Mrs Hamilton. I'm sure you understand that. And I really do need to speak to you."

"You already are."

316

Again an indecipherable noise. I'm sure he finds me very exasperating but so do I, him.

"I'd like to share some new information with you and I'd prefer to do it in person if it's not inconvenient."

"As I told you, I'll be working but you're welcome to pop in. We have an excellent crime section, fiction and reference."

He catches the smile in my voice and rewards me with a small laugh.

"Shall we say around 10am?"

"That'll be fine. We're just off the High Street in Baker's Lane. Drive slowly or you'll miss us."

Again, a small laugh.

"I do have sat nav, you know."

"I'm not sure our little shop'll show up."

"One way to find out! Ten o'clock then."

He hangs up and I prepare breakfast for the four of us.

10am

They must teach punctuality in police college because at 10am on the dot the shop door opens, the bell tinkles and in walks DS Cox, casually dressed in jeans, sweatshirt and leather bomber jacket.

"Bang on time. Would you like some tea?"

He nods and I beckon him to follow me upstairs, calling out to a couple of customers to tell them where I'll be if they need me. They scarcely look up from their serial browsing.

While we wait for the kettle to boil I gesture for the DS to sit down.

"Dress down Saturday?"

He smiles.

"Actually I'm off duty."

I raise an eyebrow.

"DI Bhadri decided to shelve the case for the foreseeable future. She's not convinced we'll ever find the culprit and in truth we do have a huge backlog of unsolved cases to wade through."

"And yet here you are."

He nods.

317

"So I am. Actually I volunteered to try and wrap it up on my own and my boss agreed, on the proviso that it didn't eat into my other case load."

"So you're on your own time? Impressive."

He glances at his feet for a second.

"You were quite right about you're having been a person of interest. In cases like these it's usually someone well known to the victim and close family members are always at the top of the interview list."

"Present perfect?"

He looks non-plussed.

"Having been'. Which implies I was but no longer am."

"That's correct."

"So why have I been crossed off the suspect list, might I ask?"

His eyes light up.

"That's the thing. Our tech guys went over it with a fine tooth comb and they could see that there'd been a dent on the passenger-side rear fender which was straightened out. "

I look and nod.

All this time I have been leaning against one of the kitchen units, looking over DS Cox's shoulder but all of a sudden my knees buckle slightly and I move to sit down before he notices. Pictures of Steve flash in front of my eyes and it's all I can do not to cry.

'Get a grip, Fiona. You are not going to break down in front of this man whom you hardly know.'

"My instincts tells me there's more to the whole incident."

"Accident."

"Possibly."

He sounds far from convinced. To my mind he's blowing it out of all proportion but I keep my counsel.

Sunday, 3rd November

9am

I leave the house early, determined to make Edgbaston by 9am. The morning is foggy and I have to take it slowly but I've always enjoyed driving and I like being out on the open road. Once I hit the southern suburbs of Birmingham I find Edgbaston Royal Infirmary is well signposted and I arrive at half past nine. I follow the signs to the spinal unit, park and enter through a small side door. Once inside I find my way to ICU without difficulty and present myself to a nursing sister at her station. I explain who I am and who I am here to visit and that I was given permission by Mr Reddy. She rises and gestures for me to follow her through the glass door into ICU proper.

"Mr Prentiss is still on strong medication and he is in a spinal brace to restrict his movement. But he is awake and talking. There he is."

The unit is more like a computer lab than a hospital wards. Each of the 4, curtained-off beds are connected to a battery of electronic equipment, all with LED monitors which hum and beep rhythmically and softly. The sister draws back part of a curtain around one of the beds where Oliver is prone and protected by a full-length brace. He looks up as we enter and manages a smile. I notice that his skin is almost alabaster white, where once he had a weathered, country complexion and he has a few cuts and bruises, some covered with tiny strip plasters others left exposed.

"Fiona. You're a sight for sore eyes."

His timbre is low but his smile is genuine.

"I'll leave you two alone. No more than 10 minutes please."

The sister turns retreats, closing the curtains behind her, bar a small gap.

"How are you feeling?"

"Hard to tell. They've got me on morphine, so I'm told."

"It must be hard for a workaholic like you to lie still."

"Torture. I told Mr Reddy when he came around last night that I'd no intention of staying here a day longer than necessary."

"That sounds like the old Oliver."

I fill him in on Skipper and the horses and he nods gratefully.

Keep a track of anything you spend and I'll be sure to reimburse you once I'm up and about."

319

"I wouldn't hear of it. You're not to worry about anything back at the house. I spoke to a PC Wharburton at the local nick and he's promised to keep an eye on the place and I'll pop in occasionally just to tidy round."

I hold up the holdall.

"I've brought a few of your things for when you're more mobile"

I cross my fingers as I say this. I'm determined to stay positive but at the same time I don't want to tempt fate. I pull out the picture of him and his wife and prop it on the bedside locker, placing the bag inside.

"Wonderful. There are a few people I ought to let know I'm here. Tradespeople, mostly."

"What about your son? Do you want me to contact him?"

His face clouds over a little.

"We largely go our separate ways. He's very busy."

Oliver has only mentioned him a couple of times but I gather he's a vet in a busy practice in Adelaide.

"I'll call him myself. Just to let him know where I am."

I nod.

"Can I bring you anything?"

"Something to read would be nice."

"Now that I can definitely manage."

We both smile.

"Glad to see you're keeping my patient cheerful."

I swing around and see a rotund, pleasant-looking Asian man standing by the drawn curtain.

"That was the idea. Do you want me to leave?"

"No, no. I'm just here to make a quick round check."

I'm Mr Reddy. Ish. We spoke on the phone."

He walks over to the bank of monitors and gives them a practised eye, then he turns his attention to Oliver, rolling up the blanket at the bottom of the bed to expose his feet.

"Have you been practising moving your toes like I asked."

"I certainly have. Want to see?"

"I do. Start with your right foot and try and wiggle each toe, one by one."

In his prone position, Oliver can't see his own toes but I am transfixed. Mr Reddy, too, is watching closely. Try as I might, I can detect no movement.

"Very good. Now the left."

Again I can see the concentration and effort on Oliver's face but it doesn't seem to be translating into movement.

"Excellent. Keep at it."

Mr Reddy beams and rolls the blankets down again.

"I'll pop in again this evening, Oliver. Mrs Hamilton, I'll wait for you outside."

"I think that's a hint for me to go. I'll sort you out some reading material and pop back again tomorrow while the shop's closed."

"You don't have to…."

"I want to."

I squeeze his hand, bend down and give him a light peck on his cheek.

"Bye bye for now."

He waves the fingers of his right hand at me and I leave. Outside the unit, Mr Reddy is waiting.

"His toes didn't move. He's paralysed, isn't he?"

Mr Reddy smiles indulgently at me.

"Rome wasn't built in a day, as they say. The resultant inflammation from a fall such as he had can take weeks to subside enough for the nerves to regain function. You have to give it time. And in the meantime he needs to work the muscle memory."

I am relieved at his words and his easy manner. I had thought the worst watching Oliver strain and fail to move his toes even a little but this amiable surgeon's casual optimism is infectious and reassuring.

"I thought…"

Again the smile.

"You know what thought did! Take a look at this."

He walks over to a wall where several images, similar to x-rays, are hung up and backlit. He points.

"This is his MRI of his lumbar vertebrae and I can see no obvious signs of a break in the spinal cord. Same thing here."

He points to another picture.

"This is the coccygeal region and again, no clear sign of severance, though there is still considerable swelling. Now, it's possible that that inflammation might be hiding a problem but I prefer to wait till I know for sure before leaping to a premature diagnosis and I suggest you do the same."

He pats me on the back in a kindly fashion.

321

"We're one of the best units in the country, Mrs Hamilton. Mr Prentiss is lucky he lived so close and also that he was moved here so fast. I gather we have you to thank for that?"

"All I did was call for an ambulance."

"You found him timeously and that can be crucial in such cases. Now, off you go and enjoy the rest of your Sunday. I'm hoping to get in a round of golf if that wretched fog clears up."

I bid him farewell and leave the building and it's only when I get to the car and go to take my keys out of my bag that I realise my fingers have been crossed for the past 5 minutes. And as I glance at the VW logo, that and Mr Reddy's reference to a round of golf, bring Steve's cold case file back into sharp focus. Once again someone is walking across my grave.

Monday, 4th November

True to his word George decided to take himself off to Oxford this morning, travelling up on the early train and phoning me just before lunch to advise me he had arrived safely, was ensconced in the comfortable lodgings of the incumbent Master of Balliol and that he intended to remain there till Saturday. As ever, he is hugely apologetic for having left me alone but I assure him that both myself and the shop will be fine. This is quite true but I have to admit I am happy that Oliver's horses have been moved, thus relieving me of the added burden of daily travel to attend to their care.

Tuesday, 5th November

I'm up early in the November dark, once again setting off for Edgbaston. On hearing Oliver's request for reading material Mattie offered up his e-book reader. On seeing my blank look he explained that you could load whole books on it to read. I was about to say I had access to a whole shopful of them but anticipating my stating of the obvious, Mattie explained as if to a stubborn child that the device could store many volumes of compressed files. He also made the cogent argument that it would be much easier to manipulate manually in Oliver's prone position and given his limited movement. So last night he helped me select a few titles I thought he'd enjoy which we uploaded (get me!) and this is now tucked into my handbag, along with a mains charger.

On arrival at the unit I am pleasantly surprised to learn that Oliver is now out of intensive care and is in a private ward. I am led to the door by a male nurse who introduces himself as Dev. He taps lightly on the door and enters. Oliver is no longer completely prone, though he is still restrained with a surgical collar and chest brace. Is it my imagination or my wishful thinking that a little colour appears to have returned to his face? I approach the bed, calling out a greeting and Dev discreetly backs out, calling out a 'Buzz if you need me, Ollie boy!' as he does so.

"Thank you, Dev."

His voice, in response, is definitely stronger than yesterday, displaying more of its old timbre. As I approach the bed he presses a button on a switch lying next to him and his electric bed moves gently up a little so that when I take a seat next to him we can look each other in the eye.

After giving him a perfunctory peck on the cheek and a suitably upbeat greeting, I bring Oliver up to speed on his menagerie as well as filling him in on the family situation and George's peregrinations, the trivial type of chatter we have so often engaged in on our hacks out, all the while keeping my back resolutely turned away from his immobile lower limbs. He listens attentively, chipping in with the odd comment or question and tells me in his turn that he has spoken to his son and told him not to be concerned and not for a single moment to consider dropping everything to be at his side.

"I nearly forgot. I brought you this."

I reach into my bag and retrieve the portable library, holding up the charger and placing it in the bedside locker.

"And that's what, exactly?"

"An electronic book store."

I switch it on as instructed by Mattie and demonstrate how to access the menu.

"I've loaded some Dick Francis and John Grishams; also a couple of volumes on military history that you might enjoy; and some PG Wodehouse for light entertainment. Mattie says to let him know if there's any others your specially need and he'll put them in for you. Oh, and he put these on too."

I show him the photo storage file where there are some pictures of Skipper and our dogs in the garden and a couple of his 2 horses looking over the doors in their new, temporary looseboxes.

"Thank you so much. For everything."

"It's really no bother. I brought you these as well."

I delve into a carrier bag and pull out a bar of chocolate, a small tin of toffees, the obligatory bunch of grapes and a copy of The Times, along with a pen.

"For the crossword."

"You know me too well."

He is shaking his head and smiling as the door opens and Dev walks in with his box of diagnostic tricks.

"Time for your vitals, Ollie boy."

"I'll leave you to it. Anything you need, call me. Which reminds me."

Now I pull out his mobile which I retrieved from the cop shop.

"I'll pop in as often as I can."

He raises his hand in farewell as Dev takes my place on the chair and begins to check his blood pressure. I leave them to it and walk away, once again crossing my fingers for a happy ending.

Wednesday, 13th November

Today began with another bombshell communication from Michael, or more correctly, from his solicitor. It was in my inbox in the form of an email attachment from Claire. I'm up to speed with those now, too—needs must when the devil rides, so the saying goes - and the devil was definitely having the ride of his life. I opened the attachment and read.

'My client has professed himself to be emotionally and nostalgically attached to the property known as 'Lionsgate'. In view of this deep attachment he is generously offering to pay for a suitable property of an equivalent value of Mrs Hamilton's own choosing. Acceptance of this new property would be on condition that Mrs Hamilton would henceforth cede any further claim on the aforementioned Lionsgate.

This exchange would be separate from, and not related to, any additional apportioning of goods and chattel and is to be effected as soon as is reasonably possible.

Please submit this proposition to your client soonest and revert with her decision. Her co-operation in this matter will be regarded in a most favourable light in terms of final and speedy settlement'

"What the hell, Michael!"

There's no-one around to hear me, alone in the study at this early hour but the ejaculation is involuntary and heartfelt.

Accompanying the attachment is a short message from Claire

'Hi Fiona—FYI! It's outrageous, of course. You and your children have lived in the property for over a decade and as a mother you naturally have far more than mere residence invested in what is your home in every nuance of the word. That would apply equally to your two daughters, for whom it is effectively the only home they have ever truly known. I'll write a strongly worded letter to Mr Hamilton's solicitor to that effect. I just need your emailed rejection of the offer for legal reasons.

He's a piece of work, that husband of yours. I get the feeling he is using the house to make a point that you need to suffer somehow when it should be the other way around and I shall tell his solicitor so in no uncertain terms! Regards. Claire.'

I type a quick response, advising her that the offer of an alternative property is rejected absolutely, not least because it would certainly distress both the girls and Sarah is no state for any further emotional upheaval right now.

That done, I light my first cigarette of the day, my chemical crutch of choice.

I am about to set about my duties when the computer beeps to advise me of another incoming mail. It's from Alex.

'Hey, Guin. I read your mail and I'll keep a look out for the redoubtable George around college. Don't forget to send me some mug shots.

This next one's a bit delicate so please don't say anything to Jude and Sarah. They've been dropping fat hints about me coming to visit and believe me, I really do want to meet you all but I don't think this is the right time. The truth is I've been putting it off because of the split between you and your husband. I'm pretty sure I factor in there somewhere so I'm deliberately keeping a discreet distance.

I hope you understand.

Love

Alex'

And there it is. Somehow I knew it wasn't for want of a formal invite—he doesn't seem the type. Just another deprivation for which I have Michael to thank. He's partly right of course—his presence on earth was always a thorn in Michael's side and my desire to find him went down like the proverbial lead balloon. That said, it's scarcely any of his business anymore. And suddenly a thought strikes me—maybe that's what's behind Michael's obsession with the house. It's not an emotional attachment at all, just that same Soames Forsythian love of property and somewhere in the devious depths of his mind he probably thinks that if I'm granted ownership in the split, somehow, somewhere, sometime, Alex might end up as a beneficiary. That explains a lot. It also hardens my resolve to stay put.

Monday, 18th November

The weather has been grey, drizzly and overcast for days which dovetails with my gloomy mood precisely. Sarah's improvement has plateaued out which Professor Turner has now definitely attributed to something in the past she's either unwilling or unable to share. Michael is digging his heels in about the house but so am I and I have letters from Professor Turner to back up my defence. Claire assures me it is only a matter of time before he's forced to capitulate which can't happen soon enough as I am finding the entire process enervating and mentally exhausting. Happily Jude seems to be taking it all in her stride, Amanda too, and Mattie is seemingly imperturbable. George is positively thriving, back in the city of dreaming spires, popping back occasionally to pick up a change of clothes and check in at the shop.

And now I'm on my way to Edgbaston to visit Oliver, knowing full well that there has been no change in his condition since he left ICU.

I find him deep in conversation with Mr Reddy and they both look up as I enter, Mr Reddy with a face both bland and amiable simultaneously and George looking somewhat perturbed. Mr Reddy turns to me as I enter.

"Welcome, Mrs Hamilton. Our friend here has some good news to share."

Oliver's face looks as though the news is anything but.

"I'm being discharged."

His voice is flat, confused. My mind is racing.

"Already?"

"As I've been explaining to Oliver, the purpose of hospitalisation is for any necessary surgical procedures and stabilisation, not for recovery and rehabilitation. Mr Prentiss is now fully stable and further bed rest would hinder, not help. The best thing now is for him to either return home or if that is not practical to enter a care facility so that he can begin the process of physiotherapy and recovery. The former will assist the latter but of course, only time will tell the extent of his recovery."

This sounds to me like a gentle let-down but I try not to show it in my face. Mr Reddy smiles reassuringly.

"Only 1% of spinal patients leave hospital fully recovered. Further progress can take 6 months to a year, though a complete recovery cannot be guaranteed."

My stomach lurches. He's saying Oliver could end up confined to a wheelchair. He catches the look and points to an iPad on Oliver's lap which he swings around to show me. It is from a Swiss website.

"I advised Mr Prentiss to read up for himself. This research team carried out extensive studies on patients with acute traumatic injuries to the spinal cord and compared them with healthy patients over a 2 year time period, measuring loss of myelin—that's the insulation around nerve cells—as well as accumulation of iron in the brain and spinal cord tissue. That gives an indication of levels of inflammation and degeneration."

He points to the text on the screen.

"What they found is very relevant in Mr Prentiss's case."

He reads aloud.

"....'It then emerged that there was a direct link between the recovery levels of patients after two years and the extent of neurodegenerative change within the first six months after injury. The smaller the overall loss of nerve tissue across the neuroaxis at the beginning, the better the patients' long-term clinical recovery'. Meaning patients such as Oliver here who showed very little nerve tissue loss in the initial stages stand a very good chance of complete or significant recovery, providing they receive sufficient and effective physiotherapy and steroidal treatments."

Oliver still looks less than fully convinced.

"Do you think I could speak to Mrs Hamilton alone? There are a few things I need to discuss."

"Of course. Someone will pop in with the brochures and information to get you sorted."

Mr Reddy exits, still beaming and nodding his head happily. Once the door is closed, Oliver turns to me anxiously.

"He seems very hopeful but I'm not sure I share his optimism."

"You heard what he said—only one percent of patients walk straight out."

Oliver looks slightly shellshocked, as well he might. I think we both assumed he'd be in hospital for quite a while.

'He did sound quite hopeful."

There is a tap on the door and a chirpy-looking young woman enters.

"Mr Prentiss? I'm Ayesha. You're probably wondering how on earth you're going to cope on the outside but I promise there's loads of help out there."

She pulls up a chair, sits down and begins pulling out a selection of brochures from a big box file.

"These are a few care homes in your area which you might want to consider, especially in the short term. These…" She shuffles around and pulls out some more "…are nursing agencies…" She rummages some more"…and these are some approved local mobility assistance installers."

She pauses and catches our confused looks.

"Stair lifts, wheelchair access ramps and various other home applications. I'll just leave them with you so you can look them over and choose your options and if there's any questions you have, just give me a shout. This is my mobile number."

She hands over a card, beams broadly and exits. Oliver spreads the brochures out like a conjurer laying out a pack of cards and shrugs his shoulders in bewilderment. I decide it's time to play Pollyanna again.

"I'm sure you'll only be needing these temporarily but you need to make a plan. Can I ask, is finance going to be a problem?"

He shakes his head.

"I do have very good medical cover and if anything's not included, I should be all right."

"Great. Next question, do you want to go home or would you prefer a care home for now?"

He doesn't hesitate.

"Home. As soon as is practical and possible."

"Okay. Let's make a list." I pull out paper and pen from my bag. "No. 1. Home help."

"I do have a lady who does. But she only comes in a couple of times a week." He pauses. "She did come in full-time when my wife was ill. I'm sure she'd do the same if I ask her."

"Excellent. You might also need a day-care nurse. We can contact one or two of those agencies in the brochure. Second. Wheelchair access. I'm sure I can get Mattie and his mates to rig up some temporary ramps but you're going to need a stair lift." I pick out another brochure. "Do you want to give them a call or shall I?"

"I can do that. It's not like I've got anything else to do all day."

Oliver waves his arm around to indicate his surroundings.

We chat for a while and discuss other arrangements and agree that we'll attend to other difficulties as and when they arise and I offer to run him to and from Edgbaston for his specialist physiotherapy. By the time we are done he is looking a lot happier.

Tuesday, 19th November

The post arrived just before I left for work, bringing a batch of envelopes from local estate agents, some proffering a selection of Black Country properties, others volunteering their services as selling agents. Bloody Michael! I chuck the lot in the bin and head out.

George calls mid-morning to enquire about Oliver, Sarah and Patti so I fill him in on current events, including the realtor brochures. He tells me he is relishing the reliving of his student days and thoroughly enjoying his research. The Bodleian contains a plethora of ancient herbal treatises and he is already forward planning all the spring planting projects for the revival of the Featherington monastic kitchen garden.

I then make a few phone calls of my own, referencing the pamphlets given to Oliver and manage to arrange for the hiring of a day-time carer cum nurse from an agency in Birmingham. This information I relay to Mr Reddy who confirms that Oliver will be discharged first thing next Monday. I assure him that we will all rally round to make sure he is comfortable and that Oliver can count on us all for help and home visits.

Thursday, 20th November

Professor Turner calls to confirm that I'll be visiting Sarah this evening. I find this odd—he's never done that before. I tell him we'll all be there around 6pm.

'Perfect. Would you mind popping up to my rooms when you come? There's something I wanted to discuss with you."

I tell him I'll give Sarah some alone time with the teenagers while I chat with him, we exchange pleasantries and I hang up. Obviously he must want to talk about Sarah's progress, or possibly lack of it but he was playing his cards close to his chest and giving nothing away. I have an uneasy feeling that I attempt, unsuccessfully, to ignore.

6pm

At 6 on the dot I dutifully make my way up to Professor Turner's rooms, knock on the door and am welcomed in in his usual affable manner. After summoning a tray of tea we sit in the usual cosy corner and he wastes no time in coming to the point of the tête à tête.

'I think we may be getting somewhere with what it is that's troubling Sarah."

"That sounds positive but you don't?"

"There's not much gets past you, does it?"

He gives me a wry smile. I do the same in response.

"I wonder if you could fill me in on someone called Steve."

My head jerks up involuntarily, as do my eyebrows.

"I'm sorry. I didn't mean to startle you."

"It just wasn't quite what I was expecting to hear."

"That's the thing about psychiatry. It almost never is."

That wry smile again.

"Of course we don't have to discuss this now if you'd rather not."

"Do you mind if I ask in what context his name came up?"

"That's just it. I can't contextualise it but Sarah has made a few references to a Steve and I have the distinct impression that it's a big issue with her. I asked her if he was a boyfriend or someone from school but all she'd say was that it was in the past."

I look at his face, mildly impassive, well-intentioned face and make a decision. I've never discussed Steve with anyone except Patti since he died. Even in my conversations with Her Majesty's finest I've been careful not to say any more than the bare minimum but I know that this room is what is referred to as a 'safe space'. I also know that the man seated opposite me has

330

my daughter's best interests at heart. All of these facts I process at lightning speed and I come to a decision.

"What I'm going to tell you stays between these four walls."

"You have my word."

"Steve was…" I hesitate as I search for les mots justes. "Steve was the only man I ever loved."

I pause and look at him to gauge his expression but it is completely impassive, non-judgmental.

"When Sarah and Jude were small Michael and I were separated for a couple of years. Steve gave me a job on the paper he edited. We hit it off and started seeing each other after hours." I pause again. "We became very close."

"And was there a relationship between him and your daughters."

"He adored them and they adored him. We were like a family."

"You're speaking in the past tense. You broke up?"

"In a manner of speaking."

My protective shutter comes down. There is a longer pause while I secure the padlock.

"I'm sorry, Mrs Hamilton. I believe I've touched a raw nerve and that wasn't my intention."

"There was no way you could have known."

Another Pinter-esque pause as I briefly wonder why Sarah would suddenly be fretting over Steve and then it dawns on me that it must be the cold case investigation. Even though she's not living at home, she knows all about it and she's undoubtedly worked out that it's another cross I have to bear right now. My brain races as I try to decide how much I want to share with Professor Turner in Sarah's best interests and what I want to keep sacred and secret.

"It seems like a lifetime ago now. When he er…left us, it was very painful but it's not something we've ever talked about. They were both very young at the time…. But recent events have rather brought it to the fore." I tail off.

"But there's no special reason why Sarah would feel it more keenly than her sister?"

I shake my head emphatically.

"Definitely not. But being that bit older, her memories are probably that bit more vivid than Jude's…I'm not helping much, am I?"

He smiles warmly.

331

"In a way, we're like artists. We start with a rough sketch, not much detail. Then we stretch out a fresh canvas and begin filling in some background. Then slowly, very slowly we add more detail, more colours until it starts to take shape."

"That's a good analogy."

"Sarah's picture is still very much a work in progress."

I nod.

"Thank you for coming in."

We both rise, I take my leave and walk outside to clear my head. The weather is chilly but dry and the grounds are cheerily lit, unlike my mood which is much more gloomy. I am aware that I wasn't as forthcoming with the Professor as I might have been but I feel very certain that Michael is the main cause of Sarah's malaise, not Steve, and that I've disturbed his bones more than enough of late. Nevertheless, as we are driving back I replay the conversation in my head and resolve to probe Jude with a few discreet questions to see if she can shed any light on the matter.

Monday, 24th November

Oliver's discharge day. I'm out of the house early, driving to Fordham to open up for the care assistant and of course to wait for Oliver himself. Over the weekend the ever-resourceful Mattie and his mate, Jake, fashioned make-do ramps on the front and back doors from some bricks and wooden planks. I look at them and think they will suffice for now but if Oliver's condition is for the long-term we might have to make something more solid and permanent. And just as soon as the thought passes through my mind, I metaphorically shake my head and banish it. At such times a glass half-full is called for.

Carole, the newly appointed nurse-carer arrives promptly at 8 o'clock and I give her the guided tour, pointing out the bedroom I have prepared for her to occupy and the new stair lift, complete with a lightweight, folding wheelchair which attaches neatly to the side. With a little practise this will allow Oliver to be both mobile and independent in and around the house. Carole admits to being only a passable cook, which probably places her several grades above my level and more than adequate for Oliver's immediate needs. Also that she can rely on the auspices of Maggie, Oliver's daily, for all the cleaning and to help with shopping and cooking. As we stand in the kitchen, a feeble, grey

November light straining through the window that overlooks the rear stable block, we catch sight of a people carrier coming up the drive. I open the back door to call Skipper but with that curious sixth sense that dogs have, he is already bounding towards the vehicle, wagging his tail furiously. It comes to a stop, a driver and a nurse emerge, open the sliding doors and helping a seated Oliver to manoeuvre into a wheelchair, they lift it, and him, onto the gravel, much to the delight of Skipper.

I'm almost as thrilled as the dog to see Oliver home again and rush over to give him a hug. Then I leap to the back of the chair and push him to the back door, up Mattie's ramp and into the kitchen where the offer of fresh coffee is gratefully accepted by all. I can't help but notice that under a blanket, his legs lie inert and immobile.

One hour later and Carole is up to scratch with Oliver's current condition, therapies and treatments and I take my leave so they can get properly acquainted and into what will become his regular routine for the foreseeable future, promising I'll be back as often as I can, with Jude and Mattie when they are able.

Thursday, 27th November

We—that is me, Jude, Mattie and Amanda,—are making our customary visit to the Avon to see Sarah. I had a vaguely disturbing phone call with Professor Turner yesterday in which he said he'd had a one-on-one session with Sarah where he'd subtly steered the conversation around to Steve, casually mentioning that he knew from me that we had all been quite close when we were living in Bath. Her reaction was one of reticence but also, he said, one that was clearly quite painful. My response was that of course she would be upset under the circumstances but he seemed convinced that there's more to it than mere childhood trauma and that somehow it's at the core of Sarah's problem. He also said he surmised a feeling of guilt which made no sense to me. After the call I turned the girls' reactions over and over in my mind. Of course they were sad but children process death in a very different way to adults and as I thought and remembered, something long buried came suddenly back to me. In a recollection of my stupor of grief and loss and my Zombie-like PTSD, I recalled a 6-year old Sarah saying to me over and over again whenever she saw me looking sad or trancelike 'I wish he'd wake up, mummy', not once but over and over again and over and over again I would smile, kiss her and say 'Me too, darling', or words to that effect. My precise response may have differed from time to time but Sarah's litany never altered—'I wish he'd wake up, mummy'.

And then I began to wonder, did she somehow think it was her fault that Steve couldn't wake up and why was it playing, if not on her mind, then at least on her subconscious?

Sunday, 30th November

Today is Carole's day off and we're all going over to visit Oliver. After work yesterday I popped in to Pricerite, a store I usually avoid like the plague but this time I was on a mission. I made a beeline for the Gourmet Foods section, piling a trolley up with microwaveable haute cuisine meals for one and finishing with a large, general shop for invalid fare, anything to perk up a jaded appetite. Carole and Maggie are doing some cooking for him and on his own, though he can't properly reach the stove to fend for himself, he can manage to access the lower oven and the microwave, now sitting lower down on a hostess trolley borrowed from the dining room. I know how much he valued his independence and how he must hate having to rely on a stranger for assistance so any small way in which he can be helped to help himself will be a psychological boost.

On an impulse I phone Professor Turner's cell and request dispensation for a day pass for Sarah so she can join our expedition. Through force of circumstances she is forced to only ever participate in family life second hand and even though our expedition today is hardly the stuff of great excitement, I think she'll enjoy being a part of Oliver respite crew. Professor Turner readily agrees, saying that a change might be as good as a rest in terms of recent counselling revelations and so it is that with Mattie and I in the front of the bug and the 3 girls playing sardines on the back seat, we all five set out from the Avon at just after 10am en route for Fordham.

En route I can't help noticing that Sarah seems somewhat quieter than usual, answering questions put to her directly but contributing little herself. Then again, she's always tended towards the introspective so perhaps I shouldn't read too much into it.

By the time we reach Oliver's house a light rain has begun to fall. I park the bug by the stables and we all pile out, heading towards the kitchen door. Clearly Oliver must have heard the car because the door opens just as we reach it. He is sitting in his wheelchair, still holding on to the door handle. His skin has a grey pallor which I attribute to a combination of the cold weather and his being housebound but he looks absurdly pleased at our invasion. Jude impulsively hugs him, I offer to put the coffee pot on, Sarah and Amanda unpack all the Pricerite goodies and Mattie offers to check around the property to see what, if anything, needs doing, accompanied by Skipper. Oliver protests mildly at this latter offer in view of the rain still falling but Mattie just laughs and says as fellow riders they're used to being out in all weathers.

Over coffee Oliver anxiously asks me if I'd be able to drive him to Birmingham tomorrow for his first out-patient therapy session, to which I respond "Of course!"

"Apparently I'm getting something called nerve stimulation. That and some massage."

"I suppose they don't want anything to atrophy. I'm sure it's a good sign."

I metaphorically cross my fingers as I say this. I know the possibility exists that Oliver may never properly recover but I can't, no I won't, accept that outcome. Why do bad things always happen to good people? And as this thought races across my mind I have a fleeting vision of Steve, so full of joie de vivre, taken so suddenly and pointlessly. And then I think how cruelly coincidental it is that both tragedies were caused, in part, by careless drivers.

Monday, 1st December

I drive Oliver to Birmingham and remain in the waiting room with a copy of Wilkie Collins' The Moonstone, widely regarded as the first English detective novel. I am making my own reading study of the genre so that I can hopefully add something to Alex's treatise. We exchange email notes on his progress and direction and I like to feel in some small way I am making a useful contribution. God knows, I never put anything in to his first couple of decades on the planet, the guilt for which I know I can never hope to assuage.

When Oliver is done, his colour looks better but his expression is glum.

"Nothing. I didn't feel a thing. Couldn't even feel the electrodes when they switched on the power and zapped me!"

335

I smile. One of us has to remain positive.

"Give it time. Mr Reddy said it could take months, remember."

"At my age I haven't got time."

At this I burst out laughing.

"Good grief, Olly. You're still a young man."

At this he laughs uproariously, the way he did when we were out on our rides and something tickled his fancy.

"You're very diplomatic, Fiona, but I am very nearly a pensioner, remember."

"Scarcely."

We smile at each other and the subject is closed.

Wednesday, 3rd December

The shop phone rings mid-morning. It's Patti.

"Just to let you know we're moving on Saturday."

"In your condition? You need locking up for your own safety!"

"If I had a quid for every time someone had said that to me I'd be rich as Croesus."

"Very funny. Seriously, Patti, you're 7 ½ months gone with a small litter inside you!"

"Can't be helped. We put this place up for rent and a lovely couple of guys from work want to move in and spend their first Christmas here together."

"I've never taken you as a sucker for a sob story!"

"Now who's being the Grinch?. Anyway, that's what's happening. And to be honest, Ross and I want to spend New Year with our new family in our new house too."

"I think I hear the hormones talking. The nesting syndrome. I don't suppose there's anything I can do to change your mind?"

"Nope!"

"Fine. Anything I can do?"

"Since you asked......"

"Spit it out."

"Those 3 strapping teens who hang around your place eating you out of house and home. I couldn't borrow them, could I? I'll make it worth their while."

336

"I'll have to ask but I think they'll jump at the chance of a weekend away. Maybe I just won't mention the move!"

"It'll be a nice surprise!"

We laugh and hang up.

In the afternoon George also calls with news of his own. He's coming back at the weekend, planning on staying a few days to do some more research at Featherington, before returning to Oxford. He sounds very animated which I attribute to all the excitement of his new purpose in life. He says he'll stop by the shop first and then go to his apartment on Saturday morning. I tell him that in all probability I'll be alone so if he doesn't mind an early start, I'll drive him over before I have to open the shop.

6pm

Back home I prepare a fish pie for supper, with the weather being so miserable and the dish being a firm favourite of all 3 teens. Hopefully that will soften them up for the Bath bombshell. I cheat a bit with a large tin of pink salmon for the base, my metamorphosis from cuisine-a-phobe to kitchen goddess not yet being complete but I think it will pass muster. If not, the Simmonds Bakewell tart for pudding should clinch it.

8pm

We are all in the kitchen having supper, it being the cosiest room in the house in winter. I wait till everyone is served and making 'Mmm, nice'-type noises, then light the blue touch paper about them helping to pack up the flat and retire behind a glass of wine. I needn't have bothered going to so much trouble. They are all thrilled at the prospect of a weekend down south in the company of Patti and Ross and declare that they can slope out of school after lunch on Friday, catch the Bath train and be down there well before 5pm.

The only problem I foresee is that I know Sarah would love to be able to go with them but that would be an ask too far. Leaving them to clear up and load the dishwasher, I phone Patti with the good news about the removals crew.

Friday, 5th December

2pm

I dropped the 'crew' off at the local railway station at lunchtime, having sorted them out with rail passes and some cash. Jude and Amanda were raving about Bath's boutiques but I cautioned them that they might not have too much time for shopping. Patti said she'd arranged a split move, with one lorry in the morning and another in the afternoon which sounded like a lot of last-minute packing to me, not to mention the unpacking at the other end. Sunday would be spent sorting out and settling in and Ross said he'd drop them all off at Bristol Temple Meads at some unearthly hour on Monday, their new house being out in the Somerset boonies and he had an early meeting in the city. I consoled the girls with the promise of a major shopping expedition before Christmas.

As luck would have it, George's train got in half an hour later so I hung around, even though the sign I'd left on the shop door had optimistically read 'Back in 30 minutes'.

I was so pleased to see him. It felt like an eon since he left and the premises had seemed somewhat forlorn in his absence. We arrived back to find a small group of regulars waiting around outside, in spite of the cold, word having got around that the proprietor himself would be back in situ, if only for a short time.

Over tea I fill him in on Patti and Oliver and then he gave me the sly, sideways look I know so well which means that he knows something I don't.

"Spit it out then. I can see you're dying to tell me."

He beams.

"Good news." Pause. "I bumped into Alex."

My jaw drops and my eyes grow wide.

"When? Where? Did you speak to him?"

"In the corridor outside his tutorial room."

I raise an eyebrow.

"Did I say 'bumped into him'? Perhaps 'waylaid' might be more accurate. I made some enquiries, found out the name of his tutor and engineered a meeting, accidentally on purpose."

"What did you say? What did he say?"

"I simply asked if he was Alex and that we had a mutual friend. He was a bit startled but said you'd told him we might run into each other and I said we had!"

"Was that it?"

"Certainly not. I insisted we go into the town, find a local hostelry and celebrate our chance encounter."

"I've said it before. You're a wily old trout, George Fitzsimmons. So what happened next?"

"He took me off to a student bar just around the corner, I ordered a couple of pints of Guinness and we chatted for about an hour. First thing I asked was why he hadn't been to visit you, being so close and he looked a bit embarrassed and said he thought it might be a bit awkward. So I told him in no uncertain terms that it would be a damned sight more awkward if he didn't."

"George!"

"It had to be said, young Ffion. You've been hoping and praying for him to put in an appearance ever since you tracked him down and I told him so."

"How did he react?"

"He sat and mulled it over for a bit and then asked me if I thought it'd be cheeky if he popped in over the Christmas vac and I said that would be the best Christmas present ever for you. I also told him you were a very special person which he'd find out for himself when he comes."

"Thank you."

I'm trying very hard not to cry as I give George a huge hug and mutter 'Thank you' somewhere in the vicinity of his left ear. He pulls away slightly.

"I also said I'd like to be the bearer of good news and not to spoil the surprise with a message on the computer which is anyway hardly the appropriate medium for such a proclamation."

I hug him again and reluctantly move away to serve a customer.

Saturday, 6th December

I'm probably up as early as the house party in Bath, driving to the shop to collect George, dropping him off at Featherington, then heading back to open the shop for the day's business. And all the way back, the only thing I can think about is the prospect of Alex visiting over Christmas. I mentally shop for appropriate gifts and wonder if I should have one of the spare bedrooms repainted and restyled in a format more becoming to his age and sex. I'll consult the girls and perhaps it can be a little project for them.

I am tidying bookshelves in the shop around 11am when I look up to see DS Cox in the doorway, once again wearing his trendy, civvies leather jacket.

"Is it convenient?"

I want to tell him no, we're too busy but that's patently untrue.

"I guess. We're never all that busy till after lunch on Saturdays."

I come around from behind the counter and we both sit down on the old sofa in the corner.

"I hadn't heard anything from you and I felt like a drive."

"Sorry. I've been really busy recently and it looks like it's going to get worse over the next few weeks."

"Christmas?"

"That too."

I brief him in broad strokes on the family situation, leaving out Alex whom I consider none of his business, and mentioning Oliver's accident and current arrangement to illustrate how my time is being taken up.

"Where was that?"

"Just outside his village. Place called Fordham."

He nods.

"I went to see that Gregson character again. Shifty little so and so!"

I smile

"I don't think he's our man, though. He remembers the accident all right and being interviewed after the event. But he insists he was at home with his wife all that weekend. He also admitted he did bear a grudge for the exposé but more towards you than the editor."

"You think he could have done it to spite me?"

"It crossed my mind so I asked him straight out if he'd ever thought of doing something about it."

"What was his reaction?"

"He just laughed. Sardonic, like. Said it wasn't his style. I have to say I believed him. He's a bit of a spiv but I don't think he's the violent type."

"So where does that leave us?"

"No further forward, I'm afraid."

"My hopes weren't high."

"I'm not giving up. It's just a setback."

340

"If you were a dog, you'd be an annoying little Jack Russel, yap yap, yapping and never giving anyone a minute's peace."

He laughs, rises to leave and shakes my hand.

"I'll be in touch."

"Thanks."

I watch as he closes the door behind him, then turn my attention hack to a bit of shelf sorting.

Sunday, 7th December

On an impulse I call the Avon and beg a day pass for Sarah which is readily given. I drive over to pick her up, telling her that since she missed out on Bath, I thought she deserved a little treat of her own. Without giving anything away, I carry on to Fordham where I surprise Oliver as much as Sarah by insisting he come out for a drive. Sarah and I manoeuvre his wheelchair into the boot of the bug and settle him into the front seat, next to me and I then head off to our local stables. Once there, we wrestle Oliver back into the chair and manhandle it across the rough, cobbled yard and over to the adjoining stalls where Cloud Dancer and Captain are stabled. I inform Sarah that we're going to ride the horses in the arena as a bit of therapy for their owner, telling her that her jodhpurs and boots are in a bag in the car.

Though not as keen or competent as her sister, Sarah is happy to oblige. We tack up and with her on Captain and me on Cloud, we walk, trot and canter them both in the large arena, to let Oliver see that Captain is clearly none the worse for his adventure and Cloud is coming on very nicely with his schooling, after such a long lay-off.

As we dismount in the yard, I fish in my pocket and take out carrots for Oliver to feed them. While all this is going on, Bethany, the yard owner, walks up.

"Sarah, it's been a long time since we've seen you on a horse."

"I've been away."

I catch Beth's eye and she changes theme. Looking first at Oliver, then me she says

"You must be Oliver? I've heard a lot about you from Mattie and Jude."

She proffers her hand which Oliver accepts, shaking it politely.

"Will you still be leaving the horse here now that you're out of hospital?"

341

"I think it'd be best. I'm in no fit state to take care of them right now."

"You can ride them if you want."

We all stare at her.

"Didn't Jude tell you? I'm a qualified Riding for the Disabled instructor so it wouldn't be a problem. Also it's very therapeutic."

"I've heard that. What do you think, Oliver?"

He looks a bit shell-shocked at the suggestion.

"It's mental and physical, you know."

I look up at Sarah as she finishes speaking.

"I really enjoyed my ride this morning and honestly, I was feeling really down this weekend, then mum popped up without telling me. I've had some fresh air and exercise and I'm feeling much happier."

Oliver still doesn't look convinced but Bethany has clearly made up her mind.

"No time like the present. Captain's still got his bridle on—he's the one you usually ride, isn't he? I'll just pop into the tack room for my special saddle."

And brooking no dissent, she strides off, coming out a couple of minutes later with the saddle and accompanied by a young man she introduces as Ajay.

"He'll be helping us."

Half an hour later, Oliver himself is back in the saddle, both literally and figuratively, and Bethany and Ajay are walking him around the yard, helping him readjust his balance. In spite of his mild protests, Oliver looks happier than he has for weeks. Clearly he and Captain have a very special bond and the pair of them easily mould back together.

The five of us form a phalanx and we head off down a bridlepath towards a wooded area, threading through the trees, wet, winter leaves squishing underfoot, taking a circular route bring us out the other side and back to the stables. As Beth and Ajay help him down and back into his chair, Oliver has colour in his cheeks and looks almost like his old self."

"Thank you so much, both of you," he says, several times over.

"Any time. Really."

Back in the bug I pull into the car park of a country pub we passed on the way in which I thought looked inviting and had a sign outside advertising their Sunday Lunch special. It's too chilly and damp to sit outside but there are plenty of willing hands to help amongst the clientele and staff and we are soon ensconced in a cosy spot near the open fire which feels like bliss after a morning in the biting open air.

Sarah has her 'rabbit in the headlights' look at the prospect of a menu and eating in front of strangers but the table is secluded and I assure her there is a vegan option. Thus it is that Oliver and I tuck into excellent rare roast beef with all the trimmings, washed down with half a pint of draft bitter each and Sarah nibbles into her seasonal nut cutlet and vegetables and sips on local cider, chatting about our impromptu but hugely successful outing. I assure Oliver that both Mattie and I will be happy to drive him to the stables a couple of times a week for more equine therapy which I silently am sure will do him far more good than all the professional sessions he undergoes at the clinic.

After dropping off home and settling him in, I tell Sarah she might as well come home and stay the night and I'll take her back to the Avon early in the morning. I don't tell her immediately that I have an ulterior motive but leave that till we are in the house.

"I have some news and since you didn't get to go to Bath, I thought I'd even the score and let you into the secret first."

She looks at me, drinking in my cat-that-got-the-cream expression and raising her eyebrows. I blurt out

"Alex is coming over Christmas."

She squeals.

"Are you serious? He never said a word."

"George arranged it and I told him not to mention it to anyone on pain of death."

"How did George get involved?"

I explain everything and, like me, she marvels at the ingenuity and cunning of the old fox. Then a dark cloud passes over her face.

"Dad'll be livid."

"I wasn't planning on telling him."

"He'll find out."

"None of his business."

"Try telling him that"

Knowing she's quite right, I steer the conversation away from Michael.

"I was hoping you'd have some ideas on redecorating. I thought one of the attic rooms—they're quite big and there's the adjoining bathroom so he can be a bit self-contained if family life gets a bit too much."

343

Her dark expression suddenly clears. She squeals again and claps her hands like she did as a small child.

"What?"

"You finally said it. You called him 'family.'"

So I did. I say it again to myself, then I catch Sarah's eye and we both grin.

"Can I tell Jude?"

I nod.

"After she gets back tomorrow. For now, let's go up and see what needs to be done."

Monday, 8th December

I'm up early in the pitch dark, waking Sarah with a cup of black coffee and hustling her up and about to take her back to the Avon. She dawdles, deliberately, but even so we make it there before 7am, then I drive to Featherington, collect George, take him to Birmingham New Street to catch the early train to Oxford and wait around for an hour till the first train from Bristol gets in.

"You should see Patti and Ross's new place. It's like something out of Jane Austen."

We are all 4—me, Jude, Mattie and Amanda—in the bug on the way back, they to school and me to a rare day alone and at home.

Amanda chips in.

"Seriously! I half expected to see Mr Darcy appear out of the library at any minute."

"Gonna cost them a fortune to heat."

The ever-practical Mattie.

"How's Patti?"

"Super-fat! Looks like she's ready to pop."

"Heavens, I hope not. Her gynae's booked her for an early C-section because of her age and carrying two but her real due date is in January."

"Ross was fussing over her like a mother hen but she wasn't having any of it. She was directing operations and bossing the removals guys around like there was no tomorrow."

"Sounds like our Patti."

1pm

With Michael's computer long gone, I've been using an old laptop, kindly donated by Mattie's father. I have to send a message to Alex and it needs to be both diplomatic and casual at the same time, even though my stomach has been in knots ever since George told me the news. After staring at a blank screen for several minutes, I write

'Hi Alex. George was back for the weekend and told me he'd hooked up with you and that you might be dropping in over the Christmas vac. That's brilliant news and the girls are over the moon'

A bit of poetic licence here—I know I've only shared with Sarah so far but I'm pretty sure she'll have already messaged Jude and that she'll be as excited as her sister

'George does have a very persuasive manner sometimes—he's ex-military from back in the day and he knows how to wheedle out the results he wants! I must warn you it might get a bit hectic around that time. Patti's booked in for a C-section on the 28th and I've promised to be there for the birth and a couple of days after. But I'll be back New Year's Eve latest and Sarah will be home with us as well. Both the girls will stay here while I'm down south so you're welcome anytime.

Really looking forward to having you here for however long you can manage—I know you'll want to spend time with your family as well so whatever and whenever works best.

Love Guin'

I re-read it a couple of times, decide it's sounding the right note and hit 'Send'.

Friday, 12th December

There are several customers in the shop, browsing and reading, none of whom look like they're in any hurry to leave. In George's absence I have committed the cardinal sin of bringing in the laptop with a view to making a back-up stock catalogue, transferring all the information on the plain postcards George insists on using onto a single file. It's mind-numbingly tedious and I'm sorry I started. I hate to admit it, but he may have been right all along about his hardcopy system being easier and more accessible. Irritated, I take a break.

345

Looking around, it occurs to me that the shop interior has taken on an aura of a Hollywood interpretation of the Old Curiosity Shop'. There is scant light coming through the two tiny windows in the December, late afternoon gloom and the subdued indoor lighting from a few reading lamps dotted around strategically put me in mind of old theatrical gaslight. And those thoughts in turn, along with the Dickensian reference, direct me to recollections of the ghosts of Christmases past. I recall the artificial tree back home in Chester which was ceremoniously retrieved from the attic every year on the 20th of December and decorated with the same box of miscellaneous ornaments which had been garnered over the years of my parents' marriage. Not many people had designer trees and themed yuletide décor in those days, especially not in the north of England. But after marrying Michael, that all changed. Beginning with our very first family Christmas, when Sarah was just a few months old, he'd gone the whole hog with a pre-decorated tree from an upmarket interior design store. It came complete with tartan bows—an homage to his Scottish roots, lights in the shape of red and green candles and miniature wooden soft fruit—strawberries, raspberries, cranberries, blackberries and Scandinavian snowberries. I remember being utterly bemused, not to mention slightly embarrassed when any of my friends dropped by, I could see them taking it in and trying not to reference it, all except Patti, of course, whose immediate reaction was

"I'm confused. Is it a Christmas tree or the harvest festival offering from Balmoral?"

The pair of us completely cracked up and Michael had icily responded by asking how she could possibly know anything about the royal estate since she'd never stayed there.

He had, of course.

And every Christmas after that was more or less on the same lines. As Sarah and Jude grew up they would eye up pretty baubles or tacky ornaments in the shops and beg to be allowed to buy them for the tree. Sometimes I relented and let them have their way. Their little treasures would join the vogue display ordered in, pre-dressed, but next day I would always find they had been quietly removed and binned.

And as all those memories flooded back it suddenly occurred to me that this would be out first, post-liberation Christmas, free at last. Free of making the right impression, free of designer tableau scenes and free of all of Michael's stuffiness. And best of all, it would be the first Christmas, actually first anything, when I'd have my long-lost son to share it with. So right there and then I decided this would be the year when the girls finally got their wish—I'd put them in charge of garlanding the house and I'd even try my hand at a metaphorical festive fatted calf instead of the annual gourmet Pricerite hamper, selected with the express purpose of distancing me from the kitchen.

A proper family Christmas. There's that word again.

Sunday, 14th December

6pm

Jude, Mattie and I had fetched Oliver and taken him to the stables for another therapy riding session. He was still bemoaning the loss of feeling in his feet and legs which dangle limply at the side of the horse and won't stay in the stirrups but Beth was patience personified and pointed out that at least his upper body and arm muscles were being exercised and that he must persist.

Now we are all in the kitchen and Mattie is preparing supper when my phone rings. I glance at the screen. It's Ross.

"Patti went into premature labour. I'm driving her to Bristol Royal Infirmary. We didn't want to wait for an ambulance to get to us out in the sticks."

He's on the speakerphone and Patti cuts in.

"I've told him it's Braxton Hicks. Big fuss about nothing."

"I'm coming down."

"Don't be melodramatic."

"Don't you be so Harry casual. You were due your C-section next week anyway. I'll phone about trains and call you."

The kids' mouths are all agape.

"You heard that?"

They nod.

"Jude, phone and find out when the next train to Bristol Temple Meads is. Mattie, will you drive me to the station?"

"Sure."

I rush upstairs, throw some clothes and toiletries into a small bag and am down again in 10 minutes.

"There's one from New Street at 9.15. You can catch a connection in 40 minutes. That'll be there in plenty of time."

"Thanks. You will be all right on your own for a couple of days, won't you?"

I am rewarded by withering looks all round, then we are out of the door, piling into the bug, supper forgotten about in the rush. I pull up outside the local station, Mattie slides into the driver's seat and I thrust some money into Jude's hand.

"Go and get a takeaway."

"Go and get your train."

I smile, hug her through the window and rush off.

4 hours later I disembark from a taxi outside the maternity wing of the hospital and rush inside. Patti is in a private room on the ground floor and as I enter I see she is hooked up to a drip, a harried-looking Ross sitting in a chair by the side of a bed. Absurdly, the first thing that went through my mind was that this was the third hospital I'd visited in less than 6 months.

"So what's the plan?"

I address the question to both of them.

"The obstetrics chief was called out and said she's in danger of pre-eclampsia. So he called her gynae who drove over from Bath, she's just had an epidural, they're prepping the theatre and she'll be going in any minute for an emergency C-section."

"I prefer to call it a lumpectomy."

Patti looks pallid and uncomfortable but clearly it'd take more than a medical emergency to stifle her slightly sick sense of humour. I go closer and peck her on the cheek.

"Trust you to cause a shed-load of shit on a Sunday evening."

"Why not? I pay enough for it!"

She laughs, then visibly winces and clutches her stomach. Ross jumps up, presses a button and a young nurse comes hurrying in.

"They're ready for you now, Mrs Badger."

"I don't think your magic mushroom injection is working."

"Give it a few more minutes."

The nurse beckons to an orderly just outside the door who enters and introduces himself as Clayton and the two of them deftly manoeuvre Patti, her bed and her drip out of the door.

"Ross?" "Fee?"

Patti looks at us and holds out an arm.

"You're welcome to watch. We'll find you both a gown and a mask."

Ross nods, relieved, and we both move to follow the procession.

Monday, 15th December

3am

Patti's babies were safely delivered at half past one this morning, a girl, 3lbs 3oz and a boy, 3lbs 5oz. Being so small they were immediately installed in a single incubator where they promptly fell asleep. Ross filmed the entire process on his phone and as they emerged into the glare of the theatre spotlight, he beamed at the babies and at Patti and told her she deserved an Oscar. Patti being Patti responded by saying in her book she deserved a glass of Krug. Ross got out his phone and by some miracle managed to locate an off-licence which was willing to deliver right to her room half an hour later. Her exhausted gynae had popped in and stayed long enough to wet the babies' heads, before leaving, saying he needed to get some rest and advising Patti to try and do the same. She is under instructions to remain in hospital for 48 hours but the twins will have to stay until they gain enough weight and strength to come out of the incubator. This was a blow to both of them but he assured them they were both doing well and it should only be a matter of a few days.

Left alone, the three of us polished off the bottle back in Patti's room as her epidural wore off and the reality of being a mother to two miniature infants set in.

"How long can you stay, Fee?"

"Till the end of the week. Jenny has promised to take care of the shop till then."

"I hope they'll be able to come home for Christmas."

I nod and Ross squeezes her hand.

7pm

We finally left the hospital at 5pm. The day was spent in a muddle of medical check-ups, several visits to the paediatric ICU to gaze at the babies, snatched meals and the drawing up of copious shopping and to-do lists in order to fully prepare for the care of two infants, each the size of my hands till at last Patti metaphorically pushed us out of the room saying she needed some sleep and we needed to go home and make ready.

The girls weren't kidding when they described the house. I think 'Palladian' is the architectural style, a huge country house of grey, Cotswold stone, on generous Jacobean lines and sitting in a few acres of rolling Somerset lowland. Inside, it had retained all of its original features and elegance and was furnished in perfect period style, courtesy, I was told, of a team of the Beeb's finest historical set designers and a generous budget. Ross gave me the grand tour, proudly showing off the nursery with its matching pair of dappled wooden rocking horses and wicker cribs suspended from the ceiling. It was utterly charming and so un-Patti, apart from 'no expense spared'.

Then we repaired to the vast downstairs kitchen, also in the style of its time, bedecked with copperware utensils and period cookware and even the original cooking range, converted to run on oil. Ross made omelettes and oven chips and we sat at the below-stairs table, basking in the warmth from the range and marvelling over and over again at the pictures of his new-borns and his radiant wife. Then we both repaired to bed where I slept the sleep of the dead.

Tuesday, 15th December

Ross and I were both up early, anxious to go back to the hospital. As I drank tea in my vast bedroom complete with four-poster bed, I took time to send some of Ross's pictures of the twins to Jude, along with an account of the events of the past 36 hours, then Ross and I were back on the road. Coming into Bristol from the south side, I instructed him to drive to my old haunt of Whiteladies Road, telling him we needed to buy baby clothes. He reminded me that there were drawers full of them in the nursery but I just smiled. As soon as we parked we walked around till we found a charity shop where I unearthed exactly what I was looking for—an extensive children's toy section with loads of second-hand dolls clothes. Finally the penny dropped for Ross—all of the baby gear they'd bought would swamp the two tiny beings in the incubator and together we cleaned out as much of the stock as seemed suitable. That done, we sped off to the hospital.

"Have you thought of names yet?"

I address the question to Patti who is sitting up in bed tucking into croissants and strawberry jam—clearly not even major surgery will put this girl off her stride. She and Ross exchange glances and a small smile plays around her lips.

"Tell her, Ross."

As she takes another bite of a very flaky croissant, Ross grins.

"We didn't ask about the sexes. Wanted it to be a surprise. But we'd played around with a few names to cover all bases."

"Ross phoned me last night and we both agreed. Christopher Stephen for the boy. Christopher after Ross's grandfather and Stephen…"

She falters and I nod.

"And Emily Georgina for the girl. A nod to your George."

"He'll be tickled pink and blue. And while we're on the subject…"

I tip the bag of dolls' clothes onto the bed. Patti has a fit of the giggles, then winces. "Stitches."

There is a tap on the door and the handsome - 30-something gynae whom I had at first taken to be a media colleague when I met him 2 nights ago—walks in, being greeted by 'Hi, Gy' from Patti.

"Patti, you look fabulous."

As he speaks, he parks himself on the edge of the bed and begins examining her pupils, taking her pulse and finally lifting her gown to check the neat row of C-section stitches. Satisfied, he looks up.

"Good news. Both babies are breathing independently. I've recommended they stay in the incubators for a couple of days for observation but if all goes well, you should all be able to go home on Friday."

Ross beams and exchanges a little smile with Patti.

"And for now, feel free to go give them a cuddle. Start getting acquainted."

"I'll need a wheelchair."

"You need no such thing. Off your lovely, lazy bottom and take a walk. Doctor's orders! I'll look in again tomorrow."

And with that he saunters out.

In the paediatric ICU they make us don gowns and masks, then lift both the babies out, handing one to Ross and the other Patti. Each was only the size of Ross's hand but in every other way they were perfectly formed. I stay long enough to allow them to squeeze my fingers, then make my excuses and leave the new family to it.

351

"The cupboards are barer than Mother Hubbard's. I'll nip into town and do some shopping."

"You don't have to do that."

"It'll be fun to revisit some of my old uni haunts."

"Call me when you're done. I'll come and pick you up and we can go home together."

I nod, take a last look at the tiny humans and leave them to bond.

Friday, 18th December

I call home to let Jude know I'll be back by early evening. She is in what can only be described as an ebullient mood.

"We went into town and ransacked a few stalls and charity shops for decorations. They're all in the sitting room. We're going to get some more stuff for some of the other rooms today. And Sarah phoned and said she's got a 7-day pass, starting Sunday."

"That's fantastic news."

"Isn't it?"

She sounds more excited than if it were her first-ever Christmas.

"There's something else?"

"Isn't that enough?"

I hear giggling in the background and guess that Amanda is lurking.

"Got to go, mum. The crowds in the shops are shocking."

"I'll see you tonight then."

"Okay. Love to Patti and Ross and the babies."

"We're just off to bring them home now."

"Have you checked your messages this week?"

"No time. Why?"

"No reason." She pauses, then continues. "This is going to be the best Christmas ever. Gotta go. Bye!"

She cuts the call abruptly. Jude the Impatient.

At the hospital Patti is waiting, bag packed, her progeny tucked up tightly in a wicker carry cot. We process slowly to the main doors, Patti ambulatory but cautious, and wait while Ross brings the car round, then the cot is safely strapped in the back of the spacious, German SUV, alongside Patti while I ride shotgun up front with Ross.

352

On arrival their mutual joy in introducing their slumbering family to their new home is palpable and infectious. The nursery is warm as toast and the twins are put down in their cots, still sleeping. With neither parent able to take their eyes off them, I offer to go and rustle up some toasted sandwiches for lunch which I take back upstairs and we squat around a tiny table on nursery chairs, eating and drinking more Krug. Then all too soon the taxi I ordered is outside and I take my leave.

"We'll come up for New Year. Promise."

"I guarantee you won't be short of babysitters. The girls are all dying to meet their proxy cousins."

We embrace, I step into the taxi and drive away.

7pm

"Supper's ready whenever you are. I expect you want to check your emails first?"

Jude is giving me a look I can't quite interpret but there's the ghost of a smile playing around her lips.

"I really need a shower."

"You can do both. Amanda's done a veggie lasagne and it's in the oven on low."

"Smells lovely. Shower first, I think."

The piping hot shower is bliss after the somewhat antiquated and temperamental plumbing at Brigham House and I linger, letting the water warm my bones. Then I pull on jeans, socks and a sweater and head to Michael's study (note to self, stop calling it that—it's yours now) to catch up with my correspondence.

As I reach the door the desk phone rings.

"Ffion? Jude told me you were due back about now. Just to let you know that Alex and I plan on travelling down on Sunday afternoon. Apparently he's got a term-end party on Saturday which he doesn't want to miss…"

George is saying something about last minute Christmas shopping for his upcoming Ireland sojourn but I'm only half-listening. I'm finding it hard to concentrate after the announcement that after more than 2 decades I am finally to be reunited with Alex in just 2 days' time.

"He said he'd emailed you on Wednesday?"

"I haven't logged in since I went to Bath."

I'm doing just that now with me free hand and sure enough, there's a message from Alex. This must be what Jude was hinting at.

"Just let me know what time you're leaving. Are you going to be staying at the shop or will you need a lift to Featherington?"

"Shop, definitely. Charles and Diana are picking me up there on Monday morning and we're hoping to catch the 1pm Dunloghaire ferry. Alex says he'd be happy to help out while I'm away."

"Jude says it's going to be the best Christmas ever. I think she may be right."

"I must say I am rather looking forward to it myself. They think I'm the Prodigal Son, you know, so hopefully we can expect a fatted goose, if not an actual calf."

"Gosh, that reminds me. I'd better do a mammoth shop to tide us over. Hopefully Mattie could fetch Oliver over so he won't be alone."

"I'm sure he'd appreciate it. I'd better go. Alex is taking me to a pizza restaurant for supper."

"Have fun."

With both hands free I pull up Alex's message.

'Hey Guin. George and I plan on arriving sometime Sunday evening. Hope that's cool? Jude tells me Sarah has been festively furloughed so she'll also be there? Is it okay if I plan for a week with you? I may go up to Cheshire for New Year—not sure yet. Wow, this is weird but in a good way, I think. George has been showing me his plans for the Featherington garden and I've promised him that Paulo and I will come down at Easter to give him a hand. I think I should warn you I eat a lot and I'm definitely a carnivore!

Love Alex'

As I formulate a response I find my hands are shaking and there's a knot of excitement in my stomach that seems to be stopping me breathing properly.

'Alex. That's wonderful news. I expect Jude has told you that Patti went into labour prematurely but she's home now. I know she wants to meet you at some point—she claims proxy aunt-hood on you and says that gives her visitation rights so I don't think you have any choice! Jude & co have been buying loads of decorations but they won't put them up till Sarah's sprung so I guess you'll get roped in too. Anyway, this is the best news ever and I can't wait till Sunday. Amanda's veggie lasagne, on the other hand, won't keep that long so I'd better go.

Much love, Guin'

I push 'send' and head for the kitchen, grabbing a bottle of red wine as I do.

Saturday, 19th December

I drive to work with all three teens as passengers. A Christmas shopping expedition is planned and as soon as I park the car, they shoot off towards the high street.

I am catching up in the shop and it has been non-stop all morning with people looking for Christmas gift books or just something to read over the holidays. The teens had included it on their decoration list and I have to admit their efforts have brightened the December gloom, lighting up our quirkily shaped premises with rows of lights tacked up above head height and more framing two small, mullioned windows. I am putting the finishing touches to a display of vintage Christmas annuals when the phone rings. I break off to answer it.

"Fiona?"

DS Cox.

"I've called a few times this week but you weren't available."

"I was down south. What was it you wanted?"

"It's a bit delicate."

"Luckily I'm not."

"Em… You had a friend at uni."

"I had quite a few in those days."

"His name was Alan Naseby. "

"We called him Pip."

"I understand he died."

"After he graduated. He….had some issues. Why is that of interest to you?"

"No reason. I just wanted to talk to some of your old friends and his name came up."

"You think a jealous old flame might have killed Steve?"

"We have to consider all possibilities."

"Impossibilities, you mean. He died before I even met Steve."

"Why Pip?"

355

"He was hooked on apples. Cox's Orange Pippins, particularly."

Inappropriately I laugh.

"What's so funny?"

"Nothing, I just realised he was the Pip and you're the Cox." I sober up. "He was a gentle soul."

"So you were close?'

"Not in a romantic way. Just really good friends. Me, Pip and Patti—we did everything together till…."

I break off.

"Till?"

I hesitate.

"Till we all left uni. Left Bristol, actually."

"I'm just exploring avenues."

"More of a dead end, I'm afraid…that's black humour, by the way."

"We get a lot of that in our line of work."

"Sounds like you need a break. Any plans for Christmas?"

"I'm on call. You?"

"Just Christmas with the family."

"No 'just' about it. It's a family time. Sorry to keep bugging you."

"It's fine. Really."

I hang up and make a mental note to send a card to Pip's parents and let them know Patti's good news.

I spend the afternoon making lists and trying, but failing, to suppress the butterflies in my stomach. I menu-plan and write shopping lists. I jot down gift ideas. I work out a schedule for who needs picking up or dropping off. I even come up with some old parlour games from my childhood in case the weather takes a turn for the worse. In the midst of this I am interrupted with a visit from Jude who carries in her hand a list of her own.

"I need some books."

"You're come to the right place."

"Ha ha. Very funny."

She moves off and begins pulling selected volumes off the shelves, glancing at her list for confirmation. I leave her to it and attend to other customers. When done, she informs me she will write up the sales herself, which I take to mean the selection is a state secret, then, after depositing some money in the till, she gives me a quick hug.

"See you at home, Guin."

Clearly the Camelot nickname is less of a secret than the book list.

As soon as the last customer leaves, I rush off, stopping off to cross as much food and gift items off my lists as possible, after which I drive home.

Inside the house I am greeted by an animated Jude who tells me that Mattie and Amanda are spending the night at their respective homes out of filial duty. Meanwhile she is anxious to show me something upstairs.

I follow obediently and am led to one of the big attic bedrooms which has undergone something of a makeover. With help from the other two, Jude has designed what she describes as a 'guy wall', a montage of random objects— varsity scarf, cricket bat, rugby shirt, movie posters, a playbill for an RSC production of 'The Merchant of Venice' and some of the old prints I picked up at the Featherington sale.

Jude has her grandmother's artistic eye, noticeable in her clever collages and very eclectic yet somehow aesthetic style of dress and she has put all of that panache and creativity into the wall. The effect is unconventionally cohesive and looks amazing. I tell her so and she is pleased but tries not to show it.

"That's not all. Look."

She waves at a bookshelf above the bed so I move closer. On the shelf are her purchases from this afternoon—a history of Alexander the Great, a Victorian copy of Jude the Obscure, Lancelyn Green's King Arthur & the Knights of the Round Table, an autobiography of Sarah Bernhardt, a collection of poetry by Matthew Arnold and some old Milly-Molly-Mandy books from Jude's own childhood.

"Get it?"

I nod, then pause. Something has been bothering me and I feel this might be the ideal time to broach it.

"Has Alex ever mentioned his mother?"

Jude looks genuinely surprised.

"He hasn't told you?"

"Told me what?"

"She died. When he was about 10. Ovarian cancer."

"So it's just his father at home?"

She shakes her head.

"He remarried. Some woman he met on a cruise. I don't think Alex likes her very much. That's why he doesn't go back home all that often."

I let this sink in. All this time I have been harbouring jealous thoughts about a dead woman. I feel guilty, yet somehow relieved at the same time. I decide I'd better keep that last bit to myself.

"I'm glad you told me. I wouldn't want to put my foot in it when he's here." I take a last look around the room. "You've all done a great job. Thank you. And now I'm going to have a quick bath then rustle up some supper."

"I'll get it started. Can we collect Sarah really early tomorrow. I think she'll want to leave ASAP."

"Definitely."

We leave the room together and I head off to my room.

Sunday, 20th December

I wake to pouring rain and limited visibility but weather won't defeat me today! It does literally put a damper on Oliver's riding but nevertheless Jude and I collect him and Skipper for a bit of an outing on the way to the Avon where, as predicted, Sarah is packed and waiting by the entrance. Still painfully thin, she looks chill but cheerful.

"Out of chokey for a whole week!"

"I know just how you feel, young lady. I couldn't wait to leave hospital too."

Sarah joins Jude in the back of the bug.

"Tree farm first. That way."

I turn in the direction she is pointing and half an hour later we are squelching down a dirt track towards a wooded area accessed through a 5-bar gate on which is a sign reading 'Black Country Firs'. Jude opens the gate and we proceed with caution through the mud to a small wooden hut, outside of which are small fir trees of varying sizes and shapes, their roots wrapped in hessian and tied up with thick string. Presumably hearing the engine, a young man in jeans and thick parka emerges from the hut.

"Dig your own or pre-packed."

He waves towards the stack of trees. It's still bucketing down and I take the easy option.

"Pre-packed, definitely."

"'Elp yourself."

Sarah and Jude leap out and begin wading through the pile while I ponder the practicalities.

"Maybe we should have borrowed the horsebox. I didn't think they'd be quite so big."

"We could strap it to the roof."

Oliver winds down his window and calls to the young man.

"Could you find us some baling twine?"

He nods and goes into the hut. Meanwhile Jude and Sarah have made a unanimous choice.

"This one."

They point to a bushy affair about five feet in length.

"Good choice. I wish I could help…"

"We'll manage."

And we do. The young man ties the tree branches tightly to its side, then hoists it onto the roof of the bug where he fastens it on top with twine threaded through the car windows. I thank him, pay for the tree, add in a generous tip and we drive off, even slower this time as I test the security of the load.

Back home by 11am, Mattie and Amanda have let themselves in and are waiting in the kitchen. Mattie first helps Oliver into the house, then unpacks the tree and plants it into a wooden bucket. It is then carried ceremoniously into the sitting room and the now four teenagers set about decorating it with Jude's vintage ornaments, helped by Oliver who pronounces himself in charge of the lower branches. I leave them to it and head off to the kitchen, accompanied by Skipper and Cromwell where I began prepping my version of the fatted calf, namely the fillet for the Beef Wellington I have been trying to perfect. When satisfied, I cover it in foil and place it in the fridge, to be completed by Sarah and Amanda. I am still relieved of my pastry chef duties on account of my total incompetence. I then rustle up some soup and rolls for lunch.

2pm

Apparently there is more decorating to be done so I busy myself setting up a heater in the small conservatory that currently houses the garden furniture and where a few green pot plants make a sorry semblance of summer. I am trying, unsuccessfully, to quell the butterflies and I am relieved when Patti calls to

359

wish me luck and update me on the progress of the babies who have now gained several extra ounces each.

"You could have warned me how much work parenting would be."

"Not my fault you spawned a litter."

"Nervous?"

"Sick as a parrot. What if we don't get on?"

"Of course you will. You've been cyber-chatting for months."

"Not the same."

"Better. Oh, Lord, they're both crying. I'd better go and give Ross a hand."

"Admit it, you've loving it, really."

"Not all the time."

We hang up companionably.

Going into the kitchen, now festooned with bunches of holly and ivy from the bottom of the garden and copious candles, I am informed that they have heard from Alex who says he and George will be leaving Oxford around 4pm and estimate their arrival time at around 6.30pm, depending on traffic. At the mere mention of an actual ETA my stomach lurches again and all I can manage is a weak smile in acknowledgement. Jude the Intuitive crosses the room and gives me a hug "Sarah and I are pretty nervous too, you know. Meeting our half-bro' for the first time."

"Good nervous?"

"Oh, yes."

Sarah and Jude exchange a look, high-five each other and turn to me, hands raised, palms outstretched. I join in the mini celebration and then rescue my cigarette which is rapidly burning down, only to stub it out. The girls smile in approval and then Jude and I set to to prepare some vegetables to accompany the Beef Wellington whilst Sarah begins prepping something with chickpeas and tomatoes as a veggie alternative. Being so close to Christmas we lay the table with red candles, antique festive wreaths Jude found in some junk shop or other and a box of crackers. Including George, we will be 8 for supper and with the places laid the effect is warm and inviting.

Jude's phone pings, she glances at it then frowns and flashes it in front of me. It's a short message from Alex reading

'Change of plans. Family flap. Have to head home. Put G on the 3.45, arriving Brum 5.20. Explain later. Big bro'.

The phone is passed around the room. Sarah immediately tears up and excuses herself. Amanda gives Jude a hug, as does Mattie, and Olly shoots me a sympathetic look. I put on best Mary Poppins face.

"There's always next time."

Then I walk briskly out of the room and head for the conservatory where I chain-smoke 3 cigarettes, trying to calm my rising feeling of mild panic. My only thought is that Alex got cold feet about the impending reunion at the last minute and conjured up an excuse about a family crisis. That would explain why it was short on detail and very eleventh hour. Then I ask myself what else could I expect and what right had I to thrust myself back into his life after abandoning him at birth and leaving it for so many years to try and make contact. And just as I am sinking into my Slough of Despond, Olly taps on the door and wheels himself in.

"It's not the same, I know, but I haven't seen my son for over 7 years. He didn't even come back for Eleanor's funeral. Said he was too tied up in the practice."

I glance at him and see genuine grief and empathy etched in his face. I cross over and squeeze his hand.

"I hope you like Beef Wellington. There'll be plenty to go round."

"Love it."

"In the meantime how do you fancy a trip to New Street Station? Someone needs to pick up George and the teenagers can run the kitchen while we're out. The weather's awful and I'd like the company."

The weather can only be described as filthy. It's a slow drive and off the main roads, the surfaces are quite treacherous. By the time we reach New Street, George is waiting just inside the entrance, looking positively grey with cold so I bundle him quickly into the back seat and we retrace our snail-like steps. En route George explains that Alex received a cryptic SMS from a number he didn't recognise saying 'Borrowed phone. Explain at home. Can you come urgently? Dad' He seemed a bit puzzled but thought he'd better check it out."

"Quite right too."

I'm not sure I really mean that.

7.30pm

We arrive home to a warm kitchen, redolent with the scent of roasting potatoes and browning pastry. The teens have clearly decided to make the best of a bad job. Supper is sorted and, we are informed, ready whenever we are. The candles on the table have been lit and as we enter there is Christmas music playing somewhere in the background. I mouth 'Any word?' to Jude who shakes her head and shrugs her shoulders and we all set to, sorting out Oliver, taking George's coat and stowing his bag away. I lift out a couple of bottles of Rioja and the three girls begin lifting food from the oven and placing it on the table. Mattie passes plates around and Oliver, seated in his wheelchair at one end of the table, deftly carves the meat, then we all sit and dishes are passed around.

"He doesn't know what he's missing."

I smile weakly. Around the table there is desultory chatter but also an unmistakeable air of disappointment. This wasn't how it was supposed to be.

Later, after shop-bought mince pies and whipped cream, we play Pictionary and paper charades and apart from the elephant not in the room, it was almost fun. Almost.

And all the while, Jude's phone remained resolutely silent and her attempts to contact Alex went to voicemail.

"He'll get in touch as soon as he can. I know him. Don't worry."

Jude whispers these words to me and I smile and nod but deep down I am convinced it was just a case of cold feet.

12pm

George, Oliver and I head off to bed, George bivouacking down on a camp bed in the other attic bedroom, directly opposite Alex's newly decorated room, and Oliver on the old sofa in the kitchen, the warmest spot in the house with easy access to the downstairs cloakroom. The teens opt to stay up and move into the conservatory where I suspect they were having their own council of war on the Alex situation now the adults were out of earshot.

For my own part I lie awake, fretting. I had pinned my hopes on finally seeing Alex again, built it up in my mind till it overtook everything else and then, at the very last minute everything imploded. I tried to convince myself that there really was a family emergency and he needed my sympathy and support, not my approbation, but it seemed too much of a coincidence, a convenience, even. He had second thoughts at the thought of coming finally face to face so he bowed out as tactfully as he possibly could. Probably asked a mate to send the text.

1am

"Mum, wake up."

Jude is shaking my shoulders, thinking I must be fast asleep when in fact I have scarcely closed my eyes.

"Alex just called!"

"Really?"

I sit up immediately.

"Where is he? What happened?"

"What didn't! He says he was driving up the motorway and he had an electrical problem with the Jeep. So he was going to call but his phone died. He managed to hitch a lift home but when he got there the house was closed up, no sign of his father or Alice. So he traipsed over to the Deputy Head's house— guy called Malcolm—to find out what was going on. He was worried his father had been taken ill or something. But according to Malcolm his father had gone off to Portugal with Alice for Christmas a couple of days ago. So Alex begged a bed for the night and finally managed to finally use the landline to call. He feels terrible."

I shake my head, trying to digest this tale of woe.

"But if his dad's in Portugal, who sent the note?"

"He doesn't know. Thinks it must be someone's idea of a joke."

Not funny, I think, but say nothing.

"Anyway he says Malcolm's going to help him tow the vehicle to a garage tomorrow and he'll see about getting the problem sorted. But.......he thinks with it being so near Christmas he might not get it done in time so he probably won't be able to come."

Jude's tone turns flat at those last words and she looks at me anxiously. I'm desperately disappointed but my head tells me it can't be helped.

"I suppose it is a bad time. Maybe he'll manage to find someone. You never know."

I keep my own tone bright though I feel anything but.

"Maybe. Night."

"Night, sweetheart."

Before settling down to try and finally catch some shut eye I resolve to call Patti first thing tomorrow for a sympathetic ear. She's bound to be up early with 2 new-borns to tend to.

Monday, 21 December

5am

After practically no sleep at all I am on the phone to Patti who has had an equally disturbed night, albeit for very different reasons.

"I was just about to call you. I've been online for the past half an hour looking for a nanny."

As flat as I am feeling, I laugh.

"Can't take the heat, heh?"

"No sleep for three consecutive nights. I adore my babies but I know when I'm beaten. I've found 3 possibles online and I've mailed them to call for an interview."

She pauses.

"I'm being totally selfish as usual. How did it go with Alex? Tell me you hit it off?"

From laughing one minute, I now burst into tears. Very adult, Fiona.

"It couldn't have been that bad, surely?"

364

I go through the sequence of events with her, stressing that I'd been sure he had second thoughts about actually meeting me.

"I'd convinced myself that if it was just the girls he'd probably have come. They all seem to be getting on like a house on fire."

"Bollocks! I've seen his messages and I know genuine from fake. I see it all the time in my business. As for what happened, it's not like you to turn a minor mechanical setback into a full-blown Elizabethan tragedy."

"I suppose I just pinned too much hope and glory on the big reunion and the metaphorical fated calf."

"You can always freeze the leftovers for later."

"How much later, that's the question."

"Christmas won't be Christmas without any of his presence!"

"Very funny."

"I thought so. Now bugger off while I sort out my childcare issues."

"Same to you."

In spite of my blue mood I manage a giggle.

1pm

After I put the phone down Oliver, George and I left, dropping George off at the shop where he was planning on packing and preparing for his Christmas sojourn in the Emerald Isle, then doing a big supermarket shop with Oliver to tide him over for a few days, though I insisted he come and stay over Christmas proper so he wouldn't be on his own.

The teens were also up and about just as we were leaving, readying themselves for a pre-arranged outing to Stratford where I am informed there is a Christmas market with mummers, music and street theatre. The party should have included Alex but the collective decision is to carry on without him. I have instructed them all, in time-honoured tradition to 'wrap up warm'. I also reminded Jude to keep her phone on at all times in case Alex calls or messages to which I am rewarded with a withering look and a sarcastic 'You think?

2pm

The shop phone rings and I answer it. I wish I hadn't—it's Michael.

"Feef? I'm not calling at a bad time, am I?"

It's always a bad time when you call, Michael.

"I thought we could call a Christmas truce. I suggested to Lulu we should spend the holiday weekend down there."

Over my dead body.

"Down where, exactly?"

"I hadn't firmed up on that."

"We've all made plans, Amanda too. She's spending Christmas Day here and Boxing Day with her father. And I have a houseguest."

"Really?"

His tone is odd.

"Just think it over."

"I don't need to. It's too late for Sarah and Jude and too soon for Amanda. Goodbye."

I replace the receiver abruptly. Angrily. I'm upset enough over Alex's non-appearance. Michael, even just on the phone, is more than I can tolerate today.

Almost as soon as I have replaced the receiver, George appears with 2 cups of tea on a tray and a plate of biscuits.

I tell him about Michael's call.

"Sounds like he wants to have his cake and eat it."

"With a bit of luck he might choke on it."

George smiles and wags a finger at me.

"Speaking of fathers, Charles phoned and he and Diana should be here early tomorrow morning. They're staying with friends in Warwick tonight so it won't take them long to drive over. With a bit of luck we'll make the ferry."

"I hope you all have a wonderful Christmas. Irish hospitality is legendary."

"And the Fitzsimmons are renowned for honouring that tradition." He groans theatrically. "I can feel my liver complaining already." He pauses. "I'd better finish my packing."

He smiles, pats my arm and moves away.

6pm

I am in the kitchen preparing supper when I hear the bug drive up. This is quickly followed by car doors opening and closing, muffled chatter and the opening of the back door. I look up from my vegetable peeling to see all 4

366

teens entering, laden with festive gift bags and other carriers bearing the names of some of Stratford's many quirky shops. Judging by their faces and voice tones, the day has been a successful one. Jude holds up a couple of the bags.

"These are all for our eyes only."

She grins.

"Did you...."

She interprets and jumps in.

"Yeah. He called this afternoon. Good news is he found a garage open. Bad news, the jeep needs a new fuel pump and the mechanic says even if he orders online, it might not arrive in time to fit it before New Year."

I'm disappointed but not surprised.

"So what's his plan?"

"Going to stay with one of his uni friends in Paris. Says it's one place you don't a car to get around."

"That's true enough."

I put on my best Mary Poppins face.

"What's for supper, Mrs H?" (Mattie)

"Toad-in-the-hole. I have some pork sausages and some veggie ones."

"You know I don't eat batter?" (Sarah)

"You can eat this one. It's soy milk, flour and apple sauce."

I know she'll just nibble her way around it so it doesn't much matter if it works out or not.

"Do you need a hand?" (Amanda)

"No, it's all under control."

"Good. We've got loads of wrapping to do." (Jude)

I nod and smile, resolving to make the most of Christmas with or without Alex. And the Michael bombshell can wait till later.

Wednesday, 23 December

1pm

George, Charles and Diana departed for Holyhead just before nine. The teens all came into work with me to see them off and stayed on to help in the shop which has been even busier than yesterday. I've just shooed them out to the stables where Beth and Ali have organised an afternoon of gymkhana

367

games followed by a Christmas party. They said they'll call me this evening for a lift home.

2pm

"Feef? Just to let you know Louise and I are driving down. We're spending Christmas in London but we've booked into an hotel in Stratford for tonight so Louise can see Amanda tomorrow morning."

He pauses, ominously.

"And I'd like to see Sarah and Jude."

"Have you asked whether they want to see you."

He laughs, in a dry, hollow sort of way.

"I'm their father. I was thinking I could come to the house...just for old time's sake."

"You are joking, aren't you?"

"God, Feef. Can't you drop the hostility for once. Peace on earth and goodwill to all men and all that."

"Not all men."

"Just think about it."

"I don't have to. I don't want you anywhere near the house, do you understand? And if you don't mind, I have to get to get back to work."

I slam the phone down and inwardly curse him for calling and me for reacting. I want to swear and slam something but the shop is full of customers and it might be a tad unseasonable.

10pm

All five us are in the bug driving home. I am told that a good time was had by all at the stables and accordingly the mood is light and festive. I hate to put a damper on the occasion but needs must. I glance briefly towards to Sarah who is sitting next to me in the front.

"Your father called this afternoon. He and Louise are on their way to London, stopping off in Stratford tonight. Louise wants to see Amanda...and he wants to meet you both."

"No chance."

"That's what I told him." Over my shoulder I speak to Amanda.

368

"Are you okay with it?"

"I'd like to see mum. Give her her presents. But she can't come to the house. Dad'd be really upset."

I nod.

"Maybe call and find out what their plans are. Offer to meet her for coffee or something?

"I s'pose."

"I'll come with you if you want." (Mattie)

"That'd be great. Thanks."

"Good idea. Do I drop you guys off or are you coming to Lionsgate?"

"With you, if that's okay. But I've promised dad I'll be home tomorrow."
I nod.

"Home for me. I'd better put in an appearance."

"Okay." Forced brightness. "So who else was there this evening?"

Hopefully that will divert the conversation away from the bad penny about to turn up again.

Thursday, 24 December

8am

I'm finishing my tea and toast, fortification against what I know will be a hectic day at the shop when I hear a car pull up outside. Thinking Mattie may have borrowed his father's car and effected an early escape, I glance outside And then my stomach lurches and it's as much as I can do, not to retch. It's Michael's blue BMW

"You cannot just pitch up here. You know that."

I am standing outside on the porch, front door shut firmly behind me. Michael is outside the driver's door and Louise is sitting in the front passenger seat fussing with her make-up in the visor mirror.

"Feef. Louise was hoping to see Amanda."

He is all smiles and smarminess. Butter wouldn't melt.

"She's asleep."

"Can we come in and wait?"

"You are joking, aren't you?"

"Oh, come on. Surely we can be civilised?"

Words are forming in my head which are anything but. I take a deep breath.

"You rock up uninvited and unannounced on Christmas Eve, no less, and expect to just walk in as though nothing has happened?"

He makes a small movement towards me and instinctively I recoil slightly.

"To be honest there's another reason."

I stare at him, my face a mask.

"It's about the house. I thought if I asked you in person, I might persuade you to change your mind. I'm prepared to pay you well above market value."

"I don't believe this."

"It's just bricks and mortar."

"Then why are you so invested in it?"

"It is in my name, you know."

His tone has changed from wheedling to harsh and hard.

"You are perfectly well aware that ownership is a mere technicality. The house is part of the settlement and it's non-negotiable. Now please leave."

"What about Louise?"

"What about her?"

"She really does want to see Amanda."

"Does Amanda really want to see her?"

"It's her only daughter."

"A fact she conveniently forgot when she ran off with you to Manchester."

I glare at him, then look over to Louise. She half-smiles and waves tentatively.

"I'll tell Amanda to call her when she gets up."

"Please tell the girls I'm here. I have presents."

He is smiling, beaming even. I glare at him.

"You don't live here anymore. If you'd sign the bloody papers I wouldn't even be your wife anymore."

"It's Christmas, Feef. It was always such a special time for all of us."

I stare at him, recalling the theatrical set dressings and colour supplement catering.

"It was an illusion, Michael, like our marriage. And my name is Fiona."

His smile is more rectal now.

"We've just popped in to drop off gifts for the girls. Amanda is here, isn't she? We don't plan on staying long."

"I don't plan on letting you in the front door. Amanda said she'd call Louise to meet somewhere in town."

"Well we're here now so we might as well kill 2 birds with one stone."

"Leave the packages on the doorstep. The girls don't want to see you at the moment, They made that quite clear. And you can't come in the house. Ms Rowley made that quite clear."

"Just five minutes—that can't hurt, surely? And I was hoping to grab a bottle of something fizzy from the cellar."

"It's not on, Michael. And if I stand here talking to you any longer I'm going to be late for work. Please leave."

He locks eyes with me and I stare back unblinkingly. Then he leans into the car and says something to Louise who merely shrugs, then winds her window down.

"Tell Amanda to call me as soon as she gets up. We'll stop somewhere in town for brunch and she can meet us there."

"Of course."

Michael says nothing but opens the boot and lifts out two large festive gift bags which he deposits at my feet, after which he turns on his heel, strides back to the car, starts the engine and reverses in a semi-circle, revving the engine and sending bits off gravel flying like shrapnel. I wait till the car goes through the gates at the end of the drive, then pick up the bags, unlock the door and walk inside.

Leaving the bags on the kitchen table I write a note.

'Your father left these for you. Please keep the doors locked and if he comes back on no account is he to come inside. Ask Amanda to call her mother—she wants to meet up for brunch in town later.'

The I pick up my bag and keys, exiting through the back door and locking it behind me. A shop full of last-minute Christmas shoppers will be a breeze compared to the last quarter of an hour.

8pm

The girls had prepared a vegan baked pasta dish which filled the kitchen with a welcome aroma when I finally arrived home, shop now locked up for the

371

holiday, feet killing me. I opened a bottle of Valpolicella and poured small glasses for Sarah and Jude, a larger one for myself and having missed lunch, I devoured the pasta with gusto. Now we are sitting around the cleared table and there's only one topic of conversation.

I am advised that Amanda met up with her mother but that Michael was not present, after which the girls did some shopping, caught a movie, then they split up and returned home separately. Sarah emphasised that they had locked the house up meticulously when they left and there was no way that Michael could have effected entry. I smile and raise my glass.

"Well done."

Then they show me some pictures from Alex of him, his friend Paolo and a few other young people in and around Paris—Christmas stalls on the Left Bank, the Eiffel Tower lit up in coloured lights, a boat ride on the Seine, the boat similarly festively bedecked.

"Lucky duck." (Sarah)

"Wish we could have gone with him!" (Jude)

I nod, wistfully.

"Still, we're all together and Olly will be joining us for lunch tomorrow. I thought I'd catch the early service at the village church. You coming?"

The both look at me as if I had suggested we rob the local bank.

"Just me, then, I'll take the bug and go straight to Oliver's house afterwards."

Friday, 25 December

10am

They sky was overcast and ominous when I woke up but the church was bright with electric light and several dozen candles and though not of a particularly pious bent, I enjoyed the camaraderie of the communal service and the singing of familiar carols. If the priest was surprised to see me, he hid it well and on leaving, I do feel slightly more festive than when I set out.

I am now on my way to Fordham to pick up Oliver and bring him back to spend the day en famille. The plan is for a light lunch, a lazy afternoon and then a quasi-traditional supper of roast duck for Olly and me and a gourmet nut roast from a recipe Sarah found on an online vegan website for the girls. It was decided that Olly would stay over again and of course Skipper is also invited.

This was scarcely the day that we had originally planned-exchanging of gifts and life stories, my three offspring together around a table, old movies on the television, a proper family Christmas-but as my grandmother used to say 'man proposes and God disposes'.

'For fuck's sake, Fiona, that sounds like Charles Dickens, Bing Crosby and a tableau from a tin of Quality Street all rolled into one. The only thing missing is waking up to snowflakes outside the window. Admit it, you never really believed it was going to happen anyway, did you? That's not how your life goes.'

Monday, December 28th

The past week is beginning to feel like a dream. Though Amanda did catch up with her mother last week, Jude and Sarah were steadfast in their refusal to see their father, in spite of his proximity. When he called to remonstrate and asked again to stop in on the way back north, I told him the entire situation (actually, I said 'affair') was of his own doing and I remained deaf to his wheedling to reconsider his offer on the house.

I wonder if his masterplan is to reclaim the property, have me removed, then invite the girls back 'home'? It wouldn't surprise me at all if that were the case, so twisted his thinking seems to have become.

11am

I drive to Oliver's house and pick him up, then we proceed to the stables to meet up with Mattie and the girls. With the shop and schools closed we have arranged to go for a gentle hack, all 6 of us, plus the dogs. The weather is damp and cold, with patches of ground frost in shaded areas but the threatened rain holds off. Tacked up, I help Oliver to mount, then I hop onto Dancer and we slowly process out of the yard, crocodile-style behind Jude. It's so good to be out riding, all the stresses and strains of the past few weeks—Patti's C-section, Alex's non-arrival, Oliver's incapacity, Michael's intransigence over the house—draining away. We sight pheasant in a copse near a stubble-covered cornfield which take flight in a blur of autumnal colours against the leaden sky and several rabbits which the dogs chase and attempt, unsuccessfully, to catch. Keeping vanguard, I see the mood is infectious as the teens chatter and joke amongst themselves and Oliver turns to give me a smile and a 'thumbs up'. We spend a good 2 hours in the saddle, taking a meandering path back to the yard and I feel invigorated and re-charged, albeit chilled to the bone when we dismount. As I help Oliver back into the front seat of the bug he thanks me and tells me he thoroughly enjoyed it, though he is quite quiet on the drive home. My fault—I think we may have overtired him with such an extended ride.

Tuesday, 29th December

I re-open the shop, though I am not expecting a brisk trade and I make use of the lull to stock-take and tidy. Mid-morning DS Cox calls. We exchange pleasantries and I tell him about Christmas with Oliver, omitting any reference to Michael. He in turn tells me he was on duty. I commiserate.

"The car was a bit of a disappointment. Nothing in the way of evidence."

"So that's that, then?"

"I'll keep on digging. You never know."

'Give it up, why don't you?' I think, but do not voice.

7pm

Jude and Sarah video call Patti to discuss arrangements for New Year. She looks simultaneously sleep-deprived and smugly self-satisfied as she tells us Ross is putting the babies to bed and she's about to make supper. Also that they'll drive up on Friday morning and will be with us in time for lunch. The girls inform her that they'll be in charge of the twins, no arguments and Patti says there won't be one from her or Ross.

"Will Alex be around?"

"I doubt it. From the sounds of it, he's having too much fun in Gay Paree."

"I'll keep my fingers crossed. I am his proxy aunt, after all. It's about time I met and vet him as well."

"You're not that poxy."

She pulls a face, we both laugh and I leave her to her kitchen duties.

374

Wednesday, 30th December

Mattie and Amanda are both back in situ so I delegated all four of them to prepare the house for our guests. Before leaving for work I left a long 'to do' list, everything from airing and prettifying the big, first-floor bedroom and scouring the attic for their assorted old toys, (yes, I know the babies are only a few weeks old but it will still give a nice nursery feel to the place) to checking the fridge and pantry and mapping out some menus. This last task I know Sarah will attack with gusto—she relishes the planning and preparation of food, so long as she doesn't have to eat it. Ironical, isn't it? Alex is still a maybe but I'm keeping my fingers crossed. I leave the bug for them to go shopping and I take the bus to work.

Business again is slow which is to be expected. I phone Oliver and he asks if I could possibly take him to Birmingham for a check-up with Mr Reddy, whom he now calls 'Ish', their being on first-name terms and old friends, almost. I tell him it should be fine if we go early. I'll ask the teens to look after the shop for a couple of hours and we can be there and back before lunch.

"I'll see if they can fit me in. It's not urgent."

He calls back five minutes later to tell me Ish can see him at 8am and I promise to drive over and pick him up no later than 6.30am. With the extended holiday hopefully the roads in should be fairly empty.

Thursday, 31st December

5am

I'm up and about, anxious to be on the road. It looks a bit foggy again outside so the drive to Brum will take a bit longer than usual. I arrive at Oliver's more or less at the allotted time, his nurse helps him into the front of the bug and we set off for the hospital. Visibility is poor and it's slow-going but as I expected there's precious little traffic around.

Oliver's appointment is in Ish's rooms in a small wing off to one side of the spinal unit. I wheel him in, exchange pleasantries with the ever-cheerful Mr R and wander off to find a cup of tea. When I return half an hour later the consultation is over.

"Oliver tells me he has been doing some horse riding?"

375

I nod.

"Excellent. Fresh air and exercise. The perfect combination."

I murmur agreement and Oliver acquiesces and smiles.

"I've booked him in for some more tests on Monday. Just to monitor progress."

"Will that be convenient?"

"Perfect. The shop's closed on Mondays."

"Thank you."

We bid the genial surgeon farewell and head off home for Oliver and back to work for me.

2pm

Patti phones to say they're on their way and should be with us around 5pm. I'm really looking forward to the visit and I tell her so.

4.30pm

My phone rings again and I assume it's Patti with a travel update but instead it's DS Cox.

"Don't you ever take a day off?"

"I wanted to ask a favour."

His voice is odd, sombre, official.

"Ask away."

"Did your husband leave any belongings behind?"

"Quite a lot, actually. It's all packed up and stored in the garage. He was supposed to send a van to pick it up."

"But he didn't?"

"No."

"Would you mind if I took a look?"

"Why should I?"

"Some people don't like that sort of thing."

"I'm not 'some people' ".

"I've noticed! So it's okay if I pop round?"

"I'll be home by six. I'll open the garage for you."

376

As I drive up to the house I see the German SUV parked outside the garage and behind it, DS Cox's official squad car. I leap out, anxious to see Patti and Ross, fumbling for the garage key on the bug key ring, and turning it in the lock.

"The light switch is on the right. Come in for tea or something stronger when you're done."

"Thanks."

I head for the front door, then half turn.

"What exactly are you hoping to find?"

"No idea. Between you and me, it's a fishing expedition."

"Have fun."

I leave him to it and head inside.

Patti, Ross and the babies are installed in the room the teens had prepared, the infants sleeping peacefully in their travel cots. After oohing and aahing over the little bodies, I fill them in on Cox and Box, or rather boxes.

"There's nothing very exciting in them. We packed them, remember?"

I nod.

"So what's he hoping to find?"

"More interestingly, why's he looking in the first place?"

"Perhaps Pricerite's been doing some dodgy dealing in it supply chain. You know, like that Gregson's business back in Bath."

"Or insider trading?"

"Possibly."

Ross didn't sound convinced.

"I thought you said he was from the Cold Case unit?"

"He is. That's what made me think of Gregsons."

"Maybe they found something out 'in the course of their enquiries'? Isn't that the phrase they use?"

I ponder the implications.

"And if there is some incriminating evidence on his computer or in some of those files, that would explain why he's been so keen to get his hands on the property and get you to move out."

"But if that were the case, surely he'd have collected the stuff long ago?"

377

I stare at Patti as she speaks but it doesn't quite fit. It also just doesn't seem like Michael's style.

None the wiser, we all troop down to the kitchen, then sit around drinking tea and trying to get back to normal, whatever that is these days. Sarah and Jude chat with Alex who says he is ensconced at an outside table in a café in Montmartre, along with a group of other young people. Sarah reminds him that she is due to go back the Avon first thing Monday morning and he jollies her along, promising to visit in term-time, thesis permitting. She smiles but I know her too well and I can tell she is acting. And for the first time I wonder what the effect of all the recent turmoil will have on her illness and recovery.

Patti, who can read me like a book, catches my eye, and understands.

"I'm no expert but I bet you won't be in there too much longer."

"I'm not going back."

Wow. That came right out of left field and was almost shouted.

"We can talk about it later."

"There's nothing to discuss. I've been thinking about it and I've made up my mind. I'm 18 and you can't force me."

I look in panic at Patti who shrugs imperceptibly but Ross pauses, halfway through refilling his tea cup and smiles at Sarah.

"Works for me."

Patti raises a quizzical eyebrow at him. He adds sugar and milk to his cup and returns to his seat.

"I know I'm new to this parenting thing but with everything that's been going on here recently you three are going to need to lean on one another. Plus what would be the value of sending Sarah back to hospital to complete her treatment when she'll probably spend most of the time worrying about you two back at home."

We all take a moment to consider what he said.

"That's exactly what I was thinking. How can I leave when everything's in this mess?"

I look directly at Sarah, trying to gauge her motive and meaning.

"We can speak to Professor Turner. He needs to know what's happened since you left last week anyway. I'll phone him tomorrow and he'll probably want a word with you too."

"Okay."

Supper is pork chops and mash with a few root vegetables for the carnivores and quorn cutlets for the faddy eaters, well, eater, to be more accurate. I send the girls out to the garage and instruct them to drag DS Cox to the table, kicking and screaming if necessary. It's a cold night and there's no source of heat in the garage, it being part of what was originally the old stable block. They reappear a few minutes later, shepherding a far from reluctant Cox with them.

"Thanks for the invite."

"You're welcome."

I introduce him to Patti and Ross.

"We spoke to your colleague on the phone a couple of months ago."

Patti's tone is mildly disapproving.

"I remember."

"Did you find anything useful?"

"Hard to tell. Is it okay if I take the computer away?"

"Help yourself. Michael appears not to want it. Where are you staying, by the way? "

"I thought I'd try the local pub."

"On New Year' Eve? You'll be lucky."

"You'd better stay here for the night."

"I don't want to impose."

At which point Jude interrupts.

"There's heaps of room so I wouldn't worry. Now can everyone please sit down? This food's getting cold."

And very obediently we all sit and begin passing around plates and dishes while Ross does the honours with a bottle of something red, French and expensive from downstairs.

Monday, 4th January

DS Cox departed early on Friday morning, after coffee and croissants, complete with Michael's old computer and a few assorted boxes of files and the rest of our house party spent the long weekend eating, drinking walking in the country and what I believe is known in current parlance as 'chillaxing'. On Saturday, I phone Professor Turner to advise him of Sarah's decision. I can't say he was happy—he is still convinced there's something she's not saying, either because she can't or won't. But he conceded that there is still a good chance of getting to the bottom of it with her as a day patient and agreed to consider a trial run after he's had a chance to discuss it in detail with Sarah.

Ross, Patti and family departed early this morning. Ross has to be back at work on Wednesday and he was anxious to begin prepping his new project. We were all up at the crack of dawn, me to see them off and Sarah and Jude to catch a lift to the local station to hook up with Mattie and Amanda, where they plan on going ice skating in Stratford.

8am

I am paying a hospital visit, once again sitting in a waiting room in Birmingham while Oliver has his physio.

En route to Brum Oliver surprises me by saying he's had a visit from the Old Bill.

"Nice young chap by the name of Cox."

My head swivels around.

"What did he want?"

"He mentioned my cell phone. From the accident. Said the local police had had it in their evidence drawer and he wanted to make sure I had it back."

What the hell was he doing at Fordham cop shop?

"Is that all he wanted?"

"Pretty much."

"He certainly spends a lot of time away from his patch, that one."

"I don't follow."

"He's supposed to be a cold case officer from Bath. Now he's on lost property in the Black Country."

Privately I wonder what exactly he's up to now.

Back in the now-familiar waiting area, my mind decides to preview the ordeal to come this week—the looming appointment on Wednesday with Professor Turner to map out Sarah's external programme, assuming he okays the new arrangement, and on Friday a crucial milestone in the impending divorce. Claire has applied for a court order to prevent Michael from harassing me over the house anymore and assures me I do not have to attend—it will be a formal hearing between her, Michael's lawyer and a judge and she is confident that his counsel will see sense and persuade his client to accept that legally,

380

whilst his daughters are in situ in the family home, he hasn't got a leg to stand on.

Before going home I drive to the stables for a bit of equine therapy for both of us. It is bitterly cold but the sun is out as we take Cloud and Captain on a short, circular route which skirts the village, edges around the back of the local church and winds up almost back where we started. It's utterly relaxing and exactly what we needed. I drop Olly at his house, pick up some groceries and head home myself.

7pm

The skating party has returned and is helping to prepare supper. I remind Sarah that we have an appointment at the Avon tomorrow.

"I'm not going back in."

"So you've said. But you do need to discuss it with Professor Turner and if he agrees, he'll have to give you a treatment schedule.

Thursday, 7th January

Sarah and I had a long heart-to-heart with Professor Turner yesterday concerning the home situation. I'm sure he secretly believes the whole family totally delinquent and thus little wonder that one of the progeny has flown over the cuckoo's nest. Not that he would ever express it in those terms. In fact what he actually said was that under the unique circumstances (psychiatrist-speak for internecine implosion) it might actually be preferable for Sarah to become a day patient for the time being and a timetable was mapped out whereby she would attend the Avon three times a week after school and on Saturday mornings. She wasn't too happy about the weekend session but caved in eventually, more to bring the meeting to a close than with any real commitment.

The fine weather of three days ago has given way to heavy, leaden clouds, threatening snow so when I get back to Ink-an'-Abulia to relieve the others who have been shop-keeping, I send them all home in the bug and tell them I will take the bus later. The shop is almost deserted, save for a few regulars, seeking refuge from the January gloom and chill. The doorbell tinkles and I look up, expecting another winter refugee but instead it is DS Cox. I look at him quizzically as he traverses the shop floor and approaches.

"Back so soon?"

"The thing about searches is that most of the time you don't know what you're looking for, you don't always recognise it if you do find it and more often than you'd like, there's nothing to find."

"You'd do well to heed the words of my father-in-law's ghillie. 'It's called fishing, not catching'."

He smiles and points his finger in that 'You've got me' manner.

"Where might your husband have kept important papers? Title deeds, house insurance, bank details, that sort of thing?"

I pause to think.

"There was a little grey safe he had. He bought it years ago to keep his company papers in. I think it made him feel important."

"So where is it now?"

"No idea."

"Did he take it with him?"

"Not that I know of but I suppose it's possible. He might have kept them in his office at Pricerite"

"What about a safety deposit box?"

"What about it?"

"Did he have one?"

He spaces out the words as if talking to a half-wit.

"I have no idea. We led very separate lives, as I'm sure you know."

"Let's start again. He bought a safe?"

I nod

"He moved here and then what?"

"Haven't a clue."

"So he might have found somewhere else to store the safe and whatever he had in it?"

"You still haven't told me what you're looking for."

"That's because I don't know."

"Or why."

"I'm nosy. It's part of my job description."

"I'll think about it.

He looks at me enigmatically.

"Think about where they might be or whether you'll tell me?"

"The first one."

"I'd better be off. I just popped in in passing."

"Bye."

"You won't forget?"

"I said I'll think about it."

He nods and exits.

Tuesday, 12th January

It seemed utterly unreal to see the three girls once more in uniform, pressed and polished, more or less, and giggling like the eponymous maids in the Gilbert & Sullivan song. We all piled into the bug—now apparently trés chic—and processed to the school gates where I dropped them off and carried on to the shop.

9am

I call Patti. She tells me the twins are thriving and have now almost caught up with their full-term counterparts.

"They're still sleeping. It's bliss."

I brief her on Cox's visit and his obsession with finding wherever it is that Michael stores his papers.

"Let's hope the house deeds are in it."

"Somehow I don't think that's what they were looking for."

"Which is what exactly?"

"Incriminating documents, I suppose. I did wonder if they thought he was people-trafficking, that time last year when they impounded the lorry with those illegals."

"I wouldn't put anything past that slime ball but that doesn't strike me as his style."

"What then?"

"The stuff in the cellar. What if it's not legit? That might explain why he's never mentioned it to his lawyer."

"But how would the filth know about it?"

"They get intel."

"Get you with the jargon!" Pause. "I suppose it's a possibility."

"So that's my problem. Do I tell him about it or not?"

383

"Why not fish around a bit on your own. Play him at his own game."

"Neither of us knows what we're looking for."

"You were a helluva investigative reporter. Use your initiative."

"I was, wasn't I? I had a good teacher."

"Yes, you did."

And lost in thought, we both hang up.

Friday, 15th January

3pm

George phones to say he's back on the mainland, en route to Featherington Hall. Charles and Diana are going to drop him off and carry on to London, he to sort out some sundry affairs and she no doubt to shop till she drops.

A message from Alex this morning confirmed that he too was on the move. He's taking the Eurostar to London and then up to Oxford. I responded with another off-hand reference to our extensive, eclectic book stock but stopped short of asking him outright when he might be able to visit us.

Saturday, 16th January

Sarah reluctantly caught the bus to the Avon this morning for her weekend check-in, check-up and counselling session. It was decided that it would be easier this way, taking the bus straight from school during the week and again on Saturday morning. She's still none too keen but I remind her that Oliver is also an outpatient and it's either that or she checks back in full-time. Time for a bit of tough love.

From Amanda we hear rumblings that all in Louise's garden is not rosy. Apparently she's finding life in a Mancunian flat, albeit a very upmarket, penthouse affair, not to her liking and she assures her daughter that she 'misses her dreadfully' but since she's neither especially outdoorsy nor especially maternal, I rather think it's just a case of regret for burned bridges. Also I wonder if she's starting to rumble Michael's act? He certainly wasn't very complimentary about her that time on the phone. In truth, I couldn't care tuppence either way but Amanda clearly needs a sounding board and sympathetic ear sometimes and it's not information she can share with her

384

father. Poor kid. She's become an unwitting casualty in a mess not of her making.

And it strikes me that all three girls in the same boat.

Saturday, 16th January

10pm

I stand at the counter in case I am needed, pondering Patti's challenge about playing the fuzz at their own game. My first thought is 'why should I?'. Why would I care what Michael might or might not have gotten up to? And my second thought is that Simon Cox is not going to give me a minute's peace till he has a definitive answer one way or another. So it is that I return to my journo training, taking out a large legal pad and beginning to jot down facts and hypotheses in order.

i)   The cops seem to suspect Michael of something. What? They're not sure. Maybe grey vintage wine and spirit dealing?
I pause
Maybe fraudulent provenance or mislabelling?
ii)   Michael has requested the return of 'personal
items and documents of no intrinsic value'. But
he hasn't bothered to have the boxes in the garage
collected so if he is into dodgy dealing,
presumably there's nothing incriminating there?
iii)   Is that why he's never specifically mentioned the stuff downstairs?
iv)   Is there incriminating stuff somewhere else in the
house.
V) If so, where? _BASEMENT?_
vi) Maybe there is no paper trail? Or maybe it's on his other laptop?

I resolve to poke around downstairs when I'm on my own. That means Monday when the teens are all safely in class. I've seen a lot of the wines, of course. The walls are lined with stone and wrought iron racks, put in place when the house was first built for the precise purpose of storing bottles at just the right temperature. So much so that I know Michael often undertook to keep some special reserves belonging to premium Pricerite clients. But there's also an inner room that's always kept locked. I make another notation

vii)   Where the hell would I find a key? Presumably Michael has it with him

I pause again. Don't think I've seen a set of spare keys around but something is nagging at the back of my mind. It will come.

1pm

Sarah enters, freshly back from her morning session at the Avon. She looks unhappy. Knowing she's just had a one-on-one with Professor Turner I resolve not to ask any probing questions.

"Just in time. I was about to pop upstairs for lunch. Would you like something?"

"I'm not hungry."

"You know it's important that you eat regularly. That's one of the conditions of your out-patient arrangement."

I keep my tone light but firm.

I can't just force food down when I don't want it."

Actually, you can. That's exactly why mealtimes are supervised at the clinic. I think this but do not say it out loud.

"There's some tomato soup in the cupboard. Go and buy a small brown loaf from Simmonds."

I hand her some money

"I hope you're hungry because you'll be eating it all yourself."

I haven't heard her this moody and miserable for a long time. Maybe it was a mistake allowing her to come out early?

Reluctantly Sarah departs in the direction of the bakery, leaving me to only guess at what's upset her. Logically it's something that was either said, left unsaid or discussed with Professor Turner and I am reminded of his conviction that there's still something deeper underlying Sarah's condition. Maybe psychiatrists and police officers alike should learn not to disturb sleeping dogs and long-dead family skeletons?

With this thought, I pop upstairs to heat up the soup, though I'm probably in more than enough of that already. Let battle commence.

Sunday, 17th January

7pm

I'm lying in the bath, going over a few things in my mind. Such as the fact that Sarah's mood hasn't improved much all weekend. I know the other teens all picked up on it, though they didn't mention it to me. I'm hoping a day of school routine tomorrow might help bring her out of it but I'm not overly optimistic.

And such as the issue of house keys. Why do I have this nagging feeling that somewhere, sometime, I've seen some old keys.

Think, Fiona

And then it hits me. It was that time Michael had the kitchen remodelled a couple of years ago. At some point in its chequered history, someone had bricked up the original hearth with its spit roast and black lead range. And with Michael at work and no-one to contradict me, I'd insisted they un-block it so we could have an open fireplace in the kitchen. And when we'd tried to clear the flue which was full of old birds' nests and bits of other detritus we found an old metal box on a ledge just inside the chimney. It had contained a few old coins, a notebook with some hand-written recipes, a faded picture postcard from Bognor Regis and... a few assorted keys! As I recall, I'd given the recipe book to George, Jude had bagged the coin collection, Sarah had taken the postcard and I'd put the keys...I'm wracking my brain...got it—at the back of the boot cupboard in the scullery, still in the old tin box! Of course there was no telling what keys were there but it was a start.

387

Part IV
"Barren Winter, with His Wrathful Nipping Cold"

Monday, 18th January

I'm trying to quell my butterflies as I drop the girls off at school and head back home. I have no idea if any of the keys in the box will fit the cellar doors: I also have no idea if I will uncover incriminating evidence against Michael and that even if I do, will I hand it over to DS Cox, at this point in time, at least. No doubt, it would have an impact on the ongoing divorce and also it's likely to lower the girls' opinion of their father even further than it is already.

The box is just where I left it. I lift it out, take it into the kitchen and sort through them on the table. They are variously made of brass and iron, not much different from their modern counterparts but with more intricate locking teeth. I lift out a cloth and lubricant spray and clean them up, then I take the box and go down into the wine cellar. With no Pricerite stock in temporary storage, a few of the racks are empty and the full ones are more recent, easy drinking acquisitions, basically superior table wines as well as Michael's personal collection. Behind are wines in cases, bought for long-term keeping, higher priced but unlikely to be worth anyone's while trying to pass them off as something they're not. I am now right at the back, facing a heavy, oak door and the first thing I notice is that it has two locks, top and bottom. Damn. I start with the bottom one, painstakingly trying each lock in the box till I find one that not only inserts but turns. I repeat the process up above and go through them all. The very last one I try slides in and clicks free. Turning the doorknob and opening the door, I realise I had glimpsed inside this room on my first visit with Michael and the girls, though I hadn't taken much notice. It's a compact space and has yet more wine racks and shelves. I see immediately that the entire room has more of the appearance of a museum than a storage area. There are wine and champagne bottles wrapped in tissue, the traces of foxing on the papers and labels testimony to their age. Some offerings are in individual wooden cases, some in cases of a dozen. I glimpse some of the names— Macallan, Chateau Latour, Chateau d'Yquem, Domaine Romanée-Conti, J.S. Terrantez, Heidsieck. I pick bottles at random and glimpse dates, 1955, 1895, 1920. I have no idea of what these sorts of bottles fetch at auction but my guess is that the entire collection must be worth a small fortune. If it's all genuine, of course. In a space between the racks is an old-fashioned bureau. I pull up the cover and find a ledger and some neat files, some marked with familiar names of prestigious auction houses—'Sotheby's', 'Christies' others I don't recognise. Again, I open one at random and see what appear to be authentic bills of sale. Some of the amounts are eye-watering and there are several that have been bought directly from source, deceased estates and the like, including one from the agents for the sale at Featherington Hall. Presumably that lot came courtesy of Louise. Yet another file is marked 'Sales' and opening that I see receipts and shipping waybills. It would appear that Michael is not only buying but selling, presumably at a profit.

I pause to think.

I'm not an expert but on the face of it, this documentation appears completely kosher, so my theory of fake bottles doesn't seem to hold up. But what if this wheeling and dealing has been done without the knowledge of HMRC? That might explain his reticence to bring it up in the divorce negotiations and would definitely dovetail with his keenness to get his hands on Lionsgate. He presumably hoped to keep the secret from everyone, me included.

There is one more item of interest in the room which is a heavy Victorian safe in a corner at the back. It must have come with the house as it seems to be cemented in place. I wonder if that's what he meant with his old litany of 'safe as houses'? Some sort of secret joke? And that makes me wonder what could be in there? Some extra-special bottles, perhaps? Or the incriminating documentation Patti and I talked about? I bend down and examine the safe. It is certainly sturdy and has a formidable-looking locking and lever device and something similar to a modern combination dial.

I sit down on the chair by the bureau and wonder what a bottle of 120-year-old champagne would taste like. Also I wonder how I'm going to get into that safe. I consider calling Patti. She has all sorts of contacts but somehow I doubt there's a safecracker in her little black book. I briefly toy with the idea of calling DS Cox but quickly reject that idea too. I'm sure Her Majesty's finest could rustle up a competent lock picker but somehow I don't want him involved till I've found what's going on. And then it suddenly hits me— George. I bet somewhere in his military intelligence past there may be someone with just the set of questionably legal skills I'm looking for. And the old fox will be discretion personified. I stand up, leave the inner sanctum, locking it behind me and head upstairs to the kitchen and the phone.

"There's a safe in our cellar."

"And you're sharing this information why?"

"I want to get into it."

I explain briefly what my quest is all about.

"What sort of safe?"

"Very big, very old and set into the wall and the floor. I'm guessing Victorian or Edwardian. It has a seriously impressive-looking locking system."

"The old Treble Clef, eh? Seems like you need a talented musician."

"That sounds like a euphemism."

Pause

"You are mindful of the story of Pandora?"

"The myth, you mean."

"There's many a truth hidden in ancient folklore."

"I'm willing to risk it."

"Let me give it some thought. I can't promise anything."

We hang up.

1pm

I phone Patti and fill her in. When I mention some of the names on the wine and spirit bottles she gasps.

"Jesus, Fee, I think you're sitting on a goldmine there. We did a feature on it a couple of years ago and some of those bottles change hands for tens of thousands."

"I know. I've seen the invoices. But it's not really mine to sell."

"He hasn't asked for it back."

"I'm not supposed to know about it, remember."

"Nor's anyone else, presumably. You're probably right about tax evasion. So what do you think's in the safe?"

"I'm hoping there's some paperwork that'll give him away."

"That'll mean a hefty fine. He might even go to jail."

I consider this observation for a moment.

"Somehow I doubt it. He'll hire an expensive brief and wriggle out of it."

"Still worth it, though."

"Damn right!"

4.55pm

The shop has been quiet all day and I'm just about to close.

George is still at Featherington so I'm on my own. It's been snowing lightly this week but he's hard at work in the greenhouse, planting seedlings in batches, to be ready to go into the ground in March.

I'm just putting on a jacket when the door opens and a man in his thirties, wearing a tailored three-quarter coat and preppy slacks, enters.

"You're just in time. I was just about to shut up shop."

"Then I am definitely lucky to have caught you."

His accent is plummy, his smile genuine.

"Were you looking for something in particular or would you prefer to browse?"

He beams again.

"Not something, somebody. Are you Ffion?"

Only one person ever calls me that.

"You're a friend of George?"

"More a son of a friend of a son of a friend."

"I'm guessing you have a specialist interest?"

"I do, indeed."

I look at him quizzically.

"Actually I have quite a combination of interests." Pause. "I believe I might be of assistance in that regard?"

Light finally dawns. I have no idea what a safecracker should look like but I'm pretty sure this isn't it.

"I do need some help at home."

"Well then, lay on Macduff! I'm Rupert, by the way."

"You'd better follow me."

6pm

Sarah has just arrived back from her session at the Avon and Jude will be back from the stables at any moment. Rupert is unpacking an overnight grip upstairs in a spare bedroom, the story being that he's an old friend of George, just passing through and hoping to beg a bed for the night. Tomorrow, he'll have the house to himself and he can ply his trade without awkward questions from the teens. As luck would have it, all four are staying tonight so I hope Rupert's handy with a back story. I don't doubt it, somehow.

7.30pm

We are all assembled in the warmth of the kitchen. Rupert has introduced himself, vaguely referencing his doing something in the city, 'a sort of civil servant'. In the department with the motto 'Semper Occultus', I suspect. The teens are all agog, slightly overawed by his air of urban sophistication and over a supper of vegetable biryani and rice, he regales us with comic tales of red tape, royal escapades and gaffes and apocryphal Whitehall farces, offset with an intimate knowledge of the capital's pubs, clubs, theatres and museums. Sarah is totally entranced and announces there and then that she's going to apply to read English at King's College, Jude and Amanda quiz him over his flat and Mattie learns that he plays polo, is a member of the Hurlingham Club and can procure complimentary tickets for matches. By the end of the evening, his stock is sky high.

Friday, 22nd January

I drove all the teens to school before heading to the shop. Rupert was suitably vague when asked about his plans, telling me that he hoped to be done in a day but that sometimes these things took a little longer. I was desperate to be able to watch a master at work but it was politely made clear I'd be persona non grata so I had to make do with a promise to be immediately advised when he had completed his task.

The call came at 4.30pm. It was agony waiting till I could reasonably lock up and leave, drive the bug as much like a bat out of hell as I could squeeze out of the old engine and rush inside the house, only to find him in the kitchen, leisurely drinking a cup of tea.

"Want one?"

I shake my head. He finishes his tea and rises languorously.

"Come on then."

I follow him down to the cellar, into the inner room, right to the back. He bends down on one knee, twists the dial a few times, then grasps two locking levers, one in each hand and pulls them down. I hear a series of clicking noises and then the great door opens a crack. I see that the door is easily five or six inches thick.

"There you go. My work here is done."

Rupert stands.

"Give the kids my regards and tell them they're welcome to look me up anytime they come down to The Smoke."

He hands me a business card and I glance at it. It must be the most understated design in the history of all such cards, bearing only his name in a tiny, handwritten font—Rupert Cholmondeley-Rose—along with a landline and cell phone number. He also gives me a small piece of paper with a series of numbers written on it—the safe combination. And with a wave, he turns on his heels and leaves. I wait a few seconds, then through a high window, I hear the unmistakeable roar of his Morgan driving away. Shaking my head, I turn back to the safe and with an immense amount of trepidation I open the safe door fully and squat down to inspect the contents.

There are several items covered in thick layers of bubble wrap. I lift one off at random and, just as I expected, it reveals an antique wooden box, presumably an especially rare and sought-after vintage. There are also two large metal boxes, one large one, the size of a microwave oven, the other shoebox size and shape, both locked. Damn. I tug at the lids but to no avail and toy with the idea of taking them upstairs to try a few suitcase keys and the like or even to try and jimmy them open with a hairpin, like they do in the movies.

And that is all there is. No dodgy dossier, no metaphorical smoking gun. Just some very valuable vino and a couple of boxes holding what I assume must be a working float.

I stand up and move to push the safe door, leaving it slightly ajar when my eye is caught by something small, right at the bottom of the safe and right at the back. I fish it out and once more am disappointed to find only a matchbox—for candles if the power goes out or a light bulb pops, I assume. I idly slide it open and stop short. Inside are two small keys tucked under the matches. Can it be that simple? Did Michael really leave spare keys in the matchbox? Answer, yes! They each fit one of the boxes. This must be where I hit paydirt, as the Americans say, the incriminating paper trail and presumably cash that can't be accounted for. My hands tremble with anticipation as I lift the lid on the first box which contains nothing more exciting than Michael's old set of volumes of the corporate Pricerite bible from when he was first inducted, Mason-wise into the sect. I've heard of industrial espionage but I'd hardly have thought it was worth locking a few manuals away in a safe. Then I remember that's why Michael bought that old grey portable affair back then but now they're years out of date and surely of no use to anyone? Must have some sort of kinky sentimental attachment for him, I assume. I turn to the second which also holds no hoard of banknotes, merely a single leather pouch. Tipping the contents into the box I gaze first at an art deco pill box. Lifting the lid I see there are some small pills inside and I wonder, somewhat absurdly, if they could be some form of Class A drugs—uppers, downers, Es or.... Actually that's as far as my druggy vocabulary goes. I turn to the next object—a thin aluminium case which I recognise immediately as the sort used for hand-rolling cigarettes, containing a couple of thin specimens rather the worse for wear, along with a packet of papers and a small twist of tinfoil. I unwrap the foil package to reveal something that looks like part of a Bovril cube and give it a practised sniff which confirms my suspicion that it's marijuana. The roll-ups have the same aroma, along with a trace of tobacco. Next to that are a generic vehicle cigarette lighter and a silver flip-top Zippo with a Jack Daniels insignia on the front. I slide them around, much as you might move pawns on a chessboard, baffled as to what they are doing there. They could be some sort of drug dealer or user's kit, I suppose, but I can't imagine what Michael would be doing with them. He's never smoked a tobacco product in his life, much less anything more hallucinogenic.

Double-checking I haven't missed anything else, I again feel carefully around the inside of the safe but find nothing more. Rising to my feet, I retrieve the auction ledger and check the names and vintages of the items in the safe against entries in the book and they are all there, literally present and accounted for, albeit at amounts akin to a king's ransom. I return the boxes to the safe, close the door, exit the inner room, locking it behind me and make my way upstairs to the kitchen, somewhat disappointed and also extremely puzzled.

When the teens dribble in later, I give them the bad news of Rupert's untimely departure to which they react as though a favourite pet had passed away but they are slightly mollified by the business card and open invite. They are also far more impressed than me by the enigmatic calling card which they all agree is 'super cool'.

10pm

"Drug paraphernalia? From the sainted Michael!"

Patti is hugely amused by news of my find.

"What do you think I should do?"

Shop him, of course. To your friend in the filth."

"Hardly my friend. Anyway, I think he must be keeping it for someone else. Odd, though, the packet of weed and those reefers seem very stale."

"I don't think that matters. Look at this way. The fuzz has been buzzing around looking for something to nail him on so give it to them. Okay, it's not exactly big time but if they caution him for possession, it'll take him down a peg or two."

I ponder for a moment. She's right. On the karma scale this is fairly near the bottom but it would serve him right for thinking he could keep it hidden till he got his hands on the house.

"There is that."

"Also, even if he did buy all that wine legitimately, who's to say he hasn't squirreled the money away in a safety deposit box somewhere so the taxman doesn't find out."

"Funny you should mention that. Cox was asking much the same thing."

"Well there you are! Great minds and fools and all that. Anyway, I'd better hit the sack. When do babies start sleeping the night?"

"Three or four months, usually. But I heard that twins take much longer. They wake each other up."

"Thanks for nothing."

"You're welcome."

397

Saturday, 23rd January

1pm

Sarah returned from her Avon session clutching a large diary and looking fractionally happier than she has done recently.

"Professor Turner gave it to me. He said if there was something troubling me that I couldn't properly remember, I should just jot down anything that comes into my head, even if it doesn't make sense. And eventually he thinks it will come back to me and then we can deal with it together."

"Good plan."

I've been considering what to say when I call DS Cox and I decide I'll just show him the pouch and the box and let him decide what to do with it. I give him a quick call and ask him to pop into the shop on Tuesday.

"Can I ask why?"

"I've got something to show you."

"Oh?"

He sounds cool, dispassionate.

"I don't think it's what you were looking for but you might find it interesting."

"Can I ask where you found whatever it is that you found."

"No."

"I'll be there at 10."

"Fine."

Sunday, 24th January

I picked up Oliver and brought him to the stables. It's cold and wet but he insists he wants to ride so we opt for the indoor arena.

"I'd like to use Captain's old tack. I don't need that training saddle. I'm quite capable of using the reins and I think my back's strong enough to sit up straight on my own."

"Fair enough."

I tack up Captain and Dancer, help him up into the saddle with Ajay's help and arrange his feet in the stirrup irons. Then I mount up and we spend 10 minutes walking around.

"Can we trot for a bit?"

"I turn round, surprised.

"You sure you're up for it?"

"I'd like to try. Sitting, of course."

"Okay. Just shout if you want to stop."

I squeeze Dancer into a gentle trot and we go around the arena once, very slowly, with me turning anxiously every few yards. Oliver's face is set in a determined grimace and I can see he is using all his upper body strength to stay upright, his left hand clamped firmly under the pommel of the saddle.

"I'm going to walk now."

"Fine."

I come down to a slow walk and allow Captain to move up beside his stable companion.

"How was it?"

"No problem."

"Liar! Your face was a picture of painful concentration."

"I need to push myself."

I nod.

"I get it. But that's enough for today."

We walk to the side of the arena, I jump off, quickly unsaddle Dancer and put her in an empty stall, then turn to Oliver, helping him down with Ali's aid and settling him back into his wheelchair. He looks tired but contented.

Tuesday, 26th January

10am

The shop bell tinkles on the stroke of ten and DS Cox walks in, as irritatingly punctual as ever. I glance over to our two browsers—both regulars—and call out to them that I'm popping upstairs if they need anything. They both nod imperceptibly, much too engrossed in their singular searches to notice or care.

'Follow me."

DS Cox obediently takes up the rear and I lead him into George's sitting room which he refers to as a parlour, being too small to constitute a proper 'withdrawing room'. I motion for him to sit down, then reach for the cashbox, sitting on the occasional table where I placed it earlier. With just a touch of the theatrical, I unlock it, lay out the contents and sit back. Young Simon takes the objects in at a glance and looks at me, a suspicion of an eyebrow raised.

"I know it's probably not what you were looking for but it's something, surely?"

"What was I looking for and what am I looking at?"

"Evidence."

"Of what?"

Why are cops always so cagey?

"You suspect Michael of something. Some sort of fraud but it's all completely legit."

"What is?"

"His rare wine trading. Every bottle's provenance is all down in black and white."

He is looking at me intently but he doesn't say a word.

"Of course, he might not have declared it all to the taxman. But you could get him on this."

I open the cigarette roller.

"Smell that. I'm pretty sure it's weed."

I proffer it. He takes it, sniffs and nods.

"I think you're probably right."

"Michael had it locked away. Funny, though, as far as I know he's never so much as smoked a kipper."

He puts the roller back on the table and studies the rest of the haul.

"And those pills might be illegal, mightn't they?"

He shrugs, noncommittally.

"Where exactly did you find the box?"

"I can't tell you."

"Can't or won't?"

"Lexically and grammatically speaking, both."

I am reminded of our conversation about where Michael might store important documents but remember that I said only that I would think about what or where that might be. There was no commitment to disclosure.

"Do you mind if I borrow them for a bit?"

"Help yourself."

I put everything back in the box, lock it, push it towards him and hand over the key.

"I did wonder if they belonged to one or more of his female friends. The petrol lighter's a bit butch for one of Michael's types, though."

He smiles wryly, tucks the box under his arm, we both rise and I lead the way downstairs. The browsers are still browsing and DS Cox takes his leave, tapping the box lightly.

"I'll be in touch."

I nod and he closes the door behind him.

As soon as the shop is empty I call Patti.

"I think he's taken the bait."

"Your fuzzy friend."

"I keep telling you he's not my friend."

"So what now?"

"He said he'll be in touch," Pause. "He didn't look wildly enthusiastic."

"A bit of weed and a few poppers is hardly County Lines drug dealing."

"I s'pose not."

"But even a caution from the Old Bill might bring that prig you married down a peg or two. Which reminds me, what news from the formidable Ms, Rowley?"

"She's just waiting for Michael to officially surrender his claim on the house to draw up the final settlement."

"Which presumably he won't do."

"Maybe I should tell him I've found his secret stash?"

"No, don't do that!"

Patti's tone is imperative, strident.

"Why not?"

"Just better to leave him in ignorant bliss."

"You're probably right."

"Anyway, he'll presumably find out soon enough."

"Mmm. How are my god-babies?"

"Monsters. Slave drivers. Torturers."

"Admit it, you're loving motherhood, really."

"Which would make me a total masochist. Anyway I've hired an au pair. He's Swedish and…"

"He?"

401

"That's very judgemental of you."

"Not at all. I just had a flashing image or a blonde, Nordic demi-god emerging from the water like a modern day Mr Darcy."

"What are you talking about?"

"It's the girls. They think your place looks like something out of Jane Austen."

"Darcy was dark and mysterious. Nils is blond and butter wouldn't melt. Anyway it's icy out here in the Cotswolds this time of year."

"I know what you're up to."

"Which is?"

"You want to get back to work asap."

"First of Feb."

"You're incorrigible."

"Look who's talking!"

"Give everyone a kiss from me."

"Sure. Does that include Nils?"

"Goodbye Patti."

"Bye."

6pm

An email from Alex.

'Hi Guin. Sorry again for Christmas but I have to admit Paris was a blast and coming back early to an empty house did wonders for my reading so I'm pretty much back on track, thesis-wise. I still need to check out that shop of yours sometime—I'm a sucker for an old book shop.

Love

Alex'

That's almost a definite statement of intent to visit! I smile to myself and quickly formulate a suitable response.

'Hey Alex

That all sounds great. George has been closeted away working on his garden project so I'm literally minding the shop full time but it's a quiet time of year.

Keep me posted on the thesis

Love Guin'

Friday, 3rd February

Nothing from Cox about the box. I'm mildly disappointed but still hopeful that Michael might be charged or at least cautioned about some misdemeanour. Maybe he has but it's protocol not to inform me? Then again, I'm sure I'd have heard from Michael as soon as he worked out how word got out. Yes, I know it's petty but I'm at the point-scoring stage.

True to her word, Patti went back to work on Wednesday. She's researching a new project, something to do with small business enterprises in food and drink—micro-breweries, organic farming, artisan cheese factories and the like. It won't go into production till early autumn but apparently there's a lot of ground work to be done beforehand and as usual, she's throwing herself into it, body and soul. I should have known she was never cut out to be a full-time mum. Thank heavens for Scandinavian male nannies.

7pm

Just Sarah, Jude and me for supper—mock cottage pie made with shredded tofu. It tastes like grated cardboard but that might be the way I prepared it so I tuck in and keep schtuum. The conversation turns, as it sometimes does, to Michael.

"Mandy says her mum hates Manchester. She wants to move out of the city."

"I assumed your father would be buying somewhere for them both to live."

"He told her he can't afford it because of the divorce."

I force my eyebrows to stay in place. This is such a blatant lie, even by Michael's standards. Claire was given copies of his onshore and offshore assets, and the numbers made my hair curl. True, it might not be in ready cash, but he could purchase a sizeable chunk of Mancunian real estate and not even notice. Which makes me wonder what his motive is behind the lie. Is he perhaps tiring of Louise already or does he still harbour ambitions to somehow reclaim Lionsgate? If the former, it was easily predictable but if I'd tried to tell her she wouldn't have believed me. Probably have viewed it as a pathetic attempt by a cuckolded wife to rescue her failed marriage. And if the latter, I wonder if he still thinks that collection of fine wines and spirits is his little secret and anyway, if it means that much to him, why not come right out and say so?

Also there's an implication that Cox hasn't approached him about the contents of the box. Damn!

Meanwhile Jude and Sarah are looking at me and waiting for a response so I have to think on my feet.

"It takes a while to sell stocks and bonds. It's not like money in the bank."

They nod and return to their plates, Jude eating as though she hadn't seen food for a week and Sarah playing hide and seek with the peas in the ersatz cottage pie. I reach for the bottle of Chablis and refill my glass.

Saturday, 4th February

8am

Sarah left to catch the bus to the Avon half an hour ago, just as Mattie arrived. He, Jude and Amanda were planning a long hack this morning but it's bucketing down outside. They debate the pros and cons of riding in the rain and decide against it, opting instead to school in the indoor arena. I suggest they swing by and collect Oliver for his regular equine therapy and they readily agree. That decided, I head off to the shop.

Friday, 10th February

4pm

I'm ambushed by a posse of all four teens crashing into the shop straight after school. Mattie is propelled to the fore, clearly having been delegated spokesperson.

"Is it okay if we borrow the bug. We need to run an errand?"

"Of course."

"We might be a bit late back." (Jude)

"No problem. I'll take the bus."

"I mean late for supper."

"I'll put it on hold till you get home."

"Thanks, mum,"

Presuming the purpose is on a need to know basis, I hand over the keys and the four barrel out, intent on their secret mission.

6pm

I'm at home alone, wondering what I can cook that's veggie and won't spoil. I settle on ratatouille and baked potatoes with some pork sausages for the carnivores, veggie for the rest and once prepared, it all goes into the oven on a low light. That done I head down to the cellar to treat myself to a bottle of something posh from Michael's stash, settling on a Burgundy I remember him crowing over when he acquired a case last year. Back upstairs I pour a generous glass, drink in the bouquet—it does smell exceptional—take a small sip and settle down with the house phone for a good gossip with Patti. I learn that Nils is a superstar, the babies are thriving, work is frantic but utter bliss after her enforced absence and Ross has been promoted. In turn I brief her on Sarah's progress, really more of an impasse, and the filched bottle of claret from downstairs.

"I'll set a couple of bottles aside for your next visit."

"I'll hold you to that."

8.30pm

The teens arrive home, mission presumably accomplished.

"Sorry it took so long. We had to go to Stourbridge and we got a bit lost on the way home."

I am none the wiser but again forbear to ask probing questions and we all sit down to devour the supper which, though plain and simple, is warming and welcome on a chilly evening and dovetails nicely with the wine.

Sunday, 12th February

8.30am

I drive to Fordham to pick up Olly and take him for his riding session. Driving over he asks if not too much of an imposition could I take him tomorrow morning for a consultation with Ish Reddy which I assure him will be fine. At the stables we opt for a hack, the day being dry. The bridle paths are soggy from the recent rains so the going is slow but it's still good to be out and about on horseback. When we find a dry patch, Olly insists on trotting.

"Are you sure it won't be too much?"

"I sincerely hope it is. If I don't push myself I'll vegetate."

So I push Cloud into a gentle trot, rising for me and sitting for Olly, turning around every couple of minutes to check he's okay. His face shows the effort of balance but he insists on carrying on till we hit another boggy area and to my relief, we are allowed to slow to a walk.

Monday, 13th February

9am

I am again in the waiting room at Edgbaston while Olly has his consult. There is a filter coffee machine provided and a barrel of biscuits so I help myself liberally and read a few chapters of Josephine Tey's Daughter of Time which I intend recommending to Alex as a detective story but with a very different twist. I only manage a chapter when Olly emerges with Ish.

"That was quick."

"I'd like to see my patient again same time next week if that's not too much trouble?"

"Of course not."

He turns to face Olly.

"And I'll definitely pop out to watch you in the saddle when I can."

I wheel Olly out.

Tuesday, 14th February

6.30pm

The teens are all at the stables and I am making supper, a mock spag bol with soy mince, when I hear a vehicle in the drive. Looking out of the window I catch a glimpse of something red and assume they have caught a lift home. A few seconds later the back door opens and Jude bounds in.

"I'll grab a shower and come and give you a hand."

"Thanks. Where are the others?"

"In the garage putting something away."

A few minutes later the other three emerge, give me a cursory greeting and also head off upstairs. The fake bolognaise sauce now simmering, I decide I might as well slip away for a wash and change myself.

7.30pm

Coming back down I find Sarah watching over a boiling pot of spaghetti and Jude and Amanda laying the table.

"We're nearly done here. You might as well sit down."

"We need a salad."

"I'll do that." (Amanda)

"Okay, I can take a hint."

I sit on the side-lines and pull out a cigarette which I'm about to light when Mattie appears from the direction of the conservatory.

"Happy Valentine's Mrs H."

He produces a rose bush with several dark red buds in a brass pot from behind his back and presents it to me with a flourish. February 14th—the significance of the date had eluded me. I smile and rise to accept the floral gift.

"It's from all of us." (Jude)

"The pot's Victorian." (Sarah)

"We found it in an antique shop in…town." (Mandy)

"What a lovely surprise. Thank you."

I move to place it on the table as a centrepiece, only now noticing that it has been surreptitiously laid with a theme of red—our Christmas candles, some paper napkins with a heart motif and a brocade table runner which I don't recognise. Amanda sees me looking at it.

407

"We bought that today as well. Jude found it in a charity shop."

"It all looks fabulous."

The girls beam and we all sit down to our bogus bolognaise supper in a convivial mood.

Wednesday, 15th February

6am

Opening the garage door to back the bug out for the school run I am surprised to see a red Jeep parked next to it. Presumably that was what I caught a glimpse of last night. Going back into the house I find Mattie pouring himself tea in the kitchen.

"Was there something you were going to tell me?"

He gives his familiar infectiously disarming grin.

"Sorry. We forgot about it last night."

He goes on to explain that the mysterious trip to Stourbridge last week was to check out the red Jeep outside which Alex had found online, having decided it was time his old one had a new home. They had taken it for a test drive, sent a video and favourable report to Alex, he in turn had paid for it with a phone transfer, made while they waited with the seller. The plan was that he and the girls would drive it up to Oxford at half-term so they could spend a couple of days with Alex.

"That is okay, isn't it?"

I assure him that it's fine but warn him to clear it with his parents, Amanda's too if she is to join the party.

3.30pm

George phones and advises me that Alex is entranced by the ambitious gardening project and has now officially committed to coming to stay during the Easter vac with Paulo to quite literally put in some spadework and when I say 'stay' I mean at Lionsgate. For a month! I am more thrilled than I can say and I know the girls will be equally delighted, Mattie and Amanda too as they have all become firm friends, albeit somewhat vicariously. I don't even care that the forecast is for heavy snow by Friday, meaning that riding for all of us

408

will be curtailed. As Byron so succinctly put it, 'If winter comes, can spring be far behind?'

Sunday, 19th February

10am

The forecast was correct and heavy snow set in late Friday afternoon and didn't let up till Saturday lunchtime. The roads were cleared by early this morning but the fields and hedgerows are blanketed in white as I drive with Olly to the stables. The redoubtable Ish Reddy was so determined to make good on his promise to come and watch Olly ride that the two of them insisted, Olly asserting that he could still work in the indoor arena, in spite of the inclement weather. Accordingly, with both of us wrapped up warmly, I tack up Captain straightaway and Ish arrives as I am leading him out to the arena and the waiting Olly. Ish stands by and observes as Ali and I manoeuvre Olly into the saddle and we both accompany him on foot around the arena as horse and rider amble around. Then we stand back and watch as Olly makes a torturous circle of sitting trot without stirrups, his face a study of effort and intense concentration. After a little more gentle walking, he walks Captain to where we are waiting on the side-lines.

"You don't mind if I have a quick word with my patient, do you?"

"Of course not."

Ali deftly lifts Olly down and into his chair and I lead Captain back to his stall so doctor and patient can chat in private. The pair confer confidentially and laugh like old friends. After a decent interval I walk up to join them.

"It's very good for the soul, riding."

"I can see that. Good for muscle tone and posture, too. Very important, those, in spinal cases."

"Makes sense."

"Thank you very much for allowing me to observe."

"Any time."

"And now if you'll excuse me, I shall be off to my golf club."

"In this weather?"

Mr Reddy guffaws.

409

"The course may be snowbound but the clubhouse and the 19th hole are still open. And the restaurant does an excellent roast lunch on a Sunday."

We take our leave, I thank Ali and we go our separate ways.

Wednesday, 1st March

4.30pm

Sarah, Jude and Mattie come bursting into the shop straight after school. Both girls' faces are flushed and as soon as they see me they exchange a glance.

"You'll never guess what's happened." (Jude)

"No point in trying then, so why don't you tell me?"

Another glance. Mattie holds up his hands in a backing-off gesture. Clearly this is girly stuff.

"Amanda's mum's back!"

Sarah half shouts out these words.

"For a visit?"

"Dunno. She was waiting at the gates when we got out. Amanda had a word with her, was told she had to go home and they drove off."

"Home?"

"I know! She moved out, right?"

"She's probably sorting out some stuff with Gerald. Or maybe picking some more stuff up."

"Told you." (Mattie)

"In that case why did she need Amanda?"

"She is her daughter."

"Left it a bit late to start playing Mother of the Year." (Jude)

"She texted to say she'll call us later." (Sarah)

"So presumably all will be revealed then."

"You don't sound very interested." (Jude)

"I just think we shouldn't jump to conclusions."

"That's what I said. Anyway let's get out to the stables. I want to get a ride in before it gets dark." (Mattie)

"Do you want to borrow the bug?"

"You sure you don't mind?"

"Of course not."

I hand them the keys and they troop out, the girls with heads together, presumably still speculating. Privately I'm also wondering what it's all about.

8pm

"She's saying going away with dad was nothing more than an itch she had to scratch."

We are seated around the kitchen table post supper and I am being regaled with tales of the return of the prodigal wife. As soon as the teens came back from the stables Sarah and Jude closeted themselves away upstairs to gather the gossip from Amanda whilst Mattie helped me get supper ready. As it has been told to me, Louise swept back into the house almost as though nothing of any consequence had happened, telling the hapless Gerald that the affair was something she had to get out of her system, she was over it now and she had never intended it to be anything more than a frivolous fling. Gerald, poor hapless sap, had swallowed it hook, line and sinker, telling her in turn that he had brought it on himself by his frequent absences and promising to pay her more attention in future.

I opine that we knew she wasn't happy living in the company flat and that I'm sure it must have been difficult for her being separated from Amanda, for the last part of which statement I am regaled with withering looks from Jude and Sarah while Mattie busies himself clearing a few plates.

11pm

I lie in bed and mull over the events of the day. I had given Patti a call and we threw a few theories back and forth but concluded that any attempt to fathom Louise's action was mere speculation and there was now't so queer as folks. I told her I hoped it wouldn't give Michael any ideas that he too could waltz back home and expect to be welcomed with open eyes. Her response was 'Set the Doberman on him', by which she meant Claire Rowley. My reply was that we didn't want her catching rabies and with that thought, we had hung up.

411

Sunday, 5th March

1.30pm

I picked Olly up earlier and we went for a short hack, after which he insisted he make himself useful by cleaning some tack. I joined in and we soaped and polished till it was time to leave for our lunch date. Once we were loaded into the bug we drove to Featherington under a faded denim-blue sky, flecked with fast-moving cumulus, still wintry, temperature-wise—but with a promise of spring in the greening hedgerow bottoms. George seemed delighted to be playing host and proffered glasses of tawny sherry by way of an aperitif, followed by an excellent Irish stew, a recipe from the resident cook at Wellington House when he was a child, which benefited from a generous amount of Guinness and whole white peppercorns, just the thing to keep out the cold, especially as we washed it down with a bottle of rather superior claret which I'd selected from Michael's extensive cellar. Helping to clear, post prandially, I fill George in on the cellar contents, the priceless vintage wine and spirit collection and the box with its curious contents.

He rinses the last glass, dries his hand on a tea towel then turns to look at me.

I did warn you about opening Pandora's box."

"Technically, Michael's."

My tone is facetious but there's an uncomfortable feeling in the pit of my stomach that wasn't caused by Irish stew. We are both silent for a moment, then the door is pushed open.

"I thought I'd better make myself useful."

Olly has wheeled himself into the kitchen, some placemats and items of cruet balanced in his lap. I relieve him of them and stow them in cupboards.

"How about giving Olly a tour of the old monastic garden?"

"Delighted."

And with that, Michael and cellar are set aside and we all don warm clothes and trek out to view the progress on George's pet project.

412

Friday, 10th March

On Monday Sarah presented me with an elaborate diet sheet which she then pinned to the cork board in the kitchen. I say 'elaborate' but 'rigid' would probably be a better word. For example, each morning for breakfast she has specified fruit, half a piece of wholemeal toast and tea, a different fruit for each day, organic honey on the toast and a tiny spoonful of glucose and a dash of almond milk in the tea. I am under strict instructions that if it's a mango day, that and only that fruit will do. By the same token, lunch is a single cup of soup, from a flask on schooldays or from a small teacup at home and if the menu specified minestrone, that and nothing else will suffice. The supper menu was equally meticulous. A small bowl of salad followed by a single cooked vegetable, a spoonful of rice or pasta or a small boiled potato and a serving of her choice of raw nuts but at that I drew the line. She would eat what the rest of us were having or a vegetarian option when appropriate and if she wanted nuts, that would be as well as, not instead of. Battle Royal ensued, followed by a few days of sulking but I remained steadfast. As did Sarah, of course, who can be as obstinate as me and then some. I phoned Professor Turner who told me such behaviours were common and it was simply another manifestation of maintaining control over her diet when other aspects of her life were dictated by others and he advised me to acquiesce to what was convenient in the household and to reject that which was unreasonable. I thanked him and was about to take my leave when he interrupted.

"Sarah is still a very troubled young woman."

"I thought she'd be feeling happier, what with her father gone and her half-brother so much of a part of our new life. They all seem to get on really well, Sarah, Jude and Alex."

"I really feel that for Sarah to be happy in the present she must confront whatever it I that's worrying her in her past."

"Which is what?"

"I wish I knew. She's holding something back inside and I don't think she realises it herself. Something from when she was quite young, which is probably why she has no clear recollection of it, just an uneasy, buried memory."

I hesitate. There's something I have to ask but I don't want to vocalise it.

"It must be Bath. When I left Michael. I know the girls both missed him but they were far too young for me to even try to explain why I did what I did."

"Sarah and I have spoken about that on several occasions and I don't think that's quite it."

"And of course she was very cut up when Steve was killed. She felt my grief much more than Jude. She kept trying to tell me he was only sleeping and he'd wake up soon. Like Sleeping Beauty, she used to say."

"I am working on getting her to open up her memory box but it's a delicate process. I encourage her to write and draw in her diary and she knows that if there's anything she doesn't understand or she wants to talk about, she can bring it up in complete confidence."

I echo George's prophetic phrase.

"Pandora's box."

"In a very real way."

"I was accused of opening one myself recently."

"Indeed?"

"I'm on a little journey of discovery too and I'm not sure I'm going to like the destination."

"I've said it before but you really are welcome to talk to me about anything, anytime."

"I might just take you up on that."

There is a short but not uncomfortable silence as we both gather our thoughts. He is the first to break the quiet.

"I am utterly convinced that Sarah's issue lies with the death of your partner."

"Can't you just ask her."

He laughs, wryly.

"I'm afraid it doesn't work like that. She has to be the one to unearth the memory of whatever it is that's bothering her."

"What about hypnosis."

I blurt out the words, not knowing quite what prompted them. There is a long pause as he considers.

"It might help. I've occasionally used it with patients in the past but it doesn't always yield any useful results."

"Surely it's worth a try?"

414

"It's not without risks. Some memories are so painful that their recollection can have a detrimental effect."

"Sarah's anorexia is already having a detrimental effect. I'm worried she's going to completely regress and she'll never recover."

I'm trying hard not to cry here. I think he hears the catch in my voice.

"Let me sound Sarah out and see how she feels. It has to be up to her."

"Of course."

We agree that he'll speak to her tomorrow and before then he'll contact a colleague of his in London whom he feels would be the right person to handle the situation if Sarah agrees.

"Meanwhile how do I handle the dietary demands?"

He laughs.

"Negotiation and compromise."

I also laugh and hang up. As I do so I resolve to be slightly more accommodating towards Sarah's dietary demands but only so far.

Saturday, 11th March

8.50am

I am in the shop doing my usual pre-opening dust and tidy when the phone rings. I answer it eagerly, hoping it's Patti. We haven't spoken for a few days and I'm feeling guilty. Grabbing the receiver I hear an all too familiar voice, not Patti but Simon Cox. After the usual peasantries, he pauses, clears his throat, then speaks.

"I have a question and I don't think you're going to like it."

"So why ask it?"

"I need the information."

I don't reply.

"Mr Driscoll. Steve. What happened to his car?"

"Isn't it in the file?"

"It says it was examined forensically. That there were was a fresh dent on the driver's side rear fender, marked with some red paint which was identified as from a VW—that was the Golf. Nothing else."

"What else do you need?"

"Not sure."

415

"Fishing again?"

"But hoping to get a bite." Pause. "So what did happen to it? It's usually given to the next of kin."

"Steve didn't have any that I knew of. His parents were both dead and he was an only child."

"You're going to tell me you didn't want it."

"Of course I didn't."

That came out sharply.

"In that case it would have stayed in the police pound and eventually would have been scrapped."

He sounds disappointed. I hesitate, unwilling to take this further. No use. I have to 'fess up.

"I told Bill to take it."

"Bill?"

"Bill Bailey. Sub-Editor. He and Steve were friends as well as colleagues. And he'd always admired the SAAB so I told him to take it."

"Might he still have it?"

"Maybe."

"Do you know how to get in touch with him?"

"We exchange Christmas cards. And I've spoken to him on the phone a few times since…He left the Gazette just after me. Said it just wasn't the same anymore. He took a job on a local rag in Weston-Super-Mare. I can give you his address and phone number."

"That would be helpful."

"Helpful with what?"

"With our inquiries."

"He's probably sold it by now."

"Worth a try."

He rings off and I go and open the shop door, irritated about yet more raking up of a past I try to forget. Outside it has clouded over and is starting to rain quite heavily.

1pm

Sarah flounces in, simultaneously shaking her hair loose whilst shaking raindrops from her umbrella. She looks around the shop where only a scattered few customers are quietly browsing and whispers conspiratorially.

"He wants me to be hypnotised."

I feign ignorance.

"Professor Turner?"

"Who else?"

"What did you say?"

"I told him I thought it was hocus pocus and mind manipulation."

My heart sinks but I say nothing.

"Anyway it won't work on me. I'll prove it."

I keep my voice casual.

"You're going to give it a go?"

She shrugs.

"Why not? Try anything once." Pause. "I need some stuff for an essay."

She walks off and begins to browse our British history section.

7.30 pm

We are five for supper again tonight. Mattie is staying the weekend, his mother being both sober and self-sufficient for the time being and Amanda is having a sleepover. She reports the home atmosphere as 'cloying' and says that Lulu is being ingratiating to the nth degree, that she's all over Gerald like a bad rash and that he is lapping it up. Amanda, on the other hand, is convinced it's all an act and will not last long before she gets that same old itch back again and needs to scratch it. Her cynicism is understandable.

In view of the inclement weather which has persisted all day, the girls have made a vegetarian curry which, though it might not pass muster in Jaipur, is nevertheless warming, tasty and filling. Sarah makes a thing about using a fork to eat her portion of rice grain by grain and paying lip service—pun fully intended—to the curry. She also nibbles on a grilled poppadom, then declares herself full. The others tuck in and Mattie shows off by swallowing some Scotch bonnet chilli peppers, a party trick I've seen before.

"They're going to put Sarah under." (Jude)

Sarah pulls a face at her. Amanda waves her necklace chain back and forth in front of Sarah.

"You're getting sleepy."

"Look into my eyes, look deep into my eyes." (Mattie)

"You're all just jealous."

Clearly Sarah has shared her news and is revelling in it. I'm glad she's taking it so lightly and I also hope it doesn't go spectacularly wrong. It's a big risk but surely it has to be worth a go?

The conversation moves on and they all make plans to ride tomorrow, provided the rain eases off and promise to pick Olly up for his equine therapy.

While they clear the table and load the dishwasher I take the opportunity to phone Patti. She tells me that she can't wait for the twins to start school and that Nils has requested a week's leave over Easter and she has no idea how she's going to manage on her own. I suggest she brings the babies and Ross up here for a few days r & r and she jumps at the chance.

In turn I fill her in on Simon Cox's quest to find Steve's old SAAB.

"What on earth for?"

"He wouldn't say. I think he's clutching at straws."

"So the Golf angle didn't work out?"

"Nope."

"What will you do if he does manage to find out what really did happen?"

"I've told you I'm not interested. Steve is gone and he's not coming back. I came to terms with that a long time ago and it was the hardest thing I've ever had to do in my life."

"I know, kiddo."

Thinking about it brings me back to Professor Turner and Sarah and I fill Patti in on the hypnosis.

"Can't hurt."

"I hope not."

"Hey, now. She's going to come right."

I ignore the sick feeling in the pit of my stomach.

"Hug the babies and say hi to Ross from me."

"You mean the merciless brats?"

"You're not fooling anyone with that act. You adore them."

"Of course. But that doesn't mean they're not driving me up the wall."

"Wait till they start crawling!"

"They'd better not till Nils gets back from leave!"

"I don't think it works like that."

We hang up on a good note, as ever.

Wednesday, 15th March

12 noon

I receive a phone call from Claire to say that Michael is still dragging his heels over signing the divorce papers. She had received a letter from his solicitor stating that his client was still fervently hoping for a change of heart on my part and a reconciliation.

Unbelievable! Her word, not mine, but I share the sentiment. I truly believe he's either having some sort of mid-life crisis or Lulu's departure has finally tipped the scales between sanity and madness in his psyche. We agree that Claire will compose a strongly worded response telling him politely to jump in a lake.

6pm

Alone in the house, Jude being at the stables and Sarah not yet back from the Avon, I write a lengthy email to Alex. I know that he'll be well up to date with family gossip from the girls but I enjoy our correspondence and still get a thrill when I hear from him. I metaphorically chew the end of my pen, then begin.

'Hi Alex

The weather here has been horrid for the past week or so which means only riding in the arena for me and library and greenhouse work for George. Let's hope it improves by Easter—I assume you and Paolo are still planning on coming up? Pattie, Ross and the babies will also be here for a few days and she's dying to meet her nearly nephew! Ross will probably enjoy lending a hand with you guys at the Hall and Mattie has also been press-ganged into providing extra labour with all the spring planting George has planned. All those years of garnering his historical botanical book collection has finally paid off in a way he couldn't possibly have envisaged this time last year!

So although Christmas turned out to be a bit of damp squib, festivity-wise, we can make up for it with a fabulous feast in honour of the goddess Oestre and in absolutely the best of company. According to the Venerable Bede, she was a pagan goddess of fertility, dawn and light so Patti and Ross have a lot to thank her for—something else that they definitely hadn't envisaged this time last year. Come to think of it, it's been a twelvemonth of flux all round—I never imagined I'd have found you after all those years or that all our lives would have been tossed around in such a maelstrom, some bad, some good and you definitely fall in the latter category.

Only a month to go—I can't wait. I will light a candle to Oestre and task the girls with planning a suitably festive and fertile feast!

Much love

Guin'

The sending of this prompts another quick call to Patti to pre-warn her that we'll have a houseful for her visit. As predicted, she's over the moon as the prospect of finally meeting Alex and she also suggests a suitably pagan blessing of the old monastic kitchen garden in the name of Oestre to ensure that each and every planting comes to fruition. I point out the anomaly of a pagan rite on a Christian site and she retorts with references to the many pseudo religious relics in Christian festivals, not least of which the spring fertility symbols of eggs, bunnies and baby chicks. She's right, as usual and I give the nod to the prospect of some pre-planting goddess worship.

After this I turn my attention to supper, spaghetti a la Carbonara, it being quick, easy and store-cupboard, with a vegan option of pasta and mushrooms for Sarah, a salad of tomatoes, peppers and grated carrot and a loaf of ciabatta bread from Simmons. Both girls arrive before I am done and help with chopping the vegetables and stirring the spaghetti while I nip down to the cellar for another bottle of something red and expensive courtesy of Michael.

Over this scratched but delicious repast I regale the girls with full details of the Easter plan and as I expected, they are immediately invested in the whole kit and caboodle, wanting to know if there are any extant remnants of the old monastery where the ceremony could take place, to which I answer yes, there are some ruins. This triggers a flurry of phone calls to Mattie and Amanda firming up plans for a site recce at the weekend and initial thoughts on decoration and food. I leave them to their plans, load up the dishwasher and head off to the conservatory with the remains of the bottle of wine and a packet of cigarettes.

Friday, 17th March

8am

I drive over to Featherington to pick up George who wants to spend a couple of days in the shop, returning to the hall on Sunday. I find him pretty much locked and loaded and looking forward to a brief respite from his intensive gardening project.

On the drive back we both admire the burgeoning signs of spring in the fields and hedgerows. The weather is still cold but there is the proverbial bit of blue—enough to make a butcher's apron—in the sky to promise a dry day and fair-weather cumulus clouds are scudding along at a great rate of knots, propelled by a stiff breeze. I describe Patti's pagan plans for a blessing ceremony for the garden which enchants him, adding that the teens are all on board and have taken over the organisation, though I'm sure Patti will want to add her professional touch once she's here. For his part, he confirms that Alex and Paolo will be here for more or less the whole of the Easter vac.

"That will mean a lot of extra work for you in the house."

"I've got plenty of willing helpers to assist. I can't believe I'll actually have Alex under my roof for a few weeks. I'm fit to burst with excitement!"

He clears his throat and glances casually out of the window.

"I've also had a letter from Diana saying that she and Charles would love to be there to see it all come together."

I look sideways at him and raise my eyebrows.

"They can stay in my spare bedroom. They won't be any bother."

"Rubbish. Diana is always a bother. Super-high maintenance and you can't possibly look after her and Charles while you're so busy with the project."

I do a quick mental calculation. Patti, Ross and the twins in the big first floor bedroom. Alex and Paolo can bunk up in the two attic rooms, the blue room is more or less Mattie's by default now. That leaves Michael's room which is more than big enough and comfortable enough for Charles and Diana.

"We'll be fine. And Diana will be in her element organising menus and schedules!"

421

"If you're sure?"

"I am."

Privately I wonder if the Michael situation won't make it just a tiny bit awkward with his parents staying with us but I promised them they'd be welcome anytime and so it shall be.

Saturday, 18th March

Noon

It's a pleasant change to have George for company in the shop again. Clearly I'm not the only one who's missed him as he was monopolised for much of the morning with his regular coterie of fellow bookworms. In a quiet moment he glances across at me with his 'something up his sleeve' look that I've come to know so well.

"Ffion, what say you to the idea of an Ink an'Abulia website?"

Whatever I was expecting, that wasn't it.

"The internet? You?"

"Don't sound so surprised. I might become a late convert. Alex told me about a fellowship dedicated to reviving lost native plant species and they share information on the line. He signed me up for membership."

"Online. You'll need a computer to join in."

"You could give me lessons."

"I'm hardly an expert. We'd be the blind leading the blind."

"I expect we could muddle through. And there's always the young generation to call on for assistance."

"I suppose so. But where does the website come in?"

"That's Alex's idea too. He tells me that lots of students purchase their course books that way and that we should be able to sell a lot more books by mail order."

I pause to allow all this to sink in. The mental juxtaposition of George and a computer seems so incongruous as to be comical. That said, we already offer a mail order service for our stock and it would be foolish to turn down the chance to increase business volume. Plus unbeknownst to George I've already made e-listings of most of the stock so it won't take too long to complete the inventory

"Who could set it up?"

"He says he's got a friend who does that sort of thing for extra income. He gave me a quote which I found very reasonable. I just wanted to sound you out before I said yes."

"Fine by me."

"Capital! I'll telephone Alex this evening."

We are both smiling when the shop door opens and Sarah enters, having just arrived back from the Avon. She looks troubled, her default post-Professor Turner session mode. She started her hypnosis sessions earlier in the week but all attempts to elicit and information on how they are going results in a noncommittal 'okay'.

"How was it?"

"Fine."

Her tone and expression tell me she's anything but, though I know better than to say so.

"I'm going to rustle up some lunch. Just beans on toast. Do you want to join us?"

"Can't. I'm meeting the others in town."

On impulse I take two twenty pound notes from my purse and proffer it.

"That should pay for lunch for everyone."

"Thanks. We'll probably go the stables afterwards. See you. Hi George, bye, George."

And with that she is gone again. I resolve to call Professor Turner before she gets home to find out if they have any further insight as to why she is so troubled.

6pm

I prepare a vegetable and bean casserole which I split into two, adding some bacon chunks to one and leaving the other as more or less vegan. With them both now simmering in the oven, I pour a glass of Bordeaux and call our tame Professor to quiz him on whether the sessions have yielded any revelations. He tells me these things take time—I wish everyone would stop saying that to me.

"I can tell you that Angela is managing to coax some memories of Bath from Sarah but she's treading very carefully. If there is anything that's bothering her from that time it has to come from her."

"I understand, really. It's just that patience isn't my strong suit."

"It's our stock in trade. If it means anything I have the feeling we're on the right track."

"It does."

I put the phone down feeling slightly less uneasy. Slightly.

3 out of the 4 teens are back for supper, having dropped Olly and Amanda off at their respective homes. Olly is now insisting on riding on his own, though he still has to submit to assistance in mounting and dismounting. He and I still hack out occasionally on a Sunday but it's a big help to have the teens organise his excursions on Saturdays when I'm at the shop.

Jude and Mattie are making plans for the upcoming show season with plans to make good use of Mattie's box to travel to as many local events as possible, as well as a few farther afield. Olly, I am told, is keen to come along and has offered his services as Chef d'Équipe, insisting that he is more than up to the task, despite his disability. Sarah, never one for competitions, also promises to attend a few of the shows as a spectator, A-level coursework allowing. The atmosphere at supper is light-hearted and if Sarah only manages a saucerful of the casserole and half a thin slice of dry bread, at least that's something.

Sunday, 19th March

10am

Mattie, Jude and Sarah have just left to collect Amanda. They have a shopping expedition to Stratford planned and as luck would have it, the day dawned bright and sunny, though still with that biting March chill to stamp out any thoughts of Tuesday's spring equinox. The landline rings and answering it to hear Simon Cox's voice.

"Am I disturbing you?"

"Not more than usual. Don't you ever take a day off?"

"This is it. I told you I'm pursuing this matter on my own time."

"And what matter is that exactly?"

"Good question."

"Which you haven't answered."

"That's because I'm not sure. I have some puzzle pieces that I'm trying to fit together."

I sigh.

"So which piece are you looking at today?"

"I know whose cigarette case it was."

He pauses but I say nothing.

"They lab guys managed to lift a partial print off the old packet of papers and traced it to an Alan Naseby."

I almost cry out but manage to say nothing.

"He was one of your friends at Bristol, wasn't he?"

"Yes. We called him Pip. You asked me about him before."

"Ah. I hadn't made the connection."

How do you know it was him?"

"He was busted for possession of some marijuana in Cardiff a couple of years after he moved there. His prints were still on file." Pause. "I have to ask why you think your husband would have his cigarette case in his possession?"

"You'd have to ask him that. He didn't approve of Alan, Pip. Referred to him as a dope head."

"Which presumably he was."

"He was a lot of other things as well. He played the guitar and wrote beautiful poetry."

"Were you sleeping with him?"

"None of your business."

"I'm wondering if Michael was jealous?"

"Again, you'd have to ask him that."

"But you were in a relationship with this Alan?"

"He wasn't 'this Alan'. He was my friend Pip. Mine and Patti's."

"Were you in love with him?"

"You sound like…."

I early said 'Michael' but catch myself in time

"…an interrogator."

"I'm just trying to work out why your husband was holding onto that cigarette case."

"Not that it's any of your business but like I told you, Pip, Patti and me were really close friends. We were all a bit older than the other freshers in our year and we just bonded. After a while we were like family—siblings."

There's a brief pause.

"Can I have it?"

"Not right now."

"Only I think his parents should have it."

"I'm not quite done with it yet."

"When you are."

"Sure."

We hang up and I immediately redial.

"Remember that box of junk I told you about? The cigarette case was Pip's."

"Fricking hell!"

"Michael must have been holding onto it all these years. What the hell for?"

"Probably thought depriving him of his weed would teach him a lesson. He never liked him. Remember he couldn't even be bothered to attend the funeral."

"I didn't really want him there."

There's a moment of silence as we both think back to that poignant visit to Hebden Bridge.

"Maybe he has some sort of weird anti-smoking/druggie fetish?"

"God, you're right. Pills, lighters, roll-your-own. He was always on at me to quit from the time we met."

"You didn't find a little effigy with pins stuck in it, did you?"

"He probably hid that somewhere else. I wonder if Cox has worked out the theme in the box?"

"Shouldn't think so. All plods are thick as bricks."

"He thinks it's all part of some big mystery he can't get to the bottom of. Shall I tell him?"

"And spoil his fun?"

We giggle conspiratorially and I ask for an update on family life. I learn that the babies are smiling regularly and that Nils is convinced Emily is trying to say his name. Also that Ross is trying to do more work from home whilst Patti is signing up for as much OB and location work as she can get.

426

"I love coming home and finding Nils in the kitchen slaving over a hot Aga, babies bathed and in bed and Ross thrusting a great goblet of wine into my hand as I head for a soak in the bath."

"Sybarite."

"Damn right!"

We laugh and ring off.

Monday, 20th March

9am

Olly has booked me for an expedition. I am to go to his place and then he wants to start up his car so I can drive it and him to the dealership for some spare parts. I call ahead to let him know I am on my way.

10am

Olly is waiting for me inside the garage. He has managed to open the bonnet on his car—a rather expensive-looking Jaguar—and is busy attaching jump leads to the battery. I manoeuvre up so we are bonnet to bonnet and attach the other ends then slide into the leather-covered driving seat and turn the ignition. The engine roars into life, scaring the life out of me but Olly doesn't bat an eyelid. Leaving it running, I park the bug by the stables, then help Olly into the passenger seat, fold his wheelchair into the ample boot and we set off for Solihull.

"I've never driven one of these before."

"Super, isn't she?"

"Scary."

I am driving as cautiously as a learner, the horsepower and price tag making me nervous. Olly is watching me with a twinkle in his eye.

"Put your clog down! We don't want to be all day."

"I'm not in any hurry, thank you."

All the same, I speed up a little and begin to enjoy the sensation of so much power in my hands. We reach the dealership in what seems to me double-quick time and as I park in the forecourt, an immaculately dressed, middle-aged man comes out, beaming at the passenger.

"Oliver! Welcome back."

"John! Are you well? This is my very good friend Fiona."

John and I shake hands and then, seeing me begin to heft the wheelchair out, he moves swiftly to assist, simultaneously summoning a waiting technician.

"Take Mr Prentiss's car to the workshop, Terry.!

The technician obediently hops into the driver's seat and shuttles the car towards the rear of the complex. With Olly now ensconced in the chair, we process inside past the display of current models to a very well-appointed client waiting room overlooking the floor. He proffers coffee and biscuits from the highly technical Espresso machine on a credenza and as soon as we are seated and sorted and pleasantries are exchanged, he takes his leave, assuring us that the work will only take a short time and that he'll be back in a jiffy.

Olly and I chat amicably amongst ourselves about the upcoming grand opening. I tell him that a tenants' meeting had been convened and that there was considerable interest in the garden launch of George's project.

"Are you going to use an outside caterer?"

"No need. The girls and I will be able to manage. And Patti will be helping out as well."

"I hope I'm on the guest list?"

"You most certainly are!"

At this moment John returns, beaming like the Cheshire cat.

"All done. Terry will take you for a test drive."

"Excellent."

John guides us outside where Olly's Jag is sitting, engine running. To my amazement, John and Terry help Olly into the driving seat. He looks at me and smiles.

"I thought I'd better sort the car out if I'm going to act as Chef d'Équipe for the youngsters."

"We've fitted a hand-held throttle and brake controls for Oliver to be independent. They can easily be installed or removed as needed. Show them, Terry."

Terry obliges, demonstrating how the controls work and how the device is attached and removed. Then he hops into the front passenger seat and encourages Olly to take the wheel and try it out. I am knocked for six.

"You and George are a pair! Both as sly as foxes!"

"I wanted it to be a surprise."

"You certainly succeeded."

John and I stand on the side-line as Olly guides the car around the rear car park with Terry instructing from the passenger seat. It only takes Olly a short while to master the hand controls and he beams as we watch him drive forward and back and steer expertly around the parked vehicles, then pull up next to us.

"Terry is going to accompany me on a drive around town. Would you like to ride along?"

"Why not?"

I slip into the back seat, still astonished to see Olly exhibiting such independence and obvious competence as he confidently pulls out into busy mid-day traffic.

7.30pm

During supper—moussaka with soy mince—I fill Jude and Sarah in on today's surprising turn of events. After dropping Terry back off at the dealership Olly insisted on taking the wheel all the way home, including a quick detour to the hospital at Edgbaston to show off his new-found skills to Ish Reddy who reminded him not to slacken off with his riding rehab.

"So he's serious about helping us out at shows in the summer?"

"Seems like. It'll be good for him to have something useful to do."

"What about you, Sarah? How did your session at the Avon go?"

In reply she grunts noncommittally. Jude flashes me a quick glance which I interpret as 'eggshell country—change tack'. What am I not being told? I quickly change the subject to the safer territory of Easter and both girls enthusiastically fill me in on set design (Jude, in conjunction with Patti and her props department resources), mediaeval menu planning (Sarah) and costumes (Amanda and Patti again). I had no idea it was going to be such a major production but when I question the elaborateness of the arrangements I am dismissively told not to worry and that everything is being taken care of.

Friday, 24th March

3pm

My cell phone rings and I see it's Professor Turner

"Mrs Hamilton. Fiona, I'm afraid Sarah's...."

My heart skips a couple of beats and my stomach lurches.

"What's happened? Is she okay?"

"Yes and no. She's a bit upset. I didn't mean to worry you. It's just that I don't think she should travel home on her own. Is there any way you could come and collect her?"

"Of course."

I drop the call, redial Jenny's number and ask her if she can fill in at the shop. As luck would have it, she's already in town and she promises to be along in 10 minutes so I grab my bag and car keys, call out to the few browsers that I have to pop out and rush off.

4.30pm

Sarah is with Professor Turner in his office. Her eyes are red, her face blotchy and as soon as I walk in she flings her arms around me, clinging on for dear life in a very uncharacteristic manner. I pull her over to the sofa in the corner and just hold her for several minutes while she sobs, dry-eyed on my shoulder. In response I hug her but say nothing. Eventually she subsides and pulls away. I look across at the good Professor.

"Sarah, why don't you show your mother what you drew?"

She looks over at him, hesitates for a second, then pushes her sketch pad towards me but says nothing and doesn't meet my confused gaze. I open the pad and page through. Each sheet is filled with random pencil sketches of what I take to be her recollections from Bath, many depicting what must be herself and Jude. There are some toys which I recollect from memory and family photographs, the flower clock in the park, what looks like Patti and Ross's garden, some playground swings and slides. As I look through them I turn to Sarah with a wry smile.

"Bath?"

She nods.

430

"Most of them are from photos in the box in the attic. But every so often something pops into my head and I draw that from memory."

I smile nostalgically and continue perusing the book. Then I see some images that almost causes me to cry out but I check myself in time. A man, face down on the ground. Darkness. Car headlights. And the words 'I wish he'd wake up-', written over and over again. I lay the book on my lap and turn to Sarah.

"Steve?"

She nods.

"It's my fault. I tried to shield you and Jude but I was hurting so much. I was in such a dark place and you must have felt it."

She shakes her head vigorously and looks appealingly at Professor Turner He in turn looks over at me.

"Sarah thinks she was there. She believes she saw it happen."

"That's impossible, Sarah."

Again the shake of the head.

"You were with your father that night. You and Jude."

"I saw it. It started coming back to me a couple of weeks ago. Just bits and pieces that didn't make any sense. But this afternoon it was much clearer. I saw him lying on the ground in the car park. It was dark so I couldn't see very well but I know I was there. And dad kept telling me he was all right, he was only sleeping."

"Perhaps it was a nightmare and that's what's coming into your head?"

"I look questioningly at Prof Turner

"That is possible, Sarah. You would have heard a lot about it and it might have played on your mind. So much so that you began to have bad dreams about what happened?"

Sarah looks doubtful.

"It seemed so real."

"Dreams often do."

"I remember you telling me you wish Steve was like Sleeping Beauty and he just had to wake up. You kept saying it when you saw me looking sad."

"I'll talk to Angela and ask her what she thinks but I believe we may have had a breakthrough today, Sarah. This is most probably what your mind had buried for all those years and now that you've remembered we can begin to work through it and bury those demons once and for all."

431

He gives Sarah an avuncular smile.

"Nightmares for a young child can seem very real."

Sarah nods and gives him a weak smile in return.

"Perhaps?"

"Let's go home."

I hand her the sketchpad, put my arm around her shoulder and shepherd her towards the door, turning my head to the Professor Turner.

"Let me know what Angela says."

He nods, pats Sarah on the back and opens the door for us.

6.30pm

We are driving home. For the past 25 minutes neither of us has spoken.

"I must have imagined it, then?"

Sarah has broken the silence.

"Children have very vivid imaginations."

"I really want to get better."

"I know."

"Don't tell anyone. They'll think I'm crackers."

"They won't but no, I won't either!"

I mentally cross my fingers as I say this because of course Patti is on the 'need to know' list. Then I turn and smile wryly at her and am rewarded with a weak one in return. I think we really have turned a corner.

8pm

Jude and Mattie had prepared supper—a vegetarian chilli with baked potatoes. Not quite like the real thing but tasty and I was grateful to be relieved of the cooking for one night. At the start of the meal Sarah announced to the assembled company that she had made a breakthrough in her treatment and that she was determined to get better before summer, though she did not elaborate. Jude and Mattie made suitable noises of encouragement and the atmosphere over supper was light. Sarah even consented to eat half a small potato along with a tablespoon of the chilli.

I am now sitting with a glass of Bordeaux while the three of them clear and load the dishwasher. Jude's cell phone pings and she glances down at it.

"Message from Alex. Uni went down this afternoon and he and Paolo will be here on Monday evening!"

My stomach lurches, but in a good way. I hadn't exactly forgotten he was coming, it was just that it had sort of snuck up on me with everything else that had been happening.

"Can you do some food shopping tomorrow?"

"Sure."

"I'll make a list."

And I put down my glass, pick up a pad and start scribbling.

10pm

I phone Patti and fill her in on Sarah's progress and prognosis.

"Poor kid. So she's been bottling that up for all this time?"

"Somewhere deep in her subconscious, so Prof Turner says, and when it finally came back, she was sure she must have seen it all happen. And I suppose it all got a bit fuzzy in her 6 year-old mind and she was convinced he was only sleeping except he wouldn't wake up. And somehow that was her fault. The Prof says that now she's finally brought up that memory, she will begin to remember more and be able to work through it and make sense of it all. I'm massively oversimplifying but I think that's the gist of it."

"Wow. She always was very deep."

"It's a huge relief for all of us. And it couldn't have come at a better time."

I explain about Alex arriving on Monday and she says she, Ross and the babies will drive up sometime the following week, depending on her filming schedule.

"I can't wait for Easter."

"Me too. All those tame babysitters and I get to meet my proxy nephew!"

And on that note we hang up.

Saturday, 25th March

10am

I called George earlier to fill him in on the calendar and to invite him over on Monday. He was very diffident and diplomatic, protesting that it was a

433

purely family affair to which I reminded him that he was extended family and his presence was required. So with that settled I said I'd drive over and pick him up in the morning and bring him back to the house where he could help me with all the food prepping and other odds and ends. Still protesting but secretly pleased, he agreed.

Now I'm writing out an ever-increasing shopping list and waiting for the teens to come and pick it up. I have no idea what Alex and Paolo eat but I can guess that their appetites will be voracious. And of course I plan on Beef Wellington as the pièce de resistance for the first supper. As I'm metaphorically chewing the end of a pencil, trying to think of every possible food contingency, the shop door opens and the 4 teens crash in, having picked up Amanda en route.

"I have no idea what they eat?"

There is a mild note of panic in my voice.

"Anything and everything, according to Alex. Relax, mum."

"I've made out a list but just add anything you want. You can get most of it at Pricerite and charge it to the account. But use the butchers on the high street for the meat. And fresh veggies from Dysons."

I am rewarded with a withering look from my younger daughter, who snatches the list from my hand, glances at it and holds it up for the others to see.

"Not sure the bug's big enough for that lot. Maybe I should go and get the horsebox?"

Mattie is grinning and I know they're all having fun at my expense. I don't care. This is a biggie for me.

"Pricerite will deliver. Now just go!"

"See ya."

They troop out and I calm my nerves with some overdue cataloguing.

3pm

Oliver rings to say he would be riding tomorrow but that with the modification on his car, he will manage to get to the stables by himself. He also informs me that he also did some shopping on his own this morning. I ask how he is managing to get in and out of the car and he references the Tennessee Williams quote about the 'kindness of strangers'. He is clearly relishing the return of a level of independence. I invite him to join our supper party on Monday and insist that he stays over so as not to have to drive home late and in the dark. He laughs at my concern and after a short argument he concedes defeat.

"It will be the Christmas we didn't have."

"I'm sure you'll have a lot more to look forward to in the future."

"I hope so."

5.30pm

I am once more riding the bus home and enjoying the familiar experience. As the bus exits the town and we pass the large Pricerite premises my mind flashes back to the day last spring when I saw Michael and Lulu together in the car park and it occurs to me again what a lot of water has passed under the proverbial bridge since that day less than a year ago. High up I am able to view the burgeoning signs of spring in the fields and hedgerows—primroses popping up and green shoots appearing on tree branches. It's a pleasing sight after a long, hard winter and I speak metaphorically rather than meteorologically.

6pm

Walking up the drive I see a mini mountain of cardboard boxes outside the garage, two of which Mattie has tucked under his arms and is hefting around to the back.

Once inside, I find the girls in the kitchen, stowing items in the cupboards and fridge.

"We stocked up on cleaning stuff as well."

Amanda waves a large packet of washing powder at me.

"Thanks."

"And we've bought heaps of Easter goodies and decs."

Sarah shows me eggs in baskets, eggs out of baskets, pastel-coloured flowery tree hangings, rabbits in all manner of materials, decorative and edible and a host of other spring-themed ornaments and table dressings.

"The narcissi are coming up in the garden. We'll pick them tomorrow. And we can get Pussy Willow from the trees down by the river."

"And your fillet is in the fridge."

435

Jude opens the door to show me. A huge piece of meat wrapped in greaseproof paper.

"It was the biggest one in the shop. Two and a half pounds."

"But **we're** making the Beef Wellington. Your pastry is rubbish."

Sarah is quite right and I offer up no protest. Rather, while Mattie ferries the boxes in and the girls empty them and stash it all away, I begin prepping supper, beef lasagne for the meat eaters and a la funghi as a vegetarian alternative, plus a spring salad. I can manage that!

"Mattie, when you're done, go down to the cellar and find something French and fizzy."

"Righto, Mrs H."

I feel like seriously celebrating.

"And Diana phoned. She says she and Charlie will be here on Wednesday afternoon."

I force a rectal smile and resolve not to let the impending arrival of my erstwhile in-laws spoil my mood.

"She'll want to take charge." (Jude)

"She's welcome."

I catch Sarah and Jude exchanging raised eyebrows and small smirks but I choose to ignore it. Tonight is for fun.

Sunday, 26th March

6am

I rise early and leave the house as everyone else is sleeping. I am going to ride Dancer and I want to be alone. I need to think, to plan, to savour and anticipate and hacking out on the back of horse is the way I know how. Once done I'll drive over and fetch George. He is adamant about staying in the flat above the shop but is happy to muck in with the house-warming plans and preparations.

Dancer and I are sauntering through the woods and I swear he's enjoying the spring weather and the scenery as much as me. Cromwell and Dottie dart about looking for early rising rabbits, also into the spirit of the outing.

With the terrifying combination of Patti and Diana to plan and plot the minutiae of the Easter weekend and George's Oestrus Festival, I can concentrate on keeping the house ticking over and of course taking care of shop business. The important thing is that I'll have Alex staying under my roof for the next month. I am sick with anticipation and yet…something is niggling at the back of my mind, a thought I keep trying to push away but it scratches away at my sub-conscious until I have to unleash it. It's Michael's box and the assorted and extraordinary contents. Why on earth would he have kept Pip's cigarette roller all that time and what's with all the other smoking paraphernalia? I know he hated the idea of my smoking but why the collection? And where did those lighters come from? The Jack Daniels Zippo and the one from a car. That must also be quite old. There's one in my bug but I know for a fact that his fancy BMW doesn't have one, nor most other new cars, as far as I know. It's pretty peculiar yet PC Plod AKA Simon Cox doesn't seem to share my curiosity. I shake my head to rid myself of all thoughts of Michael and his bizarre box. It's far too lovely a morning to worry about whatever peccadillo he may or may not have and anyway, this is going to be the best few weeks of my life apart from…… and with a fleeting vision of Steve, of Bath, of the four of us and how good it all was, my mood is all but broken. I take up Dancer's reins and urge him into a fast canter along the bridle path, drinking in the cold air and pushing everything else out of my head, bar the speed, the air whistling in my ears and the feel of Dancer as he flies along the empty track.

Monday, 27th March

I was press-ganged by Jude and Sarah into allowing them to take the day off school and the three of us, plus George, pooled our resources to have the house shipshape and Bristol fashion. I bribed Jenny with double wages to come and assist and the place is now not only spotless from top to bottom, but brimming with spring décor, from the wooden tree in the kitchen festooned with Sarah's pagan artefacts, the bowl of crocuses just about to bloom in the sitting room and the bowls of wooden and ceramic eggs which have popped up all over the place. In the garden, John has also been hard at work, mowing the lawn which is just starting to come back to life after its winter sulk and tidying up the flower beds. Now the whole place is literally done and dusted, Jude has heated a couple of tins of soup and warmed up some rolls in the oven and we are in the kitchen, about to partake of our light lunch, just waiting for Alex and Paolo to arrive. They sent a text half an hour ago saying they would be here about 3pm and all that's left to do is for me to try and not look too much like the cat that's got the cream!

3.15pm

I am in the conservatory with a nerve-calming cigarette. It occurs to me that I am smoking much less these days but needs must when the devil rides or your long-lost son's arrival is imminent. Jude pokes her head around the door to say that Alex's Jeep just turned into the drive. Both girls have been looking forward to the visit but with their frequent trips to Oxford, spending time with their half-brother is run-of-the-mill to them by now. I stub out my cigarette and we make our way outside and walk around to the front of the house where Sarah and George are already waiting, just as the red Jeep pulls up in front of the garage.

The two young men emerge and I make no attempt at playing it cool, rushing up and hugging my son. Then remembering my manners, I do the same to Paolo.

"Welcome to Lionsgate."

"Amazing place, Guin."

Alex grins disarmingly, moves forward to give George a manly hug, then he and Paolo embrace the girls casually.

"Yo, bro. Hi Paolo."

"Bellissima Sarah and Jude!"

Paolo gives them both a Latin greeting, embracing them and kissing them on both cheeks. Then he turns and does the same to me.

"Come on in. We'll give you the Grand Tour."

Jude the Imperious.

"Sounds good."

438

He and Paolo heft couple of bags out of the bag of the Jeep and we all walk inside.

"Inside first and then the garden. We've got an orchard, you know. It was laid out when the house was built in 1792. It's got quinces, mulberries, apples, pears and there's a bramble bower. And this is Cromwell.'

Alerted by the strange voices, Cromwell has appeared from the back of the house.

"Roundhead?"

"Spaniel, silly. A King Charles, so we called him Cromwell."

"Figures."

"We'll start upstairs and show you where you're sleeping and work our way down."

And the four make their way to the main staircase, chatting and laughing, so easy in each other's company you'd think they'd know each other for years. I turn to George.

"Seems we're redundant. We might as well go and make some tea."

"He might not say it but he's pleased as punch to be here, you know."

I nod and grin like the Cheshire cat.

11.30pm

"The Beef Wellington was superb. Sarah made the pastry and Jude and Amanda assembled it."

"It was supposed to be your signature dish."

"Last time I signed it, it turned out to be a Death Warrant!'

I am on the phone to Patti, regaling her with the events of the evening. Olly had arrived just as George and I were drinking tea and the two sat talking about Irish hunters, Dublin alehouses and classic Jaguar models. The teens, plus Alex and Paolo, had all congregated in the kitchen and when I took the tea tray, through I was shooed out and instructed to 'take a chill pill'! With neither George nor Olly having seen the wine cellar, it was decided that they should both get the guided tour so Alex and Paolo made a makeshift bo'sun's chair to carry Olly down the steps and Mattie followed with the portable wheelchair.

"They spent ages down there—I'd forgotten that Olly was a bit of a wine buff—and finally emerged with a selection of some of Michael's priciest purchases, white, red, dessert and port. George just winked at me and said 'We thought this occasion called for the best'."

"Quite right, too. How was it?"

"Superb! Olly really knows his stuff. I was a bit worried about the guys having to start metaphorically toiling in the fields in the morning after so much vino but Paolo's response was—I affect an exaggerated Latin accent—'In my country, the farm workers carry a bottle of vino rosso with them to take with their lunch. A big bottle."

"I hope you left some for Ross and me!"

"Just a few cases! Seriously, Patti, it's like a bonded warehouse down there!"

"No wonder King Rat wanted to keep his hands on the place."

I fill her in on the gist of the evening, she brings me up to date on the babies' progress and we hang up, agreeing that neither of us can wait to see each other on Wednesday.

Tuesday, 28th March

The plan is that Alex and Paolo will clear, dig and plant to George's specifications and come and go from Lionsgate as time permits. The teens will also be there, Mattie offering a bit more muscle and the girls working on the Oestrus Festival set dressing, as it's now their Easter school break. Olly will also be in attendance during the week, to do whatever he can—I think he just needs some male company and a useful occupation and I am sure it will good for him mentally and physically. In the meantime and in between shop duties, I'll be preparing the house for Patti, Ross and the twins and of course, Charles and Diana. I assume that somehow or other, their visit will have come to Michael's ears and I am certain he won't be happy about it, especially if he also knows about Alex being here.

Wednesday, 29th March

6pm

I have taken a few days off work, sending in the redoubtable Jenny to take my place. Patti, Ross and the babies arrived just in time for a lazy lunch, followed by a gossipy catch-up and fussing over the infants who are nearly caught up to their full-term counterparts and are both utterly adorable. Right now Ross is upstairs on bath duty and Patti and I are attacking the mammoth task of preparing supper. We are 13 in total, excluding the twins but including Charles and Diana, they having first called in to Featherington to touch base with George and inspect the garden work, now due here any moment, and I trust that is not a bad omen. To keep things relatively simple, Patti and I settled on pasta, a massive pot of spaghetti, another of genuine Bolognaise sauce for the carnivores and a mock alternative with red lentils for the veggies. With the addition of a big bowl of salad and Simmonds' excellent Ciabatta bread that should feed the 5000 satisfactorily and keeping to the quasi-Italian theme, this will all be washed down with some genuine vino rosso from the cellar which Paolo pounced on yesterday, declaring it to be 'Bene, bene and giving us a lecture on the grape, the terroir and the vineyard.' And to complete the Latin theme, Ross also nipped out earlier to buy gelato from the little deli next to Dysons to accompany a shop-bought cherry Genoa clafouti.

11pm

Patti and I have just finished loading the dishwasher for its 3rd cycle. Supper was rowdy, chaotic and curiously relaxing. I was afraid there might be a little initial awkwardness with Michael's conspicuous absence, his ghost occasionally haunting the banqueting table, but it proved not to be. Diana, having been given the royal tour of the nursery and introduced to the twins, oohed and aahed, pressed Patti and Ross for a full briefing on their short lives to date, to my amazement and Patti's complete disbelief. She even went so far as to offer her services as a babysitter tomorrow to free up Patti to help put the finishing touches to the Oestrus ceremony. Patti, needless to say, accepted with alacrity. She may adore her babies but the mundane mechanics of childcare hold no attraction for her whatsoever.

The seating arrangements at supper had been designated with generational separation but with the newly formed alliance of Patti and Diana, not to mention Paolo who was charm personified with the self-appointed matriarch, the placements went completely awry and seating was an unlikely free for all that seemed to work. Alex sat next to Sarah and surreptitiously encouraged her to eat by tempting her to taste this titbit and that, Ross commandeered Jude and

441

Amanda and Matti, I sat between Olly and George and Charles paired up next to us. The teens acted as servers, Paolo was a very knowledgeable and efficient sommelier and Alex and Mattie cleared between courses.

And now George and Olly have just left to drive to Featherington, Diana has retired, Ross and Charles are sampling what I am given to understanding is a very old and expensive port from Michael's cellar—damn, his ghost just wafted through the kitchen again—in the conservatory and Alex, Paolo and the teens are playing billiards in the basement games room.

After checking in on her sleeping infants, Patti has poured 2 glasses of the port and we have collapsed at the kitchen table for a proper girly gossip and catch up.

"So you've finally got Alex under your roof."

I smirk.

"And Sarah looks almost radiant."

"Doesn't she? That awful pallor is gone and she's regained some colour."

"We just need to get King Rat to sign those papers."

"Claire says he's still being stubborn over the house."

"He must be livid at the thought of you guzzling his liquid gold!"

We giggle.

"I wouldn't dare touch any of those bottles in the back room."

"No such scruples for me!"

We giggle again and clink glasses. It really is an exceedingly good port.

Thursday, 30th March

10am

Since everyone else is otherwise occupied I thought I might as well come into the shop to relieve Jenny for the day. Diana and Charles have taken the babies off for an outing, the boot of the Bentley stuffed to the gills with Patti's top of the range Italian double stroller plus bottles, wet wipes, toys, packets of nappies and changes of clothes, and with the baby restraint installed in the ample back seat. Everyone else is over at Featherington, either labouring in the garden or organising Saturday's ceremony. Diana has put herself in overall charge of catering supplies and supervision and insists she can pull it all together tomorrow.

442

"Entertaining on a large scale is second nature to me, Fiona. And Charles and I will pick up everything that's needed while we're out today."

I don't doubt it.

1pm

Patti rings to say that her Pebble Mill friends have expressed an interest in covering the ceremony as a local interest, news actuality item. She spoke to George, who consulted with the residents' committee who in turn raised no objection. So one of the producers and a cameraman would be popping in to Featherington tomorrow for a quick recce.

This is all taking on a life of its own!

7pm

The teens, Alex and Paolo all decided to head off to town this evening, George is staying at Featherington and Olly is at home so it's just Patti, Ross, Charles, Diana and me for supper. Pork chops—even I can't mess them up—accompanied by new potatoes and spring vegetables. Patti was exhausted from toiling on the Oestrus set all day, as was Ross, unused as he is, to working as a son of the soil. Diana, in stark contrast, breezed in as though she'd spent a day at a spa when in reality she and Charles had taken the twins to Birmingham zoo, followed by a shopping spree in the city's most upmarket department store. Judging by the parcels they uploaded from the Bentley boot, it would appear they more or less cleaned out the entire children's clothing and toy sections, almost single-handedly. Diana also announced that she had ordered everything she needed for the Oestrus lunch and it would be arriving promptly at 9am tomorrow morning from the same source, whereafter she would be monopolising the kitchen, if that that was all right with me. It was, I informed her, as I planned on manning the shop again, wanting the arrangements at Featherington to be a pleasant surprise on Saturday. Patti, now bathed and somewhat rested, is helping me with supper and we are both making short shift of a bottle of excellent Chablis from the cellar.

"Your mother-in-law never ceases to amaze me."

"What's she done this time?"

443

"Only asked if she and Charles could be stand-in grandparents! She said they'd both fallen in love with the kids today and they want to keep in touch and watch them grow up."

My jaw dropped.

"The same Diana who nearly swooned at the sight of your belly ring last summer?"

"The very same!"

"What did you say?"

"Yes, of course. Ross's folks are in Guernsey so we don't often see them. And you know my backstory."

I did. Patti's mother was a junkie who'd died when she was a toddler and she never knew who her father was. Her maternal grandmother had taken her in but the two never hit it off and Patti had left her house when she was 15, moved in with an older girl friend, found a job as gopher for a theatrical costumier and studied for her A levels at night school. It was right after that that we met up at Bristol Uni.

"Judging by today's capital outlay, your children are going to be spoiled rotten."

"Didn't do yours any harm. And you've forgotten the best bit."

"Which is?"

"King Rat will spit blood when he hears!"

"You're not wrong!"

We clink glasses and put the finishing touches to supper.

Friday, 31st March

10am Good Friday

A dark green, liveried van drew up at the house this morning, just as I was about to leave. Diana was already up and dressed, a butcher's apron covering her Gucci shirt and skirt. Eschewing my offer of help, she was in full Colonel-in-Chief mode, shooing me off to work and marshalling the van crew towards the kitchen, bearing large cardboard boxes from which bunches of vegetables, unleavened breads and bottles of olive oil protruded. There were also cooler boxes whose contents I could only guess at,

Having been given my clear marching orders I drove off and left her to it. She looked completely in her element.

My cell phone rings. It's Jude.

"Mum, you don't know what you're missing! There's a television crew here, getting some background footage, they said. They shot the guys weeding out the vegetable beds, did a long interview with George, all about the project and then they took shots of Sarah, Amanda and me in our costumes!"

It's a while since I've heard Jude quite so animated. At this last comment, I butt in.

"What costumes?"

"The ones they brought. They came in this huge van with loads of electronic equipment inside. And another with stacks of costumes, Mediaeval, all sizes, for men and women. Patti insists we all dress up tomorrow and there's even some for the other residents if they want to get into the spirit of the thing. So everyone's been trying stuff on and picking out what they like. I've chosen one for you. I hope that's okay?"

I digest this new development. Knowing Patti, I should have guessed as much.

"I don't suppose I have much choice, do I?"

"It's going to be bitching!"

"I'm pleased for George. He's worked so hard on this whole thing."

"And it's partly because of him that Alex is here now."

She's right, of course,

"It's all coming together really well."

There's an inflection in her voice that implies she's not only referring to the garden project and tomorrow's ceremony.

"I need to ask you something."

"Ask away."

"Amanda wanted to know if it's okay if her folks come to the ceremony."

I hesitate for a millisecond.

"Of course. Tell her they'll be very welcome."

"Thanks, mum. Only she's pretty embarrassed about the whole dad thing."

"It was hardly her fault."

I can't say I relish the prospect of seeing Lulu again but I keep it to myself. And without prompting, the vision of Lulu in Edinburgh at the Pricerite store opening flashes uninvited in my mind's eye. Was that really only 6 or 7 months ago? It feels like a lifetime.

7pm

A large easel housing an equally large flipchart has appeared in the kitchen. Sarah is standing to attention next to it and Jude, Patti and Diana are seated at the table. The twins are in their buggy which is strategically placed between the latter. Glancing at the chart I see it is a battle plan for tomorrow, with timings and random jottings, everything meticulously planned, from the costumes, to the catering, the filming schedule and running order, garden tour and offerings to Oestrus for good luck, with flowers, poetry and music.

"We're all going to be there from 6 o'clock." (Jude)

"I've organised for a wardrobe and make-up crew for everyone on camera." (Patti)

"The guys are all going to be dressed as monks, George will be an abbot and Diana an abbess. We're going as nymphs, Patti will be Oestrus, you'll be her handmaiden. All the guests will be mediaeval villagers and gentry. And the twins are going to be cherubs."(Sarah)

"You hope!" (Patti)

"I hope mine's not a speaking part."

"You just have to stand behind Patti and strew a few flowers."

"I suppose I can manage that."

"We'd better get this table cleared for supper. As it's Good Friday, I've made fish a la Portuguese. I hope that's all right with everyone?" (Diana)

I glance anxiously at Sarah, a look that is not unnoticed by Diana.

"Oyster mushrooms instead of fish for the vegetarians."

Patti and I exchange a look with slightly raised eyebrows, one that clearly says 'Who is this woman and what has she done with Diana?' At that strategic moment Emily Georgina wakes and begins to cry which wakes her brother who joins in.

"Bath time!"

Patti stands up, scoops up a baby in each arm and heads for the door. Sarah and Jude make a beeline to follow her, leaving Diana and I alone. I began lifting out cutlery and laying the table but pause. Diana has her back to me as she gently stirs her fish dish.

"I'm really glad you and Charles are here."
And I actually mean it,

Saturday, 1st April

10am

I drive into Featherington to find it a total madhouse. There is a phalanx of vans, one from Diana's food hall and four from the BBC's OB unit. What I take to be broadcasting personnel are swarming over the house and grounds like an invading army, laying cables, setting up cameras and mikes and rounding up the troops, in the guise of residents dressed as Chaucerian extras. Not without difficulty, I find a parking space and set off to locate Patti et al. I track them to a motorised caravan where 2 young women are artfully dressing hair and adding make-up to the waiting main protagonists in the upcoming feature. George, in his abbot's habit, looks somewhat embarrassed but Sarah, Jude and Amanda, clad in velveteen and silk mediaeval gowns and with garlands of flowers in their hair, are taking it all in their stride and appear to be enjoying themselves immensely. I am informed that Mattie, Alex and Paolo are all suitably costumed as Franciscan friars and are working in the vegetable garden being filmed for background footage at this very moment. And whilst I am taking all this in, Patti thrusts a handmaiden's blouse and kirtle at me and orders me to costume up and report for hair and make-up. Sensing that she will brook no argument, I meekly obey.

1 pm

With the costumed residents gathered around a lectern set up by the garden project, George delivers a short speech cum sermon beseeching Oestre to bless its bounty and increase his yield through her beneficent auspices. Then Patti, standing close by, framed in the ruins of the old monastery archway, responds as the goddess herself, giving her blessing and summoning the Earth's fertile bounty, the girls wave long, silken ribbons and strew catkins and spring blossom, chanting lines from William Blake's poem 'Spring', which they have been learning over the past few days. Once finished, I hand Patti/Oestre a leather ewer filled with water which she scatters over the soil whilst the 'friars' deliver a Gregorian-style chant which sounds amazing—they must have been practising in secret. And while all this was going on, the BBC crew was moving hither and hither with cameras on dollies and large, muffled microphones, capturing the entire proceedings.

Finally the 'cast' takes a bow, George thanks the goddess for her blessings and bounties, the extras applaud excitedly and the ceremony is complete. A handbell is rung from the vicinity of the Hall and we all make our way to what looks like a marquee from a mediaeval jousting tourney, another BBC prop, where trestles and benches are laid out for lunch. To one side, Charles, Olly and Ross are manning a bar, already attracting a jostling crowd of thirsty peasants and to the other Diana is in command of her buffet lunch, including a suckling pig on a spit conjured up from heaven knows where, plus all manner of salad items, cheeses, breads and sundry savouries. The girls, still in costume, don makeshift aprons and begin serving the waiting guests. Marvelling at Diana's organisational skills, I too duck behind the buffet table and lend a hand. I even manage a sort-of convincing smile, when Lulu and Neil Sinclair approach and tell me how well I'm looking and what a lovely ceremony it was.

6pm

The festivities carried on all afternoon and even now, the buffet marquee is still full of Hall residents, drinking, talking and snacking on the remains of the lunch. Patti reclaimed her babies from an obliging BBC gopher who had been assigned childcare duties for the duration and we are now packing up our belongings and preparing to head home. I am packing odds and ends into the bug when a familiar Ford drives up and parks close by. DS Cox.

"You're too late."

"I know."

The look on his face makes me wonder if we're talking about the same thing,

"How did you know I was here?"

"I told you, I'm a detective."

"We're just leaving."

"It won't take long."

He pats the passenger seat. I hesitate, then make a quick decision.

"Patti, can you take the girls home with you? I'll follow on in a bit."

"No probs."

She shoots a look of disdain at Simon Cox, then moves away to her SUV. I open the passenger door and fold in, onto the seat.

"I'm absolutely bushed so this had better be quick. And worth my while."

"I think it should be. I was burning the midnight oil last night, going over Mr Driscoll's file."

"You can call him Steve, you know."

He nods and smiles wryly.

"I thought there had to be something that was overlooked and I think I might have found it."

He pauses and looks at me. I open my hands in a 'so what' gesture.

"The statement from the kitchen commie, the one who went out for a smoke break and said he saw the red Golf."

"He said he thought the driver was male but he didn't get a clear look. So what?"

"That wasn't all he had to say. In his written statement he also stated he couldn't make out the passenger!"

He raises his voice to emphasise this point and looks at me triumphantly. I look at him blankly.

"So there was a passenger? I'm not sure where that takes you."

"Listen to this."

He pulls sheet of paper from out of his glove compartment, opens it up and reads.

"At about 8pm there was a bit of lull in the kitchen so I nipped outside for a cigarette. I went outside the back entrance which overlooks the car park. I sat on a stack of beer crates and lit my cigarette. I heard some tyres squeal and saw a little hatchback, Golf, I think, screaming off. The one on the passenger side hadn't even closed his door properly. I assumed they were a couple of boy racers. I didn't get a good look at the driver but I'm pretty sure it was a white male. And I think the car was red. That's what it looked like when it passed the street light."

"I still don't get the point."

"Remember you said in your statement Mr Driscoll—Steve's Rolex was missing? You mentioned to me and DI Bhadri when we first spoke to you."

I nod.

"That's probably who took it. Suppose they knocked him over as he was getting out of his car. Either one or both gets out to check and sees he's not moving. They panic. But they're a couple of wrong 'uns and they just can't resist grabbing the watch before they hightail it out."

"Makes sense but it still doesn't solve anything."

"Maybe not but it's another lead. The original investigation always assumed it was just one person because they were working on the commie's initial verbal statement which just talked about the red Golf. Now we know there were at least two, the driver and a front seat passenger. And also no-one took the absence of the Rolex as a factor. I'm thinking the passenger got out to check on Mr Driscoll, realised he was unconscious, possibly dead, saw the Rolex and nicked it, then he and his mate took off. We've made extensive enquiries and come up against a brick wall in our searches for the Golf driver but now we've got a much better lead. There were a lot fewer Gold Rolexes in the country back then than red Golfs so we just might get lucky."

"I would like to have that watch back."

He nods, understandingly.

"Thanks for stopping by."

"My pleasure."

Impulsively, I lean over and give him a half-hug, before exiting. It's been quite a day.

Part V
"Whan That Aprill with His Shoures Soote
The Droghte of March Hath Perced to the Roote,
And Bathed Every Veyne in Swich Licour
Of Which Vertu Engendred Is the Flour"

Sunday, 2nd April

10am

George had insisted that Alex and Paolo take a break from the garden today and since Paolo had expressed an interest in visiting the RSC in Stratford, he had miraculously procured tickets for them and the teens for a matinée performance of The Taming of the Shrew. Wanting to make a day of it, they had all set off in Alex's Jeep straight after breakfast, their expedition oiled with a generous cash donation from Charles. My in-laws, too, had plans to meet up with George and do lunch so their departure was imminent. And I persuaded Patti that she and Ross needed some chill time together so they have decided to take the twins for a long, invigorating walk. For my part, I'd arranged to meet Olly at the stables in an hour but there was something I needed to do first. I picked up my phone.

"Why did you want to know about Steve's Saab?"

"I'm not at liberty to say."

"If you were a girl, I'd call you a prick tease."

"That's blunt! I really can't say anything at this stage. I have a hunch, that's all."

"So tell me about your hunch."

He sighs and pauses.

"Okay. I think your husband is a serial stalker and a very jealous individual. I think he keeps tabs on any man who means anything to you, whether real or perceived. I think he's done it for a long time and I think he's probably still doing it. And when he does it, he likes to collect a souvenir to remind himself."

His tone is sombre, cautionary.

"I'm sorry I bothered you on a Sunday morning."

"It was no bother."

"Thanks, Simon."

"That's the first time you've ever used my first name."

"I know."

I put the phone down and check my watch. Time to leave for my ride. I hope Olly's up for long hack—I need to think.

Olly is in great spirits this Easter Sunday morning. As I hoped, he was up for riding out and we have plotted a meandering route around the back roads, through the woods behind the stables and along the banks of a tributary of the Avon which runs close by. The weather is glorious, what Keats must have had in mind when he penned Home Thoughts From Abroad. That bit about 'Oh to be In England, now that April's there'. Daisies are brightening the verges, spring violets and wild pansies poke out from under small bushes in the woods, daffodils adorn the banks of the river and the late morning sun is warming my bones. Olly chats about an upcoming 3-phase competition in Gloucestershire which Mattie, Jude and Amanda have all entered and he, true to his word, has signed up as their personal Chef d'Équipe. Then we lapse into a companionable silence and I turn over my conversations with Simon Cox and come to a decision. It's long overdue.

"Shall we canter?"

Olly is pointing to the grass track along the bank of the river.

"If you're sure you'll be okay?"

He nods, I kick Dancer into a brisk canter and Captain follows suit. And not for the first time I wonder what on earth could have caused that seemingly bombproof animal to spook and lose his rider that night. I turn to check on Olly and he is grinning broadly. Equine therapy.

Part VI
"For There Is Nothing Either Good or Bad, but Thinking Makes It So"

Monday, 4th April

Easter Monday. Tomorrow Ross, Patti and the babies are off back to the West Country, Patti anxious to return to work and Ross's presence required at an important production meeting. Nils, I am told, is missing his young charges and after his weekend in London, he is re-energised and keen to resume his loco parentis duties.

Charles and Diana, too, will set out on a leisurely drive back to Scotland, having impressed upon the Badgers that not only would they be welcome at Carnegie Castle at any time but that the old nursery will be spring-cleaned and spruced up along with an adjoining suite of rooms, to be put at their disposal at any time. Furthermore, Diana managed to extract a promise from Patti that their visit would be sooner, rather than later. Wonders will never cease.

Meanwhile, while the twins are still in the arms of Morpheus and the house is still quiet, I have a private call to make. I pick out the card still lying in a porcelain dish in the kitchen and tap in the number.

"Rupert? It's Fiona—Hamilton—George's friend. I hope I'm not calling too early?"

"Fiona, what a pleasant surprise. How are you and your young companions?"

"We're all very well, thank you. How is life in London?"

"I must confess to having snuck away to the boonies for the Easter weekend. I have a little pied-a-terre, well more a pied-a-mer, really! I have a little lighthouse that I'm doing up."

Of course you do!

"All those stairs!"

"Keeps me fit. So to what do I owe the pleasure?"

"I need to find someone and I thought you might be able to give me some suggestions as to how to go about it."

"I see. And is this someone a stranger or an acquaintance?"

"An acquaintance. Someone from my dark and distant past."

"And will this someone want to be found?"

"Possibly not but it's important."

"Hmm. I could probably make some enquiries on your behalf."

"You'd have to be discreet."

457

"Fiona, 'discreet' is somewhat sine qua non in my profession. We civil servants are supposed to be deaf, dumb and blind."

He is laughing

"Do you have a name for this someone?"

"It's James Greville."

"French Huguenot family. And if it's not too intrusive a question, when and where did you last hear of Mr Greville?"

"He was a friend of a friend when I was doing my 'A' Levels. He was reading astro-physics at Liverpool Uni but his family was from Shropshire."

"Age?"

"Early forties."

"And how urgent is it that you track him down?"

"Very."

"Give me a few days. If he's still alive and living in the UK it should be quite simple. If he's overseas or deceased it might take a bit longer."

Deceased? The thought had never occurred to me but of course it's perfectly possible. A lot can happen in twenty-something years.

"I really didn't mean for you to do it. Just to point me in the right direction."

"It's no bother, I do have a few resources I can call on to facilitate the matter."

"That is very kind of you."

"Not at all. I'll be in touch as soon as I have anything to report. In the meantime do remember me to those charming young people and remind them they are welcome to visit anytime once I'm back in the Smoke."

"I will. They'll be thrilled."

I click off my phone with more than a frisson of excitement. Part 1 of my plan has now been launched.

Tuesday, 5th April

5am

I've been up for half an hour and am bathed, dressed and in the kitchen preparing breakfast for my departing guests. I plan on resuming my duties in

458

the shop once they have left and Jenny has promised faithfully to come and give the place a bit of a spring clean once everyone has left.

As perceptive as ever, Patti is convinced I am up to something and did her level best yesterday to wheedle it out of me but honestly, I don't really have a proper plan per se, just an inkling of an idea which may or may not come off. But I promised her on pain of death that I'd let her know if anything came of anything.

8.30am

The two parties are all packed up and ready for the off. There are hugs and handshakes all around and as Patti and I embrace she hisses in my ear.

"Keep me up to date or die!"

I smile conspiratorially at her, give Diana a continental air kiss and plant real ones on each of the babies' heads. They blink at me without emotion as Ross deftly lifts them out of their double-buggy and into the car seat. The buggy is then expertly stowed in the back, Patti and Ross get into the front seats and they head the procession down the drive, between the stone lions and off home, Diana and Charles following closely. Sarah and Jude joined us a few minutes ago and both wave madly at the departing row of vehicles. It is only after they have all disappeared from view and we turn to go back into the house that I notice Sarah has a handful of nuts and raisins in her palm and is nibbling them. I honestly can't remember the last time I saw her voluntarily eating a snack.

Thursday, 7th April

7pm

I am in the kitchen with all 4 teens for the first time since Saturday, Amanda and Mattie having both been spending some time at their respective homes. Louise, I am told, is on her best behaviour and Gerald is soaking up the saccharine sweetness. He has seemingly bought her a diamond eternity ring to symbolise their renewed romance and she has traded in her mini for a Mercedes. The symbolism is not lost on me. Mattie's mother has spent the past

459

fortnight in another drying-out clinic and is so far still on the wagon but Mattie, as cynical as Amanda, is certain it won't last.

All this gossip is exchanged in the quasi-familial atmosphere of our motley group whilst I try my hand preparing a dish of Eggplant Parmigiana, setting aside a small one sans cheese for Sarah, served with pasta. I have also taken the precaution of popping some thick pork chops into a separate pan with some sage and onion for the gardeners who return each day from their toils claiming to be starving and proceeding to pack away enough food for a small army. I have it on good authority that in a few short months I will have fresh sage and a multitude of other herbs from the garden at Featherington so I am garnering as much pre-knowledge as I can from a useful book from our culinary section at the shop. Once I have all my dishes in the oven and simmering on the top of the range, I decide the time is right to pass on Rupert's invitation. The reaction is that of a large pebble tossed in a mill pond. The ripples immediately begin radiating outwards.

"Did he really remember us?" Sarah

"He asked after you especially."

"Does he actually mean it?" Mattie

"Absolutely. He strikes me as very much a man of his word."

"We've still got another 2 weeks off school. Can we go before we go back?" Jude

"I'm not sure that would be convenient. When I spoke to him he wasn't in London."

"Did he really say we could all go?" Amanda looks anxious.

"Yes, he was quite specific."

"Was he on holiday?" Sarah

"As it so happens, he was taking a break. Apparently he owns a lighthouse and he's doing it up."

This last statement draws a cacophony of half-shouted comments, including 'Cool', 'Boss', 'Wow', 'Wonder where it is?', 'Maybe he'll let us use it' and others in the same vein. And whilst they're still digesting and marvelling at knowing someone who not only has a pad in London to which they have an open invitation but also an actual lighthouse, Alex and Paolo are heard driving up. As soon as they come into the kitchen, they are waylaid and regaled with these pieces of news and in spite of their superiority of age, they too are suitably impressed.

460

As they head off upstairs to shower and change, I make the finishing touches to tonight's supper and the others lay the table, open wine and light candles, as has become the norm these days. And I am relieved that in all the excitement of the life and times of Rupert, no-one thought to enquire as to the circumstances and substance of our phone conversation.

Saturday, 9th April

10am

I finish writing up a sale receipt for one customer and with others happily browsing I make a call.

"A couple of quick questions. The first one's a bit delicate. You asked me a while ago about your real father. If I did have any information, would you want to know?"

I hear an intake of breath.

"Yes, I think so. It's just a question of filling in some blanks. My adoptive dad is still my father."

"I think I understand. Okay.

"Secondly, just out of curiosity did you ever find out who sent you the crank message telling you to go home just before Christmas?"

"Not really. I suspect it was one of my housemates' idea of a joke but no-one's owned up. And what with the car breaking down, it was probably just as well George took the train, otherwise we'd both have been stranded."

"That's true, I hadn't thought of that."

"And 'Noël en Paris' was hardly a punishment, no offence."

"None taken. Perfectly understandable that you'd find it agreeable in the land of your forefathers."

"I have French ancestry?"

"Peut être."

"What are you not telling me?"

"His first name only, for now! It's James. Au revoir."

I laugh and put the phone down.

He probably thinks I'm one step away from the funny farm but it can't be helped. I am now firmly back in my investigative journo mode.

461

Monday, 11th April

9am

Sarah and Jude left early to ride with Amanda and Mattie, Sarah is just there to potter about but the other three are putting in practise time for the show that Olly was talking about. Alex and Paolo, of course, are still assisting George in the garden project so I am alone in the house which suits my plans.

While Patti was here over Easter we'd had a long girly gossip that first evening, after everyone else had gone to be. Over a glass of one of his better ports, we'd discussed Michael's secret box and its strange contents.

"That has to be why he was obsessed with getting the house back. He wanted the box."

"Maybe."

"You sound doubtful."

"That was my first thought too but it's not against the law to have that stuff, even if he did nick poor Pip's roller box. No-one's going to charge him with petty theft, years after the event"

"Bit embarrassing, though."

I shake my head.

"Still not worth all the fuss he's still making about Lionsgate. I've gone over and over it in my head and I think I missed something."

"Downstairs?"

I nod.

"But you said there was nothing else in the safe."

"I didn't think here was, But there must be. I need to go down there again."

"Now?"

"Two heads and all that."

She had needed no second invitation.

I had showed her the collection of ledgers and we'd sat by the bureau going through each and every one, looking for any scrap of incriminating evidence which might prove that Michael had been cooking the books or perpetrating some sort of fraudulent activity in his wines and spirits dealing but after an hour and a half of microscopic scrutiny we came to the same

462

conclusion that I had originally drawn—the books looked clean and the transactions legitimate. There was no way of telling whether the taxman had been appraised of the recent accounts but there were tax clearance certificates for previous years so even that was hardly promising.

We re-inspected the collectable bottles in the racks at the back of the cellar and they too looked like the genuine articles so finally we moved on to the safe. Patti picked a few of the bottles at random and was suitably impressed with their antiquity and value when I matched them to their entries in the purchase ledger. Together we went over the entire interior of the safe with a fine tooth comb and satisfied ourselves that there was absolutely nothing more to be seen there, bar the remaining box, the one containing the corporate manual. At her insistence, I opened the box and lifted it out. It weighed a ton and was arranged like a set of mini encyclopaedias, each volume emblazoned with the Pricerite name and logo, their titles clearly indicating content—Corporate Philosophy & Values, Store layout—Exterior, Store Layout—Interior, Marketing—Vols 1 & 2, Corporate Dress Code, Staff Hierarchy, Staff Functions, HR Policy, Emergency Procedures, Storage—Non-Perishables, Storage—Perishables, Vols 1—4, Just In Time Stock Control, Customer Relations, Store Directory', 'Addenda'

I looked at Patti, shrugged, replaced the box, then we left and went to bed. Whatever I'd hoped to find had still eluded me.

Today I mean to revisit the cellar. Something that Michael wants very desperately is down there and I will find it. That box of corporate manuals has been nagging at my psyche. I know Michael used to refer to it as his 'Bible', pretty fitting since he treated the job like a religion with Francis as its leader. Maybe there's an incriminating note tucked away somewhere. Unlikely, I know, but I'm clutching at straws here.

10am

Again I lift out the heavy box. Last time I had picked out a couple of volumes at random and flicked through them. Each page carried the word 'Confidential' in bold, at the top but the text was as dull as ditch water, just instruction manuals on Pricerite's rigid operating policies. I suppose they are all stored digitally these days and they must have been updated as methodologies advanced but I remember how absurdly pleased Michael was when he first brought them home and locked them away in that little old, grey safe. Could he really have just hung on to them for sentimental reasons and even so, why keep them locked away when the information must be hopelessly out of date?

I lift out the first book and begin leafing through it, page by page.

4.30pm

It is when I lifted out the last volume, the one marked 'Addenda' that I finally find something that seems out of place. Tucked into the back of the ring binder-style volume are several clear plastic document holders where the user can store additional notes, into which are a number of envelopes containing photographic negatives. They are similar to those in our old family photo albums from before Bath and the break-up and I wonder what they are doing here and what is on them, though logic tells me they're most likely just a photographic record of the store projects he's worked on. Lifting out a sheet or two, it is hard to make out exactly what is depicted without positive prints. And I wonder where on earth I might find somewhere where that obsolete skill might still be practised. I lift out the envelopes, lock the tomes back in the box and retreat upstairs, lost in thought,

5.30pm

Still in contemplative mood, I round up Dottie and Cromwell, load them into the bug and head off to Featherington. I know George appreciates me taking an interest in the progress of the garden, not to mention Alex and Paolo, so I will do my duty, inspect the beds and give the dogs a run at the same time.

6pm

It is just light enough for me to be given the royal tour of the vegetable patches and large herb garden where some small shoots are already beginning to show. George tells me that now all the donkey work has been done on that side, he can begin reviving the main landscape, replanting flowers and shrubs and repairing hedges. We walk around the grounds companionably, whilst the dogs run wild, and he waxes lyrical about the overall effect he hopes to achieve by June. I consider whether to tell him that I have been in touch with Rupert and explain the task I set him and decide to wait till I hear back, whether the answer is informative or fruitless. Then I load the dogs back in the car, say my farewells and head off home via Dyson's to pick up some vegetables for supper. George's endeavours have prompted me to take an interest in traditional British cooking so I plan on trying my hand at braised celery with baked potatoes. I shall also pop into the butchers for some of their home-made house sausages for the sons of the soil and myself and as I drive I wonder if my previous lack of prowess in the culinary arts was only through lack of interest or perhaps it was a deep-rooted antagonism to playing Earth Mother and nurturer to my soon-to-be ex-husband?

Saturday, 16th April

6am

I am getting dressed when my cell phone rings.

"Hope I didn't wake you."

"I'm an early riser."

'A girl after my own heart. I have some information for you. That person you were looking for is in Houston, Texas. I have a landline number and a street address."

He reels off some numbers and I write them down.

"That's brilliant. I owe you."

"My pleasure."

"How's the lighthouse?"

"Getting there. Why don't you come and have a look. It should be a bit more habitable in a couple of months."

"I'd love that."

"Super. I must dash. Urgent meeting at HQ."

"One quick question. Sorry to keep pestering you."

"Not at all. Spit it out."

"Would you be able to have some old photographic negatives printed for me?"

"Easy peasy. Just pop them in the post. How absurdly retro that sounds!"

"You're a godsend."

"That's not what my mother says! Keep in touch."

And he is gone. I try and calculate the time in Houston. I know they're behind us but have no idea how long. I suspect this is not a good time to ring, though and resolve to look up the time difference. In truth I'm not quite ready to make that call just yet. I need to psych myself up for it as it won't be easy. I can call one other person, though. With 2 infants under 6 months I know she's bound to be awake.

"Rupert called.'

"Who's Rupert?"

Patti sounds groggy. Maybe she was sleeping.

"You remember. The safe cracker."

"Spy, you mean."

"Civil servant."

"Yeah, right."

"He tracked him down to Houston."

"I hope you know what you're doing. It's going to come as a helluva shock after all these years."

"I can't help that. I really need to ask him something."

"Is this anything to do with King Rat?"

"Just the opposite. If there's anything to tell after I've spoken to him, you'll be the first to know."

"Damn right. Now buzz off and let me sleep. Ross is feeding the brats and Nils will take over at 8."

She drops the phone.

10am

I lift down a huge old atlas from our geography section and locate Houston on a mercantile map of the world. Then starting from Greenwich I count back along the lines of latitude and conclude that Texas should be 8 hours behind London. Today bring Saturday, I wonder if 4pm is a good time to call, decide to give it a go anyway and that means midnight our time.

466

6pm

I close the shop, having spent all day composing, recomposing and rewriting my script for the transatlantic phone call in my head. I knew it would be hard but not this hard. Do I really want to do this? Definitely not. Do I need to do it? Absolutely.

'Just screw your courage to the sticking point, Fiona, and you'll not fail.'

Sticking to my new theme of traditional British fare I had also leafed through some old cookbooks in the shop and come across a casserole from the Lake District involving lentils, fresh vegetables and bacon chops which seems quite simple to prepare. Figuring I could make a large one with meat and a small one without, I settled on this for supper tomorrow. I will stop off at Dyson's for the dried pulses and I am sure the butcher will know what bacon chops are as I certainly don't. I wonder if Michael has any English wines downstairs, and resolve to have a look. Anything to keep my mind off the phone call.

7pm

The girls were all very enthusiastic about the British food theme and offered to try their hand at some sponge puddings and fruit pies. With Alex, Paolo and Mattie working up massive appetites after their labours in the gardens, a single course is never enough. So tonight it is a traditional roast-pork for the carnivores and nut-loaf as the veggie option—followed by treacle tart. Whilst rooting around in the cellar not only do I find a few cases of English wines but also some of a rather superior Frascati which I think will pair well with the roast pork and also please Paolo greatly.

11pm

Supper passed well enough. The food was good, the wine even better and Sarah managed a whole slice of her nut loaf as well as veggies and a (very)small roast potato. She declined the treacle tart but did accept a taste of the tiniest morsel that Alex offered her from his plate. Mattie had downloaded the programme for the horse show and between discussion about who was entering what and when and chatter about Alex and Paolo's return to the city of dreaming spires in a week or so, no-one noticed my lapses of concentration, worrying again over what on earth my opening gambit in tonight's transatlantic phone call was going to be.

And now I am sitting in the conservatory with the remnants of the Frascati and a packet of cigarettes. I know I had vowed to cut down but tonight is a justifiable lapse. Checking the ashtray I see I have smoked 3 since I sat down.

Midnight

I pick up my cell phone, check the number Rupert gave me for the umpteenth time and tap the keypad. A far-off beep indicates the number is ringing.

"Ola!"

I am startled to hear a female voice with a decided Hispanic accent I clear my throat.

"Hello. Is this the right number for James Greville"

"Si. I call him."

The receiver is placed down and the voice calls out

"Jeemmy. Someone she is asking for you."

I hear random muffled noises, then the receiver is lifted and my stomach lurches.

"Hi there!"

A southern drawl. I wonder if Rupert found the right James?

"Hello. I'm looking for James "

"You found him. What can I do for you?"

I clear my throat again.

"I'm sorry to have bothered you. The James I was looking for was English. From Shropshire."

"That'd be me."

He sounds upbeat, amused.

"Sorry, your accent...." I trail off, try again. "You probably don't remember me. I'm Fiona. Dobson, was my maiden name."

"Fiona?"

He sounds puzzled. Oh god, he has no recollection whatsoever. Well, what did you expect after all this time?

468

"It's a bit awkward. I knew you when I was still at school. Chester Grammar. You used to call me Filly. You said I reminded you of a mare on your father's string."

There's a long pause. A pregnant pause.

"I thought that name sounded familiar, somehow. Jeez! This is a surprise." Another pause.

"Look, I'm real sorry about what happened back then. But it was a helluva long time ago."

"Yes it was. And you don't have to apologise. I made my choices." Pause. "So you're in Houston? How is it there?"

'Pretty good. I work for NASA. Climate's great and the pay's not bad. How about you?"

"I'm still in England. The Black Country. Near Stratford."

"You married?"

"Not really. You?"

"Never settled down. Big disappointment to my folks!"

"Have you been in the States long?"

"Yeah. Must be….about 18 years, I guess."

"What made you choose there?"

"While I was at Liverpool studying, I learned that Harvard had the best astrophysics department anywhere. I went out there in my summer vac for an interview and a bit of a look around America. I got my acceptance letter before I went home so I just stayed on and transferred."

I take a deep breath. This small talk isn't getting us anywhere and I'm sure he's wondering why the hell I phoned.

"Sounds exciting. I took up my place at Bristol reading English after…"

I falter, not quite how to phrase what I want to say.

"It must have been pretty rough."

"It was."

"Not that I know anything about it but I've heard women who've gone through a termination saying it's never easy."

My jaw drops at this last sentence. An abortion? I fall silent.

"Filly? You still there?"

"Er…yes, sorry. You caught me off guard."

"That makes us even!. Sorry, I kinda interrupted. Carry on."

469

"Oh, Lord. This is going to come as more of a bombshell than I thought, You see, there was no abortion. I was brought up strict Catholic."

It's his turn to be lost for words. I let it sink in.

"You had the baby? Christ! Why the hell didn't you tell me?"

"It was such a casual thing between us. And I was afraid you'd think I'd got pregnant on purpose."

"I asked a few of my friends if they knew where you were. Nobody seemed to know. I can't believe this."

"I went away. To a residential 6th Form college in Lancaster. I didn't tell a soul" Pause. "I'm really sorry. I didn't call to lay a guilt trip on you."

"Girl or boy?"

"A boy."

"Did you ever tell him about me?"

"That's the thing, I …er…gave him up for adoption. I didn't want to but I was sort of boxed into a corner."

"Jesus. You poor thing. So he didn't have either parent growing up?"

He falls silent.

"I really wish you'd told me."

"I'm sorry. Truly. I never should have let me him go. I agonised over it back then and it haunted me over the years."

"I bet." Pause. "So I have a son out there somewhere?"

"Not exactly 'out there'. That's really why I'm calling. You see, I met up with him recently."

"Jesus! This is the weirdest Saturday afternoon of my life."

"Sorry. I know it must be an awful shock but I gave it a lot of thought and decided you needed to know."

"So where is he? He must be what 21, 22?"

"22 last birthday. And he's staying with me for Easter."

I briefly explain how I got in touch with Alex, what little I knew of his life with his adoptive parents and the fact that he'd asked me about his birth father.

"I didn't give him any details, other than your first name and the fact that you were a science student when I knew you. And I haven't told him I'd tracked down your phone number in case you didn't want anything to do with him. Which is absolutely your right."

"Wow. Look, Filly, I'm going to have to give this some serious thought."

His accent has reverted to received English.

"It's such a stunner. I honestly don't know what to think or say."

"I understand."

"Give me your contacts and I promise I'll come back to you once I've processed it all a bit better."

I give him phone numbers and email.

"Jeemmy. You want I make coffee?"

The same voice that answered the phone.

"Sure. I'll be right out."

This is slightly muffled. He must have covered the mouthpiece.

"Look, I'll let you go and I promise I'll call you. Soon."

"I get it, really. It took me a while to come to terms with actually finding him after all those years, much less meeting him." Pause. "He's really nice. My daughters adore him."

"Honestly, I just can't think straight right now. It's a bit early for strong liqueur so I guess I'll have to settle for caffeine. Preferably intravenous."

He laughs, sardonically.

"I know the feeling. I'll leave you to your coffee. Bye."

We hang up and I exhale deeply. A long-suppressed picture of a 19 year-old James has come into my head and I suddenly realise that he and Alex are almost mirror images. How could I have pushed that picture away for so many years? The mind is such a complex organ. And with that thought I switch tracks to poor Sarah and her own buried mental snapshots. I pray she doesn't have a relapse as I head to bed and ponder that she and I have more in common than she probably thinks.

Monday, 18th April

9am

Back to school for the 4 teens this morning but Alex and Paolo don't go back till Saturday, with college classes resuming next Monday.

With the house to myself I find a large, padded envelope into which I place the packets of negatives. There are 24 in all. I seal it up, copy Rupert's name from his business card and the Whitehall work address he gave me and head off to the village Post Office. I will send them by registered post.

1pm

Sitting in the kitchen with a ham sandwich and a glass of Russian tea, I call Patti and fill her in on the James situation.

"Weird how I completely forgot what James looked like, when he's the spitting image of Alex?"

"Bit of a dish then, your teen lover!"

"I suppose he was."

"And he honestly never knew you had the baby?"

"Nobody did. That was all part of mum and dad's plan. Hide the skeleton in the family closet and throw away the key. Do you know, I don't think they've ever so much as mentioned it since."

"So which way do you think he'll jump?"

"I truly don't know. It must be a pretty heavy bomb blast to his system."

"Little bit." Pause. "Just as well he never married. Imagine what his wife would think!"

"He had a female there but I don't know what the relationship is."

We fall silent for a few seconds, then I remember to tell her about the cache of photo negatives.

"What do you think's on them?"

"No idea and I couldn't make much out when I tried holding them up to the light."

"They must be important for King Rat to have locked them away."

"Maybe just more soft porn, like those ones of Lulu."

"If that's the case, poor Rupert's going to get a helluva shock."

"Something tells me Rupert doesn't shock easily."

"I need to meet this spy guy. He sounds intriguing."

"He's very charming but he gives me the impression of a human iceberg. Mostly hidden under the water."

"Now I definitely want to meet him—try and plumb those depths."

"That sounds so racy when you put it like that."

"It was meant to! Keep me posted on James and the photos."

"Natch!"

We hang up.

Friday, 22nd April

6pm

With Alex and Paolo all packed up and preparing to return to Oxford tomorrow, it has been decided to throw a farewell feast in the garden, weather permitting. My Victorian table and chairs are being manhandled out of the door, to be set under the big mulberry tree in the orchard, to seat the family, the teens, our soon-to-be-gone house guests plus George and Olly. The cooking is being taken care of by Sarah and Amanda, supervised by Paolo who has coaxed some special Venetian recipes from his mother. I am advised that we are dining on an antipasti selection of cured hams, Italian cheeses and insalata from the delicatessen in the village, followed by Risotto Congli Asparagi and Chicken Cacciatore, Paduan style, with fresh fruit and gelato for dessert and I am under strict instructions to touch nothing unless specifically requested, though I may help plate up the antipasti. In between his supervisory duties, Paolo has been down to raid the cellar of some Italian wines, of which he appears to have an encyclopaedic knowledge, having been drinking them ever since he came off the bottle, or possibly before, as he tells it.

7pm

Mobile again and increasingly independent, Olly drove to Featherington to collect George and they arrive just in time for the serving of aperitifs and the antipasti. The weather, though cool, looks set to stay dry and everyone is directed to make their way to the orchard where the table has been laid beautifully by Jude and Mattie, decorated with a cornucopia of fresh fruits and flowers, along with enough candles to light Westminster Abbey. Though I can scarcely bear the thought of Paolo and Alex leaving us tomorrow, I have to admit this is the perfect send-off.

11pm

One more surprise was awaiting me after supper when, accompanied by some excellent white port from downstairs, Paolo and Alex produced a laptop and portable screen which they propped against a couple of tree branches and

473

treated us all to a PowerPoint pictorial tour of their Italian adventure the previous summer, from the shabby chic of the family farmhouse, the 13th century University of Padua which Paolo was at pains to point out, made Oxford seen positively modern, and the world-renowned 16th century Botanical Gardens. No wonder his help was so invaluable to George. From there it was a whistle-stop tour around Italy as the pair tried their hand at glassblowing in Venice, worked in a vineyard in Tuscany, swam and fished on the Puglian coast and paid a visit to La Scala. It all looked fabulous and I quietly resolved to see it for myself, hopefully in the not too distant future.

George and Olly headed off half an hour ago and I came inside, leaving the younger set to party on.

Saturday, 23rd April

9am

The boys left early this morning so they'd have time to settle back in and sort themselves out over the weekend. It was tough seeing them off but I am still counting my blessings for having had my long-lost son all to myself—well, sort of—for a whole month and am consoling myself with the thought that Oxford is not that far away and he has promised he will be back in the very near future.

My cell phone rings and I check the caller. Simon Cox.

"Those pills in the box.... The results from the analysis came back."

His voice sounds not flat but not keyed up either.

"They're common-or-garden birth control pills. 60, all told."

I briefly consider this odd piece of news.

"He's had other women. Several, I suspect. Probably belonged to one of them."

"That's a possibility. Odd things to hang on to, though."

"He's an odd person."

"I agree. Anyway, I just thought I'd let you know."

"Thanks."

I forbear to mention the photographic negatives I found. I'll keep those on a need-to-know basis and right now he doesn't.

"I'll leave you to it. Enjoy your weekend."

"You too."

We hang up and I turn my attention to a customer who is looking for our historical section, all things WWII, to be specific. I lead him to the relevant shelves and leave him to browse happily amongst our extensive and, if I say so myself, superior, selection.

Sunday, 24th April

5am

I wake to the sound of the bedroom landline ringing. Shaking the sleep from my head, I reach for the receiver.

"Filly?"

"James! What time is it there?"

"9 pm. I hope I didn't wake you?"

"Don't worry. I'm an early riser."

"I've been thinking about....you know."

"It's a lot to think about."

"You got that right. Anyhow, I was wondering if you had any photographs."

"Plenty." I prop myself up on the bed and pause, ever so briefly. "He looks the spitting image of you. I hadn't realised it till I spoke to you the other night. Hearing your voice, I suddenly pictured you so clearly."

"Same here." Pause. "Since your call I've been trying to imagine what your son would look like."

"Yours too."

He gives an embarrassed half-laugh.

"I guess so. Could you send me some? Email or phone."

"Of course. I'll do it as soon as I've made some tea."

"So I did wake you?"

"Only just."

He laughs. More genuinely this time.

"It was good to hear from you again. Even in spite of that earth-shattering news."

"You too."

I say it and mean it.

"Talk to you soon."

"Bye."

He drops the call and I swing my legs out of bed. It's what George would classify as an Irish Breakfast blend morning. As I do so I resolve to forward him the collage of pictures Alex sent me in what now seems like an age ago, along with some of the recent ones from the Easter trip. As I do so, I realise it's suddenly become important to me as well as Alex that his genetic father makes contact.

Wednesday, 27th April

1pm

Sarah has been in an odd mood this week. She's back to her picky eating, finding excuses to reject anything put in front of her on very spurious grounds. Jude thinks she's just pining over the departure of Alex and Paolo. I hope she's right and it's not a more serious relapse. At any rate, I wait till the dribble of customers had left the shop and phone Dr Turner to ask his advice.

"My staff haven't mentioned anything and they're a pretty perceptive bunch. I'm inclined to agree with Jude. Having had her half-brother home for all that time and all the company and excitement over Easter, it's all bound to feel like a bit of an anti-climax. And for a young woman in Sarah's condition she'll probably be feeling the loss more acutely. My advice for now is not to make too big a thing out of it. Just keep coaxing her to keep up her calorie goals but don't force the issue. And ask Jude to include her in whatever she has planned."

"They're all working hard towards the summer competition schedule. Sarah's not much of a one for competing but she does enjoy her leisure riding."

"A the risk of sounding a bit old-fashioned, I'm all for a bit of fresh air and exercise for my patients, so long as they don't take it to extremes and provided they make up the effort output with an increase in their calorie intake. And I'll tell the staff to monitor and observe, just in case."

"Thank you. Sorry to be a nag."

"You're a protective parent. Nagging's in the job description."

We say our goodbyes and I put the phone down feeling reassured.

7pm

Mindful of the doc's instructions to keep her busy, I called Sarah before she left the Avon this afternoon and suggested she meet the other three at the stables. Mattie and Amanda are both spending some time at their respective homes, having been away so much over Easter so it's just the three of us for supper tonight. I opted for a vegetarian curry with brown rice to please Sarah as well as sambals and poppadom's.

"I'm not really hungry."

"Still, you need to keep your strength up after being out all day and riding this evening."

I keep my tone light.

"I'm going to shower."

She leaves the room. I glance at Jude who shrugs her shoulders.

"I need to clean up too."

8pm

I am about to serve supper when the phone in the hallway rings. Sarah springs up to answer it, probably a convenient ploy to delay the eating ritual. I pour myself a glass of Chablis and Jude and I nibble on poppadom's while we wait for Sarah. A few minutes later she positively bounces in.

"That was Rupert. He wanted to know if we could put him up on Friday night. He's on his way up to Carlisle and he thought it would be nice to pop in. I told him it would be fine. It is, isn't it?"

Her eyes are shining and her mood has shifted a hundred and eighty degrees.

"Of course."

Privately I wonder what has prompted Rupert's request but since it appears to have geed up Sarah I don't voice my curiosity.

"Wow. That's great. Wait till Mattie and Mandy hear."

Jude is just as enthusiastic. Rupert certainly made quite an impression on his last visit. Both girls help themselves to curry and rice and though Sarah's portion is much smaller, she tucks in with enthusiasm and even accepts a spoonful of mango chutney. Dr Turner's instinct was spot on. I refill my glass and eat.

Friday, 29th April

11am

Since Wednesday there has been little other topic of conversation in the house other than Rupert's impending visit. Whatever he has, if anyone could bottle it, they'd make a fortune. I have been quizzed a dozen times as to the exact time of his arrival but I have no more idea than my interrogators. I turned down their request to take a day off school 'in case he comes while we're out' and with no further communication from Rupert himself, I will expect him when I see him. In the meantime I busy myself with the thankless and seemingly endless task of transferring our shop stock from cardex to computer, courtesy of a discarded unit from a fellow tenant of George's at Featherington who, I am given to understand, has 'upgraded'. I am sure this will all be worth it in the end but that seems a long way off right now as I laboriously type up each remaining stock item. Once this is executed, Alex has promised to hand it over to his friend for the website, along with some photos which the teens are to supply. For a former died-in-the-wool luddite I have to confess to being quite excited at the prospect of being 'online'.

1pm

I leave the shop in the capable hands of Jenny whom I conscripted to fill in for me for an hour while I pick up food for tonight's supper. In keeping with my recent resolve to source old recipes and home-grown produce, I venture in to the local fishmongers, a family-owned business on the high street which also stocks poultry and wild game in season. I have a recipe for baked cod with capers which calls for thick fish steaks and wild fennel which I show to the middle-aged woman behind the counter. She obligingly cuts the steaks from a large cod and asks if I need the head for stock, which I decline. The steaks, 6 in all, are wrapped in greaseproof paper and I am advised that wild fennel is literally and figuratively thin on the ground these days but she assures me the cultivated variety in the greengrocers will do just as well so that is my next call. On enquiring about seasonal produce, I am advised that there are new baby potatoes freshly dug and ready-podded peas, both of which will perfectly complement the fish. For pudding I decide on fruit crumble, partly because it's

478

quick and easy and partly because it's foolproof and I can rustle it up from what's in the pantry, to be served with whipped cream. These errands run, I return to the shop to relieve Jenny and continue with my cataloguing.

4.30pm

The 4 teens descend en masse, the girls demanding the whereabouts of Rupert, to which I can only shrug my shoulders. The reaction is utter desolation. I hand the bug keys to Mattie and suggest they all head off to the stables and I'll see them all at home later. I also remind them that Olly is expecting them there early tomorrow morning to put in some show practice which they'd all clearly forgotten. This is obviously going to eat into their Rupert time so I suggest they call Olly, explain the circumstances and reschedule.

"I'm sure he'll be fine with switching to Sunday. And that way, Sarah can go with you."

At these words, it dawns on my elder daughter that she is due at the Avon for her regular Saturday session in the morning and as the full implications dawn on her I suggest she too requests a cancellation. Using the shop phone both Olly and Nurse Dakin are reached, arrangements postponed and the four leave for the stables, content in the prospect of a whole day in their idol's company.

6pm

Back home, I clean up, don an apron and start first on the apple crumble which is then put into the fridge for baking later. That done I whip the cream which joins the pudding, scrub the potatoes and set them aside whilst I scour the small herb garden for fresh mint. Last but not least I arrange the cod in a large baking dish along with the fennel and seasoning, cover with Devon cider, season and dot with butter, as per the recipe instructions and cover the dish with a lid, ready for baking in the oven later, along with the tart. The recipe says 40 minutes in a hot oven so for now I have nothing to do bar scouring the cellar for more English wine to accompany the meal. I am still downstairs when I hear a car outside. Thinking it might be the elusive Rupert I head back upstairs only to find it's the bug. All four occupants rush off in various directions to scrub up and—at least for the girls—put on some glad rags.

7pm

I hand over the kitchen to the four of them to set the table while I take the opportunity to have a quick bath and find some fresh clothes. In what is now a well-rehearsed routine, Mattie sets to laying out cutlery, glasses and plates, Jude goes out to the garden to search for suitable foliage to dress the table and Sarah and Mandy take over the cooking. Leaving them inspecting the fish and the tart I go upstairs.

8.15 pm

The candles on the table are lit and the food is ready to be served. Rupert phoned while I was in the bath to say he'd been delayed at work till 6 o'clock and had only left London then but he hoped to be there within the hour. Sarah had taken the call and assured him that was fine, there was no need for him to apologise and sure enough we hear his car pulling into the drive. The teens all rush out to form a welcoming party and I hold back, leaving them to enjoy the moment.

Dressed in a suit that fitted so perfectly and hung so immaculately that it must have cost a pretty packet, Rupert breezes into the kitchen, shrugging off his jacket and carrying a small, leather overnight bag. Confirming he's in the same room as last time, he begs leave to shower and change before supper, promising to be done and dusted in 10 minutes.

8.45 pm

Everyone is seated around the table, save Sarah and Mandy who are placing the baked fish and side dishes on the table. As guest of honour Rupert is served first, Mattie pours wine and everyone begins to eat, even Sarah who naturally declined the fish but accepted a serving of everything else, adding a sprinkling of walnuts and almonds.

"Cheers, everybody."

Rupert takes a mouthful of the wine, swills it around his mouth adeptly and swallows, pronouncing it excellent.

"Tell us about your work, Rupert." (Mattie)

"Not much to tell, really. Spend most of my time on a computer."

"Monitoring foreign chatter and playing no small part in keeping the country safe", I think but don't say out loud.

"What's in Carlisle?" (Jude the Observant—straight to the point, as ever)

"What is there not? A castle, a cathedral, Hadrian's wall. Very ancient city. We've got an office up there and they want me to take a look at something."

He manages to turn evasive responses into a conversational art form.

"Mrs H says you have a lighthouse. That's so cool." (Mattie)

"I'd call it a work in progress but I don't seem to be making much! It does come with a lovely sea view, though."

"Do you have pictures?" (Mandy)

"I most certainly do. I'll give you the full virtual tour after we've finished this splendid supper. But you have to promise to show me yours in return."

"Our what?"

"Your mother told me about your spring ceremony at the hall. It sounds charming and very imaginative. A lot of which was down to you, I believe."

He casts a smile in Sarah's direction and she positively melts.

"It was all of us, really."

But she is reaching for her own phone and looking thrilled."

He shoots me a quick smile and a wink and everyone turns their attention to the food.

9.30pm

The teens are clearing the table and stacking the dishwasher whilst Rupert and I sit and finish the second bottle of Kentish Chardonnay.

"You must be dying for a cigarette."

I open my mouth to say 'Not really' but he gives an imperceptible shake of his head.

"You read my mind. I think I'll go through to the conservatory."

"I'll join you."

We walk out together.

"You might need a smoke."

481

I glance at him. His jovial face has changed to one more serious.

We sit and I look at him expectantly.

"I had those photographic negatives developed."

"And?"

"They're not the usual sort of holiday snaps."

"I didn't think they would be."

He is silent for a long moment.

"In my line of work I see a lot of...shall we say, sensitive footage."

I frown.

"What sort of sensitive footage."

"Just routine CCTV stuff, mostly. There's a lot of security in Whitehall these days."

I bet there is, especially where you work.

"Just to be on the safe side. We wouldn't want our elected officials put in any danger. The point is, those negs look an awful lot like surveillance footage."

He pauses and glances at me. I frown.

"I don't understand."

"Who took the pictures?"

His tone is insistent. I sidestep the question

"What do you mean, 'surveillance footage'?"

"I mean long lenses, grainy footage, awkward camera angles."

I'm starting to feel queasy.

"What's in the pictures?"

"The pertinent question should rather be 'Who's in the pictures?'"

"I haven't seen them, remember."

"The question was rhetorical."

He looks deadly serious. This is a side of him I haven't seen before.

"Where did they come from?"

"The safe you opened."

"And who used the safe?"

"Michael."

He nods as though he knew all along. He just wanted me to admit it.

"So why do you think he'd have pictures of this person?"

He pulls out his phone and hands it to me. I look at the man in the picture and gasp. It's James.

"Your friend in Houston, I believe?"

I nod.

"There are quite a few of him. Harvard, Boston, Kentucky, a few other places. And some in the UK."

He swipes his phone screen, giving me brief glances of the pictures. Changing landscapes but always James and mostly taken from a distance. I feel increasingly queasier.

"What about this one?"

He swipes again and now shows me pictures of Pip in Bristol, in what I assume is Cardiff, some up in Yorkshire and some more in London.

"A friend from uni."

And how about this one? There are quite a few of him?"

I look again and my stomach somersaults.

"His name's Steve."

"And he died." His tone is softer. "He was important in your life?"

I nod.

"How do you know?"

"That he was important to you or that he died?"

"Both."

"Number one, you're an intelligent woman. Why do you think your husband is taking pictures of your male friends?"

"Jealousy."

"To the point of obsession. This is not healthy."

"But it's not against the law?"

He looks directly at him but I can't read his face.

"What do you know about Steve's death?"

I hesitate.

"It was a hit and run. In a pub car park of all stupid places."

"By a VW Golf."

I stare at him.

"It was captured on film."

My eyes grow wide and I feel even sicker.

"Michael was there."

He nods.

My mind is racing. Michael had the girls that night. He claimed he'd been at home all evening so how could he been near the pub taking photographs?

483

Who was looking after the girls? Then lightning fast, it hits me. Sarah's mantra, 'He's only sleeping, mummy.' and the picture in her journal. Steve lying on the ground by his car. Did she dream it up from hearing the grown-ups talking or is it possible she might actually have seen it?

Rupert sees my stricken face.

"Bad memories."

"Show me the pictures."

"Tell me what's going through your mind?"

I explain as best I can the circumstances of Steve's death and my concern about the girls.

"There's no way of telling from the photographs. He was parked some way away and took pictures of the Golf leaving the car park. You can just see…"

"Steve's body?"

"A figure prone. In the background."

My mind is still flying around in different directions.

"If he was there why did he never say anything to the police?"

"Possibly because he wouldn't want to admit he was stalking your friend."

I nod.

"There is another possibility."

He looks at me.

"That he knew it was going to happen?"

"Oh, Christ. You think he….arranged it"

"I'm only hypothesising. That sort of obsession can spill over into violent action. Revenge, if you like. But I'm only saying it's a possibility. It could equally well be wrong place, wrong time and he couldn't openly admit he was there."

I fall silent, examining different scenarios and explanations.

"Wait here."

I can hear the teens in the small parlour watching something on television so I skirt to the back of the house, run up the service stairs, sneak into Sarah's room and pick up her journal. I feel guilty at invading her privacy but it's all in a good cause. Then I nip back down the same way. Back in the conservatory I open the book at the page with Sarah's drawing of the accident.

"We, her psychiatrist and I, both thought she must have conjured it up in her imagination from what she heard or maybe she dreamt it. But what if she really there. What if she actually saw it?"

Rupert takes the book and studies it for a long time. Then he closes it, picks up his phone, selects the photograph he withheld and pushes it towards me, face down.

"I'm no psychologist but that looks to me a childlike depiction of something your daughter heard." He pauses. "Maybe you should look at it."

I stare hard into his eyes. His expression is neither encouraging nor discouraging. I hesitate, my hand hovering over the phone, then I turn it over and glance quickly at the photo, before thrusting it back. Contrary to what I had always mentally envisaged, Steve was not lying by his car but several feet away. And in this picture frame all that can be seen of his prostrate figure are his feet and legs tucked up as if asleep in bed, his left hand slightly above and behind. Centre of the picture is his car, shot from behind and the left hand side. The Golf, slightly out of focus, is moving away. That Steve's head and face are out of the frame, I am more relieved than I can say.

"Let me give the pictures to a colleague. Get him to see what he makes of it and poke around, anything he can find out about the pair in the Golf."

"Like I said, that Detective Sergeant is still investigating."

"I won't spoil his fun. But we have a few more resources than he has access to. There are more pictures. Some of you."

He proffers a few more which are clandestine photos of me as a student in Bristol and others from in and around Bath, some with the girls, some of me at work, or shopping. He must have begun following us around pretty much as soon as he found out where we were.

"And what about these?"

He pushes more pictures and I recoil. They are of Pip's funeral in Yorkshire. The one he refused to attend.

"And who's this wild child?"

More pictures, this time of Patti in Bristol and Bath.

"My best friend."

"That figures." Pause. "It's a fly-on-the-wall montage of your life. That's one sick bastard you're married to."

"Not for much longer."

"He won't stop, you know."

"The detective was thinking on much the same lines."

"His sort need a bit of gentle persuasion."

This is said in a tone and look anything but gentle.

485

"I don't want you having to get involved."

"Too late, I already am."

I look straight at him. He looks back, jaw set. Then he smiles.

"It will be my pleasure. Honestly."

I say nothing, just wonder what on earth he might have in mind. Then I pick up the journal.

"I'd better put this back where I found it."

"And I'll go and say goodnight to the gang. They might be wondering what's taking so long."

He smiles wryly and taps the photo from the pub car park.

"We're very discreet and I'll let you know what we come up with. In the meantime let's not speculate."

I nod and try to quell the dark thoughts going around in my head.

Saturday, 30th April

3am

Well, that didn't work—the quelling, that is. After some fitful sleep in which images of Steve's body on the car park tarmac running around in my head, alongside one of Michael driving past, pointing it out to Sarah and Jude, like a noteworthy landmark, I woke with a start. Of course I don't know the girls were with him in the car that night. I don't even know for sure if he took the pictures himself. What if he paid someone to kill Steve and gave them the camera for proof. I know it sounds fanciful but I also know these things happen and if what Rupert said about him stalking my male friends for years, surely that's proof enough of some sort of psychosis? I want to scream, yell, howl but I can't do any of those things without waking the other occupants of the house and having them think I'm the mad one. I need to talk to Patti desperately but even she might not appreciate being woken up in the stilly hours by her half-crazed friend. Sisterhood only goes so far.

4.30am

After trying, unsuccessfully to get back to sleep I rise, shower and dress and go downstairs to make tea.

5am

Did tea ever taste so good? I have added the honey I bought for Sarah and which she never touches, on the basis that hot, sweet tea is supposed to be good for shock. I gulp it with the desperation of a heroin addict pushing the needle into their skin. It tastes like nectar and I feel marginally less like a corpse but it does nothing to ease my troubled mind. I open the laptop on the kitchen counter and half-heartedly check my email, more for the distraction than out of anticipation or enthusiasm. There is a mail waiting from James and I click to open and read it.

'Thanks for the photos. Not sure I see the family resemblance—the kid's too good looking! Anyhow I've given it a lot of thought and I guess it's only natural he'd want to look into his genetic roots so go ahead and give him my number. You can give him the landline you used and my cell phone is 214-8198733. You might want to put that in your phone too, just in case.

Fond regards,
James'

I ponder this cyber missive. I'm glad he wants contact with Alex, even if it's just box-ticking and the pair find they don't have much else in common.

6.00 am

Rupert appears in the kitchen, bandbox fresh as though dressed by his valet. I don't know if he has such a person but it wouldn't surprise me.

"I thought I'd get a jump on the day. Any tea mashed?"

"I'll make some fresh."

"I made an early call and set the wheels in motion. Those clowns in the car should be easy to track and trace. And someone will have a quiet word with them."

He smiles though it doesn't reach his eyes. There is a steeliness under his suave external demeanour that I wouldn't care to cross.

"Those pictures you showed me yesterday….the ones from America. Can I see them again?"

"Sure."

He whips out his phone, swipes the screen and hands it to me. I roll the sequence and find the picture I glanced at last night. It's a distance shot showing a young James standing in the shade of a tree lighting a cigarette. I look long and hard at it.

"Can you make that bigger?"

"No probs."

Rupert runs his finger over the screen and eliminates the background, till only James is in shot. I look again. He is using a Zippo lighter and I can't be a hundred percent sure but it looks awfully like the Jack Daniels lighter in Michael's box. I hand the phone back.

"Can you print that out for me? There's a printer in Michael's old office. Down the corridor, last door on the right."

"Old flame?"

I look at Rupert who is smiling. He makes a gesture mimicking lighting a cigarette with a flint lighter.

"Joke."

I smile weakly. Steeliness or not, he does have a very calming influence.

2pm

The teens persuaded Rupert to accompany them to Featherington to meet George and tour the mediaeval garden, after which he will head straight on up to Carlisle. As I left he promised me he'd fill me in as soon as he had any news on the occupants of the Golf and assured me that his department would have no problem tracking them down if they'd picked up so much as a speeding ticket at any time. It's really good of him to get involved but I still feel sick and shell-shocked at the idea that Steve's death was caught on camera and by Michael of all people and my mind goes around in circles wondering if or how he night have been involved. And that thought leads me on to the possibility that the girls might have also seen it happen and that that's what's behind Sarah's muddled memory and disturbing drawing. As luck would have it the shop has been quite hectic all day, up till now and this is the first moment I've had to myself. I pick up my phone and call Patti. She needs to know.

"I bloody knew it!"

Patti is expressing her certainty that Michael was somehow involved in Steve's accident. I know she'd always harboured her suspicions—'cherchez le man' and all that—but even to my sceptical mind that had seemed far-fetched, notwithstanding the fact that he's always maintained, even to the police, that he'd never left his flat that night as he was looking after the girls.

I in turn tell her I'm just as horrified but that in spite of myself I had no option but to wait and hear what Rupert's people uncovered.

"I think he's in some pretty hush-hush department. He as much as told me they have resources way beyond the capabilities of the cops."

"And if he is in it up to his scrawny little neck, what then?"

"I think I'd kill him."

The words are out of my mouth before I have time to really process what I'm saying.

"No jury in the land would convict you. But Fee, what about the girls?"

"I have no idea."

There's a catch in my throat, not missed by the ever-perceptive Patti.

"We'll get through it, Kiddo."

"Thanks."

"Call me the minute you hear anything. Promise."

I mutter something in assent and hang up. The shop is thankfully empty and for the first time in a long time, I allow myself to weep.

5pm

Faking a calm I didn't feel I buried myself in work, dealing with customers as and when and sorting shelf stock when the shop was empty, all the time trying desperately to compartmentalise Rupert's revelation. Now I lock up the shop and head off home.

6.30pm

The gang is still out at the stables so I go into the study and dash off a quick missive to Alex, telling him that I managed to contact his natural father—I don't go into detail as to how—that his surname is Greville, he lives in Houston, works for NASA and add his contacts.

'I spoke to him on the phone and to say he was taken aback is putting it mildly. No-one ever told him I'd gone through with the pregnancy and he'd drawn his own conclusions but once he'd processed that rather earth-shattering news, he called me back to say he'd like to touch base with you. I sent him those pictures you sent me—it's uncanny how alike you are and bizarre that I'd completely blanked it out.'

I want to add that I've seen some photos of his birth father quite recently but decide that might lead to too many questions and even worse, he might mention it to the girls so I keep that to myself.

'How is the website coming along? George is quite excited about it—you've made a complete convert of him!

Much love
Guin'

9pm

The talk at supper all centred around Rupert—his impeccable clothes sense, his flat in Chelsea, his lighthouse, his cloak and dagger work. Clearly he's the closest thing to a superhero any of the teens have met in real life. I let them chatter and made the odd noise to indicate I was listening, all the while playing out various black scenarios in my head and half-wishing I hadn't gone poking around in the cellar in the first place. Well, George did warn me about opening Pandora's box—as it turned out, hers wasn't the one I had to worry about.

Sunday, 1st May

Another sleepless night with a sick feeling in the pit of my stomach that just won't quit. The clock reads 4.30am but since the arms of Morpheus continue to elude me I rise, shower and make my way downstairs.

5.30am

With more fortifying tea, I log on to the computer, more to keep occupied than in the expectation of finding any messages. To my surprise there are 2 one from Alex, the other from James. I open Alex's first.

'Guin—you are amazing. I don't know how you tracked him down but made a call to Houston as soon as I read your mail last night. James is a really cool dude and we chatted for ages, swapping life stories and experiences. Dad will always be my father in that sense so it was more like talking to an older brother I never knew I had and we found we had more in common than I expected. For instance he's a big fan of detective fiction and was super-interested in my thesis. And we've both done a bit of sailing—he says he has a small boat in Galveston that he keeps to go fishing when he feels the need to get away from work.

Loads of other things too numerous to mention but it was really cool to touch base with him and we've agreed to keep in touch.

Big, big thank you
Love Alex'

I ponder this missive briefly, happy for Alex to find another missing piece of his genetic jigsaw and wondering what James would think if he knew his every move had been stalked and photographed while he was at Harvard and even back in the UK, on holiday presumably. I also wonder if I should tell him and that brings on that butterfly sensation in my stomach again, praying that there is some sort of, if not innocent then at least reasoned, explanation to Michael's presence at the pub the night Steve died and not believing it for a second. I take a deep breath and click on James' mail.

'Hi Filly. Alex called me this morning and we just fell into conversation like old friends! So weird to think he's my flesh and blood but on balance it's a good 'weird'! I'm really glad you got in touch—I won't deny the news came like a thunderbolt but I guess I'm mature enough to accept it, embrace it, even. I'm a dad! Well, sort of! And to be honest, it was pretty cool to hear your voice again. Brought back a lot of good memories. Can we also stay in touch?

Fond regards,
Jack'

I looked twice at his sign-off and then I too had a bit of a flashback. I remember back then when we were seeing each other, most of his friends always used to call him Jack. I knew it's often used as a diminutive of James but I never used it myself, especially after he told me his father winced every time he heard it. I smile at the memory, the first time I've done so since Rupert dropped his photographic bombshell into my lap.

Tuesday, 3rd May

9am

I'm in the shop, still trying, and failing, to keep my mind off Michael's seedy stalking pictures and his presence when Steve was killed. Part of me wants to believe it was pure coincidence—he was just being a creepy stalker of which there is ample evidence; but another part of me wonders if he could have had something to do with arranging it and he was there to watch the dénouement. It makes me feel physically sick. I always knew he had a jealous streak where I was concerned. I just had no idea how far he was prepared to take it so from there it's not too much of a leap to take it to its ultimate conclusion.

The shop bell tinkles and I look up, surprised to see George entering.

"I thought it was time I put in an appearance. Olly came to pick me up and dropped me off on the way to the stables."

"I'm really glad to see you."

I say it and mean it. He smiles, walks towards me and his smile fades.

"Whatever's the matter, young Ffion?"

Oh, Jeez. Is it that obvious or is it just his uncanny intuition? I shake my head.

"I can't talk about it. Not right now."

He studies my face for a few seconds, nods and moves towards the stairs.

"I'll just go and hang my coat up. Shall I put the kettle on while I'm about it?"

I nod and smile wanly. The bell tinkles again and I am relieved to see a customer walking in. I need to keep very, very busy.

"Are you okay to browse or can I help you with something specific?"

"I'm actually interested in lepidoptery. You wouldn't happen to have a section here, would you?"

"Quite an extensive one as it happens. Over here."

I lead him to our science section and point out the shelves covering entomology, including butterflies and moths around the world. He takes in the selection and beams.

"I'll leave you to it."

George comes down the stairs carrying a small tray of tea, along with a bottle of single malt.

"A bit of a nip in the air despite if being May. I thought you might need something to warm you up."

He sets the tray down by the counter, and pours a generous tot into my cup, before proffering it to me. I make no remonstration. It may not help much but it can't hurt.

Thursday, 5th May

2pm

The shop phone rings and I answer it. I'm quite taken aback to hear DS Cox's voice. In the midst of the new-age Elizabethan tragedy that's playing out around me, I'd completely forgotten he was still a bit player in the plot.

"Not much further forward, I'm afraid but I thought I'd just let you know I'm still on the case."

I feel a twinge of guilt for knowing what I know which anyway isn't nearly enough. I need to cut this conversation short before it becomes awkward but still go through the motions of acknowledging his efforts.

"No luck with the Rolex, then?"

'Not so far. It would probably have been fenced on the black market but someone may have insured it. We've been contacting a few brokers who deal in that sort of thing and they're checking records but it's a painstaking process after all this time."

"I s'pose so. Well, thanks for letting me know."

"I'm determined to see this through."

'Good luck. Bye."

I put the phone down quickly, guiltily, ashamedly. Then in a fortunately empty shop and George upstairs, I slump down onto the old chintz sofa and give way to the deepest, darkest state of mourning over the loss of Steve, poor Sarah's troubled mental state, for my sorry self and for the mess that is my life.

Wednesday, 11th May

Prior to last week I had heard the phrase 'living on ones nerves' but I'd never really understood. But for the past 10 days I've actually been its flesh and blood embodiment. I have started smoking again big time. Not that I ever completely stopped but somehow quite organically I'd just cut back to next to nothing. And now I've long overtaken my former personal best and am consuming a pack a day, as furtively as I can manage so as not to arouse comment from awkward quarters. As for my appetite, I can easily give Sarah a run for her money in self-denial. My food intake has shrunk to a size scarcely noticeable to my body or brain and it's me now who's making a show of doling out a normal portion on my plate, then concealing how much of it I actually ingest. I check my phone constantly in the hope of finding a missed message from Rupert and when not so doing, my mind plays out a series of possible scenarios to explain Michael's presence at that pub on the fateful night, none of which are in any way edifying, all the while desperately trying to convince myself that the girls didn't, couldn't have witnessed what happened and failing miserably. If Michael was there, they must have been with him in the car. And every time I have this vision I scream out loud if I'm alone and in my head like the creature in the Munch painting if anyone is near. I'm a complete and utter wreck.

Saturday, 14th May

3pm

I am in the shop when my cell phone rings. I check the caller and it's Rupert. I rush to answer it, my hands shaking so hard I can scarcely swipe the screen.

"We located Tweedledum and Tweedledee without too much trouble. Rap sheets as long as a bog roll. A colleague had a friendly little chat with them and they were very helpful. They were a little surprised to see their ugly visages caught on camera in the car that night and it only took a little coaxing in the confessional for them to admit their sins."

His words are casual, his tone harsh, sarcastic.

"Just a pair of small-time purveyors of non-prescription medicine to the clientele of the hostelry. Only trouble was, they'd both been sampling their own merchandise too freely and their faculties were somewhat impaired. And with trade a bit on the slow side they'd decided to try their luck somewhere else. And the driver put his clog down just as your friend was exiting his vehicle."

"They couldn't have been going that fast, surely?"

"Uh uh. I had a colleague take a look at the pictures. He's absolutely certain those goons could only have given him a glancing blow with the car's fender. But somehow he must have fallen awkwardly and died as a result of hitting his head on the tarmac."

He pauses.

"Seems you were right after all. Just a tragic accident."

Something in his tone….an element of doubt?

"You don't sound completely convinced?"

"It would explain why there were no visible injuries on the body apart from the minor head wound."

"What about Michael?"

"They both swear on their grandmothers' graves they never seen him or heard of him. As for the accident details, they admit they were both so stoned they didn't even know what happened, apart from hitting the car and seeing someone on the floor. The one driving stopped, the other one got out, thought they'd killed him, got back in and scarpered asap. After a bit of arm-twisting they did finally admit to removing the Rolex to feel his pulse, so they said, then accidentally forgetting to put it back on again."

I try to digest this news. What sounds like no more than a swipe from a car driven by a couple of dumb dope-heads. What a waste. What a tragic, senseless waste. I try to speak but my voice comes out in a whisper.

"Thank you."

I am silent for a few seconds then recall my conversation with Simon Fox.

"Did they say what happened to it? The Rolex."

"Popped it for a pony apiece. Too stupid to realise its true value. We can put out feelers so that if it ever surfaces on the open market we'll get an alert but I wouldn't set your hopes on it. Sorry."

"The detective on the case said much the same thing."

"Ah, yes. DC Cox, wasn't it? Somerset and Avon."

"How did you know......."

I tail off, realising I am asking a stupid question.

"What happens now?"

"Professional courtesy normally dictates we hand over his collar and the photographic evidence so they can decide whether it's worth pursuing further."

Again, the sceptical tone.

"What about Michael?"

"Not much they can charge him with, short of withholding evidence. I suspect he was just parked somewhere – probably across the road -stalking your boyfriend out of habit. I could have a word with him if you like."

"Let me speak to him first."

I find myself echoing his steely tone.

"Maybe best if I hang around in the background."

"No." That came out quite sharply. "I need to do this on my own."

An idea is forming in my mind as I speak.

"Fair enough but I'm at your disposal if you change your mind. Meanwhile I'll give your little DC Cox a call. Tell him we've turned up some evidence in his case whilst on an unrelated enquiry. I think that's how they phrase it in Plod-speak."

"Be nice to him. He's one of the good guys."

"I shall be chivalry and courtesy personified."

"You're another one."

He laughs.

"Not everyone would agree with you. Certainly not the two guests holed up at Her Majesty's pleasure in our basement. Speaking of whom, I want to have one more little chat with them before I knock off for the weekend."

He rings off and I stand in the middle of the shop, staring blankly at the few customers dotted around as I digest all that I've just heard. That my darling Steve was cruelly taken from me and the girls by careless driving from two drugged-up lowlifes and that Michael knew all along pretty much what had happened but chose to keep quiet for all this time. I still don't know if the girls were in the car with him and if they were, could they possibly have seen anything but I intend to find out and soon.

Sunday, 15th May

7am

Another sleepless night but this time a productive one. In my head I solved a long-forgotten mystery, after which I formulated a plan and now I intend to put it into action. I sit in the kitchen, reach for the landline and dial a number. It rings twice and is answered.

"Michael."

"Feef. It's so good to hear your voice."

"We need to talk."

"You've had a change of heart. I knew you would. That's great, We can put it all behind us. Start over."

I keep my voice neutral.

"I want to meet up tomorrow. In Stratford. The RSC rooftop restaurant. One o'clock."

"That sounds perfect. We can make it work, Feef. I know it. There's too much between us to stay apart."

"Tomorrow. 1 o'clock."

I ring off.

Monday, 16th May

12 noon

I gave some thought on whether I should be waiting for Michael to arrive or the other way round and decided on the latter. It will take an hour or thereabouts to reach Stratford, a little longer to drive to the theatre and park. I will be what is politely termed 'fashionably late'. I dressed carefully half an hour ago in a summer frock, one of the few dresses I own, a linen jacket and sling-back shoes with kitten heels. My make-up is light but I paid careful attention to my lashes and selected my pale fuchsia lipstick with care, then finished with a floral spray which I know Michael loves. Now about to leave, I take a large, leather shoulder bag from the wardrobe, pop in some items carefully laid out on top of my bed, add a packet of cigarettes, close the bag, pick up the keys to the bug and leave the house.

1.30pm

The weather is perfect spring sunshine with a few scudding clouds. I enjoyed the drive in spite of the occasion and easily found a parking space outside the theatre. I pick up the bag and head for the rooftop restaurant.

1.35pm

Michael is sitting at a window table, facing the door. He sees me enter, half rises, smiles and waves. His dress, I note, is smart casual and even from a distance I note his hand-made cotton shirt, loosened at the collar tucked into expensive chinos set off with a canvas belt. I also note a bottle of champagne in an ice bucket at his side.

"Feef!"

He steps away from his seat and embraces me, whispering in my ear.

"I began to think you'd changed your mind."

I push him away and duck my head as he attempts to kiss my cheek.

"I wouldn't have missed it for the world."

He holds my chair out, I sit and he takes his seat opposite me, reaching for the wine.

"Champagne?"

"Iced water, please."

He nods and clicks his fingers to attract attention from one of the staff.

"We can open it later."

He nods towards the ice bucket, leans his elbows on the table, links his fingers, looks long and hard at my face and smiles.

"I'm so glad you called."

I say nothing as the waitress places a glass of iced water on the table and hands me a menu. I smile and thank her, laying the menu down in front of me. Then I look up at Michael and affect a smile that doesn't reach my eyes.

"You stole my pills."

"What?"

He looks at me blankly.

"In Bristol. Just before you went to Harvard. You stole my birth control pills and presumably substituted them with some sort of placebo."

"You're being ridiculous."

498

I stare at him, keeping my face expressionless.

"No, Michael. I'm following the investigative thread. I never could work out how I got pregnant with Sarah when I'd been so meticulous about taking my pills. The ones you hid in the box in the safe."

His eyes widened, just a fraction. 'A hit. A very palpable hit'.

"What the hell were you doing going through a locked box that didn't belong to you."

No denial, just a counteraccusation. I re-load.

"And I found your photographs."

He looks momentarily nonplussed.

"Sorry?"

"Or should I say negatives. The ones in the basement."

His smile has faded completely away, replaced by a hardness in the set of his mouth and narrowed pupils. He is looking at me trying to read my expression. I reach into my bag and lift out the photo of James in Kentucky, along with one of Pip in Cardiff and another of Steve outside a delicatessen in Bath. He unclasps his hands and makes a bewildered, dismissive gesture.

"Okay, I admit it. I was jealous. That's not a crime."

"Stalking might be."

"It was harmless.'

"Was it?"

My tone is hard. I pull one more photo out of the bag, one from the car park, showing the red Golf leaving the scene. It was the only one Rupert would let me have.

"So I was there. You surely don't think I had anything to do with... what happened?"

"I wouldn't put it past you."

He makes a snorting noise.

"Why else would you not report it? At the very least you were a material witness, Michael, yet you said nothing." I raise my voice. "Nothing!"

Some other diners turn their heads at the sound of my raised voice. I glare at them and they turn away. I turn back to Michael.

"And explain this."

I reach into the bag again and lay down a photocopy of Sarah's drawing.

"What's that supposed to be?"

"Isn't it obvious?"

499

"Not to me."

I lean across the table.

"Were the girls with you that night? I want the truth."

He looks at me, looks down at the table, then back at me.

"No."

I jab Sarah's drawing.

"They must have seen what happened"

I sound mildly hysterical.

"That's ridiculous."

"How could they not?'

"Because they were home the entire time. I used to pay my cleaning lady to babysit when I needed to be out of the flat."

"Then how do you explain this?"

I stab again at the picture. He shakes his head.

"The girls were home with the sitter. I didn't want them getting in the way or asking awkward questions that might get back to you."

I look long and hard at him. It makes sense. The girls would have given me chapter and verse if they'd been driving round with him after their bedtime. Prof Turner must have been right—Sarah probably fed on the atmosphere around Steve's death, piecing together what she overheard and letting her imagination run wild. It is small relief but it doesn't let him off the hook.

"Why didn't you do something? Call for an ambulance? Just because you weren't driving the car that hit him doesn't mean you had nothing to do with arranging it. You are an unspeakable human being. You are deceitful, insanely jealous, creepy, furtive, untrustworthy and you make my skin crawl."

He snorts again.

"You're being ridiculous. It was obvious he was dead. What good would an ambulance have been?"

"You couldn't possibly have known that. And at least he would have been found sooner. I would have known sooner."

I have raised my voice again and the room is once more straining to look. don't much care—shouting is stopping me crying.

"Why should I? I hated him. You were mine. My girlfriend, my wife. H had no right to even touch you. You were a married woman, my wife, and h defiled you. I wasn't sorry he died. And that one had you before me and couldn't bear it. I just needed to know what he looked like, what sort of perso

500

he was." He is pointing at the picture of James. "As for him", he stabs the photo of Pip, "he was always in the way, along with that interfering bitch girlfriend of yours."

"She has a name."

"You know who I mean."

I can't believe the words I'm hearing. 'Had me', 'Defiled', it's the vocabulary of a Victorian bodice-ripper.

"I was never your possession, Michael. You think you bought me with your family money but you can't own a human being."

I pause.

"And your stalking didn't finish there, did it? I have no proof but I know it was your car that night that spooked Oliver's horse. It was you who caused his accident, your fault he's semi-paralysed."

I pause again and look hard at him. There is a flicker of defiance in his eyes but I am sure I am right.

"That's attempted manslaughter. And you who sent that bogus message to Alex at Christmas. That's why you were hanging around with Louise then because you knew he wouldn't be at the house. You made sure of that."

I study his face again. The same defiant look and fleeting contraction of his iris which confirms my accusation.

"And you removed the cigarette lighter from Steve's Saab. Some sick souvenir, no better than grave robbing. You might hide it well but you're completely deranged and demented."

I pause to let my words sink in. But not for long.

"Which brings me to the fact that two out of the three men are dead. Co-incidence?"

Another thrust of my foil. I study his face for reaction.

"You can't blame me for that. I had nothing to do with either of them kicking the bucket."

I wince inwardly at the crude expression but keep my expression deadpan.

"I'm not the one you have to convince, Michael. The negatives and the rest of the prints are already in the hands of the authorities."

I pause, dramatically. His iris widened, albeit imperceptibly. Another hit.

"You had no right...."

"I had every right, you despicable apology for a human being. You invade my privacy and that of my friends, you obsessively stalk and spy on them. You were there the night one of them died—there's undeniable proof. How do you think that will look when I pass on the details?"

"No-one would ever take it seriously."

A defiant response, I call his bluff.

"They would be duty-bound to follow up. You'd be questioned, undoubtedly taken into custody. How do you think your stalking portfolio will look to one of Her Majesty's finest? You'd be under a cloud of suspicion and they might even charge you."

"Don't be ridiculous. On what evidence?"

"Circumstantial evidence is still evidence."

Another palpable hit. He stares at me, glares at me for a long time. I meet his stare unblinkingly till he is forced to look away.

"You have no conception of how angry I am. Not just tricking me into getting pregnant so I'd have to marry you. Not just because you were driving round at dead of night spying on my lover through green-eyed, twisted malice. That was bad enough. But keeping quiet about it for all that time, then moving into Lionsgate and coercing me into agreeing to the sham that was our marriage. All those wasted years when the girls and I could have been building a life of our own, away from you and your evil machinations and your obsessive jealousy. For Sarah's birth, I can't be sorry, But everything else, for those lost years, for all the stalking and spying on me and my friends, for watching my lover die, I will never, ever forgive you."

I reach again into my bag, lifting out a sheaf of documents and a pen. I push them across the table.

"Sign the papers, Michael. Now. I assume you no longer want the house since your grubby little secret has been exposed, figuratively and literally."

"And what if I refuse."

Still defiant. I anticipated exactly this reaction.

"You won't. Unless you want me to make a formal statement to the police which, make no mistake about it, I will."

I look him directly in the eye again. He stares at me for what seems like several minutes, his expression that of a whipped cur. Then slowly, reluctantly, he picks up the pen, scans the documents, adds his signature and initials and pushes the papers back to me. I collect up the pictures and papers, replace them in my bag and rise.

"Goodbye Michael." I nod towards the ice bucket. "Enjoy your wine."

And I turn and leave the restaurant.

2.30pm

Sitting in the bug in the car park, in dire need of a nicotine fix, my hands are shaking so much I can scarcely light a cigarette. I want to cry, scream, shout and laugh cathartically, hysterically but I content myself with one cigarette whilst trying to compose myself and a second, chain lit, as I pull away. There's a time and a place for cutting back on my smoking and this here and now is neither.

I drive towards the town centre till I spot a post office, park and enter, purchase a large, manila envelope, inserted the signed papers, address it to Claire and send it off by registered mail. As I put the bug in gear to head home, my cell phone rings. It's Olly.

"Fiona, I know it's your day off and I wondered if you'd have time to pop out to meet me at the stables. There's something I want to show you."

I check the clock on the dashboard. It reads 3.05pm.

"I'm not at home but I could meet you there about half past four."

"Perfect. See you later."

4.25pm

I arrive at the stables to find Olly waiting in his wheelchair near the tack-room. He was smiling warmly and absurdly, just for a fleeting moment, I wondered if I was somehow unwittingly transmitting some post-Michael euphoric vibe. I shake my head and the thought fades. I note his attire.

"You're riding?"

He nods.

"I'll help you tack up."

I lift out Captain's saddle and bridle and we proceed to the stable. Once tacked up I look around, catch sight of Ali and call him over to assist. A minute later Olly is ensconced in the saddle and with the weather being fine, I lead Captain into a small outdoor arena. I hand him the dressage whip but he shakes his head.

"This is what I wanted to show you."

"What am I looking at?"

503

He glances down at his foot, encased in a tan paddock boot, I follow his glance and see his heel move almost imperceptibly, nudging Captain in the ribs. The import doesn't occur to me immediately and then it hits me like a sledgehammer. His foot can move! He sees my astonished expression and smiles again, turning Captain to face me.

"Both feet. See."

He gently clicks his heels and Captain obediently walks off. Then he clicks again and the horse moves up into a trot.

"Now you're just showing off!"

I find myself laughing and crying at the same time probably as much for myself as for Olly.

"That's all I can manage for now but Ish assures me I'll be walking again before too long."

He pulls Captain up to a walk and then halts next to me.

"Remember that hack we took just after Christmas?"

I nod.

"While I was riding I thought I felt one of my toes. It was just a tingling sensation and I didn't want to get too excited in case it was some sort of phantom feeling. That's why I asked you to drive me to Birmingham the day after for that consult with Ish. He confirmed that it was indeed muscle movement, albeit minute and that it was a positive sign that feeling was coming back. So that's when I started upping my therapy sessions and little by little I regained small movements, just in the toes at first. That was how I was able to maintain some balance on the horse. And now it's the whole foot and the ankle. I can even pull myself upright using the physio bars."

He is beaming, as am I, whilst managing to blub a little at the same time. Perhaps a surfeit of emotion for one day but I am so genuinely pleased for this kind, decent man who has become such a good friend to the whole family.

"Anyway I wanted you to be the first to know, outside of the physio staff. And to let you know that I intend pushing myself as hard as I can so that hopefully I'll be on my feet by the time I'm needed as Chef d'Équipe."

"Olly, this is wonderful news. The best. I'm so pleased for you."

"Thanks. I'm pretty pleased myself."

I smile at the understatement.

"This is proving to be quite a day."

He looks at me questioningly,

504

"I had a bit of a milestone moment myself earlier."

He raises an eyebrow.

'It's complicated—a family matter—but I can tell you a huge weight has been lifted from my mind."

"So we both have something to celebrate?"

I nod.

"Let's make a plan for this Saturday. You, me, the teens and George and we can let them all in on the secret at the same time."

"Mine or yours?"

"Mostly yours but I can share the non-classified stuff."

"I'd like that."

"That's a date then. Meanwhile are you planning on exercising this horse today or just sitting there gabbing?"

He grins and gestures for me to hand him the whip. Then he squeezes again with his ankles, Captain trots off and with a feather-light touch of the whip, the horse moves off into a working canter. Olly's legs are still inactive, with an observable lack of muscle tone akin to a beginner rider but his back is ramrod straight, his balance perfect and he looks completely at home and happy. Captain, too, by the way he is moving out.

What a landmark day this has been.

6.30pm

On my way home from the stables I suddenly realised I was starving, the first time I've wanted to eat in over two weeks so I stopped off down the road to pick up something for supper. And now I'm in the kitchen peeling potatoes and making up a salad to accompany the home-made Scotch eggs from Dysons, along with a vegetarian ersatz facsimile for Sarah. There's also a cherry tart with real ice cream for dessert. I might be ravenous but today is no time to be slaving over a hot oven.

7pm

"What smells so good?"

Jude and Sarah enter through the back door. Sarah heads straight for the door and announces she's going to shower. Jude lingers, smelling the air like

505

Mole coming up for air after his spring-cleaning session. She follows her nose and opens the oven where the Scotch eggs and pie are both warming on a low light.

"Ready-made food at last!"

"My cooking's not that bad."

"It's not this good either. Jude grabs an oven glove and half lifts the cherry tart out the oven with more appreciative sniffing noises.

"I was suddenly hungry and didn't feel like cooking for once."

"About time too. You've been as bad as her."

She nods towards the door and fixes me with an old-fashioned look and I know she is referring to my semi-fast of the past couple of weeks, the one I thought I'd concealed so well. Jude the Observant. She is looking at me presumably expecting an explanation. I ponder how much to reveal and decide on not too much right now.

"I've been a bit stressed and food hasn't seemed that important. But I'm feeling a bit better about life today."

"Does that mean you'll be cutting back on your smoking as well?"

Dear lord. Is there nothing that gets past her all-seeing eye?

"Probably."

"Okay. I'll get washed and changed and come back to help."

She too heads for the door and I take a bottle of Californian Chardonnay from the fridge. A glass of cold white wine will really hit the spot.

9.30pm

I call Patti and fill her in on the revelations of the past couple of days— Rupert tracking down the guys in the Golf, my close encounter with Michael and his signing of the divorce papers and last but not least, the great news about Olly.

"And does he think King Rat had anything to do with Steve's accident?"

"I had the impression he hasn't decided one way or another on that."

"What does 'on that' mean"

Sharp as a tintack.

"I don't know. I just had the feeling he thinks there's a piece missing in the puzzle."

"But you said his colleague came to the same conclusion."

"Not exactly. He said his colleague thought the photographs backed up the police report and the two dope-heads' story."

"Same thing."

"Not quite."

"It does make sense, though."

"I s'pose."

"And if they were stoned out of their pea-brained minds, they might not even know exactly what happened, just the bullet points."

"That's true. I'm just so relieved that the girls weren't there."

"And King Rat probably couldn't believe his luck. His rival dead, the field clear for him to step back in and you a basket case."

"I can't believe I was that naïve, that stupid."

"You were a wreck, an empty shell, kiddo."

"I'm getting my life back. Patti."

"I can see that. I'm really happy for you."

We hang up and I call Rupert, just to let him know that I'd hung a Damoclean sword over Michael's head and forced him to sign divorce papers.

"If he gives you any trouble it'll be the easiest thing in the world to let slip who took the photographs to your tame 'tec and drop a few hints as to possible involvement in your friend's accident. He deserves to have his collar felt a bit."

There's a tone of sadistic enjoyment in his voice. That steel core again.

"I can't pretend I wouldn't enjoy it."

"We'll just keep it in abeyance then." He pauses, momentarily. "I thought I'd head off to the West Country tomorrow. It's rather lovely this of year." He pauses again. "Keep your pecker up, old girl."

He affects a clipped, World War II accent. Is he implying a battle has been won but not yet the war, or am I reading too much into it?

Tuesday, 17 May

10am

I slept like the proverbial log last night, a thankfully deep and dreamless sleep, just like the little town of Bethlehem. It was a blessed relief after the mental torture of the past couple of weeks. I had lived for so many years with the gradual acceptance that Steve's death had been a tragic accident and the

507

apparent confirmation gives me no more nor less peace than before. Part of me died with him that night and nothing can change that but I am at least comforted by the knowledge that Sarah's long-buried secret was simply a childlike vision and that with the continuing help from the Avon team she will work through her problem and hopefully come out stronger on the other side.

Prior to leaving the house I read an email from Alex in which he said the Ink an' Abulia website is now ready to go live and he sent me a link to click on to view it. So with the shop quiet, now's the perfect moment. The site opens with a header picture of our shop sign, flanked on one side with one of an extant volume of Dickens' The old Curiosity Chop and on the other a page from an illuminated monastic scroll. The homepage contains photographs of various shelves, nooks & crannies of the shop, along with a description of the business, its potted history and a few paragraphs describing George's passion for incanabula, along with his Featherington project and accompanying photographs. It also carries a satellite map giving directions to the shop, contact numbers and my email address which, to my mild horror, also has a head and shoulders portrait of me that I certainly don't remember having been taken. Also on the home page are category headings for out various sections. I click randomly on Pastimes & Hobbies and am directed to a page with a photo of the relevant section, along with up-to-date stock listings and prices. Back on the homepage I also note that there is a 'Search' facility which responds to either author, publisher or book title, a trolley icon and a checkout button. At this a feeling of mild panic washes over me but I recall Alex's assurance that any or all of the teens had been fully briefed and would talk me through the checkout, payment and shipping processes and that then and only then would the site go live.

So George and I, along with our delightfully quirky bookshop which has been my sanctuary and salvation for so many years, have officially entered the internet era.

Thursday, 19th May

11am

Clare calls on the shop phone to confirm that she has received the signed documents and that she'll be lodging them with the court immediately.

"He took his sweet time but he finally caved in."

I refrain from revealing the exact circumstances under which he signed and just murmur "Yes, thank goodness."

Saturday, 21th May

7pm

The forecast was set fair so I decided on an al fresco feast for Olly's and my celebration and revelation. I informed the teens that their collective presence would be required at supper and that both George and Olly would be joining us but said no more and gave no hint as to its import. For the menu, still sticking to my current traditional British theme, I decided on roast beef, roast potatoes and veggies. There will also be individual Yorkshire puddings, a task I have delegated to Sarah who will make a better hand of it than me. For her and Jude if she's in a veggie mood, which I doubt, there is a terrine of nut roast and I cheated with a Simmonds Black Forest Gateau for a ceremonial pièce de resistance to mark the significance of the moment.

My Featherington table has been manoeuvred outside again under one of the mulberry trees and is being laid by Jude and Amanda who decided to revive some of the Oestre decorations to tart it up. And Olly is picking George up on the way and the pair should be here any minute.

9pm

The roast was a triumph, if I say so myself, perfectly pink in the middle and expertly carved by Mattie and washed down with vintage Châteauneuf du Pape from the cellar. Plates having been cleared and the cake brought out, I catch Olly's eye and metaphorically give him the floor. He taps a knife on the side of his glass to demand attention, conversation dies down and everyone dutifully looks in his direction.

"Ladies and gentlemen, please charge your glasses for the toast."

We all obediently fill up.

"First a toast to our gracious hostess for that superb supper."

"Hear, hear". (George)

"And next I have a little announcement to make. Or rather, something to show you all."

All eyes are expectantly on Olly who has drawn his wheelchair closer to the table and now firmly grasps the edge, his fingers placed on the top. As we watch he slowly, and clearly with huge effort, pulls himself upright, to yelps of excitement from the girls, an 'Oh, wow' from Mattie and a 'Well done, that man' from George.

'I'm still not too steady on my pins but I'll give it a go."

Olly then lifts first one hand then the other and achieves a wobbly balance for several seconds. Once secure he grips the table edge once more and with what is clearly some considerable effort, shuffles a foot to the right, stops to catch his breath, then moves left to his starting point. That done, and perspiring a little, he re-balances himself before slowly sinking back into his chair to a table of open mouths and a spontaneous round of applause.

'To Olly.'

George raises his glass and we all copy him and take a sip, echoing his words.

'That's bril.' (Jude)

'Fabulous!' (Amanda)

'The best news.' (George)

'Time to cut the cake.' (Mattie)

'Not so fast, Matthew. I think Fiona also has something she'd like to say.'

Everyone turns their face expectantly towards me. I look first at Jude and Sarah and give them an intimate, reassuring smile, then at George.

"Mine's not nearly so exciting as Olly's but I have to confess it's a big relief." I look again at the girls. "Your father has signed the divorce papers and they've been lodged with the court. He's dropped his claim on Lionsgate so we can start making plans for the future properly."

"I'm very happy for you, young Ffion."

"Good riddance to bad rubbish." (Jude)

"You deserve better." (Sarah)

Everyone falls briefly silent. Amanda is first to break the silence.

"I don't know about anyone else but I can't wait to get stuck into that cake."

"Right with you on that." (Mattie)

"George, will you do the honours?"

"Delighted."

I hand him the knife and he begins to slice up the gateau. It really does look delicious.

"Just a tiny piece for me. I'm so full after that nut roast."

Since Sarah only had a minute portion of the main course this is unlikely but some things take longer than others to fix. I'll be happy to see her eating any cake at all. George obligingly cuts her a small sliver and plates and cake forks are handed round.

As we all take forkfuls of what is certainly an excellent confection, Sarah also lifts her fork, slices off a small section of her sliver and pops it into mouth, chocolate frosting and all. That's the second best sight of the evening.

Wednesday, 25th May

It's not that I really care but I am somewhat surprised not to have heard from Simon Cox. If Rupert paid him a visit at the weekend, as it sounded like he planned on, and if, as he previously promised, he'd passed on one of the pictures of the Golf and its occupants, along with their names and locations, I would have thought he'd have been eager to share his news with me. But he is curiously silent. To be fair, though, I told him often enough that I didn't care. Perhaps he finally took me at my word.

Olly has now embarked on a programme of extreme physiotherapy, with Ish's full support, meaning what he said about being ready and as mobile as possible for the upcoming show season and his Chef d'Équipe duties.

Plus after my own crash course in web management, the shop's site went live yesterday and I am already dealing with our first online orders which I will take to the Post Office at lunchtime.

And best of all, I spoke to Prof. Turner on Monday and he advised me that Sarah seems free from her major hang-up after the art and hypno-therapy, though he was careful to stress that this is by no means a cure for her anorexia

511

and it's still a long, hard road ahead to persuade her to normalise her eating habits.

As for George, he is now up to his Wellington boots in the Featherington garden as many of his plantings are growing in earnest and needful of lots of TLC.

Everything in his garden is metaphorically rosy, my situation has also seemed to turn a corner so why do I still have a feeling of disquiet that I can't shake?

Saturday, 4th June

11am

It was an early start for all of us this morning. Jude, Mattie & Amanda are all competing in a 3-phase event near Aylesbury so they were up before the crack of dawn to groom horses, box up and drive down. Olly also insisted on going along. Even though he'll still be mainly in his wheelchair he is adamant there's plenty he can do to help. And Sarah brought forward her Avon session after which she's catching a train down to watch and offer support.

I was glad of the early start at work. The website is attracting a huge amount of business, mostly from students, and I'm becoming a high roller at the local Post Office. After dealing with the latest enquiries and assisting a few hard-copy customers, I take advantage of the lull to call Patti.

"How are the twins?"

"You mean the creepy-crawlies? Driving me up the wall. How can anything that's on its hands and knees possibly be so fleet of foot?"

"Piece of advice. Remove anything breakable below knee level."

"Now she tells me." Pause. "You didn't call to give me childcare advice so what's up?"

"I don't know. Something Rupert said about the accident."

"You thought he was holding something back."

"Not intentionally. More that he had some doubts."

"Me too. I still think King Rat shouldn't get away Scot free from his nasty voyeuristic film noir crap."

"I'd happily expose him myself if I didn't think it would have a devastating effect on Sarah's recovery."

"How's she doing?"

"Surprisingly well. She ate some cake last week."

Patti whistles down the phone.

"In that case let's just hope she never does hear what he got up to."

"I'd still like to kill him with my bare hands."

"I bet."

The shop bell rings and a small group of young people enters.

"Have to go. Duty calls."

"Keep me up to date."

"Will do."

Sunday, 5th June

8am

The teens got back really late last night, whacked out but happy with their day. All three had a clear round on the cross-country, but Mattie had a few penalties in the show jumping and they all agreed their dressage left a lot to be desired. Olly had gone straight home after dropping Sarah off but I gather he's insisting on some serious schooling under his tutelage over the next couple of weeks before the next show comes up.

Monday, 6th June

11.30am

After a morning spent doing much-needed chores around the house I'm in the kitchen wondering whether to make a grocery run when I hear a car in the drive outside. Looking out of the window I see a small hatchback which I don't recognise. The driver is out of view. Then the doorbell rings so I get up to answer it. I'm a little taken aback to find Rupert standing under the portico, immaculately dressed in a cashmere polo-neck sweater, chinos and leather loafers.

"You're like a will-of-the-wisp the way you pop up."

"I was just passing and thought I'd drop in."

"Liar."

He grins disarmingly.

"Perhaps I did have to make a slight detour. Are you frightfully busy?"

"I was but I'm taking a bit of a break."

"I'm on way back to London and I wondered if I could buy you lunch?"

"That's not your car."

"Company run-around. Is that a yes?"

I regard him for a few seconds. As always it's hard to gauge his mood or get a sense of why he would be dropping in on a Monday morning.

"Come in. I'll need a few minutes to change."

"Take all the time you want."

He sits on the old settle in the hallway and I head upstairs. Once in my bedroom I take a lightning-fast shower and dress in semi-formal Capri pants with a matching jacket over a cotton blouse.

"You look very summery."

Rupert rises, moves to open the front door and we both walk through. Then he holds the passenger door open, I slip into the front seat, he gets in the other side and we drive out. On the road, he turns left.

"Where are we going?"

"I passed a lovely little hostelry on the Banbury side. Should be quiet on a Monday."

As we drive he enquires about the horse show and I tell him as much as I know. He also wants to know how George's garden project is coming along, how Sarah's treatment is progressing, the health of the dogs and other assorted, safe subjects. I in turn ask how the work on the lighthouse is faring and how is life in London, realising that although he apparently now knows a great deal about me and my life, I still know virtually nothing about his.

Eventually, after a forty-minute drive, he points to a tiny roadside inn that looks like it might have once been a coach stop in days gone by. He turns off the road, pulls into the car park and we both enter. Inside the low beams and old spit and sawdust-style wooden floor tells me I was probably right about the inn's origins. We approach the bar, he asks me what I'd like to drink and orders 2 halves of lager. There is a limited luncheon menu on a chalk board behind the bar and I opt for home-made tomato soup and a garden salad, whilst he selects beef pie and chips. He then requests that the food be brought outside and we make our way through a side door to a rear garden where the old coaching stables have been converted into a covered seating area, the floor still retaining its original cobbles. We sit, both take a sip of our drinks and I look at him expectably, my brow slightly quizzical.

"So what's the occasion?"

He frowns slightly, lifts his glass and takes a sip, carefully puts it back down and purses his lips.

"I went to see your DC Cox."

"You told him about the drug pushers?"

"Not exactly." He pauses. "Actually I asked to see the file." Another pause. "He was happy to oblige."

I bet, consider who was doing the asking.

"And?"

"I needed to go through it myself. You'll appreciate that up to now I've largely been basing my input on conjecture and second-hand information."

"Sorry. That's probably my fault."

'Not at all. Merely that I needed to see the full picture, in this case literally and figuratively, principally because there was something about Cox's working assumption that didn't quite fit that picture."

"And now you have a better idea?"

"I think so. It all comes down to the car door. The report stated that it was open."

I nod.

"And so it was and the investigating detectives at the time concluded that your friend—Steve—must therefore have just stepped out of the car and he was hit by a glancing blow from the Golf. But looking at the photographs that didn't seem to quite fit the scenario."

"In what way?"

"The position in which he was lying on the ground. It seemed to me he was walking away from the vehicle when he fell, in the which case, presumably he'd have shut the car door behind him."

"So they hit him while he was moving?"

He shakes his head.

"The Golf hit the rear right fender of the vehicle. The paint marks showed that and those clowns confirmed it."

"So they hit the car first and then hit Steve."

Again the shake of his head.

515

"I did consider that. After all, by their own admission they were high on coke and weed. But from the pictures taken the following morning and which were in the file, the tyre tracks clearly show that after hitting the vehicle, they braked sharply."

"But they also said they hit him."

"That's what they thought and what the police concluded."

"I don't understand where you're going with this?"

"Neither did I. That's why I needed to see the file. Specifically the autopsy report and photographs. And that's what I was doing in Oxford this weekend. My godfather is Emeritus Professor in surgical trauma at Magdalen and he kindly agreed to have a look at them."

He pauses again and looks straight at me.

"And he found something that the police pathologist missed. A minute clot, not visible to the naked eye, in the brain cortex which he said would almost certainly have brought on a cerebral venous sinus thrombosis. A stroke. In would have been very sudden and it proved fatal."

I am staring at him, trying to understand what he's telling me.

"As incredible as it appears, Steve's collapsing and dying had nothing to do with the two Stooges and by inference, nothing to do with that scorpion you married. It was pure coincidence that they hit his car at almost the exact moment he suffered his stroke. They were so high they assumed they must have hit him, panicked, tried to check his pulse, realised he was unresponsive and took the opportunity to steal his watch. It was one of them who opened the car door, probably hoping there'd be something else of value there, didn't find anything and took off, all in the matter of a few seconds."

He stops, looks hard at me again and takes a deep breath.

"Steve's death was a terrible tragedy but it was from an undiagnosed medical condition, not being hit by a car or even falling on the ground and hitting his head. All of that was just a massive coincidence."

He stops again and takes hold of my hands.

"No-one is to blame for his death, Fiona."

My eyes have filled with silent tears. He hands me a napkin with which I dab them dry. He sips his drink and allows me time to unpack the narrative he's just laid out. Several minutes pass while I take it all in, trying to accept that I've been living under a false black cloud for all these years.

"But that's not to say there is no wrongdoing."

The tone and timbre of his voiced had changed completely. The soft, sympathetic sound has gone, replaced with a harder, harsher note.

"Your husband's serpentine, sly behaviour, for instance. He needs to be held accountable for those years of stalking and spying."

"I threatened to expose him. Forced him to sign the divorce papers."

He cocks his head slightly and smiles wryly.

"Good for you."

"I told him never to come near any of us ever again."

He nods.

"There's no guarantee that he won't. Leopards rarely change their spots."

He breaks off as a young woman approaches with a tray of food. She places a bowl of soup in front of me and in front of Rupert she sets down a large plate holding a pie, generous portion of chips and salad garnish. Adding cutlery, napkins and a small basket of bread rolls she asks if we want a refill on our drinks. We both nod and she walks off towards the building.

"As I was saying, he needs to be taken to task."

"But you said yourself that the police won't be overly interested in some clandestine creeping around with a camera."

He nods.

"What I had in mind was that he should disappear."

My eyes grow wide. I know he's some sort of government agent but surely that 'license to kill' phrase is the stuff of Fleming fiction?. I smile nervously.

"You don't really mean that?"

"Oh but I do. I think for the sake of you and your family, it would be better for all if he were out of the picture permanently."

He takes a large forkful of his pie and looks at me over the top of his food. I'm confused and slightly disturbed.

"I don't know that that's necessary, surely?"

'Only answer to your problem. Leave it to me."

And then he actually winks. As though he were offering to run a small errand. He must be pulling my leg so I smile back.

"Sounds like you've got a magic wand you can wave."

He smiles and winks again.

"This pie is excellent. Have a chip."

He proffers his plate but I decline and take a spoonful of soup, putting his suggestion down to sick spy humour.

6pm

I'm home and on the phone to Patti.

"So it could have happened anywhere, anytime?"

"Pretty much." I pause. "I know it doesn't bring him back but at least it was no-one's fault."

"That doesn't let King Rat off the hook for what he did and what he put you through."

"Rupert offered to get rid of him."

"Let him!"

"Part of me hopes he would or could. But I'm sure he was just joking."

"You sound doubtful."

I giggle.

"No. Just wishful thinking."

'I'll drink to that."

"At least he's signed the papers. Claire said the Decree Nisi should be granted in a couple of weeks."

"You're moving on, Kiddo. Good for you."

And I realise she's right.

Part VII
"Full Many a Glorious Morning"

Monday, 8th August

7.30 pm

Heathrow Airport

I'm here with Alex waiting for our overnight flight to Houston. Over the past couple of months, we have both been in regular communication with James, albeit quite separately, eventually both being cajoled into making a visit to the United States, a first for both of us. I have it on good authority from James that southern Texas is hot as Hades and horrendously humid in August but there is much to see and do. Personally, I'm looking forward to seeing a real live rodeo whilst Alex, though eager simply to meet his blood relative face to face, has plans to join him fishing for marlin in Galveston Bay. As for James and me, we've been rediscovering a little of what drew us together in the first place— his anti-establishment attitude, dry sense of humour, love of animals and a passion for the cinema, in view of which he's also scheduled a visit to Archer City in north Texas where Peter Bogdanovic famously filmed The Last Great Picture Show.

Somewhere in our emails he reminded me that his middle name was Daniel and that's why his friends all called him Jack, rather than James, hence his obligatory visit years ago to the eponymous bourbon factory in Tennessee. So tucked away in my bag is the Jack Daniels lighter that I retrieved from Michael's trove of trophies. I haven't decided whether or not to give it to him yet, much less explain how I came by it. I'll see which way the wind is blowing.

And remember when Rupert said it would be best all around if Michael were to disappear? Well he did, in a manner of speaking. Seemingly Pricerite wants to expand into the lucrative Russian market and Michael was dispatched to St Petersburg to search for suitable premises and oversee the construction and opening of the company's first branch in Eastern Europe. I have no idea how Rupert pulled that off but also no doubt that it was at his behest.

As for the others, the teens are all on a week's break in Rupert's lighthouse, on the proviso that they do their fair share of repainting of the living accommodation. They have taken Dottie and Cromwell with them and though I suspect there will be more partying on the beach than painting I think they all deserve to let their hair down.

522

Oliver is now walking fairly well, albeit with the use of a cane—an appendage he is determined to abandon as soon as possible.

George is still tending the revived monastic vegetable and herb garden with a view to an autumn harvest of mellow fruitfulness and the garden is looking quite perfect in the summer sunshine.

Patti, Ross and the twins are off to Scotland at Charles' and Diana's invitation for the start of the Glorious Twelfth. Neither is in the slightest inclined towards blood sports but Ross is keen to try his hand at some trout fishing as well as visiting a distillery or two to sample some fine single malts whilst Diana has promised to show Patti the delights of the Edinburgh social and retail scene whilst spoiling the babies rotten.

Best of all, Sarah has set her sights on a degree in art history at the Courtauld Institute at London University from September next year. Rupert's sister has a small flat in Chelsea and works for Sotheby's and Rupert assures us that she'll be delighted to have Sarah as a flatmate and keep an eye on her. That's the strongest incentive she could have for making a good recovery. Her stated aim is to put on one whole extra kilo by the end of this year, my and Prof. Turner's study permissions being dependent on her achieving it.

All this is flowing through my head as I sit in the departure lounge, trying to ignore the butterflies performing acrobatics in my stomach, precipitated by the upcoming reunion. In an effort to distract myself I force myself to view the bigger picture.

"Texas isn't too far from Kansas, is it?"

"Not sure. Why?"

"Truman Capote. In Cold Blood. About the mysterious murder of an entire family in a tiny town in Kansas called Holcomb. It's masterful."

"Never read it."

"You should. Might be good for your thesis. I know it was a real-life crime which had already been solved but he covers it like an experienced investigative reporter, the incident, the search for the killers, the dearth of either evidence or witnesses, the painstaking search for the perpetrators and the complete lack of any apparent motive. Hence the title."

"I'll give it a read."

"I know a good bookshop that has it in stock."

He grins at me.

"It was his Magnum Opus, you know. Once he finished it he never wrote anything again."

As Alex digests this snippet of information my phone beeps and glancing at it see it is an SMS from Rupert. Anticipating a bon voyage message I click and instead find a link to a Reuters stop-press. Puzzled I click and read:

'Local sources are reporting that an unnamed British subject has been detained by Russian authorities on suspicion of spying. Though unable to confirm or deny the report, our own correspondent believes the charges relate to sensitive material found in the subject's possession. It is not currently clear where he is being held, but it is suspected that he is being interrogated by the GRU, Russia's military intelligence unit, somewhere in the Russian capital. British authorities declined to comment when contacted by our Moscow correspondent and the detainee's name has not yet been released. '

I gasp involuntarily and Alex glances sideways at me. Rupert surely means me to understand the unnamed man is Michael. Why else would he be sending me the stop press? I return to his message which goes on to say

'Those pesky Reds are notorious for jumping to conclusions and do rather delight in locking people up and throwing away the key willy nilly, as opposed to our rather more liberal form of justice which assumes a man innocent till proven guilty. Unfortunately such misunderstandings, if such it is, often take years rather than months to sort out.'

I am in no doubt whatsoever that this is a continuation of his plan in orchestrating Michael's transfer to Russia. My jaw drops open in shock at the chutzpah and I gasp, then inappropriately giggle, recalling Rupert's stated intention that it would be better for all if Michael were to disappear. Alex looks at me quizzically.

"Interesting message?"

"Unexpected."

He raises an eyebrow, inviting more details but I shake my head.

"Need to know. Sorry."

Time enough to share this information when more details emerge and when I have had time to take it, and its wide-reaching implications, in.

And now they're calling our flight and Alex is hustling me to join the queue for boarding. Seems he's an old hand at this sort of thing whilst I haven't been on a plane for years.

"Time to go."

And he propels me forward.

As I obey, it occurs to me that I will have to have a serious heart to heart talk with Diana on my return. Somehow I suspect she will take the news stoically, in spite of Michael being her only son. Precisely how much I will be able or willing to share remains to be seen.

Shuffling along in line my phone beeps another message. This time it's from James assuring me that he'll be waiting at the airport to collect us both. The message signs off

'King James awaits her lady's pleasure.'

I giggle again, this time more appropriately. It's a private joke from a long time ago and that's as much as I'm saying.

I switch off my phone and look at Alex.

"Let's go."

And as we board, my thoughts are also travelling; to a book in our foreign literature section—Fyodor Dostoevsky's Crime and Punishment. I resolve to pack the copy up and pass it on to Rupert on my return. I am quite sure it is easily within his purview to send it by diplomatic pouch for onward delivery, Red Cross parcel-like, to what are probably his counterparts in the GRU. I am equally sure that Michael will know immediately from whom it comes and that the title and its content will not be lost on him.

Revenge, as they say, is a dish best served cold.

END